Cheater

a stalker romance
by DD Prince

Copyright

All rights reserved. No part of this publication may be reproduced, distributed, or transmitted in any form or by any means, including photocopying, recording, or other electronic or mechanical methods, without the prior written permission of the publisher, except in the case of brief quotations embodied in critical reviews and certain other non-commercial uses permitted by copyright law.

© Copyright: DD Prince http://ddprince.com. 2024.

This novel is the fictional product of the author's imagination. Copyrights are the property of their respective owners.

Thank you for respecting the author's work and copyright.

While certain places in this story exist in the real world, creative liberties have been taken.

Contents

Content Warning — vii
Foreword — ix

1. Chloe Turner — 1
2. Chloe — 15
3. Chloe — 21
4. Derek Steele — 31
5. Chloe — 39
6. Chloe — 45
7. Chloe — 51
8. Derek — 53
9. Chloe — 57
10. Chloe — 65
11. Chloe — 77
12. Derek — 91
13. Chloe — 99
14. Chloe — 119
15. Derek — 125
16. Chloe — 127
17. Chloe — 137
18. Derek — 143
19. Chloe — 151
20. Derek — 163
21. Chloe — 173
22. Derek — 179
23. Chloe — 185
24. Derek — 189
25. Chloe — 191
26. Derek — 195
27. Chloe — 207
28. Derek — 221
29. Chloe — 233
30. Derek — 245

31. Chloe	255
32. Derek	285
33. Chloe	301
34. Derek	315
35. Chloe	319
36. Derek	351
37. Chloe	367
38. Chloe	393
39. Alannah Fisher	401
40. Derek	409
41. Chloe	421
42. Derek	431
43. Chloe	433
44. Derek	459
45. Chloe	467
46. Derek	477
47. Chloe	487
48. Derek	495
49. Chloe	499
50. Chloe	505
51. Chloe	511
52. Derek	523
53. Chloe	533
54. Chloe	545
55. Derek	561
56. Chloe	563
57. Derek	569
58. Chloe	581
59. Derek	599
60. Chloe	603
61. Derek	623
62. Chloe	627
63. Chloe	633
64. Derek	639
65. Chloe	641
Epilogue	653

The End	661
Want More?	663
Book Report	665
End of Book Notes	667
About the Author	671

Content Warning

CHEATER'S CONTENT NOTICE:
This story deals with difficult subject matter and a toxic, obsessive, stalking, morally dark male lead who makes threats to get what he wants. If you're not a dark romance and antihero lover, this book won't be for you. Further information is available on the author's website.
http://ddprince.com

Zero baby unicorns were harmed during the writing of this book.

1

Chloe Turner

"Hall pass granted," my fiancé Adam announces as he hands me a piece of paper.

"Huh?"

Adam used to drop one-liners constantly. For a beat I think his sense of humor is returning. But he's not wearing that silly smirk that I miss so much.

"Read it, Chloe. Marinate with it today and we'll talk it over tomorrow." He presses the joystick on his wheelchair and motors away from me, out of the bedroom, leaving me holding the piece of paper with the words *Hall Pass* on top, underlined.

He's not joking.

He actually handed me this piece of paper and said what he said before wheeling away like he'd handed me a menu and told me to pick what I want for dinner.

I force myself to swallow as I take in the list and ending paragraph.

<u>Hall Pass</u>
<u>Who</u>? Chloe and anyone I don't know.*
<u>What</u>? Just sex.
<u>Where</u>? Just not in our home.
<u>When</u>? When you need it.
<u>Why</u>? I don't want to lose you.

*I ask that it's never the same person twice. Nobody you've been with before, so no emotional attachments. We won't talk about it and discretion is sacrosanct.

He signed the bottom with his actual signature and today's date.

I'm rooted in place while reading the paper a second time with trembling hands. And now I'm angrily stuffing it into the nearest drawer, which happens to be the drawer of my nightstand.

This means it's beside my vibrator, which lies there innocently despite the fact that the vibrator was the catalyst for all this.

I slam the drawer and aggressively finish making the bed instead of doing what I want to do – follow Adam and pick a fight with him.

We haven't fought in over half a year. Because Adam was in a horrific accident and suffered a spinal cord injury, I tiptoe around, trying to make everything sunshine, flowers, and rainbows.

But the reality is that I'm not sure if our relationship will ever be anything close to what it was. And the piece of paper he just handed me makes me feel like a complete asshole.

It's been six months and three weeks since we've had sex. I made a wine-fueled mistake two nights ago by pulling out the vibrator while he was in bed beside me, and now here we are.

He didn't want to help by using it on me. He didn't want to watch me use it. Doesn't want anything to do with anything sexual. Doesn't want anything to do with any intimacy at all. Because things don't *work* for Adam the way they used to.

I asked questions about intimacy at a doctor's appointment a few months ago and was given a stack of literature that Adam refuses to read or discuss. He gave me the silent treatment for three days afterwards because my questions embarrassed him. While the doctor says he might eventually regain sensation, might gain full function (and if not, there might be things we can do to help), Adam won't talk about it.

Sperm collection and IVF could also be an option if we want to have kids. The doctor was very willing to answer my questions, was

Cheater

the one who encouraged me to ask questions. But Adam cut him off, so the doctor handed me the pamphlets.

And now he wants me to marinate on him giving me a license to cheat on him?

And I absolutely will not.

He gets himself from his chair into bed and I stop myself from remarking on how fast he's getting at what used to be much more of an ordeal. He's getting more and more independent. Moving here almost a month ago has helped significantly, since everything is calibrated for accessibility.

Since he dropped the hall pass into my hand a few hours ago while I was changing the sheets, I've been cleaning our spotless townhome needlessly while he's been in his office. He wanted to eat his dinner in there, too, telling me he wanted to work on his novel. Funny how the last two days he's so entrenched in writing that novel that he's been blocked on for as long as I've known him. I suspect it's a tool to avoid me.

Adam is a journalist, and the novel has been something he's talked about working on since we met a year and a half ago. He won't let me read it, won't tell me what it's about, and I don't know if it's dozens of pages, hundreds of pages, or a series of paragraphs because he won't even say.

He barely looked up when I put his plate down beside him, but he did switch screens so I couldn't see anything in the document he had on screen.

I ate my dinner over the sink, did the dishes, and watched some television alone while mindlessly scrolling on my phone after that. And now I'm on my side of the bed, he's on his.

"Goodnight," I say softly, but it sort of comes out like a question.

"Goodnight," he replies without turning over to kiss me.

The chasm between us has never been more gaping.

"Are you marinating?" Adam asks a while later.

He knows I'm not asleep.

I clear my throat.

"Well..." I start.

"Keep doing it. We'll talk tomorrow."

"I just-"

"Chloe, please. Do what I ask. Think about it. We'll talk tomorrow."

I bite my tongue. Literally. I'm not going to be able to fall asleep any time soon. I'm going to toss and turn because he put this out there and won't talk about it. And this is typical Adam.

It's not the first time I've gotten exasperated with Adam always being the one to decide when we do and don't get to talk about things. This isn't a new problem. He's been like this since the beginning. I used to point things like this out and he'd listen. Sometimes he'd compromise. Sometimes we'd agree to disagree. I know this is one of his character traits, but until six months ago, it never stopped me from standing up for myself.

Of course I've outwardly had the patience of a saint these last months as we've adjusted to a new reality. I've avoided things escalating into an argument at whatever cost.

I stare at his back. In less than ten minutes, his breathing evens out. He's always been able to fall asleep in a snap.

I, however, stare into the void between us for half the night. I do it missing how we were together before the accident. I miss the closeness. I miss the banter. I miss our life and I miss who I was, too.

But this isn't Adam's fault. The accident changed everything about our lives, who he is, and what life will be like going forward. And it's nobody's fault. It's just... life.

I've been unwavering in my commitment to finding the same happiness we'd have had if Adam's world hadn't blown apart when his car rolled multiple times after he lost control on an icy night after working late.

But tonight, staring at his back, I've allowed a small amount of

Cheater

bitterness to creep in. And now that I've done that, I'm worried that the dam might burst.

I set his coffee mug and bowl of oatmeal on the table and ask, "Fruit today or just plain?"

He doesn't answer straight away; he's got his eyes on his phone.

"Oh, I got more of those blueberries you like yesterday," I add, but he still doesn't look up.

"Hm?" he asks belatedly, then looks at his oatmeal and lifts his mug. "Oh, thanks."

"So, what's on tap today?" I ask. "Writing for money or pleasure?"

"If I ever get this novel done, maybe writing will become both."

"Making progress with–" I start to ask, but he cuts me off.

"I don't want to know about it when it happens, Chloe, but I just want to know you'll do it. Accept my offer."

"Adam," I say and massage my temples, deflating.

He sets his phone down. "Just tell me you'll accept my offer. Say it and then we can get on with our lives."

"Oh, am I allowed to address this now?" I fire back, impatiently.

He looks taken aback. This might be the first time I've been coarse with him since the accident.

His eyes search my face.

"You're angry with me," he says.

"I'm not accepting an offer to cheat on you, Adam. Give me a break." I spin to rinse the blueberries, turning the water on full blast over the pint.

"It's not cheating if we come to an agreement. If you follow the rules I laid out," he calls over. "I don't want anyone to know about it, but... can you turn that off and sit with me a second, Chloe?"

I grind my teeth.

"Chloe?" he prompts.

I slap the lever down and tuck a plate under the fruit pint so I can carry it to the table without getting water everywhere.

"It's not gonna happen, so might as well drop it." I dump some blueberries into my oatmeal and nudge the pint his way. "Anyway, you did well this morning," I change the subject the way he often does when he wants to shut a topic down. "Progress. You're getting more and more ripped, too." I plaster on what's probably a poor attempt at a smile and run my hand along his bicep.

He's got a great physique, always has. I've seen more definition in his upper body in the last few months because he's working so hard at physical therapy. Although he's worried about retaining muscle in his lower body, so maybe I shouldn't have remarked on it. Heat floods my face and I worry his mood will take a dark turn. Not that his current mood is good either, but Adam's dark moods are quiet. He doesn't yell. He doesn't pick fights. He just shuts down for long periods of time. And with all he's been through, I've been doing my best to keep things light so that if a dark mood descends, it's not my doing.

He moves back an inch to escape my touch. "Pick one friend to talk about it with if you must. Alannah maybe," He goes on like I didn't even speak. "Though she's a lot to take, she isn't a blabbermouth. But I don't want it widely known and make sure whoever you pick to tell doesn't bring it up around me. Ever."

I do my best to tamp my temper down while simultaneously feeling the twinge of physical rejection. Again.

He raises his blond eyebrows in challenge. Neither of us says anything for a long moment.

"Are you even here?" he asks.

"What?" I whisper.

He huffs like he's exasperated with me. And I'm shocked at his attitude.

"I'm trying to have a conversation with you," he states.

"Why do you think I'm *that* shallow? Because I pulled out a sex toy you think I want to have an affair? I already explained that I was trying to open the door for us. *Us*, Adam." I gesture between us. "In all that literature your doctor gave me–"

He cuts me off with another huff of exasperation. "And I already told you how I feel about... *that*. I told you long before the other night that I'll let you know if and when I might be ready and yet you're pushing the issue anyway, despite what I asked of you."

I blink hard and jolt in surprise.

He goes on, "That's why I've come up with the alternative. Because I'm tired of being pushed."

"Forget it," I whisper, my voice trembling. "I won't push you anymore."

He shakes his head sharply. "No. You can't un-ring a bell, Chloe. Obviously it's weighing on you. So you have my offer. Think about it."

God, this is mortifying.

When I pulled out my vibrator, I was looking to open the door to intimacy between us, not have him push me into other men's arms. I wanted him to participate. I wanted him to take over, or watch. Something. Anything. Anything but agitatedly asking me to take it to another room so he could sleep.

The moment felt like a record scratch. I didn't take it to another room. I turned it off and put it in the drawer before bursting into tears and apologizing. Explaining. He kept his back turned and didn't offer any sort of comfort, muttered for me to go to sleep, told me I was drunk.

I took a hot shower and then crawled back into bed. I called his name. I touched his back. He pretended to be asleep. The next day he told me without eye contact that he wanted to have breakfast in his home office and get an early start. He barely looked at me and we didn't speak all day until dinner time where he talked about his job and an article he was working on. He acted like nothing at all had happened, but I know I don't have a good poker face.

And then a day later, we're still not talking much, and he hands me the handwritten hall pass.

"I'm okay to wait," I insist. "Or I will be if you stop this silliness."

"I need your needs to be met, Chloe," he presses.

"Then maybe do something to help meet them," I mutter.

He jerks back like I've slapped him, then says, "I wish I could."

I shove my chair back as I fly up to standing, then I drop to the floor by his wheelchair, putting my forehead to his knee. "I don't mean it like *that*. You know I don't. Not that way. By letting intimacy back into our relationship. You can touch me. You can kiss me. You can hold me and use one of my toys on me. Or watch me and hold me afterwards. I could try touching you in places and see how you feel about it, too. The pamphlets had some suggestions for bringing intimacy back into our relationship."

He sighs like he's absolutely exasperated with me.

"Then we can fall asleep together cuddling afterwards, Adam, like we used to do. We don't even snuggle anymore. We don't even kiss other than a quick peck. I don't need the whole nine yards to be satisfied. I was just trying to open the door for something... not meaning for it to turn into... *this*. I just need some kind of intimacy between us. Just... a..."

I want to crawl into his lap, but of course I can't. I realize I'm leaning on a body part he can't even feel and he's making no move to offer comfort whatsoever, so I straighten up.

He's gripping the arms of his wheelchair. He's gritting his teeth.

Seeing me this upset, he doesn't even have it in him to stroke my hair or offer some words of comfort?

My belly pitches and I feel a chill creep over me slowly. Reality sinks in. And it doesn't feel nice.

I don't bother to finish my sentence.

Finally, he says, "I feel nothing from the waist down. I can't fake that, Chloe."

He's not willing to try. He's unwilling to try any level of intimacy with me but wants me to have it with someone else.

I'm crushed. I'm embarrassed. I don't know how to fix this.

We were happy. Okay, sex wasn't as often as I'd have liked and it

Cheater

was kind of predictable, but we had intimacy. Talking quietly in the dark about our future with warm, naked bodies pressed together. Affection. Snuggling. And he looked at me with lust or at least appreciation when he saw me undress or wearing something new. All that's gone now, and after six months of hoping it would come back to some degree, any degree, I try something to stir things up and wind up hurting him.

I feel like garbage.

Selfish garbage.

And also hopeless. Because he's not even reaching for me right now.

I've done my best to be a supportive partner to him, to be the partner I'd want if I were in his position.

I slept in a chair at the hospital, not leaving for days. I've been to every specialist appointment. I've been at his side constantly. I took a leave of absence from work and my job was more than accommodating to ensure I could be here to look after him by letting me take months off without canceling my medical benefits, which he's on as well, and which were crucial for Adam's recovery. They've been very flexible about my hours and workload.

We cleared both of our savings out to buy this modern townhome because his mom knew the realtor who told her about it – that it was built for someone in a wheelchair who passed away before the closing date. It's nothing I thought I'd ever live in, all modern and sterile feeling with not much of a yard, but it works well for Adam's mobility issues with wide doorways, an accessible kitchen and bathroom, with everything on one level.

I do my very best to be here with empathy and support, along with hope in my heart. Hoping I've been a comfort to him through the worst days of his life. Because they've been some of the worst days of my life, too, tied with when I lost my brother in my teens. I've done my best to hide the pain and strain. I've been more than patient when he wasn't easy to be around. Forgiving when he got frustrated and took those frustrations out on everyone around him. I've been willing to do whatever I can do to be a supportive partner to him. Because that's what you do. That's what I'd hope for if the roles were reversed.

After six months in this new reality, I can't help but count that I haven't had more than a peck on the mouth from him even after my hinting at making out a while ago, which was met with a chilly eyeroll. As much as it hurt, I've tried to be understanding, to let it go.

All these pamphlets they gave me talked about how he might have some sensation return, that we should experiment and not get discouraged. That medical aids and even procedures exist that could help if he doesn't get to a point where he can get an erection on his own.

I've been trying so hard not to be selfish, but I guess I've failed. Maybe the idea of me getting sexual pleasure when it isn't in the cards for him is just unthinkable, but it's about so much more than sex.

"Don't look at me like that, Chloe. You don't know what it's like."

"I know that," I say softly. "Sorry."

And I've apologized for not being able to see things from his perspective on a variety of issues at least a hundred times.

"I didn't intend to make you feel bad, Adam. I wasn't trying to be cruel. I was trying to open the door for us to try things. I didn't mean to insult you."

He's been in counseling since almost the beginning. I went to a session with him last week at his counselor's request. She point-blank asked if my needs are being met in our relationship. I stammered something to the effect of being more worried about Adam at the moment than myself and she asked if I wanted to see her separately, if I wanted to explore my feelings, since I'm allowed to have them. She asked me if I've become someone I'm *not* in order to support Adam in his recovery. Adam snapped at her stating I'm who I always was, that I've always been supportive and caring and giving in our relationship. She let it go, but handed me her card at the end of the session in case I wanted to explore my feelings.

Cheater

And Adam has been almost edgy ever since. It's like he didn't even consider my feelings until she brought up the fact that I must have some, too. That I might have emotions around the fact that our lives are now different than what I'd signed up for. He's been so focused on his recovery, on his new reality that I don't think he's had a chance to think about me. And admittedly, her words probably, at least in part, spurred action from me with the vibrator the other night.

I haven't agreed to attend counseling on my own yet. Maybe I should.

Maybe it was partly her words, but also, maybe the fourth glass of wine the other night helped me grow bold. And now that vibrator sits in the drawer beside a piece of paper that he thinks will solve everything.

I have a secret, anonymous sexual fantasy blog I called *My Sexy Bucket List* that I've had for almost a decade, though I hadn't logged into it since Adam and I got serious, but I thought about that blog after the therapy appointment and re-read some of my old posts in my wine-addled state. The wine and reading my old posts centered around sexual fantasies I used to have were fuel for this firestorm, I guess.

"The hall pass will get you what *you* want," he says.

"Adam..."

"And it'll take the pressure off me."

"I don't mean to pressure you," I say, staring at my feet.

"Nobody does, Chloe."

Our eyes meet as he continues, "But everyone does. My parents. My physical therapist. My shrink. My editors. You. Friends and relatives. Everyone's pushing me in whatever way, asking questions, or disappointed I'm not hitting their expectations and I'm tired of being pushed. Of being prodded. Having no privacy or personal space. And not having the ability to go for a run or even a walk to clear my head like I used to do. I've got too many people pushing, and I don't need any more of it, especially not sexual pressure from you when I don't... when I can't..." He lets that hang.

"I'm sorry," I whisper. "Forget it. All of it. I won't..."

"Stop being a fuckin' martyr!" he shouts, physically startling me. "God, just stop." He rakes his hands through his hair with frustration.

I stare, shocked as he blows out an exasperated breath before continuing much more calmly with, "You've always had a higher sex drive than me. Frankly, you were hard to keep up with. Now I have no hope in hell of keeping pace. Accept my offer. This way, you get what you need."

"You're making me feel like a sexual deviant," I whisper hoarsely.

He rolls his eyes.

And this feels like insult added to injury. I say nothing for a minute, before I manage to rasp out brokenly, "What I need so much more than orgasms is intimacy with the man I love."

"Chloe..."

"Connection," I add, voice getting stronger. "I need to know that I matter to you as much as you matter to me."

"Are you for real right now? Like I haven't had enough to deal with. Making it about you?" he mutters, looking at me with disappointment, "When my life won't ever be the same."

"You've had too much to deal with, I agree, more than anyone should have to deal with. All I need to keep me going is some intimacy. I need to occasionally be kissed in a way that doesn't leave me feeling like I'm your cousin. I need to know you might someday read those pamphlets and see that there might be options to help. Things worth exploring. For intimacy. For us to have children down the road, to–"

"Try it my way," he says, "See if it'll fill the gaps in our relationship for you." He shrugs.

I frown.

This feels blasé in a way that's frankly infuriating.

"Try an affair?" I croak out.

He shakes his head. "Not an affair. Hall pass. An affair would be behind my back, against the rules of our relationship. This is like a backscratcher. Try it before we get married. See if it would be enough."

"I love you, Adam. I..." How do I express that what I need is much more than to simply *scratch an itch*.

"I know that. I love you, too. And that's why I'm looking for a solution. I don't want to lose you. This takes the pressure off me and gives you what you need. I don't know when or even if I'll ever be ready to be anything in the realm of intimate when I can't... I... I just don't have those urges and I'm not about faking it. You know that about me, don't you? I'm not fake."

I feel like I've swallowed broken glass.

"I want you going into our marriage prepared for what our future will be like, Chloe. It's not all about sex is it? Think about this."

I swallow down the jagged shards, reality bleak before me. No intimacy, ever? Nothing? Living like roommates? The words *why bother* bounce around softly, but I fear the volume might suddenly get deafening. And I hate what that might say about me. I've had to fake plenty of things to try to be supportive to him. Fake smiles. Faking that I'm okay. For him. But is this what life is from here on out?

"Please," he whispers. "I need you to think about it. Sweetie, you've been a saint throughout all of this. Thank you for that. I don't know what I would've done without you. But now that we're moving forward and life is hitting a new rhythm, we have to be realistic about what I can and can't give you. I'm trying to think about you instead of just me here."

Silence stretches between us.

"Chloe, please."

"I just need some hope, Adam. Some..."

He shakes his head. "I'm not gonna bullshit. If I say yeah, gimme six months, it'll feel like more pressure on me. A ticking clock. I need to know if you can live with things *this* way. Not saying things will be like this forever, also not saying I can give you any more than what we have right now. Because I just don't know. I'm taking it minute by minute because that's all I can do. That's how I can keep myself from thinking dark thoughts about offing myself."

I jolt in shock.

He keeps talking like he didn't just drop a bomb, "What I *can* do is be okay with you getting what you need if it means you and me are still together, still planning to move forward and be a couple. I'm working on being okay, Chloe. I'm not there yet, but I need to work on it without pressure from the person who means the most to me."

"I'll... think," I manage to say, chin wobbling.

All I want right now is for him to open his arms so I can sink into him. I want him to tell me everything is going to be okay, that we'll figure this out. I want to tell him those things too. That as long as we have one another and as long as we're open with one another, it'll all be okay.

But Adam doesn't say any of these things. And neither will I. Just a few of the right words would go a long way right now for me, but I know I won't hear them so there's no point in saying anything else. He classifies himself as a realist. And right now he's also being a pessimist, which shouldn't surprise me after the hand he's been dealt. But I can't help but feel devastated when instead of putting his arms around me, he turns his focus to his phone as he dumps the rest of the pint of blueberries into his oatmeal bowl.

I guess this is his way of dealing with things. Of keeping the dark thoughts at bay.

I'd describe Adam *before the accident* as pragmatic, practical, but still full of life, love, and affection. We were always doing things – biking, hiking, adventuring. I used to tell him he should've been a life coach. He was that much of a motivator.

I'm starting to think I don't know who *this* Adam is anymore. That the Adam I love is gone.

And it's not his fault.

Three Weeks Later

For the first time since Adam's accident, I've got a night out planned. A few friends are celebrating my best friend Alannah getting a fat bonus and landing a big account at her job. We're hitting a popular nightclub on the ground floor of her office building.

I hesitated to go, but Adam insisted, reminding me that life needs to move forward, and that Alannah and I are always there for one another's milestones.

He's right. She's been my bestie since we were in fourth grade. We call one another 'breast friends' because we were the best of friends since just before we both grew breasts. I grew them first; Alannah was jealous. But I stopped growing at an average sized bra, she kept going until she hit the territory where people wonder if her boobs are surgically enhanced.

"Are you sure you don't want to come?" I ask Adam, who is lingering in the doorway of the bathroom while I get ready.

"I'm good. And don't worry about me tonight. Have a good time. Don't be tempted to even check in."

"I'll set things up for you for the morning before I go."

"Let me take care of myself. I'm perfectly capable."

"I know you are," I whisper and try to smile, but it's got me feeling a little emotional, so I hold my breath while I do it.

Frankly, he didn't need to push too hard because I've been thinking about a night out to let my hair down for a while.

He insisted I take a cab and stay over at her place.

If I'm honest, I'm relieved he doesn't want to come. But I also feel guilty about these feelings.

"How do I look?" I ask, capping my lipstick and turning to face him.

"Good," he says. "You always do. Uh... so?" he keeps going. "Have you thought about it?"

"Thought about what?" I ask even though I know exactly what he's about to bring up.

My face goes hot.

"Chloe," he chastises.

The hall pass has been the elephant in the room with us for the three weeks that have passed since he passed me the piece of paper.

A few days ago, I tried to deepen a goodnight kiss and he turned away. It made me angry, and I know I made that known in a passive aggressive way, which isn't very mature of me, so I forced myself to bury my emotions after a day of sulking.

While communication has been a no-go, he's trying to do more things on his own. This has me worried that he's preparing for an eventuality without me in it, trying to not need me because he thinks I won't be able to get over the intimacy issue.

"I mean it, Chloe. I don't want to lose you," he says. "And I feel like I might."

"You won't," I assure.

"If you don't do this, I feel like I *will*. I see it in your eyes. I feel it, Chloe."

I want to scream. I want to scream for him to show me just an ounce of what we used to have. I don't need his dick to work. I need him to look at me like I'm more than the roommate who cooks and cleans and does his laundry for him. Who drives him to PT appointments and answers the door to the lady who clips his toenails. I need eye contact. I need to not feel invisible around here.

Cheater

I don't know what it's like to be told you'll never walk again; I can't possibly put myself in his place. Lord knows I've tried. I've tried to be patient, to hope for patience with the intimacy stuff.

"Oh, so you think I'm *that* superficial?"

It sounds like a lighthearted jab, but it's not. I'm hurting right now. Even as I tell myself I need to get over it, give him more time, try harder, I'm deep-down terrified that time won't do a thing. That I need to become a-sexual and live like roommates. And I've been feeling like that's the only solution, that's what I need to try to do. Because what's the alternative?

The alternative is to be the type of person who would leave her fiancé after he had a life-altering accident. That's not who I want to be as a human. And I don't have to be that way. I feel perfectly capable of seeing the glass as half-full if he gave me a bit more than what he's giving me. And then of course I feel guilty because it's not fair for me to put timelines on his emotional recovery.

"It's not about being superficial," he denies, "It's about your needs being met. It's about me realizing I can't meet them myself, but I can make it so that you still have a full life. So that you won't cry yourself to sleep because I can't..." His voice cracks.

He clears his throat.

My heart swells with love for him. "I don't need that. I need you. I need intimacy way more than intercourse, Adam."

I take a step forward, but he lifts his hand to halt me.

I pull a handful of hair out of my hairbrush and whip it into the toilet before flushing it and pushing the lid down so I can sit.

Tell me to come to you. Hold me on your lap and whisper into my ear that we're going to be fine. That you love me. That you still want me. That we'll find a way to have the life we want, to find something new since we can't have what we were supposed to have.

"And I'm not capable of giving it to you at this point, Chloe. It's all still... new."

"I know," I whisper. "I'm so sorry to make you feel like this. I don't mean–"

He shakes his head sharply, cutting me off. "You've stood by me. You've been here in every way I've needed you. I need to return that favor by giving you my blessing to make sure your needs are met."

I don't know how to respond to this. We stare in silence for a long moment. It's a longer eye lock than we've shared in a long, long time. I see his pain. His frustration. It's etched into him. I've seen it all along and felt for him. But maybe Adam is finally taking a closer look at me. Is that what this is? Am I being unfair by resisting here?

"You hovering in the doorway of the bathroom while I'm getting ready to go to a bar suggests you want me to do this *tonight*, which would be breaking one of your rules because you'd know about it."

"Tonight might bring an opportunity. If you talk to someone... if you meet someone it might work with, you know..."

"I don't know. That's just not me."

"Get Alannah's take."

"This is so fucking weird," I mutter.

"So, you're thinking about it."

I sigh. "I told you I would think about it. And I have. I just don't know it's something I can even do."

"You've got my permission to do this, Chloe."

"Adam..."

"If I hadn't lost use of my legs, I'd never push you toward other men. I'm trying to do what I think we need here so we can move forward, to make sure you marry me because you can see a life with me, a life that includes you having everything you want. Even if I'm not the one who can give it all to you, I won't be the man in the way of you getting it. Does that make sense?"

"And what about you?"

"If it starts working again, that's another story."

I straighten up. "That's the thing... I can totally wait. If you'll consider reading those pamphlets or let me read them to you, there's even an implant that–"

"Sweetie," he says dolefully. "I read the pamphlets a long time ago. It was like alphabet soup. Sex is the last thing on my mind. I'm trying to cope with so many other things, it's not remotely on my radar, other than talking this out with you to make sure you're okay. Our relationship is about a lot of things and as time goes on, sex becomes less and less important in a relationship, you know? This is the only stumbling block for us, but there's a solution. My hall pass."

I do my best to clear my expression. "I've thought about it but I'm still not sure I'm even capable of a hookup."

"It's just sex. It doesn't have to mean anything. You and I still have everything we have. We still mean everything we mean to one another. Then before we walk down the aisle... I mean, before *you* walk down that aisle, you'll know if it's something you can truly do. Because you won't be feeling like you're walking the plank." He swallows, looking emotional. "I'm working on getting back to who I am, but it's taking time. I don't know if that part of me is gone forever, and I need you to be prepared that it might be. But that doesn't mean you can't get what you need somewhere else."

There's no point in me repeating my speech about only needing intimacy from him, although if I had that, I really do think it would be enough to last me for a while. Sex is an important part of a relationship. Clearly more important to me than to him. But he doesn't seem to understand that I want closeness and connection the most.

"Our life together is about so much more than sex," he says. "We can still have an amazing life together, can't we?"

I nod, biting my lip.

"Think about using the hall pass, Chloe."

"I'll think about it," I agree. "But clearly you'll need to know if I've done it or not by the way you're behaving and that doesn't fit with what you wrote."

"I amend the hall pass, then. I guess I'll need to know once and just once. And maybe you can take up a couple of your old hobbies again, so you're not home so much. That way it won't stand out blatantly if you decide to take me up on my offer on a regular basis."

He gives me a tight smile, but emotion flares in his eyes. He's such a good guy. He's been through so much.

I've given up a social life and all my *me-time* to be his caregiver. He wants me to start having a life again. Will me moving forward with my life help him do the same? Maybe we're in a rut together.

But I can't help but wish he'd understand it's about more than sex. He just doesn't seem to get it.

"Before you walk down that aisle to a man in a wheelchair who can't give you everything you need, be sure that what I *can* give you is enough."

We can't hike a mountain the way we used to do. But maybe we can get an RV and spend time outdoors in accessible locations. Campfires. Camping. Fishing. Boating. Kids together with medical intervention. Board games. Making memories. And maybe he'll get into the groove and decide he *does* want to explore options for intimacy.

But what if me being intimate with someone else changes everything for him? What if it changes me in his eyes?

"What if I do this and you can't live with it?" I ask. "What if you can't look at me the same way because I'm having sex with other people?"

He gives me a sad smile and I know now that this has already crossed his mind. "Better that we know now, don't you think? A lot of people open up their relationship, Chloe. Some make it past that, and some don't. I'm really hoping we do."

The emotion in me wells up to near overflowing.

This is a test for both of us. Me, to see if a life with him without sex from him is enough for me. And him, to see if he can spend his life with me knowing I'm having sex with other men.

If I agree to do this, even if I find I'm okay with it, Adam might not be.

Everything could change. Whether I take him up on this offer or not.

3
Chloe

"He's right," Alannah says, after flashing a smile at the bartender who hands us each another drink. "Thanks, Alex."

"My pleasure, Alannah," he replies, flirtation clear. He instantly strikes me as the type that would flirt with anyone and everyone to boost his chances of getting a better tip.

Her eyes bounce back to me. "Best to find out now if you can live with life as it is before you put on the one and only white dress."

I give her a pointed look as I stir my drink with the plastic stir stick.

"You said you only wanted to wear the dress once. No, not said it, *swore it*."

She's right about that.

"Besides," she continues, "You were worried about a boring-ever-after with Adam. This solves that problem. You've got a free pass to get all the kinky sex you want. Bright side?"

I just about choke on my tongue as I shoot her my best effort at an evil eye.

The fact that I bitched about our sex life being repetitive and vanilla one time, not long after we got engaged, feels like forever ago. Things were so much simpler then.

"I certainly did not refer to my relationship as a *boring ever after*."

"It's what you meant, though," she says, then takes a long sip.

I've just spewed a long monologue at her with all my feelings about Adam's hall pass idea, including telling her about the vibrator incident and the crying myself to sleep, and him turning his head away when I tried to slip him the tongue. How I can't even make a dirty joke around him these days. How I feel like a sexual deviant. How he barely even looks at me and when he does, I know he doesn't *see* me. I told her I look at him sometimes and get a big burst of affection, but I'm afraid to show it to him and get rejected. I'm feeling like the maid more than the fiancée.

As mortifying as it was to spill all that, I feel a little lighter, like I needed to get it out. Alannah has always been here for me, but I've been clammed up about life in general since the last several months have been so overwhelming.

"And it'll let him know if he can handle it, too," she adds.

"Yep. If I actually did go through with it, which I'm still not sure I could ever... it might be okay with me, but it might not actually be okay with him after all."

"Mm," she agrees, taking a sip.

"I mean... I don't even think I can," I whisper. "That's not me. A hall pass. An unemotional hookup. Like... what?" I laugh.

She doesn't laugh. "This could be a good place to sample your potential future," she jerks her chin toward the space at large.

I scrunch up my nose.

She wiggles her blonde eyebrows.

"Not tonight," I say.

"Tonight," she corrects. "It's perfect. He's not expecting you home tonight, so..."

I scoff. "As if I can go from planning a lifetime of commitment to one man, a man who had his whole life blown apart, to fucking a stranger I meet in a bar just like that?" I snap my fingers. "I know it's too much to ask that he factor intimacy into our relationship with all he's gone through, but I can't help but wish–"

"That he'd still wanna rock your world? Of course. And it's not too much to ask, Chlo. This didn't *just* happen. It's been over half a year."

Cheater

"I don't just need mind-blowing orgasms, Lan. I can get by for now with hand-holding and cuddling. Forehead kisses and for him to look at me like... like I'm more than his caregiver. He's needed my help so much that I know it's changed the way he looks at me."

"You poor thing. Hate to say this, but Chloe... maybe it's better if you do this and he decides he can't live with it. Or if you do this and you decide it's time to move on. On your own."

"Don't say that," I breathe. "I love him. He didn't deserve this. And he doesn't deserve me abandoning him. Seven months isn't that long in the grand scheme of things."

"Babe." She grabs my hand and squeezes it. "No, he didn't deserve to lose the use of his legs. But, you're loyal to a fault. Not a lot of girls would even hesitate before taking him up on his offer. In fact, a lot of girls might not have stuck around. I don't know if I could've."

"He's Adam," I say, feeling protective over him. "Everyone loves him."

He's a good guy. He's the first person to help someone in a crisis. He's funny and fun to be around. He's competitive in a sporty way and the type to encourage others to do their best. A cheerleader and motivator. He was a good boyfriend before all this pulled the rug out from under him. He didn't deserve this. He doesn't deserve any of it. I'm about to choke up. I push it away.

"And," I add, "His penis isn't a sex organ anymore. He has to catheterize multiple times a day. He doesn't have any sensation in it, doesn't have any urges whatsoever. He does a daily routine to train his bowels to empty at the same time every day, but he has to wear an adult diaper, Alannah, just in case."

She winces. "I hadn't thought about that."

Everything below the waist is a chore for him. Moving his body without controlling his lower extremities. He even had to deal with colostomy bags in the early days of recovery.

"I've been feeling so guilty for the past three weeks about pulling out that vibrator. I'm such an asshole."

"You're not," she tells me, jiggling my hand. "It's been hundreds of days, Chlo. Your life has been on hold. You've lived and breathed for him for all this time. And there's nothing wrong with wanting handholding and forehead kisses and to be told your ass looks great today, which it does."

I roll my eyes.

"We both know you, though. You really want him to kiss your forehead just ahead of giving you a hand necklace while railing you against a wall. Or... what was that fantasy you told everyone about that night at the campground? The 24/7 total power dynamic for a weekend thing? And he never did any of that. He looked like he wanted to clutch his pearls when you suggested it. He's Mister Vanilla. No, more like Mister baked potato without butter, salt, or pepper. Now's your chance to get yourself a *loaded* baked potato. Sour cream. Cheese. Bacon and chives. All kinds of butter. The works. I know... join that hookup app for kinky people."

I snicker derisively. Adam talking about being unable to keep up with me was sobering. And I know he was embarrassed when we went on that group camping trip last summer and played drunken truth or dare around the fire. He muttered, "Grow up, Chloe" instead of getting a hard-on and whisking me to our tent to dominate me. The next day he acted like nothing had happened but from then on, he seemed to get bitchy if I went beyond one or two drinks at a party, occasionally even asking me to remember to have some decorum.

"Imagine what'll happen to you in ten years when you hit forty and your sexual peak? Imagine having no ability to do anything about it other than dream about it, fantasize about it while being afraid to even do something about it because you don't want him to hear the buzzing?" Alannah raises her eyebrows pointedly.

I shake my head. "It's too soon. I shouldn't have done what I did. I was a little tipsy and I'd been reading something sexy that I wrote years ago on an old fantasy blog of mine, and it was an asshole move. Thinking he'd reach over and want anything to do with helping me come when his parts don't work anymore? It was selfish. And probably insulting."

Cheater

"Stop it," she hisses. "Don't do that. You're not an asshole and it's not selfish to try to move forward with life after half a year, Chlo."

I sigh.

"You are not an asshole," she repeats firmly. "His fingers aren't paralyzed. His tongue still works, right? He's working again. He's working out. He's hanging with his boys. Playing fantasy football and telling jokes and dropping F-bombs on their Discord chat while playing video games with his buddies."

"How do you know that?" Adam almost never drops F-bombs around me. He thinks it's rude to swear around women. I asked him to dirty-talk when we first got together, and he told me it would be demeaning to me.

She shrugs. "I crashed at Craig's the other night. Woke up at three in the morning and heard them talking on chat in the other room. He sounded like *old Adam*."

I gasp. And she knows it's because she spent another night with Craig, Adam's best friend.

"Just a booty call." She waves her hand.

Yeah. Booty call number five if I haven't lost count.

"Could it be? Is my breast friend in danger of finding herself in a situationship?"

"Hush; this is about you. Adam is living life in his new life. It's absolutely fair to expect forehead kisses and clit kisses and whatever else he can give you to make sure you're fulfilled."

I palm my face in exasperation. "Inside voice!"

"Sister, you've been his live-in nursemaid and chauffeur for months. Asking for more than a peck on the cheek from the man you're planning to marry doesn't make you an asshole. He's given you permission to get your freak on, so now... let's get this show on the road. You're getting laid tonight."

"No way. Shush."

"Yes way," she declares. "I can see you shaved your legs today. But what about your pits? Your hoo-ha?"

"I've kept up on the lady-scaping. Out of pure hope. All along. Nothing to do with the hall pass."

"So, no baby unicorns need to die today. It's been a genocide lately thanks to your dry spell. Let's save some lives."

"Stop it. You're not the boss of my vagina," I say, too loud, too.

She tries to fight off laughter while she sips her drink. I take a gulp of mine, followed by another gulp.

And now we're exchanging looks loaded with feelings.

I look away so we don't dissolve into puddles of emotion. If I shed a tear, she'll bawl. If she does, I'll bawl. It's better we avoid eye contact for a minute.

"Seriously," I go on, staring at my nails. "I just wanna celebrate with you tonight. Enjoy having my hair down for the first time in months. Have a girls' weekend with zero stress. I'll think on that hall pass stuff later. I just wanted to vent about it a bit; not act on it."

"Well, I'm here any time. Sounds like you've been holding back on the venting, and you know that's my job as your breast friend to be that ear, right?"

"Right. Ditto," I say and give her a look, which she immediately reads.

"Craig's just a booty call. He has a big dick and he doesn't have any expectations, so it works."

I raise my hands. "Fine, I'll drop it."

"And I'll drop it about the hall pass too. But before I do... if you meet a hall pass contender tonight you could use it, couldn't you?"

I massage my temples and sigh with exasperation.

She gets right up in my face. "Answer?"

"Technically, yes. And he wants me to. He gave me a list of guidelines. But I won't. It's too soon. I'm still processing. Personal bubble, sister."

She takes a step back and smiles. "And what are these guidelines?"

"He doesn't wanna know about it. Other than knowing I'm going to accept the offer, so it takes the pressure off him."

Cheater

"Which puts pressure on you. Man, he pisses me off sometimes."

I freeze.

"Forget it," she waves her hand. "Tell me the rest."

"Um... he doesn't want it to be anyone he knows. I also can't use the hall pass on the same person twice."

"He doesn't want emotional attachments to happen," Alannah surmises. "Makes sense."

"And he doesn't want it happening in our house, either."

"Reasonable."

"Can we drop it? I wanna have fun tonight and celebrate with you. I didn't mean to hijack your celebration. I'd like to forget about all my drama for the night. Let's let the rest of the night be about Alannah who just got well-deserved recognition in a male-dominated environment. Alannah, who I'm so, so proud of."

"No problem." She waves her hand. "I'm more than happy to be the center of the universe. But just sayin'... if you do happen to meet someone with Hall Pass potential tonight, even better."

I roll my eyes. "Not happening tonight."

She aims a big, beaming smile at me and then puts her hand on mine with affection. "Ready to dance?"

"*So* ready."

"One more thing." She leans in closer.

"What?" I ask.

She smiles, looking me right in the eyes, not blinking as I feel her grip my engagement ring and pull it off my finger.

"Alannah," I mumble.

"Just in case," she says, and then she puts my engagement ring onto her finger and extends her hand, admiring it.

My eyes roll.

"You never know. You might at least collect a phone number or two. Right? So, let's go dance and see if there's any filet mignon on offer."

This place *does* feel like a meat market.

She and I slipped away from our group to the quieter section at the long, sleek, sparsely populated bar ten or fifteen minutes ago, but the place is filling up, the lighting has gone dimmer, and the thump of the bass is rising in volume and intensity.

I'm ready to succumb to that bass, realizing just how much I need a carefree night. To laugh with my friends, getting lost in a world of fun instead of feeling trapped by a bleak reality ridden with guilt and uncertainty. I down the rest of my drink before I hop off the bar stool.

I'm gonna have fun tonight. Celebrate life with my friends. Tonight, I'm just Chloe.

Not Adam's caregiver.

Alannah reads my smile, gives me one back, and tugs on my hand, shaking her ass all the way to the dance floor. Our three friends are already there, dancing together.

Alannah, though perpetually single, is the default person I would talk to about this. She adores Adam. She's proven again tonight that she's a great sounding board. Though I've been clammed up about all of it until now, she's been here for me throughout this ordeal. Making me go to mani-pedi appointments so that I have some self-care time, too. Calling me or showing up when she hasn't heard from me. Bringing me a fancy coffee. Dropping a care package on the doorstep when she knows I'm overwhelmed.

And another good thing about Alannah – she tells it like it is.

She won't hold back the truth if you get a bad haircut. She'll commiserate with you, fake-plotting the demise of the bitch that cut your hair. She'll then buy you hair clips and headbands or help you find a style for it so you can live with it while it grows out.

If you ask her if your jeans make your ass look big, she won't lie about that either. Be ready for the truth when you ask Alannah Fisher for an opinion.

But her friendship is loving and supportive, too. If she can't stand the guy you're dating, she'll tell you the truth in a gentle way you can stomach.

If you're being a whiny bitch for too long, you'll know it. Everyone needs a friend like Alannah. She's ambitious, caring, moti-

Cheater

vating, and honest. She's excelling in her field as a professional arbitrator as well as a social media influencer on the side with her "single, successful, and sultry" makeup tutorials channel. She's great at motivating people to go after what they want in life.

I'm stoked that her career is accelerating. She's worked her butt off for it and I'm glad I came out with her to celebrate her achievements tonight. To reciprocate friendship and be here for her.

Also, to let my hair down a little. Move my body a lot. Let myself feel a little sexy with my extra effort on my makeup, taking down my dark, shoulder-length hair that's been in a ponytail or messy bun pretty much every day since Adam's accident. Dusting off my curling iron and using it. Wearing a cute little black dress that I bought just before the accident and hadn't had a chance to wear.

Of course Alannah thinks I should take Adam up on his offer. He had to know she would when he suggested I talk to her about it. She's not the type to turn down a license for some fun.

I don't know if I *will* do it. I don't know if I *can*. If it'd be fun for me or if I'd feel like a cheating whore. If I did use it, how could I stand at an altar making promises to Adam in front of everyone we love knowing I'm lying my face off about promising fidelity?

I *am* the monogamous type. I don't know if I can have sex with someone without feelings involved; I've never tried. I'm thirty years old and I've had sex with a grand total of six men in my life, including Adam. Feelings were involved each time.

All I know tonight is that the cocktails are tasting good, I don't have to drive home, and I don't have to even *go* home. I don't have to let Adam see me get sloshed. I don't have to hold back so that he doesn't see me get what he calls "sloppy drunk".

Tonight is a night with no decorum required.

I learned the hard way in our early days of dating that instead of thinking it's adorable, looking after me, taking the opportunity for extra-dirty sex like his predecessor did, he gets disappointed in me. Embarrassed. I get lectures about it. My own dad never lectured me about booze the way Adam does. My parents don't really lecture me period. They've always let me go my own way. That's a nice way of saying I was always pretty invisible to them.

But Adam is Mister Responsible. Mister Decorum. He messaged me after I left to suggest I stay at Alannah's all weekend. And I suspect it's because he hopes she'll talk me into things tonight and then I'll do something about it tomorrow night. Since he won't even see me until Sunday, I can get as loopy as I want tonight.

And I've decided I will.

No, it's definitely not in me to just have sex with a stranger tonight, to switch gears from being in a committed relationship, spending eighteen months with one man, almost a year engaged to him, and seven months caring for him after his whole life got swept up into a tornado to simply falling onto a stranger's dick my first time on a girls' night out. *Not* who I am.

But having a bit of freedom, having no responsibility for the next forty-eight hours? Having the option to just be me? It sounds pretty damn good.

4

Derek Steele

Although my eyes are on the security feed, my veins are being flooded by an adrenalin surge.

I track the movement of her hips, then watch the hypnotic sway of the curtain of thick, shiny dark hair that frames her face in fat curls and dances across her shoulders with every movement. My finger flexes, causing the screen to zoom in on her face. Her thick-lashed eyes are closed and it's as if she's part of the music as her friends surround her while she moves to the beat.

Everything falls away but her. Sounds. Images. She's all I see right now.

I want to reach through the monitor and touch her. I want to know the sound of those silver rings looped through the series of straps above her sweet tits on her black dress, as they clang on my bedroom floor.

Something has woken up in me. Something I didn't know had been there – dormant, perhaps.

I don't get fixated on females; I get focused on goals. But something about her has me intrigued enough to want to know more. To want to be the one she chooses to use that hall pass on.

I've learned quite a few things about her in short order. That conversation I overheard paints a vivid bird's eye view of who she is. I know why this is the first time in half a year she's dancing. How this is the first time she's *let her hair down*, using her words. And the way she said it, she loves to dance and let loose and has denied herself the pleasure. She announced she'll dance like nobody's watching tonight. But I'm watching. And the only reason I'm about to tear my eyes away is because I'll be going out there and starting something. Starting something I suspect won't move at the pace I want.

But I'll do the calculations and decide the best way to get to my end goal. As soon as I know what that goal is. All I know right now is that I'm interested. Very.

Her eyes open. They're light blue. So light they're like ice on the monitor. I'm looking forward to gazing directly into them with my dark brown ones. Seeing how she responds to me. My vibe. My voice. My touch. No eye contact from her fiancé? Tired of feeling invisible? Well, I see you, Chloe. And I like what I'm seeing.

I don't generally fuck around with club patrons. In fact, I haven't felt the need to fuck around with anyone in a while. I wouldn't likely linger on her this long and from multiple camera angles if not for the conversation I overheard between her and the blonde who works upstairs.

I've long believed things don't happen by accident. When an opportunity presents itself, I assess moving pieces around me and determine whether they're true opportunities or warnings. And then I'll act, depending on the situation.

She's the reason I'm here tonight, now, watching, readying myself. She doesn't know it yet, but I'm about to react to this opportunity. To insert myself to become her new reason.

Looks like she's a reason to stay in Columbus a while.

This club is on the ground floor of one of the larger office buildings in the city. It's one of the many buildings my family owns. I own nightclubs here in Columbus along with Cincinnati and Cleveland. I divide my time between the three cities, preferring Cleveland as my home base. And that's mostly because my family leaves me alone there. They insert themselves into my life far more often when I'm here.

My clubs are upscale, trendy. And they stay that way because I'm

Cheater

proactive. I calculate and then I act. I operate in business districts and near the airport of each city and my clubs are also wired for surveillance. Because the conversations picked up in bars in business districts, blue collar areas, as well as airports can be valuable for a variety of reasons, none of those reasons wholesome.

Surveillance is why I know as much as I do about Chloe. It's not usually me that's listening and we don't generally listen live, but tonight was different. A staffing issue required my personal attention, so I tuned in to the bar area in order to pay attention to a bartender who's been stealing from me and my patrons.

I had grounds to fire him within twenty minutes of paying attention. He's fucking with the drinks and skimming cash as well as ripping off our customers. Watering down booze for some, switching shelves without charging accordingly, and diluting drinks to grog once he figures a patron is half in the bag while pocketing the difference. I've got audio and visual proof the greedy fuck is even screwing some customers for change. Someone half-snapped or distracted hands him a bill and he gives change for a smaller one. Saw him do it twice tonight. Once, it was missed, the second time the customer looked embarrassed when she called him out on it, probably feeling like she appeared cheap. He played it off like an innocent blunder.

I can fire him with cause. When I overheard the accusation from another staff member, I looked over the background check we ran on him when he was hired. He graduated high school in the same class as my brother Ash. This means he would know better than to fuck with anyone in my family. As my father always says, *steal from a Steele and you'll lose much more than you took.*

I take theft personally.

I was just about done paying attention to the bar when the conversation happening between the brunette my eyes are on now and her friend piqued my interest. This girl was pouring the depths of her longing out to the busty blonde from upstairs who slipped me her number about a year ago. I tossed the number. A woman making a move on me isn't something I find sexy, and I prefer not to shit where I eat.

I clued into the conversation by the tragedy and the longing, getting fully snagged when it turned sexual. And now my eyes have been on the brunette, Chloe, on the dancefloor for the length of three songs.

My phone rings, pulling my focus away.

Grace calling.

I reject the call and fire a text off to a guy I use for security and investigation services that need a little extra finesse. For background checks that need a deeper dive. Kenny lacks a typical moral code of conduct and loves money. He comes in useful from time to time.

Go deep. Subjects: Adam in Columbus. In a car accident seven months ago that resulted in paralysis. He's in journalism. Writes for a local magazine and news website. I want a dossier on him and his fiancée. Chloe. Deep on both. Chloe: close friends with a blonde named Alannah who works somewhere in the offices above the Downtown club. Give me the basic rundown on Alannah too. Priority 1 on Chloe. P2 on Adam. P3 on Alannah. Photos coming.

He responds about two minutes later, despite the fact it's 10:30 on a Friday night.

Deadline? More info?

I reply.

Whatever you can get in one hour via text on Chloe. The rest, by the end of tomorrow in a file. I'll be at Downtown tomorrow night, too. Bring

Cheater

me dossiers directly. Contact Shep for surveillance as Chloe and Alannah are here now. Gimme five mins to give him a heads up.

I take a few snapshots of the monitor in front of me and forward them to him. One is of her dancing. One of her laughing. The third, she's twirling.

He responds.

1 hr without a last name?

Yeah, I'm a demanding client. But I pay well.
I write back.

I'll get you a last name. Hang tight.

As I ponder my actions and my upcoming few moves, my phone alerts me to a voicemail message.

Grace can wait.

I eyeball the monitor again and see a guy touch Chloe's shoulder. Something foreign invades my system and I'm immediately craving violence, bolting to standing.

I forcefully shove the sensations away as I grab my handset and press the digits for my head of security, who answers on the first ring.

"Shep," I clip into the phone.

"Yeah, boss?"

"Dance floor. Dark hair, strappy black dress dancing with that blonde from upstairs who comes here regularly. See?"

"I see them."

"The goof talking to her in the red shirt? Show her he's a goof who's been hittin' on women all night."

"Has he?"

"Shouldn't you know the answer to that?" I fire back.

"Don't think he has. Think he just got here."

"You have your orders," I advise.

The phone is silent for a beat before Shep asks, "Reason I should know about?"

"My private eye is gonna get ahold of you for surveillance on them. Particularly the brunette, Chloe. I'm coming up behind you. Wait thirty seconds before you approach."

"Ah," he replies knowingly, despite the fact that this is the first time we've ever done this. "On it," Shep says and hangs up.

I put the phone down and pull air into my lungs before releasing it slowly, rolling my shoulders, flexing my jaw. I tip my head to the left until my neck cracks, pocket my phone and a business card, and make my way out of the office, into the club.

I'm this pretty thing's hall pass. No way is that honor going to the schmuck in the red shirt.

Her words, how much it sounds like she gives a shit about this guy. And more than that, the sound of the utter and complete longing in her voice? It's lit a match in me.

Tired of boring and repetitive sex but wanting even that after not being touched in seven months? Spends all her time looking after a guy who can't even bother to get her off when she's spent seven months loyally looking after him? Didn't feast on her offered pussy when it would've cost him just minutes of his time to keep the girl who was standing by him feeling desirable, wanted?

He doesn't deserve it. I don't know him, but I know if he did deserve it, he wouldn't leave a question in her mind about how much he wants her. About how much he appreciates that she's sticking by him.

People who don't know me well think I'm ice-cold and unshakable.

People who know me well know I've got a few screws loose. I hide it pretty well otherwise. Yeah, takes a bit to rattle me but once you do… results aren't pretty.

Me and most of my siblings are a little damaged. Rich and powerful prick of a father who clawed his way to the top through a

Cheater

blood bath, getting organized crime hooks embedded deep with an unstable drama queen retired supermodel of a mother who requires a whole lot of attention to keep her out of emotional spirals. My father sees what he wants, and he takes it. In life, in love. Flat out. Anyone who's tried to steal from him has paid the price, either dished out by him or one of his kids.

We were raised by nannies under the critical eyes of busy parents who are fully focused on one another. They've got high standards and rules for their offspring that results in frustration from my siblings. I'm handled differently. Probably because I'm more damaged than most of my siblings. Thad excepted, though Thad is no longer anyone's problem.

I'm probably as twisted as I am because of being abducted and held for ransom for two weeks by my child psychologist who played mind games with me as he spiraled even deeper into madness.

It was mere minutes before the deadline. No one was coming for me. He was melting down. I got my hands on his gun.

Though not sure that was all that cracked me, because why send a kid to a psychologist if he's well-adjusted? They all say Thad was the psycho. Nobody says anything about me. They pretend everything is all right with me, except Grace, who is the youngest of the seven of us but who tries to mother us all.

I don't trust people. I keep hookups unemotional. I don't do emotions in general, because my default emotion is best served to make shitheads pay for their sins.

Tonight... after being a fly on the wall for that conversation and now watching this girl dance, foreign sensations have woken in me. Maybe they're emotions.

I want to give this tight little brunette the hottest night of her life. What I'll want after I give her that remains to be seen.

I get to the dance floor just as Shep is ready to walk the dick who's got the nerve to touch her out of my club.

5
Chloe

While dancing with my friends, I'm tapped on my shoulder. I turn to see a nice-looking blond-haired, man-bun wearing guy in dark jeans and a red button-down shirt smiling at me.

"You wanna dance?" he asks.

"Thanks, but I'm having a special night with my friends," I reply.

I feel bad as the smile falls off his face, so I add, "You can dance with all of us for a song or two if you really wanna just dance."

Alannah gives me the side-eye. Our friend Coraline sees her do this and her head jerks back slightly, her nose wrinkling. She's giving Alannah a look like... *what's the side-eye about?*

Cor knows I'm not the type to tease and lead someone on. Alannah is either giving me that look because she's annoyed I'm inviting him to dance with us or because she thinks I should go for it. Probably the latter.

"Dance with us, man," Jeff, another friend of ours invites.

He's a lawyer at the firm Alannah works at, and he's tall, built, dresses well, and presents himself as very metrosexual. He pings gaydar and leaves many unsure which way that cookie crumbles. If you ask, Jeffy will tell you he loves cookies in all forms. He loves to come out when we dance and it makes us feel safe because he's big, strong, and protective.

He also swears that in addition to being into buff, attractive metrosexual men like himself, he especially loves curvy, dark-skinned high-maintenance girls a lot, too. He's currently trying to get out of the friendzone with the curvy Black beauty Coraline, but whether he wants her for a night or a lot longer than that is a mystery we've debated. At length.

As far as Cor and Jeff go, she's not having it and keeps telling us that although dating him could be a dream come true since she's attracted to him, she's sure Jeff is going to either realize he prefers men over women, or he'll never settle down because he wants to keep helping himself to both. And she's not only unwilling to share, she says she's also completely unwilling to ruin their friendship.

While Jeffy knows Coraline's stance, he told Alannah, me, and our married friend Maddie who is also out with us tonight, to "watch and see" him accomplish his goal with her. He swears he'll wear her down eventually. He's not giving anyone a clue as to whether he's got real feelings or if it's just a challenge to him as he's definitely the competitive type, so we're all trying to stay neutral on the issue.

The guy in the red shirt looks at Jeff with concern. "Thanks, but I'm more interested in one-on-one." His eyes ping back to me. "Can I buy you a drink instead? Chat by the bar? I won't keep you from your special night with your friends for long."

I give him what I hope is a non-bitchy but also non-flirty smile. "Thanks anyway, but I'd prefer to spend the evening celebrating with my friends. Thanks, anyway." I then add, "And... I'm engaged, so..."

The guy's eyes rove over my empty left hand. I see the diamond on my ring practically wink at me from Alannah's hand.

Now Coraline's eyes are on Alannah's hand, too.

Shit. She's gonna ask questions. No, more like she's going to stare at us until we spill. Cor's superpower is that she can often make you spill your secrets with one of her long stares.

A guy dressed in a suit with the vibe of a secret service agent and the build of a side-by-side refrigerator is suddenly in our little huddle and clapping his hand on the red-shirted guy's shoulder with a serious expression.

Cheater

He states, "That's it, pal. Already warned you. You're officially barred from Downtown, effective now."

The guy in the red shirt looks thrown. "Huh?"

"You heard me," the guy in the suit advises aggressively, like he's looking for a reason to throw this dude on the floor, step on his back, then handcuff him.

"You're mixing me up with someone else, man," Red-shirted guy defends. "You and I have never had a conversation."

"When a woman doesn't welcome your advances, you back off, sir. Anywhere and everywhere, but especially here because this place is under *my* watch."

"You've got me mixed up with someone else," Red Shirt asserts. "I just got here, I'm on my first drink, and I haven't approached any other women tonight. Miss, was I bothering you?"

He looks at me for help. But before I'm able to answer, the security guy clips aggressively, "Ah, so you've got a twin? A twin who's here tonight?"

"No." The guy looks like he's about to piss his pants.

"You're outta here. Don't make me get physical, pal."

"This is bullshit," Red Shirt retorts, looking toward me again. "Right? I'm not bothering you, am I?" He looks back at the guy in the suit. "Man, call a manager over here. I haven't done anything wrong."

"He's not-" I start, about to say he's not bothering me, but the security guy already has the red shirt-wearing guy in a hold where his right arm is bent unnaturally behind his back as he grips the guy's other bicep and moves him away from us.

"A manager? You're outta here, Karen."

"Somebody call for a manager?" A man's voice sounds from behind me.

Most people nearby are no longer dancing, instead they're staring.

"I'm the owner," the voice adds. "If you're bothering other guests, you're no longer our welcome guest."

"I wasn't," Red Shirt calls over his shoulder as the security guy continues to march him toward the door.

The owner turns his back on the red-shirted guy and looks directly at me. And I'm awestruck as his dark eyes slowly coast over my body from eyes to toes, then back up to my eyes again. It's like it happens in slow motion.

This guy is one of those head-turners. Heads turn everywhere he goes, I'm sure of it. My body tingles as my spine straightens.

He's tall, built, somewhere in his thirties, dressed in an impeccable suit with a navy-blue shirt. His inky-dark hair looks soft, tousled in that stylish way that screams *rich guy who doesn't give a shit if he needs a haircut*. His lips are full. His jawline is chiseled. He looks like he belongs either on a soap opera or a red carpet with a supermodel in a designer dress as arm candy. He's a walking, talking thirst trap.

"Sweet baby Jesus," Coraline says from behind me. "Five movie star hotties had an orgy thirty-odd years ago and made a pretty baby."

"I'm sorry about that," the club owner says to me, and I suspect he had to have heard Coraline, but he doesn't visibly react. "We endeavor to ensure guests feel safe here at Downtown and all our establishments. I regret that you were harassed." His hand is pressed to his chest with what looks like sincerity as he stares straight into my eyes.

"I..." I swallow and shake my head. "Actually, he just asked me to dance. Nothing bad happened. If he had plans to harass me, he didn't have time because your security was here quickly."

The man's eyes are on my mouth as I speak. And it's making my face burn hot.

He hands me a business card. "Glad to hear Shep's doing his job. I'm Derek Steele."

I look at the card in my hand, not seeing anything on it because my eyes are bouncing quickly up to meet his again.

"Of course you are," I hear muttered. Cor again.

He not only looks like a soap opera star; he's got a soap opera star name.

Cheater

"For legal reasons, we write up a report whenever we bar somebody," Derek Steele goes on, "so would you come with me to the office, please? I'll get all the details so I can write this up." His hand lands on the small of my back and my eyes hit Alannah's briefly while on the move. She's nodding with a positively delighted look in her eyes.

"The bar or a table out here should do," Jeffy pipes up. "Unless I'm coming with."

Derek Steele smiles wide at me. "Protective friends. Good stuff. The bar it is."

Although that hand on my lower back should feel fairly benign, it's not. Because although my dress has spaghetti straps on top in front, it's also crisscrossed over most of my back, which means his hand is touching plenty of bare skin. I'm exceedingly aware of its presence and grateful for the fact that the dress is velvet because hopefully the thick fabric is hiding that my nipples are now erect. He doesn't let go until we're at the bar in front of the two empty seats Alannah and I sat in earlier.

6

Chloe

"You're on break," Derek Steele says to the bartender without looking at him as he removes his hand from my back and reaches out to take my hand as if I need help climbing up onto the barstool.

I don't take the extended hand; instead I climb up without assistance, eyes bouncing between the club owner and the confused-looking bartender, who asks, "I'm... *on break*, Mr. Steele?"

"Take your break in my office," Derek says without looking at the frowning bartender whose expression changes to one of alarm. "Right now would be ideal," he adds.

The bartender sidesteps past him and slips out of the opening at the side of the bar as Derek gestures with his left hand. I see a suited guy by the front door look our way and then he's on the move, approaching us.

"Escort Alex to my office, Mel, and ask Tamara to come look after the bar, please," Derek says to the man approaching who's obviously another security guy.

Mel nods and quickly moves past us, disappearing down a hallway that presumably leads to the office.

My eyes bounce back to Derek as he takes his jacket off, lays it across the bar beside me, fiddles with his sleeves, then rolls them halfway up his well-veined forearms. His eyes are on me the entire time, though mine have been rather... bouncy. His shirt showcases his muscles quite well. I tear my eyes away from his defined shoulders and the ink that crawls up one of his arms. Heat creeps from my neck upwards as I try to behave as if I'm not checking him out.

"What can I get you, Miss..." He lets that hang.

"Chloe."

"Miss Chloe what?" he inquires and gestures to a passing waiter. "Can you take Tamara's section while she runs the bar the rest of the night? Alex has been relieved."

"Sure, boss," the young guy says. "I'll bus that table and be right back."

Derek jerks his chin at me.

"Chloe Turner," I reply. "And again, that guy in the red shirt wasn't bothering me. He asked me to dance, and your security got there immediately, before he even had a chance to misbehave."

"Did you have plans to dance with him?" Derek asks. "Did my head of security ruin your night by giving him the boot?"

His dark eyes feel like they burn into me. And it makes me feel strange. Exposed. That was probably meant to be a lighthearted comment, but the way he delivered it – with what felt like accusation – I'm a little flummoxed.

"No," I advise. "I invited him to dance with the group of us, making it clear I'm here to spend the evening with my friends dancing. And then I told him I'm engaged."

"Hm," he responds, grabbing an empty glass from the mirrored shelf behind himself. "What to drink, Chloe Turner?"

He pulls his phone out and is doing something on it as I answer.

"Rum and Coke with lime in a tall glass, thanks." I reach into the slit pocket along the side seam of my dress, which has enough room to keep my phone, some cash, and my keys at my mid-torso, which is another reason why I bought it. I pull out my wad of twenties, fives, and tens and pass him a ten.

"On the house. For the trouble," Derek lifts a hand.

"There was no trouble," I advise with a smile. "Your security guard got it wrong, so maybe you should be inviting the guy in the red shirt back in and giving him the complimentary drink."

Cheater

Derek looks surprised for a beat and then leans forward. "You want him back in here?"

His jaw muscles flex and it's sexy while also being unnerving. He looks almost... angry?

Caught off guard, I reply, "No, not that. I don't know him and had no plans to get to know him. But maybe he also didn't deserve to be turfed out of the club. Maybe your security guy mixed him up with somebody else."

"Shep doesn't make mistakes like that," Derek denies.

"Well..." I say, and then I don't know what to add to that, so I let it hang. "I guess I'll accept the free drink then."

"His friends at the first table to the left of the door are still sitting there, so they watched him get escorted out of my establishment and didn't go with him. Aren't rushing to finish their drinks, even. That probably says something about the guy." His eyes bounce that way as he takes down a bottle of rum from the top shelf. "Don't you think?"

I shrug. "I... guess?"

Pretty observant of him, actually.

"If you were kicked out of a club because you broke their rules and your friends were with you, what would they do? Come with you or let you find some other fun on a Friday night?"

"My friends? If I broke a rule, they'd still come with me."

"Even if you were in the wrong?"

"Even then. But if they thought I was unfairly kicked out of an establishment, not only would they not hang back to spend money lining the pockets of that establishment's owner, they'd probably plot to set the place on fire in my defense."

His brows shoot up.

Oh shit. That's probably not a good thing to say.

I giggle, shaking my head. "I mean... not that they'd set your place on fire here or anything. We'd just plot about it."

"Best not kick you out so I don't have to find out," he says, eyes lighting with humor as he pours rum from the top shelf and then uses the soda gun to fill my drink with Coke. He drops in a lime wedge, then slips a straw and stir stick in before he extends his hand, holding out the drink.

"Thank you," I say and take it from his hand. Our fingers brush and something exciting ignites in my belly. Low in my belly. Derek Steele's eyes are on my mouth again.

I slip the ten back into the little pocket and pull the zip up. "Thank you, Mr. Steele."

A smile slowly spreads across his face and our eyes stay connected for longer than they probably should.

A woman slips behind the bar. "Excuse me, Mr. Steele. I'll handle everything."

"Well, I'd better re-join my friends," I say, looking over my shoulder.

My friends are all at a table watching us. Coraline looks concerned. Alannah looks positively delighted. Maddie and Jeffy are whispering to one another while watching.

"You forgot the card," Derek says.

"The card?" I ask, eyes bouncing back.

I quickly look at the bar top where his business card sits. I must have set it down when I sat on the stool.

"Oh. Not sure I need it," I say, intentionally not looking at his face.

"Chloe," he says simply.

I feel like I have no choice but to look up and I'm afraid my eyes might be saying more than I intend for them to say.

He leans forward. "If you wanna give me a card, I'm pretty sure I need it."

Heat floods my face. "I don't have any business cards with me, and I'm engaged to be married, so even if I did have cards, I'm afraid they'd be given out for business reasons only."

"That's a shame," Derek says, though heat and humor are both still lit in his eyes. "Shame for me. Not for the fiancé. Lucky man to have your loyalty."

Cheater

My expression drops as a hundred thoughts about Adam flit through my brain.

"Hope that man shows you every day that he feels how lucky he is to have it," Derek tacks on.

Face burning, I manage, "Thanks for the drink. Have a good night."

I hurry back to my friends, not taking Derek Steele's business card, also not looking back, because it feels like his eyes are still on me.

7 ♡ Chloe

Two Hours Later

"Pizza," Alannah calls out.

"Big Mac," Coraline counters.

"Donairs!" Jeffrey casts his vote.

Maddie took a cab home half an hour ago or she'd probably have a fourth idea.

Cor and Jeffy are coming back to Alannah's for a sleepover. And Cor has been trying to give me 'the stare' all night long. I know she's dying to get me alone. I figure I'll just tell her Alannah wanted to borrow my diamond ring as a social experiment.

I pipe up. "We never agree on post bar food options, so we almost always wind up in someone's kitchen with me drunkenly cooking for everyone. Let's skip the rest of this dance. What's in your fridge, Lan? Or do we need to hit the store on the way home?"

She twists her lips. "Probably not much. What are you in the mood for, Chlo?"

"It's your night, so why don't we go with what you're craving?"

Coraline and Jeffy don't look happy.

"I like the way you think," Alannah says. "But I want everyone happy."

"I know!" I grab Alannah excitedly. "We'll swing by the all-night grocery store and I'll grab naan bread and the fixings to make all your..." I twirl, pointing at the others, "drunken post-bar food fantasies come to life."

All eyes light up.

"Naan bread pizzas. I'll do yours with hamburger, pickles, and thousand island dressing, yours I'll add some tzatziki and whatever meat and vegetables you want, and yours the traditional way."

"And this is why we invite Chloe to the meetings," Jeffy says, sagely.

"Finish up our drinks and I'll order us a rideshare," I suggest, reaching for my phone.

8

Derek

I'm both appeased and unhappy at the same time.

Appeased because I got a preliminary report from Kenny an hour ago on both Adam Hallman and Chloe Turner. He'll have more information for me in a day, then even more a few days after that because I want an extra-deep dive. But I've got enough for the moment. Enough to know I'm moving ahead with a plan.

I'm unhappy that Chloe is drunk. It means I'm not making my move tonight. Because I want her one hundred per cent sober when I rock the foundation of her existence.

I had Shep and Mel watch her group all night. Two other men tried to approach Chloe on the dancefloor; they stopped it. I think her friend, the Black woman in her group, glommed onto it after the second one as she kept her eyes pointed at my men suspiciously after that.

It's last call, and I've had my ears on their table so know they're going back to Alannah's apartment. I can already tell Chloe is the nurturer. Trying to please them all. The tall guy that's been with them all night is going, too, but I don't sense he's got a sexual appetite for Chloe, rather for her friend, so that's all that matters to me for tonight.

She's on the move to the ladies' room and none of her party joins her, so I slip into the hallway a moment later, ensuring I'll catch her on her way back.

By design, she slams into me coming out of the bathroom.

"Oh! Omigod!" she gasps, then tries to move back, but stumbles on her high heels and I catch her before she falls.

Arms wrapped around her, I look down into her eyes.

"Whoops. So sorry about that," she breathes out, eyes glassy from alcohol. Her eyelashes flutter and she sinks her teeth into her bottom lip in a way that I know is from our proximity. "Hello again," she adds, voice a little husky.

My cock goes immediately erect and presses into her stomach. I don't generally spring hard-ons like this, but my brain is already poring over plans including all the ways I'm going to fuck her and now that I've got her in my clutches, clearly it brought my cock up to speed.

We're trapped in one another's gazes for a long moment. And I feel something odd. Something jagged unfurls in me as I stare deep. Whatever it is I'm feeling, it's new and it's big.

"Careful," I advise on not much more than a whisper, continuing to look into her eyes as I make a smooth move that she doesn't notice, sliding down the zipper of that side pocket on her dress.

"Sah-sorry..." she stammers, wide-eyed, blinking adorably at me. She swallows as her eyes slowly rove my face, then she gives her head a shake and steps back. "First time wearing heels in a while... while imbibing," she explains.

I don't immediately let go. I take a step forward so she's pressed against me again.

"You good?" I ask. "Need some help back to your table? To your cab? I can have a driver take you home. A hundred per cent above board and chivalrous here. I've got two sisters."

She shakes her head. "I'm okay. I'm not totally trashed. I just wobbly. I mean, *I'm* just wobbly a little bit. The shoes are to blame. Lucky sisters." She gets a wistful smile that piques my curiosity.

Cheater

I flash her a wide smile and whether she realizes it or not, she's melting into me.

"If you're sure?"

She seems to snap out of a daze, so I covertly slip my business card into that side pocket on her dress and pull the zip up a second before she backs away.

I catch her hand and give it a squeeze. She looks at me with panic.

"Sorry for the trouble tonight. Get home safely, Chloe Turner."

"Thank you very much, Derek Steele. You get home safe, too." She shoots me with a finger gun and winks exaggeratedly. This surprises me. In a good way.

I smile, stuffing my hands in my pockets. As she takes two steps backwards, I add, "Might wanna watch where you're goin'."

She salutes me and turns, but nearly trips so I lunge and catch her by the hips.

"Easy there," I say, my nose grazing the shell of her ear.

She stiffens and presses her hand to the wall, then walks away slowly. That Jeffrey guy has stepped into the hallway; his eyes land on me shrewdly.

Platonic protectiveness. Good. I'm glad she'll get safely to her friend's place tonight in his company.

I step back into my office, switch the monitor off, and call Shep in.

"You know Alannah Fisher? She's in here often."

"I do," he confirms.

And the way he confirms it has me curious.

"You friends with her?" I ask.

"Hooked up once. Not on company hours of course, boss."

"Of course," I reply. "Good terms?"

"Good terms," he confirms. "Cling factor zero."

That's what Shep prefers. Non-clingy types. Same here. Previously.

"Good. Would you make sure she and her party safely get where they're going?"

Shep looks perplexed. My returning expression lets him know I don't want to be questioned.

He nods and leaves. I send a text message to Kenny who already knows I want information on Adam Hallman and Chloe Turner. But my message lets him know I want her followed around the clock, beginning tomorrow morning from Alannah Fisher's home.

9

Chloe

Sunday Night

I feel like I'm tiptoeing when I get into the townhome, but instead of things being quiet, Adam still has company. They're lounging in the living room watching sports on TV. The coffee table is littered with beer cans, a stack of pizza boxes, and four chip bags. And the drink coasters sit, unused in their coaster holder.

I wave to the room which includes Adam, his brother Paul, best friend Craig, and our former neighbor Lawrence.

I get multiple greetings including hugs and cheek kisses from Adam's guests, who each get up to hug me. After this, I move to Adam who is on the recliner. His chair is parked beside him otherwise he'd look like the Adam of seven months ago.

I haven't seen him lounging on the furniture like this since it all happened. The only time he's not in his wheelchair outside the bathroom is when he's in bed or in the car. I lean over and he puts his hand to my jaw and kisses me. I drop a peck and am about to straighten up when he hooks his hand around the back of my neck and keeps me there to deepen the kiss. It lasts a few seconds before he looks directly into my eyes.

"Hi," he whispers. "Welcome home."

"Hey you," I say.

I feel my chin wobble. I feel like I'm about to burst into tears. Because he hasn't kissed me like this in months. Months and months.

"Have a good time?" he asks softly.

"Yeah, I did. I guess I kinda needed some girl time," I say, somehow managing to keep my voice from completely cracking. It definitely trembles, though.

"Lots of food here if you're hungry, Chloe," Craig invites, gesturing to table. "We ordered your favorites, too."

"Jalapeno poppers and mozzarella sticks?" I gasp with enthusiasm. I'm laying the enthusiasm on thick as these are Craig's favorites and I've always ordered his favorites in the past, but the diversion is welcome.

"Of course," Craig says and tugs my hand so that I fall onto the couch beside him. "Fried pickles, too. Stay with Alannah?" he asks me with his puppy dog eyes.

I smile. "You probably already know the answer to that, Detective. What do you wanna know?"

"She take anyone home from the bar this weekend?" he asks.

I snicker and zip my mouth with a pretend zipper.

"Killin' me, Smalls," he mutters, throwing his head back.

Craig is a cop. He's pretty hot. And sweet. A little immature, but he's had a thing for Alannah since day one and they started their little thing right after Adam's accident. Adam complained a while ago about hating the idea of her stringing him along, but I set him straight. Alannah lays it all out on the table, wouldn't pretend, wouldn't let Craig think they were going to be something if they weren't.

My guess is that she told him she was up for strictly *friends with benefits,* and he wants to change her mind but might be afraid of getting shot down.

"Nobody took anybody home from the bar this weekend," I advise pointedly.

"So, Coraline and Jeffrey are still doing that dance, are they?" Lawrence asks, popping the tab on a beer and passing it to me. "For Adam," he says. "You want one?"

Cheater

I wave and shake my head as I pass Adam the beer. "No thanks. I've had enough alcohol poisoning this weekend, thank you very much."

Adam takes a big gulp of the beer. And then he belches and doesn't even excuse himself.

"Oh, I'm here for boys' night so I don't get manners?" I quip.

"You hang with us, you can't be mad if we let 'em rip, too," Adam's brother Paul warns.

"I neither want to smell your ass air, nor hear your ass fluttering to make that noise, thank you very much."

The guys laugh.

Adam's eyes slice to me. "We don't make boys' night rules, woman, just live by them. You're here, you can't get all judgy."

There's light in his eyes so I get to my feet, lean over, and blow a raspberry on his neck, which makes his eyes light up even more. I twist to lean over the coffee table and while I'm nabbing a mozzarella stick, Adam swats my butt.

I look over my shoulder at him and smile wide before I dredge my cheese stick in the open container of marinara sauce, and take a bite on my way to the fridge for a can of root beer.

∞

I'm feeling hopeful when I get into bed. Adam's already here, eyes on his phone. His friends left and he called out that he was heading to bed while I was cleaning the kitchen, which hadn't been cleaned all weekend.

I know Adam's still finding his way to independence and household chores have fallen on me, but Paul was here all weekend, too, so I didn't expect to have to come home to such a mess. Almost every dish in the kitchen was dirty, so I ran a dishwasher load and still had to wash a whack of dishes by hand.

Even still, I'm in a good mood so I don't even bitch about it.

I finish working lotion into my elbows and then fall onto the bed with a bounce. "Ah, a comfortable bed," I say with relief. "Alannah's guest room mattress has got to be at least forty years old."

His eyes hit me and then go back to his screen.

"Did you have a good weekend?" I ask.

It's a few seconds before he puts the phone down and looks at me. "Missed you," he says, "But yeah. It was good."

I move closer and put my head on his shoulder, then run my hand up his chest.

He doesn't turn away, doesn't stiffen up. This feels natural. This feels right. God, I've missed this.

Is it possible that a weekend apart was what we both really needed for perspective?

"Did you use it?" he asks.

He means the hall pass.

I stiffen as I look up at him. "No."

"You had Friday *and* Saturday night."

I stare with surprise at what has come out like a procrastination accusation. I move back and put my head on my own pillow, still looking at him.

"I don't even know if I want to," I say.

"But we talked about this."

He's pissed off?

"Yeah, and I listened to what you said. I thought it over. And I still don't know if I want to do it. I don't know if I *can* do it."

I hate the look on his face. Like I've done something wrong by not having sex with someone this weekend.

"I've been in a committed relationship with you for a year and a half, Adam. I can't just switch that off. Just suddenly start looking for fuck buddies."

He makes a face of distaste. "You don't need to be crass, Chloe."

I throw my hands up in the air in exasperation. "I can't believe you're being so blasé about this."

"I just thought you'd take the opportunity, like we discussed."

"I've taken the opportunity to think about it. That's what I agreed to do. I've never, not ever in my life met some guy at a bar and hooked up with him the same day. Never."

"Whatever." He repositions himself so I've got his back.

I stare for a minute in shock.

"Adam," I snap.

"I'm tired, Chloe."

"This is bullshit!" I snap. "Fucking bullshit!"

He doesn't make a move to look at me. He says nothing, so I repeat, "Bullshit," as I grab my pillow and storm out to go sleep on the couch.

Fifteen minutes or so later, I'm flicking the channels irately and needlessly, because I wouldn't be able to focus on the TV even if I found the most amazing program ever created.

Adam rolls out and stops in front of me. "I'm sorry," he says.

My eyes search his face. I don't know what to make of all this. It's like I don't even know him anymore.

"You do realize we're fighting because you're mad that I didn't fuck someone this weekend, right?"

"I just... Chloe... this is gonna sound screwed up but if you'd do it, then I can get through the mental shit attached to it."

"Are you serious with me right now?" I sit up and gawk at him in shock.

He drags his hand through his hair frustratedly. "I know how it sounds and I'm sorry. But all weekend I was trying to come to terms with this. All weekend. Then you come home and tell me you didn't do it, which means I get to keep waiting for the shoe to drop so I can figure out if I'm gonna be okay with it."

"If you're gonna be..." I tilt my head. "You? This... this is just all about you, is it? Do you realize you're bullying me into doing something that's out of character for me and you want me to hurry up and do it so that you can figure out if you're okay with it?"

He looks away with remorse before he responds. "And you. You've gotta figure out if you're okay with it, too. It's late. We'll talk about it tomorrow. Come back to bed. I'm sorry, okay?"

"No. Let's talk about it now," I amend. "I wanna know... what was all that when I got home? The playfulness. The sweet kiss. The ass swat. Was that all for show? For the guys? Not for me?"

He says nothing, just grinds his teeth.

"Yeah. That there?" I point at him. "That behavior tonight when I got home after being gone for forty-eight hours? That's the kind of thing I'd be happy with. A nice kiss. Playfulness. Looking at me like I'm more than your fucking roommate."

He looks like I've struck him. The pain etched into his features hurts me, too. "So... you want me to fake it?"

I huff. "Wow, Adam. Just wow."

"Explain yourself, Chloe."

"You faked it tonight for them, you can't fake it once in a blue moon for me? Sadly, though, I wouldn't call it faking it. I'd call it trying to be supportive, affectionate, and caring to your partner. Trying to give them some intimacy. But what do I know, right? I'm the selfish one. Right? Because I want to feel wanted. Because I didn't run out and cheat the minute you gave me permission like a goddamn machine."

He shakes his head with disgust. "You don't know what I'm going through. You can't possibly imagine what I'm going through, Chloe."

"I know," I say softly. "I've tried really hard, Adam, but I *can't* know what you're going through. All I know is that I've been trying really hard to be everything you want, everything you need, everything I think I'd want if I were the one in your position. And that's all I can keep doing. I know you're still going through it and I'm not trying to add to your stress, which is why I told you to forget the whole thing. Why I apologized to you for the vibrator incident. I fucked up. And I apologize for it."

"But I've told you... I've told you that I don't want to fake it. I need to wrap my head around how my life's gonna be. And I want you beside me for it. I do. I want that as much as I did before."

"Do you?" I ask, tearfully, feeling like my chest is about to cave in.

"Absolutely. I love you."

Cheater

"I love you, too. But I don't need to cheat on you. I just need you to put in a little effort with me. I know it's hard with all you've got going on, but I'm just asking for a little bit of effort."

"Please, honey," he pleads, "Try. Try it my way. Use the hall pass sometime in... say... the next two weeks. If you can, if you find someone to do that with, we'll talk about it again in two weeks. Two weeks from tonight, you tell me you've done it and then we'll both take the week after that to see how we feel about it. See how we both feel about setting a wedding date."

I say nothing. Because he's still pushing despite everything I've said. And it hurts. It hurts and it's confusing.

"Deal?" he asks. "I'm not trying to bully you into doing something you don't want. I think that if you can get over the idea of it meaning you're a cheater you'll see it could be the answer. I've thought about it a lot and I think it could work for us."

I stare at him for a long moment through the tears in my eyes.

He waits while my heart twists up in knots.

"My parents have an open marriage," he blurts.

I'm taken aback.

"Dad cheated. They almost split up. She wanted to work it out. He told her he couldn't promise he'd be faithful. Asked her to leave the marriage open. He told me he was ninety-nine per cent sure she didn't fool around with anyone. He also told me not feeling trapped with one person made it so he only occasionally stepped out. He said it saved their marriage. He loved her even more once they changed things up. Can you think about it? I know you've tried hard to put me first and I'm not trying to bully you. I'm trying to hold onto you. Think about it?"

I blow out a long breath.

"Deal?" he asks.

"I've thought about it. I'm still thinking about it," I whisper.

"Try? Please try it my way."

"I'll try. But if I-"

"Just try."

I nod.

"Thank you," he says softly, pain in his eyes. "I know you don't want to accept what's happened to me, how it changes things, but you need to do that, Chloe. You need to understand that I'm asking you to do this for you, for both of us."

I sigh.

"Coming to bed?" he asks.

"In a while," I say softly.

He stares at me for a long moment before he nods and then motors away from me.

10
Chloe

Thursday

I close my laptop down for the day with a big smile on my face. My boss just had me jump on a video call to tell me I've earned a ten-thousand-dollar bonus, that my recent contributions to a campaign made a client so happy after their profit quadrupled their ad spend this month that they not only renewed their contract but also boosted their budget, insisting I get a cash bonus. They want me to be their primary point of contact and the potential for this client is so huge, my boss wants me working only on them instead of continuing to handle the half a dozen clients I manage now.

And I'm tickled pink.

Considering that most of my savings got eaten up buying the townhome with Adam a whole year before we planned to buy a house, this is great news and I'll be tucking it away to help me re-boot my nest egg.

I've been working hard, trying to show my appreciation for all the company has done for me throughout the ordeal that has been my life for the past seven months and it feels great to be rewarded. I've been worried I asked for too much flexibility. Worried I haven't been present enough, so I doubled down and really threw myself into work as a distraction from my reality.

I'm ready to celebrate this little win and decide I'm treating myself, taking myself on a date.

A trip to the mall, to the bookstore, and then a dinner date with whichever book I buy myself at my favorite soup place. *Alone.* I used to try to do it once in a while. Shop for a book, go to a restaurant, and enjoy reading while eating. I always get dessert when I do this and I'm looking forward to one of my favorite treats.

In fact, I haven't been to the gym in seven months, let my membership expire, and it's part of the same mall I'm going to, so I think I'll stop by tonight and renew it.

Adam wants me to take up new hobbies anyway. We've rarely even eaten dinner together lately and if I'm out of the house more, he can pretend I'm cheating on him which might boost his mood.

I roll my eyes at my inner sarcasm.

My home office is on one side of the master bedroom, Adam's is on the other. I rap on his office door and open it. He immediately closes the laptop lid and looks over his shoulder with irritation, asking, "What's up?"

I feel the smile die on my face.

His expression is one of impatience, so I answer, "I'm going out. I probably won't be back until late. Gonna wander the mall. Renew my gym membership. Eat while I'm out at that coffee shop with the soup so... do you mind eating leftovers? There's lasagna there. Or would you like me to get something delivered. I could bring back–"

"I'll figure it out. Have fun."

"Need anything before I go?" I ask.

"I'm good. Hit a rhythm here with my story, so wanna keep it up. Sorry."

"Oh. Okay."

"Thanks. Have fun." He turns his back to me and opens his laptop again.

I would've shared my good news, but his reaction completely halted me. *Dismissed.*

That bitterness that's been creeping in lately is picking up steam.

Cheater

Now it's seeping in through multiple foundation cracks. Of course I don't want to mess up his writing rhythm, but he's been like this non-stop. Irritated or at the very least *terse* with me.

He's in his office from morning to night and lately we're lucky if we have more than breakfast together.

Not tonight. Tonight, I'm celebrating alone. And I'm looking forward to it. I'm pushing away the urge to fully consider my future. To think about what *I* want for a change. To think about whether this is what I want for the rest of my days. Walking on eggshells. Being bullied into cheating. As much as he says it's not cheating if he's sanctioned it, it's not how I'm built.

I pull my thoughts back, afraid to go further down that road. Because there might be no turning back. And to abandon Adam and our plans isn't something I ever thought I was capable of.

I shake it off, deciding not to let him get me down today. I want to celebrate my work achievement and get out of this house, so I shove the negativity away and change out of my typical work-at-home comfy clothes into jeans and a cute top. I put on some makeup and jewelry, spritz some perfume, and take the ponytail down before I grab my phone and keys and head out.

∞

Twenty minutes into my bookstore wander, I see none other than the hot nightclub owner from last Friday night. I feel my face flame with heat; I'm sure it's bright red.

It's weird, too, because I could've sworn I'd left his business card on the bar, yet found it in the pocket of my dress when I took my stuff to the drycleaners yesterday. I'm guessing that's courtesy of Alannah who mentioned him and suggested I use him as my hall pass about half a dozen times over the weekend.

I tucked the matte charcoal card with raised glossy black letters into a pocket in my purse for no logical reason instead of tossing it into the trash.

I duck out, abandoning my planned purchase on a table. Derek Steele probably wouldn't remember me, but for some reason, I don't want to run into him.

I pull in a big breath when I get outside and let it out slowly as I make my way across the parking lot. In broad daylight he looked just as sinfully attractive as he did under the lights of his dim nightclub. Tall, built, with that sexy dark and disheveled hair. Those dark eyes.

He's got a five o'clock shadow today and he's in jeans and a black shirt under a leather jacket instead of an expensive suit, but he looks just as much like sex, money, and power today as he did the other night.

∞

In the coffee shop down the street from the mall, I'm kicking myself for not buying that book. I'm scrolling my phone while I eat and while the soup is as good as always, the experience feels a little underwhelming without a fresh new paperback.

I often read e-books, but this dinner and a paperback date for one has a different feel to it for me. Cracking the spine. Smelling the paper. Drooling over a sexy cover.

I decide to read the e-book sample of the paperback I'd almost bought. Maybe I'll go back to the bookstore and get it after I eat and read it in my office at home tonight.

I'm deep into reading reviews of the book when I hear something being set on my table, so I look up, expecting a refill for my green tea. But it's the book I had planned to buy. And resting on top of it is a masculine, attractive hand with an expensive-looking watch on his wrist.

My eyes take a slow journey up to the perfectly sinful face of Derek Steele.

"Worried I'd bite?" he quips, a mischievous sparkle in his eyes.

My mouth drops open.

"Good call," he adds, then sits at my table.

Cheater

"Excuse me?" I rasp.

"You saw me and took off like your sweet little ass was on fire. Like a terrified little bunny rabbit. Thought I'd buy this for you and see if I could find you."

I tilt my head to the side. "How *did* you find me?"

He shrugs. "Luck, I guess."

My expression drops. "No way."

"Followed the trail of your alluring perfume?" he tries.

I give him a bitchy look.

"Okay, I stepped out after you rushed out, then watched you bunny-hop across the parking lot and down the street."

He gestures to the elderly owner. "Hot and Sour soup for me, please, Mr. Nguyen. And maybe some more tea for this little bunny."

The owner waves. "Sure, Mr. Derek. Where you been?"

"Out of town. But I'm here a while."

"Good, good," Mr. Nguyen says.

His wife pokes her head out from the swinging door into the kitchen.

"Mr. Derek! Hello! We didn't see you for a long time!"

He waves. "How's the most beautiful lady and best cook in the world?"

She smiles wide and waves at him like he's a naughty boy before disappearing back into the kitchen.

Derek turns his gaze back to me.

"You're a regular here?" I ask.

"Oh yeah," Derek says, leaning back in his chair. "First sign of a tickle in the throat in my family, someone's comin' over here to pick up soup."

I'm surprised.

It's a little independent donut shop. The décor is still circa 1980-something, but it's famous among the locals. You get house-made-from-scratch soups for cheap from the sweet, elderly Asian couple who get wounded if you go too long between visits. When me and Alannah moved to Columbus for college we practically lived on this soup. It suited our *broke college girl* budget quite well. And I could swear the Nguyens put extra wontons in it for us.

When I came in a while back (after not coming for three or four months) they laid grandparent-like guilt on me. When I told them why I hadn't been by, they reacted as if they knew Adam themselves even though they've never met him. They sent me home with two family-sized containers of won ton soup.

Adam wasn't in the headspace to find the gesture as sweet as he normally would. Since he isn't much of an Asian soup person, I froze the soups in individual serving sizes and had them twice a week for several weeks.

"You grow up on this stuff, too?" Derek asks.

I shake my head. "Moved here for college from Dayton with my best friend Alannah, who works upstairs from your club in the offices. We decided to stay. Got hooked on this place back then and still come as often as we can."

"What's your favorite?" Derek asks. "That one?"

"Definitely."

His mouth splits into a wide smile.

"What about your favorite donut?" he asks.

"Hm?" I ask, eyes on his smiling mouth.

"You save room for dessert?" His head tips toward the counter. "You should. If you get too full on that soup, get something for later."

This is technically a coffee shop and is known for not just the soup, but also for their donuts and pastries which are still made from scratch.

"I always take a chocolate éclair to go. When I'm lucky enough to get here before they run out, of course," I tell him. "They're out today so I'm trying to decide between a powdered jelly donut and a sour cream dipped."

Still smiling, his eyes move over my face in a way that has me feeling like I'm under a microscope.

"Pro tip?" he offers.

I jerk my chin up.

Cheater

"Their éclairs come out at one o'clock every day. Or they did. Been a few years since I had one."

"Thanks for that tip. Explains why I almost never get one when I come for dinner but why I sometimes score at lunchtime. I take it you grew up here?"

"Technically, yes," he says. "When I wasn't away at school. Nowadays I split my time between here and Cleveland mostly."

He's leaning forward, hand still on the book, and he's looking at me as if I'm the most fascinating creature he's ever laid eyes on. It's a strange sensation.

"You don't mind if I eat here with you, do you?" he asks.

"Oh. It's... um... fine," I say, tucking my hair behind my ears.

He moves the book a few inches toward me. "Here."

"You didn't have to buy that for me. I wasn't sure I wanted it anyway. I didn't leave because I saw you."

He leans forward even more. "We both know you did, Chloe."

Heat floods my face, and my mouth drops open at the bluntness of his statement.

"Is it because you feel guilty for being attracted to me?" he asks.

The nerve!

"Who says I'm attracted to you?" I scoff. "Maybe I just really wanted soup. And we had a five-minute interaction. Yes, I recognized you, but didn't think much of it."

My face is blazing hot.

He smiles wider again. And it's almost condescending the way he's doing it. He's convinced I'm lying through my teeth. Not that he's wrong.

"Cocky, much?" I ask.

He leans even closer, so close his face is hovering over my soup. "Much," he confirms.

Mr. Nguyen delivers Derek's soup, so he straightens up in his chair and thanks him.

As Mr. Nguyen shuffles away, I take the opportunity to reach for my bag and pull out my wallet with one hand, flipping the book over to see the price with the other.

"Here," I pull out some money. "For the book."

He shakes his head. "The book is on me. A caveat though."

Mr. Nguyen is back, refilling my tea and bringing Derek a cup too so I'm left in suspense until he walks away.

My eyes roll. "A caveat. Of course," I say.

"I expect a report afterwards."

He puts his teacup to his mouth, eyes on me while I gawk at him.

"Very funny," I finally break the awkward silence.

He takes a slow sip and then sets his cup down thoughtfully. "I'm absolutely serious. Book report. Due as soon as possible."

My eyes roll.

He continues the ridiculousness. "I'm intrigued to learn about a wolf shifter who's... what did it say?" He flips it over and reads the back. "even wilder as a man than he is as a wolf." His gaze bounces back to me with his eyebrows up. "Let me ask you a question. Does the knotting reference mean what I think it means?"

My face burns scarlet. "Oh my God. Yes. Yes, it does." I bury my face behind my hands in absolute mortification.

Derek laughs. And even his laugh is sexy. "I begrudge everybody their literary choices."

When I peek between my fingers, I see his expression has changed. The laughter is gone. Not even a smile remains. I think he's looking at my engagement ring.

I'm sure he's about to make an excuse to leave at the visual reminder of what I've already proclaimed, that I'm engaged, but instead, he lifts his spoon and dips it into his soup bowl. "So, tell me about you and what you do for a living, Chloe." He spoons some into his mouth and his face mirrors what everyone's does when they get their first mouthful of soup here.

"I'm an account manager for a marketing company."

"You don't work in one of my family's office buildings, right?"

"Pardon?" I ask.

Cheater

He shakes his head. "I know your friend works in the building my nightclub Downtown is in."

"She works for a law firm on the eighth floor. How'd you know?"

"She's a regular. Slipped me her number once."

I blink in surprise.

"Never considered using it," he adds.

I stare at him and say nothing.

"Your marketing company is where?" he prompts.

"I telecommute. They don't have a bricks and mortar location. The team is sprinkled throughout North America, the UK, Australia."

"Ah. My father isn't too happy the work-from-home trend is picking up steam. He has a number of commercial real estate holdings."

"Is the current trend making him evaluate what he uses his buildings for?"

"Yes, in fact. He's selling his largest one in Cleveland to be repurposed for low-income housing. He's having one of the buildings here converted to condominiums as leases run out. Something I'm not thrilled with."

"Why is that?"

"My siblings and I have suites on the top floor. Means we'll have neighbors."

I laugh. "Not a fan of neighbors that aren't your family members?"

He wrinkles his nose. "Not a fan of neighbors, period, particularly my family."

I nod. "Small family so I can't relate. Big family?"

"Too big," he says, spooning up more soup.

"I always imagined living in a place where you could see but not hear your next-door neighbors. Like my parents. All the homes on their street have one acre lots, they're old homes with character, from back before developers put people on postage-stamp sized lots with all the houses exactly the same. Still close enough to say hello to people, though. To look out for one another. For kids to grow up playing together on a street. For neighbors to look in on one another if someone's alone or elderly, you know?"

"Hm," he murmurs, "Tell me about your digs here in Columbus. Not like your folks' place, I take it."

"Oh, uh, my fiancé and I just bought a townhome together. Not really my style. Kind of too modern and small, only a little patio for a yard. Front porch not big enough to put a nice swing on. No room for all the fruit trees out back like I'd wanted, but it was for practical reasons." I shrug.

"I see," he says, and takes another spoonful of his soup.

He doesn't ask questions and I'm relieved. He probably thinks we just bought an entry-level home we could afford. I don't typically blurt my business and I'm surprised I've said as much as I've already said. I'm stopping myself from explaining that my fiancé lost the use of his legs recently and that's why we bought a one level rowhouse when I've always dreamed of living in a big home with all sorts of character including a wraparound porch, grand staircase, and a yard big enough to have a football game in. Like that house I've been watching that we can't afford and that's come off the market. Just as well, I guess. I've stopped dreaming about raising a family there.

I eat more of my soup, but I'm feeling self-conscious. He's eating his soup, too, but he's also studying me.

I feel a little stumped. Because if I encourage conversation, will he think the wrong thing? I can't just sit here and say nothing.

My phone buzzes and I quickly reach for it, relieved that I've now got an excuse to make a quick exit.

"Excuse me a second," I say to Derek as I read it.

Dad: What's my Wi-Fi password, kiddo? Got a new phone.

I reply.

Cheater

I taped it to the upper inside of the drawer in the table where you keep the remote controls.

I stare at my screen a moment, waiting to see if he replies. He does.

Dad: Thanks. All good with you?

I reply with a smiley face and another line saying,

We should catch up soon.

He replies with a thumbs up.
I tuck my phone away and loop my bag over my shoulder.
"I'm gonna have to go. Something's come up." I wave to Mr. Nguyen and move in that direction with my wallet. "Could I have a take-out container and a raised chocolate donut to go, please?"
"Of course," he calls out and rings me up.
After I pay for my food, three people come in, so he tells me he'll bring me the container and my donut in a moment.
I move back to a watching and waiting Derek Steele, who has his elbow propped on the table, his chin resting on his palm.
"Don't forget your book," he says.
"I'd like to give you the money for it," I tell him.
He shakes his head. "Book report."
I roll my eyes. "How am I supposed to deliver a book report to you?"
"It won't be difficult," he states with a salacious look in his eyes.
I laugh it off, feeling uncomfortable. I'm not sure what that means, but I don't ask. Instead, I put the book into my bag and sop up stray soup drips from the table with a napkin, studiously avoiding Derek's eyes, even though I know he's still watching me.
More people have come in, so it takes a minute, but Mrs. Nguyen stops by with a container, lid, and a paper bag. I thank her as she lifts

my soup and pours it into the container while Derek gets up and holds my jacket out for me.

He helps me into it and the proximity means the heat is again rising, not just up my face and up my neck, but also in other places too.

He steps around to face me and begins to button up my coat for me.

I stand still, sort of statue-like, sort of deer-in-the-headlights like, eyes on his face while his fingers work their way up my coat.

Why is he buttoning my coat? Why am I not backing up and taking over?

He's got fascinating bone structure. Cut jaw. Really great skin. Grooves in his bottom lip that have me licking my lips for some reason. After doing up my top button, he straightens my collar for me and looks straight into my eyes while still holding it. "Get home safely, Chloe Turner."

He remembered my last name.

"Thank you for the book," I say, awkwardly. Because this whole situation is beyond awkward.

"You're welcome."

"Gonna let me go?" I ask.

He smiles so wide and so attractively with something sparking in his eyes that manages to set my panties on fire. He doesn't answer.

I back away and he releases me.

Blushing, I grab my takeout bag, wave at the Nguyens, and move out, hearing him say, "Book report," before I'm outside.

11 ♥ Chloe

Friday Night

Exercise is kicking my ass. It's been way too long. I'm in a pitiful, breathless state as I turn the incline and speed back down two notches on the treadmill, doing it painfully aware of the fact I'm nowhere near ready for anything more than a brisk pace. I've already spent time on the elliptical machine and on some weight and resistance training and feel like I'm about ready for some ibuprofen and a nap.

Something catches my eye as I reach for my water bottle and now I'm taking in the shocking vision of a shirtless, shiny, Derek Steele who is doing bicep curls with his eyes on me. As our gazes connect, I stumble, crash to my knees, and of course the conveyer belt sends me backwards until I wind up flat on my back, on the floor.

My eyes are closed tight, but the place is busy so I'm sure there are multiple sets of eyes on me. Could I just lie here on the floor behind the running treadmill, until everyone leaves?

Sadly, not.

Must open eyes and covertly get out of here, avoiding the urge to do it on all fours pretending no one sees me. Pretending Derek Steele didn't just watch my treadmill fail which I will probably see later on in a compilation on TikTok or YouTube.

What are the odds of him being here tonight?

Granted, I haven't been here in over half a year, but this isn't the only gym in the city. This is definitely not another coincidence.

I open my eyes, expecting a view of the rafters and *lord have mercy*, Derek is standing over me, looking down at me, with his hand extended to help me to my feet.

I shakily accept it and one of his muscled arms goes around my waist as I get to my feet. Now we're face-to-face and far too close.

"Hurt?" he asks, concern etched into his features.

"Just my pride," I whisper.

His lips slowly split into that very nice smile of his as he looks me over. I look him over, too, which provides an added benefit of me not looking anywhere else to see who might be gawking slash laughing at me.

"Muscles. So many muscles."

He's laughing and I realize I've just whispered about the muscles aloud.

It's true, though.

Gorgeous shoulders. Neck. Chest. Abs of steel. And his skin is all shiny from sweat. He's strong. Muscled. But not steroid level. And his skin tone is a beautiful golden color. Tan. But not fake-tanned.

And he's still holding my hand. He's still got an arm around me.

"You done, miss?" An elderly lady with purple hair, in full makeup along with a headband around her head asks and then cracks her gum.

"Oh yeah, I think I'm beyond done. One second." I take the opportunity to move out of his orbit, grab a sanitizing cloth, wipe down the machine and grab my stuff.

"Sure you're all right?" Derek asks, following me.

I drop the cleaner and cloth on the ledge by the changerooms. "I'm fine," I say, failing to hide my embarrassment. "Stuff like this happens to me all the time. I'm like a cartoon character or something. Bye." I escape into the locker room out of his view.

When I'm done showering and changing, I'm unsurprised to see

Cheater

him sitting in the lobby on a bench, eyes on me as soon as I emerge. Of course he's waiting for me.

"Fancy meeting you again," I say with sarcasm. "If I didn't know better I might think you're stalking me."

"And you know better, do you?" he asks, a wicked gleam in his eyes that is not only a little dangerous, it's also *a lot* hot.

"How long have you been a member of this gym?" I ask, a hand propped on my waist. I know my stance oozes accusation.

"Just joined," he says, shamelessly smirking.

I tilt my head. "Coincidence? I just re-joined last night after leaving the soup place."

He continues smiling.

My eyebrows go up. Of course he knows that somehow. Did he follow me?

"Confession?" he asks.

I wait, braced.

"I'm gonna be making Columbus home base for a while. Saw you walk over here from the soup joint last night and... lightbulb went off."

"Uh huh," I nod sagely, "So, Derek... I don't typically like to make assumptions, but I'm thinking my assumption here about you is probably not far off."

"Probably not," he returns, then casually sips from the water bottle in his hand. I watch him twist the cap back on and then he volleys with, "Just like my assumption probably ain't wrong either. That you ducked out of the coffee shop pretending something came up because you were uncomfortable with the chemistry between us."

"I'm engaged," I state. "Though I know I've made this fact clear to you directly more than once as well as to someone else in front of you another time, so..." I give him a pointed look.

"How's the book so far?"

"I don't know. I haven't dug in."

"Have a drink with me, Chloe."

I blink, taken back. "A drink?"

He rises and takes a step forward, putting us toe to toe. I look up at his face. He's so close I can smell his soap on his freshly showered skin. So close he's all I see.

This feels dangerous. Wrong. And yet ... something else. Something I'm not sure I have the capacity to acknowledge fully.

"I'm not sure I'm in a state to be seen outside a gym," I say self-consciously instead of doing what I should do. Walk away without responding.

My hair is wet, I have no makeup on my face. I'm in jeans and a plain tee.

He smiles. "I disagree." He touches a tendril of hair that's hanging over my ear. "But we don't have to be in public if you're not comfortable with it. We can have a drink at my place instead."

I blink a couple times and then I shake my head. "I can't. I... I'm-"

"Engaged. I know."

"You know but you just don't care?" I ask.

"There's something here." He gestures between us. "I think we both know it. And I want to explore it."

"Meaning?" I ask.

"Meaning, come for a drink with me, Chloe," he says, dark eyes searching mine.

I'm against the wall beside the locker room door and he's close enough to kiss, if I get up on my tippy toes and lean forward just an inch.

"Not your place. Somewhere public," I amend.

He smiles wider. "One of my clubs isn't far. You know The Fifth?"

I nod.

"I'll follow you there," he tells me.

I nod again.

"Yeah?" he checks, like he doesn't quite believe I'm agreeing.

"One drink. No promises of anything beyond that."

He jerks his head toward the exit, so I move in that direction.

Cheater

He gets to the door first and holds it open, gesturing for me to go ahead.

Heart pounding hard in my chest, I walk ahead of him. After I hit the button to get my car unlocked, he gets ahead of me to open the driver's door. I climb inside. He looks dead into my eyes and something... that something he spoke of that's between us, it pulses. Throbs. My heart is racing.

Derek skims his bottom lip with his front teeth and shuts my door.

∞

I pull into a spot outside The Fifth; I've been here before. Twice, I think. I remember it as fairly dim, with plenty of high-backed booths. Should be a safer bet for discretion, though that's never a guarantee in public.

Derek pulls up beside my six-year-old Jeep Cherokee with his swanky new-looking Mercedes SUV. He crooks his finger and then drives past me, so I follow him around to the opposite side of the parking lot. He stops in a reserved spot outside an entrance to the office building part of this location. This is another office building with a nightclub on the ground floor like last Friday's spot.

I pull into the reserved spot beside him. By the time I turn my car off, he's outside my door, opening it for me.

I'm not dressed for a club like The Fifth, being make-up free, damp-haired, and in jeans and a basic T-shirt with slip-on sneakers.

Despite this, it's obvious by the carnal look on Derek's face that he's attracted to me anyway.

He'd look attractive if he, too, looked like he just came from the gym. But he doesn't. While his dark hair is damp, he still looks amazing. He's clean-shaven, in nice jeans, the same leather jacket he had on last night, and a snug wine-colored Henley hoodie that I'm sure will show off his defined upper body under that jacket. He takes my hand and pulls it to his mouth, touching his lips to my knuckles. "The club's that way." He points across the parking lot, still holding my hand. "My place is this way." He points to the door in front of us. "Which way are we going, Chloe?"

I'm taken aback by the kiss on my hand, by the way my hand feels in his. By his eyes on my face. By all of it.

While holding my breath, my feet move us toward the closest door. The door to his place.

His free hand moves to the small of my back the way it did in his nightclub a week ago, and then he lets go to reach ahead to touch a door sensor with his thumb. I hear it unlock, and then he opens and holds it for me. When I'm over the threshold, his hand lands on my lower back again. And I can't stop my mind from focusing on the feel of his hand on the back of my jacket, wondering what it would feel like to have his hand on my bare skin again.

He grabs my hand again as we move down the long, swanky cream-colored marble-walled shiny-floored hallway toward an elevator. This entrance is obviously private. There were no other cars in any of the reserved spots that bordered the entrance, so I take it this is the building his father is re-purposing, and that Derek's siblings are currently absent. The elevator is waiting, so Derek walks us in and presses the PH button on the panel. We take an express ride up with our hands still clasped together. And my heart is pounding hard.

Am I really about to do this? Am I really about to use the hall pass? It feels illicit. It feels like I'm a cheater. But Adam has been encouraging this.

Should I tell this insanely hot man why I'm doing this despite the diamond on my finger?

He's a rich, insanely attractive man. But I don't know the protocol for this sort of situation. Do I bring it up? Do I assume it's understood?

My eyes are fixed on the elevator lights showing our ascent above the door, but I'm pretty sure his are on me.

Shit. Does he have condoms? Of course he'd have condoms. He's a rich, attractive man.

Cheater

Does he have a girlfriend? A fiancée? A wife?

Why didn't I do a quick internet search on him?

I know why I didn't. Because despite the fact that he's crossed my mind plenty in the past week, I never expected *this* to happen so there was no point looking him up. I also didn't want to become fixated on the idea of hooking up with him so of course I pushed him out of my mind every time I thought of him, which was more often than I'd care to admit. Except that time when I was in the shower and indulged a fantasy while I took care of my... *ahem*...needs.

The elevator halts and when the door opens, something ignites in my veins. His too, I think, because now he's powerwalking and I'm jogging to keep up until we get to the second-to-last door on the left side of the elevator in a hallway that looks the same as the one on the ground floor. He puts his thumb to another sensor on this door and when I hear the click of the door it feels as ominous to me as the sound of a gun being cocked. Not that I've ever heard one of those in real life.

And another thought surfaces, too. The fact that it doesn't matter if I go home tonight or not. Adam is spending the weekend at his brother's place. I know he's done it on purpose. He did kiss me before he left at four o'clock this afternoon, kissed me the same way he kissed me in front of everyone last Sunday, which probably wasn't supposed to feel like being stabbed in the heart, but it did because he did it in front of his brother. I didn't even fake a smile as Paul wheeled him out the front door toward his van.

I decide here and now that I won't be thinking about Adam at all for the rest of whatever time I'm here in Derek's penthouse apartment. I'm only here because Adam pushed this. And if I'm honest with myself, maybe I do want this, too. Because this man right here is the ultimate Hall Pass type. If I'm going to actually do this, why shouldn't it be with an insanely attractive man who has put effort into pursuing me?

He opens the door and gestures for me to go ahead.

I take four or five steps into the dim, large, open-concept space that feels like a swanky hotel suite. There's a great view from up here and the full-length windows show off that the sky is dappled with city lights. There's a lamp lit in the corner beside a white leather sectional couch. I take in a large wall-mounted television, some monochrome art on the walls, the modern, spotless kitchen done in black, white, and chrome. There's a glass dining table for four with tall black and silver chairs. The only splash of color in the space beyond the jewel-toned kitchen backsplash is a vase of colorful flowers in the middle of the table.

I hear the door click shut behind me, so I look over my shoulder. Derek is leaning against the door, hand still on the knob, eyes on me, and he's sucking on his bottom lip.

As he releases his lip, he releases the doorknob too before reaching out and grabbing my hand. He tugs, pulling me to his body.

My eyes bulge as I absorb his body heat.

"Give me permission to make your fantasies come true," he requests gruffly, looking down into my eyes.

I blink twice. "Fantasies?"

His hand slides across my jaw, his thumb grazing my cheekbone. "You could tell me what you want tonight or..." He pauses both in motion and in talking and smiles, "you can leave it to me and fulfill my fantasies instead. Choice is yours. Tell me which way you want it."

My stunned silence lasts what feels like a long minute before his other hand snakes down and he grips my behind as he pulls me tight to his body, his erection pressing against my stomach.

"Maybe we oughta talk. I should tell you that I don't usually–"

His hand on my jaw moves to cup my mouth, stopping me from speaking.

And while my heart skips three beats, my panties are flooded.

"Do you feel how much I want you?" he asks, placing my hand on his erection.

My eyes take in his face, the dark and carnal expression in his eyes. And with where my hand is, what I feel there, the thrill racing through me is something new, something potent.

I feel strange. Foreign. Alive. I haven't felt this level of alive before. Because it's supposed to be forbidden, maybe? I shove that thought away. Because I have an actual license to do this tonight.

"Your fantasies or mine?" the gorgeous man who wants me asks, keeping one hand firmly on mine while flexing his hips. "That's all we need to discuss right now. Be in this moment with me Chloe. Here. Now. Everything else can wait. What do you want? What *you* want or what I want? Whose fantasies? The choice is yours."

He moves his hand away from my mouth.

I swallow and say something I've never dreamed I'd ever get to actually say out loud.

"Do I get a safe word if I pick your fantasies?"

His eyes light up and he grabs my jaw with both hands, mouth descending on mine.

Electricity races through my veins as he kisses me hungrily. And I show my hunger, too. Starving. Fucking starving like he would not believe.

Months of pent-up sexual frustration are unbridled. Maybe even years of it. While he's kissing me, I pull his leather jacket off and toss it, then my hands dive under the back of his soft Henley and the feel of his muscular, hot back nearly undoes me. I might come before he even gets me undressed.

The shirt goes up over his head with both of our help and he tosses it as I reach for his belt, getting it undone as he kicks off his shoes. He's lifting me at my waist. My legs wrap around him and we're going right, down a hall with a few closed doors, through the open one that's got a light on. Our eyes are locked the entire short journey until I'm put down on the black, white, and silver comforter.

We lose eye contact as he pulls my slip-on sneakers off and then his eyes are locked with mine again as he climbs up to hover over me. As soon as he's within reach, I'm grabbing for his jaw with both hands, so that he'll kiss me again, so that I can kiss him back while feeling his weight on top of me, pressing me to his bed.

A hundred thoughts flutter through my mind. None of them are stop signs or red lights. Everything is green. Everything in me says *yes*. No, *shouts* it. **Yes!**

This sexy man wants me. This incredibly attractive man is a hundred per cent focused on me right now. And it feels exhilarating.

"Mine? My fantasies? Wanna ask you once more. Be sure." He asks this against my lips while undoing my fly with his right hand.

My fantasies or his? I'm beyond interested in knowing what his are. And maybe that's dangerous given that I don't know him, but I'm in the moment.

"Yes, *your* fantasies, Derek," I say while nodding enthusiastically.

He groans with what looks like supreme pleasure. "I was hoping you'd pick this option."

"Do I need a safe word?" I ask again.

He caresses my face gently, with what feels like affection in his expression. "No, my little bunny rabbit. I'll keep you safe at all costs." He drops a kiss on my mouth, then adds, "Guess what?"

"What?" I whisper breathlessly. My chest heaves up and down like I've run a marathon. My panties are drenched. I'm about ready to come out of my skin, I'm *that* turned on.

And the look in his eyes excites me. Because not only is it carnal, it's also playful.

"My fantasies about you are wide and varied and include giving you the hottest night of your life tonight. Ready?"

"You have no idea how ready I am," I say. "But Derek—"

"We can talk later," he cuts me off. "I know what you want to talk about but I'm asking you to table it for now. Okay?"

I hesitantly nod because his eyes seem full of understanding, somehow.

He continues. "I'm clean and healthy. Tested three days ago and got results already. Haven't been with anyone in a few months. And you'll be safe. I won't harm you. Okay?"

Cheater

Relief floods my veins. I believe him.

"I'm clean, too. And I'm on birth control," I say.

"That's all we gotta talk about this minute. Yeah?"

I nod hesitantly.

"Nervous? I'll take good care of you, Chloe. I promise. You want to message a friend and tell them where you are? Or have you already done that?"

The offer gives me a reality check that I hadn't even thought about. I should have done that on the way here. I'm smarter than this. I need to remember that. Despite how insanely hot this man is, I can't let it make me stupid.

I nod, ignoring the little voice telling me to decline his offer so we can get to the good part sooner, because it's an offer I should absolutely take.

"Right back," he says.

I stare at the ceiling, trying to catch my breath, hoping he gets back here before common sense returns. Or guilt. Without looking at it, I slip my engagement ring off my finger.

He's back with my purse. I sit up and covertly drop it in there as I pull out my phone.

I send a text to Alannah.

Safety check-in. Hall Pass getting cashed in - in T minus 1 minute. Derek Steele. Don't swoon but I'm at his penthouse condo in the building the 5th nightclub is in right now. Message you later.
Don't make my phone beep for the next 2 hours at least. Love you. Xoxo

The message zooms through cyberspace and instantly I see that it's been delivered, so I slip my phone back into my bag and put the bag on the bench at the end of the bed.

"You need a drink?" he asks.

I swallow and shake my head. I don't need a drink. What I need right now is this man's tongue in my mouth, his hands on my body, and for his penis to pound me into this very comfortable mattress.

At that thought of being filled after so much emptiness for so long, everything south of my waist reacts. And my breasts feel heavy. If I weren't on birth control, I'm sure I'd drop an egg.

He climbs up from the bottom of the bed again as I recline. As I'm seeing is the norm with Derek, our eyes are again locked. Eye contact during sex is rare in my experience. And I feel like it should be a requirement, because it is sizzling hot.

His eyelids lower as his mouth gets to mine. Mine close, too, and I'm avidly participating in the kiss. It's an eager kiss that's deep and passionate, with his hands roaming my face, my jaw, my shoulders. And then he's got the hem of my shirt and it's being peeled up and off. He's down to unbuttoned jeans and I'm down to my bra and jeans when his focus goes back to my fly.

The floor lamp in the corner seems to be staying on. I find I'm okay with that, with seeing what's about to happen in addition to feeling it.

He stands beside the bed and my jeans are shimmied off and my socks are gone before he's moving between my parted thighs, dropping a kiss on my knee. I jerk with surprise and excitement. His eyes light with amusement as his hand glides up my torso, stopping to caress my throat and then resumes the journey as fingers glide through my hair. It feels great. His eyes on my skin feel amazing. Suddenly he's over me, but moving back down, kissing his way down my shoulder, then his lips land on the top of my left breast.

The cup of my pink lace bra is savagely ripped down so he can take a pull on my nipple. I hear the fabric strain and am surprised it hasn't ripped. I let out a breathy sound as my back arches.

Derek works his way down my body, lips pressing to the skin of my ribs, then my stomach as his fingers hook into the waistband of my underwear. My heart picks up pace yet again as the black Spandex slides down my legs.

I feel a little spinny with arousal, so I pull in a deep breath and

Cheater

close my eyes, exhaling slowly while absorbing the way Derek's mouth feels as it touches down between my legs in a gentle kiss. My legs are lifted and thrown over his broad shoulders a little roughly and I squeak in surprise.

I'm glad I just took a shower. I'm also glad I didn't give up on lady-scaping like I was tempted to do with lack of attention to my nude body lately. Many baby unicorns have sadly vanished as they do when a woman goes to the trouble of lady-scaping and then getting zero action. Or so me and my friends say. Not today. Today, thanks to this hot man, baby unicorns get to thrive.

He thrusts his tongue into me while suckling my clit and *yes* - good Lord, I'm in heaven. It feels amazing, and I'm dying to watch, so I get up on my elbows and it looks like he's devouring his favorite meal. It's insanely hot to watch a man give you head and see that he's enjoying what he's doing.

I should feel shy, apprehensive about this perfect stranger having his perfectly sinful mouth between my legs, but instead, this feels like the most exciting thing to happen to me... maybe *ever*.

Derek's gaze moves back up to mine and he winks. I smile and reach down, my fingers weaving into his dark, thick, still slightly damp hair. He takes a hard pull on my clit and then rams what feels like more than one finger into me and crooks it, hitting my g-spot. I jolt.

He does it again, applying suction to my clit and it makes me cry out.

I cover my mouth.

Hot damn, he knows what he's doing.

Derek looks up and says, "Let it fly, baby. Don't muffle your sounds. I'm earning those right now and believe me when I tell you I wanna hear them."

Okay, but this is about to be embarrassing. Because I'm going to come in about thirty more seconds if he keeps this up.

He's fingering me like a pro while working my clit with his mouth and then his free hand snakes up and pinches my nipple to the point of pain. But because of everything happening to me right now, I don't complain, instead I detonate, crying out "Omigod!" as my head slams back onto the pillow. It's the only part of my body touching the bed as Derek has the rest of me in the air, my trembling legs still draped over his shoulders. This feels so incredible, I could fly straight into the sun or the sea without a care in the world.

While I'm still lost in sensation, spiraling upwards to some heavenly plane, crying out shamelessly, filled with his expert tongue and fingers, at least some of his attention turns to a hole that has not ever gotten attention from anybody. A digit – his thumb, I think – slips in the back door just a little. And I fly to a sitting position, grabbing his shoulders. He freezes and looks at me. His thumb is still in there and I think he's assessing my expression to see if I want him to stop.

I don't.

His mouth crashes into mine, his thumb vacates anyway, but I can't complain because he's falling on top of me, so my legs instinctively wrap tight around his thighs to help guide a hard and impressive part of him inside me. But he adds strength to it and slams his hips forward to hit the end of me before I'm entirely prone.

God, yes.

And it feels incredible. I've missed *this*. I've missed this so much. He's well-endowed and he knows how to move. Not just that, there's still eye contact. It's like he's not just fucking some random chick. Derek is fucking me. Me. He's looking at me like he's got every intention of making all of my fantasies come true.

This is good sex. This is great sex. This absolutely *is* the hottest night of my life.

12

Derek

She feels exactly like I hoped she'd feel. Right. Real. Like she was meant for me. I'm so glad this wasn't underwhelming. It's the polar opposite of that.

And to make it even better, it's not just about how good it feels to me. It's also about how she's into this in a way I've never experienced, because her enthusiasm is easy to see. And maybe that's because I've never paid this much attention, I don't know, but I *do* know I'm absolutely fascinated with Chloe Turner. I've done research. I've got a thick report on this girl, so I know a lot about her.

I know she was adopted as an infant, that she's an only child because her younger fifteen-year-old brother died when she was sixteen. I can tell she's a nurturer who puts others first. She's a good worker. She's intelligent.

And even more importantly, I know things about her fantasies that put me in the perfect position to make tonight more than she expects and all that she's wanted and never had. To make it something she'll quickly get addicted to. I know what she wants and how she wants it. And bonus: I'm into all of it.

She's squeezing her tight cunt around my cock. She's milking it so hard, it's like her life depends on it. It's never felt this good to fuck anybody before. The sounds she's making are sexy as fuck and she's kissing me like she can't get enough of me. She's like a tiny, pretty, wild animal that's finally been unbridled.

She meets my gaze with her teeth sunk into her bottom lip and staring into these light blue eyes makes me feel new things. I've already become addicted to looking into them to see how she'll react to things I say and do.

I never expected it to feel *this* monumental to be inside her. To feel like this because she looks at me this way. To be inside her with nothing between us. I haven't fucked ungloved since I was sixteen years old and that whole shit show happened with my father's twenty-four-year-old secretary, who tried to worm her way into the family with a fake pregnancy scare.

I have a strong suspicion I'll never fuck gloved again, because this is the only woman I can see myself fucking going forward.

I wondered if my fascination with her would wane after I got a taste. I wasn't prepared for how this would feel. For what it would wake up in me. Things are shifting on my chess board even as I fuck her hard, swallowing the sweet cries my cock pulls from her. My focus has sharpened and if it weren't for the fact that I don't want to spook her yet, I might otherwise not *ever* let her out of my sight.

I feel urges coming on. Urgent urges.

I turn her to her belly and fuck her harder. Faster. I don't hold back. My fingertips are going to leave marks. So are my teeth. And she fucking loves it. She's gonna love *me*. Yearn for only me. And get what she yearns for.

On that thought, I grab her hair tight and erupt, coming inside her with a roar that sounds mostly animal.

When I catch my breath, I examine her face. She looks absolutely sated, happy, gorgeous. I want to pound my chest and give her everything. Put her on my shoulders and shout to the world that she's mine. I want things right now I've never wanted.

These emotions surging in me? They're huge. I need a minute with them, to tamp them down, so I tell her I'll be right back and then slip out.

After a solid two minutes of pacing the length of the floor to ceiling windows in the living room, I come back with two bottles of

Cheater

cold water. No sooner has she put her bottle down before I'm hard again, so I toss my empty water bottle somewhere and lift her up out of the bed and put her against the bedroom wall, fucking her there, my hand around her throat possessively while my cock pumps in and out of her slippery pussy that's dribbling my cum. And she cries. Weeps. It's not from fear or protest. It's emotional. She cries big fat tears of release as she comes on my cock while our gazes are still locked. And then she limply snuggles into me as I carry her back to the bed, not nearly done yet. I continue fucking her in missionary position while rubbing her clit until she comes yet again.

She's so wet that I use her juices and the leftover cum from the last time I fucked her to lube up her ass and then moving her to her belly, I gently press my cock against the entrance and get what I want - resistance.

She winces.

"Want me to stop?" I ask, hoping she's the miracle I think she is.

"No," she whispers. "Just... go slow. Careful."

Damn right she is. She *is*.

I press my fingers to her clit and rub tiny circles while guiding my cock in just past the head.

Fuck, that's tight. And hot.

"It's okay, Chloe. I'll go slow. You okay, baby?"

She's clenching my sheets, but she nods.

"Relax, baby," I whisper. "I'll take good care of you. I'll make you feel so fucking good. Yeah?"

I advance a little more, feeling that tight ring milking my cock as I advance.

She squeaks and clenches, so I slow down.

"Relax, beautiful. Relax." My palm skates up and down her back. Her body relaxes marginally. She's ready for more. I move in further.

She lets out a slow exhale.

"There. You're okay, baby. Doing so good. Fuck, do you ever feel incredible. You know that?"

She whimpers.

I'm fully seated. "There. Take it. You're taking every inch of me, Chloe. Feel good yet?"

She whimpers again, then rotates her hips just a little. She's ready for me to move.

"Ready for me to fuck this tight, hot hole harder, Chloe?"

"Mm hm," she groans, biting the pillow.

I slide my middle finger into her pussy and crook it. She jolts.

"Fuck, you're such a good girl." I kiss her shoulder and then pick up pace as she relaxes entirely, giving in.

I fuck that hot, tight hole while pressing her g-spot with two fingers over and over while kissing her back, neck, and shoulders as she whimpers into my sheets.

I bite her shoulder as she whimpers my name; I feel triumphant.

I read on her sex fantasy blog (that she hasn't updated in a year and a half) that while she's never had anal, she finds the idea intriguing. Given the conversation between her and her friend about the guy whose ring she wears being vanilla or an unseasoned baked potato ... without having much of a sex drive ... I'm confident I've just been the first to take this sweet little ass. No protest. Letting fear melt into trust at my urging. She just gave it up and cried my name into my sheets while I claimed her ass.

I pull back and then slowly drive to the root one more time, feeling her tremble as I shudder out my orgasm, grabbing a handful of her beautiful hair.

Fuck, that was hot. So fucking hot.

My brain is mush for a minute. As I pull back out of her body, I have to slow because she whimpers, "Ow, ow, ow."

"Shh," I hush her as I get the rest of the way out before I turn her over, cradling her to my chest and pressing my lips to her head as I lift her and take her to the shower to clean both of us off.

She's limp in my arms, blowing out long breaths.

I wash her from her head to her cute little toes. She's pliant, smiling, and her eyes tell me she's still hungry for me. The hunger I see there mirrors my own. Never have I looked into the eyes of another person and seen something that makes me feel like this. I've never seen hunger that I understand so fucking well before. She's as into this as I am.

Almost as gone for me as I am for her. Not quite though. And the rest of that'll come.

I dry us off and carry her back to bed, placing her on her back.

"You good?" I ask.

She giggles, then nods while biting her lip.

Fuck. Cute.

"Stay still," I order, and climb up to straddle her face, pressing my knees into the headboard.

She's staring at me with shock, but she's not protesting.

"Gonna fuck my little bunny's pretty mouth," I advise. "Give your other sweet little holes a minute to recover."

Her eyes light up eagerly as she licks her lips, readying herself.

"My perfect girl," I praise and watch her melt as I run the backs of my fingers across her cheekbone.

My cock is harder than it's ever been as I slowly feed it to her eager, sweet mouth. She grabs my ass cheeks with both hands and hungrily opens wide as I slide in halfway. She swallows around my cock, and I go deeper.

Her eyes are glued to my face as I fuck her mouth slowly, gently, going two thirds of the way in before pulling back out until she surprises me by pulling me even closer, hands tightening on my ass cheeks, digging her nails into my flesh as she manages to take me to the root, showing she wants all of it. She gags, but doesn't try to get out of it.

Go time. She wants this. And so do I. Everything in her body language and especially in her eyes tells me to go for the gusto, not to hold back.

So, I don't.

I take a handful of her hair and increase my pace. The gagging sounds she makes are like music because as her eyes water, she completely submits to it, taking all of me as I rock my hips forward over and over, filling her sweet mouth.

"Look how absolutely fucking beautiful you are, full of my cock like this, Chloe. I'm not ever gonna forget how you look right now."

Her eyes are on me, I've got her full, eager, hungry submission. Submission changes to participation as she engages with her tongue, slurping, applying suction while I continue to rut her face. And now the little vixen's fingertips rub down my asshole and press on my taint. This makes me blow my load so hard I see spots as I moan, pressing my forehead into the wall. She chokes. I pull back and help her to a seated position as she coughs and sputters a little bit, looking out of breath.

I use a handful of her hair to pull her forehead to my chest "Fuckin' fuck, Chloe," I sigh before I grab her jaw and tilt it so I can look into her eyes. "Fuck, baby." I blow out a hard exhale and then move sideways, legs dangling off the side of the bed while still using my grip on her hair to urge her forward, then holding the back of her neck to drag her across my lap. I pull my right hand all the way back and land a hard slap on her bare ass.

Her ass shakes with the slap, and she cries out, spit and cum all over her chin soaking into the sheets.

Moving my hand enough to admire the stark pink handprint across her cheeks, I plunge three fingers into her sopping wet pussy.

She grunts and fists my sheets hard, her face on my thigh, her little tongue darting forward to lick at my cock. I pull my fingers out, slap her ass again and demand, "Open your legs wide, Chloe. Right fucking now. Show me what's mine." I shove her toward the bottom of the bed and get to my knees behind her, spreading her ass cheeks wide as she opens her legs like the good girl she is, gripping the bench at the foot of the bed.

Her asshole is swollen. Her cunt is soaked. Looks raw. Well-used. She's panting. She's loving every minute of this.

Cheater

A phone rings. Not my tone. It's coming from her bag. She makes no moves to go for it as I bury my face in her ass cheeks and slurp all I can get into my mouth, licking from her clit to her asshole. I slap her ass again and flip her to her back before I drag her up a foot so she's fully on the bed instead of half hanging off the bench.

I land a hard slap on her pussy making her squeak. Her mouth is open and her pupils are blown as she watches me slap it a second time. She jerks as a reaction but makes no moves that make me think she doesn't want more.

"Legs wider," I order.

She complies, fisting the disheveled bedding with both hands. She spreads them as wide as they'll go. I move up and take my hard-again cock into my hand and slap her clit with it.

She arches for me, whimpering.

I slap her with my cock again. "You like that?" I ask.

She nods, eyes closing.

"Eyes on me, baby," I order and hers snap open obediently.

"Fuck you're beautiful," I tell her. "Beautiful spread wide for me like this. Taking whatever I plan to give you. Giving me whatever I want. Such a good girl."

She whimpers again, looking drunk on me, looking like I've just told her I'm gonna buy her anything in the world she wants.

My lips meet hers and I slide inside her pussy again, this time giving it to her slow, deep, with our mouths connected as I pump and pump until I spill the last load I've got in me for at least a couple hours.

She clings to me like she needs me. And it's heady as fuck. I've never wanted this feeling I've got, never knew *this* existed.

I turn to my back, bringing her with me so that she's on top of me and haul a corner of the comforter up and then flick it so it billows out and covers us. The sheets are half off the bed, and that would normally irritate me. But I don't give a fuck tonight. I could stay here like this for eternity with her. She's got my cum in her pussy, her ass, and down her throat as she falls asleep on top of me. Nothing has felt more right.

My eyes coast over her body in the moonlight and land on her left hand, which is on my chest. She took that engagement ring off sometime after we left the gym. A smile spreads across my face. And I know it probably looks sinister. With good reason.

13
Chloe

I wake up to the muffled sound of my phone ringing.

I manage to pry one eye open, feeling like a zombie.

I take in the sharpening image of what's in front of me. An expanse of muscled torso.

Derek Steele.

We're lying on our sides, my head tucked under his chin, most of me plastered against his body heat. I move back a little. Both of his arms are around me so one of his arms is my current pillow.

Many illicit images assault all my senses at once. Images of last night. Of the things he did to me. Of the things I did to him. So. Much. Fucking.

My belly takes a nosedive at the memories. I ticked several boxes on my sexy bucket list last night. My belly takes another dip. Wow, that was some dirty sex. And though it went on and on and on, every minute of it was amazing. I never got bored, it never felt monotonous, I didn't want it to end.

This room is drenched with light, which means I stayed all night and slept like the dead. Did he want me to leave afterwards? I don't know the etiquette for a hookup.

If he wanted me gone he probably wouldn't have cuddled with me afterwards. He did more than cuddle me. He pretty much swaddled me like a baby. I fell asleep on his chest, his arms around me, and I slept deeper than I can recall sleeping in months.

The phone stops and I'm guessing it's Alannah since I dropped a pretty hefty bombshell into her phone last night and it's been way more than two hours. It was probably her calling in the middle of our final round.

Funny... because last weekend at her place on Saturday, she told me if I was smart, I'd pursue Derek Steele as hall pass material. Rich. Sexy. Would probably be happy to do it once and never ask for my phone number.

I bite my lip.

I'm sure she never thought I'd actually do it.

And I definitely never thought it was a possibility when she suggested it.

She certainly never told me she slipped him her number once.

I'm suddenly flipped to my back and covered by the hot, hard body of Mr. Hall Pass himself, who pins my wrists to the mattress and in one thrust, enters me to the hilt.

Ooh.

Our eyes lock.

His are sleepy. Sexy. And as always, kind of irresistible. Mr. Hall Pass loves eye contact, it seems. And it's insanely appealing.

His jaw and cheeks are covered by faint stubble, and it looks good. His hair is a mess and that looks good, too. I can only imagine what my hair looks like after me falling asleep on it wet, without even combing it after that shower we took. After all the times he tangled his fingers in my hair and used it as a handle last night.

Hot.

He's clearly not mad that I slept here, certainly not done with me. I lost count of how many times he made me come last night; how many times he came. He came a lot, though I came two or three times as much.

And here he is as soon as his eyes are open, fucking me again. A man with stamina such as this isn't something I'm familiar with.

My legs hurt. Everywhere he put his dick kinda hurts.

And I'm a little shocked. It's as if he had a cheat sheet or some-

Cheater

thing. Notes on his hand that I didn't notice. Bullet points telling him what would turn me to goo for him. A panicked thought hits me. Did Alannah get to him?

My mind races and I see spots for a beat while I ponder this.

Did she tell him I'd melt for a bunch of kinky stuff? Did she suggest I'd like it if he fucked me while holding my throat? Tell him to boss me around and talk dirty while he fucked me? Did she fill him in on just how badly I needed my dry spell to be broken and for me to use the hall pass on someone who really *really* knew what they were doing? Is that why he's pursued this? Is Alannah the reason I'm here right now?

His mouth is on mine, taking a deep drink of me, bringing me back into the moment. My mind becomes all about sensations instead of intrusive thoughts and I wrap my arms and legs around him and go for the gusto.

But it doesn't take long before other thoughts begin to flood in. Adam wouldn't kiss me in the morning until after he'd brushed his teeth, especially considering the fact I swallowed cum last night. I've been kissed by guys with bad breath, so I always appreciated that about Adam. But Derek tastes amazing first thing in the morning. Just as good as he tasted last night. By the way he's kissing me, I must not taste half bad either.

More visions wash over me, thinking about where his tongue was last night. How he kissed me after I went down on him. How he thankfully had the sense to get us both clean after the butt stuff before we went another round. My belly dips as he plunges into me again and again for a good few minutes before he moves to his back with body language that tells me to ride him. I get to my knees and give it my all, despite the fact that my body is sore. Between the first gym workout in over half a year and the most energetic sex of my life until the wee hours, I'm not sure how I'm even doing this.

It doesn't take long for my limbs to go numb. When I wince and slow down, without missing a beat Derek rolls us, does a push-up, then slides out of me so he can flip me to my belly. He rams back in, hard, making me cry out.

His lips move to my earlobe and as he takes it between his teeth, he demands, "Make that sound again."

"How about you make me make it," I fire back, breathlessly.

He chuckles deviously and does exactly that. He pounds into me over and over like it's a competition. And we're both winning because I'm quickly close to coming undone under his weight, amid the sinfully good sound of his skin slapping mine. And does it ever feel good. Length and girth and rotating hips.

And now I'm thinking *ooh, bonus* because his fingers slide under my hip until he finds my clit and works my magic button, which doesn't take long to detonate. When I majestically explode, moaning a garbled string of vowels into the mattress a few minutes later, I'm ready for another snooze. And the vagina hospital, if such a thing exists, because mine probably looks like minced meat at this point.

He's not done, though. He continues to pound into me for a long time.

"Another one," he growls against the back of my neck and his fingers find me again.

I don't think I have another one in me. That last one was pretty fucking spectacular.

"It's okay," I offer. "I'm good. You go ahead." I clasp the sheets to hold on while he brings it home.

"Nuh uh. You, too," he demands, and then he's got my clit in one hand, a breast in the other, and he sinks his teeth into my neck just a little while gyrating his hips, making more magic happen between my legs, making it happen all over.

Okay, so maybe I *do* have one more in me. Though I have no idea how.

I'm almost there when I realize he's suckling my throat.

I panic. "No hickeys!" I demand.

He releases my neck, flips me to my back, then kisses his way down to my pussy and gives me more phenomenal head with all sorts

Cheater

of suckling. It's good. Very good. He can put hickeys *there* all day long if he wants to. And what's also good is watching him fist his thick cock while he does it.

And it's a combination of the two along with the knowledge that this is all coming to a close that takes me over the edge again.

Because this insanely hot man is eating me out like he's dining on the finest meal while fisting himself, and the vision is beyond pornographic. So, I burn it into my memory knowing it's the sort of vision I'll absolutely want to refer to during self-care in the future.

As I'm coming down to Earth, he turns me to my stomach again and slides back inside me. Gently finger combing my hair over to one side, he kisses my neck and rams once, twice, three times, and then spills into me on the fourth, groaning my name in a husky, sexy tone.

My heart is working overtime, and it feels like his is too as we catch our breath.

Derek kisses my neck and then in his sexy, deep voice asks, "What does my little bunny want for breakfast?"

A record scratch moment.

Breakfast. Daytime. Reality.

I've done this. I used the hall pass. I actually did this. And it was...

W*ow*.

I blink a couple times as it all sinks in.

I can't let it sink in here. I need to do that at home.

I should get home. Get home and take the opportunity to spend the next twenty-four hours or so alone. Process. Figure out how I feel about this, about what I've done. About the fact that I, Chloe Desiree Turner, took a hall pass from my fiancé and used it. I *really* used it. I even had anal for the first time. And although it's sore back there, my curiosity about it has finally been satisfied and I know one thing for damn sure – anal is hot! At least with Derek Steele it is... I've heard plenty of women complain about their first time being awful. Not for me.

But technically speaking, have I broken the rules of the hall pass?

Because it happened with Derek more than once. Many more times than once. On two different calendar dates, in fact. But maybe that doesn't count if I consider that this could be technically counted as one session. I bite my lip pondering if the sleepover is a loophole or if I'm kidding myself.

He rolls off me and now he's watching me. He's trying to read my expression. And I don't know how to read his because the warmth is gone. His expression is almost icy. Does he see I'm trying to plan my exit?

I should stay for breakfast. End this on a good note with him. After all, he joined my gym, and he goes to the soup place I love. Not to mention the fact that he sees Alannah at his business since that's her favorite place for after-work drinks.

And... last night was incredible. It was beyond expectations and after the interactions he and I have had up until this, I had big expectations of what he might be like in bed. He absolutely did give me the hottest night of my life, *bar none.*

But I've got to go soon. Decompress. Deal with my feelings about all of this. Sit in an Epsom salt bath for my muscles and my poor butt. Also, consider all the sex I've been missing out on and think on whether I want to actively look for more sex like this. Or not. Whether I'm okay with living with Adam and building a life with him while doing things like this.

And then have a talk with Adam, after which he'll then process how he feels about me having done this, too. Me doing this will change things. Absolutely.

Because he'll either lose his attitude with me and we'll move forward or... I already know I'm not about to put up with endlessly being ignored and neglected. I can't let that be my life even if it makes me a bad person to give up on him. If I give up on Adam, it'd be because he gave up on us first. Because I'd like to think the Adam I fell for wouldn't want me to live half a life. I know I wouldn't want that for him. So, I've got to find a way to have a conversation that's both logical and factual, as well as heart-to-heart.

Cheater

Heart to heart, brain to brain, to figure out if we have a future together.

I've had all the empathy in the world for what he's going through, but the way things are these days can't be our life together permanently.

It feels like dismissing me has become a habit and habits can be hard to break. I'm not going to let being treated like a doormat become my own habit. He seems happy around friends and family, but when it's just the two of us, he's not. And I won't live like this indefinitely. It'll suck the life and joy right out of me.

I'm feeling too much right now. And I didn't want to start feeling things here. But I do feel a sudden clarity about my relationship that sort of frightens me. I'm feeling so much.

And it appears I'm wearing my heart on my sleeve right now – or would be if I weren't naked – because Derek's eyes are exploring my face like he's trying to read my mind.

He reaches over and sifts his fingers through my hair with what feels like affection, the iciness thawing, and he says, "Hey, come back to me here. Those troubles can wait."

"Sorry," I say, shaking my head.

He leans in and kisses me. It's sweet, gentle. And it feels a little... inappropriate. Like I need to switch gears.

"I need the bathroom," I announce. "Coffee would be appreciated. I'm not fussy about food. You don't have to go to the trouble, but if you... uh... really want to, I'm game for whatever you wanna make." I shrug and roll away from him, pulling a sheet with me that I wind around my body as I rise.

Oh... it's the fitted sheet. We've totally un-made the bed and slept on the mattress cover.

"Little late for modesty, no?" he asks with a serious look on his face as I toy with the fitted corners.

The tension is broken by me giggling. He flashes a gorgeous grin at my laughter and I rush toward the bathroom embarrassed, but look over my shoulder as he laughs and my shoulder slams into the doorframe. He's looking like a billion dollars lying there naked, on his side, watching me. But the smile falls off at seeing my klutziness.

"Careful," he warns.

"Oops," I quip and flash him a smile.

∞

A hickey. He gave me a fucking hickey. I thought I stopped him in time, but nope. It's faint, but it's pretty obvious that's what it is. And Derek seems like a mature adult so far, so I'm kind of surprised he pulled a teenager move like this.

It's low on my neck and thanks to Alannah's tutelage, I'm semi-pro with concealer, so I'll deal. But I'm not happy about it because hiding it will feel like deception toward Adam and that's not at all what I want.

There are purplish bruises on my hips where he gripped me, too. They don't hurt, but they're here, plain as day.

Shuffling out of the bathroom, I find my handbag on the floor under the bench at the foot of his bed, so I fish out a hair tie to throw my hair into a ponytail. Rifling through the bedding on the floor, though, I can't find my clothes. All that's here among the mess of the bedding is the shirt he wore last night, which doesn't make sense because it got taken off by the door when we first came in and I could swear it was thrown out there.

I put his shirt on. It's big on me so it'll do for a modicum of modesty.

I resist the urge to make his bed, figuring he'll probably change the sheets anyway. Or have a maid do it. We certainly did dirty them last night.

Besides, I don't live here, and don't need to be my hall pass's maid the way I'm a live-in maid at home.

This thought vibrates in me for a brief moment, and I acknowledge it. Yeah, I have felt like a live-in maid lately. The townhome isn't large, but I like my space to be clean and organized. I hate clutter. I

Cheater

have standards and I'm busy, so maybe it's time to have someone in once a week for deep cleaning since it's not like Adam can do all those things.

Though, if he started pitching in a little with the things he *can* do, like putting things away after he uses them, a cleaning service might not even be necessary. Even a little help from him would make a difference.

I jokingly sang Barney the Dinosaur's *clean up* song the first time he stayed over for a weekend. He laughed it off like it was a joke as he tidied, but I worked at a daycare center part-time when I was in college and that song worked like a charm to get toddlers to put things away. I was half-serious because although Adam seemed to have it together pretty well, it was like I fit the default role of cleaning up from early on. And that isn't what I'm about. Or... it wasn't. I grew up in a house where both parents worked, and Mom didn't have to come home and do it all. She and Dad took turns cooking and once we were old enough, me and my brother were added into the rotation. We all cooked, we all cleaned. There weren't girl chores and boy chores, either. Dad taught me to use the snow blower and lawn tractor and he ironed his own shirts. Until Bryan got really sick. Then I took on everything for a while. I shake those old thoughts off.

Adam and I bought one of those robot vacuum cleaners when we moved into the house, and I can keep up with the mopping. We have one of those furnaces with the air cleaners, so dusting is manageable, but maybe it's time for him to pitch in on laundry. Would it be too much to ask for him to wipe the sink down after he shaves in the mornings? To not leave toothpaste in the sink? To bring the dishes out of his office when he's coming to the kitchen anyway? I've seen him fit snacks on his lap on the way to his office, why not use the same lap for the dirty dishes when he comes back out instead of letting them pile up until I decide to clear them out?

I'm feeling so neglected in my relationship that I'm starting to feel bitter and petty about things I wouldn't have cared so much about before.

And here I am, still in my hall pass's apartment, letting petty thoughts invade. I shove those thoughts away, grab my purse, and venture out of Derek's room.

He's frying eggs while wearing just a pair of tight, blue boxer briefs.

Mercy!

He catches me ogling him. I clamp my mouth shut and smile.

"Coffee?" He gestures to a single serving coffee maker. "I put a cup there for you. Plenty of choices in the drawer."

I put my bag down and pull on the drawer under the coffee maker, revealing a variety of tea and coffee choices. I pick a dark roast Colombian pod and open the top of the coffee maker.

"Good choice," he says as I pull the exact same used pod out of the coffee maker before putting the new one in.

He sips from his mug and then leans over and kisses me quickly before turning his attention back to the eggs he's scrambling.

My brain feels a little scrambled, too, as I look around.

Definitely a corporate apartment / hotel suite feel to this place in daylight, too. Kind of sterile. But it is spotless and drenched with light, which is nice.

I press the brew button and watch the coffee pour into the mug for a few beats before I ask, "Oh, where are my clothes?"

"Threw them in the washing machine for you," he says.

"That probably wasn't necessary."

He shrugs. "How else would I get to admire you wearing my shirt? Seein' you in my shirt all sleepy and cute was part of the fantasy."

I laugh.

He goes on, "Seemed like you were ready to bolt so figure doing the laundry will keep you here another hour at least." He shrugs.

I bite my lip and wag my finger at him.

"So? You ready to bolt, little bunny?" he asks and abruptly hooks an arm around my waist, yanking me to him.

Cheater

I wince, placing my palms on his chest hoping it'll soften the blow. "Um... about last night, Derek? We should talk."

He throws his head back and laughs as he lets go of me and twists the burner off, moves the frying pan, and pushes the button down on the toaster. "Let me guess," he says, "You don't usually do things like this."

As I shake my head, heat floods my face. "No. Never."

This man did things to my body last night that were entirely new. I'm not sure my booty hole will ever be the same. But I liked everything he did. Beyond a lot. I felt like I was finally having sex with someone whose appetite matched my own. And he actually surpassed it, exceeding expectations. But I can't let myself dwell on just how incredible it was because it might make me want more.

And that's not allowed.

He leans back against the counter and regards me for a moment. He's still smiling. And still so, so attractive. "I figured you'd say this."

"Did... um... Alannah put you up to this?" I ask.

He moistens his lips, but doesn't say anything right away, so I keep talking. "She knows I've been going through some stuff, so it wouldn't surprise me if she did. Don't worry, I'm not... not mad or anything if she did."

I wait. He gives me nothing.

"Are you just gonna keep me guessing here?" I ask.

"Nobody puts me up to anything, Chloe. And no, I haven't talked to your friend Alannah about you."

"Oh," I whisper.

He sips his coffee and then opens a cupboard door and pulls down two plates. I watch him divide the scrambled eggs between them. He reaches into a mostly empty fridge and pulls out a small store-bought fruit tray and a bottle of orange juice.

I frown as I watch him move to the table, which he's already set with cutlery and napkins.

"Ketchup for your eggs?" he asks.

I wrinkle my nose. "Eww."

"Thank God," he mutters.

"Hm?"

He smiles. "Just can't stand that. Glad I won't have to watch you debase your eggs like that."

I scoff. "Kind of ironic considering the degradation that happened in there last night, don't you think?" I hook my thumb over my shoulder.

"No," he denies, a serious look on his face. "Nothing ugly about any of what we did last night as far as I'm concerned. Did any of it feel debasing to you?"

I'm taken aback. Heat creeps up my cheeks and I shake my head. "Not at all."

"Then why say it?" he asks.

I shrug. "I don't know. Never been in this position before."

He studies me for a too-long moment. I'm saved from his study when the toaster pops. He looks mildly irritated as he moves back to the counter and drops two pieces of toast on each plate. He grabs a knife and butters them sort of aggressively.

"Can you grab the jam from the fridge, baby?" he mutters and walks them to the table.

I open the fridge and see a jar of jam on the otherwise empty top shelf. The only other things in this fridge are a quart of cream in the door and a carton of eggs on the middle shelf along with some condiments in the door of the fridge.

"Good jam choice," I say in an effort to lighten the mood. Because I think I've pissed him off.

I sit across from him and look at my plate. Perfectly scrambled eggs. Perfectly toasted marble rye bread.

Realization sinks in.

"You sure you didn't talk to Alannah about me?" I ask.

"I already said I didn't."

"Then how'd you know I like rye toast?" My eyes hit the jam jar. "And seedless raspberry jam?"

Cheater

"Do you?" he asks. And there's light in his eyes. Like he's got a secret.

I frown.

"Don't overthink it, little bunny. Just enjoy."

"If you knew me you'd know I overthink everything," I joke, then get up and go back to the fridge to fetch the cream for my coffee. I add sugar and cream to my mug, stir it, then bring it to the table.

He's poured me a glass of orange juice and is digging into his breakfast.

After my second bite of eggs, I wipe my mouth.

"Seriously, Derek. How did you know I like marble toast and raspberry jam?"

"Don't believe in coincidences, obviously," he states.

I take a sip of my coffee and study him for a moment.

He smiles and takes a bite of buttered toast.

No jam on his toast. This jam was bought for me.

"Alannah didn't contact you? Or stop by last night after I fell asleep to drop off breakfast supplies?"

"Is that something she'd do?" he asks with twinkling eyes.

Ah. That's it.

"Absolutely, she would."

His smile widens.

I roll my eyes and slather jam on my second piece of toast.

Turns out I'm hungry after all. We eat in silence. I'm mostly checking out the view from his windows and thinking about my exit plan. About what I need to say. This isn't exactly an easy conversation for me. I'm a novice. If I'm going to do things like this in the future, I need to be clear and concise about what I want, what my rules are, including no hickeys.

Am I going to do this in the future?

He's done eating first, still sipping his coffee and watching me as I finish my breakfast. When I'm done with my last bite of toast, he rises and takes my plate.

"I'll clean up," I offer.

"No need," he says. "Relax and drink your coffee. You want some music or the news, or… round three?"

I chuckle. "I think it'd be a lot bigger of a number than three, but actually, I need to get going."

"Your clothes are still in the washer. Should be ready for the dryer now. I'll go do the switch. You're here at least another half hour, my guess."

I wag my finger at him. "Fine. But I'll do the dishes."

"There's a dishwasher. Don't worry about it." He disappears down the hallway.

I eyeball my bag and ponder checking my phone. I decide to wait until I'm out of here.

He's back and he's now in a pair of trackpants that sit low on his hips. Still no shirt. He turns the stereo on low. A *Jackson 5* song plays as he grabs our coffee mugs from the dining table, takes them to the matching coffee table, and pats the couch beside him. I'm still behind the kitchen island, wiping down his stove, so I rinse the cloth, wring it out, and drape it over the ledge between the double sinks.

His eyes are on me with intensity as I dry my hands and move to the couch, tugging the back of his sweater down to cover my butt before I sit.

I twist sideways to face him, adjusting the shirt so that I'm not flashing him indecently.

"So, last night was wonderful, Derek," I say, looking into his eyes. He twists sideways, too. "It really was," I emphasize.

"Yeah," he says softly, eyes sparkling as he runs the back of his fingers along my cheek sweetly.

Gosh, this guy is swoony.

"And it's not something I've ever done before," I go on, "A casual one-night thing. Especially when I'm already in a relationship. But… I actually didn't technically cheat on my fiancé. I'm not the cheater type. At all. I actually had permission to do this, and I didn't even know if I could, but you kind of made yourself irresistible."

I'm hoping the honest compliment will soften things here.

Cheater

He cocks his knee as he adjusts his position a little, and props his elbow on the back of the couch, putting his chin on his palm. He patiently waits for me to continue.

With intent, I get up and walk to the counter to grab my bag and fish around until I find my engagement ring. I slide it back on my finger and then I look at him. He's staring at my hand.

I stay where I am.

"Late last year, my fiancé was in a bad accident. He suffered a spinal cord injury and to say things have been tough is an understatement." I moisten my lips.

Derek doesn't visibly react, so I keep talking. "He can't... um... you know..."

"Fuck you," he finishes for me, straight-faced.

The harsh way he says it feels a little off, but I nod. "No. He can't. He–"

"I know," he states.

I frown.

"You know?" I parrot.

What?

"How do you know?" I ask, coming back to sit beside him.

He scratches his jaw and rubs his lips together for a second while I fix the shirt after accidentally flashing him.

"The night we met? I heard your conversation with your friend. I know all about the hall pass."

The room twirls. I grab for the edge of the couch cushion to steady myself.

He keeps going, "I was listening in on and watching the bartender. He was stealing from the club, also from patrons, so I was gathering proof of theft and I happened to overhear what you and the blonde were talking about. It caught my attention."

I blink in shock. Utter shock.

I try to recall my and Alannah's exact conversation. It's a little foggy, but snippets wash over me. And those snippets make bile rise up into my throat.

Shit, I do *not* want to face him, especially not like this. I try to dash the tears away with his shirtsleeves.

I guess I have to face him, since I'm in his apartment.

"Chloe, I'm coming in."

I've still got my back against the door. Before I can move, he's opening it and it opens out into the hallway, so I stumble backwards. He catches me and as I try to shrug him away, he hangs on firmly, so I squeeze my eyes tight and cover them with my hands. He's got both arms wrapped around me, my back to his front. While I don't want to let this guy see me cry, I can't help it. I've deteriorated into ugly-crying. And he's gripping me like he wants to offer me comfort. As if.

"Don't be embarrassed." He squeezes me and kisses the side of my head.

"It doesn't matter," I say. "Because it was a one-off. You never have to see me again if you avoid the soup place and the gym."

I try to break free, but his grip tightens.

"Can you let go?"

He doesn't let go.

"I like soup," he says softly.

"Fine. You can have Tuesdays, Thursdays, and Saturdays. I'll take Monday, Wednesday, Friday. Same with the gym. Though you probably don't need the gym since you have equipment here. Let me go."

"What about Sundays?"

"Not funny." I try to move away but his grip tightens.

"I was fascinated by you," he says. "I don't know that I can articulate just how much. At how much you do for someone who doesn't appreciate it. How easy it would be for him to take five minutes out of his day to make you happy. Ten to make you ecstatic."

"Don't," I plead brokenly.

"You deserve more than what he's giving you."

"It's not his f-fault. You don't know him. You don't know me. Let go of me."

Cheater

"I wanted to give you what he should've given you. I wanted to give you more. Give you everything you deserve."

"Let go."

"You need space right now, so I'm gonna give you some. What I will say first is that what I wanted most last night was to give you the night of your life. And baby, it was the night of my life, too."

I wince.

He must feel it because against my ear he says, "I mean it. It was fucking incredible. We both know that. And I want more of it."

I shake my head. "Stop."

"I want more of it, Chloe. No, little bunny, I want all of it. *All of it.*"

I shake my head, saying nothing.

"I'm gonna give you space right now. Leave when you're ready. And I'll be in touch."

"No," I whisper. "You can't. This was a one-off."

He puts his mouth to the top of my head. "No, it won't be a one-off. Last night you agreed to make all my fantasies come true, Chloe. And that's what you're gonna do."

He squeezes again before he releases me. I sway with the loss of his stability, but I don't turn around. Instead, I stay still in the hallway, staring at the digital number ten on the dryer's display as my clothes continue to tumble.

And I don't know what to think about what he's just said, or how to process any of what's happened in the past ten or twelve hours. So I simply stare at the display on the dryer through blurry eyes, while it slowly counts down the minutes until I can get dressed and get the fuck out of here.

∞

The button and zipper of my jeans are so hot they're burning me, but I don't give a shit.

I don't see him on my way out and don't know how to lock up, so

I don't worry about it since he got in with his fingerprint, anyway. And I shouldn't worry about his stuff, his property, after what he's just admitted to doing to me.

The elevator is waiting for me, so I get in, press the button and leave. His car is gone when I get to mine. He must have sent the elevator back up to wait for me because the parking lot is empty other than my car.

I cry all the way home, grateful I don't have to face anyone for at least the next twenty-four hours, though I'm sure twenty-four hours won't be nearly enough.

14
Chloe

Sunday Evening

My door opens and Adam motors into my office without knocking. I peer over my shoulder at him, thinking I should remark that I'm implementing the same rule he has. I still remember the sting of him snapping at me when we first moved here because I walked into his office without first knocking.

But I don't say anything. And right now I don't think I even feel anything. Not guilty about sleeping with someone else. Maybe a bit of anger, though. Maybe like what I've just been through is Adam's fault because I didn't want to use that blasted hall pass, but he pushed and pushed.

"Hey. Um... I'm home," he says expectantly, looking a bit confused.

Maybe because I didn't come to greet him when he arrived a few minutes ago, loudly announcing his arrival.

"Good weekend with Paul. Missed you, though. How are things here?"

I unclench my jaw. "Hey. Good. I'm just trying to get some work done," I tell him. "Talk to you in a bit?"

He looks surprised at my dismissal. "Oh. All right."

I turn my back to him, lift my phone and pretend to do something.

He's gone.

Pressing my forehead to the desk, I let out a heavy sigh. That was probably me giving him a taste of his own medicine. And it doesn't feel good that I've sunk to this.

I keep my head down for at least five minutes before I get up and close the door, then drag myself to the little sofa bed in my office that we figured would work well for overnight guests. I'm thinking I'll sleep here tonight.

I wrote a text to Alannah this morning after a sleepless Saturday night, telling her I couldn't talk about what I did, that I need space to process. She'd sent a bunch of texts and called several times. After I finally messaged her, she wrote back telling me she had a feeling I was in GuiltyVille, that I have nothing to feel bad about, and to let her know when I'm ready to talk. I responded with a simple OK because I knew I had to in order to get her to give me time before messaging, calling, or showing up here.

Thirty-odd hours hasn't brought me any perspective. I don't know how much time it'll take for me to come to grips with my night with Derek Steele.

∞

"Chloe?" The door opens and light from the hall illuminates Adam's face. "Why are you sleeping in here?"

I haven't slept yet. It's after midnight and I'm lying on the pull-out bed in the dark, staring at nothing.

"I'm not feeling great so no point in disrupting your sleep," I say.

He doesn't answer right away, but then he moves his chair and stops close to the bed.

"You okay?" he asks, voice laced with concern. "You sick or... what happened?"

What happened? What happened?

My dam bursts and I crumble into a heap of emotion, covering

Cheater

my eyes, unable to swallow the ugly sob that comes from the depths of me.

I feel weight on the bed. He's pulled himself onto it. He pulls me close, wrapping his arms tight around me.

"Chloe, hey... talk to me," he requests softly, and this makes things worse, because he sounds like the old Adam. He feels like the old Adam.

He's holding me tight, whispering into my hair. He actually gives a shit. And he hasn't had the capacity to give a shit about me lately. I've missed it.

"I'm not built this way and I don't think I..." I start to cry even harder, making it hard to speak.

He presses his lips to my forehead and squeezes me tighter. "God, I'm sorry."

I weep into his chest, wrapping my arms tight around him, too.

It should feel right that he's holding me like this, but instead, it feels strange. I don't know how we move forward from here, if we even can move forward, but getting this reaction from him, it feels... hopeful?

I let it out. I cling to him and let it all just pour out of me. All the pain, the embarrassment, the missing him I've been doing for months because as hard as it is to miss someone who's gone, which I know from losing my brother, it's also really hard to miss someone who's right there with you.

"You did it or you couldn't go through with it?" he finally asks.

It takes a while for me to manage to say, "I did."

He goes rigid and silent for a minute.

I'm about to pull away, feeling like it's what he wants, but his grip on me tightens.

"I'm sorry, sweetie," he says gruffly into my hair, "Please, please forgive me. I'm so sorry I pushed you."

I reach for his face. It's wet. Adam's crying with me.

And this rocks my entire foundation. Because through all the anger and frustration he's dealt with these past seven months, he hasn't shed a tear, not in front of me at least. In the eighteen months we've been together, I've never seen him cry. He doesn't cry during sad movies. He once told me he felt bad that he didn't cry at his grandfather's funeral despite that they were close, but said he just wasn't a crier.

But he's crying with me while he holds me.

"Do you want to talk about it?" he asks.

I shake my head vigorously. "Never. Not ever."

He doesn't say anything, so I say it louder.

"Never ever *ever*, Adam. Never."

"Okay," he whispers and kisses my forehead. "If you change your mind, I'll listen. I owe you that."

I nod, but brokenly repeat, "Never."

"I'm sorry I've been so fucked up. I'm trying. Trying not to be. I promise I am."

I nod again, unable to form speech.

"I don't know if I'm gonna be able to give you what you need. And it kills me. It really kills me," Adam adds. "I owe you so much, Chloe. You've been incredible all these months since it happened."

I squeeze him tighter.

He keeps talking. "You're too young, too vibrant for the life you're stuck in now with me," he says softly. "This broke me. I know a lot of people bounce back and find new purpose, but this really fuckin' broke me and I don't know who I am anymore. I don't know if I can be the man you deserve."

Hearing him choked up, vulnerable, it cuts like a knife.

"W-we d-don't have to figure it all out tonight, Adam. You'll bounce back; I know you can do it. Just can't shut me out. I'm here for you, okay? But be here for me, too. Please. Even a little."

He lets out a long sigh. "I hope you know that I love you."

I manage to nod. But I don't know if I'm being honest here, because I don't know if he *does* love me. Like he's just said, I don't

Cheater

know if he's capable of the love I need after all he's been through. I just don't know.

He says nothing for a minute, so I put my hand to his face and give him a soft kiss.

"What can I do to make this better?" he asks.

"Just this is enough for tonight," I manage and snuggle in closer.

15
Derek

I'm holding the arms of my office chair so tight my knuckles are white. My eyes are on my screen and I'm seething at seeing him hold her like that. I want to rip his fucking face off. I want to take her and keep her where nobody but me can touch her like that. I want his blood. I want to ruin him.

I pull air in and let it out slowly, counting backwards from a hundred. Dr. Jones used to tell me to count back from ten when I felt like I would snap, that I'd find calm before I got to zero. Ten won't cut it tonight.

Kenny told me the fiancé left with his brother with an overnight bag on Friday, so I had him slip in while she was with me so he could wire the place. Not only do I have their cells bugged because of a remote hack, now her house is bugged, too. He wired her office, his office, the bedroom they share, and their main living space Friday night. He also installed software on both their computers that'll be helpful going forward and slapped a tracker onto her car when it was parked at the condo Friday night.

I've been watching her mope since yesterday. Mope. Cry. Pace. Clean. Right now I can make them both out easily with the night vision setting and the sight of her sleeping in his embrace is making my goddamn skin crawl.

That she's pouring emotion into him infuriates me. All that emotion isn't about him anymore; it's about me and what I admitted to doing. That emotion is mine. She's mine. And I don't want his fucking hands on her.

I'm mostly calm by the time I get to thirty, because I manage to tell myself she needs time. She needs more proof of who I'm gonna be to her. She needs things she'll get from me. Only me. I finish counting down anyway and then I keep my eyes on the screen until there's no noise or movement for half an hour before I switch it off. I shed my clothes and get into the shower, staring at the drain with my hands braced on the tiles as the water hits my skin.

Adam Hallman doesn't get to keep her.

Chloe Turner is going to be mine. Wearing my ring on her finger. Sleeping in my bed. I'm gonna fulfill every sexual fantasy in that blog and beyond. She won't want for anything. Not affection. Not emotional support. Nothing.

I don't want to wait. I want her now. But I need to play this the way I play everything. Like chess. But instead of winning for bragging rights, I'm going to take my queen. And keep her.

16
Chloe

"Can you just... there. Like that, yeah," Adam grunts.

I feel my back twinge with protest as I help him the rest of the way into his wheelchair.

"I got it," he says, then pulls himself the rest of the way in.

Getting onto the convertible couch bed wasn't as difficult for him as getting him back into his chair proves to be. There's a height difference to our calibrated-for-Adam bed and the fact that the handles installed there are fixed, not something I could bring here to my office for him to use.

I open the door so he can easily maneuver out. I put the couch back the way it belongs and fold the blanket.

A new day. New attitude? New chapter for Adam and I? I don't know. I really don't.

We lay together for a while cuddling this morning and something in the air feels different, but I haven't got the capacity to figure things out at this point.

He's going to physical therapy this morning and said his brother Paul is taking him, that Paul has a surprise for him. He's being sweet and careful with me. He offered to skip PT, but I insisted he go as well as find out what Paul's surprise is. I told him I just need to throw myself into some work for the day.

We've left things unsaid, I know, but it feels like we've crossed over a threshold. There's just no telling yet where it'll take us.

∞

My doorbell rings just after 1:30, so I answer and find Alannah standing on the step with a cardboard tray holding two coffees and a paper bag.

"Chocolate éclairs," she states, and pushes her way past me.

"I'm working, Lan," I mutter.

"I said chocolate éclairs," she repeats with more than a bit of attitude. "In other words, I'm paying a toll, so you get your ass in here and talk to me."

She goes directly to my office, sets the bag and coffee tray on the floor in front of the convertible couch, then parks her behind on it. I sit beside her, folding my legs under myself and cradling my elbows.

"Background noise needed?" she asks.

I shake my head. "Adam's out."

"Good. Now, spill."

I haul in a big breath and let loose. "Derek Steele overheard our conversation in the club that night I met him. He heard all about the hall pass, all about my kinky wannabe status from the things you said, and then he proceeded to run into me multiple times. I actually thought you set it up after it happened because he knew just what to do and how to do it. So, short version is that I slept with him and then before I left the next morning, he told me he overheard our conversation."

She stares, mouth agape.

I say, "He played me, Lan. Got what he wanted, and I don't ever want to hear his name again. Ever again."

She blinks a couple times with her mouth still open.

"I'm so embarrassed. I can't believe he told me, too. Like... he used the information he heard and got what he wanted, so why tell me? Why not just let me leave and work another notch into his bedpost with me none the wiser?"

"That's... that's wild, Chlo. I'm..." She shakes her head, folds

Cheater

forward to grab the éclair bag, and then pulls one out before passing it to me. She takes a giant bite from hers.

I set the bag down on the little table beside me.

"You probably need that more than I do," she says, gesturing toward the bag.

I shake my head. "I've barely been able to eat since that lovely breakfast he cooked for me Saturday morning." I shoot her a poignant look.

She takes another bite, then says, "Wow," with her mouth full.

"Yeah," I say. "Even thought for a minute you might have put him up to the entire thing."

"Me?" she points to herself.

"It's not above you to try to fix my problems for me by talking to a hot guy about fulfilling a big chunk of my kinky sex bucket list."

"I'd never break trust like that, sister. You know me better than that. Don't you?"

"You're right. Sorry," I mumble.

"But shit, Chloe, I *am* sorry I got so personal in that bar. So sorry, sister. How the fuck did he overhear that? That place is bugged? Shit... the conversations I've had in there. Yikes."

"Evidently. He says he was spying on a bartender who was stealing. It checks out because when he walked me to the bar to get my report about the red-shirted guy who got kicked out, he sent the bartender to his office with a security escort."

"Holy shit. I'm really sorry for the shit I said."

I shake my head. "You didn't know."

"God. I'm just... wow. So it ended badly after good sex?"

I frown, not answering.

"Decent sex at least?" she nudges, running a finger through her éclair and then licking the whipped cream off her fingertip.

I give her an incredulous look. "I know you're not *seriously* asking me about the sex right now."

She gives me a slow shrug.

"I mean... when you throw out terms like fulfilling my kinky sex bucket list you can't be surprised I'd ask questions. The dick moves aside, was the dick good?"

I throw my head back out of frustration, but do it too hard and don't hit the back of the couch like I would've in my old living room. This couch is low backed, so my head bonks off the wall. I hiss. So does Alannah.

"I don't want to talk about that night with Derek. Not ever." I rub the back of my head.

"Okay," she says softly, but then adds, "Never ever?"

She nibbles her lip while waiting for my answer.

I scoff. "You've got three."

She knows I mean I'll answer three questions and that's it.

"Was he good?" she asks, then takes another bite of her éclair.

"On a scale of one to ten?" I pause, then say, "forty-four thousand and sixty-nine."

Her eyes bulge.

She chews what's in her mouth, swallows, and asks, "Does he want to do it again?"

"Yes. But it won't happen. It can't, not even if he didn't prove that he was a dick of the highest degree. Because the terms of the hall pass state that I can't use it on the same person twice. But that doesn't matter because I'm done with this hall pass business. It was a disaster. I've had a mental breakdown in the past two days because of it. I blubbered to Adam about not being cut out for this."

Her eyes boing. "You told Adam?"

I nod and tilt my hand with a so-so gesture.

"This doesn't count as my third question, Chlo. That's a part b."

I snicker, pull my black band out of my hair and then I redo my ponytail. "I burst into tears when Adam came home yesterday and didn't want to talk about it but told him I'm not cut out for it."

"So, you're swearing off sex for the foreseeable future?"

"Is this your third question?" I ask.

"No. Second question, part c. Duh," she says and takes another bite of her éclair.

Cheater

"I don't know. I don't know anything right now. I'm taking it minute by minute. What's your third question? Adam could be back any time."

She considers this for a beat before asking, "What did he make you for breakfast?"

I blink a couple times. "What?"

She laughs. "I didn't have three questions. I know we'll talk about this later; you just need time with it." She shrugs and opens the tab on her takeout coffee cup.

"Alannah?" I query.

Her eyes bounce to me.

"Did you not drop off breakfast to his place?"

She frowns.

What the fuck?

"He made me scrambled eggs."

"Okay..."

"And rye toast."

"Hm."

"He had a jar of raspberry jam in his fridge."

Her eyebrows go up.

I add, "Seedless raspberry jam."

Her mouth forms into a letter O.

"And nothing else other than a fruit plate from the grocery store and the stuff for coffee along with some... like... random condiments. So I figured you got my text and dropped breakfast groceries at the door in the morning while I was still asleep or something and either you must have told him I'll only eat eggs scrambled or he took a lucky guess. But the marble rye toast? The seedless jam? I figured that had to come from you."

"No," she whispers.

We stare at one another for a solid five seconds.

"You know much about him?" I ask.

"No. I do know he's from one of the richest families in the state."

"Can you look into this guy for me?" I ask softly.

"I'll do that, hon."

She looks freaked. And this tells me I have reasons to feel a little freaked, too.

Because how the fuck would Derek Steele know what sort of jam I like, what sort of toast I like? Who told him? Why would he go to that much trouble? And again, why tell me he knew things? His words before he left me crying in his laundry room ring in my mind.

"You deserve more than what he's giving you."

"I wanted to give you more. Give you everything you deserve."

"I want more of it, Chloe. No, little bunny, I want all of it. All of it."

"You agreed to make all my fantasies come true, Chloe. That's what you're gonna do."

"Alannah..." I whisper and meet her gaze. "I think I've stirred up some sort of hornet's nest here. He said some things that were a little..." I wince.

"Concerning?" she asks.

I nod.

"Like?" she prompts.

"Like when I told him I didn't want to see him again he told me he'd give me space, but that he'd be in touch. He made a reference to the fact that I agreed to make all his fantasies come true and that it's what I'm gonna do."

Her eyes bulge.

My phone rings and it's a jump-scare for both of us. I move to my desk and lift it.

Adam calling.

"Adam," I mutter to Alannah and answer it.

"Hello?"

"Come outside!" he exclaims.

"What's wrong?" I ask, panic spiking in me at the volume and pitch of his voice.

"Nothing! Just come. Hurry." He ends the call.

Cheater

"He wants me to come outside," I say to Alannah, getting shoes on. "Not a word to Adam, okay?"

"No problem. I'll report back ASAP with what I'm able to find out."

"Be careful," I whisper.

"You, too," she says, squeezing my hand with a dark expression on her face.

When we get outside, Adam is waving at me from the driver's seat of a van. He has a huge smile on his face. Paul is in the passenger seat.

My mouth drops open.

Adam lays on the horn with his palm, the biggest smile on his face I've seen since the day he proposed to me on the side of that mountain we hiked, when I said *yes* to his offer of a lifetime of adventure, side by side.

Paul says something to Adam, then hops out. "Hiya, Alannah! Hey, Chloe. Hop in!"

I rush to the passenger side and climb in. Adam is in his wheelchair. There's no driver's seat.

"Hand controls," Adam says, then puckers for a kiss. I lean in. "Don't even need help transferring in and out of the chair. Cool, right? The door opens up instead of out. There's a swiveling ramp and everything."

"Whoa!" I exclaim. "I had no idea there was a local rental company that had these."

I realize Alannah is recording us with her phone.

"It's mine. Paul did a fundraiser with our friends and relatives to get it for me."

Adam looks emotional.

"I had no idea," I say.

"He wanted to surprise us both. Get your seatbelt on, sweetheart." He rolls his window down, "Hey Alannah, can you drive Paul back to his car? I was gonna ask Chloe, but now I can take my beautiful fiancée to lunch instead."

133

"Of course," Alannah agrees. "Nice ride!"
"Did you know about this?" I ask her.
She smiles, still holding up her phone.
"She's one of the benefactors," Paul states.
"Surprise!" she shouts.
"Thank you, Alannah. I can't even…" Adam starts.
Alannah waves. "Don't mention it."
"Drive-thru all right?" Adam looks to me.
"A drive-thru sounds amazingly perfect," I say softly.

He kisses me again. He's got so much light and happiness in his eyes that I'm choked up.

I look at Paul and he's smiling from ear to ear.

I place my palm against my chest as I give Paul a look that I hope shows my appreciation.

He looks away and chews his cheek; he's biting back emotion, I can tell.

My eyes bounce to Alannah. She's got watery-looking eyes, too.

"Lock up?" I ask.

Alannah gives me a thumbs up.

∞

We're in the parking lot of a nearby drive-thru burger place.

And sitting while eating burgers and fries, he tells me that having his independence back will make a huge difference to him. He tells me that the fundraiser didn't cover everything, though, that Paul took on a loan for the rest.

"How much of a loan?" I ask.

"Twenty-eight K," he says. "I'm gonna make the payments. I won't let him do that. Things will be tight, but I can't let him go into debt like that."

"I got a ten-thousand-dollar bonus from work. I want you to put it toward that loan," I say.

He looks surprised.

"I was going to tell you about it on Thursday. That's why I came into your office before I went to the bookstore and..." I shrug.

"I was unapproachable," he says. And then he reaches across and grabs my knee. "God, how have I hung onto you this long?"

I frown. "Don't do that."

He shakes his head. "My brother gave me a reality check on the weekend about you. Wasn't the first time, either. I think it just took a minute to sink in."

"A reality check?"

"He told me you were an angel, that I'm taking big chances by taking you for granted. He was right."

"Tell me more," I quip.

He laughs and then holds out an onion ring. I open my mouth and he feeds it to me.

After I swallow, I see a sober look on his face. He says, "Paul said everyone's worried about you because I'm so closed-off. They can all see it's taking a toll on you. I'm sorry. I'm gonna be better."

I give his hand a squeeze.

∞

We get back into the house and as I'm locking the door, he's looking at me expectantly.

I raise my eyebrows in question.

"You're more than just the person I wanna marry. You're also my best friend," he tells me. "No matter what. I love you and I don't ever want you to forget how much you mean to me."

"Stop being so gushy or you're gonna make me cry," I warn.

"If we don't work out, Chloe, I just want you to know how much you being here for me through everything means."

"Stop," I say.

He doesn't say anything for a minute. He's searching my face. And now I'm wondering if he wants reassurance from me on the 'if we don't work out' bit.

135

"You okay today? Better, or?"

"I'm hangin' in," I tell him.

"We're gonna make it, I think," he tells me. "If you haven't given up on me, that is."

Yep, he's fishing for confirmation. For guarantees. And I'm feeling a little...numb. But he needs something here, so I answer softly with, "Of course I haven't." But my chin trembles and I think he sees the fear, the uncertainty in my eyes. I see it in his, too. But I see more emotion than I've seen, ever, too, and I'm hopeful that it means something good.

"If you change your mind and want to talk about the weekend, I'm here," he tells me.

I nod.

"If you decide you wanna try that again, you can. I know how upset you were, but I want you to know that for now, those terms still stand. If you decide you don't, I won't push."

"Okay," I say after a minute of stunned silence.

"I still think we should sit down Sunday and talk about setting a wedding date. Talk about how we both feel at that point. Work for you?" he asks.

"Yeah," I say softly.

But I'm not sure it does. I'm not sure of anything right now.

Seeming satisfied, he smiles. "Good. Okay, gotta go call my editor. Can I have a kiss?"

I lean down and kiss him softly. He holds my hand while I do.

"Love you," he whispers.

"Love you," I parrot. "I'll transfer you the ten thousand for Paul now, okay?"

"You sure?"

"I'm sure," I say.

17
Chloe

Tuesday

After loading my groceries into the trunk of my Cherokee, I get the shock of my life. Because when I slam the trunk, I realize my SUV is nose-to-nose with Derek's swanky Mercedes SUV. And he's in the driver's seat, eyes pointed at me.

I'm frozen in place for a beat when he crooks his finger.

I don't think so.

By the time I'm opening my door, he's coming this way, a tall drink of water in his leather jacket, dark jeans, and boots. I quickly get in and lock all the doors.

He raps on my window with his knuckle.

I shake my head and start it up.

He pulls sunglasses off his face and gives me what I think is a stern look as he knocks a little louder.

"Unlock the door and let me in, baby," he orders, then he rounds the hood and goes to the passenger door and pulls on the door handle. It resists as I've already locked it.

I take this opportunity to put it into reverse and back out.

He's staring at me with an unreadable expression on his face as I swing out of there.

I'm practically vibrating with anger as I take the short, four-minute trip home.

When I pull into my driveway, I see Adam has already gone, which isn't surprising; he told me he's going out to meet some friends at a sports bar for wings and to watch a game. He's pretty stoked about his new wheels and newfound independence after selling his car six months ago to Lawrence, our old neighbor.

I'm still shaky as I unload the groceries.

"Chloe," I hear and startled, I drop a bag, sending vegetables and fruit tumbling onto the driveway.

Derek squats and begins picking things up. His SUV is parked directly behind mine, still running.

"You can't be here," I whisper-hiss.

"You didn't give me a choice," he says, filling my reusable grocery bag with the food. "That wasn't very nice, little bunny."

He flashes a little grin and eyes me from head to toes. I'm in jeans and a light sweater. Nothing fancy. I don't even have make-up on. But he's looking at me like I'm dressed for a night out or something.

I don't return the smile. "This isn't funny."

"I wanna talk," he says.

"I don't," I return.

He scratches his jaw thoughtfully as I pull the other bags out of the trunk, move aside and hit the button to shut the hatch.

"I'll rephrase then. I need to talk to you. Can I come in?"

"No way can you come into this house. Are you crazy?" I huff, then add, "I have nothing to say to you."

"But, I have things to say to you."

"I don't need to hear what you have to say."

"You do," he counters. "Am I helping you bring these in so we can talk? Or would you rather meet me at my place?"

"Neither," I snap.

He leans forward. "Refusing me is not wise."

"What's that supposed to mean?" I ask.

"Chloe, I want to talk," he says searching my face.

"Go fuck yourself," I snap and storm toward the house with grocery bags dangling from each hand.

Cheater

He halts me by catching my wrist. "Chloe," he warns.

His grip isn't painful, but it is tight.

Our eyes meet.

"My fiancé is in there," I hiss.

"He's not," he corrects. "He'll be out until at least midnight. That gives us five and a half hours."

I'm now frozen in place.

"Take your groceries inside and drive to my apartment. See you in twenty minutes. It's important."

I frown. "Important?"

"Yes," he says simply. "And don't lie to me again, baby."

"Don't *baby* me, Derek. I told you I don't want to see you again."

"Come over. Don't call anyone first."

"Why can't I call anyone?" I ask. "I think we both know you've done some pretty shady stuff to get me where you wanted me the other night, so that comment sends up a major red flag."

His expression softens. "We need to clear the air. I promise, you want to hear what I have to say to you."

"I don't think so," I say simply.

He stares at me for a moment, saying nothing, so I try to pull my arm out of his grip. He doesn't let go. Instead, he pulls me in so he can get his mouth to my ear.

"I didn't want to play it like this, but you're not leaving me a lot of choices."

I wait for him to elaborate, but all my senses are suddenly about to hit fight or flight mode.

"Meet me at my place in twenty minutes. If you don't, I'll have to come back."

My jaw drops as he delivers the threat.

"I'll come back when he gets home," he adds, releasing me.

His eyes coast over my face, over my entire body. His top teeth skim his lower lip before he whispers, "Twenty minutes, Chloe. Don't make me wait longer than that."

He relieves me of all the groceries, carrying them to my front step before turning around, giving me a look loaded with... I don't know... something that feels sexual... before he walks to his SUV and leaves.

The lady across the street is watching from her front window.

I don't know most of the neighbors yet, but I'm sure most of them certainly know who we are having seen us come and go with Adam's wheelchair.

I manage to pry my feet from where they're glued on the driveway and press my entry code into the smart lock before I hurry inside with my bags. I lock the door before I lean back against it, body shaking, heart hammering against the wall of my chest like it's about to take flight.

Am I overreacting? Does he just want to talk? No. What could he possibly want to talk about that would have him threatening to come back here when Adam gets home?

My phone dings so I pull it out of my bag. It's a number I don't recognize.

20 minutes, Chloe. I won't harm you. Use your thumb to get into the building. The condo will be unlocked too so come right in. I'm waiting.

My thumb will get me in? What?

I quickly call Alannah.

She answers on the second ring. "Hey, girlie."

"He showed up here," I whisper.

"Derek Steele?" she asks. "No way!"

"He wants me to meet him at his place in twenty minutes or he's threatened to come back here when Adam's home later. He swears he won't harm me but why would he threaten me?"

"Oh shit!"

"What have you found out?"

"Not a lot. That family is very guarded. Nefarious reputations, some of them. Three of his brothers, but one in particular. Thaddeus Steele. He got shot to death not long ago and that made the papers,

Cheater

but... then nothing about who did it or why. I'm coming up without much so I'm gonna ask Jeffy to help. He has some investigators that help him with some of his cases and he seems to know everyone in this city."

"No. Don't! Don't involve Jeffrey."

"Don't worry about how I gather information, I'm careful. What are you doing about tonight?"

"He told me not to even tell anyone. I'm calling you to ask you what to do. I'm flipped out and I can hardly think."

"What if you go over there, leave your phone on record in your pocket, and record everything that he says to you. Bring that bear spray we got for that camping trip last summer. You still have it?"

"Yeah."

"Bring it and if he pulls anything, use it. Don't turn your back on him. Stay in the hall if you can, if not, stay close to the door."

"Do you think he's dangerous?"

"What's your gut tell you?"

"My gut tells me he's probably going to try to convince me to have sex with him again."

"Tell him when you get there that you've notified people of your whereabouts."

"Good idea."

"Bear spray," she says. "Call me afterwards. Chloe, if it's actually harmless and he just wants more..."

"That's breaking the rule."

"Girl, it was 44 thousand and sixty-nine out of ten. Maybe he just wants to keep fucking. Maybe he's just... quirky about investigating women he wants to fuck. Rich guys have the means, so it's not such a big deal to them. The toast and jam thing – maybe it's not that bad if he just investigates women he fucks beforehand. Maybe he just wants to explain himself. Would it be the end of the world if you broke one teensy little rule in order to get one more kick at that kinky can?"

I roll my eyes.

"Be careful, but trust your gut. You're smart. Savvy. Hear him out, maybe, but don't be a doormat though. Follow my advice and stay safe. Let me know what happens."

"He threatened to come back here when Adam is home, Lan. What are you even talking about right now?"

The phone goes quiet for a moment.

"You're right. You're right. I think I just wanted this to be a fairytale, not a Dateline special."

"Who are you?" I ask.

"You're right. Sorry. Do you want me to come with you?"

"Yeah, maybe."

"Shit. I don't know if I can get out of this meeting. It should be a quick one. Can you wait an hour?"

"You know what, I'll do this. Figure out what he wants and make sure he knows I'm not some pushover. I'll keep you posted."

"You sure?"

"Yeah."

"Tell him if you don't report to someone within fifteen minutes of arriving, they'll call the cops. When you message or call me, if you say you're totally fine I'll know you're not and to send help. Say the word *totally* in a text or a phone call and I'll know things are not cool and you need me to call the police."

"Okay. You'll hear from me in half an hour, forty minutes tops."

"I'll be waiting."

After shoving the ice cream I bought into the freezer along with the chicken breasts and ground beef I purchased into the fridge, I decide everything else can wait until I get home. I dig through the closet in my office where we've stowed our camping gear and find the bear spray.

But surely, he's not a psycho, right? He's a businessman from one of the most prominent families in the state. This has got to be a misunderstanding. I'll remind him I want nothing to do with him, let him apologize if that's all he wants to do, and then walk away.

18
Derek

I'm sitting on the couch facing the door when it opens.

She takes me in, looking concerned.

While I'm in a relaxed pose with my feet on the coffee table, my arms resting across the back of the couch on both sides, I'm shirtless, shoeless, in just a pair of jeans with the button undone.

"Close the door and come here," I say.

She backs up. "This was a mistake."

"Chloe, stop," I order. "Come here."

She backs away.

She's halfway down the hall when I get to her, walking backwards, clumsily fumbling to pull the bottle of bear spray from her pocket.

She drops it before she hurriedly squats to grab it and then points it at me. "Don't come any closer or this will burn your eyes badly. It might even blind you permanently."

I stop two feet away. She's full of it, but I need to calm her down.

"Why does my fingerprint get me in here, Derek? How do you know where Adam is? How did you know about the jam and the rye toast? You're kind of freaking me out with this creepy shit, but I'm giving you a chance here to give me a reasonable explanation why I shouldn't report you to the police. And before you make another move toward me, someone I know knows I'm here right now and the cops will be called if they don't hear from me in fifteen minutes."

"Creepy?" I ask.

"Yes, creepy!" she cries out, her pitch now soprano. "Why the fuck did my fingerprint open your doors, Derek?"

"You shouldn't have called your friend. Pass me your phone."

She jolts in surprise.

"Send the blonde a text message and tell her you're good. That everything's cool, you overreacted and misunderstood the threat, and you'll call her later. You don't want her or that lawyer buddy digging into me. I'll forgive you this time for making that call, but don't disobey me again, Chloe. And if you use the word *totally* in your text message I'll have to act fast to do damage control and believe me, you don't want that."

Her body trembles. Her eyes widen. My cock hardens.

"Don't be afraid. I won't harm you," I assure.

"I don't understand why you're doing whatever you're doing," she whispers, eyes filled with fear. She begins to back up again.

"Do what I've said, little bunny. I'm about to make another of your fantasies come true," I tell her.

"Derek, you're freaking me out. Let's be rational here."

"I'm as rational as I can be, believe me. Give me your phone. Here." I reach out and snatch the spray and scoop her up into my arms.

She pulls in breath and I'm sure she's about to scream, so I cup her mouth with a hand.

"Shh. Don't be afraid. You're okay. I'm not gonna hurt you."

Grace's car was outside when I got back, and I don't need to run into her in this hall.

She tries to struggle in my grip, but I rush into my place, placating, "Don't be afraid. This isn't like that," I tell her. "I'd never harm you, Chloe. Never." I sit, tossing the spray to the other side of the couch while keeping her on my lap and reaching into her coat pocket, fetching her phone myself.

She watches me stop and erase the recording she's been making of our conversation. I open up a message to Alannah and begin typing a reply while she stares at the screen.

So he wants more of what we had the other night and he's making a good argument/being kind of irresistible so I'm gonna listen to what he has to say and talk this out with him. I misunderstood the threat and you're right. He does investigate anyone he hooks up with to make sure they're not bunny boilers. Call off your search for now. I'll let you know if I want you digging further. K? I'll call you later to explain more. Just messaging you from his bathroom. XOXO

Yes, I know the way she signs off. I've read her blog, a lot of her emails, her social media statuses and text messages, and I know how she writes texts to her best, rather *breast* friend. I can see she's coming to grips with some things as I set the phone down on the coffee table and reach for mine.

I phone Kenny on speaker.

He answers on the first ring.

"Yeah, Derek?"

"You're on speaker. Chloe will be leaving here at eleven. You'll follow her to make sure she gets home safely?"

"Got it."

I end the call and wrap my arms tighter around Chloe's trembling body.

"Now," I say, "I know you're upset and confused, but I really wanna take you to bed and fuck you senseless for the next three or four hours."

"No," she whispers, looking terrified.

"Yeah, baby, I do. You're lucky I even let you out of here Saturday. I wanted to keep you in bed all weekend. I knew you weren't quite ready for that. Based on your behavior since then, I can see it's time to take the reins here, so it's what I'm doing. Let's go to my bed so we can take the edge off. We'll talk specifics after."

She blinks at me, panic all over her pretty but currently pale face.

"Be my good girl, Chloe, or things will move at a pace you're really not ready for."

"What does that mean?" she asks.

"One step at a time. Tonight, we're gonna have some fun. From here, I'll figure out the pace. Your actions will dictate it at least partly. Okay?"

She shakes her head. "No. Not okay. None of this is okay. You're freaking me out, Derek. I don't understand what's happening here. Why you've done all these things."

"I promise you're safe with me, Chloe." I drop a kiss on her forehead, get up, and carry her toward the bedroom, leaving our phones where they are. "Nobody will keep you safer than I will."

"Put me down. I'm leaving."

"I've got plans for you."

"Are you crazy?" she whispers.

I tip my head. "Dr. Jones called it antisocial personality disorder, though he proved himself to be a quack, so... We can talk about that all later. I don't like talking about it so let's build up to that. I'll tell you whatever you wanna know about me eventually. But let's get you on board first."

"I'm not doing this," she tells me as I set her down on the bed.

"You are," I whisper and run my fingers through her hair.

"No, I'm not!" she shouts in my face. "And you need to leave me the fuck alone."

"You are staying here for at least a few hours, Chloe," I say calmly, "otherwise... something you don't want to happen could happen."

"Such as?"

"For example, the recording I have of you and Alannah Fisher talking at Downtown *could* be played for Adam Hallman."

Her eyes widen with horror.

Cheater

I ask, "You want him to hear you and your breast friend discuss him being your boring-ever-after? A potato with no seasoning? And beyond that, you want him to hear you tell your friend that I'm what was it? Forty-four thousand and sixty nine out of ten?"

Her jaw drops.

"Gotta say, that made me smile. I don't do much of that. But every time I look at you, think about you, I find I'm doing it." I run my hand up her leg. "It's taken a lot of self-control to give you space until today."

My fingers wander to undo the bottom button of her blouse.

She swats my hand. "There's something seriously wrong with you."

"Not gonna disagree," I put in. "Now, are you gonna be my good girl or my bad girl tonight?"

Her gaze narrows.

I continue, "I know all about the good girl and the bad girl fantasies too, Chloe, and I'm more than happy to punish you for your transgressions in a way we'll both enjoy."

She's perfectly still. Wide-eyed.

"Love your blog by the way," I tack on.

Her lip trembles and I watch her eyes get shiny, then pretty tears drip out and trail down her cheeks.

"I'm fascinated by you. When I become fascinated by something, I need to dig deep, get well-versed. Now, are you my good girl, my bad girl, or will you be my punished girl tonight? You pick."

Little lines appear over the bridge of her nose. "Punished?"

"Decide if you're good or bad. Cooperate because if I choose *punished* because you don't choose, I'll take you to RJ's Bar to meet up with Hallman and the three of us will have a chat."

"You're blackmailing me for sex," she states.

"Like I said the other day, I want more of what we had. It was everything I didn't know I was missing in life. So you're gonna cooperate and give me more. You're not gonna fuck anyone but me. No hall pass with anybody else, and I mean that. You don't wanna test me on that. Although I think we both know that's not who you are."

"You really are certifiable," she whispers.

I undo another button on her blouse. She doesn't stop me.

"Yeah, you're gonna be a good girl tonight, Chloe. Know what I think? You wanna be bad, deep down, but you don't know how. You're too sweet, too good. So guess what?"

She says nothing as I undo the third button.

"Let's make this easy. This is my fault. Right now, I'm gonna *make* you be my good girl. So, blame me, curse my name after you scream it into my sheets or my skin, but you and me will know the truth." I pause for effect. "You'll secretly love it."

I'll bind her in my chains so she can actually be free. Give her everything she wants. And what she needs. Show her how much I want her, how far I'll go to have her. Show her what she's missing by staying with him.

"Are you wet for me, Chloe?" I shove her chest and she falls to her back on the bed.

"No," she whispers the lie I'm about to prove.

"You don't want him to hear all about you using the hall pass, do you?" I pull my zipper down. She watches. "Break his poor, fragile heart especially now that he's so ecstatic about that new ride that gives him some freedom back?"

"You're a terrible person," she whispers.

"A terrible person who dropped twenty grand toward that new ride." I stand up and drop the jeans and underwear, then climb back into bed. My cock is rock-hard. "Thirty if you count the ten grand you forked over to him."

More shock registers on her face.

"Yeah, another sign pointing to how pure and sweet you are. Giving your bonus to him when you're down to just four thousand and eleven dollars in your savings account. Only a little over two grand in your checking. Did you know he's got more than triple what

Cheater

you've got saved right now? And that he's got around forty k in bonds he didn't cash in when you guys bought the house?"

She frowns.

"Didn't think so. Didn't think you knew you cleaned everything out to make your mortgage as low as possible when he held money back."

"Why are you doing this? Why me?"

"Don't know. Never been fascinated with another person this way before." I shrug. "I get fixated on goals. Overheard that conversation in my bar and you became the goal."

"Just like that?" she asks.

"Just like that," I confirm.

She shakes her head skeptically. I watch her eyes, knowing she's working through all the facts running through her brain right now.

"You're not gonna do that to him, are you? Force my hand and make me play those recordings for him?"

Her expression contorts like I've said something hurtful.

"Naw. You're gonna let me do what I want to you tonight, so I don't tell him what you really think about his skills back when his dick still worked. Right?"

"You're despicable," she says sourly.

I chuckle. "Maybe. But I don't feel bad about it. Especially not after the shit Hallman wrote about my family for one of the local rags he writes for. And anyway, an attractive, bad man making you bend to his will is one of your fantasies, after all, isn't it? Serendipitous that you happened to be there intriguing me that night. You don't believe in coincidence, do you? But you *do* believe in serendipity. You wrote that in your blog, too. One of the early entries when you didn't know what the blog was about yet. Back before you loosened up and focused on sharing your sexual fantasies, including having an attractive bad man making you be a good girl..."

"It wasn't real. I wrote most of what's on there before I even met Adam. It no longer applies."

"Lots of capture fantasies. Being taken hard. Talked dirty to.

Being with someone who can't get enough. Not what you wound up engaged to at all, am I right?"

"That's an anonymous blog so nobody was meant to read it and I never intended to act on anything that's in there. It's just–"

"Bullshit." I undo her jeans. "You'll look back on this soon and realize you love it. I saw that fire light in your eyes last Friday when I did dirty things to your body, things you've wanted but never expected to happen outside the saucy books you read, those dirty fantasies you write down. You'll feel bad about this a time or two, but my guess: it won't take long before me commanding you to come to me will instantly soak your little panties."

She shivers as I caress her face.

"You'll come to me wet, Chloe, even as you pretend to be angry about me blackmailing you. I'm sure you can't wrap your head around the fact that this is really happening to you, that your fantasy is coming true. You'll get there. One day you'll admit that your friend blurting all those personal secrets in my club was the best thing that ever happened to you. Right now, I'm gonna make you come. Hard. You already know what I can do to this sweet little body, don't you? And I've gotta tell you, all those things we did barely scratch the surface of all the fantasies I've got, all the ways I want to fuck you."

I shimmy her jeans down, pressing a kiss to her hip. She doesn't protest, doesn't move. But she's got tears in her eyes. She looks sad. Afraid. It won't last. I'm about to make her body light up.

"My good girl. You're about to get two-for-one here, too, because I seem to remember an old blog post about a very demanding boss with big muscles making you do naughty secretary things in order to keep your job. Since I just bought the company that's your biggest and now only client, here we go..." I flex my biceps, shooting her a wide grin.

19
Chloe

He's crazy. For some reason, he's decided to play this little game. He keeps saying he's not going to hurt me, but he's dug so deep into me, seems to know so much about my life... too much about my life. And to threaten to tell Adam?

What did Adam write about his family? Was it that bad? Is that what all this is about? Targeting me to get revenge on him?

It wouldn't be wise to just believe he won't hurt me. At all.

If he's as crazy and diabolical as I suspect, he could snap and hurt me at any moment. He could do so much more than just devastate Adam by blowing the lid off my fantasies, by playing the recording of me venting to Alannah about how Adam's been treating me. Alannah's words about our sex life from before the accident. But of course the last thing I want beyond being harmed physically is for him to do what he's threatening to do.

Adam has turned a corner in his healing progress in the past few days. I can't imagine what hearing all that could do to him. He's been having dark thoughts about offing himself... I can't let it happen. I won't let Derek set Adam's healing back.

Derek has obviously bugged my phone. Bugged the house. He's got someone following me. He's done some deep diving on my computer and he's even pulling strings at my job! My boss told me that Cavalier Commerce is my baby, that my hard work has paid off.

Derek Steele has dug into multiple layers of my life to get leverage.

Sex? He's done this for more sex? I don't get this at all. He's rich. He looks like a fitness model in regular clothes and a movie star when he's in a suit. He's charming. He knows how to make a woman feel desired. So, why me? Why be this methodical and devious? Why, when there's no way he has any trouble finding women willing to have sex with him? Even kinky sex, I'm sure.

I need to think. I need to assess my options. But right now, he's undressing me, and he's determined to have sex with me.

I close my eyes and a tear rolls down my cheek as I tell myself I'll have to just let it happen. He could overpower me easily, he's made threats. This feels like the safest option: do what he wants and get out of here.

The man he phoned will make sure I get home safely at eleven o'clock, so obviously I get to go home in time to greet Adam. Just a couple hours and then I can go home and think about how to deal with this. Maybe after this, he'll be done. I'll just lie here and he'll get what he wants and maybe he'll move on.

He dusts kisses down my body as he takes my underwear off.

"Legs wide, please."

I'm frozen in place, thinking no. No, no, no.

I can't. I can't just let this happen. No. This isn't right.

"Now, little bunny," he urges.

Our gazes connect and he gives me one of his beautifully dazzling smiles. The smile he used on me so many times to disarm me and lure me in.

"Please don't do this," I plead, entire body quaking.

"Now," he says simply.

And his eyes look cold. He looks cold, sinister, and just as handsome as he always looks. If I don't do this, it could be catastrophic.

If I do allow this, how can I even look in the mirror at myself?

He takes my non-answer, my non-movement as a cue to do what

Cheater

he wants. He parts my legs and I don't struggle. I shakily close my eyes tight.

And I feel his tongue swipe through my folds before he zeroes in on my clit, sucking hard.

I jolt and this makes Derek laugh. Deviously.

"Sopping wet for me, just like I knew you would be. You're perfect, Chloe."

I squeeze my eyes shut tighter, as if it'll shield me further, fisting the bedding as he settles in between my thighs. His fingers spread me apart and then, nothing.

Nothing happens for a long moment, so I open my eyes. And I immediately wish I'd kept them shut, because he's staring at me down there. Staring at my exposed private parts with a look on his face that would make me blush if this were last Friday. Our eyes meet and he flashes me a grin then moves back in, immediately sucking hard.

I tell myself it's just mechanics, biology, as I'm quickly shuttled into sensation. Both of his hands snake up and grip my breasts.

"Let me hear you. Don't you dare hold back," Derek demands, then drives fingers inside me, crooking them against my g-spot. "Hold back and it'll force me to pull out some moves before you're ready for them, Chloe..."

My hands cover my face and I lose it. Lose complete control and begin shuddering as he takes me over the brink.

He's slurping, plunging with fingers of one hand, and twisting a nipple with his other while I convulse. It's lewd. It's wrong. And the sensations just go on and on and on.

"Stop, too mu-much," I finally cry out.

"No. Never too much," he denies, then barks, "Eyes on me. Now!"

I move my hands and he looks like a man possessed as he fingers me harder, sucks harder, and suddenly, with our eyes locked, my body bucks even harder as his fingers move fast in and out of me. I see white spots as everything becomes drenched between my legs, including Derek's face before the edges of my vision blurs.

I try to catch my breath, but now he's driving that thick erection forward, slamming it deep while moaning before one of his hands wraps tight around my throat with his eyes holding mine hostage.

"Fuck, baby, fuck, fuck, fuck, Chloe!" He pounds and pounds and finally comes with a roar before he collapses on top of me, giving me all his weight.

I'm bawling.

He's lifting me, carrying me into the bathroom, setting me down on the vanity between the sinks.

I stare at him through blurry eyes as he wipes his face with a towel and then leans over and turns on the taps for the big, soaker tub.

He made me squirt. I've never done that before. His face was absolutely drenched, and he wasn't disgusted by it.

And now he's trying to take care of me. He dries my tears with a clean towel and I'm trembling all over as I watch him pour from a bottle of foaming bath. I know it's no coincidence that it's the exact same blue bottle I have at home with Epsom salt and coconut oil in it. I bought one on the weekend on the way home from his place. It seems I was followed even then.

I'm still trembling when he lifts me up and steps into the tub with me, sitting down and arranging me in front of him, between his legs.

He leans back and cradles my head against his chest as I continue crying while he lifts a folded washcloth from the niche in the wall, wets it, and squeezes the water out before he dabs my cheeks with it, murmuring something I don't make out over the roaring water as he presses kisses to my forehead while tipping my face up to look at him.

He's searching my face as he continues to dab my cheeks with the cloth, staring into my eyes the way he did before, no iciness, only warmth. Warmth with a smitten expression on his face.

I say nothing. I just keep crying.

He doesn't look unhinged. He doesn't look dangerous. But he is. Sitting here smiling at me with that tender expression while I cry in the bathtub with him.

Cheater

Why is he doing this to me?

When the water is just about to the rim, he moves us upright so he can reach the taps and turn them off.

And he lounges in the hot, bubbly water with me like we don't have a care in the world, nowhere else to be, and nothing to talk about. He runs the wet washcloth over various parts of my body, snuggling me, dotting my hairline with little kisses.

My tears have dried. I'm staring off into space when he says, "Hungry? You skipped dinner, didn't you?"

"Not hungry," I manage to rasp.

"Come on, I got something you'll like." He nudges me so I'll stand and takes my hand, helping me out of the tub before wrapping a thick towel around me.

He grabs another towel for himself, dries off quickly and wraps it around his waist, tucking the end in while casually saying, "I'll leave your bathrobe on the end of the bed for you. Got it for you today. Got you some slippers, too. See that you always have a pair on when you're *there*." He kisses me softly, holding my jaw with one hand.

"Mm," he adds and then runs the backs of his fingers down my cheekbone. "You're beautiful, Chloe. Fucking you is my new favorite thing."

I do nothing until he leaves. When he does, I close the door and shakily sit on the toilet.

I blow my nose and do my business, then while washing my hands I examine my red, puffy face before I sigh and move out to his bedroom, where he's already made the bed and folded my clothes, putting them on the end of the bench beside a very soft pink robe. On the floor beside my sneakers are slippers that match the robe.

I put them on, hang the towel up, and dreading what might happen next, I leave his room and find him setting the table.

It's dark now but instead of turning lights on, he's lit the dining space with multiple candles. There's wine. And there's a platter of taco shells along with taco fixings in the middle of the table.

Derek looks at me, smiles, and pulls a chair out for me.

"Taco Tuesday," he announces.

Adam isn't a fan of tacos, so I usually go out for them with Alannah or Coraline. Or I used to go. I haven't had tacos in months. I can only guess he's surmised I love tacos because I've probably gushed about them online.

I sit and he pours me a glass of my favorite sweet frizzante wine. I haven't bought a bottle since I finished that one that led to pulling out my vibrator. I certainly don't want to drink any right now.

I stare at Derek as he sits opposite me.

"If this were a date instead of blackmail, I'd be getting lucky tonight, wouldn't I? Oh wait..." He flashes a devious grin then throws his head back and laughs.

My face flames as my blood boils with an onslaught of anger.

He sobers. "You're pissed now, but just wait. I'll win you over." He pours himself a glass of wine and starts to put together a taco.

"I'd make one for you, too, little bunny, but I don't know what you like in yours. Show me."

I remain still.

Derek leans forward slightly and orders, "Show me, Chloe."

"Fuck you," I manage.

He stares for a moment and I'm wondering if I've just made a grave error.

He takes a bite of his taco.

"Mm." He chews, swallows, and wipes his mouth. "Pretty good. We have a girl who drops food off when we need it. Me and my siblings here, I mean. One of my sisters cooks, went to culinary school, but she doesn't use her condo here much. Lives in Phoenix with her husband. My other sister doesn't cook at all. Paulina's versatile, can make pretty much anything, so I use her whenever I don't feel like going out while I'm in town. Whatever you're in the mood for, I can have done in a few hours most days. I've already got plans for our next dinner. Have some."

He takes another bite and chews, makes more sounds of enjoyment, then sips the wine before looking at the glass. "Too sweet," he

Cheater

mutters and then he takes the last few bites of the taco before going to the fridge and pulling out two bottles of water. He sets one in front of me and kisses the top of my head. "I'm already sweet enough. You should eat some tacos. It's Tuesday, baby. They're good."

"No thank you," I mutter, uncapping a water and taking a long drink.

"You want, we can fuck again now. We've still got a few hours," he suggests, way too casually, eyebrows up high as he jerks his thumb toward the bedroom.

I say nothing, so he asks, "What do you want, Chloe? Tell me what you want most right now. Maybe I can make it happen."

"I wanna go," I croak out, on the verge of tears again.

He reaches out. I stare at his outstretched hand.

He wiggles his fingers.

I frown.

"Chloe?" He wiggles them again.

I reach out and he takes my hand in his, stroking my knuckles with his thumb. "You wanna go?"

An ugly sound comes out of my mouth as I fail to hold back an ugly-cry sound.

"You don't want tacos? Don't wanna fuck again?"

Another sob comes out of me.

"Okay, beautiful," he says gently. "*This* time. Because I can tell you're overwhelmed."

I get to my feet and try to pull my hand away, but he doesn't let go. He stands and uses the grip to pull me to his body, wrapping me up in a hug.

I'm stiff. I'm flustered. I want to bawl my eyes out some more.

"I want you to stop this, too, Derek," I say brokenly.

He leans back to look at my face, then his fingertips are moving down my temple and tucking my hair behind my ear.

His head tips to the side and he leans down and touches his lips to mine. "No, you don't. You just don't realize it yet. I'll message you with instructions when I'm ready to see you again. Don't disappoint me, Chloe."

I swallow, staring at his face.

"You're a sexy, smart, capable, woman. So don't do something stupid," he warns in a gentle tone, touching my nose with the tip of his index finger. "Don't tell Alannah what's happening here. You can let her think we're going to continue to fuck, but for the moment, nothing else. No texts about me. No notes. No sign-language or hiring skywriters, using carrying pigeons, or anything like that. Be smart." He taps my nose with his index finger a second time. "Don't test me, baby. I'm a hundred per cent serious. Our little arrangement is between just you and me. I mean that. The only thing you can talk about regarding us with her or anyone else is how incredible the fucking is. Because it is. Isn't it?"

I try to break out of his hold, but he tightens his grip and moves in, so his mouth is just a few inches from mine. "You don't want to defy me. Clear?"

I nod slightly, more fear spiking.

"No attempting to remove any of the surveillance equipment, no attempts to lose the tail I've got on you when you're out. I am not joking. You don't want me to get anxious about not knowing where you are or what you're doing. That would be very, very bad. And I'm not talking the type of bad that earns you an erotic spanking, little bunbun, because there will be times where you get those... making me worry about you is different. I'm talking about consequences. Big." He gestures with both hands in the air. "Big, Chloe. Understand?"

I step back.

He steps forward.

I step again and find myself against the wall.

"Tell me you understand," Derek demands, gaze sharpening.

"I understand," I reply.

"Okay," he says, looking satisfied. "I'll tell Kenny you're getting ready to go." He cages me in with both hands on the wall on either

Cheater

side of my face and then he drops his voice to barely above a whisper, mouth right by my ear. "Until next time, baby. It probably won't be long. I don't know how long I can stand to be without you. Good work on the Cavalier campaign. Keep up the good work. I'm replacing that ten k bonus. In fact, I'll add a zero. Hallman didn't deserve it. You do. I'll drop it into your savings account tomorrow."

He backs up, turns and goes to the table, lifting another taco shell and filling it while I stare, more than a little dumbfounded. He flashes me a smile and I manage to unglue my feet to get away from him.

After throwing my clothes on quickly, leaving the robe on the bench, kicking the slippers off, then getting my shoes on, I rush to the living area where I grab my coat and my phone.

"Don't forget your pepper spray," Derek calls over from the kitchen.

He's cleared the table and looks like he's putting food away. I don't dilly dally. I grab my shit and rush out. I run to the elevator, press the button, and feel like my heart is on fire waiting for it to come.

When it does, I collide with a stunning blonde.

"Oh sorry," I say, backing up.

She steps out of the elevator and looks me over, frowning.

"Who are you?" she asks.

"Nobody," I tell her.

"Which suite were you visiting?" she demands.

I probably look like something the cat dragged in. The tips of my hair are damp from the bath and my eyes must be puffy from all the crying.

"I..." I start, then back up into the elevator. "The one before the last door over there." I gesture and press the button. She tilts her head curiously and I'm pretty sure she considers sticking her hand in to stop the door from closing so she can ask more questions. Mercifully, she doesn't.

I cry all the way home, followed by a navy-blue SUV that continues past me when I pull into the driveway.

I'm awake when Adam gets himself into bed beside me and although I'm pretending to be asleep, I'm physically startled when he rolls into me and spoons me from behind, kissing my shoulder before settling in. He hasn't done this in seven months. Longer than that, even. And it feels like a knife twists in my heart as a lump of emotion clogs my throat.

I got a return message from Derek's fake message to Alannah.

I don't blame you. He's hot AF. But gurrrrl... be careful. His behavior is definitely suss. I think we need to talk this out. Love you lots but you might just be the flavor of the month. Don't fall in love, gf.

I replied with:

Don't worry. Love is 100% NOT gonna happen. And you're prob right about the flavor. Love you. XOXO.

Not two minutes after I sent the message to her, my phone buzzed with a message from Derek.

You'll love me. Not soon enough though.

I saved his number as *DS Cavalier* even though I wanted to throw my phone. A helpless feeling enveloped me instead as I realized I was putting him in my phone under a code name. And it felt eerily similar to the feeling I got when I was told about Adam's spinal cord injury.

But in addition to feeling helpless, I feel deceitful. Like a cheater. I slept with someone tonight out of fear, but I still did it. I might have tried to just lay there and take it like a corpse, but that's not what happened. I came harder than I've come in my life. I squirted. But it doesn't count as part of the hall pass. At all.

Five minutes after Derek's text, something dawned on me, so I wrote back.

Are there cameras or microphones in my bathrooms?

He replied.

Of course not. But that can be remedied if you force my hand.

I angrily cleaned the faces of my kitchen cupboards, organized the coat closet, and did it feeling like I was being watched. Because I was. I wondered where the cameras were. My eyes kept scanning to see if I could spot them, but nothing. After a long, tearful shower, I dried and dressed for bed behind my shower curtain as it was the only place that felt private. I was in bed with the lights out at 10:35 in case Adam came home early.

I see four o'clock in the morning before I finally fall asleep, spending all night staring into the void, no idea what to do about any of this.

20

Derek

I won't stop myself from watching to see how she reacts to my actions. I want to know. I want to see. I anticipate her responses, look forward to seeing how she'll respond when I push a little harder. I know I'm becoming addicted, because I need to keep reminding myself to check my pace.

I'll ramp things up a notch at a time to give her everything.

I want her longing. I want to see it, feel it. When I enter a room, I want her focused on me. I want to know her nipples have gone hard, that her panties are wet. I want the sight of me to make her body react in ways that astonish her.

I know women find me attractive. I want something much deeper than what I get from most women this time. How deep? Each time I see her, each reaction I get leaves me wanting even more.

I saw some of the yearning before, *and* while I fucked her the first time. It was even more potent the morning after, though it hasn't gotten to the level I want – the level I heard in her voice before we met when she talked about what she wasn't getting from him. Intimacy. Eye contact. Physical affection. She wants to feel seen. Appreciated. Wanted.

She'll have all those things from me and more. Because she'll get to live out all her fantasies while she has my utter and complete devotion and attention. I'll pamper her. I'll worship her.

The physical attraction was there for me from the moment I saw the longing in her eyes. Hers was evident for me when we met. Things shifted and the budding affection that built for me disappeared when I revealed that I overheard her and her friend in the club that first night. Her eyes changed. Hurt, I guess. Betrayed, probably, because although we didn't know one another well, she let me in physically and I already see she doesn't give that away without consideration. Physical intimacy isn't throw-away for her like it's always been for me. Until now, it was all about urges. Release. For Chloe, it means something deeper. And I respect that. She feels disappointed that she let me in physically because I disappointed her emotionally.

I won't skirt the facts. She needs to know just what she gets with me. She'll soon understand just how fucked up the man who's fixated on her is. It's beyond a fixation; I already know I'm traveling down the chain of addiction with her. And I'm taking things slower than I want to – because it's necessary.

People around me get concerned when I pursue my interests at my preferred pace.

My father always told us your strategy is important. Before you devise one, learn all you can through research and observation so the most logical course of action with the minimum amount of risk will reveal itself.

My father had plenty of advice for his sons as kids. Continuous lectures. Nowadays I don't have much to say to him and he's given up on saying much to me. But I've remembered all his lessons well. Too well.

I'll work to get Chloe's longing aimed in my direction. Until she wants me a whole lot more than she ever wanted Hallman. Or anybody. With a big difference. She'll get everything she wants from me. I'll do more than make all her sexual fantasies come true. She will not have a doubt in her mind that I want her. She'll feel worshipped, treasured.

Cheater

I stand in the shower fisting my cock with her face in my mind. I see her on her knees taking me – eyes watering but still full of lust and submission the way they were that first night. It's only been eleven hours since I had her. And I already crave more.

I crave fucking her with those looks, those reactions from the first night. But until things progress emotionally for her, I'll take what I can get.

∞

I make it to noon before I send her a text message with a demand. As I send it, I switch to the screen with the set of windows showing me the wired rooms in her house. She's in front of her computer in her home office. Hallman is in front of his computer in the other office. He's playing a video game. She's replying to a work email, but immediately lifts her phone at the alert.

I watch her read the message.

I want you at my place at 7. Wear your hair in those big curls like you wore the night we met. Same red lipstick. Wait for me in my bed wearing the clothing I'll leave on the end of the bed. I'll be there soon after you. Bring your appetite.

She puts her phone down, shoves her keyboard back toward her monitor, and rests her forehead on the edge of the desk for a good two minutes before I send another message.

Acknowledge you received this message, Chloe.

She doesn't move to check it despite that I hear the ping.
I send another one.

Don't disappoint me.

She's still face-down on the desk, so I phone her.

She picks it up, looks at the screen and sighs before answering. "What?"

"When I message you, I want replies. Prompt ones."

"Whatever," she mutters.

"Chloe," I warn.

She says nothing.

"Be here at seven," I order. "Put the outfit on and I'll be along soon afterwards. Don't disappoint me."

She holds the phone and looking at her profile on my screen, I see fire in her expression. And it sparks something in my blood. Something I like.

"I need a response, Chloe."

She thrusts her middle finger up in the air.

I chuckle, letting her know I see her. "Be my good girl, baby. I'm not sure you're ready yet to see what I do to you when you're my bad girl."

She deflates but says nothing.

"You'll be here at seven," I tell her. "Don't eat dinner before you come. I have something planned."

She doesn't reply.

"Chloe?"

"Fine," she rasps.

"Bunny," I say, "I'm gonna fuck you so hard tonight. You're gonna cry out my name as I lap up all your sweet juices. And guess what?"

She doesn't answer me.

"Don't worry, I'll feed you, too. With dinner and I'm also thinking I'll paint my name down the back of your throat tonight, too. Seven o'clock, baby."

I hang up and fire off two text messages. First, to my personal shopper. Second, to my sister's chef friend.

Cheater

∞

Excitement pulses in my veins as I enter the apartment and set the two thermal bags of food on the table. The food will keep for an hour while I spend time with Chloe, which I'm anxious for, but I deny myself for a moment longer, long enough to pour two drinks at the kitchen counter. I carry them toward where I know she's supposed to be waiting.

And she's here. Waiting on my bed on her knees, sitting with her hands fidgeting nervously in her lap. She's wearing a little white and silver mostly sheer spaghetti-strapped number that immediately makes my dick hard. Her nipples are hard. My eyes travel to see the straps of matching panties underneath the layers of fabric that comes to her thighs. I notice there's an open box containing a pair of matching silver heels on the bench at the end of the bed.

Her eyes are downcast, and her teeth are nibbling on her bottom lip. She followed directions with the lipstick. With her hair.

"I'm very pleased my good girl followed my directions. And on your knees, too? Mm."

I set both drinks on the dresser.

She shifts so that now she's sitting, legs folded on one side instead. A little bit of defiance. Her cheeks are pink.

"Fuck, you're beautiful, Chloe," I tell her as I shed my suit jacket and undo my cuffs. "Brought you a Jack and ginger."

"No, thank you," she says without looking at me. "I don't drink when I need to drive."

"Good girl," I say, then add, "Gonna want another sleepover soon, though. We'll schedule that."

Her eyes meet mine with fire in them. "You don't need to do this, do you? I mean... for real, Derek. Please help me understand why you're doing this."

"Because I want you," I say simply.

"You can't tell me you have difficulty finding women who want to..." she trails off.

"I don't want just any woman, Chloe. I don't want random. I just want you."

Her forehead crinkles with confusion.

"You have no idea how under my skin you've gotten." I take a sip of my drink, then remove my shirt as I kick off my shoes. Her eyes are on my torso. I stretch my neck and then go for my belt.

Her expression is filled with distress.

"Guess what's for dinner, bunny."

She shakes her head while shrugging and doesn't meet my eyes. She'd rather be somewhere else. Anywhere else, I'd guess. But I'm going to change how she feels.

And the fact that my hands are on my fly hits me.

"Ah. That's not what I meant but I like how you think. Prime rib. And..." I leave it hang for a moment, before answering, "we've got baked potatoes and a bunch of toppings. Know why?"

She says nothing, keeps her eyes focused on her hands.

"Look at me, Chloe."

Her eyes come up slowly.

"Because we both know you like your baked potato loaded, don't you?" I chuckle. "Sour cream. Butter. Cheese. Bacon. Chives. You want flavor, baby, so I told the chef to season the potato before she baked it, too."

She sighs and squeezes her eyes shut tight.

And it hits me that I'm going to eventually learn things about her that don't come from me overhearing them, that don't come from watching her live her life without me right there to witness it in person. I'm going to learn things about this girl firsthand. Soon. And I look forward to it.

"Check your bank account?" I ask.

She frowns.

"I dropped the hundred k for you this morning."

She shakes her head. "Why would you do that?"

"I told you. It's your bonus."

Cheater

"What, like I'm your whore or something?"

I sit beside her and take her face into both hands. "Don't call yourself that unless you're saying it with confidence. That you're my whore because it turns you on to say it. Not to say it like it's a distasteful thing."

"I'm nobody's whore," she whispers. "I don't want your money."

"You're someone who deserves to not worry about money. I can tell you're conscientious and non-materialistic by how you live your life, by how you spend your money. Not to mention the fact you gave that ten thousand dollars to him. So I gave you more."

I'm interested to see what she does with it. I can see she doesn't carry a balance on her credit card. She pays her bills on time. She's got a good credit score. She also didn't have much after she put nearly everything toward her house down payment and she's been living lean while trying to save twenty per cent of each pay.

"Why does he send you less than half the grocery money?" I ask.

She frowns. "Pardon?"

"You and Hallman split bills down the middle. You put the grocery receipt on the side of the fridge yesterday and then this morning, he sent you half, but he shorted you by fifteen bucks from his half. Why?"

"He probably didn't reimburse me for my tampons. I underlined them so he'd know they were just mine."

I frown. "That's bullshit."

"Why do you care?"

"I can't wrap my head around how he isn't taking care of you."

"I don't need him to take care of me."

"You don't. Because from now on, I'm taking care of you."

The alarmed look mixed with confusion makes me realize I'm showing my hand too soon.

"I can take care of myself," she says softly, looking perplexed.

"And you've done that for far too long," I reply.

"I don't want your money. I'm returning it."

"No, you're not."

And now I'm wishing I hadn't said anything about the money. I could've just watched to see what she'd do with it. From everything I've surmised so far, she'd probably use it for good.

I reach out and she flinches.

I caress her shoulder with my fingertips.

"You're very beautiful," I tell her.

She swallows hard and stares at her lap. I loop my finger under the strap over her shoulder and it falls. The lingerie is tight enough across her breasts that nothing further is revealed.

"I've been thinking about you since you left," I add.

She moistens her lips and blows out a long exhale, saying nothing.

I regard her for another moment, how perfectly still she is, wondering if it'd disappoint her if I didn't fuck her right now. After a long moment, I announce, "Let's go eat."

I get up and hold out my hand.

She flinches, looking confused. I'd hoped she'd look disappointed, but I'm not getting that.

"Take my hand, Chloe."

She does and I help her up.

"Don't like the shoes?" I ask, staring at the box on the bench.

"They seemed a little unnecessary," she says.

"Do you like them? I notice you have some nice shoes in your closet, though you rarely wear them."

"I work at home. I don't need to wear expensive shoes every day."

"Do you like those?"

"They're nice."

"Put them on," I say, then I take them out of the box and set them on the floor in front of her. "Here." I gesture to my shoulder.

She places a hand on me while she gets into the shoes, which raises her up a few inches.

"After you," I say and gesture for her to walk ahead.

She does, and I get to admire the sexy lingerie while she walks ahead in very high heels that make her legs look even hotter.

Cheater

"Didn't get a chance to set the table. Have a seat. I'll take care of that."

She sits at the table, looking pensive.

I grab two plates and some cutlery, then unload the food. She watches, saying nothing.

I fetch her drink from the bedroom, then give her a bottle of water before serving her.

I unwrap the foil over the potato and steam curls up. The room is filled with the fragrance of the spices.

"Oh, roasted corn," I add after inspecting an extra container. "Load up your potato, baby."

I open a container of what looks like spiced butter.

She shakes her head. "I'm not playing this game with you, Derek. I'm not going to sit here and get excited about you bringing in food that I like as if it actually softens the blow of what you're doing to me. You can take all this food and choke on it."

"Guess I made the right call not ordering dessert. I was gonna do up a sundae bar. Thought we could eat those in bed after round two. Should we get started on round one then, since you're not hungry?"

She stares at me hatefully.

"There was that sexy Sunday sundaes post you wrote about fucking all day and eating sundaes together in bed. Remember? Would you prefer to leave instead?" I ask.

"Of course I would," she snaps.

"Fine. Go." I gesture.

She looks surprised.

She doesn't wait for me to say it twice, doesn't risk me changing my mind. She rushes back to my room and in a matter of minutes, she's gone. No goodbye.

After I eat alone and clean up, I find the discarded lingerie on my bench, including the little G-string, which I inspect.

An adorable little wet spot on the crotch.

Yeah. I thought so. As much as she's angry and embarrassed, she can't help but want me.

I put the fabric to my nose and inhale, then smile as my cock hardens.

She's gone home and she's probably denying she's a little disappointed that I didn't fuck her tonight.

She'll lie there in bed, wondering what I'd have done to her if she'd stayed.

21
Chloe

Thursday

When lunchtime hits, Adam knocks on my door and pushes it open.

I turn around to face him.

"Hey," he greets excitedly.

"Hey," I return.

He sent me a text message half an hour ago asking me to not interrupt until he said so. He said he had to do a video call. A week ago I'd be asking right now how that call went. But today, I've got other things on my mind.

Alannah tried to get me to meet her for lunch today, but I've made an excuse. She knows me so well, so she's going to know things aren't okay when she talks to me or heaven forbid, sees me, and I'm not supposed to tell anyone what's going on. My brain has been working in overdrive and not giving me answers.

He scratches his temple thoughtfully. "I, uh... got a last-minute assignment to cover a story in Bowling Green."

"Oh?"

"Uh huh. I told them at work I have wheels now and said I'd wanna be considered for more assignments where it's accessible, you know, and they had someone interview me just now on the fly through video call for their morning show tomorrow, which is why I asked you not to come in for a while. And that's done and they're running a clip tomorrow on the local news about how that fundraiser got me mobile even though it didn't hit the goal. They're adding the link to the story so it might even go viral and help cover the rest of the cost."

"That's great," I say, and my mind flashes to how much of the costs Derek covered.

Both directly and indirectly. And also... the fact he told me he dropped a hundred thousand dollars in my bank account. I've been afraid to look.

"The magazine wants to do a trial run on a new accessibility column, so part of it means me covering a story up there, attend a town hall where some issues are being brought up and... I wasn't sure I wanted to become the poster child for it but... I figure it's an assignment. A lot better than the crap they've handed me the last few months since I've been housebound. The column could take off. Could help me get my book published, too. When it's ready, I mean. Who knows?" He shrugs.

"That's great," I say, genuinely pleased for him. "Exciting stuff."

But he looks uncertain. His mood has been great the past few days with his newfound freedom that came with the new van.

"I don't want to get too excited," he says.

"Get excited, Adam. It'd be good to get excited about work again."

"Yeah. I guess. So, I won't be back until tomorrow night. The company is gonna have assistive tools sent to the hotel in Bowling Green for me. Things I can use going forward. I told them I need portable stuff to help me when I travel, so they're footing the bill for that. And they're talking about sending me to do a story at a related expo in Cincinnati next week, too."

"That's great. Congratulations."

"Thanks," he says, not seeming overly thrilled.

"Are you not happy about this?" I ask.

"I am, I think. But, I don't know if I should be. Catching a break on this new column and doing away assignments when they've only

Cheater

had me covering local just because I lost use of my legs seems a little strange, doesn't it?"

"If they didn't think you could do it, they wouldn't give you the opportunity, would they?"

He shrugs. "Maybe."

"If you do a few assignments and it's not for you, you don't have to keep doing them, do you?"

"Don't know. Don't know if I wanna be known as the paralyzed journalist. Not sure if this'll mean they start pigeonholing me."

"Don't let them. And I say for now, be open-minded. This could be good for you. You're new to this world but that doesn't mean you can't use your voice and your writing skills to be a champion for others in your position, right? It doesn't mean you only need to write about accessibility issues. It'll increase your audience, too, won't it?"

He smiles. "Guess so. Yeah."

He used to be so confident.

"And you can make the most of it. Seize the opportunities that come and don't let them pigeonhole you. When do you need to leave?"

"Soon."

"Need help packing?" I ask.

"That'd be great. Thanks, Chloe. This helps."

∞

I'd be relieved about having the house to myself tonight if not for the fact that I'm being watched. I don't know if Derek watches recordings of everything happening here, if he's watching a live feed, having someone else watch it and report things to him, or if he just watches me when he feels like it.

I do know that I know a little more about him than I did before, but it's still not much. Because I've been doing internet searches about him and his family. He probably knows about that too, or will if he's got someone watching my internet browsing history.

One of the stories I found online was one Adam wrote before we met. Derek's father Michael Steele wasn't painted in a very positive light. It was the last article in a series about the wealthiest men in the state. In fact, there were undertones that eluded to organized crime ties. Derek's father's self-made money comes from real estate, mostly, but his father was a wealthy shipping magnate.

The organized crime accusation wasn't blatant, but there were seeds planted there about not only Michael Steele, but also his sons Elijah and Thaddeus as well. Reading it left me even more unsettled. Michael Steele's older brother did two years in a minimum security prison over tax evasion a couple of decades ago.

I'm sure, though, that Derek's obsession with me has got to be about more than the article Adam wrote because Adam certainly isn't the only journalist in town that has written negative things about his family.

And there's a lot of negative stuff out there about Derek's recently murdered brother. And gossipy stuff about an ugly divorce happening for the oldest sibling, Elijah. The now-dead Thaddeus was second-born. Derek is third. He has brothers named Jonah and Asher as well as two sisters, Naomi and Grace.

Grace Steele, who I know now is the blonde I saw in the elevator the other day, got some tabloid coverage not long ago as she dated a guitarist in a mid-level rock band.

I couldn't find much about Derek, other than pictures of him with some of his family at charity and other press events. Derek's mother is a retired supermodel and was a TV actress for a while. I recognize her, remember watching a sitcom she was in when I was in grade school, but there isn't much press about her.

Adam's announcement about work interrupted my sleuthing, so after I pack his suitcase for him while he showers and shaves I think about getting out of the house this evening.

I've pondered reaching out to Coraline or Maddie for a night out, but it's a weeknight. I'm too gun shy to meet up with Alannah because she will see everything the minute she sees me. But after

Cheater

turning down her lunch invite, if she finds out I met up with Cor or Maddie, she'll march her fine ass straight here to confront and interrogate me. Finally, after Adam leaves, I decide to go to the gym and then to the soup place and bring the shifter romance Derek bought me.

I can't figure out what to do about him at the moment. I don't know what to make of the way he dressed me up like his own personal sex doll with that lingerie, presented me with an elaborate meal, and then just let me leave.

He seemed pretty blasé about the fact that I again didn't fawn over his efforts to woo me.

I could call his bluff by breaking his rules and telling people, but everything in me is telling me not to do it. If he's gone to these extremes financially as well as having me followed and installing cameras in my house, I need to be cautious.

I've told myself I can hope he loses interest in a way that won't end in my disappearance without a trace, but I'm beyond stressed out. Because if he gets bored, aren't I a loose end?

When I leave the house, the blue SUV follows me.

After the gym, the donut shop is busy and I'm grateful there's no small talk with Mr. Nguyen or his wife because I've been worried they'd ask me questions about my last visit, about Derek, who they seemed fond of.

I eat my soup from the corner table, facing the window and doing my best to pretend I'm not being watched by some guy out there named Kenny in a blue SUV. I don't see it, but I'm sure it's out there. I surprisingly get hooked into the book I'm reading. Before I know it, I'm a few chapters deep and my soup bowl is empty. I didn't get an éclair this visit since they're sold out, but got a cherry cruller for later.

Once home, I take a hot bubble bath with the curtain closed tight (just in case) and then I change the sheets and get into a fresh bed with the book and my treat and a grateful feeling that I haven't heard from Derek today.

I'm feeling strange being alone, but it doesn't take long for the book to hook me again and make me forget about the fact I'm likely being recorded or watched. After a few more chapters that get pretty steamy and leave me feeling a certain kind of way, I shut the lights out and then under covers, I stealthily fetch, then start to use my vibrator. I work at it for a while, but release is elusive. Probably because Derek's face keeps showing up behind my eyelids. His face. His body. His voice.

I try to send my fantasies in the direction of the erotic scenes in the book I'm reading and very nearly get there, but then the character morphs to Derek, the cruel visions of him dancing in my mind like a cruel prank, so I stop, toss the vibe to the side refusing to come with Derek Steele's face, mouth, hands, cock, or other body parts playing in my mind.

An hour and a half later, I slip into the bathroom and take sleep medicine that I use once in a while when a bout of insomnia hits me. Mercifully, it works quickly.

22

Derek

After pressing the four digits marking the date Chloe and Hallman got engaged into the smart lock on the door, I slip in and lock it behind myself. It's just past one o'clock in the morning and the house is dark and quiet.

I've seen them enough times in the past week that I know what these shadows on her nightstand represent. Hand cream. Kleenex. Tablet. Charging station. A small dish for jewelry that currently holds a pair of hoop earrings, a bracelet, and two earring backs.

It's fascinating to be here, in this space that I've been watching. Now I know what it smells like, and that's a craving I had while I watched. To know the scents of this space. To feel the textures with my fingers. I run my hand along the wall and my finger hovers over the hall light switch. I smell Chloe's perfume. And something foreign. Something that does not fucking belong. A primal urge coasts over me, the urge to mark with my own scent. Erasing his. Blanketing her.

I touch the light switch outside her door and leave the bedroom door open wide.

The hall light doesn't disturb her, and it provides me with a great view of her sound asleep in the middle of the bed, one shapely leg outside the blanket, bent. Waiting for my touch.

Before giving in to that urge, I look at the drawer on the table at her usual side of the bed as it's halfway open. I reach in and immediately find the piece of paper I suspected was still here. Not because I've seen surveillance of it, because of that first conversation I overheard where she told the blonde that the hall pass is in the bedside table drawer with her vibrator. I hold it out toward the light coming in from the hall and seeing it's what I wanted, I slip it into my jacket pocket.

Again, I look down at her slumbering form. Her angelic face. Her dark hair fanned out across the white pillow. Her chest rises and falls steadily.

I touch her face.

"I'm going to give you everything," I vow.

She doesn't stir.

Emotion swells up big in my chest. Each time it happens, it strikes me as odd, but it's happening more frequently, emotions welling up in me. For her.

I sift my hand through her silky hair. My girl is a deep sleeper.

I run a fingertip across her bottom lip. Still no stirring.

My cock twitches and then it drips, knowing what's about to wrap around it. Chloe's tight heat. So fucking tight and beautiful in there. Fuck, I could *live* there.

I grab my aching erection and squeeze it.

After a long moment, my eyes adjusting well to the dimness, I kick my shoes off, undress, and get into bed beside her. She immediately rolls into me, cocks her knee over me and moans in her sleep as her hand skates up my torso and stops over my heart.

She's wearing the oversized T-shirt that I saw her wearing earlier on my screen, but it's ridden up to mid-thigh and rises higher as my hand glides up underneath the soft cotton to caress her hip. No panty line. Goosebumps rise on my beautiful girl's skin as my fingers slip between her naked ass cheeks and slide through her silkiness. Wet already? I get to my knees and throw one over her to straddle her body as I move her to her back. My knee presses against something hard. After digging into the bedding to find it, I lift it and inspect it. Is

Cheater

this what I think it is? I lean to the side and twist the switch for the bedside lamp. A rabbit vibrator.

"Ah. Little bunny," I say and laugh low.

This sleeping girl makes me smile. She makes me laugh. She makes me feel things other than irritation or anger. I'm going to give her everything. And maybe one day I'll know by how she looks at me that I've made her happy.

Setting the vibrator beside her, I line up as I move her legs further apart then slam straight inside.

Her back arches as she hoarsely mumbles, "Derek."

This surprises me; she's still asleep. This hot body knows it's mine already.

And fuck, is it satisfying.

I balance on one elbow as I rock into her while caressing her face.

"Dreaming about me, bunny?"

She arches sleepily, "Mm hm."

I pull out and wait. How can she sleep through this?

"Gonna make it a good dream, okay?"

"Mm hm." She rubs her nose and slaps her chin before her arm flops.

"You use this because I didn't fuck you yesterday, Chloe?" I grab the vibrator and fiddle with it until I figure out the bottom is a dial to turn it on. I crank it to max and then press it between us so it's against her clit.

I fuck into this girl loving that asleep, she called out my name. *My* name, not his. I want to roar in triumph. I'm fucking her in his bed, and this is the first and last time I'll fuck her here. It's not easy to wait, to stop myself from making her mine now. I can barely fucking wait. But waiting is better. I want her choosing me. I want her to come to me voluntarily.

Now I've got a better idea, so I hold the shaft of the toy against my cock while pushing into her, stuffing her with both me and the vibrator. I increase my pace, fucking her into the mattress at a steady pace as she whimpers, clasping my shoulders. The rabbit ears are against her clit, and she's got both me and the vibrator inside her body and fuck is it tight.

"It's a good dream, isn't it, Chloe?" I ask with my lips against her throat as I absorb the sensations.

She's crying out, body shuddering, so I lift my head and see her eyes are open, and she knows what's going on.

She's disoriented, looking at me like she's not sure if she's dreaming or not.

My lips crash into hers and I sweep my tongue between her sweet lips as I groan, then murmur against her skin, "You feel so damn good, Chloe. How do you like being my little double-stuffed Oreo?"

Pressing the vibe against her clit, I continue to slam forward until I shatter, coming with a handful of her hair in my fist while feeling her body get wracked by her orgasm.

She's breathless when I roll off her, taking the vibrator with me. She immediately knifes upright and scrambles to her knees on the bed.

"You... you... omigod, Derek!" The vibrator hits the rug. It's still on.

"Mm. Come here," I say and tug her hand, so she loses her balance and falls onto me.

I take her mouth with mine despite that she's trying to pull away. She fights me, trying to detach me, but I tighten my grip and keep kissing her.

Chloe fights harder, crying out, "How dare you!" So I wrestle her to her back and pin her with my hips as I hold her hands over her head.

"Settle down."

"You... you... this is my home. This is my bed!"

"Missed you," I tell her. "Couldn't wait another minute to be inside you." I kiss her nose.

"Get off me."

"Soon as I got my hands on you, sound asleep... you were wet and

Cheater

whimpering for me."

"Off! Off!"

"No. No, baby, I call the shots here," I tell her.

"You're such a fucking bastard."

"Maybe," I shrug. "But you loved every second."

"I was unconscious! That was rape!"

"Naw. You called out my name. Lying here showing me your sexy legs. Your cute little rabbit vibrator beside you. Seemed like an invitation to me."

"Bullshit."

"You want, I can send you the recording," I offer and twirl a lock of her soft hair.

"What?" she whispers, going completely still.

"You heard me with those bunny ears. You know you did."

Her body is stiff, rigid.

"I climbed in with you and as soon as I touched you, you were calling my name. Wrapping your legs around me and clutching my back. Clutching my cock with your tight, wet hole. That wasn't rape."

"I took a sleeping pill. I was in a deep sleep. I didn't know who you were."

"Oh, you call *him* Derek? You wrap your legs around him as soon as he gets in with you here? Not what I heard, nor what I've seen with my own eyes."

"I hate you," she spits.

"Probably," I mutter and kiss her again. "But I ticked another box on your sexy bucket list, didn't I? The intruder in the middle of the night fantasy? I think you wrote the entry... two years or so ago. Got any double-stuffed entries? I haven't read the whole thing yet."

"Get off!" she shouts.

"I'll get off, but baby, calm down."

"I fucking hate you!" she shouts. "Get the fuck off of me!"

As I'm rolling off her, she slaps me across the face. So hard, my head turns.

I freeze.

So does she, staring at me, looking stunned at what she's done.

The vibrator on the floor halts, as if scared silent.

I absorb the feel of the sting on my face and take a deep breath through my nose, then let it out through gritted teeth.

I flex my fingers and stare down at my right hand for a minute as I haul in another big breath and slowly blow it out.

There's eerie silence and either she's shocked she hit me, she's terrified of what I'll do in retaliation, or perhaps both.

23
Chloe

I stare at him while my heart tries to beat its way out of my chest. I'm terrified I've just made a grave error in smacking him.

He's still halfway over me, left arm caging me in as he stares at his right hand and flexes his hand a few times.

While it's dim in here with just Adam's reading light on, the hall light also casting a glow across the bed, it's easy to see the cold look on Derek's face.

I'm braced, wondering if he's pondering slapping me back.

Finally, his eyes snap to my face. I jerk back, bracing. They rove it for a long, frozen moment before he rolls off me and sits with his back to me. I remain still, terror-stricken as he gets dressed.

I finally work up the nerve to speak, to stand my ground.

"You crossed yet another line tonight, Derek. This is not okay."

He stands, fully dressed, getting his shoes on before he turns and peers down at me.

"There is no line I won't cross." His eyes are still ice cold. "Don't forget that. And I told you you're safe with me, that I won't harm you, but I'll warn you here and now that if you strike me in anger again, baby, you might not like what happens. I'm a wildcard. You don't want to push it. I'd tell you to ask anyone who knows me, anyone who's crossed me. But you probably don't want to try that, mostly because they're either no longer around to do the talking or are too afraid to."

He looks at me for a reaction for a long moment before he continues. "I want you at my office tomorrow. One o'clock."

"I have to work," I say.

No longer around? Around where? Anywhere? Does he mean he's killed people?

"It'll be a working lunch," he answers. "I'm your only client so no reason why you can't be there."

He leans over and puts his hand to my face.

I remain as still as I can, but I'm trembling as he stares for a long moment.

"Don't change the sheets. I want him sleeping where I fucked you for at least one night. Preferably two."

I say nothing, but feel like ice-cold water is trickling through my veins.

"Dream of me some more, Chloe," he says softly, then presses his lips to mine.

He turns Adam's light off again, then leaves.

I wait a minute, maybe two before I rush out of bed, down the hall to the front door. It's locked. I look out the window. No sign of his Mercedes.

It's as if he was never here.

But he was.

He broke into my house. He was here. Here, in *this* house, having sex with me in the bed Adam and I share. Having sex with me while I was asleep.

And this means I've broken multiple rules from Adam's hall pass rules list. Against my will. But I don't know what to do to make Derek stop.

I move back to the bedroom and before I'm all the way there, I feel Derek's semen leaking down my leg. I rush to the bathroom and let the water wash away not just the signs of him, but also the tears of frustration. But all of it, honestly, feels unwashable.

Cheater

I find my vibrator not-so-innocently lying on Adam's pillow. I must have missed him putting it there before he left. I grab it and instead of putting it back in the nightstand drawer, I storm to the kitchen where I angrily step on the trashcan pedal and whip it into the garbage before flipping double birds in the air and hoping the cameras caught it.

24

Derek

I stare at the piece of paper.

<u>Who</u>? Chloe and anyone I don't know.*
<u>What</u>? Just sex.
<u>Where</u>? Just not in our home.
<u>When</u>? When you need it.
<u>Why</u>? I don't want to lose you.
*I ask that it's never the same person twice. Nobody you've been with before, so no emotional attachments. We won't talk about it and discretion is sacrosanct.

He signed and dated it. He dated it weeks before the night I met her. She sat on this for a while before she even brought it up to Alannah Fisher. She never wanted to use it. But she did. On me.

I smile to myself.

Anyone he doesn't know. He knows of my family, and he *will* know me.

Not in their home? I smile. *Check.* Not only in his home, but directly where he sleeps. She's not real happy with me at the moment for my wake-up call, but the way she moaned my name in her sleep tells me I'm on the exact right path.

Just sex? No. Not even close.

When she needs it? She needs it every chance I have to give it to her. I'm gonna give it to her a whole lot more often than she got it from him. And a whole lot better than he did it, too. Selfish prick.

And he doesn't want to lose her. Aw. Cry me a river. It's just a matter of time before he loses her entirely.

It's not easy to hold back. I want to move the chess pieces much faster so that I can take the queen. And keep her. But I'd prefer she picked me instead.

That slap she delivered across my face sealed her fate. It would've sealed it either way. It was dangerous, but I know by my reaction that I won't *ever* be done playing this game. Because the idea of inflicting retaliation on her for causing me the sting of pain is unfathomable to me.

No way will I lose focus on this goal. This woman takes feeling alive up a notch.

25

Chloe

When I drag myself to my home office at 8:30 in the morning after very little sleep, the first thing I do is go to that old blog I wrote all those sexual fantasies on and click 'forgot password' so I can reset the password and login for the first time in over a year and a half. I drum my fingers impatiently, waiting for the reset link to come to my email, then promptly login and delete the entire thing with aggression.

Gone. Just like that. He loses that ammo against me.

Adam phones me at 9:30, but I don't pick up. I just can't face a conversation with him right now.

A few minutes later, I get a text message.

Adam: Good morning! Having a really great trip. Can't wait to update you. I'll be home around 6. Maybe order something in for us? Could go for Italian if that sounds good. There's a delivery coming for me this morning, too. Can you just leave it in my office? Please don't open it. See you tonight.

I never open his mail, so that's not going to be difficult.

I'm feeling sour, too, because it's not the first time I've given myself the time to wonder if what Derek said is true – that Adam held back forty thousand dollars when we bought this place. He put in the same amount of money as I did into the house, thirty thousand each, telling me his parents lent him almost half of it to make sure he could match what I was putting in. I covered the closing costs when he ran short and didn't ask for them back. How does his account currently have three times the amount as mine?

Adam has always been frugal. But if what Derek says is true, it makes me wonder if there are other things he's held back or lied about.

I know Derek's been up to *no good* since the beginning, so I shouldn't put any stock into what he's said to me, but if it's true, it definitely leaves me feeling less than settled with where things are at between Adam and me.

My phone rings again and it's my manager, Frank, calling to tell me he got a message that I got summoned to a meeting with Derek Steele. My boss is a little off with me because he didn't know about it. And I'm not too happy as it's obvious Derek called my boss on purpose, letting me know he absolutely expects me to show up today.

When I indicate to Frank that I was just about to call to let him know, his tone changes to excitement.

He's excited. Not only did Derek Steele of the very wealthy Steele family buy Cavalier and call Frank himself instead of having one of his minions call to say how happy he is with our company, he's excited about hints dropped that mean there could be a lot more opportunities coming our way. The fact that Derek called my boss is another illustration of him obliterating boundaries, infiltrating multiple areas of my life.

My boss is panicky, asks if I'm prepared for this meeting. Tells me that if we do well for a Steele subsidiary it'd be good for business and that if we don't, it could be worse than just losing the Cavalier account. He eludes to the family being powerful with friends in high and low places, then laughs for a moment before he tells me to forget he said that last part, then he blathers on rattling off a list of businesses owned by Steele Financial, Derek's father's company, peppering his monologue with questions about my interaction with

Cheater

Derek. Three times he says he'd have preferred to head this meeting but that he trusts me. The way he says it multiple times leaves me feeling like I need to prove myself all over again with him – like he isn't already happy with my work.

Yes, I am sour after what Derek has put me through this week so far, so I do my best to improve my tone and sound excited and agreeable. I fly by the seat of my pants telling Frank I'll be spending the morning preparing for the meeting even though Mr. Steele said it would just be a casual meet and greet for lunch and a quick chat. I assure Frank I'll be *on the ball* and make a good impression.

My boss says he'll keep his phone with him from one o'clock until three o'clock, even taking it to the bathroom, in case I need him. Frank insists I should promise absolutely anything Mr. Steele wants and that he'll help me deliver no matter how big the ask is. By the time the call ends, I've had it with the whole thing and want to climb under my covers and hide from the world.

In order to get him off the phone, I remind him that when Mr. Steele bought the company, he insisted *I* get a bonus for my hard work and that my work on their campaigns has them exceedingly happy with me. I assure Frank that I'll call him the minute the meeting is over.

Frank is usually so easy-going and relaxed. But I'm typically much more upbeat and positive when I talk to him, so I guess it's not hard to fathom why he was standoffish with me.

When I get off the phone, I stare at my banking app on my phone screen. Chewing my lip, I touch the icon. I've been avoiding this, but it's time to login and look.

And yep, there's six figures in there. Free and clear. No holds, but clearly there are strings. Strings I wish I could find scissors to snip.

Feeling a little nauseous about the fact that my bank account has never seen that amount, I quickly log out and put the phone down.

26

Derek

I get a text message from Chloe at 12:57 pm.

> **Chloe: I'm parked outside your club for our meeting. It looks closed. Am I at the wrong location? I'm at Downtown. Should I be at The Fifth?**

I phone her.

"Hello?" she answers, her voice hesitant.

"I'm here. I'm unlocking the door. Come in," I tell her while on the move.

"Okay, bye," she mutters and ends the call as I reach the door, seeing her approach while sticking her phone into her pocket. She's wearing a black business suit, her hair up, and she's carrying a leather portfolio.

My pulse races at the sight of her, so when I open the door, I drop a kiss on her mouth, saying, "You look gorgeous."

She jerks back, frowns and says nothing, but walks past me.

"I'm the only one here so far," I tell her. "Staff won't be here until after three. I grabbed lunch for us. It's in my office."

"I'd prefer to be out here," she states. "Will this table do?"

She sets her things on the table closest to the door.

"No, it won't do. My office, please." I lift her bags and put my free hand to her lower back, guiding her.

She looks edible in this black blazer and short skirt business suit with her pale pink blouse, a serious look on her face. Her lips are shiny and pink. Her lashes are a thick ebony. She has little diamond studs in her earlobes. Her heeled shoes are sexy, they show her toes, which are done in pink polish. I don't recall if her fingernails were done last night, it was pretty dim in her bedroom, but right now she's got tips the same color as the toe polish.

I find myself fascinated by Chloe Turner's every facet as I lead her into my office and close the door behind us. She startles at the click of the door like she's suddenly in danger.

She eyes the table. Two large soups from the coffee shop. Two chocolate éclairs.

"I called Mr. Nguyen who very kindly baked his éclairs an hour early for me. I'm determined to feed you," I say. "If you don't eat this time, I might have to punish you." I flash a grin.

She doesn't smile. And I'm missing that. How she'd smile shyly at me before. Before she got angry with me.

"My boss called this morning and is very excited about the potential for working with you. He asked me to patch him into our meeting, so..." She pulls her phone out.

"No. This meeting is just us. And I heard the call between you. Don't fib, little bunny." I swat her ass playfully.

She jolts and as her face goes red, she states, "Don't. I'm on the clock."

"And I'm the client, so you're on my clock. And I've decided, you'll also be on my cock."

She's seething with anger. I continue talking. "We'll have lunch, talk a little business, then you'll get on your knees under my desk and suck my cock before you go home to finish up with your workday." I casually remove my blazer and drape it over the back of my chair. "If you do a good job, which I suspect you will, I'll spread you out over my desk and return the favor before I fuck you."

"No, thank you," she says as if she's not affected by the offer.

Am I affecting her? Is she imagining my mouth between her legs?

Cheater

"How about a business card, Chloe? You told me you only give them out for business reasons, so... I've given you a reason." I smile.

Her eyes flash with fire and it sends a thrill up my spine.

"I'd like you to take the bonus back, Derek. I don't want your money."

"I can't reverse it," I state. "It's your money now."

"Then I want to return it to you. I'll write you a check."

"I won't cash it."

"Maybe I'll take the money and leave town then. Start a new life. Away from you."

I step toward her. She folds her arms. I put my arms around her and pull her closer.

"I'd find you," I state, looking deep into her eyes.

The flash of emotion in her eyes gives me another thrill.

After I pull her the rest of the way into my body so she can feel how happy I am to see her, I grab her by the back of the neck and kiss her. She tries to move away, but I deepen it, sliding my tongue along the seam of her bubblegum pink lips, squeezing her neck.

I pull back, leaving her swaying.

She's affected.

"You wanna play a little cat and mouse and see what happens when I catch you, go for it. Otherwise, don't test me. You'll waste money and time. Because I would leave no stone unturned until I found you. And there's no telling what sorts of punishments I'd have to dole out to you and the folks you care about. Now, are you going to eat soup now or do you want my cock first?"

She looks at me with a blend of fear and disgust.

"If I slide my hand under this skirt, will I find you wet?"

"Don't you dare."

"About to tick another sexy bucket list line item. You, under my desk, sucking me off while I'm on a call. I think I'll make the call to your manager. Tell him how very happy I was to meet you. How very much your skills impress me." I run my hand up and down her ass. "Maybe dangle the carrot of a test project for my nightclubs and that if it all goes well, I'll consider recommending the company to my brother Jonah. He was into that line of business until recently. He sold his company, but left a lot of family businesses using it. Maybe we'll move a contract or two your company's way. There's also Eli who has some car washes, car dealerships, and some RV dealerships sprinkled throughout the state. Suspect he'd be only too happy to reconsider who he uses for his marketing."

I advance and she stumbles backwards, falling onto the small couch against the window, I'm on her, pinning her while I shove her skirt up and slide my hand into her panties.

"Stop it," she demands, struggling.

"You're wet, just like I knew you would be," I tell her. "Your body knows you want me. I just need to work on the rest of you, huh?" I smile and slide a finger into her tight, wet heat. "I could live inside this body, you know that? I could spend my life inside you and be perfectly happy. Undo my pants, Chloe. You can suck me off next time. I need inside you right now."

"Don't," she grunts, trying to shove me.

I work a second finger in and press the palm of my hand against her mound. I squeeze, pressing my fingers against her g-spot, then my thumb strokes from side to side, applying friction to her clit.

"Got 'cha. Exactly where I want you."

Her eyes grow wider and her fighting grip on my wrist loosens as I feel her body reacting to my touch. I pull her blouse from her skirt with my free hand, sliding it up her torso until I find a lacy bra cup. My fingers skate across a pebbled nipple while I taste the skin of her neck, pulling it into my mouth.

"No!" she snaps, breathlessly. "Stop trying to leave marks on me."

She shoves me again.

"Fine, no marks this time," I relent. "You can mark me, though. Nails on my back. A hickey on my neck."

"No, thank you," she mutters, but she's not pushing me off any longer.

I pinch her clit between my thumb and index knuckle. She reacts

Cheater

with a stifled shudder, eyes on my face, teeth embedded in her bottom lip. Her chest rises and falls fast.

"Wanna come, baby? Want my mouth? Or my fingers? My cock?"

She closes her eyes and blows out a slow exhale. She's conflicted. She needs my assurance here.

"I'm the bad guy, Chloe. We both know that. Just open your legs a little more and let me in like the good girl you are. This is my doing, not your fault." I remove my hand from her blouse and caress her face. "You're just doing what you're told. You're protecting what you care about from me. You don't have to feel bad about coming on my fingers, my tongue, my cock. You're just being the good girl you always are. Doing the right thing."

She says nothing, but our eyes are again locked. Her chest continues to rise and fall faster than usual. My tongue skims my lips, and her eyes drop to my mouth and stay there. She bites her lip with an expression that strikes me as pretty fucking close to that longing I'm looking for. I lean in and stroke her bottom lip with it, too. Her cunt squeezes around my fingers.

I smile.

She squirms. Her body seeks more friction. And she's about to get it.

My lips touch hers. "Kiss me," I demand. "Now, Chloe. Or else."

She doesn't. But she doesn't pull away either. She's breathing heavily.

"I want to feel your hands in my hair again, your sweet little pussy squeezing me. Give that to me, baby. Give it to me and I'll make you come so hard. Reward you for being such a good fucking girl for me."

I press my forehead to hers and pump my fingers a couple times.

She whimpers, eyes closed tight.

"Okay, fine. I'll let you keep your eyes closed this time. Just this time. So you don't have to feel bad, okay?" I whisper and then touch my lips to hers. "I'm gonna keep kissing you, keep making you feel good. You have to kiss me back, Chloe. You have to. Or else."

Her chin trembles like she's about to cry, but her cunt squeezes around my fingers again and I reward her by pressing harder into her G-spot, by rubbing faster circles around her clit as I kiss her. Her lips part and I swallow another whimper as our tongues touch.

"Let me have your sounds. Now. Do it and you'll get my mouth around your hot little clit."

She whimpers. Not intentionally, I don't think. She was holding her breath. Now, she's panting.

"That's my perfect girl." I kiss her again and our tongues touch as her back arches.

Pulling back so I can move down her body, I'm immensely satisfied by the sight of her swollen lips, by the look on her face that tells me everything I need to know. I keep moving until I'm mostly off the couch, lifting her skirt up some more until it's practically a belt. I tear her pink panties off and pocket them, then lift her right leg and drape it so her heel is resting on the top of the couch back.

She's splayed wide open for me when I dive in and taste her.

She tries to stifle another whimper, but fails.

I undo the buttons of the pink blouse and reveal the lacy pale pink bra.

"Matching bra and panties, little bunbun?" I chuckle. "It's like you knew I'd see these. Didn't you? You wanted me to make you strip for me so you could show me all this pink lace draped over these beautiful tits. This pretty, shaved pussy. No baby unicorns are dyin' today, Chloe, baby."

She posted a rant on her sex blog, the last post on there, about going to the trouble of lady-scaping for a man and having him not make a move. She ranted that baby unicorns die when that happens. They dissolve like putting candy floss into water. And then she had a sparkled image of a unicorn with a caption – *Save the Baby Unicorns*.

By my calculations, that post was written not long after she

Cheater

started dating Hallman. He was disappointing, even from the beginning.

She doesn't say anything, just keeps her eyes shut, her teeth holding that bottom lip. So I get back to business, running my tongue through her folds, dipping into her wet opening, before I close my mouth around that swollen button and suck hard, watching her back leave the couch, feeling more of her essence coat my tongue. I take both of her beautiful breasts into my hands and run my thumbs over her taut nipples while I apply suction to her clit.

Her body starts to tremble, so I keep it up. A rhythm of circles around her nipples and long, hard strokes of my tongue between her legs.

As she hits her climax, I let go of her tits and I've got her ass cheeks in each hand, massaging as I suck harder, watching her come apart under my control. Arching harder, bared tits pointing at the ceiling as she gives me all her sounds, doesn't stifle any of them, and it's like music to me.

I release her left cheek to free my cock out of my suit pants, biting down on her clit, making her squeal as her eyes jolt open to connect with mine.

"Baby," I say softly as I move up her body and then I pull back so I can slam forward, hard and to the root as my mouth again collides with hers, feeling my sweet girl's orgasm ramp up again. "Such a good girl."

Another thing that's just mine. Multiple orgasms. One of her entries was about never having the pleasure and I suspect Hallman didn't do this for her.

At the idea of him even trying, I pick up my rhythm and it turns punishing. She feels so fucking good.

"This cock is tired of not being where it belongs," I tell her, kissing her over and over. "I don't know how much longer I can last before I don't let you go, before I keep you."

She stops making sounds, she stops responding. She goes still.

"Keep you with me always, making all your dreams come true,

making you fall so madly in love with me you'll never wanna leave." I hold her face as I thrust in again and again, but her eyes are closed now.

"Chloe. Eyes!" I snap. "No hiding from me." She'll soon figure this out, even if it has to be the hard way. "He will never make you feel like this. He will never put in an ounce of effort above and beyond what he feels he has to do whereas I'll go all in to give you whatever you want, as much as you want. Because why, Chloe? I want you. The more I have of you, the more I want."

The way we look at one another, her expression stark, raw, her lips looking swollen, her eyes glassy, I know I'll never grow tired of being inside her while she comes, I'll never grow bored of exploring the facets in these light blue irises as she looks at me, while she watches me come.

I'm coming, and she whispers, "I hate you."

She doesn't.

"I... want you to l-leave me alone," she rasps, eyes closing as she tries to catch her breath.

"That's a lie," I accuse, then roll off, not happy about the lack of space on this couch for basking in the afterglow. Though she doesn't seem interested in that part at the moment as she curls up into a ball and stares at nothing while I shove my cock back into my suit pants and zip up.

I lick my lips. "Damn, you taste good." I caress her hip. "There's a bathroom right there if you need it."

Without looking at me, she gets up and the skirt falls back into place. She holds her blouse closed as she disappears into the small bathroom. She locks the door.

When she steps out, I'm at the conference table, opening my soup.

"My underwear, please." She holds her hand out.

I clap her palm and catch her hand, pulling her over until she stumbles, landing on my lap.

"Derek," she grumbles.

Cheater

I rub my nose along hers, "They're mine now." I dip, then lift my spoon and hold it in her direction.

"Eat."

She shakes her head.

"I'm sacrificing a wonton here for you, baby. C'mon. That's a gift and you know it." I move the spoon closer to her mouth.

"Don't ruin this soup for me, stalker."

"Eat the wonton, bunny. Eat the wonton or we're going to Vegas where you'll marry me."

"Don't be ridiculous."

"Is that a dare?" I ask.

She opens her mouth and I push the spoon in. She nibbles half of the wonton daintily.

I finish the other half and then kiss her neck, laughing.

"I need my underwear, please," she says.

"What underwear?" I ask, and lift the spoon again. "Have some of this broth."

She pulls away. "Seriously!"

"I'm completely serious. I'm gonna jack off with those later." I take another spoonful of soup. After swallowing, I gesture to the empty chair across the table from me. "Sit. Eat."

Chloe sits across from me and stares down at her leather portfolio.

"Plenty more ticks for the sexy bucket list today, hey?" I wipe my mouth with a napkin.

"The sexy bucket list no longer exists," Chloe states snottily.

"What do you mean?" I ask.

"Have a look," she challenges, gesturing toward my computer with a smug look on her face.

"That sass on your face makes me want to take you over my knee and spank your little ass before I fuck it," I state as I get up and move behind my desk, putting furniture between us for a moment as I rein in my reaction.

"That's become my to-do list, Chloe. Anything I've claimed as mine, I'm warning you... do not dare steal it from me. Steal from a Steele and you'll lose much more than you took."

She gives me a sour look filled with fake bravado. "There's nothing to do with me that's yours. I have to actually give it to you for it to be yours. I've given you nothing but a one-night hall pass. You used it already."

"Good point. I might have to remedy this."

She's going to give me everything. Soon.

Fire blazes in her pretty blue eyes and so does something else. I'm not sure what label to give it.

"Derek, I'm done here unless you have any actual Cavalier-related requests. I'll tell my boss we met, had lunch, and it was all very casual. That you told me you're looking forward to seeing how things go for the next three months and then you'll let us know how we're doing."

"I'm buying it," I tell her. "I'm buying it and giving it to you. You'll be the boss soon."

"That won't work for me. In fact, if you do that, I'll quit."

"And maybe wherever you find a new job, I'll buy that company and give it to you, too," I warn.

"Why?" she asks, looking absolutely bewildered.

"I'm a goal-oriented man. I'm simply working toward a goal right now."

"And what goal is that? To ruin my life? To end my relationship? To exert your power and money so much it steals my sanity and I wind up just as mad as you are?"

I shake my head in dismay. "Baby, baby, baby. You've got it all wrong."

She swallows hard, looking hurt.

I continue. "To make you happy, Chloe. To fulfill all your fantasies. So I get to watch you fall madly in love with me while I make every wish you have come true. The benefit to me being mad, as you put it, is that there's nothing I won't do to make sure I accomplish my goals."

Cheater

"I'm leaving," she states. "You got what you wanted. Fucking with my head and my body, so I'm gonna go."

"Take your soup." I gesture to the unopened soup, then add, "And both donuts."

"No, thank you."

"Chloe. Take them." I put it all into the paper bag with twine handles and hand it to her. "I insist."

27
Chloe

I'm mortified at my behavior. At how I responded to his words, his actions. Despite everything, the man knows how to light my libido on fire. And he's so unpredictable. I never know if he'll make me do something, if he'll let me go without laying a finger on me, if he'll show up in my bed, drop money in my account, threaten me, or say crazy things that make me feel so...

I shake that wistful thought off before it fully forms.

Because he's unstable. He's dangerous. He's blackmailing me! When will things turn ugly? How ugly will they get? How do I get out of this? If I can't, will I survive this?

It sounds morbid, but I'm terrified that this is going to be one of those tales where death for one of us is the only way out. Either he decides he's done, and he ends me or it goes nuclear and ends with him being shot by the cops after he completely loses it. Or a murder/suicide. The guy is unhinged.

When I get outside, my heart drops as I see Alannah by the revolving door to the office building part of this complex. She's talking to Jeffy, who's smoking a cigarette.

I glance over my shoulder while on the move and see Derek standing at the glass door. Watching.

And as my eyes bounce back straight ahead, one look at my best friend and our good friend fills me with alarm. Because they're not hiding anything. They're both looking at me with concern as their eyes bounce past me, undoubtedly clocking that Derek is still watching.

Jeffy clears his expression immediately but it's all over Alannah's face as she shoots Derek stink-eye.

Fuck. Fuck!

Clearing her expression too late tells me everything I need to know. I'm almost certain I've just caught the two of them having a conversation about me. I'm just hoping Derek hasn't read them as well as I have. But unfortunately, it doesn't seem like much gets past Derek. He might be nuts, but he's not dumb.

"Hey," Alannah greets and hugs me. "Why are you here?"

I pull back and look her dead in the eyes. She reads me loud and clear. Flinching, she whispers, "We're worried about you. I know something's up. Asked Jeffy about you-know-who and he told me things that would make your blood curdle. That was a fake text that day, wasn't it?"

"Don't give it away, he's watching," Jeffy says in a singsong voice. "Smile as you pull away, Alannah."

I let go of her.

"Honey," Jeffy says with a sweet smile as he opens his arms for me to come in for a hug. When he gets his mouth near my ear, he says low and serious, "He's very dangerous. I know who that family is, know a lot of details. Facts. Some blood-curdling rumors from credible sources. Please, please be careful, sweets." He loosens his grip and plasters on a big smile. "Don't you look pretty today!"

"Thanks," I say, tucking a loose lock behind my ear. I know my hair looks like I was just fucked, but I didn't care much about anything other than getting out of there.

Jeffy keeps talking without losing the smile. "His family is very powerful and most of the Steele brothers have a reputation. A severe one. I know someone on their legal team quite well."

I plaster on a smile as I pull back and look to Alannah. "Totally," I say.

She picks up on the double meaning.

Cheater

"Laugh or something, Fisher," Jeffy urges, then takes a drag of his cigarette, throws his head back and cackles at the same time as Alannah breaks into a fake laugh that doesn't touch her eyes.

"You really shouldn't smoke," I admonish, waving my finger playfully.

My face feels hot, but I do my best to keep up the casual act.

"It's my Friday cigarette. You know I need my Friday cigarette."

I fake another little laugh and then I look at my phone. There's a text message from my boss wishing me well with the meeting and reminding me to reach out to him as soon as I'm done.

"Oh, look at the time. I have to go." I slip it into my pocket.

"I'll call you," Alannah says.

"Maybe I oughta come for an impromptu sleepover tomorrow," I mutter.

"Sounds good," she says with emotion on her face.

"My phone and my place have electronic eyes and ears. I'll swing by tomorrow without announcing it."

Her eyes flash with understanding.

Jeffy says, "I'll come by. I'll bring wine. We'll talk. I'll tell you all I know. We'll brainstorm."

"Do nothing. I have to manage this all carefully. There's a lot at stake. Believe me. Do. Nothing."

I hug Alannah and then I hug Jeffy a second time.

"We'll figure it out," he whispers into my hair.

I nod and give him an affectionate squeeze. "It's not a good idea to get involved. I can't get into it but please. Don't. Don't let Lan go into *momma bear* mode, okay. She just can't."

"I've already told her. We need to brainstorm first. This is delicate."

"Kay. Later," I say.

My phone rings.

DS - *Cavalier calling*

I wave at them as I walk away, answering.

"What is it?"

"I don't want his hands on you like that."

"He's my friend," I state, hitting the button to unlock the door of my Cherokee.

"Next time, pull away faster."

I cradle the phone with my shoulder so I can use that hand to get the door open and put the bag of food and my leather bag on the passenger seat.

"Don't let it happen again," he warns.

I say nothing.

"Chloe?" Derek calls.

"What?"

"They know, don't they?"

"Know what?"

"Don't patronize me, baby. They're not very good actors. And you? I see straight through you."

"My friends know me. They know I'm not acting like myself because you're fucking with me. Alannah knows I've been weird since that day you sent the fake text. She saw through it; I didn't say anything. I'm texting my boss now telling him something came up, that you had to cancel our meeting. Because I can't possibly have a professional conversation with him right now."

"Your friends know something's amiss by your behavior. Yet the guy you're supposed to marry thinks everything is hunky dory. Right, Chloe? What does that tell you about your relationship with him?"

"My relationship with my fiancé is none of your business."

"I've made it my business," he clips, then warns. "If Jeff or Alannah do anything stupid about you and me, they'll be sorry. You'll be sad. I don't want you sad, so convince them everything is good. Don't make me feel like I have no choice but to upset you by retaliating."

"You've done nothing but upset me, Derek. And you *could* choose to stop fucking with my life."

"Not gonna happen."

Cheater

Frustration is practically oozing from my pores. "I'm leaving now. Starting my car."

"Don't disappoint me, Chloe."

"Goodbye, Derek."

"Next Friday," he says. "One o'clock. Weekly meeting."

Does that mean he's going to leave me alone for a whole week? I sure as heck hope so.

"Unless I can't wait that long," he adds, then laughs.

I aggressively stab *end* with my finger and put my forehead to my steering wheel.

Breathe, Chloe.

I decide to message my boss before leaving the parking lot.

Client had something come up and had to cancel our meeting after I arrived. I waited for quite a while but he said he'll be in touch to reschedule. I've got a migraine so I'm going to be offline this afternoon. I'll check in with you Monday morning.

My boss immediately replies.

Oh ok. Feel better. Have a good weekend.

I'm relieved he's not calling me, asking a zillion questions.

When I get home, I call Alannah.

"Hey, breastie," she answers fake-sunnily. "God, I'm in major need of some best friend time. I miss you."

"Derek knows you know there's something not right between him and I. I need to make sure you and Jeff leave it all be. He's probably got someone listening now or will get a recording of this call or something."

"Sweetie, what the fuck? I knew something was wonky with that text after he showed up and told you to come over. And you've been quiet ever since."

"Let's just say he doesn't want things to end regardless of what I've said, and he's been very... adamant about me doing what he wants me to do."

"Is he hurting you?" she asks. "I'll go to jail for you, sister; you know I will."

"Not hurting me," I reply. "But that's probably because I'm cooperating."

"Cooperating?" she asks.

"Yeah," I whisper.

"You're fucking him."

"Yeah," I whisper again.

She holds the phone for a minute. She's shocked. Not surprisingly.

"What's he holding over your head? Just Adam?"

"He's got the ability to blow Adam's life up and I can't let that happen. I'm just ... I'm hoping he gets bored. Finds a new fixation."

"Right," she mutters. "I'll just sit back and let him do whatever, so Adam's feelings don't get hurt. Listen Chlo, Adam pushed you to do this. Surely he'll understand that things got out of control through no fault of yours. And if he doesn't, fuck him."

"Lan!"

"No! Something has to be done. Blackmailing you into continuing an affair that you don't want? Making you lie to your friends to keep it secret? You're not alone here. We'll get you out of this."

Leaving things be is the last thing she intends to do. And I feel sick about it.

"Alannah, let me handle this. Seriously. I might catch shit for the things I'm saying, but for real, you and Jeff need to back off. He has a sex tape, too."

"A what? A sex tape? Of you?"

"He recorded us." It's all I can think to say to settle her down. She won't want that getting out. It's not like Derek threatened to use it,

Cheater

but he did admit he was recording me last night and if he didn't lie about me calling out his name that'd just add more gasoline to the fire.

"Fuck, Chlo. This is my fault. I said all that stuff. Me. I took you there. I opened my big, fat mouth about your situation. God, I'm sorry. I want to help you fix this because you're you, but also... this is *my* fault."

"You got graphic, yeah, but it was me that said all the stuff about my personal situation. The lack of sex life. Don't take this on. The only person to blame for Derek's actions is Derek."

"He's very dangerous. Most of that family is rumored to be connected with organized crime. Sketchy stuff. Links that go back over a century. I got some information from Jeffy and from Craig, and..."

"Craig? God, Lan. What?"

Craig is Adam's best friend. And a cop!

"I asked about him, said I wanted to know what he was all about for a girlfriend. Didn't say who. The shit he told me about the Steele brothers, about their father and some of their uncles... maybe we should get you out of town. Anyone who's been here longer than we have seems to know who they are, and they've got stories. Sketchy and ugly ones. Greasing palms to get what they want. Making problems go away. Cops and politicians in Derek's father's pocket and so many rumors. Even the Papalias are terrified of them."

I'd never heard of the Steele family before all this, but I've read stories in the paper and seen things on the news about the notorious local Papalia gang that call themselves The Crew with their drugs, prostitution, and chop shop.

"If he does hear this, he needs to realize he's not fucking with someone who has nobody. We'll help you. We have connections, too!"

"He'll tell Adam everything. It'll set back his emotional recovery significantly. I can't let that happen. Can't risk him using recordings he's got of me. Can you imagine if he plays the recording of us talking and you calling him a bland baked potato and a boring ever after? Sending a sex video to Adam? To my job? My parents, even? Come on, Alannah. He could leak the sex tape publicly. We both know full well the kind of damage that could cause."

She had a high school boyfriend leak nude pictures of her senior year. It was ugly. It reared its head again in college, too.

I keep going. "He could do so much damage. Promise me you won't put things at risk by messing around. This is a man who bugged my house. Who's tracking my car. Who is paying to have someone tail me whenever I leave my house."

"Fuck," she breathes. "All this for sex?"

"I don't get it either."

"We can't let him get away with this."

"So far, it's just sex," I say. And then I add, "It's assholery what he's doing but at least it's good sex." My face burns hot. "It could be worse."

I can just imagine Derek sitting there listening to this with a smug look on his face. But I'm not thinking straight. All I'm thinking about is that I need to find the words to make Alannah stand down. Downplay it. Derek terrifies me. Confuses me.

"So far, with me cooperating, nothing terrible has happened beyond being forced to have sex with him."

The line is silent for a minute, then she finally speaks up again. "This is bullshit. If he's blackmailing you, I don't care how good the dick is and you don't either. This is me you're talking to, here. I know you. This guy needs to fuck off."

"Let me handle this. I see a path."

"Yeah?" she asks.

"I do," I lie. "We'll talk later. Tell me you'll do nothing."

"Mm hm," she says.

I grind my teeth. "Seriously. Don't do anything. I'll call you later. Gotta finish up some work stuff."

"Mm," she mutters. "Yeah."

"Promise me, Lan. I need to know you won't put me or yourself in the line of fire here."

She sighs. "Okay."

"Promise me."

"I promise, Chlo. Love you."

"Good," I breathe out relief. "Love you, too. Call you tomorrow."

I end the call and hope she'll keep her word. Tomorrow night I'll go over there and talk sense into her.

I'm saying nothing until the last minute about the planned sleepover in order to, hopefully, make sure Derek doesn't try to find a way to eavesdrop on me there. I'll conveniently leave my phone behind.

Alannah and I always brainstorm our problems for solutions, but I have no idea what could be a potential solution here other than hoping he gets bored.

Jeff has clout in his law firm and knows a lot of people. He firmly believes Derek is dangerous, so he'll undoubtedly think long and hard before acting. Alannah is smart, but she's a protective mama bear type and would break her promise if she thinks she knows better than me here. I can only hope that a) she listens and b) if she doesn't, Derek's bark is worse than his bite.

∞

"Hi!" Adam is practically glowing when he comes in with his briefcase on his lap. "There's more stuff in the van. Do you think you could gimme some help?"

"Sure," I say, rising from the couch where I've been watching the local news while waiting for the food delivery, waiting for him, and wringing my hands over my problems.

I'm nearly past him when he grapples for my hand. "Chloe?"

I stop and look down.

"Don't I get a welcome home kiss?" he sheepishly asks.

I lean over and press my lips to his. I'm about to pull back when his fingers tangle into my hair that's now down from the earlier twist.

He deepens the kiss, slipping me his tongue, surprising me. "That's better," he says. "Missed you."

I straighten up and feeling discombobulated, I say, "Glad you're home. I'll... uh... go get your stuff and then you can tell me all about it. Food will be here soon, too."

∞

Adam spoke more over that meal than he's spoken in months.

And throughout, I felt strange about the kiss. Like it was wrong. That it didn't feel right. And that's got me completely disjointed. He was so excited about filling me in that I don't think he's noticed how *off* I am.

He said he can see himself doing this, focusing on accessibility advocacy and related issues for now. He still doesn't want to be typecasted, but he does see big potential for work and to elevate his profile while helping others in his position. He got a jump-start on a couple article ideas he's already pitched to his editor and says he feels inspired to write, more inspired than in many months.

He excitedly told me he made some great connections including a respected journalist who unfortunately has advancing Huntington's Disease and is expecting to have to retire due to declining health within six months or less.

Adam interviewed this journalist for an article that his editor is stoked about, and the man invited Adam to have dinner with him, which was why he only briefly texted me last night. He said they talked for over three hours and got along great. Adam says there were more than overt suggestions about this journalist passing the torch to him, recommending him for several publications that have ongoing columns and special assignments. There's even the potential for him to be on a panel for a call-in health and wellness show.

By the end of the meal, his good mood is contagious, and I find I'm still smiling while putting the food away, excited for his zest for life after such a dark period.

Cheater

I hear the motor of Adam's wheelchair coming into the kitchen as I'm wiping down the table.

"Chloe?"

I look over my shoulder. He'd gone to take care of a few work things while I put stuff away with plans to find something to watch on television together in half an hour, but now he's two feet away with a strange look on his face.

"Why don't you pour yourself another glass of wine and meet me in the bedroom?" he suggests.

"You wanna watch TV in there instead?" I ask. I can't even remember the last time he suggested we find something to watch together.

"I... ordered something and I thought we could try it," Adam says with a little smile on his face. "Shit," he adds, "I feel like a nervous virgin."

Frowning at the strange comment, I follow his eyes down to the box on his lap. This is the box that got delivered this morning that I was instructed not to open.

He smiles. "So, what do you think? Maybe instead of watching TV, you can pour another glass of wine and put on something sexy?"

He never suggests I have a second glass of wine. In fact, he was the one who suggested I open a bottle and he had a glass with me for a change. I stare as he opens the box and shows me the contents.

I don't know for a few breaths what I'm looking at. It's a tube contraption of some sort.

"It's a vacuum device," he explains. "I pump it over myself until it gets me... ready. Then there's a ring I'll put on and ... we've got thirty minutes or less."

My eyes bulge.

"Oh," I breathe.

"I... realized I wasn't being very fair to you, Chloe. So I thought we could at least ... try. When I ordered things to be delivered to the hotel yesterday, there was a catalog. And... I ordered this yesterday from there for rush delivery today."

Try. Try?

I blink a few times and rub my lips together before I blow out a long exhale as I absorb this shocking development.

My phone rings.

Adam looks over at the dining table, which he's closer to than I am. "Do you need to get this? DS Cavalier?"

"It's work. It can go to voicemail," I say, heart skipping a beat.

My mind is churning at a thousand revolutions per second. Adam wants to have sex. Adam bought a device to be able to have sex with me. In our bed. On the sheets where Derek and I–

"Cavalier. That's the big client, isn't it?" he asks.

Derek is phoning me. Derek is probably watching. This makes me angry. This is a very private moment he's watching and now he's calling?

"Chloe?" Adam prompts.

I give my head a shake. "It's Friday night. After eight o'clock. They don't expect me to answer. They're probably leaving a message for Monday morning."

It stops ringing halfway through the third ring.

"What do you think?" he asks. "About this?" He gestures to his lap.

"Well..." I say and shift uncomfortably from one foot to the other.

Adam looks hopeful. And I'm surprised. And thrown.

"Um..."

My phone starts ringing again.

"DS Cavalier," Adam remarks, lifting my phone and extending his hand in my direction.

My face burns hot.

I move over there and take it, then turn the phone off and set it on the table.

"Two calls in a row. Maybe something urgent." he says, looking concerned.

"We're having an important conversation."

I have a strong work ethic. Always have. Maybe he'd interrupt an

Cheater

important conversation like the one we're having if his editor was calling in the middle of it, but I don't think it's outlandish or out of character for me to give him my undivided attention. Even though I'm not sure he has it because my brain feels absolutely muddled at the moment.

But as for undivided attention, it's yet another one of the things between us that I've noticed.

I've put him first. Always. I haven't always gotten that back. Then again, I've never been about equality in a relationship in that way where I kept score. I've put my all into it the way I'd want the other person to do. Maybe that's changing. Maybe that's changing because of all that's happened.

"This is sudden," I say. "And I'm a little unprepared for it. I..."

My head is swimming.

"Let's just try it. I'm okay if I don't get anything out of it. I know I won't feel it, but you will and... I wanna try. Try and do this for you. For... for us. See how it goes, you know?"

I'm about to tell him a fib... that I have my period. Because I need to think. And no way would Adam want period sex. I suggested period sex in the shower once and he got absolutely grossed out at the notion. But before I get a chance to say it, the doorbell rings.

"I'll... I'll go see who that is," I say, rushing to the door. I can make out a tall man standing there with his phone to his ear through the frosted glass.

I open the door just an inch.

"Yes?"

"Chloe Turner? My name is Ken. I'm assigned to keep you safe. Please step out here and take this phone from me. There's someone who needs to speak with you privately and urgently."

There's a running vehicle in the driveway behind my car.

I frown. Keep me safe? That's a joke. Keep tabs is more like it.

"Now, please," he urges authoritatively.

"No," I deny. "Go away."

I'm about to shut the door when I realize he's inserted his shoe there. He's got a stern look on his face.

"Miss Turner, please. Don't make my job hard tonight, okay?"

I open the door wider and gesture as I move forward. He steps back as I step outside and shut it behind me.

"Listen," I say, "This is not cool."

He extends his hand, offering me his phone. "Please take the call or he'll issue another order. He needs to speak with you urgently."

I stare at it.

"An order for me to bring you to him," he says low and in a way that's chilling.

I take it and shakily put it to my ear.

"Hello?" I snap.

Ken walks down my driveway as Derek starts talking.

"Chloe!" He sounds winded. "He does not fucking touch you. It was bad enough watching him put his mouth on you. Come to me. Now."

"What the fuck?" I snap. "How about you stop watching?"

"Now, Chloe. I mean it. Make up a reason. Come here now or I'm coming there."

"Fuck you," I spit.

Ken flinches, looking over his shoulder at me briefly as if he's concerned I'm putting myself in peril.

"You will not fuck him, Chloe. Do you hear me?" Derek is yelling now. "You come here to me right now or else you'll force my hand."

"One more time, fuck you," I snap, then hold the phone out. "Here!" I call. "Take this and go away."

"Sweetie?" I hear from behind me.

Damn it! Adam has opened the door. His eyes are on me with concern.

28
Derek

When she passed the phone to Kenny and he told me Hallman had come out, I told him to keep them inside until I get there with a gun pointed at Hallman. Only at Hallman.

No way would I have anyone point a gun at Chloe.

I also told him I want them six feet apart and not to let them talk.

My impulse control is holding on by a thread here as I drive the short distance to her, flexing my trigger finger the entire way, reminding myself she's not far, that nothing's gonna happen until I get there. Kenny has the gun pointed at Hallman. He won't touch her. He better not fucking touch her, or I'll be taking Kenny's gun and...

I fly through a stop sign. *Shit.*

I will my pulse to normalize, counting backwards from a hundred.

When Hallman put his mouth on her, I wanted to come out of my skin and rip his fucking head off his shoulders. When he explained what he had in that cardboard box – and I'm kicking myself in the ass for not paying close enough attention to what he was doing when he was out of town – I knew I was about to expedite my plan. She refused to come to me so now my hand has been forced.

Strategy gets tossed out the window and instead of continuing to show this girl why she should pick a life with me by my wining and dining her, by my showing her how much she matters, by making all her dreams come true, I've now tossed it all out the window. It doesn't matter. Fuck the plan. I'm getting what I want. My queen. Because I'm done with this long-game bullshit. She's coming home with me tonight. I only lasted a week from the moment I first fucked her. I wanted to take at least a month while showing her all she'll be to me, wanted her to willingly pick me after seeing the difference between what I give her and what she gets from him. But... it is what it is.

∞

I park and rush inside, finding Kenny on a chair, a gun in his hand but resting on his knee. My eyes devour Chloe, ensuring her wellbeing. She sits on the couch, arms wrapped around herself, eyes full of terror. I have to stop myself from physically lifting her into my arms to comfort her. Because I have to deal with this first.

The asshole in the wheelchair is at least twelve feet from her and staring at me. Pale. Confused brown eyes on his pale face bounce between me and Kenny.

"Thanks, man. You can go now."

Kenny puts his piece into the back of his waistband while shooting me an angry look. I know he's displeased with me making him pull a gun and hold people. Probably unhappy I ordered he point it at a guy in a wheelchair. He prefers to be in the shadows.

"I'll make a deposit in the morning for your trouble," I say.

He scratches his clenched jaw before he looks to the captives in the room. "My apologies, Miss Turner. Mr. Hallman. Nothing personal. I hope you won't hold it against me, should our paths cross again." He nods at them and leaves, closing the door behind himself.

Chloe is staring at me with terror in her eyes. Hallman's forehead is wrinkled as he watches Kenny go, then looks at us, looking absolutely lost.

"Have you said anything since Kenny told you two to sit and wait?" I ask her.

It's only been twelve minutes.

Cheater

She shakes her head. "He told us to both stay quiet and say nothing until you arrived. Derek, please..."

"What's going on here?" Hallman asks. "Who are you? Who was that and what the hell is happening here?"

I sit in the chair Kenny vacated.

"I'm Derek Steele," I tell Hallman.

He stares at me for a second and I see recognition hit his eyes.

"You've written about my family," I add.

"A while ago, yeah. You've got a beef with me about that?" He looks at Chloe and I know things aren't adding up. "You know him?" he asks her.

"Adam..." Chloe starts to speak, but her chin trembles. She's about to cry. I don't like it.

I don't normally give a shit about tears, but I don't like this.

"I'll do the talking, baby," I state.

Hallman's eyes bounce between the two of us with confusion.

"Chloe and I met not too long ago," I explain.

"Derek," Chloe whispers brokenly. She's clasping her hair on both sides of her head. She's terrified of what I'll say to him.

She cares that much about hurting him. My beautiful, selfless girl.

I keep talking. "The night she celebrated her friend Alannah's promotion. It took about a week, but she used her hall pass on me."

"Derek, don't," Chloe says softly, eyes filled with horror, with pleading.

Hallman looks at Chloe with wide eyes. "Tell me you're not pregnant or something."

She flinches.

And my back straightens, in fact all my senses perk up at the idea of that. At the idea of Chloe carrying my child.

A series of images race through my mind. Chloe with a round belly, my hands on it. Love shining in her eyes as she holds a bundle in a white blanket. Strange sensations rise in me at the whole notion.

"No. I'm not pregnant," she says. "It's been a week, Adam. And you know I'm on birth control."

"It's gonna be okay, baby. I've got this," I tell her, then turn my attention to Hallman. "She used the hall pass and very sweetly tried to explain to me afterwards that it was a one-time thing. But I don't want it to end. In fact, more than that, I find myself unwilling to allow it to end."

He frowns.

I continue. "I'm prepared to make it very worth your while if you withdraw your marriage proposal and ask for the ring back."

Chloe stares at me with horror and she's about to speak.

"Shh," I tell her. "Please, Chloe. I've got this."

His eyes ping pong between me and her. His mouth opens and closes a few times, like he's blown away, doesn't know what to say. He starts with, "You had someone hold us at gunpoint so you can come tell me you want my fiancée?"

"In a very short time, your life has had a lot of changes, Hallman," I go on. "Until the past week or so, things weren't going very well, were they?"

He frowns and waits for me to elaborate. He's also absorbing the situation at hand. Not a total dolt.

"But things got better. You got that van and got some independence. You also had a very productive trip with that work assignment. I've put in an offer to buy the company that owns the publications Laurier writes for, by the way. If you take on the projects you and Laurier talked about, you'll be working indirectly for me. And you'll be paid very well. Better than he's been paid."

"Derek!" Chloe clips angrily.

"Just a minute, bunny." I keep my gaze focused on Hallman. "I was the anonymous donor that put in over half the value of your accessible van. I made some calls and got you that assignment yesterday. I also had someone arrange for you to meet with Sheldon Laurier last night. I had them recommend that you receive consideration to take on some of his projects after he retires above and beyond the

Cheater

magazine column. As you can see, I've got the ability to make things go well for you."

"You want my fiancée?" Adam snaps. "You think I'm gonna give up the woman I plan to spend my life with for a job opportunity and a van?" He scoffs. "And you have us held at gunpoint? Wow. You think she'll have anything to do with you?"

"Chloe has quickly become very special to me," I state. "She doesn't want to hurt you. She didn't want to sleep with me in the first place, would never have been unfaithful to you if you hadn't pressured her to do it. Once she did, feelings developed."

"Derek," Chloe warns. "Stop this."

Hallman looks at her.

She shakes her head. "I don't have feelings for Derek, Adam. I don't. He's being persistent, and I–"

"You might not be ready to admit it yet, but you are developing feelings for me," I correct.

"Hatred. That's about it," she declares, shooting a dirty look at me. "How dare you!"

My gaze bounces back to Hallman. "My brother-in-law is a neurosurgeon. He's well connected. I could pull strings to get you on probably any clinical trial you're interested in to help with your mobility. I can have Laurier recommend you for everything you're interested in writing in that field. Interested in something else? I might be able to help there, too. In fact, I can pull some strings and get you a publishing contract with one of the big five for your novels. I know you've had three rejections already, but through my family connections, I've got some pull with two, possibly three of the big five."

Chloe's eyes bounce to Hallman's face. "You finished your novel and submitted it?"

"Ten months ago," I advise. "It's not a novel. It's a series of four. He's got one left to write but he's been a little blocked since the accident. Playing video games most days all day might not help with that though, Hallman."

Hallman takes a big breath and is about to speak when I cut him off.

"By the way, the night he had the accident, he didn't come straight home from work. He stopped off at a nightclub. The Fifth."

Hallman blanches. "I wasn't drinking. I drove sober."

"Maybe, but you were upset when you left after a heated conversation in the corner with a lovely auburn-haired beauty. Coincidentally, it's a conversation I happen to have a partial recording of."

Chloe stares at Hallman in shock.

He frowns. "It was Jeannie. She begged me to meet her to talk about a reconciliation. I told her to leave me alone. Nothing happened."

"Jeannie, your ex-fiancée," I put in.

"Fiancée?" Chloe asks him. "I thought you two just dated."

"We were only engaged just over a month when we split. It doesn't matter."

She looks slain with betrayal.

Fucking goof.

"Since you'll be off Chloe's medical benefits after she marries me, I'll buy you insurance and cover everything not included. Also, I'll arrange for you to meet with the exoskeleton people you've been researching. I'll pay for that equipment, too."

"The what?" Chloe looks even more thrown.

I answer for him. "It's an expensive rechargeable suit that he'd wear and use to walk. I'll even buy you two suits, Hallman, so you can wear one while the other one charges."

"How did you know I've been researching that?" he asks. "How do you know this much about me?"

"I get daily reports of your technology habits," I admit and then I smile. "Yep. Got reports of all of your web surfing habits. Dating back about... oh... five or six years."

I lean forward and rest my forearms on my knees. "Lots of information at my fingertips, Hallman."

He flinches and blinks a couple times. "Including a recording that just happens to be from the night of my accident? That doesn't sound like a coincidence."

"It is. I have pretty good software that sifts through security footage and uses facial recognition. Lucky for me you chose to meet your ex at one of my clubs."

Chloe stares at him with concern before her eyes ping back to me.

"I know all your secrets. All of both of your secrets."

Hallman swallows and looks down, eyebrows wrinkling.

"Too bad I didn't check the last few days to see what you've been surfing and doing online. This one here was keeping me busy, if you get my drift."

Chloe shakes her head, eyeing me with disdain.

"Chloe's most unsavory secret is that she'll put up with absolutely all your shit because she thinks she loves you, Hallman. Because she's loyal. And she thinks you love her."

"I do love her," Hallman argues.

"Not nearly enough. Not the way she deserves to be loved. But that's neither here nor there anymore. You're done. I'm up. So listen, I can make things easy, or I could make them hard. I'd like Chloe to leave with me tonight. She'll marry me. We'll keep it between us maybe a month or two. Then we'll announce it. Maybe have a second wedding for the families, but she'll be my wife within the week." I look at her and flash a smile.

She's in shock.

I keep going. "Chloe needs to marry me and stay married to me for you to keep all the things I'm offering to give you. If she doesn't, you lose your job and I stop paying the medical bills, not to mention you won't find yourself anything like what I'm offering you."

I lean back and cross one ankle over my knee.

"Chloe and I... need to talk before I'm willing to make any decisions."

She stares at him in shock. "You're not considering this," she says.

The shock and pain on her face don't feel good. I don't like it. I need to stay the course, though.

"Chloe, I'm... I'm in shock over here but he's being pretty clear here about what he wants. About what might happen if we don't cooperate. He had a guy point a gun at us!"

"At you," I correct. "Did Kenny point the gun at you, baby? I told him not to. I'll fuckin' end him if he pointed that gun in your direction."

She shoots me an irritated look and then her gaze swings back to her soon-to-be ex.

"Are you saying this because you want what he's offering or because you're afraid of whatever he's holding over your head?"

"Both," I mutter.

They both look at me.

Hallman says, "I think we need time to think. Time to talk. Can we have that?"

"No," I say simply.

"I'm not doing this," Chloe states. "No way. You can't bulldoze my life like this, Derek."

"I already did, little bunny. Things are over with you and him."

"Plant cameras in our house and have someone hold us at gunpoint because you don't want me to have sex with my fiancé, and–"

"Cameras?" Hallman asks. "Here?"

"Oh yeah. I've been watching and listening for a week. Had Kenny install cameras the night she used the hall pass on me. How's this?" I suggest, "I don't tell him what you don't want me to tell him, baby, and I don't tell her what you wouldn't want her to know, Potato."

Chloe winces.

Frowning, Hallman mouths, "Potato?"

I laugh. "But Chloe comes with me tonight. Marries me. Then, she stays married to me and all goes well. And I hate to say this but to make sure there's no misunderstandings, I've got to. If either of you fuck me over in any way, shape or form, you won't like what happens."

Cheater

"You're a psychopath," she whispers.

"You're getting married just once in your life. Wearing the white dress only one time. For me."

She looks at him. "Let's take his power away, Adam. Right now. I'll tell you everything. You tell me everything. Then he has nothing to hold over us. Forget the job opportunities. You'll figure them out yourself. You're very capable."

"I can have him dealt with for you," I tell Hallman. "You'll never have to think about him again."

The room goes dead silent.

Hallman stares with wide eyes. I smile.

"Who?" Chloe finally asks.

"Or I could pull some strings and things would go very public." I shrug. "You can either make it easier on Chloe to walk away and get to have all the things I've laid out. Or I take Chloe anyway and you get nothing while your skeletons get leaked to the press."

"Let me get this straight," Hallman says. "You hook up with my fiancée, she tells you it's a one-time thing, and how do we wind up here? You started spying on us the same night she slept with you? What the hell?"

"That night was perfection," I tell him, kissing my fingertips. "She is everything I want. I've never, ever felt like this." I look at my girl and my chest swells with feelings.

But she looks ready to crumble. I can't wait to hold her, take her to my bed, cover her with my body while I whisper into her skin how I'm going to make it all better. She might not believe me at first, but I *will*.

"So it was more than just Thad Steele who was a maniac," Hallman mutters. "It's just a better kept secret with you."

My smile disappears. "Be careful, Hallman. I'm offering you some incentives here. I can rip all that away and take my girl anyway."

"Chloe and I need to talk about this," he says. "Can you give us some privacy?"

"No. Take the ring off, little bunny. Give it to him, and come with me. I'll send someone to pick up your things later."

I stand and step up to Hallman. "She's mine. From here on out. You have no more claims on her. Anything related to our agreement will be discussed via an email address I'll send you. You don't contact me directly. You don't contact Chloe." I lean toward him and add, "You don't *ever* contact Chloe. Ever." I wait and give him a severe look before I straighten up. "And you tell nobody, and I mean nobody about any of this exchange here. You tell your friends and family that you ended the relationship. She's not the bad guy here. You're just too fucked up from your accident. You need time to focus on yourself. Your career. Your healing. You realize you were being difficult to live with and you don't want that for her. Nobody can change your mind."

He blinks a couple times and then looks at her. I sidestep to block her.

"Make it easy. She's not happy but she'd never abandon you, so you end things with her. She marries me and I give her everything she wants. You get the customized robotic exoskeletons, into any medical trial you're interested in. I will pull strings to make your career go very well instead of doing the opposite. You get your fiction series published by one of the big five and you have your medical bills paid for life. I'm feeling generous here, Hallman, and I want my girl to feel good about walking away, knowing you'll be all right, so I'll sweeten the pot and if Chloe wants me to, I'll hand over a million dollars on our one-year wedding anniversary. To you. She can decide when that time comes. She's already been fucking me. Loving it, man. Loving it. I fucked her repeatedly, including in your bed." I look to Chloe. "Don't feel bad, baby. He knows it's not your fault. He pushed you into it and I'm the one pushing the issue. It's not your fault. It's his. It's mine. Hallman, she tried to stick to your rules. I wasn't having it. Any of it. Because you're a tool who doesn't deserve her."

Chloe's got tears streaming down her face as she stares at me in

Cheater

disbelief. But in short order, she'll realize this is the best thing in the world for her. She's being liberated from a life where she's not appreciated, where she won't get what she wants. With me, she'll have it all.

"I was gonna play it differently, Chloe," I explain with my palm to my heart. "Honestly. I wanted to show you what you could have. How much you're worth. How I *see* how much you're worth. I was planning things in a way you'd decide to pick me because you know I'm the man for you. But the idea of him fucking you?" I shake my head. "I had to throw strategy out the window when you wouldn't come to me. When you wouldn't take my calls. Because I can't stomach it. Can't fuckin' stomach the thought of anybody touching you but me. But you'd let him. You'd ride his dick tonight because he went to the trouble, because he was throwin' you a fuckin' bone. Wouldn't you? You wouldn't come. Neither would he. And then you'd cry yourself to sleep while I sat back feeling sick about anybody but me being inside you. No way. No fucking way. I'm not him. I'm not okay with another man fucking you."

She shakes her head with disbelief, dashing tears away.

"He told his cop buddy over here the other day that he was springing boners randomly, too, baby. He bought that pump thing but fuck, if my dick wasn't working and I was springing them randomly, I'd call you immediately and give you the option to hop on."

Hallman's eyes bounce between us. "It only happened twice. I wasn't in the headspace to do anything, to... you... Chloe, you know where my head has been at with all this. I refuse to justify myself when I'm the one who's lost use of my legs. Just me. But forget that, it doesn't matter now. What matters is you, Chloe. I don't want this guy to hurt you."

"I'm gonna give her everything, Hallman. Anything she wants that money can buy. Anything she wants sexually. And I already know Chloe better than you do after just a couple weeks. Because I know what she really needs I'll give her the emotional support and intimacy she deserves, too. Something you've never done."

I lean forward aggressively. He flinches.

"The last thing I'd ever do is hurt Chloe. I'll hurt anyone who hurts her. The only reason I haven't hurt you after all the pain you've put her through is because she'd have difficulty forgiving me for it."

"I've hurt her?" he asks.

"You pushed her with the hall pass. You had her loyalty, and you broke her by doing this. All you had to do was show her how much she means to you. But you failed, Hallman. You let her carry the whole load instead of manning up. You've been putting her through hell."

"Stop it," Chloe whispers. "Please stop it."

Her shoulders tremble and she dissolves into full-body sobs. I go to her but her hand flies up. "Stay back, Derek. D-don't touch me."

"Go spend a couple minutes talking in the bedroom and get your closure now. I'll be watching. No touching. If he touches you, it'll really piss me off. Don't piss me off, Hallman."

She rubs her temples.

"Pack a bag, Chloe. You're coming home with me tonight."

"No."

"No isn't an option," I state. "Don't test me. I'll carry you out of here kicking and screaming and I don't want to do that, baby."

She looks at him. He says nothing. I watch her examine him for a minute looking broken. And I don't like it.

"Go on. Let's get this done," I prompt.

I gesture toward the hallway and open the app on my phone that'll show me the bedroom.

Hallman puts his hand to the controls for his wheelchair and maneuvers himself around and then down the hall.

Chloe blinks a couple times, shaking her head at me through teary eyes as she gets to her feet and follows him.

29
Chloe

He had that man pull a gun on us and force us to sit in the living room to wait for him. His behavior was *that* extreme at the sight of the penis pump. And then he strolls in here and just... blows our life apart?

And he wants me to leave with him, marry him. Marry him? Did he really say that and promise Adam a million bucks on our first wedding anniversary? I can't even form a coherent thought right now.

What was Adam doing with Jeannie the night of his accident? An argument with her made him angry and he... what... drove erratically? I don't know what any of that means. We ran into her once and she was a bitch, told me she wanted him back and told him when he was ready, she'd be waiting. He laughed it off and told me she was a bunny-boiler ex. Blew it off as no big deal. He certainly never said he was engaged before me.

I close the door behind myself and sit on the bed. Adam's in front of me. Privacy is an illusion, of course.

"He's clearly very dangerous, Chloe," Adam says with a dire expression. "I guess you didn't know who he was when you decided to sleep with him."

Anger flares in me.

Adam reads it and raises his hands defensively.

"I know that's on me. Fuck. Of all the people though..."

"If I could wrap my mind around anything happening right now, I might think you're blaming me for this."

"Of course I'm not. I'm sorry. When I wrote that article on his father, I couldn't find much about Derek Steele. Whole family is secretive, but that one's the brother that's most under the radar. Clearly he's worse than even the worst of them. The shit I dug up about his brothers, though, this isn't a shocker."

I don't know what he's referring to but I'm not about to ask. I don't need to know the details to know he's right about Derek being messed up.

"And he's obsessed with you."

I say nothing.

"I'm sorry, Chloe."

I frown and say nothing again, because I'm in a state of disbelief over this evening's events. Although maybe I shouldn't be. If Derek would go to the lengths he's already gone to, how far will he go?

"I don't know what to do," Adam says. "If I say that you should go with him, and he hurts you... I can't imagine. He had someone hold us at gunpoint for god's sake. If we deny him, I don't know what'll happen. He seems like he's on a hair trigger, could snap at any moment."

"Yep," I whisper, reaching for the box of Kleenex on Adam's bedside table and blow my nose.

"How much do you know about the Steele family?"

"Not much," I say, crumpling the Kleenex.

"I don't know what to do, Chloe. I know his brother Thad was a hot-headed thug. Pulled some major shit before he got murdered. His brother Elijah has a reputation for some dark shit, too. Guy's practically a mobster. There's rumblings about Jonah Steele getting compared to Elijah. Asher Steele is a jet-setting typical rich playboy, but doesn't seem like much of a threat. Nobody talks about Derek Steele. Ever."

Bile rises in my throat.

"There are stories about the father having things go his way in

Cheater

many situations where they shouldn't have. Guy keeps getting richer and richer. About how dirty the men in that family will play to get what they want. Clearly the apples don't fall far from that tree. But if we don't cooperate, I don't know what the hell that guy will do. He's gone to a whole lot of extremes here."

"Yeah," I whisper and get a fresh Kleenex to dab wetness off my cheeks.

The look on his face says it all. He thinks I should go with Derek. He's willing to give me up. I mean, what else can he do, right? Fight for me? Fight against a rich, powerful psychotic man who has no problems making threats and showing he can make good on them, right? So, I should go with the powerful, psychotic man that's been blackmailing me and leave Adam with all the opportunities Derek has put in his lap.

"I guess it's a trade-off." I shrug, dabbing my face with the Kleenex. "Get your books published. Get access to leading edge technology to help you walk. I get to marry a psycho." I shrug. "And if it lasts a year before he does something terrible to me, I could make sure you get a cool mill. Sounds like a sweet deal for you."

"Chloe...I..." he lets that hang.

"Don't bother. No point talking about this." I let him off the hook. As always.

"I don't know what to say. I had no idea you were dealing with this. I knew something was wrong. I knew I made a mistake pushing you to use the hall pass when you fell apart afterwards. I just didn't know it was this bad. I knew you were dealing with your feelings about all that and that's why I wanted to try tonight. I've been doing a lot of reflecting. You've been really closed off since it happened, and I had no idea the guy you slept with was harassing you. You didn't tell me."

"There's a lot of things you didn't tell me, clearly." His book. Jeannie. What else?

He says nothing.

"I couldn't tell you," I defend. "He had a recording of me bitching to Alannah about you. Just venting about things. And the things I said... some of them weren't that nice. It was just venting, Adam. Girls do that sometimes when they're frustrated."

"I get it."

"Lan said some stupid shit too, and... I'm not blaming her. It was girl talk. He eavesdropped on girl talk."

"I get it."

"But I worried about how you'd react to my venting after you told me about the dark thoughts you've been having. He knew how to play me. I wasn't going to use the hall pass on him, but he played me. Heard me talking to Alannah and... and then afterward I used the hall pass, he was stalking me. I knew he was having me followed by that guy. I just... I didn't know what to do about any of it, I was trying to protect you. Maybe I should've gone to the cops, but I was threatened against that."

He shakes his head. "No. That would've been a bad idea. Not the least of which is the fact that the Steele family is rumored to have cops in their pocket. A cop friend of mine," he gives me an extreme expression, "knows a lot about them."

I sigh. He's talking about Craig and doesn't want to name him. Derek already knows about Craig, made that clear tonight already in talking about Adam springing boners. In fact, Alannah mentioned Craig's name today on the phone with me.

"I know I've been hard to live with. I don't blame you for venting. I vent to Paul and Craig about you, too. I wouldn't want you hearing those things either."

"What's he holding over your head?" I ask. "You can tell me." Though clearly he's keeping a lot of secrets from me. Publisher rejections. Seeing Jeannie the night he had the accident. The forty grand he has. That he's been getting erections.

"I can't talk about it. It'll kill me. It's something from my childhood. It's... ugly. I can't talk about it just on the fly like this, especially with him out there listening, watching." He shakes his head.

He doesn't trust me. It's sobering, to say the least.

Cheater

"It's not something I wanna talk about with anyone, Chloe. You don't have to take that on as if it's your burden. You always do that. Like this ... trying to deal with it by yourself. Clearly this guy charmed you and then showed his true colors and you didn't know what to do about it, but I wish you would've told me and then we could've talked about what to do."

I sigh. "By the time I knew how dangerous he was, he was following me, put cameras in the house. He was clearly determined we'd break every one of your rules. I couldn't tell you or he'd find out because he was watching us. It's bent. This whole thing."

He sighs. "I just... don't know what to do." Adam rakes his hands through his hair.

"He bought Cavalier and finagled me working on that campaign full-time. He's now my only client. He threatened to buy my company. I don't know how far he's willing to go. I don't know why he's so fixated on me. Why he pursued me. I really just don't get it."

"You're beautiful, Chloe. You're sensitive and caring. Nurturing. Loyal. You're also sexy as hell. What guy wouldn't want that?"

The way he says it doesn't feel nice. It doesn't feel like a compliment.

"And above you being the whole package that you are, you're my best friend in the whole world. I know I sucked at being your fiancé. I know I pushed you to sleep with someone because I thought it'd help me feel like I was doing the right thing. It didn't feel like the right thing when I found you in your office that night crying about what I made you do. I hated myself for it. I'm sorry. I... I hope you wind up with a big fat bank account when all this is over. Maybe he'll do a generous prenup and it'll end well. Be great if it lasted longer than a year so we'd both get paid. If I find out he hurt you, I don't care about me, I will do something about it. I mean that."

I gawk at him as it sinks in. This is him saying goodbye. Saying goodbye while paying lip service about doing something about me getting hurt. Reacting after the fact instead of protecting and preventing. He's wishing me well. He's ready for me to go jump into Derek's arms.

And stay for at least a year so he can be a millionaire. Derek went to extremes at the notion of Adam fucking me. Adam is giving up without any sort of fight at the idea of me being forced to marry a psychopath.

This is surreal.

He's afraid of Derek. I suspect he's also thinking about the sweet deal he gets out of this. I just don't know what the bigger motivator is.

"You never told me about Jeannie, either."

"She was trying to talk me into getting back together. There was no point. I've never been unfaithful to you. I swear it. The engagement wasn't even... she talked my gran into giving her the ring. I think she and my mother put their heads together. It didn't mean what it meant with us. She and I grew up together. It was just... she thinks that old history should've kept us connected."

"And he told me you're hiding money from me," I say.

He has the decency to look remorseful.

"I..." He blows out a breath. "I have some money aside for a bug-out fund. It's something my father preached to us as kids. Being prepared for an emergency. I wasn't trying to hide it, I just... it was there in case we needed it. In case things come out in the press about... the stuff I'm trying to keep under wraps."

"All we've been through and you're gonna let this end just like this without me really understanding what he's holding over your head?"

Adam stares at me for a long moment.

"Maybe he'll tell you anyway." He shrugs. "I don't want to talk about this, I really don't, but let's just say that my uncle is a pedophile and child killer. He's in prison. I put him there. I can't talk about it. We changed our name to get away from the press. It can't get out. Can't, Chloe. It'll kill my grandmother. My folks. My siblings. We were hounded relentlessly. I knew you were willing to clear your account out for us to have this place. I didn't want to leave us with nothing in case it leaked and we needed to get away. It'd be a circus. I took the stand, Chloe. I helped put him in prison because he did shit

Cheater

to me when I was a kid and then he did shit to other kids and a little girl died, so I spoke up."

"Oh," I whisper. "That's terrible."

"I can't talk about it. Please don't tell anyone."

"I won't. Of course I won't."

But reality is sinking in. Adam and I were never on the same page about what it takes to build a life together with an unshakeable foundation. Honesty. Transparency.

I slip my engagement ring off and set it on the nightstand.

I watch Adam's face transform from sorrow to anger. And then sorrow again. Sitting in his wheelchair but still looking so handsome, so healthy, and maybe he'll get even healthier now that he'll have everything that he wants. A publishing contract. He never even told me he had almost a whole series of books finished already. I don't understand why. Because he got rejection letters? But he'll get them published now. He'll have an exciting new career. Technology that'll give him even more mobility than what that van gave him. Financial security with new job opportunities. His dreams will come true. Without pressure for intimacy, equality in the household, for children. Two suits that help him walk.

And what about me? I don't know. I just don't know.

I feel hollow inside. Empty. And raw. I've been hollowed out with a rusty coat hanger.

"I'll just pack a small bag for now. Figure the rest out later I guess."

I don't even know Adam's real name.

I get to my feet.

Derek's having him take the blame. Derek thinks we're getting married.

Adam frowns. He's having trouble believing this drastic turn of events. I can relate.

He didn't even tell me the whole truth about the accident. That's why I saw her twice at the hospital. His mother said it was a coinci-

dence. Did his mother know the truth? Did his mother want them back together because she preferred Jeannie to me for Adam?

"I'll always love you, Chloe. I'm so, so sorry. I-"

Springing erections and maintaining that his dick doesn't work.

"I'll figure it out," I say. I can't give him the *I love you* back. It's just not in me. Because what does loving someone matter if you're saying goodbye? If they're willing to say goodbye without a fight?

He doesn't say anything else. Of course he doesn't try to touch me. He didn't try to fight for me. It's just... over.

And it hurts.

I've been fighting for him and he's not remotely willing to fight for me. He's not just biding time here. Placating Derek with plans to fight for me. He's done. He's accepting this.

I don't want anything to happen to him. I don't want him to hurt. I don't want him afraid. I just want him happy. But I now know, deep down, that marrying Adam would've left me unfulfilled in so many more ways than just sexually. And would I have stayed so that I can hold my head high about sticking by him through it all? For better, for worse? Wearing the white dress just once? Being married to a man who can keep so many secrets from me? Taking a last name that's a fabrication instead of becoming part of a family. His mom is always tepid with me. Because why? Because she wishes he'd married Jeannie instead of getting engaged to me?

I could really use some time with the feelings these revelations are bringing. But I can't have that. Because realizing Adam Hallman isn't my happily ever after is just part of the problem. Derek Steele is taking me home with him. With plans to marry me. With floating hearts in his eyes like a cartoon character.

He says he wants to focus on me, on making me feel appreciated. On making my dreams and my sexual fantasies come true. He's the whole package. The whole package plus psychological issues up the wazoo. Sexy. Skilled in bed. Rich. Doting. Extremely possessive. Scratch that: insanely possessive. I gave Derek one night and now he's demanding that I vow *forever*.

Cheater

Adam stays put while I haul my weekender bag out of the closet, then quickly shove some clothes in before I grab my phone charger and wrap it into a figure eight bunch on my way into the bathroom to toss toiletries into the bag.

I storm past Adam and down the hall where I toss the bag on the floor in front of Derek who's standing by the front door with his hand on the doorknob.

My throat is clogged. My body is numb. My chest and sinuses feel like they're on fire.

I spin around and storm to my office where I stuff my laptop, tablet, and day planner into my briefcase. I stomp back out and hand that to Derek, then grab my phone and purse, put shoes on and grab a coat.

Adam hasn't come out of the bedroom.

From my periphery, I see Derek zip up my weekender bag, so I blow my hair out of my eyes while I grab my keys and storm outside, breathing hard.

Derek catches my hand as I get to my Cherokee.

"I'll drive. Get someone to bring your car over tomorrow," he says softly.

I whirl around to face him, on the verge of something. Crying. Screaming. Using my nails on his face? I don't know.

But he senses something is about to blow and gives me a dark look. "Into the truck, Chloe. We'll talk about this when we get home."

Home?

I stare, taking big breaths, fighting warring urges in me to do something, I don't know what... scream? Run? I don't know.

He takes my keys from me, hits the lock button on my Cherokee, walks to his SUV and opens the passenger door for me before he opens the back door and puts my stuff inside, including the donut shop bag from earlier with the soup and the pastries. He must have taken it out of my fridge.

I climb in and pull the seatbelt on.

I should run out into the street. Cause a scene. Make the neighbors call the police.

But Adam is in there with his future hinging on all this.

And I'm here with my insides hollowed out by the rusty coat hanger.

As he backs out, I stare at the townhome. The townhome I didn't want to buy. The townhome I cleaned my savings out for in order to give Adam the right environment to heal in. I stare at the van Derek helped buy him and then my eyes bounce up to the sky and I stare at that while I pull in air before slowing letting it out.

Adam's in there by himself. By himself without me but *with* a whole lot of opportunity ahead of him.

Adam has bared his secrets to me as part of our ending.

And tonight, he'll be sleeping in the sheets Derek fucked me in. Just like Derek wants. I had planned to change them, to defy him, but I didn't get the chance.

I dash the tears off my face with my sleeves and pull out my phone.

I start typing into my text string with Adam.

Change the sheets before you

Derek grabs my phone out of my hand before I finish. He eyeballs the screen and then shoots me a dark look before I watch him backspace the letters away and pocket my phone.

I have no words. Thankfully, he doesn't try to make me use any for the drive back to his apartment.

∞

The parking lot is pretty full, not a surprise for a Friday night with his other club here.

When he parks, he says, "Wait there."

Cheater

He comes around to the passenger side and opens the door, leans in to click the seatbelt and then he plucks me out of the seat and sets me on my feet in front of him.

He looks into my eyes as he caresses my face.

I swallow down a lump of emotion and say nothing.

"I'll make it all better," he vows, then opens the back door, grabs my bag, my laptop bag, my purse, and the bag of food and carries them all to the door, still managing to hold it open for me.

I step inside and woodenly walk to the elevator.

When I get there, him behind me, the door opens and the blonde I ran into the last time I was here steps out and takes us in with surprise. His sister, Grace.

"Hey. What's goin' on?" she asks, eyes bouncing between me and Derek.

"Not now," he grinds out. "Go ahead, baby," he tells me.

I step into the elevator.

"Derek?" she inquires.

"Grace, this is Chloe. My girlfriend." Derek looks at me and his face transforms from annoyed, splitting into a wide smile with his eyes lit with excitement. "Chloe, my sister, Grace. Later, Grace." He loses the smile and presses the button.

"Your what?" Grace looks absolutely stunned.

I sag against the back wall of the elevator. Grace eyeballs me with concern.

The doors begin to close.

"Derek?" she tries.

"Not tonight. I'll phone you tomorrow," he states. "I mean it, Grace. Not. Tonight."

The doors close on her, so I stare at the rising lights. Before we get to the top floor, my eyes bounce his way and he's staring at me with that big smile on his face. Those cartoon hearts in his eyes.

Of course he's happy. Quite a coup tonight.

I stare at him with what must be an absolutely dumbfounded

expression, I don't know, but the ding of our arrival to his floor breaks the spell and I'm the first to depart the little box.

When I get to his apartment door, I press my thumb to the small screen and the door clicks.

30

Derek

I follow her as she marches through my apartment, throwing her jacket off as she heads down the hall. It lands on the floor in front of me.

I'm still directly behind her as she gets into my bedroom and kicks off her shoes, throws the covers back, and climbs into the bed. She buries herself under the blanket. Her entire self, head and all.

I watch for a moment and surmising she needs a minute, I set her bags down on the chair in the corner and take the paper bag containing the soup and donuts to the kitchen.

I hunt through the cupboards for the glass platter with the dome lid that I know is here somewhere.

This kitchen is well-equipped; my parents' designer saw to that to give everyone a fully functional place here in the city, but I know we won't be staying here long.

I've got many surprises in store for her.

∞

I've set a bottle of water and a glass of her favorite wine on the table beside her. She's still under the blankets.

"Chloe?"

She doesn't answer.

"I'll run you a bath," I offer.

She still doesn't answer.

"Your bath is ready, baby," I say.

A sniffle is my only reply.

I hear my phone, so I go find it on the console table by the door. Grace.

I answer with, "What did I say?"

"Who is she? What's the story? I'm shocked, Derek. Shocked. A girlfriend? That big smile on your face? The frown on hers? What's all that about? What's going on? You have to give me something. I saw her the other day and she didn't look like an escort or a porn star, but girlfriend?"

"Leave it alone, Grace."

"Not a chance."

"It's love," I say, simply. Because I think that's what this is. There's no other apparent explanation.

She laughs.

And now I'm irritated.

"No. For real," she prompts.

"For real," I state. "I can't do this right now. I'm busy."

"She doesn't look in love. That's the second time I've seen her and both times she has looked distraught."

"I can't talk. I'll call you later."

"In a fight? First girlfriend. Second fight?" she pushes.

"Bye Grace." I end the call, pour myself a bourbon, and wander back to the bedroom.

Chloe is still under the covers.

I figured there'd be a fight. Maybe some yelling. Maybe some threats coming at me. Some slaps or claws. I was looking forward to wrestling her into submission and showing her how good it's gonna be.

Cheater

But she's under the blankets like a lump.

"The bath's gonna get cold," I tell her.

∞

I undress and get into bed beside her. I've already let the water out of the tub after it sat for over an hour and made some calls to arrange a surprise for her. I prop my cheek on my hand while on my side facing the lump under my covers.

She's still. Too still. Like she's holding her body taut while also holding her breath.

I quickly yank the blanket, exposing her.

She looks completely wrecked. Beyond distraught.

And something strange happens. It lands like ice shards sinking into my chest.

I don't know what to do with it. I've finally got her where I want her. And she looks like her world has fallen apart. It has. But it wasn't the right world for her. She was in a world built on picking the wrong man. She'll see that.

I push away the urge to turn the lamp off, so I don't have to see it. Don't have to see the messy hair, the bloodshot puffy eyes, the downturned pretty mouth.

Instead I roll over and gather her into my arms, tucking her head under my chin so I can comfort her.

She struggles.

"No," she cries out brokenly.

I hush her, pressing my mouth to her forehead.

"I'm gonna make it all better," I promise her and stroke her back with both hands.

But I've probably set myself back with this change in plans. No point ruminating on it, though. Now I've got access to her 24/7 and he doesn't. He will never have access to her again. I won't have to watch them in the same bed. I won't have to see him put his mouth on her either. Nobody gets to hold her like this. Only me. And that settles something in me.

She makes a horrible choking sound and starts to wail in my arms.

I hold her tighter, pressing kisses to her forehead, her soaking wet cheeks, her nose, her beautifully soft lips.

She sobs with terrible, wet choking sounds. And I keep kissing her.

I want them to stop, but I don't want that ugliness inside her, making her feel like this. So, I'll absorb it and work on making things better.

"Chloe?" I whisper.

She doesn't answer.

"I'm gonna show you why this was the best thing in the world for you," I vow. "I know you're mad at me. I know you're sad. I have to tell you something. I've never given a shit how anybody feels about anything. Not for as long as I let myself remember. Until you. I give a shit. I care. I've always gotten fixated on goals but never something like this. Never a woman. I'm gonna make it better. Gonna make you so deliriously happy, you'll realize this is right. I promise." I kiss her again on the mouth.

She's not pulling away. She's not snuggling in. She's just crying in my arms.

She feels so fucking right, though.

I'm lost in thought a few minutes later, still holding her, when she shudders hard.

"H-he..." she stops and sniffles. "H-he..." She stops again. I caress her hair and wait.

She sniffles again and looks into my eyes. The pain in hers... it's doing something to me.

"He didn't even think about fighting for me. I know he can't. His legs... he... he's afraid of you. But... he didn't even *think* about trying. And I don't think he would have even if this were eight months ago."

She's getting it.

Cheater

And damn. I'm more fascinated by her than ever. I'm a lucky man to have found her. But things are twisting in me, peeling away, sensations rising. I can't take time to decode them, though. I need her to know she has me.

"I know, Chloe," I say, dashing tears away with my thumbs on her cheeks. "I promise you, baby, I'm gonna bust my ass to make you realize that me doing this is right. You now belong to a man who is afraid of nothing and no one. You're mine now. I might have fought dirty to get you where you are right now, but that should give you a clue about who I am. I'm a man who will fight through smoke, gunfire, even hellfire for you. I'll fight for you even if it's you I have to fight against."

"Why?" she asks in a small, broken voice. "I don't understand why."

"I don't know how to answer that. Because I don't understand it, either. You're the goal. Making all your dreams come true. Giving you everything I felt you yearned for that night when I first overheard you and Alannah. It woke something up in me. You're what I want."

She says nothing.

After a few minutes of holding her, stroking her hair, I say, "Have you ever been so thirsty when you get a drink to your lips that you can't seem to swallow it down fast enough to quench your thirst?"

She doesn't respond so I keep going.

"You have to muster control, so you don't drink so fast you choke on it. That's me with you. And I'm not sure how much control I have left when it comes to you. Lost control a little tonight when he wanted you to fuck him."

"A little bit?" she queries sarcastically.

I smirk and shrug. "I'm beyond parched for you, Chloe. So fucking tempted to give in to the urge, to choke to death if I need to because it means I get to take my fill. Consume you."

She looks up at me, fear in her eyes.

"I'm so happy you're here," I tell her.

She stays where she is, but her body is tense. I'm frightening her. I get it. In one sentence promising happiness and the next saying I want to consume her.

"I had to stop him tonight. I couldn't let him have you. Couldn't let you fuck him tonight. I can't let anyone put their hands on you that way again. You're mine, Chloe. The notion of anyone else touching you the way I wanna touch you... *no*."

She buries her face under my chin. It feels like she's snuggling in, but I know she's actually hiding.

After a few minutes, she pulls away from me and I know she's been wanting to do it for a while but is worried about how I'll react. I let go of her.

"I'm not gonna hurt you," I tell her.

"But you're doing that."

"No, I'm not. He's the one that hurt you. I'm gonna fix it. I won't ever hurt you."

"Are you sure about that?" she asks.

Good question.

I answer honestly. "Maybe not a hundred per cent sure. I'm not feeling exactly stable where you're concerned. Do us both a favor and let me make you happy."

She gets out of bed. I watch her drag the big bag to the bathroom and I hear the door lock.

I listen and hear the water running. The sound of her brushing her teeth.

She surfaces a few minutes later dressed in pajama shorts and an oversized T-shirt, so I turn my lamp off. When she climbs into the bed I smell a clean scent. Face wash. And toothpaste. She turns the lamp on the other side of the bed on and I watch her uncap the water I put down for her. She drinks some, then changes her mind, lifts the wine glass and guzzles the whole thing before she sets that glass down.

"I don't want to sleep beside you."

"Why?" I ask.

Cheater

"I don't trust you. I can either sleep here and you can go somewhere else. Or I can go to your guest room, the couch, or even better would be me leaving and going to stay with a friend."

"I've waited a long time for this night." And then I amend, "Okay, well, not a long time but it feels like it. But no. You're staying here. With me."

I'm ready for an argument, for a struggle hopefully, but she lays down and turns her back to me.

I turn over and fit myself to her back, my hand gliding across her stomach and resting there. She's rigid, but doesn't struggle or move as I kiss her neck and hold her tight.

Goosebumps erupt on her skin.

"You want me?" I ask, running my nose down her neck.

Does she want me to fuck her? Is that what she's hoping for?

"No. I'm cold."

I snuggle in closer. She's rigid still.

I'd like to fuck her. I'd like to fuck her and plant a baby in her stomach. Bring to fruition the visions from my mind tonight of her carrying my baby, holding it close and protectively. My hand skates across her stomach and I crave feeling it swelled. Because of me. My fingers slide under her waistband.

"Derek, no. Please, no," she says and sniffles.

Maybe she needs no pressure tonight. Just the knowledge that I'm here. Holding her. Ready to give her the world.

"Okay. Go to sleep. I'll just hold you tonight. You're safe, Chloe. I promise." I lean over and press a soft kiss to her cheekbone, then settle in behind her and close my eyes, my lungs filled with her scent.

∞

Two hours later, I wake abruptly, taking a minute to absorb the feeling of Chloe sleeping against me. She's now turned into me instead of being spooned by me. Her head is on my chest, her arm across my stomach, her fragrant, soft hair spread out over my shoulder.

And I feel that sensation again – that *peace* that's foreign to me.

I hate to leave the warmth and comfort of having this woman in my bed, but I need to see what Hallman is up to. I watched him for a bit after running the bath, but I want to catch up and see if I missed anything important, so I carefully move her without waking her, press a kiss to her mouth, and go out to the dining table where my laptop sits.

After we left, Hallman had a bottle of booze delivered. He sat and drank a few shots while staring into space, looking miserable. And then he was in the bathroom a long time before he emerged, showered, the lower half of his body wrapped in a towel. He got shorts from the closet, got them to his thighs, pulled himself into the bed and got them the rest of the way on before he shut the lamp off. My camera auto-adjusted to night vision and I saw him pull one of the pillows on the other side of the bed over. He put it to his nose. Smelling all that was left of Chloe. He stared into the darkness for an hour before his eyes closed.

I feel satisfied, too, at the fact that he's sleeping on the sheets I fucked her in last night.

No phone calls. No rules broken. That doesn't mean he won't pull anything tomorrow.

That scent on her pillow is all he has left. Now maybe I'm not so satisfied that I didn't allow her to change the sheets. Then he'd have no trace of her in his nostrils right now.

Those cameras will stay put for now. But after tonight, I'm having Kenny assign someone to watch him. I've got other things to focus on. I climb back into bed with Chloe and pull her close. She melts into me.

∞

Cheater

I wake up early, feeling well-rested and very conscious of that peace I've never experienced until last night. And I know it's because she's here. It's because she's now mine. And she's going to stay that way.

She's not snuggled with me; she's on the far end of the bed, sleeping in a ball near the edge.

I lean up on my elbow and look over to her face. She's not asleep. She's awake, staring into space.

"Good morning," I greet and press my mouth to her shoulder.

31
Chloe

It's Saturday, thankfully, so I have nowhere to be right now, no one to report to. Although I got zero work done yesterday.

I stare at my naked ring finger. No fiancé.

I feel strange. Sort of empty. Kind of numb around the edges, but yet full of questions in the center of me. And hurt. I feel a lot of hurt.

I cried a lot last night under Derek's covers. In Derek's embrace. I let him comfort me. Not that it did. But I didn't try to stop him from holding me tight, raining kisses all over my face. I sank into him as he whispered his crazy promises, almost taking comfort in some strange way. I cried for a lot of things. So many things.

And it might have been a cleansing of sorts. Because things feel different this morning. I have so much to figure out, but there's this illusion of freedom in not being engaged.

It's just a momentary illusion because I have a whole other set of problems now with Derek thinking what he's thinking about us, but in the forefront of my mind is the fact that I won't be Chloe Hallman. That Adam Hallman isn't even real. It's just him, his parents, his grandmother, and his brother and two sisters. He said they had no other family on either side, rarely talked about childhood memories, which makes sense now. And I don't know precisely what happened to him, but the few bits and pieces he gave me about his uncle were enough to paint a picture. A tragic one. I don't have the capacity to understand why he kept so much hidden from me. How do you fall in love with someone and not feel the urge to share your secrets? I guess we all have secrets. I guess trauma does things to you. And I guess having the ultimate trust broken by a family member can permanently scar you in ways others can't fathom.

As my partner for life though, I can't help but wonder if he would've ever told me the truth. Told me his old name. Would we be bound by marriage vows with all sorts of secrets?

I don't have a wedding date looming. I have to tell my parents. Our friends.

Or I guess I do have a wedding looming if Derek forces me to marry him. And I can't compute that. I haven't let myself even begin to fathom what that could mean for my life, my future.

I'm supposed to be at Alannah's tonight, talking her down from trying to help me deal with my Derek problem.

But my Derek problem has hit an entirely new level.

Held at gunpoint. Threatened. Adam, being told all the wonderful things Derek will give him if he makes this easy. The threats of things going very differently if he doesn't. Derek doesn't want me to worry about Adam, so he's taking care of him at the same time as destroying the remnants of our relationship. All those secrets spilling out like noxious, hot lava coming straight at me. Jeannie. Adam's uncle. How easily he gave in to Derek. He didn't even try to fight. He looked not only resigned, he was looking at the bright side of things immediately. Thinking about that million bucks. And that hurts. Is that his coping mechanism maybe? Because Adam has had to cope with a whole lot lately. How is he this morning? Did he fall asleep at the drop of a hat last night or did he mourn the loss of me? Or did he lie there thinking about how wonderful it could be to be mobile again with that technology Derek mentioned. How much was ahead of him career-wise with the new opportunities Derek lined up. How giving me up would mean he's a millionaire in a year if I don't divorce Derek and instruct him to fork it over.

I always check to see if I need to move anything he might want from the top shelf in the fridge before bed to make sure he can reach them. Is he going to have trouble this morning because I'm not there to make sure he can access his breakfast stuff?

My mind swims with a zillion thoughts until I feel Derek stirring beside me. And now I'm feeling panic set in.

What now?

This mentally unstable man has me where he wants me. For now. What if he gets bored? I have no idea what to expect from the unpredictable man who essentially schemed and connived to steal me from Adam. He says he hasn't done this before. He says a lot of things. Things some women would jump for joy about. I don't know if it's all the truth or not. And most of all, how does this end?

He says, "Good morning," in that deep timbre of his and kisses my shoulder.

"I have a surprise for you," he says a moment later, mouth against the ridge of my ear.

"I don't want any more surprises from you. I think I've had more than enough."

"We'll relax today so you can finish getting over being upset. I'll give you the surprise tomorrow."

"How magnanimous of you," I say drolly.

He moves closer. "I'd love to give it to you today. Show you something I'm excited about."

"I'm not exactly feeling up to anything where you're concerned."

"I get it. You need a little time. We'll do it tomorrow."

"How generous," I mumble. "A little time? You've derailed my entire life in a matter of how long?"

He answers, "Fifteen days since we met. I was gonna take a little longer, as I said, but you forced my hand last night."

"Oh, so it's my fault that you're an entitled psychopath?"

"No. That's not your fault. But you get to reap the rewards and that *is* your doing. Because you caught the eye of the psychopath, commanded his attention, and you fascinated him to the degree he hasn't been able to stop thinking about how much joy he'll experience as he gets to give you everything you want."

"Too bad he didn't get fascinated with world peace or eliminating child hunger instead," I mutter.

He laughs. Loud.

I turn over and face him, staring, dumbfounded at the male beauty mixed with brain chemical imbalance I'm staring at. Derek is a beautiful sight regardless of whether he's chilly or warm.

When the laughter dies off without the sparkling in his dark eyes waning, he mutters, "I'll work some of that in, too, since it's obviously important to you. My family does a lot for many causes, though."

I say nothing.

"Anything you want, Chloe. Anything you need. As long as you marry me and spend your life with me. Each night beside me. As long as I know where you are, and that you're safe, always. Keep the promises you'll make when you say your vows. That's it." He shrugs, then runs his knuckles along my cheek. "Tomorrow, there's a family brunch at my parents' house. After that, I'll show you your surprise. Monday, we'll go to city hall and get married. We'll keep that under wraps for a little while if you need to, but... not for too long, okay?" He chucks me under the chin with his index finger knuckle and then drops a kiss on my forehead before sauntering to the bathroom in just his boxers.

Family brunch? Married? I stare off into nothing for a few minutes, until the sound of the shower turning on jolts me into action. I quickly scramble for my phone, then throw on the robe he bought me. I slip out into the living room while seeing six missed calls and a text from Alannah in my phone notifications.

Alannah: I stopped by. Adam said you broke up. He wouldn't tell me where you are, but your car is there. Are you with Derek? Are you ok? Call me NOW.

I call her.

"Chloe!" she answers on the first ring.

Cheater

I talk fast. "I'm at Derek's. He's in the shower, so I can only talk for a minute, but yes, Adam and I broke up."

"I'm confused."

I rub my temples with my thumb and pinky finger while holding the phone.

"Me, too," I rasp.

"Come here or I'm coming over."

"No. Don't."

"I need answers, Chloe. I'm terrified for you here."

I choke on a sob. "I'm terrified too. And flabbergasted. And kind of crushed because of Adam."

"What happened?"

"I can't talk."

"I'm coming over. You're in the building where The Fifth is, right? Top floor?"

"I don't know if that's such a good idea. I don't think he'll let you in."

"Then I'm coming to pick you up. Go downstairs right now and down the street. There's a Dunkin' a block away. Wait there."

"I..."

"Hanging up now. If you're not there when I get there, I will call the cops on this guy. I don't give a shit."

"Lan!"

"Chloe, I'm sorry but no. I don't know what this is, but this shit isn't okay. I don't know what the hell is happening, but Adam was cold as ice with me, tells me you two broke up and that it's his fault. He doesn't wanna talk about it, won't tell me where you are. All I know is Derek Steele was blackmailing you, stalking you, and now you're there? What happened with Adam?"

Derek walks out in just a towel. Damp, muscled skin on display, eyes coasting over me with questions in his eyes.

"Fine. Come by. I'll see you in five," I say and hang up before she replies.

"Who?" Derek asks.

"Alannah. She's freaking out. She needs to talk to me. She showed up at the house and Adam told her I left, so she's having a conniption. I'll just go and –"

"I'll grab a coffee and then I'll put some clothes on." Derek moves to the coffee machine.

"Did you hear me? She's on her way here."

"Message and tell her to buzz penthouse three from the main entrance but then to walk over to our door. You can buzz her in. I'll put the app on your phone. Here. I'll message her and explain that."

He holds a hand out for my phone. "You wanna make us some coffee while I do this?" He takes my phone out of my hand when I make no moves.

I stare blankly as he walks out of the room with my phone. He comes back with his phone in one hand, mine in the other and sits on the couch, puts his phone down, and does something else on my phone.

"Please. Lots of cream and three sugars," he says.

I stare blankly for another few seconds before ungluing myself and moving to the kitchen to turn the coffee machine on.

After I make two coffees, he passes me my phone and kisses my forehead. "Thanks." He grabs the creamier coffee.

My phone makes a strange chime.

"That's it," Derek reaches over and touches my screen. "I'll open it and we'll see who's there. There are commands there to answer and speak through the intercom as well as commands to open the door so she can get in." He points to the commands as he explains and then touches one.

"Alannah?" he calls, after her face appears on the screen.

"Let me in," she answers aggressively.

She's ready for a fight.

"Go to the other door to the left. It'll open. Come up to penthouse three. I'm sure Chloe will open the door up here and watch for you."

"Right," she says.

Cheater

She looks angry.

He hits a command and walks away. I'm left gob smacked as he sips his coffee while casually moving down the hall to the bedroom.

As he crosses the threshold into the master, he takes the towel off with his free hand. I turn away and try to clear my head of the fuzzy feeling he's left me with.

I take a sip of the much-needed coffee and then set it down before I move to the door, unlock it, and open it. And just in time because Alannah is marching down the hall angrily, holding her cell phone in her hand.

Her eyes hit mine and then she wraps her arms around me. "You okay?"

I nod while squeezing her for a long beat before I gesture for her to come inside.

"Come with me," she hisses.

I shake my head and gesture for her to come inside.

"Where is he?" she asks as she takes in the space.

I point toward the hall.

He calls out, "I'm just getting decent. I'll be there in a second. I'll make us all some pancakes. You hungry, Alannah?"

Alannah turns to face me, and her eyes are practically crossed. She's got alarm in all of her features as she mouths, "Pancakes?"

I lift my index finger and draw air circles around my ear.

Derek comes out and sees this. He lets out a little snort of laughter.

He's dressed in second-skin faded jeans. He's buttoning a white dress shirt. His hair is still damp, he's barefoot, and he hasn't shaved in a few days. I know Alannah is taking all that in. It's hard not to.

"It should be a crime to look that good and be a psychopath, shouldn't it?" Alannah says under her breath.

"I'll make you a coffee," is my reply.

Because I don't know what else to say. I don't know what to expect here, because Derek is completely unpredictable.

Alannah looks around and then speaks. "Listen, pal. I realize you're accustomed to getting what you want. And we all know Chloe Turner is the whole package, but just because she's been sweet so far–"

"Let me save you some trouble," Derek interrupts, lifting his palm. "You don't have to worry about Chloe. She's going to be just fine. More than fine. I'll see to that personally. I agree, I *am* accustomed to getting what I want. Because I go after it. With purpose and intent. I wanted her and here she is." He gestures in my direction. "What you also need to know is that this girl has never been safer. She'll never want for anything. She's here because I worked to get her here and I'm not about to do anything that'd hurt her. On the contrary, I'm happy I get to work on my goal with no distractions. Doing whatever it takes to make her happy."

"Happy?" Alannah asks.

"Happy. Personally. Professionally. Physically."

My feet are still glued to the spot, though my eyes are bouncing between my best friend and Derek, shocked at his matter-of-fact declaration. I'm braced to see what Alannah does next.

"I've heard some concerning facts as well as rumors about your family."

Derek shrugs.

Alannah continues, "Most concerning that several women have gone missing when they get tangled up with the Steele brothers," she states.

"That's inaccurate," he corrects.

My jaw is about to hit the floor. Missing?

Derek gives me a sharp shake of his head. "One of my brothers had his girlfriend vanish without a trace. But it was a miscommunication. It's since been sorted. She's fine and living her own life in San Diego. But I guess Craig left that part out?"

Alannah looks contrite at the same time as pissed off. "And what about Thad's two dead wives?"

What? My eyes widen.

"They weren't missing and then reported dead. They both met

Cheater

untimely ends. Thad is dead. He was problematic. He's no longer a problem because his bullshit caught up with him, finally. You girls want pancakes?"

He opens a kitchen cupboard and takes down the yellow box of pancake and biscuit mix along with a glass jug of maple syrup. He opens the fridge and pulls out bacon, eggs, and milk. "Did you want coffee or tea, Alannah? Chloe seems a little groggy still. You drink some of your coffee yet, baby?"

I stare at the full cup in my hand and then my eyes bounce to Alannah who is watching Derek as he pulls down a mixing bowl. He turns the kitchen tap and soaps up his hands.

"I don't want coffee or tea or pancakes, man. I want you to stop this... whatever it is... you're doing with Chloe. You blackmailed her. You've threatened her."

"Yeah, I did. To get her here where I want her. Now that I have her, I can do what I intended." He stares at Alannah expectantly.

He's waiting for her to ask the obvious question, so that he can answer it.

"And what's that?" she demands.

"So I can be her loaded baked potato with all the toppings."

Alannah looks at me with her eyebrows raised.

Derek continues. "So I can continue to be forty four thousand and sixty nine out of ten on the sex skills scale."

Alannah's thrown. She grabs the counter to steady herself.

Derek isn't done. "So I can be everything she should have instead of that bland, self-absorbed, journalist." Derek puts a fresh cup under the coffee maker, opens the machine and pulls out the used pod then tosses it as if it's a basketball. It lands in the trash can in the corner of the kitchen. He opens the drawer under the machine. "Pick your poison," he offers, ironically, smiling as he says it before he glances at the side of the pancake mix box, then opens the egg carton and cracks an egg into the large mixing bowl.

Alannah helps herself to a breakfast blend pod and brews a cup, saying, "You're forcing her to be here with you."

"She'll be happy. Don't worry." He cracks another egg.

Alannah gives him a skeptical look.

"By the way," Derek says, lifting Alannah's cell phone, which she set on the counter to make her coffee, "I'll just turn this off." He does what he did the day I came in here with my phone recording the conversation.

Alannah's back straightens, and she immediately pulls a butcher knife from the knife block on the counter. She points it at Derek. "Give me my fucking phone."

He finishes what he's doing without showing a reaction, then puts the phone down and reaches into the cupboard and pulls down a Pyrex glass measuring cup.

"Go relax with your drinks while I do this," Derek says, pretending Alannah isn't standing in front of me with a knife in her hand.

"I'd rather take her home with me," Alannah tells him. "She doesn't want what you're offering and there's a lot wrong with you."

"Chloe stays here," Derek says calmly, measuring milk. He pours it into the bowl and reaches for the pancake mix. "Nothing has to change between you and her. Actually, something will change. You'll get to see how happy I make her. A transformation that'll make you ecstatic. I'd like it to be fast but as I'm getting to know her better I see how many layers I'll have to get through until she believes she's worthy of all I'm offering."

Alannah and I exchange looks. Derek pulls a whisk out of a drawer and starts mixing the batter.

"Seriously?" Alannah asks him.

Derek's eyes move over me and fill with warmth. "I'm gonna be one of your favorite people, Alannah. Guaranteed. Because you're gonna see that your best friend has what she deserves. Finally. A man who will go out of his way to make sure she's blissfully happy."

"You expect me to believe you're for real? That you're not some psycho killer who could go postal and hurt my friend irreparably?"

"I'm for real. You wanna put the knife down? If you weren't who

Cheater

you are to my girl, I wouldn't be too happy right now at the fact you're between her and I with a knife pointing at me." He continues mixing the pancake batter. "Go on. Sit down. Enjoy your coffee while I get this going."

He bends and pulls a griddle out of a lower kitchen cupboard.

Alannah stares at me for a beat before she puts the knife back into the block, grabs her phone and pockets it before nabbing the coffee cup and tagging my hand, pulling me to the couch. We both set our coffees down.

There's some clanging in the kitchen as Derek roots around. Then he resumes talking, gesticulating with a spatula.

"I didn't like where things were with her and Hallman, so last night I picked her up after having a chat with him. He agreed to withdraw his marriage proposal and take full responsibility. Which is good, because all this is his fault."

Derek opens a bacon package with a pair of scissors and separates pieces of meat, dropping them into a frying pan on the stove.

"His fault?" Alannah queries.

"If he were doing right by Chloe, you two wouldn't have had that conversation that I overheard that night in Downtown. That conversation lit a match in me and once that happens only I decide to put the flame out. Nobody else. So you won't talk me out of what's happening here, for your information, because due to his behavior I've taken it upon myself to relieve him of his duties while taking full responsibility for the breakup. Chloe won't have to feel judged by people who might think poorly of a woman who'd end her unhappy relationship because the guy lost use of his legs. As if that gives him a free pass to treat her like a piece of the furniture." He rolls his eyes.

Alannah gives me a strange look before she continues. "I've heard concerning things about your family, but also some rumors about you. How do I know you're going to be any better? How do we know you won't suddenly snap and hurt Chloe? You've got a pretty warped view from everything you're saying so far. And I've heard you have some pretty extreme reactions when you feel people wrong you."

"Have you heard of me having a history of hurting women?" he asks.

"No," Alannah replies.

"So you're letting rumors cloud your judgment?"

"Your behavior is what's got me most concerned. But I also happen to know the bartender you fired the night you met Chloe. He's not only been arrested, he got jumped by two guys when he got out on bond and beaten badly. Very badly. And then his apartment caught fire while he was in the hospital, ruining just the items in his unit, and destroying a valuable trading card collection."

"What makes you think those things have anything to do with me? Other than having him arrested. That was business. If I don't make an example of theft, I'll be a target. It's based on firing a thief that you think I'd hurt her?"

"His card collection is kept in a locked fireproof box under his bed. It was mysteriously left open on the bed. His lawyer also quit on him with no explanation."

"Why do you care about a bartender that was stealing from not only his employer, but also the patrons? Fleecing customers like yourself and your coworkers out of your hard-earned money either by fucking with the change or by charging people for top shelf liquor and serving something else? Watering down drinks."

"Okay, Alex aside, let's talk about Chloe. You've blackmailed her into having an affair with you. You've stalked her, infiltrated her privacy. You've threatened her. I don't even know all of what you've done because she's been clammed up about it."

"I've done what I need to do to win her so that I can give her the happiness she deserves. I'm gonna marry her Monday, put my ring on her finger, and make all her dreams come true."

I'm just sitting still, holding my coffee, watching these two.

I take a sip.

"Marry her on Monday?"

"That's right. I wasn't sure at first what I wanted other than to rock her world and get her to use the hall pass on me. But the more I

Cheater

learn, the more I see, and definitely the more time I spend with her, I know I want it all."

"She doesn't want to marry you. You've been blackmailing her. Stalking her. Infiltrating her privacy."

"She'll get over it." He shrugs, flipping slices of bacon.

"And when you're over your infatuation with her? She's blissfully happy and madly in love and you're over it, what happens then?"

"Until a few days ago I would've said we'd part amicably. Now, though? Now that I'm planning on putting her in that white dress and giving her my last name? I think that makes it pretty clear I have no intention of ever being done with her. I wouldn't go from wanting to make her happy and undoing all the bad in her life to making her marry me if I wasn't absolutely sure doing it would mean to me what I know it means to her."

"And what's that?"

"Forever. Wearing the dress just once for her. Saying those vows and meaning every word of them for me. For better or for worse with hopefully both of us, but definitely me working hard to make sure there's more *better*. If she'd worn that gown for Hallman, maybe she'd have sworn marriage off after that went to shit. But let's face it, it's been shit for a long time. Longer than he's been in that wheelchair, too, particularly in the bedroom department."

Sizzling gets louder. Bacon scents fill the air as he works at the stove.

She looks at me.

I again rotate my finger around my ear.

Instead of giving me a look of agreement, she has a strange look on her face.

He points the spatula at me and tsks. "Not very nice, Chloe. You wanna earn yourself a spanking, keep it up." He wiggles his eyebrows, making his meaning clear and I watch Alannah grab her own throat, like she's affected.

"You were saying?" Derek prompts.

"Huh? Oh. I mean, there's not a lot known about you," Alannah continues. "But there are some concerning rumors." She poignantly takes a sip of her coffee.

"I'm sure there are. Feel free to share."

"That you're very vindictive. That you can be violent. That most of your own family is afraid of you."

He says nothing, just keeps working on the bacon.

"Do you not see how alarming it is that you've become obsessed with her and turned her life upside down in a very short time?"

"Sometimes you have to dismantle things in order to be able to fix them," he says darkly.

Her eyes fill with more alarm. "What about fixing yourself?"

"I'm pretty content with who I am." He shrugs. "When you say you've heard I'm vindictive, doesn't that indicate that I'm retaliating? Shouldn't one retaliate if someone wrongs them?"

"Shouldn't a woman decide who she wants to marry?" Alannah counters.

"And the only thing holding Chloe back is Hallman. If he weren't a factor, she'd be all in to explore a relationship with me. The chemistry between us is off the charts, and she knows it. Don't you, baby?"

I don't answer.

Alannah continues. "You've been exhibiting some troubling signs though. You feel like you're stable? Were you on medication that you've stopped? Do you see a therapist, Derek?"

"Me and therapy don't exactly gel," Derek replies. "Been there, done that. Not interested. What I *am* interested in is Chloe. Can I make a suggestion?"

Alannah jerks her chin up.

"Watch and see what happens." He shrugs. "I'm glad you care. I'm glad Chloe's had you. She still does and I'm not looking to disrupt that. So, watch and see how things transform. It might take a little time for me to win her over, but I'm prepared to put in the work. Show your support. Come stand up as a witness on Monday. I'm sure you planned to be her maid of honor when she was gonna marry that unseasoned potato, right?"

Cheater

Alannah looks startled for a second and she looks like she's fighting laughter at how Derek's calling Adam what she first coined.

Derek shrugs again. "Give it time. See what happens."

"This should all be Chloe's choice," Alannah volleys.

"Chloe doesn't always do what's good for her. She has a history of doing what's good for everyone else. You've known her a long time. Am I wrong?"

Alannah tips her head as if she's agreeing. This makes my back straighten.

"She needed me to step in," Derek goes on, then he smears butter on the griddle and starts pouring portions of pancake batter onto it.

Alannah looks at me, sets her coffee mug on the table and grabs my hand. "You haven't said anything. Talk to me. Are you okay?" She looks into my eyes.

"No," I say simply.

"How has he hurt you?" She's looking at me like she thinks I'm afraid to answer. "You don't have to be afraid. I told Jeffy I was coming. If he doesn't hear from me soon he'll start to fret."

"Check in with him," Derek calls over. "Let him know everything's fine here."

"Chloe? You've hardly said a thing. Are you afraid to speak?" Alannah asks, ignoring Derek.

I clear my throat. "Right now I'm reeling. Mostly hurt at the turn of events with Adam last night. I don't want to get into specifics because it might make me vomit. Let's just say it's not easy to process how easy it was for him to take Derek's generous offers which include a million bucks when we celebrate our one year wedding anniversary along with a whole lot of career opportunities, medical help, and so on."

Derek waves the spatula. "That's what I'm sayin'."

Alannah jolts with shock.

I continue, "He knew he was dealing with a psycho who was very determined, especially with how the evening began. We–"

"Now, now, Chloe," Derek says. "Some things are personal."

"Are you threatening her? Because this has me concerned. Let her talk to me," Alannah clips.

"She's free to talk to you," Derek retorts. "That's why you're here. If I didn't want her to talk to anyone I could've already swept her out of the country, taken her somewhere very private. But I'm not here to tear her life apart. I'm here to make it better. But there are some sensitive topics best left between the two of us. And Hallman."

"It was dramatic. Derek seems to have a flair for the dramatic," I mutter.

He takes an exaggerated bow, rolling his hand, then he turns and flips pancakes one at a time, like he's done it a million times.

Someone knocks on the door and all three of us look that way.

Derek goes to the door and opens it just a few inches. "Not now, Grace," he says angrily.

Alannah looks at me. "Who's there?" she calls out like the pot-stirrer she is.

"His sister," a female voice calls out. "I want to meet his new girlfriend properly."

The blonde ducks under Derek's arm sideways and breezes into the apartment, looking surprised at the sight of two of us, and looking over me with concern, I guess. Derek shuts the door and seems to take stock of me himself before rushing to the kitchen to tend to the food.

Grace Steele's eyes bounce between me and Alannah. She's a gorgeous curly-haired blonde with striking gray eyes, dressed in black pencil pants and a white with black pinstripe blouse. Cute little red flats. Full face of makeup. Tasteful, expensive jewelry.

Alannah is dressed in one of her business suits. She dressed to come here and take matters into her hands and resolve matters like she'd do if this was mediation she was the arbitrator for.

I'm sitting here in the pink robe with an oversized tee and shorts, barefoot, and bed-headed. No doubt my face is still puffy from all the crying last night.

"I'm Alannah. Chloe's best friend," Alannah greets.

Cheater

"I'm Grace. Derek's youngest sibling." She extends her hand and Alannah rises and takes it.

Grace then reaches for my hand. I stand up.

"Good to meet you, Chloe. You look like you'd rather be anywhere but here," Grace very observantly states.

"That's because I *don't* want to be here." I reply.

I look at Derek and he's watching us but not doing anything about this little exchange. He's not shooting me warning looks. He's not smiling, but he also doesn't look angry. He's moving pancakes to a platter.

"Why not?" Grace asks me.

"I've derailed her life and forced her to be here," Derek answers. Now he's moving bacon from the pan to a plate covered in paper towel.

"Why?" Grace asks him.

"Because I want her," he says simply, then swipes paper towel across the griddle before re-buttering it.

Grace's eyes bounce back to me with concern before she asks, "Got enough for one more for breakfast, Derek?"

Derek grumbles something under his breath, then instructs, "Set the table."

"He always made me pancakes when I was sad as a little girl. I'm a little jealous right now that he's making them for you. Have you ever made anyone pancakes besides me, Derek?"

"Nope," Derek replies. "They always cheered you up, so I was hoping they'd do the same for Chloe."

"In that case, I guess I don't mind. But why does she need cheering up?" She puts her hands on her waist. "What did you do?"

"Derailed her life. Made her move in with me. I'm making her marry me on Monday."

Alannah and I watch this exchange with fascination as Grace takes plates down from a kitchen cupboard.

"Why aren't you wooing her the regular way?"

"Do I do anything the regular way?" he fires back.

She snorts. "Fair point. Paint me a picture, Derek."

"She was engaged. The guy didn't deserve her. Things she said had me pay attention. It lit a match in me. I intervened."

"And where is the guy now?" she asks, eyeballing us for a second as she sets the four plates on the dining table.

"He's at his home, counting all the opportunities I've put in front of him. I didn't off him, Grace. He's just no longer engaged to Chloe."

"Do you have a habit of offing people?" Alannah calls over, alarmed.

"Don't ask questions you don't want the answers to," Derek advises, deadpan.

Grace snickers. "He's being facetious. Don't pay attention to that. I wasn't suggesting he did, thought maybe he got him framed and sent to prison to get him out of the way or something like that. Not something so bloody as murder. Derek's much more creative. Most times."

"Most times," Derek parrots and pops a piece of bacon into his mouth before pointing in the air and pulling the trigger on an imaginary gun.

Alannah and I exchange wide-eyed looks before we both sip our coffees in synchronization.

"Chloe cares what happens to him, so I did things in a way that'll be more... palatable for her."

Opening a drawer, Grace pulls cutlery out, and then reaches into another drawer for a stack of cloth napkins. "Hm. Makes sense. Oh! I have fresh chocolate croissants and fruit in my kitchen. I'll go grab them." She sets the cutlery and napkins down on the island and rushes out.

"I'm gonna go put some clothes on," I mutter to Alannah.

"I'll finish setting the table," Alannah offers, looking completely fascinated by all of this.

"You message Jeff?" Derek asks her.

"I'll do that right after I finish the table," she says, separating napkins and setting them down beside each plate.

Cheater

Shaking my head at how bizarre this whole exchange is, I go get dressed.

After I'm dressed, I quickly run a brush through my hair before washing my face and getting into the pair of slippers Derek bought me. I hang the housecoat on the back of the door beside his housecoat, a navy blue one.

I'm a combination of flabbergasted and numb. And curious about Grace Steele at the same time.

∞

They're all at the table. Derek pats the empty chair to his left. He's made a plate up for me with three perfect-looking pancakes and three slices of bacon.

"Made you another coffee," he says, dropping a kiss on my temple as I sit.

Alannah is across from me, eyes on me. Grace is across from Derek, eyes on him. A platter of six chocolate drizzled croissants and a bowl of fruit salad sit in the center of the table.

"So, my brother wanted you and found a way to get you in his clutches," Grace prompts, smearing butter over her pancakes with a knife.

"Basically," I reply and watch Alannah reach for a chocolate croissant from the platter in the center of the table.

"And he's holding things over your head?" she asks.

"He was," I agree. Derek sets a croissant on my plate. "Now... now I'm not sure if there's a new threat or if he expects me to comply based on everything he's shown me so far."

Alannah's eyes bounce between me and Derek.

His expression gives nothing away.

"You're not worried about the fiancé now, are you?" Grace asks. "I mean, love doesn't just vanish overnight, I guess."

"I'm not particularly happy with my fiancé, but..."

"Ex-fiancé," Derek corrects, putting the jug of syrup in front of my plate.

"But I don't know what Derek's going to hold over my head next to keep me cooperating," I finish, eyes on Derek's face.

He forks up some of his pancakes and pops a bite into his mouth.

"What are you going to hold over her head, Derek?" Grace asks casually, sawing into her pancakes.

Derek finishes chewing slowly, looking thoughtful. He keeps chewing, swallows, and wipes his mouth with the napkin. "That'll be between Chloe and me."

"Do you really think you can build a real relationship based on threats and bribery?" Grace asks.

"Don't know, Grace. Never had a relationship before. Eat some food, Chloe. Or I'll feed you myself." He winks and flashes me a smile.

I defiantly cross my arms and lean back in my chair.

Derek gives me a look of dismay.

"Whoa. Smiles again," Grace says. "My brother never smiles. Like... never."

The room is silent for a long moment. Derek watches me while forking up a bite of his bacon.

I pull a piece of croissant off and put it in my mouth.

Alannah digs in and takes a bite of her pancakes. "Mm. Good."

"He knows pancakes." Grace says. "That's syrup from our family place in Vermont." She gestures to the syrup, and I notice the label says *Steele Family Reserve with a silver and black heart logo.* "Our brothers Jonah and Asher tap the sugar maples every year. We get about twenty or thirty gallons of syrup every year. Every family member gets one and then we send out little bottles with our Christmas cards to close family and friends. You'll love it there, Chloe. We should do a weekend soon."

"Ugh," I groan and push back from the table. "I'm not doing this breakfast thing. I'm not hanging out with your family at their Vermont place, Grace. Not marrying – " I point at Derek, "*you* on

Cheater

Monday or ever." I raise my hands and back up. "I'm not having this conversation. I'm getting my things and then I'm leaving with Alannah. This is over. It's gone on long enough." I storm into the bedroom and grab my bag and begin shoving yesterday's clothes and my pajamas into it. I want this robe. This is the best robe I've ever worn in my life, feels like a cuddly stuffed animal, and I think I deserve it, so I stuff that in.

Great. Now I can't close the zipper.

"Chloe."

I look over my shoulder. Derek's leaning in the doorway.

"I've had enough of this," I snap, pointing. "What are you going to do now? Threaten my parents? Alannah? I'm going home. After all this crap, I'd rather marry Adam and live a sexless life filled with lies than marry you."

He moves in and backs me up against the wall. His face is an inch from mine.

I'm tweaked, panicked, but I hold my ground and stare directly into his now icy eyes challengingly.

His hand comes up and closes around my throat. Not tight, though. I swallow against his palm.

"You won't marry him."

"And what could you do about it?" I snap.

Derek moistens his lips with his tongue, then says, "If you attempt to marry him, I'll burn the church down."

"You'll kill me and everyone I love?" I ask, body completely rigid.

"No," he whispers, caressing my throat with his thumb. "I'll pull you out first, then you'll watch it go up in flames from a safe distance. I protect you at all costs, Chloe. Only you."

"You're crazy," I say.

"Crazy about you," he tells me, using the same dazzling smile he used back when he first reeled me in like hapless prey.

"Back off."

"Come finish breakfast. We'll talk after they go."

"No." I grab his wrist and throw his hand off. He drops his hand but doesn't back off. "I'm not sitting at a table with my best friend and your sister while we talk about syrup from Vermont and your mental illness like it's perfectly normal. Get some help, Derek. I'm leaving. Stop following me. Stop stalking me. I'm leaving and I want you to leave me alone or I don't care... I *will* call the cops. I'll go to the press. I'll do whatever the fuck I have to do to –"

He grabs me and starts kissing me.

"Stop!" I fight as he presses me against the wall.

"I want you more right now than I did a minute ago. The backbone? It's intoxicating." He runs his nose up the side of my face. His body is pressed against mine. "Come eat with me and then when they go we'll come back here and maybe I'll eat you. After I punish you for being such a bad, bad girl, saying such terrible things."

He releases my mouth and bites my throat a little roughly, then plants a kiss on it while one of his hands gropes my breast.

I'm swaying, shocked. Heat has flared low in my belly, and I'm ashamed to admit it, but my underwear are drenched.

"Let's hurry and finish so I can kick them out and spank this pussy," he says against my throat, "Maybe tie you up and edge you for a few hours with my fingers, my palms, and my mouth before I let you come on my tongue." He presses a kiss against my mouth and then backs off, leaving me swaying.

"How wet are you right now, I wonder?" He winks and backs away slowly.

Bastard.

"Come eat. It's getting cold. You probably don't want to leave Alannah out there with me."

He gives me a loaded look. Loaded with threats.

He leaves me. Leaves me reeling.

Fucking bastard.

Not knowing what he'll do, flashbacks of the guy with the gun, of the cold look in his eyes when I slapped him across the face the other night, I decide I don't want to leave Alannah's fate to chance. I hesitantly walk out there.

Cheater

I find Alannah and Grace with their heads together while Derek is making another cup of coffee, intense eyes on me.

Both women look at me with concern.

"I'm sorry if I was rude, Grace. I'm... kind of... shattered, thanks to your brother."

She pats the chair I vacated. "Sit down. Let me fill you in on Derek."

"This oughta be interesting," Derek says, rejoining the table.

I sit down and Alannah grabs my hand and squeezes. But she's got a strange look on her face.

I don't have time to try to decode it before Grace starts to talk.

"Derek was kidnapped when he was a child. Held for ransom. It was kept out of the papers and both of you must keep this fact to yourselves. Under threat of severe consequences."

"Grace," Derek warns, giving her an icy look.

She ignores this and continues. "It was very traumatic for him. It's probably why he has some extreme reactions in certain scenarios. Most people don't know how to take him. I was very young when this happened, so I don't remember much, but I can tell you that I've never seen him get infatuated by a woman before. Never seen him with the same girl more than once. Most of them don't get past the first date. He's certainly never moved anyone in with him."

"How old are you?" Alannah asks Derek.

"Almost thirty-four," Grace answers for him.

"When was he kidnapped?" Alannah asks, now looking at Grace.

"He was eleven. Most of his life, he's had an addictive personality. When he discovers something new and gets hooked by it, his reactions can seem extreme. He works to excel in whatever he becomes focused on. I don't think you're in danger, Chloe. In fact, this is the best news I've heard in a while. Maybe best news ever where Derek's concerned. Are you not interested in him? I mean, he's attractive, wealthy. He's a catch. Right?"

"She's interested in me," Derek states boldly.

My eyes roll.

"He's not someone you can dissuade from things he sets his mind to. But that doesn't mean you need to be afraid for your safety. I think maybe you're not giving him a fair chance because of the way he went about things. His approach was probably unorthodox, but..."

I scoff.

She sallies forth, getting louder and with an even more determined look on her face, "But I'm telling you, I don't see him smile. I don't see him laugh. And I've seen him do both with you. That's something that has me hopeful. Maybe things could turn a corner for him with your help."

"I'm not looking for a project," I tell her. "He needs a therapist."

Is she delusional too?

Derek's expression turns dark, but he aims his gaze away, flexing his jaw.

We're all watching him for a minute.

"Derek was kidnapped by-" Grace starts to say gently, but Derek cuts her off, his gaze snapping in her direction with a look that must mean warning.

"Grace is the control freak of the family. She's the youngest of the seven of us and tries to mother everyone." Derek's eyes move to me, and his expression lightens. "She probably figures she'll worry about me less if you're on the job. Eat some more food, Chloe, please."

I ignore him, paying attention to Grace instead as she talks some more.

"It's true. Things are often bumpy in a big family like ours. I like things smooth. I'm the ironer-outer."

She shrugs and pulls apart a piece of her croissant, then pops it into her mouth.

She's beautiful. Very put together. A little younger than me, I'd guess. I'm now wondering, though, if she's as whacko as he is. It's like she's mediating for us along with Alannah who I'm sure is playing nice and fact-finding as part of her usual mediator process.

"You should consider dating her from a typical distance and then going from there," Alannah suggests, spooning fruit salad onto her plate.

She smiles at me. I flinch dramatically to show her what I think of this suggestion.

"Not gonna happen," he denies.

"I need to say," Alannah says, "that I'm going to have my eye on this situation very closely." She points her fork in Derek's direction and continues. "I give a shit about my best friend, and nothing is going to change that. Blackmail doesn't seem like a great way to foster a healthy relationship." She turns to look at me. "Chloe? What do you want me to do here? Call the police? Maybe if Derek gives you some space instead, we won't have to do that."

"I'll let you know what time to meet us at City Hall on Monday," Derek responds. "We'll keep the marriage quiet as the dust settles with Hallman. Then we'll do a destination wedding in a couple months. I'll fly everyone out to be there and we'll do it again as if it's the first time."

"Why not wait and see if you can get Chloe to agree?"

She's trying to negotiate, persuade him in a way to get me out of here safely.

"Woo her the regular way," Grace interjects.

"Exactly," Alannah says. "I'll take her home with me and we can take this slow."

Derek shakes his head. "I'm doing things my way."

"I'm right next door," Grace says to Alannah as if that'll help her feel better about leaving me here.

Alannah looks me over to see where I'm at with everything.

What he said about me not wanting him left alone with Alannah means I could take it that I have no choice but to go through with this with him or he might set fire to the rest of my life. Hurt Alannah?

Alannah has no idea about us being held at gunpoint by Derek's minion either. She's sitting here trying to reason with the psychopath without a full scope of understanding.

"Tell ya what," Derek says, wiping his mouth with a napkin and dropping it on his plate. "Chloe will check in with you twice a day until you're comfortable with resuming normal contact. You'll know she's safe that way. I'll send you the time and place for the marriage on Monday."

"I think you need to reconsider your stance here, Derek," Grace suggests, "Take your time with Chloe. It could work out better."

"No," Derek denies. "Next weekend we have the big anniversary party and the following weekend, we could all go to the Vermont place. You'd be welcome, Alannah."

"I'm *so* coming to that," Grace states excitedly.

"Now, I think we're about done here. Alannah, I don't like to resort to threats but let's just say that if you cause a problem, including spreading word about this situation, it would not be wise. I've got Hallman taking the blame for the breakup, which is how it should be."

Alannah's eyes narrow at the threat.

Derek keeps going. "And if you don't cause any problems, you'll skip any unpleasantness and get to see our girl here flourishing, happy, living her best life. When I set my sights on something, I don't fail." Derek looks at me. "I'm well aware Alannah is an important part of your life. I'm not planning to keep your friends from you. I'm also not giving up here just because the way I've gone about this is unconventional. I want to make you happy. I'm not wasting this opportunity."

The way he's looking at me sets me more than on edge. The idea of him derailing Alannah's life? Of him digging into her life to find dirt to use against her? Of him getting rid of her the way he got rid of Adam as a factor in my life? No. No way. There is dirty laundry in Alannah's family. For Alannah personally, too. I know her secrets and no way will I give him ammunition to punish me by hurting her. Or punish her for getting involved.

"You can go, Lan," I say softly, eyes moving from Derek to Alannah. "We'll talk. I'll message you tonight. And again tomorrow morning."

She stares at me, forehead crinkled.

"I'll walk you home, Grace. Be right back, baby," Derek says, leaning over and kissing me on my forehead and then giving me a look of promise, as if he's pleased with me and is about to give me a reward.

"I'm right next door," Grace repeats, eyes bouncing between me and Alannah. "I'll get your number, Alannah. You can check in any time."

"I've got her number; I'll give it to you," Derek states, opening the front door for his sister.

I watch them leave and then turn my attention to Alannah, who is staring at me with her mouth open.

"Ugh," comes from me. I put my fingertips to my temples.

She says, "I don't know whether I love you or hate you. I mean, I know I love you, but I hate you a little bit right now."

I rear back. "Huh?"

"Gorgeous, no,... gor-geous. Gorgeous and filthy rich man obsessed with making all your dreams come true? I mean, if you're gonna have a psycho stalker, this is the right kind to have."

"Yeah, I've hit the psychopathic hot guy lottery." I roll my eyes and then I burst into tears.

She pulls me into an embrace. "Does he hurt you?" she whispers. "Tell me."

I shake my head. "Not so far. He scares me. How the hell am I gonna get out of this?"

"I'll help you figure it out," she says firmly. "We have to play this carefully. His family? Some people make them seem like well-dressed thugs. From what Jeffy told me, that was just the brother that got killed. The rest of the Steele brothers and the father? Dangerous. Cunning. Connected. They have the money and power to make things go their way and make problems go away. They're not sloppy or careless. We can't make waves without playing this carefully or I'd have called the cops already."

I sigh.

"If you want me to leave here right now and call the police, that's what I'll do. I'll tell Craig everything. But I advise against it."

"What if you and Craig then disappear off the face of the earth without a trace?"

"I know enough between Craig and Jeffy to know this is a serious situation. I do think you need to play things very carefully with Derek. Yes, he's gorgeous and clearly smitten with you but he's obviously cracked. The sister seems like she has her head on semi-straight and she's right next door."

"She seems a little cracked, too, no?"

Alannah tips her head side to side in contemplation. "You might not be wrong, but I think mostly she's a spoiled rich princess without a grasp of how the world operates outside her circles. I think she's mostly excited about her brother wanting to get married. Acting normal. Says she thinks you're good for him. Clearly this is out of character for him but in a way that has her thinking it's a positive thing."

"Or is this part of a psychotic break that'll lead who-knows-where?"

Alannah's face drops. "Okay, let's go then. I'll call 9-1-1 right now. Your immediate safety is the priority."

I shake my head. "No. I... I need to think. You go home. I'll call you later. Big stakes here."

"What aren't you telling me?" she asks. "Why are you considering staying? What is he threatening you with? Or are you falling for this guy?"

I give my head a sharp shake. "No, definitely. Threats are mostly implied. Nothing specific."

"Then I don't feel comfortable leaving you here."

"I don't think you have a choice. I don't want you to make any ripples. I need to think about all this."

"How did it go down with Adam? How did all that transpire?"

"He could be back any second but let's just say Adam has a sweet deal if he cooperates. Big threat if he doesn't."

Cheater

"Same as what he just tried to say to me. Without specifically threatening me."

Derek walks back in and assesses us with humor lit in his eyes. "My ears are ringing."

"As they should be. So listen..." Alannah rises. "I don't know what to do about you, neither does Chloe. We realize we have to play things carefully with someone who might be on the razor's edge of sanity, but that doesn't mean you're going to get whatever you want. It doesn't mean this is all up to you."

His icy stare is unnerving.

"Chloe wants me to go," she continues. "Clearly she's worried you're gonna fuck with my life the way you've fucked with Adam's. But you should know I don't scare as easily as him. I might not come from a powerful family like yours. I might not be a billionaire with unlimited resources at my disposal. But what I am is someone who doesn't abandon her friends. What I will say here to the both of you is that there are some things you said, Derek, that I absolutely love. The idea of someone giving my bestie the happiness she deserves? That tickles me. Truly. If you deliver on the promises you've made today and my girl decides it's what she wants, bravo. Bravo, Derek. I'll be your biggest cheerleader. But she has to want it. I think you should consider doing things the traditional way with her to see where it gets you. And if it gets you nowhere, you should do what every other guy that gets shot down does. Find somewhere else to shower your affection."

"I'm not remotely bothered by being unlike everyone else."

"Clearly. So, I'm watching. Closely. And I've already gone to the trouble to inform several people that I have concerns about you. You might not like that but if anything happens to me or Chloe, there are several powerful people who are paying attention and who know you're the one to watch. You may have been the Steele brother most under radar until now, but flags have been raised in multiple places."

Derek's expression does not change.

I'm trembling, though.

"So, I'm watching. Call me later, babe. Or call me immediately if you need to." She wraps her arms around me and kisses me on both cheeks before grasping my cheeks and looking into my eyes. "I love you, Chlo. This could be amazing for you. If it's not, don't hesitate to call me. If I don't hear from you at least twice a day and know to my bones that you're okay, I will act."

"I'll walk you out," Derek says.

"No." I rise quickly, panicking.

"What's wrong, baby?" Derek asks, coming to me quickly, concern in his gaze.

He takes my face into both hands. "What, baby?" he repeats.

"I'm worried you'll walk her out and I'll never see her again."

"It's okay," she says. "I'll text you from my car before I leave and then again when I'm home safe. I'm walking out here safely and nothing's going to happen to me. Right Derek?"

"Right," he says, "Nothing to worry about right now." His thumb skates across my bottom lip.

I back away from him and wrap my arms around Alannah.

"Love you," she says and kisses my cheek, then leaves, Derek following her out.

32

Derek

I casually stroll beside Alannah to the elevator, amused at how she's consciously keeping pace so she's not ahead of me, unable to see if I'm up to anything behind her.

When we're inside and the doors shut, I press *stop*.

Her eyes fire with alarm.

"Don't worry. I just want a second to talk to you."

"A flair for the drama, indeed," she murmurs, pulling her phone from her pocket, readying it in case she needs to call for help. As if I can't move faster than she can to get it out of her hands. She's acting confident, but I've clocked the slight tremble in her hands.

"I'm a wildcard," I tell her. "Nobody knows how I'll react in any given situation, so yes like you said, even most of my family is wary of me. But hear me out, please." I pause.

"You have my attention."

"I understand your concern with the way my and Chloe's relationship has developed, but I want to reassure you. In fact, I'll harm anyone who tries to hurt her. The only reason Adam Hallman is being treated to opportunities instead of my anger is because she'd find it difficult to forgive me if I lashed out physically. I'm focused on giving her everything she wants and now she won't have to worry about him; she'll know he's doing just fine. Soon, he'll be a distant memory and she can focus on herself. It won't take long for her to realize the ends justify the means."

"What happens to Adam then?" she asks.

I shrug. "If he leaves us alone, nothing that's down to my actions."

"Surprisingly, I believe that you *think* you're doing the right thing here. I believe you *want* to do what you think is the right thing by my bestie. But I'm also being honest here when I say I will go to the ends of the earth for that girl. If you hurt her, you'll be sorry. You're clearly mentally ill, but then again a lot of people are." She lifts one shoulder in a shrug. "It just manifests in different ways, I guess. Part of me was thinking maybe if you got on medication, it'd solve things. But maybe not. Maybe you're exactly who you're supposed to be and maybe Chloe will reap the rewards. I'm not your enemy as long as you take care of her like you've promised to do. But if you decide to turn your energy elsewhere and don't end things amicably where my friend walks away unscathed, you're the one who won't like what happens."

"I can be a good ally to have," I say. "A very good ally. You'd much rather have me as an ally than a foe."

She gives me a shrewd look.

"You'll see. It's gonna work out great." I press the button for the journey to resume.

After I watch her drive away, I go back in, fully aware she's placating me. I also believe she will watch and see what happens. Because I saw in her eyes the thing I've seen in Chloe's when I've spoken about what I want.

I see the desire to believe what I'm saying. It's there in Chloe's eyes and it's there in Alannah's, too. Alannah wants her friend to have everything I'm promising.

My sister bombarded me with questions on the short walk to her apartment about how this all came about and about what I've done so far to make *that poor girl look so shellshocked*. I walked her home to tell her to mind her own business and to keep her mouth shut about the details she's picked up today.

Grace isn't a blabbermouth, but she also doesn't know how to mind her own business. It's gotten her into trouble often. She's the

Cheater

sibling that makes a relentless effort with me that I both loathe and tolerate for some reason, so I've always given her leeway.

Grace's meddling tendencies might be a good thing this time because she can become a friend to Chloe and that'll help her navigate some of the Steele family shit that's inevitable, like fundraisers, family brunches, holidays. Bullshit our mother tries to pull every so often when she has a whim to make us seem like a normal family. Bullshit she will undoubtedly instigate when she finds out there's a new daughter-in-law.

Speaking of which, I should call my personal shopper and get her to outfit Chloe for tomorrow's family thing as well as send a message to my parents' estate manager that I'm bringing a guest with me tomorrow.

That's how it goes with them. Carson facilitates their relationship with me. He's essentially a concierge for everyone in the family, making things happen, managing communications, handling day to day Steele family details.

Back from seeing Alannah out, I find Chloe washing dishes. She's already cleared the table.

"You're not the maid," I tell her, closing the door and locking it. "You don't need to clean up around here."

"Do you have a maid?" she asks.

"A service comes in Monday and Thursday when one or more of us are staying here."

"Well, I'm not exactly gonna leave dirty dishes here to fester for two days."

"I can't stand a mess, Chloe. I also can't stand having staff around all the time so I only have a cleaner come in once a week at my place in Cleveland, so I wouldn't have left them. How about you rinse, I load?" I extend my hand.

She gives me a strange look, but then passes me a dripping plate.

I put it into the dishwasher.

"Then we can move on to other, more... interesting things," I tack on.

"Interesting breakfast," she says conversationally, glossing over what I've just said.

"Yeah."

"Fucking weird," she mutters, passing me a handful of cutlery. "Do you not see how wonky all this is?"

"Unconventional, sure. Grace is curious. Not surprised she showed up. It's good I could tell Alannah where I'm coming from. Now she knows. Now she doesn't need to worry."

Chloe says nothing, though her eyes are saying it all. She knows her friend will continue to worry. And I think she's worried her friend will do something that will have me retaliating.

And she's been forced to be here, but nobody has forced her to wash the dishes. It's just who she is. She'll soon figure out that this is just who I am. And that she'll get to reap the rewards. That I'm a man who won't take her for granted, a man who will think about her needs in addition to my own, unlike that selfish prick I just saved her from.

"Did Alannah message that she's safely in her car?"

"Yes," she says.

I load another two plates. "So..." I broach, "What do you wanna do the rest of the day?"

"I need to open my laptop and do some work. I got nothing done yesterday thanks to you."

She rinses more dishes and I continue stacking them.

After a few moments of working in silence, I say, "You can change fields. Do something else if you don't like that job. Do nothing if you like. Take a breather."

"I like my job," she says. "They've been good to me."

"You didn't eat much?" I state.

"I ate a slice of bacon and a bite of a croissant."

"You didn't eat my pancakes?"

"I ate one."

I regard her. She says nothing; she looks irritated with me.

"That's not enough food, Chloe."

"I can't eat when I'm stressed. I saved it for later."

Cheater

She reaches for the bacon pan, then dumps the grease into the trashcan. I take it from her. "Leave this for now." I set it down and gather her into my arms. "I want you. Naked. Now."

She shakes her head. "No way."

"Why not?" I ask.

"If you need to ask, you're even more delusional than I thought." She throws the cloth into the sink and pushes my chest until I release her. She storms toward the bedrooms.

I follow.

"Leave me alone," she clips over her shoulder. "I don't want to deal with you right now."

"Too bad," I tell her. "I wanna deal with *you* right now."

"Fuck off," she mutters, but I catch her before she gets into the bathroom by wrapping one arm around her waist, pulling her back against my front. I lean down and suckle her earlobe before telling her, "I'm gonna fuck you, little bunny."

I feel her body react. She doesn't seize up in fear. Instead, whether she realizes it or not, she's leaned into me.

"I should edge you for a little bit, though, punish you for being a bad girl with what you said." I lick the ridge of her ear, then add, "Some things are better left between the two of us."

"Let me go," she orders, but her body is melting further into me.

"Though, then you were my good girl by telling your friend to go, so you should also get a reward as well as a spanking. How many times you want me to make you come?"

She doesn't answer.

"Three? Four?" I turn her so she's facing me.

Those blue eyes gaze into mine, searching. And I wonder for a moment what she's searching for, but she makes it clear with what she says next.

"You're even crazier than I thought if you think I want anything to do with you."

"Yet you didn't try to leave with your friend." I kiss her neck, just below her ear.

"Because I'm afraid of you hurting her," she explains.

"So, you're gonna be my good girl then?" I ask, holding her jaw in my palm. I lean in and rub the tip of my nose along the side of hers.

She says nothing. She's biting on her bottom lip. Her pupils are huge right now. She swallows with some difficulty.

"You wet, Chloe?" I ask.

She shakes her head sharply.

"I bet you are," I tell her.

"You'd be wrong," she states, looking away. "Let me go. I'm gonna go take a shower."

"After," I correct, dip and put my shoulder to her belly, then straighten to standing.

"Don't," she mutters, annoyed, but she's grabbed ahold of my shirt as she dangles over my shoulder, and I suspect it's not just for stability. I'm sure she's looking forward to the release she's about to get. That she might not realize how much she needs. I sit on the bed and adjust her in my hold until she's on my lap.

"Got 'cha," I say. "Now, what am I gonna do with you?"

"How about if you let go of me?" she suggests.

"Do you really want me to?"

"Yes!"

I tighten my grip. "Not a chance. I think you need a release. Some stress relief. I can help with that."

"What if Alannah has left and is calling the cops right now?" she asks. "What if the cops show up here and arrest you for forcible confinement? Have you already thought of a way to spin it?"

"First, you haven't tried to leave so you don't actually know if I'd confine you. Right?"

She frowns.

"I don't advise testing me," I warn, then continue with, "Second, she's not calling the cops." I shake my head. "She wants this for you. She wants what I'm saying to be legit. She's not entirely convinced, but she's doing a watch 'n see."

"Because she's afraid you'll ruin her life," she mutters.

Cheater

"Hopefully I won't have to do that," I say.

She frowns. "Would you really?"

"Don't call my bluff, Chloe," I warn.

"Did your deceased brother's wives get killed?" she asks.

I tip my head. "One, yes. Both? Maybe."

She winces. "By your brother?"

I tip it the other way. "One of them, maybe."

I feel her trembling in my arms, so I lean in and look straight into her eyes. "I'm not Thaddeus."

"Maybe you're worse."

"I *am* worse. But not in the same way. Thad was impulsive. Sloppy. I'm much more calculated."

"Your oldest brother is in the middle of an ugly divorce. It's in the papers."

"Eli's wife isn't going to go missing without a trace. She's putting him through the ringer because she believes he was unfaithful to her."

"Was he?" she asks, and I find that curious. Why would she care?

"Don't know; don't care. They won't get divorced. Steele family members don't get divorced. He's just about ready to pull the plug on all that."

"Meaning?"

"Again, don't know; don't care. I'm not my brothers. I'm not my father. I'm a whole other problem. And the solution... little bunny," I flash a smile, "is to marry me, be my good girl, and let me make all your dreams come true like I wanna do. That's what you can do. What you should do. Let me do what I want. That'll make me happy and that'll mean the fewest casualties."

"So, you were kidnapped when you were a child?" she asks. "Did you get therapy for it?"

Is she just stalling? She's probably trying to figure me out while stalling.

"Therapy was the biggest part of that problem."

"Huh?"

"I don't want to talk about that. I want to fuck you. I want to make you squirm and whimper for me."

"I don't want to have sex with you, Derek."

"But there's nothing stopping you now. No hall pass." I kiss her jaw. "No sad fiancé who'd rather play videogames on his computer all day than play with you. If I had nothing to do all day and night but play with you? Mm." I kiss her again. "Watching this hot little body bend to my will? Oh wait... that's exactly what I've got."

"Stop," she mutters unconvincingly.

"You have a new fiancé who can't get enough of you, who knows what to do with you. Don't you?"

"I haven't agreed to marry you," she advises.

"That's fair. I guess I haven't technically asked yet," I reason.

"You declared it would happen," she mutters. "I don't understand any of this, Derek. None of this makes any sense to me."

"I recognized something in you. Something that fascinated me." I move up the bed, bringing her with me. I put her on her back, pin her arms over her head and kiss her neck again. Goosebumps erupt on her warm flesh. "It occurred to me how you must have yearned." I lick the shell of her ear and then whisper, "Hearing your story, thinking about you doing all that yearning, it woke something up in me."

"Woke up what?" she whispers back. "Psycho stalker tendencies? What? How many times has this happened before with you? And what happens when you're over it?"

I lean back enough so our eyes meet, and I see something in her eyes that's new. Genuine curiosity?

I stare at her for a minute.

"Seriously, Derek. Why me?" she asks.

"I don't feel much. Coping mechanism, I guess. When I do, I get focused. Women haven't ever made me feel much. Beyond sexual release. Never connected with a woman before."

"We haven't connected."

"Don't lie," I whisper. "You felt chemistry immediately. So did I.

Cheater

I've felt sexual attraction before but with you it was more. Probably because I knew some of your secrets at that point. I felt something new when I listened to you and Alannah talking, and mostly it was you I was listening to. That yearning in your voice. It woke something new up. I wanted to fix your problems for you. Wanted to satisfy you. And I did, didn't I?"

Her cheeks pinken despite that she looks a little annoyed.

"Sexually at least. I also wanted to know what it might feel like to yearn for something as much as you. And I started feeling that way about you. Yearned to be the one who made you feel wanted. I wanted to know what it'd take to make your dam finally break. Your dam of giving so much of yourself. The yearning for connection would have to break past your filter of doing the thing that was expected of you. I was hearing so much longing. Once I dug in and found out a bit about you, I yearned even more. For more than just to satisfy you. I wanted all your good intentions, your loyalty... aimed at me."

She grimaces.

"Wanted you to want me. To be mine. Wanted you to wear things for me. To do things for me. And to never feel like a slave again. To feel noticed. Appreciated. Seen. To spend time learning more and more about you, what makes you tick, how to excite you, how to make you feel wanted and appreciated."

I lick my lips and examine her face, which is rapt with attention.

"I knew I could get your attention, make you envision using that hall pass on me. But I also knew you probably wouldn't allow yourself the luxury. Because it's not who you are. Which is an attractive quality. And I knew you weren't going after what you yearned for because you were being that good girl again. Doing what was expected of you. Staying loyal to him because of that *treat others the way you want to be treated* adage. You want unconditional love, so you've chosen to love that way. And it's what you've probably done all along in life. And pondering that... I wanted to make things better for you and I wanted to become the one you realized was the key to having what you want. If you've got to be a good girl and do the right thing, maybe you need someone to watch out for you, to make sure that being a good girl doesn't mean getting the shitty end of the stick; I want it to mean getting everything you want. Every single thing, Chloe. I want to earn your loyalty."

Her chin trembles, but she shrugs it off and tries to get bitchy.

"Marriage? Makes no sense. You barely know me. You're just infatuated with an idea, the things you overheard, solving my problems. You're pissing on the importance of marriage."

"It doesn't have to make sense to you in order to make sense to me. This will be a marriage of convenience, Chloe. It'll be convenient to me to be the only man in the world with access to this body whenever, wherever, and however I want it. For me to have the official job of making you happy. I would never piss on that. I like the sound of that. Maybe deep down, you do, too." I flex my hips so she can feel what's about to be inside her. "You said yes to the wrong man. Say yes to the right man, Chloe. And get everything your heart desires."

"Maybe I need to heal and learn how to make myself happy before I can look to someone else to help with my happiness."

"You won't. You'd go onto the next guy either one of two ways. Either you'd never let anybody fully in there again because you felt so burnt and hurt by the relationship with Hallman. Or you'd do the exact same thing, trying to make things work out better this time. Better than they did with Hallman. Better than the relationship you had with your parents."

She goes rigid. "What do you know about my relationship with my parents?"

"Not a lot. Based on my assessment, I've filled in some gaps. You don't spend a lot of time with them. Very little, in fact. I know you were adopted. I also know your brother, who was their biological child, died in your teens and he was their bio kid, so my guess is that you tried to be the perfect daughter, to be everything they'd dreamt of, making them proud and trying not to cause them any further angst. But my guess is that they mourned him in such a way that you became invisible."

She shoves with strength that surprises me. I roll off her and she bolts off my bed, looking furious.

I've hit the nail on the head. "They adopted you after trying to conceive for five years. You were given up at two months old when your sixteen-year-old birth mother decided she couldn't cope. They got pregnant several months later. Bet you've felt like they regretted the adoption when they finally conceived."

She stares at me with shock. "I was a baby. I didn't know I was adopted until I was twelve."

"Then when your brother died, it broke them. They didn't have anything left to give you. Especially your adoptive mother."

Pain slashes across her features.

"I don't want to be with you," she whispers with pain in her voice.

"Yes you do."

"I do not!" She stomps her foot on the word *not*.

"You do," I deny. "You hope I'm the man for you. Because so far I've shown you that you're not invisible to me. I pay attention. I give you what you want without you having to ache and yearn for it and that's only having a bit of information. Wait until I get to know you, baby. Furthermore, I'll take what I want from you, making you feel desired, wanted. Craved. Making you feel seen. Because I do see you, Chloe. Vividly. And I can't get enough of your body. That first night we fucked, you were wild with abandon. You finally got everything sexually you've ever wanted. You thought it was for one night only but it's not. It's for the rest of our lives. I want you wild like that with me again." I reach for her and pull her to me again.

"Let go of me," she demands.

"Never," I vow, but loosen my hold. "Not only do I want you, crave you, I also want that loyalty you gave him that he didn't deserve. I want it to be mine. Because I earn that from you."

She tries to get away. I allow her to move two steps before I catch her and pin her to my bed, wrists held over her head.

She grunts, then breathlessly asks, "You think you can earn anything from me besides my hatred when you've done all this to me?"

"After the cameras went in and I saw all the shit you did for him, all the things he took for granted, how you went out of your way to be such a good girlfriend? It ticked me off. He doesn't deserve all that."

"Oh, and you would?"

"Damn right. I'll give you everything you want from a husband. I'll fuck you daily. Any which way I can think of. Any which way *you* can think of. I'll give you babies. Take care of your every want and need. Wanna go somewhere? We'll go. Wanna do something? Just say the word. I'm young, strong, I've got the means, and I want a life of adventure with you."

She *does* want to believe me; I see it.

"I wanna give you a release right now. I think you need one," I say. "Good stress relief after last night."

"I think you need your head examined," she fires back angrily.

"Go ahead, get angry with me," I invite. "But this still ends with you coming hard, Chloe." I transfer both of her wrists to my left hand and pin them as I walk my fingers down to the waistband of her yoga pants.

She struggles, grunting and writhing, fire in her eyes.

"Got ya," I tell her, "Right where you need to be."

My fingers slip through easily and I can't help but feel triumphant when she turns her head to the side, getting a look of shame because we both know she wants this.

"Wet for me again," I state, nudging her legs further apart with my knee.

"I hate you," she snaps and fights against my grip on her wrists.

I tighten up enough she can't escape, but not enough to leave marks or cause pain.

"That's okay for now, baby. It won't be long, and you'll love me." I

Cheater

thrust a finger inside, then add a second. I crook them and watch the heat in her eyes blaze brighter.

The look in her eyes is definitely new. She's angry with me, yes, but there's something missing that was here the last few times we fucked. Maybe it's the guilt that's gone. Because I've eliminated it by having the engagement called off. Or maybe my words, my intentions, are penetrating.

I pump my fingers a few times, watching how she reacts, how her chest rises and falls faster, how her sweet lips part. She's angry, but she's feeling me. And her sweet inner walls are tightening, fluttering around my fingers.

I let go of her wrists and quickly snatch her shirt up, exposing her bra. Immediately, Chloe shoves at my shoulders, squirming in an effort to get away. But she's not fast enough and I get one of her arms re-pinned as I bite down gently on her nipple over her bra. She freezes and I take the opportunity to pump my fingers faster, adding my thumb to her clit as I suckle the hardening nipple. Her back arches and then she immediately knees me in the ribcage, which throws me off balance briefly, giving her the opportunity to squirm halfway away from me. But my fingers are still inside her. I roll her and then roll her again, quickly, so I've got her diagonally on my bed.

She loses my fingers as I undo my jeans and fumble to get my cock out while she continues to grunt and fight me.

"Want me to stop?" I ask.

She grunts in frustration, but doesn't answer.

Once I'm out, I quickly whip her yoga pants down to her knees and drive my hips forward, filling her.

"No, you don't want me to stop."

"Grr, stop," she argues but it's clear her heart isn't in it.

I caress her face.

"Nuh uh," I disagree and grab her hands with both of mine, weaving our fingers together and pinning them again above her head. "Goin' nowhere now."

"Rrr," she complains, still struggling.

"Goin' nowhere, ever," I tell her, transferring one of her wrists to my other hand so I can rub her clit while I continue to fuck her. "Eyes on mine, baby. I wanna watch you come undone."

She grimaces, angry.

"You wanna take your frustrations with your ex out on me?"

"I wanna take my frustrations with you out on you," she corrects. "But God knows how you'd react, so I can't do that. Get off me. You're fucked in the head, and I don't want anything to do with you."

"Lies," I tell her. "You feel alive right now, instead of numb, right? You won't just go through the motions with me, Chloe. Your heart will race. Your clit will throb. I'll make you feel as alive as you felt that first night we spent together. I knew I wanted to give you a wild night, a night to remember that night and that was all on me. The deceit. Stalking. Digging. The eavesdropping. But it's your fault that you made me feel so much that night. That's why you're here now. As soon as you jumped my bones when we got into this apartment that night, you sealed your fate." Holding her tight, my lips descend to meet hers. "You're perfect for me," I say against them. "And I'm gonna be everything you want. But no more deceit. Yeah, I'll still stalk you. Yeah, I'll continue to obsess about you. You're front and center in my mind, Chloe."

She turns her head away, denying me, so my mouth goes to her throat where I tongue it, kiss it, and nibble my way up and down her warm flesh while I continue driving my hips, feeling her milking my dick while my thumb circles her clit. She begins to pant harder, then she's shuddering hard, coming for me.

Her face looks full of pain, eyes squished tight, lips forming a letter O as she loses it, body convulsing under me, around me.

Yeah, she's coming hard.

"Let me have your sounds, baby," I demand, letting go of her hands and putting my palm to her throat, closing around it just a little. "I want your mouth, too."

Her eyes bolt open and I get to watch as she climbs to another level of sensation.

Cheater

I'd laugh, revel in it, but I'm too lost to my own sensations, feeling the sweet heat clenching me tight. I lose it, too, lips crashing down on hers as my cock jerks and I spill into her. I spill into her sweet body knowing to my bones that this is the girl I want, knowing I won't ever let her go. That I'll do whatever I can to get her where she realizes she doesn't want me to let her go.

She lets out a squeaky muffled sound as she comes down from the high and our teeth clash briefly before my tongue sweeps in and touches hers.

She whimpers into my mouth. Hard. Musically.

"Fuck, baby," I groan, letting go of her throat to palm both her tits while kissing her some more.

She feels boneless under me, but also breathless. She came hard. And so did I.

"But no more deceit. I promise, baby."

I wrap both arms around her and roll to my side, taking her with me. She buries her face in my throat and begins to cry.

"I want you to want me, Chloe," I say, "To crave me. I want you to want me so much, you ache for me. And guess what? I'm going keep at you until I make it happen. Be my good girl and hold me tight while you cry so I can make you feel better."

She shudders.

"Now," I demand.

She grabs my shoulders and buries her face into me.

"That's it. Just like that. I've got you." Satisfaction rolls through my veins, but she changes her mind and pulls back.

And I'm irritated. I want her. I want her to want me back. I breathe through the frustration. I won't get angry. I'll just work harder.

33
Chloe

Foiled into an orgasm once again. And the look of satisfaction on his face afterwards, you'd think I surrendered and declared I'd marry him or something.

And for a split second in that post-coital glow, I almost did. Thankfully my sense returned.

Just because there's physical chemistry and just because he's insanely attractive and swears he wants to make my wants and needs his first priority doesn't mean I'm going to be dumb enough to just fall in line.

Unless you count the sex. Yes, I've given in there. Because not only is he incredibly strong with the ability to move me how and where he wants me, he's definitely a god in bed. He makes my body betray me, but that doesn't mean I'll lose my marbles and give in. Because being able to make gorgeous, intricately-drawn but powerfully bold figure eights with your hips while inside me doesn't equate to the potential for a happily ever after. Sadly.

Because how can I give myself over to someone who's thrown my entire life into a tailspin? You don't fall for someone who gets you to do what they want you to do through threats of violence against those you care about.

After fucking me, he cuddles me and seems in no hurry to go anywhere or do anything, but lets me pry myself away when I mutter that I need the bathroom.

I lock the door and take a long, hot shower where I do a whole lot of pondering the *what ifs*.

Will Alannah play a *watch and see* game? Or is she already hard at work on a plan to free me from this?

Should I try to speak to Derek's sister on the side to see if she's someone I can reason with? Could she steer her parents and siblings to get involved and have him signed in for a psychiatric hold?

Also, how is Adam doing? Is he missing me or is he counting all the opportunities coming his way? I guess it doesn't matter anymore what Adam says, thinks, or does, does it?

My mind wanders somewhere it doesn't generally go; my biological parents. Do I even want to know anything about them? What difference would it make?

He's somehow hit the nail on the head about my family. My parents showed care and affection to me as a child. I wasn't abused. But it was evident early on that Bryan was their favorite. The way their eyes lit up with every milestone, every accomplishment. I didn't get that same light from them. He looked like a perfect combination of the two of them. When I found out on my twelfth birthday that they adopted me as a baby and that Bryan was their biological child, a lot of things made sense. But Bryan made everything better. He was the best brother I could've asked for. We were best friends. And I remembered thinking at night alone in my bed, months after finding out, that if we weren't so close, if he hadn't bonded with me as soon as he was self-aware enough to reach for me, maybe they wouldn't have kept me. Because they had their bio kid.

When he got sick, I did become invisible. When he died, I did try to make up for things by being the perfect child. Cooking. Cleaning. Looking after my parents. Trying to be the glue for our family through trying hard with my grades, with athletics, with everything. But my mom was pretty checked out. Dad wasn't much better.

My parents haven't ever been cold or mean to me, but they don't exactly make much of an effort. Really haven't since I turned eighteen and went off to school.

Cheater

So many people talk about how much their adoptive parents deserve their everlasting gratitude for giving them the most amazing childhood when their biological parents couldn't. But I rarely hear kids talk about families who seem to tolerate their adoptive kids rather than treasuring them as if they were blood.

Even though I've occasionally felt like I was a second-class family member, I know it could've been worse. They're not bad people. They're just sort of indifferent.

But even still, I've never sought out my birth mother. All I knew was that she had me young and wanted me to go to a family who couldn't have children. She wanted to go to college. She had a scholarship opportunity and didn't have a supportive family to help her raise me. My parents told me she probably wouldn't come looking for me. As far as I know, she didn't. I thought about asking about her a few times before Bryan got sick. I never did and then after Bryan, I didn't want to insult them or have them feel like they were losing me, too.

And now, feeling betrayed by Adam and that being compounded by Derek blowing the dust off the open wounds left from my relationship with my parents, I now wonder how much Derek knows about my life, my parents, my birth parents.

After the long shower, I finally have an appetite, so I dress in sweats and wander out to the kitchen to warm up my breakfast. Derek is at the dining table, laptop open, phone to his ear.

"No," he says, "Columbus for at least a few more days. After that, we'll see... Right. Right. Bye." He puts his phone down and watches me put my plate in the microwave.

I avoid his eyes while uncapping the cold water I get from the fridge.

While I'm eating microwaved pancakes and bacon at the kitchen counter, studiously avoiding meeting his gaze as he shamelessly watches me, his phone chimes with an alert.

"Oh, Nicola is here," he says and rises, eyes on his phone. "Be right back."

I don't ask who Nicola is. I continue shoveling reheated pancakes into my face. They're good, even reheated. So is the syrup from his family place.

Bottled with love by The Steele Family.

Well, bully for the Steele family with their steel heart logo. Even if it is damn good maple syrup. After I'm done, I'm still hungry, so I reach under the dome on the counter and pull out one of the chocolate éclairs and take a big bite. And then another. Even a day old, it's still the best thing ever.

Eating my feelings? Guess so.

This is, of course, when Derek's head pokes into the apartment.

"Can you hold this door for me a sec, please?" he asks.

I see he's got a rolling rack behind him.

I put the éclair down and move his way, too much food in my mouth, and not giving a care.

His eyes sparkle with amusement as I hold the door open. He backs up and then pulls in a long rack.

"That's good," he says and relieves me of door-holding duty, kissing me and then licking his lips, going, "Mm" as he shuts and then locks it.

He gestures to the seven or eight-foot-long rolling rack that's filled with clothes and stacked boxes underneath. Shoe boxes, mostly, with some brand names I recognize.

"This is all for you," he says. "I'll roll it into the closet, you try on what you like. If there's anything you don't want, leave it on the rack. Anything you do want, just move it into the closet for now. It'll all go with us when we leave. Have it all if you want."

There's a lot to unpack here but before I can even ponder where to start, he touches a sky blue dress at the front of the rack. "I'd like you to wear this tomorrow, if you don't mind. Or this." He points to another dress that's nearly the same color of blue but with black and cream mixed in. "I'd love if you'd model them both for me and let me pick, but I suspect you'll tell me to go fuck myself."

"Tomorrow?" I ask.

Cheater

"Brunch with my parents. It's their family thing for their fortieth anniversary. Next weekend is the bigger celebration."

I stare blankly. He's serious.

"This will be family only. Next weekend, it'll be about four hundred guests."

I blink a couple times as he pulls the cart down the hallway.

I'm in the same spot when he's back. "Not interested in the clothes?"

"Um…" I let that hang.

"I'm guessing you didn't pack anything for tomorrow since you didn't know about it."

"Since you dragged me here against my will, you mean?"

"You exaggerate," He pulls me into an embrace, amusement dancing in his eyes.

Irritated, I press my palms against his chest and push. He tightens his grip.

"What about the rest of it?" I finally ask.

"Clothes, shoes. A variety of things. I wanted you to have some nice things, so I asked my personal shopper to outfit you for a new wardrobe. You don't have to keep them all if anything isn't to your taste, but if you want them all, keep them all. I sent Nicola photos of you in several different outfits so she said she was getting things based on both your existing style and on what she thought would suit you."

"Several photos of me?"

"I have a file," he replies.

"A file? Can I see it?" I ask.

"If you want," he replies. "It's in my office at Downtown, though. You go check out the clothes, I'll go get it for you. Don't leave." He gives me a dark look. "I'd find you." He pokes me in the nose and then smiles as if he didn't just deliver a threat.

∞

I like nice things. I wouldn't call myself a total fashionista. I own some designer things, but I've gotten the higher ticket stuff at trunk shows, from consignment shops. I'm a big fan of bargain-hunting, so while a lot of my stuff isn't designer, some of it is. And I like fashion, love quality items, and really love getting something for a steal.

While I'm not impressed about Derek's ability to shower me with expensive things, I *am* impressed with this Nicola's abilities. Because there's not a single thing on this rack that I don't want, don't like, or wouldn't wear. There are business suits. There are designer jeans, cute tops, quality cardigans, party dresses, workout and relaxation clothes, and gorgeous footwear. There are even accessories that are my taste – to a tee.

I'll just ignore the selection of sexy lingerie, but I might not be able to resist this comfortable and cute sleepwear. These clothes are worth a lot of money. And there are also a few boxes containing expensive shoes and after looking at them, I have to curtail my inner child who dares me to get excited, who is trying to squeal like it's Christmas morning.

It wasn't difficult to squash that reaction because I'm far too logical and pragmatic to let myself get dazzled by material goods when I'm here with a psycho stalker who seems like a ticking time bomb.

While I'm still perusing the jewelry, Derek comes back with a file folder in hand. I'm surprised he's willing to give me access to the information he's gathered about me.

That didn't take long. The Downtown club is at least a ten minute drive. Maybe I got distracted by all the clothes. Any non-critical distraction with my state of mind right now is welcome.

"You didn't try to run," he observes. "Might have been fun playing hide 'n seek, but I'm glad." He kisses me, then shakes a file in his hand. "Interested in the birth mother? Background information about your adoptive parents? They've got life insurance policies willed to you, by the way. Their house is paid off. When they go

Cheater

you'll have a decent inheritance, if you're smart with the money it could've been a tidy retirement fund."

I say nothing.

"I say could've because you won't need a retirement fund because once you're Mrs. Derek Steele you'll be a multi-millionaire. I'll hit the billionaire level by the time my father dies."

I still say nothing.

"Aren't you keeping any of it?" he asks.

"Huh?"

He tips his head in the direction of the clothing rack.

"I'm keeping all of it," I state.

He looks surprised.

"If you're willing to spend five figures on clothes for me and they're clothes that match my style perfectly, of course I'll keep them."

I'm being bitchy in my reply, but it's my new strategy. I just came up with it five seconds ago. Be bitchy. See if he decides he's no longer obsessed with me.

"Here." He hands me the file folder.

"Is this everything?" I ask.

"That's what the private eye dug up for the background check on you and your family."

"What else is there?"

"I have a file on Hallman. I have a file on Alannah Fisher. I'm having a file put together on your birth parents, though there's a few paragraphs of information in there. If you don't want the file, you don't have to have it. But I ordered it in case you do."

He sees a reaction and his eyes go warmer. "I suspected that's why you were asking about the file. Want me to ask for a rush on it?"

I shake my head. "No." I set the file down on the dresser. I don't want to look this over now. I'm not sure I even want to see what's in here. A thick file that's supposed to encompass me?

"You want to see Hallman's file?" he asks.

"No," I say.

"Why?"

"Because Adam and I are history. You saw to that. His secrets are now moot."

"Fair enough. Change your mind, let me know." He looks at the rack. "You try anything on?"

I shake my head.

"Gonna let me pick your dress for tomorrow's family thing?"

"I don't want to meet your family."

"I want you there with me," he states.

"If you make me go with you, maybe I'll blurt all the crap you've pulled on me."

"No, you won't." He shakes his head.

"And how do you know that?"

"Because if I told you the consequences of such an action, you'd decide to be my good girl." He smiles, wrapping his arms around me and kissing the tip of my nose.

My hands come up to push him away, but he walks me backwards until my back is against the wall of the closet we're in.

It's a dream closet. Huge. Lots of shelves and drawers. Derek has only a small amount of the space in use, but then again I know he doesn't live here full-time. And I suddenly find myself curious about his other place.

"You don't live here," I state.

"I'm generally here a handful of days a year. When I have stuff happening at one of the clubs. When I come in for family functions. That's why I came a couple weeks ago. Things for the clubs and knowing I'd have to be here for my parents' fortieth."

"But I live here," I state the obvious.

"I know that," he replies, still smiling.

"You're expecting me to marry you and we don't live in the same city."

"You telecommute," he says. "So your location is flexible."

"No. It's not," I disagree. "I live in Columbus and that's non-negotiable."

Cheater

"We'll figure it out," he says with a shrug.

But his eyes are lit with something; I don't know what and I'm not sure I want to know.

"I need to get some work done," I state bitchily.

He takes a step back and I slip by him.

∞

I jolt in surprise when I feel Derek's hands land on my shoulders. I've been sitting at the desk in his spare bedroom working all day. It's now dark out.

"You've been working ten hours," he says. "Dedicated, even when it's work you're doing for me."

I blink a couple of times and stretch my neck. "Good point. Maybe I should sabotage everything."

He laughs.

I roll my eyes.

"Time to pack it in for the night. Get some food. Relax," he says and starts to squeeze, then his fingers start massaging. Before I search for the words to make him stop, I find I'm leaning into the tension relief his hands are capable of. He keeps going, fingers moving in circles around my shoulders, my neck.

I'm suddenly hungry.

I've put myself ahead of the game with work. It was a good distraction to get lost in something productive, something I have actual control over.

"Did your belly just rumble?" he asks against my ear, making me shiver. "I've got just the thing." He takes my hand and tugs.

Rising, I try to pull my hand away, but his grip tightens and there's no escape, so I follow him out to the living area and as the scent hits my nose, my salivary glands wake up. There's a large pizza on the table. A bottle of wine and a glass for me. A glass of something brown for him. Two plates. Napkins. A candle lit. Candle lit pizza dinner.

But there's more than that. Beside my plate is the wolf shifter romance he bought me. Beside his plate is a novel.

He opens the box and it's covered in colorful vegetables, hot peppers, and pepperoni. Just like I like it. I ignore the way it feels to have a man know what you like and get it for you without you asking for it.

"Do you enjoy reading while eating or are you doing this to make me think we're compatible?" I ask. "Because I don't do this at home. I take myself on a dinner with a book date once in a while out somewhere."

"I figure you're probably not interested in conversing with me tonight, so thought I'd give this a try," he says. "My sister Naomi bought me this series for Christmas a while back. My parents raised us getting something you want, something you need, and something to read every Christmas as kids. Grace buys me something she thinks I need every year. Nay always buys me something to read even though I'm not much of a fiction guy." He gestures behind himself, and I notice the bay window's window seat has a bookshelf under it. The door is open halfway and it's filled with books.

Instead of asking him about getting gifts he wants like I'd normally do, I ask, "You like your pizza like this?"

"We'll find out, won't we?" he sits. "Usually a pepperoni, sausage, and mushroom guy."

"And if you don't?"

Adam bitched about my hot peppers because even though they were only on half, sometimes the juice went over the border to his half and ruined his life.

"Then next pizza we get will be half what I like and half what you like, I guess. I don't know. Not a big deal, is it?" He shrugs and pulls a piece out of the box and sets it on my plate before taking one for himself.

"You went pretty far back on my socials, didn't you?"

"Gave myself something to do at night when I couldn't sleep because I was thinking about you."

Cheater

I know he has to have gone back not only because of the accuracy of the toppings, because I don't remember posting anything recently about pizza, but also because I do remember a rant post with a picture of a slice of pizza posted a few years ago. This pizza doesn't have the crust air bubbles popped and he handed me a piece with a giant bubble on the edge. That pizza slice post went semi-viral a few years ago when I posted something about loving the air bubbles and not wanting them popped with a picture of a piece of pizza with a big one.

But I do like sausage on my pizza, too, and there's none on this one. So he forwent something he likes on his pizza to try it my way.

I immediately peel the bubbled crust off and pop it in my mouth.

"This is good. Peppers add a nice bite to it," he remarks.

"I like sausage on my pizza, too," I tell him. And I don't know why I tell him. My face goes hot when I realize this.

He smiles. "Next time we'll get what you want and what I want then. The vegetables work for me." He shrugs, flips his Jack Reacher book open and starts reading.

I open my book, too, but there's no way I can concentrate on reading a love story about a bulldozing alpha male right now. Not only because of my state of mind, but also because I can't keep my eyes off him.

He's not paying lip service; he's reading while eating his pizza. I don't bother to pour a glass of wine. Instead I look in the fridge for a bottle of water but am pleasantly surprised to find a bottle of root beer. And to find the fridge is now fully stocked with food.

"Oh yeah, I got that for you. And some ice cream among other stuff," he says, glancing at the root beer in my hand.

And I'm frozen in place. The effort here is impressive. I'm a root beer float lover.

He wipes his fingers on his napkin, flips a page and then grabs another slice of pizza from the box.

I manage to put away two slices with a big glass of root beer before I'm done. He's eaten three slices and is still reading.

I haven't been reading. I've been eating and also kind of watching him.

My phone chimes. I lift it from beside myself.

Alannah: Checking in.

Me: I'm fine.

Alannah: You sure? Send me proof of life.

I take a selfie and forward it to her.

Alannah: Gorgeous. I've been doing a lot of thinking and I'm thinking maybe all this happened for a reason.

I frown and wait for her continuation for a minute.

Alannah: Don't get me wrong, he's whackadoodle, but maybe you could wind up with a happy ending anyway. Msg me in the morning with proof of life again. Love you babe.

For a reason. The reason being what? What possible reason could the universe have for putting me on the radar of a psycho stalker?

I scoff to myself. And I'm also scoffing at the *gorgeous* remark because I've put no effort into my appearance today other than running a brush through my hair this morning when we had the world's strangest breakfast, *ever*.

I put my plate and glass in the dishwasher and walk down the hall with my phone and the book in my hand. Not that I think I can get into it tonight.

A few minutes later, Derek joins me in his bed with his book, bringing in two bottles of water, setting one on the table on the side I'm on, turning on the lamp, then setting the other bottle on the opposite table.

He flicks the ceiling light off and gets in bed, then says, "I've seen him wheel into bed with his own water a few times. Saw you walk in with two bottles each time you went to bed first, setting him up on his side of the bed. Why the fuck he didn't think about anyone besides himself when you were putting effort in is beyond me."

He gets himself settled, opens his book, and resumes reading.

I set my book on the table beside me, face flaming.

Cheater

"You wanna watch TV?" he asks, casually.

"No," I snap, then flick the lamp off, turn onto my side and stare into space, feeling the grimace on my face.

"Is my light bothering you?" Derek asks.

"No," I say.

"Sure?" he checks.

"I'm sure," I answer.

And then I realize I'm supposed to be acting bitchy. I'm supposed to be behaving like a shrew who's difficult to get along with and who a man would see as impossible to live with. I guess I'll try again tomorrow.

There are a lot of things bothering me right now, not the least of which is him pointing out yet another flaw in my relationship with Adam. But miraculously, I somehow manage to fall asleep almost immediately.

34

Derek

The room is bright, and I've been awake for a while, watching her sleep. I seem to sleep better when she's beside me. I'm feeling well-rested. And big things are happening in my chest.

When I woke to her beside me, I instantly knew I'd never tire of watching her sleep. She looks like an angel. She's wearing a pair of the pajamas I had brought in. Royal blue silk ones. I run my hand up her leg and feel the silk between my fingers.

No, she didn't choose to come to me like I wanted, but she *is* here in my bed. The rest will come. I'll make sure of that.

Today, she meets the rest of my family. She also gets my surprise, which I'm beyond excited to show her.

Her eyes open and stare into mine.

"Mornin'," I greet, my hand finding its way up to her face. I rub my thumb over her cheekbone as my fingers move through her hair.

Those blue eyes stare sleepily for a moment, then seem to snap out of a daze before shooting me a look of disdain as she rolls away from me to rush to the bathroom.

After a few minutes, I hear the shower, so I decide to join her.

She's locked me out. That's okay, this flimsy doorknob lock is no match for my desire.

She's rinsing her hair when I join her wearing nothing but a smile.

"What are you doing?" she growls, trying in vain to shield her nudity with her arm and a big bath sponge.

"Saying good morning to my future wife," I inform as I drop to my knees while grabbing her by the hips and steadying her against the tiled wall so I can bury my face between her legs. And I do, just before she manages to clamp them shut. I swipe my tongue through her folds. I taste a little bit of soap and she stumbles a little, trying to protest, so I steer her until she sits on the shower bench, keeping a firm hold of her while continuing to work her with my fingers and my mouth.

She keeps trying to fight me, so I lean back and give her a reprimanding look as I smack her clit. She jolts, mouth dropping open in shock.

"How dare you!" Chloe gasps.

"I dare like this," I state and give it another smack.

"Derek!" she shouts, but the way she does it fails to hide how she really feels about it.

I smack it a third time and then lean forward and latch onto her breast, taking a hard pull on her nipple, which makes her back arch. I take the opportunity to stuff her cunt with two fingers. I get no resistance whatsoever and it's not water from the shower that grants me access.

I decide the water, bench, and the wet tiles are too much of a hassle during this struggle she's keeping up, so I grab her and throw her over my shoulder before taking her slightly slippery body back to bed, dropping her on it, falling on top of her, giving her all my weight.

She grunts in response, trying to fight me off.

"Spirited this morning, aren't you?" I ask, laughing darkly and grabbing her wrists, I pin them so I can impale her with a slam of my hips.

And I see the light burn in her blue eyes as I pull back and slam in again, keeping her pinned but transferring both of her wrists to my left hand, gripping them tight to the pillows above her head so I can slide my right hand between us and tease her clit while slowly driving into her over and over.

"This is a nice Sunday morning ritual, isn't it?" I muse and kiss her.

She bites me.

I hiss while jerking my head back in shock.

I taste blood on my bottom lip.

Alarm registers in her eyes and I'm guessing it's because of the look on my face.

I go feral and attack her mouth.

"Now you get to taste my blood too, little bunny," I tell her, as my hips slam forward repeatedly while I hold her mouth hostage with mine.

I nip her bottom lip too.

She whimpers, but instead of trying to writhe and squirm away, now she's clutching me. Clutching me with her legs and her sweet pussy.

"I wanna know what your blood tastes like too," I tell her and then I bite her luscious breast, drawing blood while continuing to thrust my cock into her tight, quivering heat over and over.

She screams as she comes, whimpering hard while I continue to thrust.

Her eyes are wild, our skin is damp from the shower, from sweat, and suddenly I want to stop rutting her long enough to mark her with my cum. Paint her beautiful, nude body with it. The idea has my balls tightening, my spine tingling, as I release her wrists, pull out and fist my cock, sending ribbons of pearly white all over her stomach, her tits, even hitting her chin.

She lies still, staring at me with shock. Her mouth is open. Her eyes are wide. I see something new, though I can't assess it because I'm feeling. Feeling my orgasm. Feeling satisfaction roll through me both physically and emotionally because she's wearing streaks of me. The blood from my lip on her chin. The print of my teeth on her breast with a tiny drop of blood where I broke the skin.

I lean over and lick the droplet away, then I collapse on top of her and kiss her again and again, on her mouth, her jaw, each of her eyelids, her throat.

"Now we need to finish that shower," I say and lift her up and carry her back to the bathroom.

The shower is still running. Perfect.

I set her on her feet, grab the sponge from the tiled floor near the drain, and soap it up again.

As I wash her, she's staring at me like she's stunned. Like she's just seen something she can't believe, maybe. I don't know.

What I *do* know is that I can't get enough of her. I might have just hit a new level of obsessed.

After I wash her off, I soap the sponge up again and start on myself. She tries to sneak out, so I catch her wrist.

"Chloe." I lift it and press my lips to her hand with a kiss. "We need to be at my parents' at eleven. We'll leave at ten-thirty. Can you wear one of the blue dresses, please? For me?"

She frowns.

I kiss her hand again and flash her a smile.

She pulls away, swallowing nervously, but doesn't answer.

35
Chloe

It's not a full on trembling I'm doing, but I keep getting hand tremors and belly swoops as I try to get ready amid lots of hot whooshes between my thighs. Because I keep getting flashbacks.

He was like an animal devouring me. He bit me. He drew my blood. Licked it. Came on my skin. If he could've written his name on me in semen, I think he would have. He looked supremely pleased with himself as he did it.

This wasn't going through the motions to do what he thought I'd like. This was what he wanted. And it was visceral, carnal, primal.

And then he carried me into the shower and painstakingly washed me clean, kissing me, smiling at me the whole time. Inadvertently tickling my feet as he even got between my toes. I didn't laugh, though. I just got increasingly uncomfortable and fidgety with the whole thing.

And now the swoony psycho wants me to wear a pretty dress to meet his parents.

This ought to be interesting.

I look through the clothing he sent and am miffed about the fact that the two blue dresses *do* seem to be the most suitable for a brunch with fancy, rich people. I wasn't planning to wear one of the blue ones and have him think I did it to please him, it's just that the other dresses are either too business-like, too sexy, or more for a vacation or an afternoon wandering antique shops or farmer's markets. The two blue dresses are both perfect for a brunch at a significant other's parents – not that I think of him as my other half – but I decide on the slightly demurer option.

I grab the dress, some of the new underthings, and a pair of the new shoes, some strappy espadrilles. As he slips out in a towel, I move back toward the bathroom, since that's where all my makeup and hair stuff is.

His eyes flash with heat as he sees which dress I'm taking in with me and he crowds me, making sure I see the smile as I try to glide by him on my way back in.

I say nothing as I close the door over, but it won't close tight, because he broke it. The latch is hanging by just one screw.

I shake my head as I survey the damage and then decide to get on with this. Today ought to be interesting, hopefully presenting an opportunity to talk to a member of the Steele family about this problem. Since I don't know what to make of his sister, I'll be assessing the rest of them in an effort to choose the one most likely to help.

∞

I'm almost done blow drying my hair when Derek comes in, dressed in a dark suit and depositing a mug of coffee beside me on the vanity counter.

He kisses the side of my head. I see his lips move as he smiles, and I can't hear what he's saying with the hairdryer going, though am pretty sure I lip-read the word *beautiful*. My finger hovers briefly over the switch but I decide against turning it off. I'm supposed to be being bitchy.

Though, being bitchy when he kissed me this morning did not have the effect of turning him off. At all.

At that thought, more belly dips ensue.

∞

Cheater

I've got frayed nerves as we leave, as I ponder how this day might go. He takes my hand as soon as I'm in the hallway, looking at a waiting and smiling Grace Steele who is standing by the elevator.

"Good morning!" she sunnily greets, "We'll go together."

"No," Derek counters. "We have plans afterwards."

"What plans?" she asks and smiles bigger, catching me staring at her gorgeous shoes.

She's looking breathtaking in a flowy ivory, red, and gold dress, which is pretty and suits her, but the showstopper is the shoes. Shoes that probably cost more than one of my bi-weekly paychecks. They're strappy platform sandals with bling-laden gold flowers at the toe strap, a blingy red flower at the ankle, and red soles.

"A surprise for Chloe," Derek says, and lifts my hand so he can press his lips to my index knuckle.

I don't react visibly, but I'm thinking I've had way more than enough surprises from Derek already.

"Drive me there, then, and I'll get someone else to drop me back off. Or I'll use Daddy's or Mom's driver." She steps into the waiting elevator.

"Nice, right?" she asks, so I look up from her shoes to her face. She knows I'm admiring them, so she bends her leg to show it off.

"Very," I say.

"Why don't you take your own car?" Derek asks, holding the elevator door and gesturing for me to go ahead of him.

"Because..." she drawls, "I plan to get snockered. Why else? You know how these SS brunches go." Her gaze slides my way. "Yes, I occasionally refer to Shannon Steele with the same acronym as Hitler's elite guard. Not making light of the holocaust – more like... describing Mom's personality when it comes to parties. Wanna get drunk with me, Chloe?" She links arms with me.

I startle in surprise.

"I promise, it'll make this brunch more pleasant."

"Maybe next time," Derek answers for me in a droll tone as the elevator door closes.

"You're no fun," she complains. "Me and Nay will definitely be snockered. So will Mom."

"When isn't she? And I disagree. I happen to be a bit of fun," he corrects, a little smile on his face and then his voice drops lower, "Isn't that right, Chloe?"

My face burns. I stare at the elevator lights.

Grace barks out laughter and it's so animated, my body shakes with hers as she's still got my arm linked with hers. "Wow. Who are you and what have you done with my brother? Girl..." She bumps me with her shoulder. "If you think about leaving my brother, I will kidnap you and bring you back. I love your dress."

Derek busts up laughing again and as handsome as my crazy stalker always looks when he laughs, my eyes are now pointed at his sister who looks both shocked and delighted to watch her brother laugh.

She follows us to Derek's SUV, and I'm grateful for the distraction of having her along for the ride.

I try to get into the back seat, but she denies me the distance from her brother, and he mutters, "Nice try," once I'm in the passenger seat, buckling up.

∞

"Everyone coming?" Derek asks as he gets onto the interstate.

"Yep," she says. "It'll be strange this year, won't it?"

Derek doesn't answer right away so she prompts, "Without Thad."

My eyes bounce to his face.

"This is the first anniversary party without him," Grace adds, for my benefit.

Seeing no change on Derek's face, I twist to make eye contact with Grace. "I'm sorry for your loss," I tell her.

"Thank you, Chloe," she replies softly.

Cheater

"I might not be happy to be here, but I sure know how strange and hard first everythings are after losing a sibling," I add.

Grace doesn't look distraught or upset at this comment, which I find strange.

"I don't know that *hard* is the right word," Grace finally says.

"You've still got five other siblings," Derek says nonchalantly.

My expression must betray my horror at how blasé he's being because Grace speaks up.

"We all had a complicated relationship with Thad. He wasn't well-liked by anyone in the family other than our mother. In fact, of course... I mean... it was a shock that he was murdered, but Thad's nickname was Thorn. He was a thorn in everyone's side. He was quite... disturbed."

I'm frowning. Not because of what she's said, because if it's rumored that he killed two wives and these two didn't like him, none of them liked him, does that mean nobody will help me? If they're all supposedly afraid of Derek, my plan might not go anywhere.

I deflate and stare out the window. I may need an alternate plan if today proves fruitless.

Do I defy Derek and share details about the stalking, the invasion of privacy, the threats?

I feel his hand wrap around mine. His thumb caresses the back of my hand, then grazes my naked ring finger. I stare at it for a minute realizing once again that it doesn't feel strange that the ring is gone. How strange that it doesn't feel strange. Maybe that's because it seemed so easy for Adam to let me walk away. A lump forms in my throat; stinging hits my sinuses, but I push away the emotion. I don't need to cry right now. I don't need to ruin my makeup before getting to Derek's parents' place, not that I want to go, but I certainly don't want to look like a non-credible walking disaster if I do manage to find someone I can talk to about helping wrangle their son or brother.

My eyes rove from his hand on mine up to his face as he drives one-handed, sunglasses on, looking devastatingly handsome in his dark suit, black and blue tie. The blue in the tie matches my dress.

He told me I looked gorgeous just before we left as he backed me up and caged me against the wall. He tried to make out with me, but I ducked under his arms and escaped back into the master bedroom closet to choose some earrings and a necklace from the selection of items *Nicola the shopper* sent.

"Chloe?"

I'm abruptly jerked out of my thoughts by Grace. I pull my hand back out of Derek's grip.

"Hm?"

"I was asking you about what happened to your sibling. Is that too painful to talk about?"

"Oh, yes, it's still painful, but... my brother died when we were teens."

"How'd he die?"

"Brain tumor."

"I'm so sorry. That must have been terrible."

"It was," I say hoarsely and clear my throat.

Bryan is a sacred subject to me, so I'm relieved when she changes the subject by asking where I grew up.

"Dayton," I say. "You?" I add belatedly.

"We were all in boarding schools with some exchange programs. Our parents wanted us to be culturally literate, so we've all done multiple continents. Well, Ash kept getting expelled so wound up doing most of his high school years here in Columbus at the public school. If he'd gotten kicked out of that last option, he'd have landed himself in a military school known for being rather... brutal. We all know he was bribing the public school's principal to overlook his shenanigans so that wouldn't happen. Technically we all grew up here between semesters, though. Have you met any of the others? Did Derek give you the lowdown?"

"No and no," I reply.

"So, there's Elijah, our oldest brother. He's married. None of us has any kids yet. Lord help whoever is the first to make our mother a grandmother. She could have a coronary when it happens." She snickers. "Then there *was* Thad born next. He... you don't need the gory details. He was very temperamental. Classic narcissist. Development delays but coddled by his nanny and our mother and then... yeah, no point going into detail. Anyway, then Derek here before Jonah. Jonah's single. Asher is single. Nay is married. Ash and Naomi are fraternal twins, but they don't get along. In fact they pretend one another doesn't exist. Then there's little ole me."

"And you're single, I take it?" I ask, just to keep the conversation going.

"I am," she says wistfully and then lets out a dramatic sigh.

I look down as I feel Derek taking my hand again.

I try to pull it away, but his grip tightens. The vibe he's giving is so sexually charged, it makes the contents of my belly take a dive.

"It'll just be all of you with your parents today then?" I ask over my shoulder. "Or other relatives as well?"

"I don't think Eli's wife will come. They're having ... issues. And she and our mother don't exactly see eye to eye so she avoids Steele family things whenever she can. Nay's husband loves being a Steele spectator and would typically come, but Joshua is a neurosurgeon and she said he had a big surgery, so he won't be there. You'll meet him at the bigger party, I'm sure. And that's where you'll meet the rest of the Steele clan. Cousins. Uncles. Aunts. So forth. There are a lot of us."

Great. All these people today and me the only outsider.

"The big party next weekend will be all sorts of family and friends, a lot of business associates and A-listers. It'll be a bash. We'll get drunk then, too."

Not if I can find my way out of this situation by then.

Grace adds, "By the way, our mom will give you a whole talk about dealing with the media. Any new love interest gets the speech. Don't let it scare you. I mean, it's a serious thing so do take what she says seriously but don't let it scare you. She can be dramatic."

We pull up to an impressive estate behind gates that open with a remote Derek has on his visor. I'm about to ask why there is a valet if there are only immediate family members expected, and those family members have remotes to get in, but don't bother. It's not like I'm truly interested in the family dynamics anyway. My goal is to figure out who to talk to and go from there.

After a valet takes Derek's car, we're greeted by a smiling man opening the front door and guiding us inside. I quickly realize that wealth at this level is not something I'm accustomed to.

"Carson," Derek greets the man who welcomes us in.

"Mr. Steele," the man greets, then his face warms as he looks at Grace. "Miss Steele. Lovely as always."

She kisses his cheek with a flourish.

"This is Chloe Turner," Derek says. "Chloe, my parents' estate manager, Devlin Carson. He oversees a whole lot of day-to-day including all their residential properties."

"Miss Turner," the man of upper sixties, perhaps, greets. He's tall, slender, and wearing a stylish suit. He has a head of thick, white hair but a dark mustache and a mostly white beard. His smile is almost disarming, and I find myself attempting to stammer something polite in return as he takes our coats and hands them off to an older woman in white blouse and black dress pants.

"Are we the first to arrive, Carson?" Grace asks.

"You're the final guests to arrive, Miss Steele. Your family waits in the solarium where brunch will be served. Follow me." He walks ahead of us, leading the way as if Grace and Derek don't know where this solarium is in their parents' house.

This place is practically dripping with money. Beautiful art adorns the cream walls of the foyer. There are gold and red accents everywhere. It feels palatial. And while I can appreciate the incredible architectural details and how the rugs from the front door to where we've walked to alone probably cost more than the house I bought with Adam, it's also a kind of disgusting display of wealth. It

Cheater

feels like we're being led toward royalty as we stroll past expensive sculptures along art-lined halls.

"This is the original homestead," Grace cheerily advises as if it's got a homey feel instead of a museum-feel. "Bought for them by my grandfather when they got married. They have six other residences in various places. Daddy went from rich to disgustingly rich, but wanted to maintain this as home base. We grew up here and this is where we spent most of our time when we weren't in school."

Her explanation seems like she's making sure I know they're too rich for the location. Even though this is the most lavish mansion I've ever been in. Not that there have been many, but I had some wealthy friends growing up.

When I see where we're being led I figure she's likely given me a heads up so that I'll realize who I'm dealing with. I see Grace is studying me as I take it all in. We're in a gorgeous, sundrenched room of people seated at a massive table surrounded by tuxedo-wearing staff.

All eyes swing to us, and everyone rises except for the woman at the foot of the table.

"Hello, family!" Grace greets loudly.

"It's eleven ten," the woman who is obviously Mrs. Steele, at the foot of the table, states.

"Happy Anniversary, Maman!" Grace adds in a fake French accent.

Her mother smiles, but it's tight.

The man at the head of the table steps up and embraces Grace. "Look who's here. Our littlest princess." He kisses her, warmth in his eyes, and then those eyes move to land on me. "Derek. This must be the young lady everyone is buzzing about."

He's inquired about me to Derek without making eye contact with him. An unpleasant shiver runs up my spine for some reason.

"Everyone, this is Chloe Turner," Derek announces. He's still wearing sunglasses, but they've transitioned in this space so they're not quite as dark but still dark enough that I can't see his eyes to try to gauge his actual expression.

My gaze skims across multiple sets of curious eyes. Some of them dark like Derek's, some of them steel gray like Grace.

"Chloe, my father, Michael Steele."

The man reaches out and shakes my hand as the rest of the table other than Derek's mother move to take turns greeting me.

"Lovely to meet you, Chloe," Mr. Steele says, eyes looking me over with scrutiny. He's a handsome man in, I'm guessing, his early sixties. He's tall, looks fit, and is well-dressed in a charcoal three-piece suit with a gray and red tie. He's graying at the temples and has dark hair and dark eyes. A chiseled jawline. Derek takes after him in a big way.

"Thank you," I say.

He kisses my hand and gives me a smile, but it's not disarming at all. Maybe because his eyes are the same as Derek's though nowhere near as warm.

"Elijah, my oldest brother," Derek continues.

And another younger, carbon copy of Michael Steele but with gray eyes steps forward and abruptly pulls me into an embrace.

"All my brothers are flirts," Grace warns, stage-whispering. "Except for Derek."

Elijah Steele lifts me up a few inches and then sets me down with a deep chuckle before his eyes travel my face.

But those eyes also look cold.

"How are you, Chloe?" he asks.

"Nice to meet you," I say, not quite ready to tell anyone how I am.

Elijah's eyes meet Derek's.

"Derek."

"Eli."

Elijah looks him over with a slight frown. "We must talk."

"Mm hm," Derek mutters.

Cheater

My eyes bounce between them, but Grace breaks awkward silence by announcing, "This is Jonah."

Eli moves out of the way.

My gaze moves to the next Steele sibling. Another dark-haired, suited, tall and incredibly handsome man. He and Derek look a lot alike, other than the eyes. Jonah's are the same as Grace's. He has shorter hair than Derek.

"Chloe." Jonah hugs me quick and steps back. Instead of cold, his gaze and his demeanor seem indifferent.

"And Asher," Derek gestures to the next guy.

He's the only one not wearing a suit. The only blond man of the bunch. He's in jeans, a black T-shirt, and motorcycle boots. He's ripped with tattoo-covered muscles.

"Hey," he says, and *this* Steele sibling's eyes and demeanor aren't cold or indifferent. They're warm and traveling the length of me as he takes my hand into both of his. "Nice one, Derek." His eyes point at my boobs as he presses his mouth to the top of my hand.

"Hello," I answer softly, feeling uncomfortable.

Derek growls low in his throat. I reflexively pull my hand back for some reason.

The energy noticeably shifts in the vast solarium, which is dominated by the large table and also dripping with flowers and other plants in a riot of colors, coming down from a variety of hanging pots.

"Clearly one of the flirtiest of the flirters," I try.

Everyone laughs except Derek and his mother, who I can see is watching me with scrutiny. There are also two tuxedoed men by the exit who don't react, looking well-versed in blending into the surroundings. As this thought occurs to me, I realize I've just tried to manage the mood of the room, which is neither my responsibility nor my place. But it's what I often do when there's tension.

"I'm Naomi," A dark-haired beauty with dark brown eyes greets, coming up behind Ash and hugging me. "So good to meet you!" she gushes.

"Hi Naomi," I say, patting her back.

As soon as she releases me, Derek nabs my hand, and we walk to the opposite end of the table.

His mother stands.

Naomi didn't greet Derek. Most of them didn't.

"Baby, my mother, Shannon Steele."

His mother was a big name in modeling and was also in a couple of older sitcoms I've seen. I might have been a little starstruck under different, more normal circumstances. She's blonde, she's still model thin, and has those striking gray eyes half of her children have. Grace looks a lot like her.

She has to be in her late fifties at minimum judging by the fact she's been married for forty years, but she looks like she's ten or fifteen years younger than that. She's had work done on her face, the lip filler is evident, but whoever did it did a good job of it. Her neck and décolleté are both as line-free as her face. She has thick blonde hair that falls to her shoulders in beautiful curls, and she's dressed in a red blazer and full, long red skirt. She has red gemstones in her lobes, at her throat and on one of her wrists.

She takes my hand daintily and gives me a sort of strange, pursed lip nod as her eyes bounce from me to her son.

"Derek, this is a surprise." She tips her head to the side.

There's a beat of silence.

"Happy Anniversary, mother," he says and kisses her proffered cheek. "Happy Anniversary, Dad," he tacks on without making eye contact with his father who is watching us from the other end of the long table with a cold expression.

"This must be a very special young lady to merit an invitation to this family brunch for our Ruby anniversary," Shannon Steele says.

"Very special," Derek replies in a husky tone, standing directly behind me, very close to my ear.

"Yes, rubies. Look at all the rubies!" Grace exclaims, leaning over and touching the gem on one of her mother's ears. "Happy ruby anniversary, Mumsy and Daddy."

Cheater

"Thanks, littlest princess," Mr. Steele says. "Why don't we sit down. Now we can begin."

The way he says it seems like what he really means is 'get it over with'.

I'm not feeling welcome. I'm feeling scrutinized. And there's a strange energy in the room that has me feeling like I'm surrounded by a combination of predators and spectators.

Derek sits on one side of his mother. Grace sits on the other side. I'm beside Derek with Naomi on my other side and Jonah across from me.

This is a very good-looking family. Asher is the only casual one as the other men are all in suits. Naomi isn't as glammed up as Grace and their mom, but definitely exudes late twenty-something rich woman in her dark conservative navy-blue dress with no embellishment other than an expensive set of wedding rings. She's polished with beautiful skin and glossy hair.

I'm feeling anxious. The vibe isn't happy or positive. It's feeling like a very stuffy occasion with a bunch of people who seem like they're either unhappy to be here or faking that they're not unhappy.

"So, how did you two meet?" Naomi asks me.

Derek answers, "I heard her voice in one of my clubs, watched her on camera all evening, and decided I had to have her. I had to make a few moves and maneuver her fiancé out of the way but now that's done, so we're getting married."

Even the staff react this time. I stare at him with shock. I'm speechless. It seems that so is everyone else.

So, I won't have to tell anyone else here what he's done to me. I can tell by their expressions that Grace hasn't spilled the beans. It's as if Derek has pulled the rug out from under me.

"You're... engaged?" Naomi asks, aghast.

"Not officially. The ex-fiancé is a paraplegic so there needs to be a suitable timeframe before our destination wedding for the sake of Chloe's reputation. We'll figure that out and let everyone know."

All eyes are on me.

"Are you...serious?" Naomi gasps.

"When am I not serious, Nay?" Derek says calmly as plates are put down in front of everyone.

Each plate is identical. Salad is arranged in an impressive floral motif with the vegetables fanned out in flower petal shapes, the center circle a mini quiche. Salad greens make up the stem and leaves.

I'd be impressed under normal circumstances, take a picture, and declare it too pretty to eat before eating it.

"Mimosa? Ceasar? Juice? Coffee? Tea? Something else?" A server asks.

"Mimosa and a Caesar and a coffee," Grace replies, throwing her napkin across her lap.

"Coffee," Derek states.

I clear my throat. "Orange juice, please? Thank you very much."

I feel all eyes on me still.

I unfold my red napkin and lay it across my lap.

"Can we back up to what Derek said?" Naomi asks.

Derek lifts the small quiche with his fingers and pops it into his mouth.

I take in everyone's expressions. They all appear wowed. Except Derek's father. He's staring at Derek.

When my eyes land on Derek's mother, she's getting a new glass of orange juice. Or more likely a mimosa, based on what Derek and Grace said earlier today.

"Derek went after what he wanted," Grace says. "Poor girl is shellshocked. He's been pretty direct about it with me."

My heart skips a beat. Is this my opening? Do I lay it all out here and ask for help?

Elijah and Asher exchange looks. Jonah looks like he's assessing Derek. Naomi's eyes are on me, and I see concern. Could she be a potential ally? I make a point of giving her a poignant look. Derek's mother is sipping her drink, eyeing me with an expression I can't

Cheater

translate. Nobody says anything, so I look back at Derek, who's casually eating his salad.

"How are you doing?" Naomi asks me, concern etched into her features.

"Not so good, to be honest," I state, my pulse racing. Hope lifting.

"When a Steele man knows what he wants, he knows," Mr. Steele says, looking at his phone. "Gotta take this. Just a minute." He steps away.

And I'm thrown. Because *what?*

"Michael swooped in and upended my life, too," Mrs. Steele says, not making eye contact with me. "And look at me now." She looks sour as she takes another sip.

I blink a few times in surprise. Surely not the same way as Derek swooped in with me. Right? I'm not sure I should ask. Being swept off your feet is one thing. Being blackmailed is quite another.

"Well, I for one, am happy for Derek and Chloe. I've never seen Derek this happy. You guys will see. Cheers to Chloe." She lifts her glass. Everyone else does the same and they all drink. I don't. I stare at Naomi and hope she sees that I need help.

Because no. Don't drink to me. Do they understand the gravity here?

"So Nay, no Josh?" Grace continues, doing it loudly, obviously looking to change the subject by engaging her sister in conversation.

"He's still in surgery, I think. This one is a long one," Naomi tells her, then has a bite of salad.

I swallow down a lump of stress as I survey the table unhappy that Grace has distracted Naomi who is no longer focused on me and my wellbeing.

Asher and Jonah are whispering something to one another and I'm wondering if it's about Derek. About rescuing me.

I see Ash snicker before he covers his mouth to say something to Eli, who scoffs. Okay, not likely they're trying to figure out how to help me. And whatever they're talking about, the way they're doing it is awfully rude.

This certainly doesn't feel like a happy family occasion.

A few moments later, Derek's father returns with an apology and five seconds after that, my untouched salad is whisked away and replaced with salmon benedict on beautiful red plates with gold rims. And it's presented just as prettily as the last course.

Derek immediately digs in, as does Jonah. Grace looks at the plate, curls her lip, and then sips her mimosa. Naomi sips her Caesar. Their mother is sipping from her glass, too.

Elijah is drumming his fingers. Jonah's now tapping away on his phone. If I'm not mistaken, Ash has been waiting for my eyes to hit him so he can try eye-fucking me.

Seeing the expression on his face, I look away, but my eyes catch Derek's jaw flexing. It seems Derek noticed the same moment as I did because he rips his sunglasses off, leans forward, and growls, "Get your own," before he grabs the leg of my chair and pulls, making a terrible noise as it's dragged a few inches, so I'm plastered to his side.

His arm wraps around me.

"Holy cow," I mutter, aghast.

Asher throws his head back and laughs. "Afraid I'll steal her?"

"I've already stolen her. Get your own, Ash."

"Maybe I'll steal yours." He shrugs. "She doesn't look too happy to be here with you."

Derek throws his head back and laughs before he says, "Try it. I dare you."

"He laughs now, too?" Naomi asks.

"Right?" Grace pipes up.

"Enough," Mr. Steele snaps.

Derek leans forward aggressively. "Don't want to ruin your brunch, Mom, by smashing your youngest son's face off the table and breaking his nose, but he's on notice."

"Please, son," Mr. Steele orders. "I have something to tell everyone."

Derek leans back in his seat, but his jaw keeps flexing. Asher's expression reads like he thinks it's hilarious.

Cheater

The server who brought my last drink comes again with a tray of drinks.

"You ready to switch to mimosas?" Grace whispers to me.

Mr. Steele says, "Let's get drinks and then I'll tell you all what I have to share."

"Don't look so worried, Chloe," Grace advises, "Ash's favorite pastime is to wind people up. He likes to make Mom and Dad have booze for breakfast."

Ash snorts.

Mr. Steele puts in, "All seven of my children drive me to drink."

"Six now," Mrs. Steele says simply, then downs the rest of her beverage.

Ouch.

The server hesitates. "Miss Turner, mimosa? Something else?"

"I'm fine. I don't need anything." I gesture to my still half-full orange juice glass. "Thank you very much."

I don't need my mind muddled more than it already is.

"So, while we wait for everyone to be served their beverages, why don't you tell us about you, Chloe? What do you do for a living?" Derek's father asks as the server moves around the table, delivering new drinks to some while clearing empty glasses away.

"I'm in marketing," I say.

"Which company do you work for?"

"Interplay Growth Solutions."

"Never heard of it," he states, and slices into his poached egg.

"It's a boutique firm," Derek pipes up. "Small but profitable. I'm in the midst of buying it for her."

"I'll quit if you do," I warn, not even trying to hide how I feel about that.

His father looks thoughtful. But he looks at me instead of Derek. "Couldn't we use her in one of our firms? We can always use marketing talent."

"She's *not* working for you," Derek states, eyes pointing at his plate as he forks up another bite of his sauced salmon, then looks at me. "It's already happening, baby. Eat some food. Don't you like salmon?"

I'm completely out of my element here. I don't want to ruin a family celebration, but I can't wrap my mind around the dysfunction here.

Derek and his father haven't made eye contact. His mother is beautiful, but looks surly and tipsy.

Naomi seems pretty normal. I don't know what to make of Jonah. Grace so far has always seemed super bubbly. But I don't know what to make of her, truly, because she knows what Derek's doing with me and isn't doing anything about it.

Elijah seems cold and calculating, but that might be that I think that because of the things I've read about him being rather shady in his business pursuits and in the revenge department. He really hasn't said or done much, but he's got a dark and almost villainy presence.

Asher is a shit stirrer and clearly by the fact that he's in jeans coupled with what Grace said about his youth, a rebellious guy.

I'm suddenly curious about the departed Thaddeus and how he'd factor into this strange vibe here. And maybe his absence is part of the odd dynamic today. They're missing a member of the family and even if everyone didn't get along with him, they must feel the absence anyway.

What's Christmas morning like with this bunch? Were things ever normal? Derek has mental health issues, for certain, but are the others well-adjusted?

"So, my small surprise," Mr. Steele announces, "I've brought in an officiant to see your mother and I renew our vows. The one you liked from that wedding we attended last month, Shan. I was just on the phone with him; he'll be here in twenty minutes."

Mrs. Steele's face lights up. "Oh Michael."

He smiles at her. And the ice in his gaze has melted. So has hers.

Conversation resumes as Naomi, Grace, and Mrs. Steele get into details about the upcoming party. Mrs. Steele lauds Grace, who has

Cheater

helped plan it down to the last detail with as many ruby red touches as possible.

I push my food around with my fork while they name drop local A-listers who are coming, including Michael's old college roommate, a Hollywood director who's coming with his third wife, an A-list actress who's a third of his age.

The scandal of this keeps the conversation going for a while, and I note Derek doesn't participate in any of the main conversations and while his brothers occasionally pull one another into mini side discussions, none of them do so with Derek.

Naomi asks me a few more questions about my job, about my family, and I politely tell her my mom is a CPA, my father is an oral surgeon. I answer when asked where I went to school. But I'm feeling like I'm not only out of my element but also like a huge weight is on me. I'm not myself. I feel unpoised, like I'm not well-spoken. I'm taking in this strange atmosphere while they've all ignored the blatant hints that I'm here against my will. While they pretend not to notice my distress.

Are these people not going to do anything about the fact that he's made it clear he's forcing me to be here with him? How can they be so lax about it? My heart is beating too fast. I feel like I can't get a deep enough breath. Maybe they don't realize how bad it really is. Maybe they think he was making a joke about maneuvering me here. Maybe my reaction to Naomi's questions wasn't severe enough.

Derek again tries to coax me to eat while showering me with public displays of affection. Temple kisses, touching my hair while his eyes travel my face, fingertips massaging the back of my neck or caressing my shoulder. I'm wincing at his touch, trying to shrink into myself. And they're all ignoring it.

His mother abruptly stands.

"We'd like the final course in ten minutes, Carson. Mimosas in my morning room now, please. I'd like a word with Cleo."

"Yes, Mrs. Steele," Carson states, magically appearing in the doorway.

Mrs. Steele grabs her mimosa, the fourth since I've arrived, and she wobbles a little as she backs up, then smooths out her flamboyant, full gauzy red skirt. I woodenly rise.

"Chloe. And Grace, too?" Grace asks.

"Grace, too. And Naynay," Mrs. Steele sings out and I nab my little handbag.

"You don't need that," Derek says, snatching it from my hand and placing it back on the table, making his point while sliding his glasses down his nose just enough to look me in the eyes with warning.

I fire back a dirty look, which makes him smile, wide. And this makes me stumble clumsily, but I manage to steady myself before landing flat on my butt. I follow his mom and sisters out of the room, back the way we came in, then down a different hall that takes us deeper into the cavernous house until we're in a beautiful teal and champagne space filled with art and comfortable furniture.

Mrs. Steele sits on one of four wingback chairs in a conversation cluster. We all take one. Grace and Naomi flank her so I'm directly across, and wondering if I'm about to be cross-examined. Maybe I'm about to get some help with Derek.

Shannon Steele eyes me with concern and hope flares until she speaks, saying, "If you're marrying into this family, there are things you need to know about, Cleo."

Carson sets an ornate silver tray with four mimosas and a large cranberry glass jug containing at least one, if not two more rounds of the same in it on the low table between us.

"Thank you, Carson!" she exclaims like she's dying of thirst and he's a savior.

Her eyes pin me shrewdly and I know instantly that this is the media speech Grace forewarned about instead of concern for the fact it's been made clear I've been blackmailed into my current situation with Derek.

"Chloe," I correct. "And I have no plans to marry into this family, Mrs. Steele. If I wasn't clear enough earlier, I'm not here willingly.

Cheater

Derek has threatened me and held things over my head to get me where I am."

Grace's back straightens. She and Naomi exchange alarmed glances.

Mrs. Steele sips her beverage. "My apologies, Chloe. You remind me of my cousin Cleo. First of all, we must be extremely careful about the press and how we handle them. We'll have you do an onboarding session with our head of PR. If the press approaches you before then, please don't engage. Tell them 'no comment'."

I blink a couple of times, absorbing how she just glazed over what I've said.

She goes on. "You'll be photographed. Often. They look for unflattering photo ops considering you'll be dating one of the coveted Steele bachelors, so if you do go out in public in sweats with a messy bun, expect to see it plastered all over social media. Also, everything you say, everything you do reflects on not just you but on us as well. Treat people well everywhere. Tip generously. Use table manners without fail. It won't matter if you get shitty service, you'll be judged on how you react to it. That server won't be. You will be. So please don't complain about poor service. Be mindful of your appearance at all times so you don't wind up photographed by a bunch of paps who will glory in catching spinach in your teeth. You'll get a full briefing as soon as my assistant can arrange it. Sometime this week. What religion are you? Tell me about your parents, please."

I shake my head profusely. "Mrs. Steele, I'm afraid I don't want anything to do with any of this. I'm only here because your son is–"

"Persistent, yes. I'm aware of how he can get when he gets his mind set on something. Like his father, there's no dissuading him. We're non-active, but if you don't object, I'd prefer some sort of Christian denomination church. What church do your parents attend? Did you say they live in Ohio?"

I reach for a mimosa and take a healthy sip. Because I need it with what I'm about to say.

The Steele sisters are saying nothing, but they both appear fascinated by this conversation.

"Please forgive me if this sounds rude, but I'm not willing to discuss a church wedding because I'm not marrying your son. He's not just being persistent. He's bulldozed my entire life. He's manipulated me into his apartment and his bed while making threats about bad things happening to people I care about if I refuse or disappoint him. He... I'm afraid he might need medical intervention. He's been spying on me, stalking me."

"So much like his father," she mutters. "Though neither of them would ever admit how alike they are. Marcie?" she bellows abruptly, startling me.

The maid who took our coats earlier appears. "Yes, Mrs. Steele?"

"Please fetch me a bottle of champagne, will you?"

"Yes, ma'am."

Marcie slips out.

"We have mimosas already, mother," Naomi says, sipping hers.

"They're weak. Too much orange juice, not enough champagne."

It's barely noon! And she's just glossed over everything I've just said to her.

I look at Naomi and shoot my shot.

"If multiple people sign him in for psychiatric observation, it could be helpful. He needs help."

Naomi's response is to drink from her mimosa, but her eyes don't leave mine.

What is she trying to communicate?

Grace puts her hand on my knee, so I turn toward her.

"Chloe," she says gently, "Derek is unique. He doesn't process things the same way as the average person. He's not easily dissuaded. With Derek, you have to finesse things to get him to see them your way. If you also tweak your expectations you'll–"

I lean forward. "He should be put in jail for the things he's done!"

My eyes dart to Shannon Steele. "I'm sorry, Mrs. Steele. I don't mean to hamper your anniversary celebration but real talk here,

Cheater

Derek blackmailed me in some very not-nice ways. I don't need a briefing on how to deal with the press or the public. I need you people to get him some help. He needs to be admitted for psychiatric evaluation. I won't have to press charges if you help me handle things in a way that I know I'll be safe. That the people I care about will be safe. That your son won't be a danger to anybody."

Marcie is back with a bucket holding a bottle of champagne and a male server follows with a tray of clean glasses.

"Put it all down," Mrs. Steele says, irritated. "We've got this."

They leave us with the table now quite crowded. Shannon tops off each of our glasses with champagne, mine overflowing until it spills on the beautiful rug that likely costs more than my Cherokee.

I gasp.

"Oh, whoops," Derek's mother says with a lopsided grin. "Marcie!"

Staff descend to deal with the rug.

"We should get back, shouldn't we?" Naomi asks.

"I'll meet you all there," Mrs. Steele says. "Chloe and I can talk about all this later. For now, I must powder my nose."

She disappears into a room adjoining the room we're in.

I'm standing out of the way of the puddle on the rug and Grace links arms with me and moves us out of the room.

I'm reeling. They're all in denial. Or they don't care.

"Grace," I whisper. "What the fuck?"

She shakes her head. "I can't get involved in that way. But I'm here if you want to talk. I can give you pointers for dealing with him."

I look over my shoulder.

Naomi shakes her head. She heard.

I stop and look at them both beseechingly. "He's making threats. He's threatening to harm people I care about if I don't do what he wants me to do. He's had me followed. Slipped into my bedroom while I was asleep and I'm sure I don't need to spell out what he did when he got in there. He's got cameras in my house. He had some guy hold me and my fiancé at gunpoint so my fiancé and I couldn't have sex. Is he capable of doing violent things? Seriously? I need to know. Because I think he is."

"Yeah," Naomi says as if the word *yeah* is an understatement.

My heart plummets.

"I need help," I whisper.

"Girlfriend," Grace says, "I know this sounds odd, but you could be really good for him."

"What?"

Grace shrugs. "He's aloof. He's unemotional. He's never displayed an interest in love or affection. He's like a different person with you. I can't get over the smiles. The laughing."

"He's probably had a psychotic break," I volley. "I don't want this."

Neither say anything. My face flames and I'm so angry I could spit.

"If you don't help me, you're both aiding and abetting," I snap.

Grace sighs. "It's not like he's not a catch. He's my brother and even I can see it. And believe me, many women would love to be in your place."

"I..." I start.

"Use your hold over him to your advantage," Naomi suggests.

"An attractive, rich, handsome husband who wants to dote on you? Why wouldn't you?" Grace shrugs.

"She's right. Things could be much worse," Naomi offers. "I can't do anything to help."

And I'm stunned at their reaction.

"You'd be lucky to wind up with any of our living brothers," Grace goes on, "They're good-looking men of means who will go to extremes to provide for and protect those they care about. But yeah, Derek is unusual, dangerous, but he's also absolutely smitten with you."

"For how long though? If I don't get out of this, do I end up like one of your brother Thad's wives? Did they ask you for help and you ignore them, too?"

Cheater

The Steele sisters exchange alarmed glances. We're back to the entrance to the solarium, so I stop talking. But I wasn't exactly whispering so might have been heard. But good! Someone needs to pay attention here. Intervene.

"I wouldn't wish Thad on anyone," Naomi says softly. "He was disturbed. As for Derek, you could be good for him. I'm sure I speak for all my siblings when I say that we'll all be hopeful that this works out well."

"Hopeful?" I ask.

"Derek's been through a lot," Naomi elaborates. "Him wanting to get married, bringing you here? That's the first mentally healthy sign he's shown anyone in years."

I give my head a shake. "It's healthy to blackmail a woman into sex? To destroy her relationship? He's threatened people I care about. If you're all going to talk this over after this, please talk about getting him some help so I can get away from him before he does more damage."

"We're allies, Chloe," Naomi says, "But there are rules in this family. Some are unwritten but might as well be carved in stone. And we all know them. We can give you advice, pointers for being part of this family, but we can't go against Derek on this. Anyone getting involved by going against what he wants? No. Not a good idea." Naomi holds the door and gestures for me to go ahead.

The fact that they refuse to get involved sets off major alarms about being afraid of him retaliating.

I'm thinking I should walk out. I should walk out of here and go straight to the police, but I see that Derek is looking over his shoulder at me. And fear grips me at the notion of what he might do if I do that, so I walk back to him. As soon as we sit, his mom comes in and sits down. As soon as her behind is in her chair, servers move in and begin to serve everyone small plate towers with three levels of tarts and chocolate-dipped fruit.

Derek puts his arm around me and kisses the side of my head, but whispers, "Naughty bunny." He tsks.

I look around and see all the men at the table staring at us. So are the servers. They've all heard some or all of what I've said.

But isn't anyone going to do anything about this?

I make eye contact with several of them. The servers look away. The only Steeles to look away are the two young females. But not their mother. Her gray eyes are like stone.

I look at Derek's father who looks straight through me. His expression is unreadable. I'm being treated as insignificant.

Clearly, I'm on my own.

Coffee is served.

So is more booze.

∞

I finish a whole mimosa. As quickly as Shannon Steele does. And it tastes too good for the time of day and the predicament I'm in so I know getting *snockered*, as Grace put it, wouldn't be a good idea. I decline the offer of another mimosa and switch to coffee.

Grace and Naomi are giggling now, Naomi sitting in Jonah's seat and Jonah and Ash are outside talking to their father. Eli slipped out to make a phone call.

Derek holds a chocolate dipped piece of melon in front of my lips with his fingers.

I fail at leveling him with a glare. I ignore the dangling fruit and excuse myself, asking for the nearest powder room.

Carson walks me there himself.

"I'm sure you heard. I could really use some help," I whisper to him before I step into the bathroom.

He looks into my eyes. "I've been a loyal member of the Steele family's team for sixteen years, Miss Turner."

"Right," I mutter. "If anything bad happens to me, it's on all of you."

He says nothing, but his expression changes. We stare at one

Cheater

another for a moment, and it seems like he's about to say something, so I wait. His expression blanks, so it's obvious he's made his decision.

I go into the bathroom and lock the door, blowing out an exasperated huff.

I stare at my flushed reflection in the mirror, feeling frustration bubble in my blood.

Derek acted like I shouldn't dare to *out* him to his family, but in truth, it doesn't matter because he outed himself and they don't seem to care.

I can't wrap my head around this dysfunction. My family isn't perfect. Far from it. My parents are barely cognizant of my existence. But this? This is like being in an alternate universe where filthy-rich elitist people only care about themselves.

Talk about a strange family...

Thad – the now dead one with two dead wives. Derek – the psychotic stalker. Talk of Elijah and Jonah being tied to organized crime. Mr. Steele's political connections. Being told Steele family members don't ever get divorced, so the dead brother had two dead wives. The mysteriously absent wife of Elijah. Is she okay?

Women survive in this environment by getting drunk at brunch.

I need to get out of here. My thoughts are all over the map. I need to take my fate into my own hands here.

Maybe I need to walk out of here and take my chances.

When I exit the powder room, Derek is waiting for me.

Damn it!

"We're going outside for the vow renewal and then we're leaving. Too bad we didn't go get a marriage license on Friday. We could've done it here today." He hands me my handbag.

I stare at him with disgust. "This isn't funny. None of it."

"I'm not telling you a joke, Chloe," he says, smiling wider.

"I've just blasted everyone in earshot about you and nobody's doing anything about it."

"I'm aware," he says.

"I'm not attending your parents' vow renewal," I tell him and attempt to change directions so I can try to find my way out.

My back is suddenly touching the wall in a move that has me pinned by his hips as he rips his sunglasses off his face. He crowds me, caging me with both hands pressed against the wall on either side of my face. He looks down at me with a dark expression. "Yes, you are. And then we're leaving. You've already tested me today with how fucking naughty you're being. Don't push me past the point of decorum."

"Meaning?" I demand.

He smiles. "You keep nudging, Chloe. Are you not concerned that one of these days you could send me over the brink."

"Meaning?"

"You don't want to find out."

"So you keep saying," I mutter, but his tongue is abruptly in my mouth, hands weaving into my hair, making my knees go to jelly.

Damn it, why is he such a good kisser?

He abruptly pulls back, tugs my hand, and now we're on the move.

Frustration floods my even-more-disjointed system as I'm led through the maze of hallways outside to where everyone is gathered in a gazebo by a massive swimming pool. The red and white rose-covered gazebo is breathtaking. Derek's mother is beaming with joy. Once we climb the two steps, Grace grabs Derek's free hand and Jonah reaches for mine and me, along with the Steele family, surround Michael, Shannon, and the officiant.

And it's like none of us are even here as Michael and Shannon Steele renew their vows. They recite them staring at one another with so much emotion in their eyes it's as if they're alone and ready to tear one another's clothes off. It's like they're getting married for the first time and it's so vividly emotional, I forget my predicament for a

Cheater

couple of minutes, unaware until they're finished kissing that Derek is holding my hand to his mouth, kissing it, watching me have the reaction as if I've watched a beautiful romantic movie.

While I shake off the stupor, Carson appears with a tray of champagne flutes.

∞

The women seem to be giving me a wide berth, likely trying to avoid me asking for help again. Not that I'm about to. They've made themselves clear and this moment is about the renewal of vows between two people who've chosen to spend their life together, as messed up as the fruits of their union might seem to my eyes.

"Time to go," Derek whispers in my ear before announcing it for all the other ears around. He kisses his mother on the cheek, and she looks at me with a strange look in her eyes as she reaches for my hand.

I hesitantly accept it. She gives me an almost maternal squeeze and smile.

"It was lovely having you here for such a special family moment, Chloe. We'll talk. I'll set up your press preparation appointment and then we'll discuss your wedding."

"Don't bother," Derek tells her. "I'll take care of that. All of that."

"But…" His mother starts but then lets it hang, looking at him strangely.

His father leans in and kisses my cheek. "Lovely to meet you, Chloe. See you both on Saturday night." He stares at Derek and their eyes meet. "Please allow your mother to help," he requests.

Derek's eyes skim his father's face and then settle on his mother's hopeful one.

"Okay," he concedes.

I stare blankly for a second, and then decide to shoot my shot one more time. "Happy Anniversary. Thank you for your hospitality today, but I'm going to do my absolute best to not be there next week. I really think you all need to sign Derek in for psychiatric help. Since

Derek's sisters and mother didn't listen to my pleas, I hope you will." I eye Derek's father who is staring at me with an unreadable expression. "I'm here under duress. He's made threats and has been relentlessly stalking me and derailing my life while manipulating me."

"We'll see you all Saturday," Derek says casually, grabbing my hand.

I look over my shoulder as he leads me away and they all watch. Saying nothing.

Eli sips his champagne.

Ash looks like he finds this funny.

Jonah, though, looks at me with concern.

Our eyes connect.

"Please," I mouth.

Derek tugs my hand a little more forcefully as Jonah jerks his chin in acknowledgement.

"Naughty girls get punishments, Chloe," Derek says into my hair and picks up his pace.

I burst into tears and am audibly sobbing by the time we get to his car.

The valet hands him keys and looks at me with concern.

"Help?" I ask the valet.

"Are you okay?" he asks.

Derek crowds the valet with an intimidating expression. The young guy swallows and looks away.

"Hold up," I hear from behind us.

I turn.

It's Jonah.

Thank God. Someone.

"A minute, Derek?"

Derek opens my door and ushers me inside before stepping to the side with his brother.

They walk about ten or fifteen paces, so I can't hear them. Derek puts his hand on Jonah's shoulder and speaks close to him.

Elijah joins their huddle and hope flares.

Cheater

Maybe these two are going to talk sense into him.

Or subdue him until the men with the white coats arrive?

Derek's father joins the huddle, as does Ash.

I swallow and watch as they all speak to one another.

Derek's father claps Derek on the shoulder and says something and I watch Derek's expression drop.

Hope sparks in my belly.

But then Derek is coming toward me again. He gets into the driver's side and starts his SUV.

Confused, I look toward his dad and brothers, but they're all walking back to the house together.

I reach for the door handle, ready to jump out, but the locks engage, and Derek angrily squeals away from the curb.

He's pissed off.

And I don't know what this means for me.

36

Derek

After I'm off the property, I reach for Chloe's hand.

"I regret taking you there. I'm sorry if all of that upset you." I lift her hand and bring it to my lips, kissing her knuckles twice, then holding her hand against my cheek.

She rubs her lips together, then her chest falls with a big exhale. She uses her free hand to dash tears away from her cheeks.

"I don't apologize, Chloe. I don't feel remorse, typically. But I do right now. I'm sorry that stressed you out. That you felt treated as insignificant."

"That stressed me out?" she asks.

"You looked at most of the members of my family like they were circus sideshow exhibits. You didn't eat. You got upset and none of them comforted you."

She scoffs, looking astounded. "*You* stress me out. Your family just shocked me because they're not going to do anything about what you're doing to me. I can't wrap my mind around that. And I've wanted to run for the exit since I found out you knew about the hall pass."

She's holding that against me. That still stands out for her. She takes deceit very personally.

"Clearly your relationship with them is weird. But I'd think they'd care enough to do something."

"My relationship with my family might not be typical, but today was the most normal family meal I've been to in years with them."

"Huh?"

She looks baffled.

"Let's forget about all that for now. I've been anxious to take you where we're going for your surprise, so we'll deal with all that later."

"What did they say to you?" she asks. "Just now?"

"Jonah told me you seem very upset. As if I'm unable to read that myself. Asked me what I intend to do about it. I told him I'm working on fixing that. Told him why I want you and how I intend to make you fall in love with me."

She scoffs. "And that satisfied him?"

"Yup. The rest came over to take my pulse on this. I advised that I'm well aware of what I'm doing and that I have the situation in hand. Asher wanted me to know he was just razzing me, that he wasn't being serious by flirting with you."

"You have the situation in hand? Meaning?"

"Meaning you're not about to run to the press or the authorities about me. That you're about to become my wife and that I know you'll come around."

"And they're... they're okay with that ridiculous idea? All they care about is that I don't go to the press?"

"It's not ridiculous. Is it ridiculous to want to spend my life with you? Making you happy?"

She stares at me instead of answering.

"My father doesn't want bad press, Chloe. He also doesn't want anything to upset my mother. Those are his priorities. He's still steamed that people are talking about Thad. He wants Steele family business kept within the family and Thad is the primary reason anyone has anything to say about us. He also wanted to remind me that Steeles don't divorce. As if I could forget."

"What happens if they do?" I ask.

"They just don't."

"Yet he felt the need to remind you of this fact?"

Cheater

"He has that conversation with anyone starting to look like they're getting serious about somebody. My father drilled into us from a young age that if we wanted to let someone into the family circle, give them the Steele name and access to the family behind closed doors, we had to be sure they'd never want out. Too much happening to have a pile of exes out there, outside the damage control perimeter that's carefully managed by his team. He wanted to make sure I know that if I do this with you, it's a lifetime commitment, so I advised I'm fully prepared for that."

"Wow," she whispers incredulously.

"He drilled it into us to only bring in people we trust enough to become permanent family fixtures. Someone willing to make lifelong commitment. You're not the only person planning to tie the knot just once. We were all raised to take marriage as seriously as a blood oath."

"Not for true love and for better or for worse, to avoid bad press and pissing off your father?"

I shake my head. "You're not a whim to me. I'm 100% serious. I've been telling you that. My father is putting pressure on Eli to fix the problems in his marriage, too."

"But left your other brother to his own devices so each of his wives were found dead? Because he wasn't allowed to get a divorce? Because he was worried about getting written out of your father's will?"

"Possibly. Most don't think he killed both of them. Just the second one. First one died in an accident and Thad was devastated. Anyway... I'm not my brother."

"Who killed your brother? Was it someone in your family?"

I shake my head. "Some of us might not have shed any tears over the loss of Thaddeus, but we wouldn't gun down a Steele family member. It was a guy who was obsessed with a girl who had him in the friend zone. Jonah's ex-girlfriend, long story, but the shooter shot Thad and Jonah. Jonah survived."

"I couldn't find much about it in the papers," she says.

"Because my father doesn't like getting press he can't control or edit before it goes to print. Shit got out before he could control it or none of it would've been publicized."

She's silent for a few minutes, then she says, "What would happen to me if I did go to the press?"

"You won't go to the press, Chloe. You know better."

"Derek, I wanna be real with you."

"Haven't you been real all along?" I ask.

"Yes... but, I mean, I want you to take what I'm saying seriously."

"I take everything you say seriously. Say what you wanna say."

"I really think you need some help. I'm not being funny here. Some real help."

She waits for my reaction. When she doesn't get one, she continues. "How about this? If you agree to sign yourself in and get a psychiatric evaluation, I'll agree to go on a date with you after you've had some counseling. Maybe we can-"

"Nice try, but been there, done that and it's why I am who I am today."

"Meaning?"

"You wanna delve deep into me? Figure me out? You can have that, all of it, when you're in this relationship *with* me and we're in a safe place. Until then, I'd rather not open that vault."

She's frowning.

I continue, "But I believe you when you say you *think* I need help. What will help me is achieving my goal with you. It's you and me, baby." I kiss her hand again.

She snatches it away and folds her arms across her chest. "If you think I'm marrying you, you're in for a rude awakening."

"If you aren't my good girl, Chloe, you're in for some sad realizations."

"And what are those?" she snaps.

"The realization that I'm not paying lip service here. I get what I want. I want you. And while I don't want to upset you or make you sad, I'll do whatever I need to do to make my point crystal clear to you. I've gone easy on you the past few days giving you a chance to acclimate, but believe this. You *will* marry me. You won't divorce me. I'll work at this as long as I need to in order to get to my end goal."

"So, you're continuing to threaten me?"

I sigh.

"What's the threat exactly, Derek? What are you threatening to do? You make a lot of threats. A lot of undefined ones. I don't actually know what's at stake right now."

"Right now, I want to focus on your surprise. I'm so excited about your surprise, I might let you away with the stunt you pulled with my family. But believe me, you don't want to test me by speaking to anyone outside my family with your 'he needs help' plea."

She lets out a long sigh and rubs her eyes. "Where are you taking me right now?"

"If I revealed that, it would ruin the surprise."

"I don't want it. And you're deflecting."

"Yeah, Chloe. You do want *this* surprise. We'll be there in less than half an hour."

She stares out the window. Sulking.

∞

I stop my SUV and look at my girl who's staring straight ahead through the gates. She hasn't said a word in thirty minutes. She's been pissed off. Fidgety. Huffing.

Now, she's altogether different. She's wide-eyed. Confused.

The house sits far beyond the tall, black gates with a long, black asphalt driveway that cuts through the lush lawn with perfect diagonal lawnmower marks. Built in 1927, the gray stone-wrapped house with four front dormers and a new gray shingled roof has a wide front porch supported by several fieldstone- covered pillars. The porch wraps around the house on the left side, going back to the large yard. I know from the photos it wraps all the way around the back of the house, stopping just before the extension that makes up a garage and further living space done in white wood siding. That extension was put on in the late seventies, consisting of living space plus a three-car garage. It's got a tall widow's walk directly behind the garages where the extension goes from utility space to more living space.

Mature trees dot the large front lawn, and the back yard is treed too, including several fruit trees and a big, old oak with a massive two-storey treehouse in it, a ladder leading up and a curved slide leading down into a sandbox. I'm guessing that's why the widow's walk was put in – direct view to the treehouse and kids playing in it.

"Wh-what are we doing here?" she asks.

"You had this house bookmarked on your web browser," I unnecessarily advise.

"I know that," she says, frowning.

"You also sent it to Hallman. To Alannah and your friend Coraline."

"I'm aware."

"You also pinned it on that what do you call... décor site."

She looks from the house to me with a perplexed expression. "You even crawled my Pinterest profile?"

I smile.

"What are we doing here, Derek?"

"I bought it," I tell her. "For us." I grab her face and press my lips to hers.

When I move back and take in her face, she's utterly still and for a change, I don't think I can read her expression.

I explain, "That first time we talked in the donut shop, you talked about the kind of house you'd like to live in. You made it clear the house you were currently living in wasn't what you wanted. I saw this place on your link list, in your search history many times as well as your sent emails, so obviously it was of significance to you. I looked into it and saw the previous owner took it off the market after four months. He bought it planning a family, bought a ring and proposed. The girl said no. So he was trying to sell it. I made an offer." I shrug.

She stares ahead at the house.

Cheater

"You visited the real estate listing forty-six times," I add.

She flinches, then whispers, "You bought it. It's yours?"

"It's ours, Chloe. It's my wedding gift to you."

Frown lines mar her forehead.

"Neighbors aren't too close. I looked into them and on one side is an elderly couple with no kids who are adopted as grandparents by their church congregation and other families on the street. The neighbors on the other side are young professionals in their late twenties. Looking at her socials just quick, she's about four or five months pregnant. I think she could be someone you'd like. She loves taking food pictures and has similar taste in food as you. We could wind up with kids who get to grow up playing together on this... a safe street that's just a twenty-minute drive to the business district. Good preschool in walking distance. There are amenities within a two-minute drive. It made sense. But even if it wasn't practical, which it is, I bought it because you love it."

When I looked at the old listing, it helped paint a picture of who Chloe is. Family spaces. Big kitchen. Playground equipment outside. Big, wraparound porch to entertain on. To watch your kids play in the yard or treehouse, on the front lawn, riding bikes on the big driveway safely behind gates where people can't get to them. It's not so big you need live-in staff who might be plotting with people to steal from you, take your kids for ransom.

It's been recently updated, too. I don't care that it's not a house my mother would choose. It's a house my mother would call cute and adorable while dropping hints about other real estate listings more befitting someone of our family's status.

This is what my girl wanted, but didn't get when Adam Hallman lost the use of his legs. It's obvious they couldn't have bought it; it was more than triple the cost of the rowhouse she lived in with him and the mortgage would've been too high on their salaries. But it's the home she described in the donut shop that day with light in her eyes and a smile on her face.

I unclip my seatbelt.

"What are you doing?" she asks, looking panicked.

"Gonna open the gate so we can go inside. I have the code for the gate and the remotes are supposed to be on the kitchen counter. I'll upgrade it soon so we can just use an app."

"No. No." She seems panicked. "I'm not going in there. You did *not* buy that for me, Derek."

"I did. It was vacated yesterday, re-keyed already. New keys were dropped at my office. Grabbed them when I picked up that file you wanted. Here." I reach into my blazer pocket and hand the keys to her. "I had our clothes and groceries brought over this morning while we were at my parents. Had it cleaned. We're moving in."

She shakes her head, staring at the keys in her hand.

"Chloe, what's wrong?" I ask, caressing her face.

She shrinks away. "Derek, you can't buy my acquiescence here."

"That's not what I'm doing. I bought you the house you should have because it's the house you want. I don't expect you to throw yourself at me. I know you better than that."

She shakes her head. "You don't know me."

"Yes, I do," I state. "I know you better than you think I know you. I also know that when you decide to stop fighting this, you'll be happy that we're living here in the house you wanted. That this is where we'll raise our kids."

Her body jerks hard like I've delivered a physical blow.

Her mouth is open as she looks at me like I'm absolutely batshit crazy.

"It's old, but it's well-made and well-maintained. Updated everything, too, so no major work to be done. The house four houses over that way..." I point, "Has three teenage girls. Babysitters, baby, for when we want date night. Let's go in."

She stares at it looking like she's about to burst into tears. I watch a swallow work down her throat.

I get out, key in the gate code and open it before getting back in and driving through, stopping so I can close and lock it behind us.

Cheater

She's got her cheeks puffed out like she's holding her breath as I park.

"I wanna see inside, see what we might like to change, then I think I'll run you a bath in that giant tub in the master with the window overlooking that big yard and all those fruit trees out back and... then what? I'm gonna want to make love to you first in our home, so I'll temporarily backburner that bad girl punishment. Don't worry, you'll still get it. Maybe tomorrow."

She doesn't answer. Just stares.

I add, "I had him leave just about everything. He took his clothes and a few personal and sentimental things, and left with the fat check I gave him. But anything you don't want that's here, we'll replace. I had a new mattress and bedding delivered this morning too. Not fucking you or sleeping beside you on a used mattress."

"Fat check?"

"A hundred k over asking to get him to leave immediately. He jumped at it."

"I wouldn't," she says, looking at the place like she's yearning to step foot inside and never leave.

"No, that's true."

"What if he didn't want to sell?" she asks, "What would you have done?"

"Thankfully, money was enough of a motivator I didn't have to get more creative." I flash her a grin.

I know it's laced with threats. And as soon as I've done it, I wish I could snatch it back, which is an odd sensation. Threats have gotten me to where I am with Chloe, but since she came home with me Friday night, I've found myself trying to find ways to not threaten her so she'll see what things can be like for us.

I don't like the crushing sensation in my chest right now as she stares at her dream house looking sad.

I cup her jaw, tilting it so she's looking at me again.

"I wasn't expecting you to instantly fall for me because I bought this house for you. Actually, everything I do is so you'll fall for me, but I know it's not money or material things that will do the trick. You've got so much more substance than that. It's the effort I'm willing to put in to show you how much you matter, how much I *see* you. How much I yearn to be the one you reach for that'll do it, Chloe. And that's not a trick."

Her pretty blue eyes search my face as her teeth skim her bottom lip.

"Chloe, this is what I want. A life with you is what I want."

"What if... right now... I decided to go for it? Be in this with you? Then what?"

A smile spreads wide enough on my face it feels like my skin is stretching. There are big emotions happening in my chest, too. But although the look on her face shows me it's just a hypothetical question, I let the smile happen fully, let myself feel what that would feel like so she can see how much it would mean to me.

It feels like warm sun isn't just on my face but also filling me. Warm sunshine with not a care in the world. If this girl starts to really love me, I can almost believe my heart will split out of the dark shroud it lives in and shine bright enough light will spew out of my chest.

"Then what if you get focused on a new goal, Derek? See a new unhappy damsel in distress who fascinates you? Or what if something else becomes your goal like work or some noble cause and I just get forgotten. But Steeles don't divorce so I'm either left in a miserable situation with someone who doesn't give a shit about me anymore or you have to get rid of me because I'm a problem you don't want to deal and can't divorce me because your father would disown you?"

"Is the promise of what I'm showing you so absolutely perfect that you can't take a chance in case it isn't real?" I ask.

She frowns but doesn't answer.

"I wouldn't stay married to you because it's my father's rule. Believe me, when I say that. I would stay with you because I believe in the sanctity of marriage, too. I've seen my folks fight to stay together through some fucked up times. As fucked as my family life was in a lot of ways, I grew up with parents who refused to give up on one another. That's what marriage is. Right?"

She winces.

I continue. "You took a chance on Hallman based on what you saw, what you thought your life might be like after spending time with him. It didn't work out the way you wanted, obviously."

I wait. She has no reply, so I squeeze her knee. "Circumstances along with his personality let you down. Should you not ever have ventured into it? Should you not venture into anything, ever, in case it might go wrong? That's not you, is it?"

"Should I venture into madness with you instead? Is that what you're suggesting?" she fires back.

"Why not?" I shrug. "It's not like you have a choice since I'm so relentless. Why not try madness on for size and see how it fits? Come on, Chloe, let's go see our house. I haven't been inside it yet. I wanted to do this with you."

She hard-blinks. "You bought a house you'd never stepped foot inside of for a hundred grand over the asking price because I bookmarked it?"

"And visited it online forty-six times. How many times you drive by?"

"Twice," she whispers, staring at the house.

"You stopped dreaming for yourself when Hallman's accident changed everything. It's time to start dreaming again, beautiful. But you don't have to just dream about this. It's yours. Come on in and see it."

She doesn't move.

"Come on, baby. Let's go fuck inside our new house."

I get out of the SUV and round it, then open her door and click her seatbelt undone.

"Derek, I..." She lets that hang.

I lift her into my arms.

"I can walk," she says, irritated.

"You're getting carried over that threshold."

"No. I don't want to go in there," she protests.

"Why?" I ask.

Her eyes are brimming with tears. She looks away from me, chewing her lip.

"What is it?" I ask.

She dashes tears from her eyes, still holding the keys.

"You gonna clue me in?" I ask after a long beat of silence.

"I can't clue you in. I can't make sense of anything right now, especially you. You've swept my life up into a tornado."

"To fix it," I tell her, setting her down.

"And I ... I feel like I'm having a nervous breakdown."

"Because you're thinking of trying this with me? Go ahead. Have a breakdown. I'm right here to look after you."

She shakes her head.

"Not now? Okay, have it later. Come on in, then." I tug on her hand. "Come walk around and then I'll run you a bath. I bet you've dreamt of using that big tub in the master while staring out at all the trees through that big picture window, huh? Thought you'd never see it outside of photographs, right? Let's go."

She follows, not pulling her hand out of mine.

When we get to the door, I lift her up into my arms again.

"Derek," she grumbles.

"Hearing you say my name always gives me a little thrill, Chloe. Even if you say it like that." I press my lips to her jaw and take the keys from her.

As I unlock the door, she pulls in a breath and holds it while being carried over the threshold.

I crave her throwing her arms around me and squealing. I crave a smile, happiness from her. I'm so looking forward to when her feelings for me are on the surface. But it feels like something is brewing. Simmering. *Maybe.*

To the left is a living room and to the right is the dining room. A staircase sits straight ahead but doesn't take up the full space. You can walk up a few steps to a landing where the stairs continue up right or

Cheater

walk past the staircase to get deeper into the house, where I remember from the online brochure is a powder room, laundry room, and the kitchen, which opens up into the massive family room and a covered part of the back porch.

The formal living and dining rooms both have fires burning in their fireplaces per my instructions. Furnishings are okay. It all looks new. The former owner furnished the place but was barely here.

We walk past the stairs, down the hall and stop in the kitchen that looks out to the sundrenched family room extension, a rounded space with soaring ceilings overlooking the back yard through the two-story back wall of mostly windows and fireplace. Past that would be lush greenery if not for the fact that we're at the tail end of autumn and winter is imminent. There should also be a fire roaring in the fireplaces upstairs per the directions I left. I wanted lit fires in all of the fireplaces for us as well as to make the place smell like lemons, which it does. Chloe used lemon cleaner, lemon dish soap, even lemon hand soap when I watched her in that rowhouse on camera, so I want it to feel like home.

"Whoever designed this certainly loved fireplaces," I remark.

"That's one of the reasons I loved it," she says hoarsely, looking emotional.

I set her on the counter beside a waiting bucket of chilled champagne and a dozen red roses in a crystal vase.

"Please, God, not another mimosa," she mumbles, staring at the counter with horror.

I laugh and she half smiles, but it slips as soon as our eyes connect. I pass her the card from the rose bouquet.

Welcome home, baby.
Love, Derek.

She sets it down, nibbling on her bottom lip.

The kitchen is recently upgraded with cream cabinetry, white and cream marble counters, and beige and cream marbled flooring.

There are pops of color with the flowers, with a few red countertop appliances, and gold and brass accented wall décor like a clock, weather station, and memo board meant for busy families. The kitchen island faces the family room.

"It's beautiful," I say, following her eyes which seem to be focused on the windows. "I see why you loved it so much."

She doesn't say anything.

"How about we tour the upstairs?" I ask, my voice dropping as I drop a soft kiss on her neck.

She shivers.

Fuck, I want this. I want to jump ahead to where she's *in this* with me. She's afraid I'll get bored when the game is over? Not a chance. I'm so fucking ready to have her in love with me. To see her look at me with love, with lust, with something other than fear, frustration, and confusion. She's worth the wait. The effort. I don't believe for a minute that I'll lose interest. I want this woman running for me when she sees me, dying to connect with me. I want it all with her.

I lift her up and move toward the staircase on the other side of the kitchen.

"You don't have to carry me up there," she mumbles.

"Yes I do, maybe I'll never let your feet touch the ground again," I warn with a grin. "Carry you from place to place?"

She rolls her eyes.

"Tie you to the bed when I can't carry you around," I add.

She chews her cheek and drops her gaze.

I laugh darkly.

The upstairs has four bedrooms and three bathrooms along with a home office that's lined with bookshelves and yet another fireplace.

I see her eyes light up at the bookshelves, which are empty but for one book. The book I purchased for her.

She eyeballs the book and then looks at the floor again.

Okay, no comment on that then.

"What do you think of the color in here?" I ask once we're in the

Cheater

master bathroom. I've set her on one of the two vanities. I look around, face likely betraying how I feel about the shade of green these walls are painted.

"It's hideous," she announces.

"Thank fuck. I was worried I'd have to live with this the rest of my life because you were in love with it."

Her eyes work over my face actively. "You'd put up with it if I liked it when you hate it?"

"No," I tell her honestly.

Her forehead crinkles with confusion.

I lean in and put both hands on her thighs and squeeze.

"Once you finish falling in love with me, you'll paint it to save me from the ongoing headache." I touch my lips to hers and back up.

"What if I did love it?"

"Then I'd have kept my mouth shut for the moment. Maybe drop some hints about a compromise. Paint your home office that color and only go in there with these shades on." I gesture to the shades tucked into my shirt. "So, bunny, what's the verdict? Do you love your house as much in person as you did in pictures?"

37

Chloe

I'm saved from answering his question by his phone ringing. He pulls it from his pocket and puts it to his ear with a little smile.

"Well, hello," he drawls, eyes bouncing to me. "She's right here. Why?"

I watch him moisten his lips with his tongue and then he says, "Ah. Yes, we've been busy. Here she is."

He passes me the phone.

Alannah Fisher.

"Hey," I say, my voice coming out scratchy.

My bag is still in his car. She probably called me first.

"You did not send your proof of life text, missy."

"Shit, sorry," I say, feeling my face flame. "I'm alive."

He walks out of the room.

"Should I assume you're fine going forward so not to expect them?"

"You should expect them," I say softly, noting the footsteps have stopped. He's probably standing directly outside the door, listening.

"Then you're not fine?" she asks.

"I'm fine," I tell her. "I think. I... I don't know. My morning was a little... crazy."

She snorts. "Crazy morning with the crazy guy?"

"Pretty much."

"Are you hurt? Hungry? Injured?"
"No, no, and no. Well... maybe hungry."
"Didn't you have that brunch thing with his family?"
"I did."
"But?"
"But I didn't eat."
"Why?"
"I don't even know where to start."
"He's there so you can't talk, right?"
"Ish. Except to say that right now we're in the house in Dublin."
"The house in Dublin?" she parrots.
"The house," I *emphasize.*

The sound of footsteps in the hall resumes, then recedes. Maybe he's gone into one of the other bedrooms.

"The house?" Alannah asks blankly.
"The house. The dream house I wanted but didn't think I'd ever have."
"Explain."
"Remember that house I was obsessing about before Adam's accident? Well, Derek bought it for me."
"He what?"
"He saw it on my bookmarks and in my web history, so he bought it for me."
"Holy fuck," she whispers.
"For a hundred k over asking to get the guy to move out immediately, leaving it furnished, so we could move in today."
"Whoa."
"Whoa is right. Fires started in all the fireplaces. Roses and champagne on the counter."
"Fire in your panties, too?" she asks.

I scoff and wander into the dazzling walk-in closet that you access from the bathroom. Yep, it's in that same neon green, but God is it gorgeous otherwise. My things are here. The few things I brought with me Friday night along with all he had the talented Nicola procure for me. I coined it my *dream gawdy green, gorgeous girl garage*. Because I would put all my favorite things in here. And it looks even better in person than it did on the real estate listing. So many shelves, nooks, and drawers. Places for my necklaces. For my not-large but very beloved and carefully bargain-sourced shoe and handbag collection. A side with plenty of storage for my dream husband's suits, his jeans, his hoodies that I'd undoubtedly borrow. Right now some of Derek's clothes are here, too. Whatever he had in that condo, I imagine.

I wonder how comfy Derek's hoodies are. I touch one that's tucked into a cubby. The arms would hang way off my hands. Like that wine colored henley of his that I put on after the first time we...

I shake my thoughts off. Hard. I force myself to clue in to what Alannah is saying. She's called my name.

"My clothes were moved over while we were at brunch. Not really my clothes, mind you. The new and perfect bespoke wardrobe Derek bought for me."

"This explains why I'm meeting you guys at the city hall, then?"

"Huh?"

"That's what he sent me in a text last night."

"Text?"

"You weren't listening, were you? 11:30. Tomorrow. Derek texted me to be there to stand up for you as your maid of honor. Not there but in a town twenty minutes from there."

"Uh..." is all I manage.

"He hasn't told you."

"We haven't discussed it, no."

"So, do I bring you the borrowed and blue and old and new? What should I wear? What are you wearing? What's the deal?"

"I haven't a clue."

Her voice drops lower as she asks, "You want me to meet you in the bathroom with a plane ticket and a SWAT team so you can get outta Dodge?"

"Maybe..." I say immediately.

"Totally?" she asks.

"One sec," I whisper.

I come out, wondering where he is.

He's come back to the master suite but is now outside on the small balcony that looks out from the foot of the bed through sliding doors. The doors are shut, and he's leaned on the railing, admiring the view, I guess. He looks casual, not like he can hear me.

I try to pull my thoughts together.

"What do you need, Chloe?" she asks, urgently. "Is there some way you can tell me so I can help you?"

"I don't know," I whisper. "I don't have a clue. I was gonna ask someone in his family to help, but they were all... out there. Way out there. I did everything but stomp my feet and scream and they don't give a fuck as long as Derek handles things so that I don't go to the press. He's got them believing he'll win me over. They're acting like him blackmailing me into being with him is the healthiest thing he's done lately. It's so fucked up, Lan."

"I'll help you get out of this."

I frown. "I don't know if you can without getting caught in his crosshairs."

"Leave it to me."

"You sound awfully confident. You have a plan already?"

"Not entirely, but no way am I going to just sit back and do nothing here. Show up tomorrow and follow my lead."

I hold the phone as my heartrate picks up.

"I've got you," she whispers.

"I can't let something bad happen to you."

"You can't let him away with this," she counters.

"Ugh," I grunt.

"Gonna go figure this out," Alannah says.

"I don't know, Lan..."

"Follow my lead tomorrow."

"Love you lots," I say. "Please be careful. I don't want anything to happen to you."

Cheater

"I'm a big girl. I know my way around drama and trauma. Tiptoed through a few minefields in my day so far. Love you, babe. You're okay though?"

"Weirded out beyond measure. Nervous about fallout no matter what I do, but I guess I'm okay. As okay as I can be."

"Right. Zero chance you're thinking of giving it a whirl and hoping for the best with him?" she asks.

"God no. What? That's nuts."

Dead air.

"Lan?"

"Tell me now if you're thinking you should consider it."

"Would you?" I quip.

She shocks me when she says, "I've been asking myself that very question, babe."

"You delusional?"

"C'mon, Chlo. You do a pro and con list yet?"

"You don't have all the facts. The threats, Lan. They're concerning. They're why I'm here."

"What specifically has he threatened with?"

Flustered, I run my freehand through my hair. "It's a general, *you won't like what happens* thing. Like what he did when you were there for breakfast. So, I really don't know."

"Hm. Empty threats?"

"The threats to Adam were... a little more specific. He threatened to share secrets. Don't ask *what* because it's not something anyone can know. But he had a bodyguard hold us at gunpoint that night he convinced Adam to end our relationship." I drop my voice even lower. "He's dug far back into me, knows a lot. Knows a lot about Adam. Told me he even has files on my birth parents. So I wouldn't say empty threats. I just don't know how far he'd actually go."

"Holy," she whispers.

"Find out anything else about him, his history?" I ask.

"About him and his family? It's all shady. Money. Power. Corruption. But nothing solid. Rumors. Lots of rumors of their ability to make problems go away in a variety of unsavory ways. Nobody wants to say anything specific."

"I'll message you tonight," I say. "But please be careful. I don't want you in his sights. Now that Adam and I are over, you're the one he's going to-"

"Don't worry about me. I'm a big girl and I'm not afraid of skeletons falling out of my closet."

"But Lan..."

"No. Really. Okay, chickie, so if you show up tomorrow at the city hall, I've got you unless you give me the high sign. If you don't do those things, I'll know to pull whatever triggers I can gather for the arsenal. Yeah?"

"Okay," I reply, doubtfully.

"Any snags or more I need to know we'll talk when you send me tonight's proof of life. Toodles."

She's hung up.

I exhale. She's determined she'll figure out a plan. What sort of plan, I'm not sure. And right now, we're on Derek's phone so is this call not being recorded? Or will he have access to everything we've just discussed? Did he wire this place this morning and has my conversation just been recorded? I don't know but wouldn't put it past him.

I step out of the bathroom; he's still outside.

He turns around, still leaned against the railing, taking me in from toes to eyes.

He's thinking about fucking me.

He's about to make a move.

I feel myself torn between retreating and... not. His expression is tied into my body's mechanics or something because I'm affected.

I'd have to be made of stone to not be somewhat affected by all the grand gestures. By all the little things, too, which add up to a lot. But the bottom line is that he's threatening and dangerous. He's manipulative. Adding that to his clearly warped view of reality and I

Cheater

just can't allow myself to slide into mania with him. It could go horribly wrong, couldn't it?

Crazy though, the only thing he'd change in this house is the same thing I'd change. I'd hoped it wasn't as bad in person as it was in the pictures, but it's worse. The neon green has to go.

I mean... it would have to go if I was committed to living here. But I'm not. I can't be.

Loving a house and being likeminded on not having the master bathroom and walk-in closet neon green isn't enough of a reason to believe anything here is viable. What sane person buys a house for me after all he's done?

Though, he has gotten what he wants so far by pushing, hasn't he? The swoony psycho wanted to bed me. He did. He wanted to break me and Adam up. He did. He wanted me to move in with him. I have. He's gotten sex every time he wants it from me. He's even taken me to the point where I'm resigned for sex and then rips the rug out from under me and leaves me on the edge and almost disappointed. Okay, more than almost. He's clearly accustomed to getting what he wants.

He wants me to marry him at City Hall a half hour from here at 11:30 tomorrow.

Will he get his way again?

What could he do to me and my loved ones if I dig my heels in and refuse? Actually call his bluff for the first time? What if I escape when his back is turned and hide?

My mind races as I consider possibilities and then I'm turning my back to him so I can go back into the bathroom. I shut the door and lock it. My eyes land on the phone in my hand, and my thumb slides across the screen to the next page of apps. My eyes do a sweep of the screen. Another swipe. A visual sweep. This last page has a folder that has my name on it. Inside are two icons. One is a car. The other is a house.

He'll expect me out in a minute, but I can't stop myself from bopping the house icon while I have a minute alone with his phone. My heart skips a beat when I realize I'm looking at a live feed of the kitchen. Of Adam and Craig.

Adam sits in his wheelchair at the kitchen table with his head in his hands. Craig stands behind him, hand on his shoulder. Adam's brother Paul steps into the kitchen and his lips are moving.

I touch the volume button on the screen and immediately hear them talking.

"...loves Gran. She'd wanna know."

I straighten up.

"Already told you we're finished, and I broke her heart. She doesn't wanna hear from me after all this. "

My chest flares with emotion.

Paul looks frustrated. "Maybe I'll call her."

"No."

"She'd wanna pay her respects before it's over, bro."

My heart sinks. Adam's grandmother is wonderful. Sweet. Of course I would want to pay my respects if she's critically ill. I like Paul. I get along fine with Adam's older sister Ruthie. I've only met his other sister Vera once; she lives in France. Adam's dad is nice to me; it's his mom who's tepid with me, but everyone else has been great.

All this with me and us and now he will lose his gran? Adam looks utterly broken. A crushing weight feels like it's sitting on my chest.

"Chloe?" Derek calls from the other side of the door.

I immediately back out of the app, then twist the lock and rip it open.

"What? I can't even have privacy to use the bathroom?" I'm about to move past him but he blocks me by leaning a shoulder against the doorframe.

"You were snooping."

I scoff, holding out his phone. "You're accusing me of snooping? Talk about rich."

Cheater

"I heard a male voice. Who was it?" He takes the phone and eyeballs it.

"I was peeking in on my ex on your camera feed, as if you couldn't guess. You have some fucking audacity, don't you? I was peeking in on my ex in my house on *your* stalker app. Take those cameras out, Derek."

"I'll take them out eventually," he says with a shrug. "And that boring little box is no longer your house. This is." He gestures.

"My name is on *that* mortgage."

"We'll get it off. Your name is on this deed. No mortgage."

"Huh?"

"I'll show you." He takes my hand and I can't wrench it free, so I have no choice but to follow him downstairs to the kitchen. He opens the roll up bread bin on the counter and there's a folder. He opens it and shows me.

"Derek and Chloe Steele?" I mutter. "I'm not Chloe Steele."

"You will be," he states, wrapping his arms around me. "Tomorrow. I got your bag if you need to check your phone." He gestures to it on the island. "What do you want me to make you to eat? Brunch portions were measly," he says. "I could eat, too."

"You don't need to make me food. I'll find something myself." I step out of his embrace, open the fridge and see the ingredients that were in his penthouse fridge. Figuring I'll eat something and then look for an opportunity to find out what's happening with Adam's grandmother, I pull out some Cajun spiced shaved turkey breast, some pepperjack cheese slices, a cucumber, mayo, and some Dijon mustard. There's a bag of buns in the bread box he pulled that file of paperwork from.

The butter got put in the fridge, so I pop it into the microwave for twelve seconds.

"You want one?" I ask.

He looks surprised and I realize I've offered out of reflex.

"I'd love one," he says softly, putting a hip to the counter and watching me root around through cupboards and drawers for plates and a knife.

Despite everything, I don't have it in me to take the offer back, so I wash my hands and get to work on the sandwiches without looking at him despite knowing he's watching my every move while standing close enough I can smell his bodywash.

"I think we should put a pool in," he states as I wash the cucumber. "What do you think?"

I give him a dark look and say nothing before I turn my attention to slicing the cucumber.

He moves behind me and takes my hair into a bunch at the nape of my neck, then presses his lips to my throat while he wraps his other hand around my waist. "Lots of space out there. Place behind is up for sale. Four acres of land and a decent house. We could get stables. Horses." His thumb goes up and down over my belly, the rest of his fingers stay still.

I hold my breath while I butter the buns. I'm not sure if he found out about my love for horses. Maybe not. A lot of women have childhood dreams of owning their own horse.

"You look beautiful today," he whispers against my skin, and I get a head-to-toe shiver that I'm unable to hide. "Covered in things I bought for you. I like that. You've taken care of yourself for a long time. I like taking care of you. Providing for you." His hand grazes my under-boob area and I find myself holding my breath as his lips dot kisses along my throat before he lets go of my hair as he announces, "I'll pour the champagne."

"I don't want champagne," I snap with irritation. "There's nothing to celebrate."

He looks amused at what he must be categorizing as my overreaction.

"I want champagne," he says. "I want to toast a celebration of buying this house for you. Of you making me a sandwich for the first time. Of the many wonderful things to come, Chloe."

He pulls the champagne out of the bucket, wraps the bottle in a waiting tea towel and twists the metal cage, pops it, and pours it into two waiting champagne flutes.

I slice the turkey sandwiches in half.

He holds his glass up and looks at the second glass that he poured as if I'm about to lift it.

"Cheers."

"I'm not cheers'ing you," I deny bitchily. " And I only offered you a sandwich out of reflex."

He sips his champagne as I grab a bottle of water from the fridge and tuck it under my arm as I walk both plates the few paces to the other side of the island where there are two stools. I climb up on one.

He brings over the two glasses of champagne and sits beside me, setting one in front of me.

"Take a sip, Chloe. Just one. Please? Isn't it rude not to?" He chucks me under the chin playfully, then taps my nose with his thumb.

I swat his hand away.

"One sip. Please?"

He holds out the glass.

Something in the bottom of the glass catches my eye and panic spikes. I refuse to wait for the details of what it is to emerge through the bubbly haze. My eyes bounce to his face instead.

He's smiling. Waiting.

My gaze narrows.

No. I am not doing this right now. He is not going to propose to me. No.

I studiously avoid looking at it. But we both know I know what's in it. There's a motherfucking diamond ring in that glass.

"You're so fucking cute when you're angry at me for doing things for you," he quips.

I lift half of my sandwich and take a bite.

Derek sets the glass down, not even trying to hide the smirk on his face. He knows I saw it, knows I'm pretending I didn't. He lifts one half of his sandwich and takes a bite. I watch his face light up as he chews, then swallows, saying, "Mm. That's delicious. Thank you, baby." He leans over and kisses me on the lips, startling me.

I'm taking my second bite when he says, "Gonna sip your champagne?"

"Nope."

"Ah, so we're gonna play this game, are we? I have a few games up my sleeve, too. I think maybe after we finish our sandwiches it'll be time to play one of them."

Ignoring the belly dip the threat gives me, I bitchily chomp off a large bite of my sandwich.

I eat while pretending there's no sexual energy in the room. Pretending not to notice how he watches me as he eats beside me. Doing my best, too, to not be affected by where I am. In *this* house. This house I thought I'd never, ever set foot in.

I'm ignoring that he's beside me in that sexy suit, chin resting on his palm as he leans on an elbow, gazing at me like I'm his dream girl. I've probably got mustard and mayo on my chin.

Many daydreams plagued me during the period where I visited the listing for this house forty-six times (according to him). Fantasies of my kids playing in that yard. Dreams of having a pool put in with a fence to keep those kids safe. Now my mind drifts to thoughts of fairy lights at night outlining the yard, and me and my man fucking under the stars on a deck chair. The fairy lights blend into the next image of a two-storey Christmas tree beside the fireplace that's directly behind me right now.

I had to stop indulging in those daydreams. Because Adam thought the house was too expensive. Too old. Too far. He had a million reasons for not buying it. He also thought it was way too much money for a starter home. I didn't want a starter home. I wanted to move into a home after our honeymoon and stay there forever.

The dream of this place fizzled to nothing when the accident happened. A few months later, Adam's mother told us about the accessible townhome she found in a price range we could afford now

Cheater

and with all the bells and whistles Adam would need as part of his rehabilitation road. And of course I put my unrealistic dreams of this house aside. It's not like we had enough money, but it sat on the market for months and up until my life had become all about Adam's diagnosis, I had hoped the price would drop. That something would work out. But then of course I didn't think about it anymore. Except the day we moved into the townhome and it was so, *so* different from what I thought would be the place I'd put down roots.

When I get to the end of my sandwich, I lift my napkin and dab my mouth before crumpling it and dropping it on the polka dotted lunch plate. Derek's plate is the same, but different colors. I own a dress that's almost a perfect match of the pattern of his plate.

The previous owner of this place even left these fabulous dishes. I loved seeing the dining room styled with these plates in the real estate listing. It took me a hot minute to find the pattern. I bookmarked a set of them online but hadn't invested in them yet.

He drinks back some of the champagne from the glass he put in front of me, grabs my face and kisses me, making sure I get some. I pull back, hop off the stool, and am about to storm off, when I'm hauled up in the air over Derek's shoulder.

"Argh!" I protest.

He slaps my ass.

"Hey!" I shout.

"We're going to bed. We're christening this joint."

"You want to wear my lunch down your back? If not, put me down."

He lifts the champagne glass, dumps the contents into the sink and I hear the clink of the ring hitting the porcelain. He sticks his hand in the sink, so he must grab it, I'm not getting the best vantage point over his shoulder. The next thing I know, he's climbing the stairs.

"If I throw up on your back it'll serve you right," I grumble.

"Serves *who* right for those ten or twenty images on a certain blog that I downloaded a full backup of via the Wayback Machine? All those images of bare-chested guys with half-naked women draped over their shoulders?"

My mouth opens in outrage at the accusation, but I clamp it shut and fire back, "So, it's *my* fault you're like this?"

"Absolutely. Your blog gave me all sorts of ideas."

We're climbing stairs now and I hold on tighter. "Clearly there's an expectation versus reality lesson here and believe me, Derek, I've learned. Put me down."

He laughs heartily as he drops me on the bed. Immediately, he reaches out and snatches my ankle and pulls me down the bed a little before he undoes my shoe buckle to get it unstrapped. He drops the shoe without dropping his gaze, which is pointed at my face. He repeats the motion with the other foot and as soon as my foot is free from the binds of the straps, he leans down and puts his lips to the top of my foot while flinging that shoe over his shoulder. It lands on the dresser with a thunk.

And I'm lying here not stopping him. Not blinking. Maybe not even breathing as I watch him toe his shoes off, shuck his blazer and undo his cufflinks, setting them on the bedside table. I see they're black with monogramed silver letters on them.

The tie gets loosened and then it and the shirt are gone. My eyes drink in the expanse of muscled chest and abs, defined shoulders and biceps and I'm momentarily hypnotized by the sight of my crazy stalker.

He drops the suit pants and toes off his dress socks and then he's got a knee to the bottom of the bed and he's moving until he's hovering over me in just his tight black boxer briefs.

"You want what was in the glass?" he asks.

I shake my head and internally cuss myself out for the intrusive thought about wanting what's in his underpants.

"Wanna see it at least?"

I shake it again.

"Hm," he muses. "Guess we'll figure that out before tomorrow. For now... we can occupy ourselves."

Cheater

I'm staring and thinking all sorts of thoughts about my Derek problem. Bitchy doesn't work. Fighting mad doesn't help; he's too strong. What if I just lie here? What if I don't react to the stunts he pulls? What if I freeze him out by being as unemotional and unexpressive as I can be? Would that do it? Would that make him give up this ridiculous game he's playing?

His eyes close and I'm fascinated by his eyelashes for a brief moment. So fixed on them I miss the descent and now his lips press to mine.

I remain still.

He backs up an inch before he moves back in, lips touching mine with the addition of him touching the tip of his tongue to my cupid's bow as he leans down and rests on his left elbow, right hand moving in, now cupping my jaw.

"This is where we're gonna raise a family, Chloe. This house, that yard out there." He tucks some of my hair behind my ear and rubs the tip of his nose against mine. "Have kids climbing in here with us on Saturday mornings to cuddle or jump on the bed, wanting me to get up and make pancakes and play outside with them while you get to lie in bed reading a book until you can't stand missing out on the laughter and join us in that treehouse."

I do my best to remain perfectly still, but despite my efforts, my nostrils flare and I really need to fucking swallow.

His hand leaves my jaw, caresses my boob, and then glides down until it's to my knee where he grips behind it and lifts, so it's cocked.

"Gonna push me away? Tell me not to?" He cups my ass.

I say nothing. I stare at him, trying to be stoic, unemotional, which is difficult. Not only because of the physicality here, but also because of the nerves he's just struck with his talk of kids and pancakes and lazy Saturday mornings.

His fingertips slip inside my underwear and move until they slide straight through the heart of me.

Damn biology, he's found me wet. Again.

Eyes sparkling with mischief, Derek asks, "Not gonna fight?"

I shrug, doing my best to give him an 'I don't give a shit' attitude.

"But I want you to fight me, baby. Because you come so much harder when I overpower you. Don't you?" He chuckles devilishly.

Smug bastard.

I keep my expression frozen somehow.

But then his hand snakes up and the zipper of my dress is pulled down. He pulls the dress up over my head and tosses it before he fiddles down below and abruptly yanks the fabric of my underwear to the side and slams forward, filling me past the brink, making me react involuntarily both audibly with a grunt and physically as my lower back leaves the mattress and I grab him by the hair.

One of his hands grips the length of my hair, too, and he devours my mouth in an aggressive kiss. He pulls his hips back before slamming forward again. Harder. And I grip his hair tighter as I arch into it, cross heels clamped just beneath his backside.

He pulls out, grabs my ankles and gets my legs up so my ankles are at his shoulders. He tears my underwear up and off before he plunges back inside, caressing my legs, slipping his right hand across my hip to get his thumb to my clit.

One leg is pushed wider to accommodate Derek's hot mouth, which closes around my nipple over top of my lace bra, sending vibrations throttling their way through me. I'm feeling it from multiple sensation points as he keeps moving, keeps circling, continues suckling.

While lost in sensation, my focus hones in on the detail of the ceiling of the bedroom in a house I spent a lot of time dreaming about, obsessing over. I gave up on this dream. I gave up pieces of myself for Adam.

I'm not materialistic, but Derek buying this for me for the reasons he detailed has my brain playing hopscotch. Because I'm dropping a rock on the sections of my brain that I don't want to land on right now because those sections are pro-Derek. And I'm telling myself those parts of my mind have got to be slipping into insanity because every-

Cheater

thing he's done, and all his convoluted logic is too dangerous to get caught up in.

Because I shouldn't be okay with any of his deceit and manipulations, and I absolutely should not be forgiving with the threats of harming people I care about. And giving him any more than this – any more than what I have no choice but to give him – is me letting the ends justify the means. And the means are so very wrong.

"You're such a wet, quivering bundle of sexuality, you know that?" he says into my ear. "You feel so fucking good. The feel of this sweet, tight pussy, the sounds you make drive me wild. The taste of your tongue? I could spend all my time fucking you, baby. Fuck you any way you want me to as much as you want me to. You hear that? You don't have to go without. Only I can make you feel like this, beautiful Chloe. I know what you want. I know how to fuck you properly. And you love every fucking minute of it. Don't you?"

"Shut up," I spit as I claw his back with both hands.

His mouth is on mine again and anger overtakes logic for me as I sink into sensation.

I let him take me into the eye of the tornado with him. Giving him my tongue. Clenching my inner muscles around him.

He groans. I clench harder. He rotates his hips. I tighten my legs, dig my nails in. His pace picks up even faster, even harder, and he's panting. Panting hard, licking my throat, biting my earlobe, pinching my nipple, swallowing my cries. Doing all of this while pumping, pistoning, driving forward in delicious, powerful strokes.

"Fuck, you're my good girl, you know that?" he asks huskily.

I'm angry. Angry that he's crazy. Angry that he's done so many things that I shouldn't forgive him for. Maybe also a little mad that he's *this* fucked up because it means I can't have any of the things he's promising me. And maybe some of them sound really, really good.

I come, in a big way, pink, white, orange, and green spots dancing behind my eyes in a swirled colorful haze as a series of loud whimpers escapes my mouth. Before I come all the way down, he turns to his back, bringing me with him, moving my hips back and forth so I can ride him.

My hair is plastered to my face, so I whip it back and our eyes meet. His hair is a mess, too; his dark eyes are full to the brim with sexual kryptonite as he bites his lower lip while moving me to and fro.

Boneless, I grab onto his shoulders and sort of melt as my orgasm starts to ebb. As I'm melting forward, into him, he pulls out and flips me to my belly, pressing me into the mattress as he slides back inside and slips his hand under my hip to again work my clit.

I chew the pillow, crying out while I wait for the rest of the orgasm to fade. But instead... it ramps up again.

"Fuck, fuck, fuck baby," he grunts, kissing the back of my shoulder.

Finally, he groans long and melts into my back.

"Fuck, yeah. That was insanely good, wasn't it?" He kisses my neck again.

Insane? Yep.

He dozes off. But I don't. He's holding me close, both of us on our sides facing one another. His steady breaths are a breeze on my forehead as I ponder things.

Finally, I slip out from under his arm and roll out of the bed before reaching to the floor to see if I can find my dress. I spy the fluffy pink housecoat on the back of the door, so I go get it on instead and go to the bathroom.

When I'm back, he's still sound asleep, so I squat and reach into his suit pants and find his phone. It goes into my robe pocket as I tiptoe out of the room and downstairs to the kitchen where my purse sits on the island. I take it with me and go to the covered porch that's accessible from the back hall where the laundry and powder rooms are. Closing the door behind myself, I call Adam.

He answers before it rings for a second time.

Cheater

"Hello?"

"Adam?"

"Chloe?" He sounds shocked.

He thought Derek was phoning.

"Hey," I whisper.

He holds the phone for a second before he says, "Are you okay?" His voice sounds choked.

"That's why I'm calling you. I probably don't have long to talk, but I got ahold of his phone and found the app attached to the cameras there and heard you and your brother talking for a half a minute, but you guys said something about your grandmother. Is she... is she sick? What's wrong?"

He lets out a big breath and then speaks quickly. "I... my uncle was found dead in prison. She got that news in the car and had a heart attack and dropped on my parents' lawn on the way in after church. They...uh... revived her, but ... it was too long before they did and now she's... the news isn't good. She's not gonna wake up. They're giving us time to get everyone here and then they'll turn off the life support."

My heart clenches. "I'm so, so sorry."

"I think he did it, Chloe. I think he took care of my uncle."

I wince.

"I didn't answer his offer when he said he could take care of that for me. I didn't... I didn't tell him to do it. I haven't talked to him at all since he ... since he took you from me Friday night."

"If he did do something to your uncle..." I swallow, "It wasn't your doing."

"You don't know if it was him?"

"I don't know," I say. "Are you okay?"

"Are you?" he counters.

"No," I whisper. "I mean I am but I'm not. You know?"

"Yeah. Same," he says. "For what it's worth, I'm sorry I took you for granted. I didn't mean to. I'm sorry about a lot of things."

My chin trembles. "That should've been between you and me.

385

And I'm sorry I said things someone else had a chance to overhear. There's no point in going over it, though."

"Guess not," he mutters.

"Which hospital is your gran at? I'd like to go see her. I don't know if I can get there. If I don't, please know I'm thinking of you. But I'm going to see what I can do."

"I don't know if that's such a good idea, Chloe. I've told my family we're over. They're dealing with all this with Gran. You don't want *him* to have a reaction either, so…" He lets that hang.

"Oh," I whisper.

"It's probably best that you don't come. They're giving time for Vera to get in and it'll probably happen tomorrow night. I appreciate the thought though." He sniffles.

He sounds far away. A million miles away from being the Adam I thought I was spending the rest of my life with.

And I'm not sure how I'm feeling about it at the moment.

"Okay. I'll let you go," I say.

"I got a message that on Tuesday, some people are coming to clear out your things. I'm… I'm guessing on some of the things we bought together about whether you'll want them or not. If something doesn't get to you that you do want, please just… tell him to get word to me."

I numbly nod, then belatedly say, "Okay."

"Take care of yourself, Chloe."

"You, too." I press *end then* pull my lips tight and fill my lungs with air before I slowly let it out.

I slip into the other app in the folder with my name on it and see it's tracking my location on a screen that uses the street maps app.

I turn my phone off. I refresh the app. It still shows my location. I do it a couple more times in case there's a delay. This means I have to pull my SIM card if I run from Derek.

Noise has me looking over my shoulder and Derek is in the doorway, wearing just a pair of dark sweatpants. His eyes are sleepy, sexy, but shifting to suspicious as I'm caught red handed holding both my phone and his.

Cheater

He comes over and holds his hand out. I hand it over.

"What were you doing?" he asks, eyes a little cold.

"Adam's grandmother is dying. She had a heart attack after finding out her son died in prison."

His expression does not change. I don't know if he's responsible or not, so I ask.

"Are you responsible for that?"

"What if I am?"

I shoot to my feet and lean forward aggressively.

"If you are, then you," I stab my index finger toward him, "are responsible for Adam's grandmother having a heart attack and being brain dead and about to have life support pulled."

"If I pulled strings to end the life of a predator of children who would never have gotten out of prison to see the light of day, would that make me responsible for the predator's mother's reaction?"

"It might not make you responsible, but if you don't feel even a little bit bad about it, you're an asshole," I snap.

"Where ending the life of a waste of space pedophile is concerned, I'd be happy to be the asshole. Saves the taxes we spend to keep him clothed and fed. Where you're concerned? I'm an asshole for very specific reasons and expected outcomes."

"If a woman is dying because you interfered where you shouldn't have, you're worse than an asshole," I fire back. "A cold-hearted sociopath, maybe."

He swipes his phone and looks at something, answering, "Probably. But maybe certain people need to know how serious I am. Certain people who aren't supposed to fuckin' speak to you."

He can obviously see I just phoned Adam on his phone.

"I called him," I snap. "He didn't call me."

Pressing his finger to the screen, he wanders off.

A moment later, still curled in a ball on the couch, I hear his voice, which grows louder as he comes back and stands in the doorway, leaning against the frame. "Me having to stop on a Sunday afternoon and call you to tell you this is inconvenient. Inconveniences irritate me. Remember that." He's back in front of me now, ending the call. His eyes slide up from his screen to my face. "That was your ex. He's been informed that if you contact him again and he doesn't immediately hang up, he'll be strung from some rafters by his ankles while watching me make you come until you pass out. You don't even wanna know what happens if he contacts you. Though you seemed to be growing weary of my vague threats. Would you like some explicit detail of this threat?"

"No," I whisper.

"I ran you a bath if you're interested. I'm gonna go use the den on the main floor to get a few things done for the clubs. Thinking you'd want the upstairs library as your office with all those bookshelves. Yeah?"

I don't answer.

"I'll make dinner around seven," he says expectantly.

"If I'm hungry, I'll get something for myself," I reply.

His eyes sweep over me and then he shrugs. "You know where to find me if you need me."

I curl up on the comfy couch, put my head on the arm, and stare out the window at trees that I know will, after this winter is over, be covered in blossoms. Beautiful pink and white ones.

And I wonder where I'll be then. Here? Or will I have gotten away from my stalker? I wonder how I'll feel about the outcome of however this goes. When those tree blossoms bloom, will I be with Derek, fighting for my freedom? Will I be alone and free of him? And will I be better or worse off than I am at this very minute?

If I've gotten away from him, will I think about all this, all he wants to give me, all the sensations he created in me? If this is temporary, which it must be somehow some way, if I've got the ability to look back on it, will be wistful? Will I wish I'd enjoyed it more? If I'm somewhere else, will I wish I was here with the ability to see those blossoms up close? Will this end in bloodshed? Whose? Besides Adam's grandma and uncle.

After a while, I take my purse and phone and woodenly walk

Cheater

back upstairs. I let the fragrant, still warm water out of my dream bathtub and instead take a long, hot shower before I put a tracksuit on and decide to check in with my parents.

Last time I called, I called Dad's cell so this time I call my mom.

"Hello?" my mother answers.

"Hi, how are you?"

"Oh, Chloe, we're fine, how are you? We're just on our way to the Keoughs' for dinner. Can we catch up later on or is there a reason you're calling?"

"Oh. Just checking in but okay, sure, we can talk later. Have a good afternoon. Say hi to dad."

"Nothing's wrong?" she checks.

"Nope," I reply, but my voice cracks.

But she misses it because she says, "Okay. Talk soon. Bye."

I don't think I've ever had a shoot-the-breeze long phone call with her. Ever. There needs to be a reason to call. Dad won't always rush me off the phone, but he's often busy. When I visit them, it seems like they're always in the middle of some big project to do with the house, often distracted.

When the three of us come together, we'll have meals together, but all the conversations are on the surface. Nothing with any depth. I wouldn't say it seems forced, just not all that warm. When I visit them, my old room is now a guest room and I generally don't stay over because a long, hangout style visit just generally isn't what they're about.

When Adam was in the hospital, they did visit. Once. Took me to dinner. Brought flowers and two self-care baskets, one for me and one for Adam. I get a text on my birthday, not a call. Holidays aren't a given with them. Sometimes I'll see them, sometimes I don't. They're busy, enjoying their empty nest lifestyle. I'm not bothered by them about when I'll give them grandchildren. They congratulated me and Adam on the engagement and my father told me they had $40K aside for my wedding. Dad asked me if I was sure, if I was happy, and that was that.

After losing Bryan. I think they walked around numb for months, semi-numb for years. Every one of us withdrew into ourselves. Losing him broke the family unit.

Adam's family is a lot closer to one another but never really made me feel like a member of the family.

Alannah's family loves me. That's where I get the lovey dovey squishy family feels fix from. I often go there for holidays. It's a loud, expressive, butt-into-your-business group. They often fight. They also laugh together a lot. It's kind of ideal.

My mind drifts to Derek's dysfunctional family as I curl up on the bed that Derek already made. I push those thoughts away while I catch up on my unread text messages. Just a few from Alannah and one from Coraline, who messaged me last night.

Alannah told us you and Adam split. She said you're not ready to talk about it. So sorry girl. I'm here if you need me day or night. Hugs.

I decide to scroll my socials and see a selfie of Coraline, Maddie, and Jeffy at brunch today, posted by Jeffy.

They'd normally invite me if they were going out as a group. Maybe Alannah told them not to. Alannah didn't go either, but she's probably busy planning how to help me out of this mess.

Panic suddenly envelopes me at the notion of what might happen. At the notion of the unknown. At the idea she could get punished by intervening.

I just don't know what to do about any of it, but Alannah has resources to get information and I'm thinking I'll get the downlow on what her plan is in the bathroom at City Hall before anything. Then I can hear her out and decide if there's too much risk.

I open the browser on my phone and type inmate+pedophile+dead. And immediately I see the results.

Alan Howard Bell was found dead in a maximum security prison in Michigan. The article was only two paragraphs, published in the

Cheater

local paper of the town where the crimes were committed, and it said that the cause of death was not yet known. He was twenty-three years into a life sentence. He not only committed sexual offences against multiple minors, but also got convicted of murdering a nine-year-old girl.

I resisted the urge to dig into the case against him, instead feeling sad for Adam's grandmother, who, regardless of the sins her son committed had to feel all kinds of pain at the idea of his death. It had to bring all the stress and devastation back to her.

38

Chloe

Monday

I wake up in Derek's warm embrace, with my head on his bare chest, his arms are wrapped around me, and I'm thinking that waking up in my dream house sleeping on the chest of a hot guy... it's quite a trip. I refuse to let the question bouncing around the edges of my consciousness take center stage, knowing it's got something to do with the curious way I keep waking up cuddled with him.

I blink the haziness away as I stare out the giant window in my periphery. It's a blustery, windy morning.

For the most part, Derek left me be the rest of the day yesterday.

I tried to work, setting my laptop up in the office down the hall from the master bedroom, but there wasn't much to do after my marathon work session of the day before, so I mostly did some online "Steele" snooping until I tore myself away from it. There was a particularly upsetting Reddit thread full of comments from people who had things to say about how crooked the family is and how they ruin the lives of anyone who dares to try to get in their way. The threads included disgruntled ex-employees, mostly. They said some not-nice things about Derek's mom. Some very blunt things about Thaddeus getting what he deserved. He would throw tantrums in restaurants. He didn't take well to his advances being rebuffed from women. He was described as arrogant, pompous, and out of touch with reality. He was compared to Joe Pesci's character in the movie *Casino*. I dragged myself out of that unpleasant wormhole and then spent the rest of the day curled up in the perfect reading chair in the corner with the sexy wolf shifter romance instead.

I moved to the bed when I got to the last chapter at around eleven o'clock. Derek was already there, reading his novel on one side of the bed with an open bag of peanut M&Ms beside him. I tried not to react to the fresh bottle of water and bag of mini white chocolate Reese's peanut butter cups laying on the table on the empty side of the bed. I didn't dig into them or the yellow bag of M&Ms, despite the sudden sugar craving.

The giant bed proved big enough for me to simply stay on my side. Him being here ruined my plan to finish the last chapter and epilogue in bed the way I usually do. Alone. I always save the end of a book for when I'm alone in bed, so I can read uninterrupted and also... in case I cry. Not to mention how *not* easy it would be to focus on reading while beside my stalker. And that's down to multiple reasons, including the fact that the sight of a hot, muscled guy reading would set panties on fire if I posted a pic in my favorite online book club.

If we were together I'd probably have tried to playfully steal some of his candy and stuff it into my shirt, hoping to distract him from his reading. Or ask him to read me a sexy passage from my book aloud. But we aren't really together, so I turned the light off on my side of the bed.

"My light bothering you?" he asked softly.

"Nope. It never will bug me," I answered and then wanted to kick myself because that made it sound like I was anticipating a lot of instances like those in our future, like I was letting him know he could feel free to read in bed beside me any time for the rest of our lives.

To blow off my mortification, I went downstairs and made another sandwich. And I sent Alannah my 'proof of life' message. She gave me a thumbs up reply immediately and as I was wondering

Cheater

what she might have planned for tomorrow, Derek showed up, read over my shoulder, and stole half of my sandwich from my plate, kissed my neck, and walked off.

I wandered the main floor for half an hour, staring out windows, snooping in the drawers, cupboards, and closets, and when I got back upstairs, the light was off, and he was on his stomach in bed.

And the thought occurred that I could just leave. Just walk out.

I didn't leave. Because what would the fallout be? I got into bed beside him and stayed as far from him as possible without dangling off the bed. The next hour or maybe hours were spent thinking about how Adam didn't want me to visit his grandmother. I was thinking about his pedophile uncle dying in jail. And I was thinking about all the things I know about Derek so far. All the things I never know about Adam.

And I woke up like this. On his side of the bed. Snuggled with him.

I'm about to roll away when I become aware of something. A ring on my finger.

He didn't!

I lift my hand and stare at it.

He did. He slipped this on my finger while I was asleep.

"Happy wedding day," he says sleepily as I take in the giant but tasteful, beautiful oval halo rock on my hand. Much larger than the ring that used to sit on this finger, but tasteful, still. Not obnoxious. Not that it matters.

"Do you like it? The wedding ring that goes with it is an eternity band that'll slide right under the diamond." He touches my ring finger. "That's how long our marriage will last. Until eternity." He squeezes me tighter, growling a reverberating *Mm* as his lips press against my forehead.

I twist to look up at his sleepy, sexy face and before I'm able to form another thought, he says, "I'll go get coffee while you shower. I'll get ready in one of the other bathrooms. Already moved my shaving stuff over. Your dress should be here by nine. I took the liberty of messaging Frank last night to tell him we're getting married today and that you're taking a couple weeks off and when you're back, you're the boss. Not to worry, he'll look after your company for you." He rolls me to my back, kisses me again, and then rolls off me.

I'm left lying on my back absolutely stunned. God, what does Frank think of me right now?

"I'll send Alannah your proof of life text for you. For reasons I'm sure I don't need to elaborate on, I'll hang onto your phone for the morning." He leaves the room and my eyes dart to the nightstand. There's the book. My bottle of water. The bag of peanut butter cups. No phone.

Panic flares in my gut. Does he know about our conversation yesterday?

∞

When I get out of the shower and into the walk-in closet, which has a cute circa 1950s retro dressing table with stool and lights, there's already a cup of coffee and a domed platter waiting for me. While lifting it to find the oatmeal, bowl of berries, and tub of yogurt underneath I spot garment bags hanging behind the dressing table with a note attached to the mirror.

I set the dome lid back on the platter and pull the note from the bag. It's written in handwriting so perfect, Derek could handwrite the wedding invitations himself and it'd look like they were done by a calligrapher.

Chloe,
Dress arrived early. I had Nicola procure 3 dress options from your wedding Pinterest board. She sent over five pairs of wedding shoe options and a selection of head pieces and other accessories. My sister's hair and makeup girl will be here at nine thirty. I'll meet you downstairs at eleven.

Cheater

**Don't worry. There will be NO bad luck for us with me seeing you before the ceremony. I made a charitable donation this morning to cancel that out.
Can't wait to marry you.
Love,
Derek**

My heart sinks as I drop down onto the chair at the dressing table and look at myself in the mirror.

My wedding day.

Against my will.

What the fuck will Alannah do? She knows my phone is bugged so she won't say anything via text, which is good, but not knowing what she has planned has anxiety climbing through my veins like a fungus.

I can't do this. I can't marry Derek Steele and live like this. Live not knowing when my stalker is going to snap and snap my neck like a twig. Not knowing when he'll lash out and hurt someone I care about.

I now know that marrying Adam wasn't right for me, but I can't marry this man who I barely know, who has shown me things about his personality that are frankly frightening. Marriage should be based on love, commitment, mutual respect, but also... consent.

Derek doesn't care about my consent. He only cares about his 'goals'. Until when? When will his goal post get moved?

∞

At eleven minutes after eleven, Derek comes into the bedroom where I'm pacing. I know I'm late, but I'm in a dither. On the verge of a panic attack. I'm running through imaginary scenarios in my head.

He stops cold, mouth dropping, eyes blazing.

"My beautiful bride. Fuck, I'm a lucky guy."

He drops to his knees and wraps his arms around my waist. "This might seem a little late but... will you marry me, Chloe?"

Stunned, I say nothing.

He's in head-to-toe black. Black tux. Black shirt. Black bowtie. He looks like every woman's fantasy come to life.

I'm in my dream wedding dress. I don't know how the *now infamous* Nicola pulled off getting it here so quickly, fitting me so perfectly, but once I put it on and saw myself in the mirror, I didn't have the heart to take it off. The one and only wedding dress I'll ever wear? That remains to be seen. The floor-length, feathery, flowing, white cloud of perfection fits like it was bespoke.

My hair is up in a twist with just a few pearl embellishments on the sides. I'm not wearing a veil. My pearly white heels are perfection. I've got on a white lace garter with a shot of blue ribbon through it and Grace's stylist, who was lovely and seemed to have a good idea of my predicament judging by the way she didn't seem to take my somber mood to heart and didn't inundate me with questions you'd expect a hair and makeup pro to ask a blushing bride, said the hair embellishments aren't new as they've been in her inventory a while so could be classed as the *"old"*. Since the dress and shoes are *"new"* she presented me with a pair of diamond earrings that are my *"borrowed"* courtesy of Grace Steele.

"Not gonna answer?" Derek asks, looking up at me.

"What can I say, Derek? That you're out of your mind? That it's not a real proposal if you're forcing me to marry you to keep my loved ones safe? I think it's better that I say nothing."

"I guess I deserve that," he says as he rises and takes my left hand into his before dropping a kiss on my freshly manicured hand. He smiles as his thumb strokes my ring finger. "Though, instead of asking you to marry me I'll amend it and give you a different proposal. No... don't get excited, you're still marrying me, but I propose this: give this a chance. Give me a chance. Let me show you how real I am. I want to be your husband. I want you to be mine. Only mine. Permanently. I want that more than anything. That's why I've so decidedly

Cheater

pursued you. I've never been surer about anything, Chloe. Let's do this. Jump in with me. The water's fine. I promise."

I stare dumbfounded.

"We'd better go," he says without looking upset that I've said nothing in response. "There are people waiting."

39

Alannah Fisher

It's almost eleven o'clock. I've been standing by this door for ten minutes waiting for Craig to get me inside through a private entrance to the building. But I spot Adam. He's parking. He sees me and looks immediately panicked.

What in the world is he doing here right now? Has he heard about Steele's plan for upcoming nuptials? Did Craig break my confidence so Adam can come swoop in to Chloe's aid? I'm about to approach when the door behind me opens.

"Psst, Alannah," Craig calls out. "Get your ass in here."

"Adam's over there." I jerk my thumb behind me, "He saw me and now he's looking at you."

Craig looks at Adam and his forehead crinkles. We both murmur *what the fuck* in unison.

Craig, Adam, and I are in a meeting room inside the city hall in a town half an hour from home. It's clear we all know what's going on with Chloe even though Adam refused to answer questions about why he was here at first.

I told him I suspected it had something to do with Derek Steele and all the shit he's been pulling, and Adam's face said it all. I pressed and pressed, and he finally admitted he was here because Derek told him to be here for eleven. Derek told me to be here for eleven thirty. And this has me concerned.

Adam looks scared. Beyond afraid. Craig went into cop mode slash best friend mode and told Adam that I'd spilled the beans to him last night, which I had to do because I couldn't figure out what else to do to help.

I swore Craig to secrecy and gave him the skinny on the Chloe situation. He went a little ballistic, filling me in on just how dodgy the whole Steele family is, how they're the bane of Craig's department's existence, but due to a plethora of issues he can't get into, the police haven't been able to do much about them.

Jeff said similar things. Derek's father and oldest brother maintain some dodgy relationships. One of Derek's other brothers is getting deeper into the shady side of their family business. Nobody knows how Derek is or isn't involved because he's rarely in town and stays under radar for the most part, but Craig has always been sure Derek's hands are less than clean. When I told Craig how Derek overheard me and Chloe talking about Adam's hall pass, it seemed like a eureka moment because Craig muttered that he bets Derek Steele has all his nightclubs bugged so he can trade information to help his father and brothers.

Craig spent the night at my place and followed me here this morning after making a few calls to make sure he could get in here and book a meeting room as well as get me inside early, so we could do a run through before Chloe gets here.

We decided I'd get Chloe to the bathroom, but Craig would finesse the bathroom nearest to the entrance as being temporarily out of order, blocked off by janitorial services. I'd move her deeper into the building to get closer to the side door and out into my car which is directly beside the entrance. Craig would distract and then detain Derek and have one of his uniformed buddies escort my car out of the area until the uniformed cop was sure there was no tail. If there was, we'd go to the cop shop. If there wasn't, I'd take Chloe out of town to my brother's hunting cabin a few hours north.

Cheater

I've already told my brother not to tell a soul where I am. I packed a bag with enough clothes for me and Chloe both. I also have half a case of wine, and two coolers filled with groceries in my trunk with this week booked off work.

I just need the sign from Chloe that she still wants me to help her get out of here. I'll know when I see her. If she doesn't, I figured I'd come up with something to get Craig to back off, though if it comes to that, it won't be easy since he knows the main facts now and to say he's pissed is an understatement.

I can't help but feel a touch envious of my best friend. Because while I've got no desire to settle down and promise to grow old with somebody, if I were in that headspace, Derek Steele is the stuff fantasies are made of. The total package.

Yes, he's shown that his cheese has slid off his cracker, that he's got toys in the attic, but I've dealt with all sorts of personality types in my dating life, including mentally unstable ones. To have a rich, movie-star-looking guy devoted to making my every dream come true? I might be able to tolerate a bit of crazy. Life could be worse. And if it all went to shit, I'm sure there'd be a decent financial outcome at least. I wonder what that pre-nup looks like.

I *get* why Chloe's acting so shell-shocked. When I saw her at his apartment on Saturday morning, she was shook. Dazed. And no wonder.

Being pursued to that degree by a determined alpha male who has gone to extremes like this? Stalking. Threats. Cameras in her house and bugging her phone? Her reference to the bodyguard and being held at gunpoint is, of course, beyond the garden variety stalker stuff. But he sure said all the right things on Saturday.

And she feels bad about Adam, but the fact of the matter is, although I like Adam, I never thought he was perfect for Chloe and I hoped, for her sake, when that whole conversation about the hall pass happened that she'd use it and it'd inject some excitement, some color into her life again to where she'd see that she could be missing out by staying with him. Sure, he's good looking. He's a nice guy. But he's a little boring. And Chloe is not a boring person. Or, she wasn't before she met him. And she complained about the sex long before his spinal cord injury and to me, sex is a pretty pivotal part of a relationship. I don't want a monogamous relationship, but I certainly wouldn't sign up for one if the sex was bad.

Adam and everything that happened to him has turned my bubbly, happy, colorful bestie... beige. Beige and sad and stifled. He can be kind of judgy. And while it started long before the accident and I made no bones about it with her, telling her she shouldn't let him dim her fire, I haven't said much in the last six months because of course his accident snuffed it out entirely and I know there's no way she'd walk away from a guy now confined to a wheelchair without it being extreme circumstances.

Derek is the extreme circumstance.

Derek's brand of crazy? Of course that sounds like a situation she should get out of. But a little part of me wants to grab her, shake her, and tell her if she doesn't go for it, I'll happily switch places with her and let him fill my life with color for a while. I'd probably sleep with a gun under my pillow in case he snapped, but I'd enjoy the fun while it lasted and collect a healthy divorce settlement when it fizzled out.

When I told Craig just the very basics, that Adam had given her a hall pass and that Derek Steele overheard the details and decided to woo Chloe and is now forcing marriage by holding things over her head, over Adam's head, Craig was livid.

He says this family acts like they're above the law, that they've got enough money and connections to get away with shit that nobody should, and that he'd like nothing more than to bring them down a peg or three. Craig got so hotheaded about it, in fact, that it made me want to jump his bones and let him take all that aggression out on my body in sexual ways. But I knew that suggestion would piss him off, so I waited a few hours and then once he had calmed down, I let him jump my bones instead.

Craig and I aren't a couple, just friends with benefits, but the benefits are pretty beneficial. The man knows how to light my body

Cheater

ablaze on a regular day. Him riled up on behalf of my bestie only made him hotter. And even better in the sack last night. Finding out that Derek Steele is the cause has him ready to go full throttle cowboy to take that family down.

Now he's here in this little meeting room, in detective mode trying to get the truth out of a clammed-up Adam. At my urging and my dropping bits and pieces of information to let Adam know that I know everything, Adam finally opens up a little.

He admits he pushed Chloe into scratching an itch since his accident has ruined sex for them, and that Chloe got tangled up with one of the Steele brothers. Adam said it was distressing to be ordered to come today, to their wedding, but he's got no choice but to do whatever Derek Steele wants him to do.

That's the strange part. If Derek wants Chloe to marry him, does he really think it'll help his cause to have Adam here? Chloe would find Adam's nose being rubbed in this completely abhorrent.

I'm confused, Adam's distressed, and Craig is even more pissed. We're in the midst of a conversation about it all when Craig looks at his watch and says, "Ten minutes until you're supposed to meet them, Alannah. What say we go ahead, as planned, and get Chloe here with you while I distract Steele and then we'll talk further? Adam, you go on and wait like he said to do. I know at least two of the uniforms here for traffic court this morning. They should be done by now and I already asked one to stick close, so I'm gonna have a word. Be right back."

Craig leaves.

I turn to Adam. "She's a wreck," I say.

"I'm sure she is," he says, looking down at his hands in his lap.

"He's treating her like a princess."

"She deserves to be treated like a princess," he says softly.

"You look like shit."

His gaze meets mine. "I feel even worse. But this guy... you're fucking with him if you try to stop this, and I won't be caught in the crossfire. When Craig comes back I'll go down there like he told me to do and then I'll leave as soon as I can. I can't get involved."

Adam is terrified of this guy. But come on... this is Chloe here! Is he really planning to hang her out to dry? To do nothing?

Before I'm able to react, to ask when he became such a pussy, the door opens. Craig comes back in with a guy that's not in a uniform but who has *cop* written all over him.

"Guys, this is Steve Benson, one of my colleagues who's well-aware of the Steele family's bullshit so I'm gonna give him the gist, and-"

"And I need you..." Steve looks at me, pulls a gun and points it at Craig, "to sit your ass down beside him." He gestures to Adam with his gun.

Craig's eyes widen and he clenches his jaw. "Fuck!" he clips. "Not you!"

"What's happening?" I whisper.

"Benson's clearly on Steele payroll."

Benson shrugs. "Hand your service revolver over, then sit down, Jenkins. Gotta keep you three here for a while."

Craig's jaw muscles flex as he passes the guy his gun.

"Explain this," he demands.

Steve Benson speaks, "Got a call that something might go down here today that'd require my help. I didn't know until ten minutes ago it'd have to do with you, man. I'm just following orders." He looks at his phone. "Gotta take your picture. Line up together and say cheese." He lifts his phone with his left hand, fiddles for a second, then points his gun at us. While that's permeating, he snaps a picture, taps on his phone to presumably send it to someone, then his posture relaxes.

"Then what?" Craig asks.

"Don't know yet. Hang tight."

Adam speaks up, "Listen, I didn't know they were gonna be here. Please tell Derek Steele that. They hauled me into this room, but I didn't know why, and I wasn't part of any plot to break Chloe free."

Cheater

"I don't know anything about any of it," the dirty cop shrugs. "No clue who this Chloe even is. Just know you three need to stay here until I get further instructions. Might as well grab a seat Jenkins. And you, darlin'." He addresses my tits instead of looking at my face.

Adam looks absolutely terrified. "Can you at least tell Derek that I–"

This dirty cop cuts him off with a wave of his gun. "Talk to him yourself when you get outta here, man. I can't help you."

I look at Craig as he clenches his jaw, enraged.

Fear is clawing its way up my spine. Not for me, Adam, or Craig. It's obvious this guy is just keeping us here so that we can't interfere with his plans to marry Chloe. He's not about to shoot us dead here in the middle of a city hall boardroom if we sit here and say and do nothing. I only hope he's not planning to take us somewhere else after this... but I can't let myself think about that or I'll start to panic.

All I know is he's definitely going to make sure we don't stop Derek from legally binding Chloe to him.

I'm sorry, Chloe. I can't save you today.

40

Derek

Our stretch limo pulls up to the city hall and Chloe's eyes are on the van parked in the disabled spot. She knows Hallman is here. And she's confused about it.

I'm sitting across from her, my back to the driver. I rap on the window and it opens.

"Park a minute," I instruct. "I'll give you the cue when I'm ready to move along to our next stop."

"Yes, sir," the driver replies, closes the privacy glass and the vehicle turns off.

She looks at me, assessing, and decides to ask her burning question. "Why is Adam here?"

Her voice drips with accusation, so she's accurate in her assumption that he's here because of me.

"Better question," I say, "Why is Craig Jenkins here right now providing backup to Alannah Fisher?"

Guilt is written all over her face, but she doesn't say anything right away.

I wait.

Finally, she moistens her lips and is about to speak, but I put my index finger to her lips.

"No. Don't say anything that'll dig that hole deeper. No games, little bunny. Before anything else happens, I want you to consider the fact that you've forced my hand here and you have choices right now."

She blanches as I show her my phone screen with the photo that came through a couple minutes ago.

Her eyes widen as she takes in the image of Alannah, Hallman, and Hallman's cop buddy Craig Jenkins sitting in a boardroom. In the foreground of the photo is the barrel of a gun, pointing at Alannah.

"Derek. What? Oh my God!" She grabs her throat.

"Because I can't be everywhere at once, I've got someone listening to her calls. Flagging me when I need to know."

She winces.

"I warned you, baby. Didn't I?"

She doesn't respond, her hand trembles at her throat as she stares out the window, pale.

"So, they're in there in a room somewhere," I say. "And they're locked down for the moment by someone who isn't afraid to get his hands dirty to stay in that coveted golden glow of my father's approval. Now, here's what'll happen. You and I are taking a drive back to Columbus, to the Franklin County Courthouse. We'll buy our marriage license and then we'll get married there. That happens, Chloe. Today. There's no monkey business. No running to a bathroom to hide, no plotting and planning to escape me. None of that. You and I are getting married in less than an hour. We have an appointment. You choose to cooperate? They get released. Hallman is in there because I instructed him to be here, knowing Alannah was cooking up a scheme."

Her eyes are now on my face, and she looks afraid. I don't like it, but it's how it has to be for the moment.

"Columbus is where it was always gonna happen. This, here today? Showing you how serious I am. You want to go back to vague threats? Be my good girl. Misbehave and things won't be vague. Okay?"

She swallows.

Cheater

"Now..." I continue, "those three stay at the other side of that gun barrel until you're legally Mrs. Derek Steele. If you don't do your part, if you don't say *I do* and kiss your new husband when we're pronounced married, and if anyone at that courthouse as much as suspects you're not there of your own free will, one of the three of those people in that room will be pierced by a bullet while the other two watch them bleed out."

The pain on her face isn't easy to watch. Her hand shakily covers her mouth.

"Don't cry now and ruin that perfect makeup, baby," I say, leaning over and dropping a kiss on her neck.

She pulls her lip tight and says nothing.

"So, I'm thinking the cop," I say, stroking her cheek with the backs of my fingers. "He doesn't mean as much to you as the other two. Not to mention he's had a hard-on for my family for the past two or three years and it'll tickle my brother Jonah's funny bone to no end if that asshole is taken out. He was a major thorn in Jonah's side over that whole missing girlfriend thing. Then they worked together to try to get Thad pinched and out of the way because they were convinced Thad offed Jonah's girlfriend, which he didn't, but it was a reasonable suspicion. Anyway, all had a fundamental impact on Jonah, who was on the straight and narrow path before all that crap, but that's off topic so I won't bother explaining. Jenkins and Jonah ended their cease fire and Jenkins has been a thorn in Jonah's side, but Jonah is meticulous, unlike Thaddeus, so Jenkins must have had quite the stiffy thinking he'd get to haul me in today. Luckily the guy in there helping out is the one who's supposed to be assigned to take Elijah down. He's been a good ace to have in Eli's back pocket. So, like I said... basking in my father's golden glow. Anyway... if there is still any doubt left in your mind after the cop, there will be-"

"Stop," she whispers.

"I'd like to stop but vague wasn't enough for you, so I need to finish. Bear with me. Second shot'd have to be fired on your ex. Not sure yet if it'll be a kill shot or just a maim. We'll see how it goes.

Might make sure he's not only lost use of his legs... could take an arm out. It'd be a shame to do since he's supposed to go to the hospital tonight to say goodbye to his grandmother. So, hopefully I won't have to mess with that. And that leaves your bestie."

"I'll marry you," she whispers.

"Good. Good, good. But let's just say I'd spare Alannah today anyway since I have the feeling I'll need a bit of leverage with you after all is said and done today."

She stares at me with horror. I'm not enjoying it, but it's a necessity to get what I want. I'll make it up to her later.

"If there's any doubt left in your mind about how serious I am about marrying you and making you the happiest woman in the world, let me just say that I'll keep on working to prove myself to you." I take her hand and kiss it. "I can't wait to make you my wife. Everything clear?"

She nods slowly.

"Any questions?" I ask.

She shakes her head.

"Good."

I rap on the window, which rolls down, and say, "We're good to go, Neil."

∞

"By the power vested in me by the state of Ohio, I now pronounce you husband and wife. Now you may kiss."

I take her face into both hands and bring her mouth to mine, tenderly kissing her.

"Chloe," I whisper, "You've made me so happy." I deepen the kiss and enjoy the fact that she's participating. Not avidly, mind, but enough to be convincing. I release her face so I can grab her hand.

We walk past my sister Grace and the family concierge, Carson, who came to be witnesses. Jonah showed up at the last minute as well, which surprised me.

Cheater

I already apologized to Chloe that Alannah couldn't be here, saying, "Sorry, baby, that your best friend can't be here today. We'll have her there for the family ceremony in a couple months."

Before we went into the building, I asked one more time, "Do I need to reiterate what's gonna happen in there?"

She shook her head slowly, nibbling her lip, hands trembling. She was frightened, I could see it, so I said, "Everything is going to be okay, baby. You'll be my good girl and it'll all be okay. Alannah can come see you when we get back from our honeymoon."

She looked breathtakingly beautiful as she walked to me carrying the white bouquet Grace brought for her. The walk was something I insisted on, despite the fact that it was a short walk and not in a church like I'm sure most brides would prefer. I wanted that bit of tradition – for her to walk down the aisle to me, to take my hand, and promise to be mine forever. I instructed her on this just before we stepped inside, so once we were past the double doors, she waited twenty feet away and then when the officiant gave the nod, she stared at me for a good thirty seconds before her feet started moving. She walked toward me, staring into my eyes.

She repeated her vows and promised to be my wife until death. And while she doesn't look nearly as thrilled to be here as I'm sure I do, she was my good girl.

The way she stared into my eyes when she said, 'for better or for worse' and 'for richer or for poorer' and 'in sickness and in health' as well as all the other parts, all felt real. She had tears in her eyes. And when I said those things to her, they absolutely *were* real.

Carson took photos of us including as I put her ring on as well as when Chloe shakily slipped the thick gold wedding band onto my finger on cue.

"Congratulations," Grace says as we get outside, kissing my cheek and then awkwardly reaching over to pull Chloe into a hug. Chloe is robotic about it, but doesn't give anything away.

Carson smiles and clasps my hand in a firm shake. "Congratulations."

Jonah shakes my hand and slaps my back with affection before he kisses Chloe's cheek. "Congrats, you, too. What's happening now?"

"Now? Now, I'm taking her to a honeymoon suite to consummate our marriage for the rest of the day and night. Then in the morning we're taking the jet to go for our honeymoon."

Jonah smirks as Grace rolls her eyes. Chloe stares at the bouquet in her hands.

"You'll have the jet back for Sunday, Mr. Steele?" Carson asks. "Your father needs it Monday evening."

"No problem," I say. "We'll be back Saturday afternoon actually, so we can be at the fortieth anniversary shindig Saturday night. We'll take an extended honeymoon later."

"Very good," Carson replies.

"Thanks for your help this morning, Carson." I say.

He smiles. "My pleasure. Always."

He, as usual, pulled out all the stops when I called him to ask him to assist me in making things happen quickly with the marriage license, with everything else I needed to organize for today.

I kiss my sister on the cheek, clap my brother on the back and say, "Means a lot you came. Thanks, Joe." I squeeze his shoulder.

"Congrats again," Jonah replies, "Welcome to the family, Chloe. It's even crazier than it seems."

Grace and Jonah exchange glances that I'm not sure about, until it dawns that I gave them affection, which they're not used to from me.

Chloe's mouth twitches in the beginnings of an attempt at a smile at Jonah's joke, but it doesn't follow through. She looks beyond shaken up.

"See you when you get back," Grace says. "Where are you off to?"

"It's a surprise for Chloe," I say.

"Ah, well have a wonderful time. Congratulations." She squeezes Chloe's hand and steps back, looking pensive. She doesn't know Chloe's here because three of her friends are being held at gunpoint, but she does sense that Chloe's not happy. And even if she hadn't been there for the Saturday breakfast or the Sunday brunch, she'd still know something isn't right with Chloe. My sister is observant.

I know Grace wants everything to be perfect at all times. She's worried about this. She'll be a good friend to her, she'll focus on her instead of me for a change, maybe.

"It's all good," I assure my sister who smiles hesitantly before hugging me, saying, "Congratulations, big bro. I hope it's as perfect as you're expecting it to be."

"It will be," I assure, then grab my bride's hand and whisk her to the waiting limo, wave Neil aside, and hold the door open for her myself.

She climbs inside.

Once the door is shut, I lean over and kiss her again.

"You're mine," I tell her. "I'm so fucking happy."

She stares at me with a difficult-to-read expression.

"What is it, baby?" I ask, cupping her cheek.

Her nostrils flare and by the rise and fall of her chest, the tautness of her shoulders, I know she's trying hard to maintain composure.

"Let," she whispers, "Them..." She swallows. "Go," she finishes.

"Ah. Yes. Not a problem." I pull my phone out and call Detective Steven Benson as we pull away.

"Mr. Steele," he greets.

"Benson. All good now. Let Alannah and Hallman go after giving Alannah a warning to do nothing else. Tell her she'll hear from us when we get back on Saturday. Have a good, long conversation with Jenkins before you cut him loose. Make sure he's fully briefed on protocol for Chloe, myself, and the others from here on out. He's now *in*. Make sure he understands."

"On it," he says.

There was a time when Detective Benson was resistant to being in our inner circle, too.

I end the call and turn to my wife.

"In?" she whispers.

A smile spreads across my face as happiness floods me. She's mine. This is my wife beside me. *My* wife. For life.

"In?" she repeats. "What's that mean?"

"Ah," I shrug. "Craig Jenkins is now on payroll."

She tips her head confused. "No. No way would he do that. He's not dirty."

"He'll be as dirty as we need him to be," I say. "It's like conscription with my family. We draft people in as needed. Now that he's privy to some things where you're concerned, he's in. Whether he wants it or not."

She looks crestfallen.

My phone chimes, so I check and see a rare text message from my father. Or maybe from his assistant.

Michael Steele: Congratulations, Derek.

I scoff with amusement and write back

Thanks, Dad. See you Saturday at the party.

I don't generally address him. He rarely addresses me. But we had a pretty poignant conversation at the curb at his place yesterday where, in the company of my remaining brothers, he informed me of his willingness to erase further problems in his family.

"I always figured there's nothing as painful as losing one of your children. I faced that when my third born son was taken as a small boy and I didn't think I could get him back."

"As if you tried," I muttered.

He went on as if I hadn't spoken, though my three brothers paid attention and looked at me with an expression that I fucking loathed.

"But I've come to realize it's even more painful to have one of your children continually and willfully make your life and your other children's lives difficult as my second-born tarnished the family name with his idiocy, hot-headedness, his inferiority complex, along with his greed and sloppiness. The stress he caused your mother..." He let that hang with a severe expression on his face.

My father then did something he hasn't done since I was a child. Laid a hand on my shoulder affectionately.

Cheater

"Not too long ago, I gave Jonah my blessing to work with authorities to put Thaddeus away for a while. To give us all a break. But since the headache of my second-born went away permanently instead and has since made all our lives much better I now realize that regardless of familial ties, the family garden needs to be kept free of weeds. Weeds strangle the health of the rest of the garden. I will no longer hesitate to weed the Steele garden, my sons. You all know your role in this family. You all know the rules. Now you all also know that my tolerance for bullshit from my children is nil. And I'm not talking about making sure people are tried for the crimes they've committed."

My father then squeezed my shoulder poignantly before letting go, stepping back, and walking back to his house.

The looks on Asher's, Jonah's, and Elijah's faces showed emotion at the display of conditional love from the man who made us.

It didn't faze me. Not a bit. Ever since I was a child and knew he wasn't going to pay my kidnapper the ransom he could easily afford, I've always known I'm expendable to my father.

∞

The hotel I chose is a five-minute drive from the courthouse and another short drive in the morning to the airport. Lunch hour traffic is still a little heavy but it's not long until we're here.

∞

I scoop her up into my arms to carry her over the threshold of our hotel suite, startling her.

Once we're on the other side of the door, I put the do-not-disturb sign on the knob, close, and lock it.

There's champagne chilling in a bucket beside a dish of strawberries and the bed is turned down.

I look at my bride, who is staring at the bed.

"Well..." I start and her eyes dart to me, "Dinner is being delivered at seven so, we've got a little under six hours to consummate our marriage."

"Are they safe?" she asks quietly, hands shaking.

I sit, keeping her on my lap and grab both hands, pressing my lips to the top of one, then the other. "They're fine."

"I... I need to talk to them."

"You can speak with Alannah. I've already told you, Hallman no longer exists for you." I reach into the inside pocket of my tuxedo and pass Chloe her phone. "Make it fast, baby. I'm very ready to consummate our marriage." I kiss her on the jaw. She rises from my lap and goes to the window, giving me her back.

I reach for the champagne bucket as she shakily touches her screen before putting her phone to her ear.

"Lan?" she whispers and then starts to weep, entire body shuddering out relief. "You're okay? Yeah? I'm so, so sorry."

She holds the phone, her shoulders shaking with her silent crying for a moment before she continues to speak. "I can't help it. I feel responsible. You're sure you're okay? For sure? Yep. Yeah, it's done. Le Meridien, but don't do anything. Don't! Okay... He said Saturday. Yeah. No, no prenup... Are you still there? No, he doesn't believe in divorce. Okay, yeah. Okay. Love you. I will." She holds the phone a minute. "I know. Bye."

She ends the call and drops her arms before putting her forehead to the window.

"Chloe?" I call.

It takes a minute before she turns to me, looking resigned.

I pass her a glass of champagne. She takes it.

"A toast," I say, holding my glass up. "To our future. To happily ever after for both of us." I touch her glass with mine.

She drinks the entire thing back. As she puts her glass down, I wrap both arms around her and pull her tight to me.

"I'm gonna make you so fucking happy," I vow.

She shakes her head, then pushes me with both hands against my chest, looking angry.

Cheater

I release her.

"The ends will justify the means, baby."

She backs away from me, shaking her head with anger emanating from her entire being.

"Go ahead and get ready for me. There's bridal lingerie in there. I haven't seen it yet. I had the staff set it in there for you when they brought our things here. Go, put it on for me."

Her eyes narrow. Her little fists clench.

I let out a little chuckle and refill both glasses with champagne.

"While it'd be fun to entertain your temper and bring you to heel, not today. Today, I want to make love to you to consummate our marriage, so please go put on your lingerie and come back to me, Mrs. Steele."

Her nostrils flare and she unclenches and re-clenches her fists.

"Now, baby. Don't disappoint me." I flash her a smile.

She stomps to the bathroom and slams the door as hard as she can. I laugh.

41

Chloe

I step out of the fancy bathroom into the lavish honeymoon suite wearing a white lace number that's the epitome of bridal lingerie while also being overtly sexual. The white lace nightie falls to my ankles with a deep slit up the front of one leg as well as a plunging neckline and delicate, scalloped straps criss-crossing over my breasts and down my back.

My nipples show, but my bikini area is somewhat subdued by the underwear that came with it.

I've taken my hair out of the updo and it's down around my shoulders in soft waves. Grace Steele's hair girl did my hair with intention in this way so that it would look good both up and later down with minimal primping from me. Not that I feel the need to primp. What I *do* feel the need to do is carefully follow my new husband's directions after today's terrifying realizations. Anger and fear take up equal space in my mind right now.

No, Derek's threats aren't empty.

Yes, he's even more dangerous, more unhinged than I thought. And I already thought it was bad.

Twice, he's had guns pointed at Adam.

And now, Alannah and Craig, too.

Thank God Alannah sounded okay when I talked to her. Her voice was shaky, I know she's affected, but in true Alannah fashion she's more worried about me than herself. Though she'd probably say the same thing about me.

I know I'm about to get dicked down because while I'm not conceited, even I can say I look pretty sexy in this getup. Then again, Derek looks at me like he would lick caked mud off my body just to prove he wants me.

He's sitting on the bed, back to the headboard, legs crossed while casually talking on his phone when I come out.

His eyes hit me and his expression changes. His face looks like stone all of a sudden, so fear wins out over anger.

"That's it. Gotta go," he says, then ends his call and puts the phone down.

He rises.

"Get the fuck over here."

My heart skips a beat; my bare feet are frozen to the plush carpet.

He doesn't wait.

His long strides eat up the space between us and I back up, but hit the bathroom door with my behind as Derek takes my face into both hands.

"Do you have a clue how happy I am right now?" He demands in a low, rumbling near-growl. "These straps... like that night we met."

And then he lets out an actual growl as he fuses his mouth with mine.

I go weak in the knees, lightheaded, and just as fast, he's released my mouth.

"You're fucking breathtaking. Beautiful. And you're mine, Chloe. Mine, baby." His expression softens. "I wanna devour you."

I swallow. Yes, I believe he does.

He rubs his nose along mine as his palm skates down my face, over my shoulder, and then down my arm until he clasps my hand in his and brings it to his mouth, pressing a kiss to it.

"My rings on your finger, my name attached to you now. Fuck yeah. The way you looked at me as you walked down that aisle to me was everything, wife. Everything. You looked in my eyes and you saw it, didn't you? You saw I'd do anything to have you. You know that, right? That I'll do anything for you? The look on your face as you walked to me made me think you've finally clued in. And I know you're scared, but I'm gonna prove to you that you've got nothing to be afraid of as long as you let me do my job of being your husband."

My heart is pounding so hard I'm afraid it's going to run out of steam.

"Being your husband is the first job I've really, really wanted, Chloe. I like goals. I like hitting them. And my goal on a daily basis for the rest of my life is providing for you, protecting you, and making you happy. Fuck, I like that. A daily checklist. Is my wife safe, happy, and have I fucked her yet today? We've got the dream, you know? Being together, being everything to one another."

He waits as if I'm going to have a response to this.

When it becomes obvious that I don't have a reply, he presses his lips to my hand again and then presses my palm to his face and leans into it. "I know you're afraid, but you don't need to be. I've talked the talk, now I'll walk the walk, little bunny. I hope you clued in on that walk to me today, that you have a man who will worship you until the day I die. Who will ravish you every fucking day until I'm too old to do it. Who will go to any and all extremes to have you, to keep you. To let you know that I take my job very seriously. I'm the luckiest man on the planet. I get to give you everything you dreamt about having when you felt all that aching, all that loneliness, the rejection. I'm so glad I get to make you happy."

"Stop," I plead, brokenly, unable to take much more of this.

"Okay. I'll stop. Instead of continuing to talk about making you happy, how about I get down to doing it?"

"Oh, you're gonna go get an annulment and stop bothering me?" I ask, but my voice is shaky.

He shakes his head like he finds me funny.

"Best get this consummated now then so annulments are off the table, huh?" He walks me to the bed, and we fall down onto it, him on his back, me on top of him. He quickly rolls me to my back and shoves the lace nightie up, growling his approval when he exposes the tiny white thong underneath. He moves down my body while gathering the skirt of the nightie up until it's fully above my waist.

"Yeah," he whispers as his mouth touches down gently between my legs, kissing over the thong. His hot breath makes goosebumps rise. He hooks into the thong at both hips with his thumbs and hauls it down before moving up my body.

"Undo my pants, wife," he whispers against my mouth.

He looks and sounds so sexy. That thick wedding band on his hand is going to attract even more attention, because women who see it are going to wonder what kind of husband he is, wonder what sort of woman could snag a man this hot.

I want to knee him in the balls. I want to scream out a primal war cry while kneeing him in the balls and raking my freshly manicured nails across his perfect face. I feel ready to wage a war against him. He'd gone too far from day one and now he's gone *far* beyond that.

But now we're married. He's ripped me out of my life and inserted me into his.

I was terrified for Alannah, Adam, and Craig. And now I'm absolutely furious.

I had no hope in hell of changing his mind, not when I tried to be bitchy, not when I tried to be cold and freeze him out. He was resolute in his determination to have me and now it's done. I've signed the contract – the marriage paperwork – I've said the vows and worn the dress, which now hangs in the bathroom.

It's over. I'm married to Derek Steele.

But what's next?

"Are you not feeling like my good girl right now? Are you, my beautiful wife, feeling naughty? Because your eyes are full of fire. And I gotta say, I kinda fucking like it. Look how hard you're making me." He presses his erection between my legs to show me. "I'm gonna spend the next few hours kissing you all over, fucking you hard. Fucking you gentle. Making you cry out over and over. You're gonna suck your husband's cock, you're gonna take it in that sweet pussy and milk it dry, then when it's hard again, I'll ram through that tight ring of your ass again while I whisper into your skin that you're mine."

How did my life so drastically change in the past few weeks? Well, it drastically changed earlier this year and now again. And I've been powerless over all of it. I want some power back.

I whimper out some frustration and try to fight him off as he kisses me, slapping his face, but he pins my wrists and his eyes prod deep into my soul as he shakes his head, his cheek pink from my slap.

"Please, Chloe, don't make our first time as husband and wife be me forcing you."

Incensed, I snarl, "No! No, you don't get this." I shake my head with disgust, "You do not get my submission right now, Derek. No! Not after what you've done today. If you're determined to have me right now, it's only gonna be with a fight."

He shrugs. "If you say so." His eyes light up with something wild before he grabs the bodice of the beautiful, expensive lace nightgown that I know from the tag came from France and cost over two grand, and he rips it down, breaking a strap and exposing one of my breasts.

I shouldn't have expected any less, but somehow I did.

I gasp, but that's all I get out as his tongue is suddenly in my mouth. He fiddles with his tux pants and then he's breaching me between the legs, ramming in hard.

I yelp in pain and try to fight, try to struggle, but his weight is pressing me to the bed and there's no escape.

"Shh," he whispers, palm covering my mouth. "Shh." He pulls out and thrusts back in slowly, fingers from his free hand sliding between us and pressing against my clit as I shove him, clawing at his shoulders, trying to push him off.

I've drawn blood with a scratch on his arm, which makes me stop. He doesn't stop though. He rubs little circles between my legs while I'm still full of him, while he continues to flex his hips, adding a rotation motion and increasing pace on both his finger circles and with his hips. His eyes bore into mine while his hand continues to cover my mouth.

I squeeze my eyes shut tight in order to hide from his penetrating gaze, but I can't hide from sensation because in addition to the penetration and the clit stimulation, his mouth closes around my exposed nipple and he pulls, making my body react against my will.

At my reaction, Derek moves his hand away from my mouth and he licks a path up to my lips before his lips tenderly touch mine as his hand takes over on my breast.

"Baby," he whispers sweetly before he pulls out of me, then tenderly strokes my cheek, wiping away the tears I didn't even realize had fallen. "Shh, don't cry, Chloe. It's okay. I'm gonna make you so, so happy. Give me a chance."

I want to scream that why should I give him a chance when he hasn't given me a choice. But there's no point.

He turns me over to my stomach and then he's back inside again, getting in without resistance with the now-present lubrication, which I can't fathom, but there is, so it's not hurting anymore. Now it's feeling good. And that's confusing to me as I bite the pillow, fist the sheets, and let the wave of sensation take me away. He's now holding both hips as he repeatedly, slowly strokes the inside of me over and over.

His mouth touches my ear. "I'm gonna make you so happy. I know you're upset right now, Chloe, but the ends are going to justify the means. You're mine. You're mine and you're safe, and you matter to me. I see you."

I'm turned to my back again. I stare to the side, not wanting to give him any more eye contact, but he tilts my chin so that our eyes are locked, then lets go of my face and puts his fingers between us again, stroking me down there.

"Guess what?" he whispers.

"I refuse to play a guessing game with you."

"Okay, I'll tell you. I love you," he says, pulling three quarters of

Cheater

the way out before driving back in to the root. "Ah! That's good. You feel so goddamn good."

"You don't love me," I whisper. "You have no idea what love is."

"I didn't. But now I do. Please don't be afraid to love me back. I can't wait for you to love me back. I know it'll happen and I'm sure you're going to try to stop yourself when you start falling, but fall, Chloe. Fall into love with me. Don't be afraid. It'll be so worth it. I promise."

As he's spoken, he's increased the friction on my clit and his words have thrown me off so much that I've forgotten to guard myself and I spontaneously come. I come hard, sensation rocketing through me. He comes with me, burying his face in my hair, groaning into my neck.

This is it. I'm married. To a man who swears we'll never divorce. I burst into sobs. My entire body is wracked with it.

He kisses my neck over and over, playing with my hair, trying to soothe me.

How can he think *this* is love?

No longer filled with him, I'm still full, but filled with hopelessness as he collapses beside me, kissing my shoulder while I lie here with his wedding rings on my finger, his cum inside me, in the honeymoon suite of a nice hotel wearing expensive, ripped French lace.

∞

He's been holding me for half an hour, my cheek is on his bare chest, my body draped over his with my naked legs tangled up with this tuxedo pant-clad ones as he traces the straps of my nightie with his fingertip, seeming deep in thought as I stare up at his face.

"What 'cha thinkin' about?" he asks, eyes meeting mine.

I say nothing.

"Wanna know what I'm thinking about?" he asks.

"No," I grumble.

He smiles a dazzling smile and laughs.

I frown.

"I'm thinking we should have a baby as soon as possible. I'm thinking you should stop taking those birth control pills every day. You have, what, three left? We have a lot of bedrooms to fill in our new house."

The look I give him must speak volumes because he has the decency to look a little contrite as he shrugs. "The sooner the better in my opinion. Have a bunch of kids now and we'll still look semi-youthful when they're all off to college and we wanna spend that next ten years traveling and enjoying the empty nest while we wait for grandbabies."

My heart twinges painfully because in a normal world, a normal marriage, it would be the perfect plan.

"Are you plotting my demise, my bride?" he asks. "Is that what you're doing?" He pokes my nose playfully. "Because no pre-nup, so... not a bad idea since it's the only way you'll get rid of me."

"How rich are you?" I ask with my best evil eye gleam.

"Very," he whispers, looking gleeful with amusement.

Feeling dejected that my bitchy little snipe failed, I roll away and go to the bathroom. I lock it behind myself and run a bath in a huge, deep tub.

I turn the jets on and lean back against the bath pillow, closing my eyes.

When it's deep enough, I sink down, going under, tuning out the rest of the world, holding my breath and just... being. Not thinking. Not feeling. It's like I'm in my very own sensory deprivation chamber.

I used to do this in the bath when I was a teenager, when Bryan got really sick, then later when he was ... no more. Turn off all the noise, tune out all the bad shit. Just, float. Float like I floated before consciousness, when I was a fetus in my birth mother's stomach. Maybe she wanted me then. Maybe she loved the idea of me. Maybe she glamorized motherhood in her mind before the reality of a crying, hungry baby overwhelmed her teenaged brain.

Cheater

Derek is rich enough to buy me a sensory deprivation chamber. Maybe I should ask for one – get something out of this marriage.

I'm suddenly yanked from the water, hauled out of my warm, bubbled cocoon of stresslessness and facing the wild eyes of my new husband. Derek's expression is stark. Fear? He's standing in the tub, in his (still undone from when he fucked me) tuxedo pants, holding me. He steps out of the tub and sets me on the countertop as if I'm breakable, dragging towels off the towel bar as he examines my face, cussing under his breath, "Fuck, fuck, holy fuck, baby, fuck."

He's winded. Panicked. His hands are trembling as he grips me.

"Stop. I was just trying to take a bath. Let go of me." I push him as he touches my face, my arms, looking wild with worry.

"You... you..." He flinches and looks back at the tub and then at me again, seeming like he's traumatized, shaking it off. "You were underwater. I thought..." He looks back at the tub and blinks a couple times.

"I was holding my breath," I defend, covering myself with a towel and climbing off the vanity onto the soaking wet tiles. "Did you think I was drowning myself? That I'd rather be dead than be your wife?"

He flinches again almost like I've landed a blow on his face. He rakes his hand through his hair, then grabs a towel and dabs at his torso as he leaves the bathroom.

I pull the plug and dig through the bag he brought for us until I find my toothbrush and toothpaste.

I don't know if he packed this for us today or if he had someone do it but nothing important seems to have been forgotten, which is good if I don't have access to my stuff for a few days.

A honeymoon. Five days alone with him somewhere after a trip on the Steele private jet? I stare at myself in the mirror as I wipe away what's left of my eye makeup and again can't fathom how I wound up here. I'm not entirely uncultured, but married to a wealthy, powerful guy like him? I guess he's not the typical, wealthy powerful guy type, is he?

I'm not the trophy wife type. What on earth must my boss Frank think of me after getting a call from our largest client who informed him that he's marrying me and that when I get back from my honeymoon, I'll be his boss?

Do I even want to be a boss?

No. Not really.

Not really able to wrap my mind around any of that, I step out of the bathroom and see Derek in the sitting area on the couch, staring out the window with a drink in his hand. A large one. He takes a big swallow and stares out the window with a bitter expression.

I dig into the wardrobe where our clothes have been hung and all that's here is one outfit and sneakers for each of us. I pull down a new soft, gray pair of yoga pants for me with a long, drapey matching cardigan, and tank top. I find underthings in the drawer folded neatly beside Derek's socks and underwear and take all this back to the bathroom.

42

Derek

I try to pull in some slow, cleansing breaths and follow them with a not-so-cleansing glug of my bourbon.

When I busted the bathroom lock with plans to join her in the tub, I was first thrown that the room seemed empty. When I saw the still water of the tub, and then movement underneath, I sprang into action and hauled her out of the water, images assaulting my mind and blurring my vision.

As I got her out, saw she was breathing, conscious, my mind was filled with reels of when I was maybe five or six, at one of our vacation homes. I hadn't forgotten the events of that day, but this was the first time in years they came to me so vividly.

I'd wandered away from the nanny; I was looking for my mother. I found her in the tub, unconscious. The water looked much like this water did, only her arm was draped over the side and red drips were dripping from her fingers, hitting the tiles.

She tried to end it all. I think if not for me walking in when I did, she could've succeeded.

After that day, we didn't see her. For a long time. Weeks? Months? I don't know. But when she came back, my father doted on her. Things changed. He spent more time at home. Glued to her. She got pregnant for the last time. With Grace. He didn't dote on us, not much changed for us, we were raised by the help, but she was his focus. He spent a lot of time with her, taking her on trips, buying her gifts. He bought her another place, the Vermont place, and we spent the best summer of our lives there when Grace was born. And my mother was different. She drank more. She was a little more manic. And I think I was different, too.

The fear that seized me pulling Chloe out of the tub is something I'll never forget. But Chloe wasn't lifeless. She wasn't bleeding. And I had the strength to pull her out unlike with my mother when I had to get the nanny, who'd been rocking Naomi to sleep.

I vividly remember the way Naomi was crying. Thaddeus had a fit. Asher was crying. I don't know where Jonah and Eli were. But I remember the sound of baby Naomi crying mixed with the sounds of the ambulance while fear gripped me that my mother's skin was so pale.

Chloe's here. Pulling me from those thoughts. She's making the bed. Now she's lying on it and pointing the remote at the television.

Our eyes meet. Her expressive eyes are filled with sadness.

It's our wedding day and she's depressed. She's depressed because she doesn't like what I did to get her here.

I need air.

I message Kenny who's got two guys stationed outside in cars in case there's any bullshit. I tell him to have someone sit outside this hotel room until I get back.

"I need air," I state. "Stay here. I'll be back."

Her eyes flash with confusion as I drop the still wet suit pants and my boxer briefs, and change into the clothes I'd brought to travel in tomorrow. Sweats and sneakers. She's wearing her travel clothes, too. I figured we'd spend the rest of today naked. No such luck.

43
Chloe

He's been gone for a few hours when there's a knock on the door.

I rise from the bed and peer out the peephole. Room service. And Ken, the guy who held us at gunpoint. Should have known I'd have a babysitter.

I open it and wave the room service guy in.

Ken gives me a nod. I don't return it. I'm not trying to be a bitch about him doing his job. Though really, what decent person takes on a job where they have to do the things Derek pays him to do?

My thoughts stray to Craig again, who is a solid guy, a good person, a friend of mine who has now been thrust into a world he's been trying to dismantle. All for trying to help me.

Maybe I can make Derek understand how fundamentally wrong that is. If I pleaded with him, would he give Craig a break and let him live his life without becoming the thing he hates? Derek wants me, clearly, could I somehow wield that into getting him to leave Craig alone?

I fetch my wallet to tip the guy who delivers the cart loaded with dome-covered plates and a bucket containing my favorite wine, which I'm sure this hotel probably brought in for me because it's not something you'd generally find at a swanky place like this.

I shut the door and sit.

My phone chimes, so I lift it seeing a text from Alannah.

I don't know how this happened but brace before you click.

There's a link. I'm feeling queasy as I click it and see a gif on a loop of Derek and I leaving the courthouse today, me in all my designer bridal gown glory, him looking like a thirst trap about to go viral.
Fuck.
Fuck!
I scan the headline.

Derek Steele Marries. But There's Dirty Laundry Here.
This JUST in. Derek Steele, son of local infamous shipping magnate and real estate developer Michael Steele, just married Chloe Turner of Dayton, OH. While they were both decked out in wedding garb befitting a lavish wedding with five hundred guests, they tied the knot at the Franklin County Courthouse in a simple ceremony today. Steele, never married, owns The Fifth, The Strip, and the Downtown nightclubs here in Columbus as well as several other establishments elsewhere in the state. Turner was engaged to be married until very recently to local award-winning journalist and accessibility activist Adam Hallman, who recently suffered a spinal cord injury after a horrific car accident.
While Adam Hallman is confined to his wheelchair, it seems Chloe Turner sure landed on her feet.
Filthy Laundry Online has it on good authority that the children of Michael Steele never requires spouses to sign a pre-nuptial agreement.

Cheater

This is a blog with no other entries. It was just created for this purpose.

Vertigo briefly attacks my senses as I calculate the ramifications here. I'll have to explain this to my parents. My friends. This means things are going to be even messier than I expected they'd be.

Derek wanted Adam to take the blame, but when people find out, they're going to be looking at me like I'm a gold-digging cheater. A monster who got a better offer than what I was looking at with my paraplegic fiancé.

Adam's probably at the hospital with his family, saying goodbye to their gran while they deal with the emotional whirlwind of their uncle's death.

As I sit on the bed, my phone chimes again.

Someone tagged me several times on Instagram.

The same gossip blog's Instagram. And it's a carbon copy of the other article, only this one has me tagged and there are a lot of comments.

"Chloe Turner is a disgusting human being. She's dumped her fiancé a respected journalist who lost use of his legs in an accident for Derek Steele. Gold digger or what?" - Anonymous

Underneath it, a commenter says, "Who wouldn't? Look at that hottie. And he's rich?"

Nested under that is a comment that says, "Yeah, but everyone knows the Steeles are practically mafioso."

I exit the app and write back to Alannah.

FML. Check Instagram. It's worse.

She sends me a broken heart emoji and then messages again.

I'm here if you need me. Love you.

The door clicks and opens. Derek is back. He doesn't look smug. He doesn't look happy.

"You'd better get a load of this," I tell him and open up the link Alannah sent and hand him my phone.

He takes it, looks at the screen, and massages his forehead with his fingers.

His eyes close for a second and when they open, he says, "Might as well pack up."

I frown.

"You don't want to go on a trip with me, do you?" he asks.

I shake my head.

"Then let's go. We'll swing by your parents' place and then we'll go home."

"My parents?"

"They need to meet me. You need to tell them. This could go viral. Someone went to the trouble to put it up, they'll undoubtedly want to spread it far and wide. Let's go." He waves toward the door.

I stare at the dining cart full of food and wine. At the flower petals all over the rug.

"Carson?" Derek says into his phone, "I need PR to take control of the gossip that's come from my and Chloe's wedding today. Yes, on the..." He looks at my phone, "Filthy Laundry site. Chloe Turner hashtag."

God, I'm a hashtag.

"Right. I'll keep my phone nearby." He ends the call.

And I get up and start gathering our things.

A few minutes later, I hear him on the phone again.

"Just Jeannie blog? Yeah, not a shocker." His voice drifts away as he steps into the hallway.

I wait for him to come back in.

"Just Jeannie?" I whisper.

"Jeannie Gilligan. Your ex's ex."

I frown. Jeannie?

"The one whose sister got murdered by Hallman's uncle. So, clearly she's feeling unhinged after his death if she hasn't got the good

Cheater

sense to realize she's fucking with my family in an effort to lash out at you."

I blink a couple times as this permeates. The little girl who was killed by Adam's uncle was Jeannie's sister? What?

I finish packing up our things, mind scattered, hands shaky. It's all I can do to make sure I remember everything.

∞

I tie my hair up into a ponytail as Derek speaks to the driver that drove us earlier. I hear him give out gate and garage door codes to the driver, who will be bringing everything back to the house, putting it into the garage until we get back later.

Someone brought his SUV here and he got the hotel to put our meals into to-go containers and pack up our wine for later, too. Derek hands the food to Neil, telling him to enjoy the meals with his girlfriend tonight, that we'll get food on the road. He opens the SUV passenger door, takes my hand, and leads me in.

∞

"What are we even doing?" I mumble after we've been on the road for a while.

Derek hasn't said a word. In fact, he seems like he's a million miles away. He hasn't tried to hold my hand or have any sort of conversation.

"I'm taking care of it," he says.

My phone has been chiming nonstop with messages from Coraline, Maddie, Jeffy, which I haven't answered or read.

Derek had a phone call come in that had him pull over at a rest stop and walk around the parking lot while I went inside, used the restroom, and purchased coffees for us.

He looked surprised when I handed him one.

He then ended his call and went inside, too, presumably to also use a restroom, and then got us back on the road. That was five or ten minutes ago.

"You'll take care of it how?" I ask.

His eyes bounce to me and travel my face for a beat before they return to the road.

He straightens up. "Not to worry," he states, reaching over and squeezing my knee briefly. "I can be quite charming when the situation calls for it."

I stare at him, a little thrown by that understatement and unsure of what to make of him. Ever since he pulled me out of the tub all panicked, he's been *off*.

He's not all smiles. All charm. No sparkle in his gaze right now. But I haven't been able to make sense of Derek since we met, so really, what's different?

He glances at the navigation screen, and I frown because it says we'll be arriving at our destination in twenty-one minutes.

How the heck am I going to explain this to my parents?

∞

He puts his SUV in park, and I cap my lipstick and shove it into my bag. I've put some light makeup on to try to make my face slightly more presentable, but I feel anything but ready. My palms are sweaty. I rub them on my legs and unclip my seatbelt.

Derek's hand lands on my knee and he squeezes gently.

"Hey?"

I look at him.

"Why are you worried about what they think? They don't worry much about you. We'll put whatever minimal issues they might have to rest by me introducing myself and explaining that when Adam ended the relationship with you, I took the opportunity to make sure I didn't let the grass grow."

I scoff. "That's an understatement."

His eyes travel my face, assessing, then he says, "We'll explain the basics and then we'll go, and things will go back to the way they were with them. It doesn't have to be a big deal."

I guess not. I'm an adult, after all. But still. I'm being painted in the media as a gold digger. Is that article going to get much attention?

He jerks his chin toward the house. "This is exactly what I pictured. I see why you fell in love with our house. It's different, but the street has a similar feel."

I look at my parents' house. At the rosebushes Mom loves so much. At the big, old oak on the lawn we used to climb when me and Bryan were kids. The swing set isn't out back any longer, but I spent hundreds or maybe thousands of hours of my childhood here on this driveway, on that front lawn, in the back yard. Living life. Playing with my brother and our friends. Being mostly carefree. Thinking about my dreams for the future. The house is quite different from the house Derek bought, but it's got the same wide front porch, mature trees and a similar feel with the manicured landscaping. No one's properties are gated here. The houses are far enough apart, most people in this neighborhood don't even have fences.

Both of my parents' cars are in their carport. Mom still drives a minivan. It's nearly new, but the same make as what she's driven throughout most of my childhood. Always maroon. Her favorite color. The same color as Bryan's football jersey in freshman year, the only year he played football. Before he started getting headaches that led to the diagnosis of the tumor.

Dad's got a newer car now than what he had on my last visit. It's a four-door silver Audi.

"Ready?" Derek asks.

I blow out a big breath. "No."

He takes my hand and kisses it.

And strangely, it makes me feel something not unlike relief. Our eyes meet. I look away quickly, feeling a pang of bitterness mixed with confusion.

"Don't worry, Chloe. We'll get through it together." He releases my hand and gets out.

I take another couple of breaths before I get out. He's come around to the passenger side to meet me, catching my hand and giving it a reassuring squeeze as we walk up the driveway to the front steps.

I pull my hand away, but too late, because my dad is watching from the family room window. He moves, then appears in the window over the door as it opens.

"Chloe? Everything all right?" His eyes ping between me and Derek.

"Hi Dad," I say, my voice coming out scratchy.

Mom appears behind him, eyes bouncing between me and Derek.

The door opens wider. "Come in," Dad invites.

"Dr. Turner, I'm Derek Steele. It's nice to meet you." Derek extends his hand.

Dad shakes it. "Call me Hal, Derek. My wife Pamela."

"Mrs. Turner." Derek shakes her hand.

"Hey Mom," I greet, leaning over and kissing her cheek. She pats my back a few times before she gestures to the family room.

"Sorry I didn't call first, but something came up and I wanted to talk to you in person."

"I'd say so," Mom says, looking rattled. "Mrs. Johanson just messaged me not five minutes ago to say her daughter saw your face on a gossip blog. Said you got married. I was just about to come talk to your father about it."

"Married?" Dad asks, eyes landing on my left hand.

"Yes, sir. Ma'am," Derek says and keeps talking as we walk to the family room. "Chloe and Adam's relationship has been over for a while now. They were keeping up pretenses for a variety of reasons, mostly because your daughter is so selfless."

My eyes dart to him with warning. "Derek."

"No, Chloe, don't take the blame here. At all. She always does this, doesn't she?" he says, looking at them like they know this about me and will agree with him.

Cheater

My parents just stare for a beat before Dad says, "I'll put on a pot of coffee."

"It's nearly nine o'clock. I'll take herbal tea. Have decaf, Harold; you know you can't drink coffee this time of night," Mom says.

"Decaf sounds fine," Derek says. "You'll have to excuse my appearance. We came here from the hotel we'd planned to stay at. These were to be our traveling clothes for the morning to leave for our honeymoon, but we hurried here when that gossip blog hit our radar."

"Oh?" Mom inquires.

"I'll explain once the coffee's done, if that's all right," Derek returns.

"Of course, please sit," Mom invites.

"Tea or decaf, Chloe?" Dad asks.

"Just water for me, thanks, Dad," I manage.

Dad salutes me and heads to the kitchen.

Mom sits on one couch, Derek and I sit on the other one that faces her.

"Pam, where's the decaf?" Dad calls out.

Mom excuses herself and joins Dad in the kitchen.

I look at Derek. "Please let me deal with the rest of this."

"Why?" he asks, looking perplexed.

"Because God knows what'll come out of your mouth," I mutter.

"Do you have a plan for how to deal with this?"

"No."

"I've got it. Don't sweat it."

I guess it all had to come out eventually, right? Instead of waiting for the right time to tell my family, no time like now, I guess. One less thing to worry about. Because I already have more than enough to stress about. Before I can ponder it further, Mom is back, Dad with her, and carrying a tray with cups, milk and sugar, along with a bottle of water.

"Coffee's on. I'll fetch it in a minute," Dad says.

"You have a lovely home, Doctor and Mrs. Turner," Derek says.

"Thank you, Derek," Dad says. "Since you're becoming part of the family, again, it's Hal and Pam."

"Appreciated. Chloe spoke so fondly of her childhood home. I see why," he adds.

My parents smile at him, but don't reply. I follow Derek's eyes, which are pointed at the mantle over the fireplace.

In the center of it sits an eight by ten framed family portrait of the four of us. It was taken when Bryan was twelve, I was thirteen. They're all light brown-haired. I'm a dark brunette. They're all brown-eyed. I'm blue-eyed. The photo wasn't taken long after I found out I'm adopted and every time I've looked at that picture all I've seen is how one of these things is not like the other.

"So... married?" Dad prompts. "That's a surprise."

"City hall?" Mom asks and there's distaste there.

And as much as it's a subject I don't want to address, I'm grateful that there's not enough dead air for Derek to bring up a taboo subject like my brother. At least I hope he has the good sense to avoid that topic. Although I'm not sure he does.

"I know it was very sudden, but..." I say, and let it hang.

My parents wait.

I'm stumped.

I've had a traumatic day. I can't think.

"But when you know, you know," Derek speaks up, wrapping his arm around me. "I knew early on. She took a bit of convincing. I just didn't want to wait."

Mom asks, "Forgive me Derek, but Chloe, when did things end with Adam? You and I just spoke yesterday, and you didn't say anything. You've only lived in that new house a short while."

"You were busy, on your way to dinner, so..." I fib. As if I might have told her all my secrets if she'd given me the time.

"Oh," she says softly.

Before I'm able to say anything further to explain when things with Adam ended, Derek speaks.

"It's only been just over a week since Chloe technically moved

Cheater

out. But that relationship was on the verge of ending long before that. He was dishonest with your daughter about a lot of things even before his accident."

I grimace and shoot him a kill look.

He sighs. "She won't speak poorly of him, feeling bad about his accident and all that, but she really hung in there much longer than she should have given all that he put her through."

"Derek, stop," I say through gritted teeth.

Mom and Dad are both rigid, staring at Derek with wide eyes.

"I don't think you guys need all the gory details. Derek convinced me to make it official with him, but we weren't planning on going public with it for a while. I'm afraid that gossip column changed everything. I didn't mean to do anything behind your backs. We kind of... it was a bit of a whim."

"A whim?" Mom checks. "That doesn't sound like you."

Dad frowns. "Well, it would have been wonderful to have a big party and celebrate, walk you down the aisle, sweetheart. But-"

"You can still have all that," Derek cuts in. "That was always our plan. I didn't want to wait. Chloe didn't want to do it without our families present, but I did a grand gesture and swept her off her feet." He smiles. "We got to put rings on today, but we're planning for a destination wedding in a couple of months. My family has a great place in the Swiss Alps. We've got a dozen bedrooms there so plenty of room to make it a big party."

"Your family?" Dad asks. "What business are you all in?"

"My grandfather had a shipping company. My father got into real estate investment when he got out of university so worked for my grandfather along with developing his own business, getting into an array of investments. The shipping company was sold a couple of years back after my grandfather passed away, but my father –"

"Michael Steele," Mom says to Dad.

"The one and only," Derek confirms.

Dad's eyes widen. And I'm not sure if it's because of how

wealthy Derek's family is or if this is down to how murky their reputation is. I'd never heard of them before, but clearly my dad has.

I hear a phone alert. Mom takes her phone out of her sweater pocket and looks at the screen. She frowns.

"And you work for your father?" Dad asks, then he looks at my mom's phone and does a double-take.

"Yes and no, not entirely. I do have interests in the business, sit on his board of directors and help out where I'm needed, but I own several nightclubs. I invested a chunk of my trust fund, and it went well. That's something my father preached to all seven of us, not to squander our trust fund money on frivolity. He worked hard for it so he wanted to see us use it to build our own wealth, build something we could be proud of. Like he did. He's one of five children and only one of two of his siblings who built new wealth instead of simply joining the family business. We've all got stakes in the family legacy but most of us have our own businesses as well."

"Seven children; that's a very large family," Mom says as three beeps chime from the kitchen. She puts her phone away.

"I'll go grab that pot of coffee," Dad says, hurrying back into the kitchen with a look of stress on his face.

"Six remaining. My brother was shot a few months ago."

"Oh my goodness. I'm so sorry," she says.

There's an awkward moment as Derek doesn't respond to that.

"And how did you two meet?" Mom changes the subject. "Oh, maybe I should wait for your dad."

"I didn't miss anything and I'm here, I'm here," he calls, coming back with the coffee pot, which he leans over with to pour into the two mugs on the tray.

I reach for the bottle of water and uncap it as my mom gets her cup of tea.

"We met at one of my clubs through Chloe's friend Alannah in a roundabout way," Derek says. "And then I admit I bought a little company in order to get closer to Chloe. What can I say? I was smitten. She was managing their marketing campaigns, so I bought it and got to get to know her better."

My face is flaming. I'm trying (and failing) to keep my cool.

Derek keeps talking as my heartrate gallops at a too-fast speed. "And I knew she was unhappy just by looking at her, let alone listening to her. Circumstances have taken a toll on her and... I'm sure as her parents you know... she's a capable, caring person but she has so much empathy for others that sometimes it stops her from seeking out things that make her happy. She's so busy worrying about everyone else."

My parents both nod but with blank faces. Faces I'm accustomed to because no, they don't really know this about me.

"Put a sock in it," I mutter, shooting him a warning look, then add, "honey..."

He throws his head back and laughs, then wraps his arm round me and kisses my cheek with affection, saying, "She cracks me up."

My parents both smile.

"So, now it's my job to make sure Chloe's happy," Derek declares, leaning forward to add sugar to his coffee. "And that's what I'm going to do. I want you both to rest assured that your beautiful, vibrant, loving daughter is in good hands. She's so good at everything she does, I just know she's also going to be an incredible wife. And mother, when that time comes. Which I'm trying to talk her into happening as soon as possible. I was very ready to be her husband and I'm thinking I'm also ready to be a father."

My parents both look thrown. Of course they are. They met him ten minutes ago.

"I'm sure you're both looking forward to grandkids, aren't you?" Derek asks.

Mom looks shellshocked.

Dad shrugs, "Well, sure. Right Pam?"

Mom doesn't look so sure. "I mean... I hadn't really thought that far ahead. I hadn't thought of Chloe as ready for that step yet. She's never mentioned plans for a family."

"She's very career-minded, yes, but she has this endless well of love and nurturing inside her," Derek adds. "As you know..."

My parents nod some more.

Oh for fuck's sake. It's taking everything inside me to not scream at the top of my lungs right now.

"So, you're based in Columbus, then?" Dad asks, sipping his coffee.

Derek shakes his head. "Most of my family is. I grew up with that being home base, but once I started building my business, I'd spent most of my time in Cleveland. I have three nightclubs there, three in Columbus, and two in Cincinnati. But Chloe likes having access to Columbus and her friends there, so we just bought a place in Dublin, Ohio, actually. I surprised her with it and then dropped the engagement ring on her finger while she was asleep. That was how I sold her on marrying me today. The place is great. Perfect place to raise a family."

Derek smiles and shrugs.

Mom looks at me with astonishment on her face. "That's very ... romantic."

"Never been one for grand gestures before, but they say that when you know, you know. I just had to make this one fall for me." Derek sips his coffee.

I glug down a long drink of my water but drink it too fast and wind up choking.

Derek pats my back as I recover.

Finally able to breathe regularly again, I say, "I'm sorry you found out through that gossip thing, Mom."

Mom nods direly. "I just got a text with a screenshot of what was posted."

"Ugh," comes from me.

Derek pipes up. "We suspect Hallman's ex fiancée runs that blog. And... of course she doesn't know the whole story, so is taking it upon herself to try to smear Chloe's good name because she thinks Chloe left him high and dry because of his disability. But the fact of the matter is that it was mostly the other way around. We found out that Adam met that ex the night of the accident. He never told Chloe about it. He was also hiding money. Telling other lies. Just... very selfish. If not for losing use of his legs I'm sure they wouldn't have lasted as long as they did."

God, Derek. Stop.

Mom is wide-eyed. "That's terrible. And it doesn't seem like him. I mean, we didn't know him very well, but from what we did know of him, that's shocking."

"Chloe was pretty shocked too," Derek mutters, sipping his drink.

"I'm not interested in getting caught up in the past," I say, grabbing Derek's knee. "Or gossiping about other peoples' business." Derek puts his hand on mine and weaves our fingers together as I keep talking. "I wanted to come and talk to you about the gossip blog. And to apologize if it causes nonsense for you to have to deal with."

Derek pipes up. "I was planning to take her on a honeymoon but with the gossip and the fact that she didn't want you both to find out from someone other than herself, we'll reschedule that after my parents' fortieth anniversary celebration, which is this coming weekend. Any chance you two can get down to Columbus and join us on Saturday night? I'd love for you to meet the whole family."

Oh God, no!

"Well, um..." Mom looks awkwardly at Dad.

I speak quickly. "No, no. I told Derek you guys would prefer to meet my inlaws in a much more lowkey, intimate way versus a party for four hundred."

"Four hundred?" Mom asks.

"At least," I say.

"Yes, that... low key is probably better," Mom says.

"Ah, too bad," Derek says, then takes another sip of his coffee. "Well, we should hit the road. We didn't intend to barge in on you both unannounced so late and it's a long drive back to Dublin."

"You could stay in Chloe's old room if you prefer," Dad pipes up. Derek looks agreeable to that.

Oh no. Hell, no. Mom shoots Dad a look that says this is the last thing she wants sprung on her out of the blue on a weeknight.

"No, no, that's okay," I get to my feet. "You both have work tomorrow. We should go."

Derek gets up. So do my parents as he says, "We appreciate the offer. Well then, we'll have to have you over for a weekend once we finish settling in at the new place."

"That sounds lovely," replies my mom, politely. "We'd love you to stay any time, but you two got married today. Surely you don't want to stay here tonight."

"Good point," Derek says with a sheepish grin.

I want to crawl into a hole and die.

She gives me a quick hug. Dad gives me more of a bear hug. And I want to sink into it and never get out of it. But I reluctantly let go, unable to stop myself from getting a little misty-eyed, feeling overwhelmed with emotion.

"I'll talk to you guys soon," I say.

"Congratulations, Chloe. Derek," Mom says.

"Thanks, Mrs. Turner. I mean *Pam*. Please do your best to just ignore any online gossip. My family's PR team is all over this. Our legal team will be, too, if needed. It'll settle down, not to worry, but if you need anything, here's my card." He passes Dad a business card. "Good to meet you both."

He must have slipped that in his pocket before we came in.

Dad accepts it and then opens his arms toward me.

"One more," Dad declares, his voice a little gruff.

I step into another hug. "Congratulations, kiddo. Coulda knocked me over with a feather, but as long as you're happy, that's all we want."

"Thanks, Dad."

Derek shakes my father's hand and kisses my mother's cheek.

Cheater

Mom's eyes hit mine and widen and then she hesitantly smiles.

I force a smile and give another little wave before I walk down the driveway.

Derek opens the door for me and then helps me in.

I wait until we're off my parents' street before I look at him and mutter, "Wow. Could you have laid it on any thicker?"

"Got a few points across," he says with a shrug. "They're a little... formal with you, aren't they? Though your father loosened up toward the end."

I say nothing. He's got a lot of room to talk when his family is so dysfunctional.

"Then again, they don't know me. Anyway, I'm fuckin' starvin'. What's good around here?"

Flabbergasted, unsure what to even say about all that, I decide to focus on my stomach, too. I managed a couple mouthfuls of breakfast this morning but couldn't get much down, stressed about the day. Turned out the day was even more stressful than I'd bargained for.

"It's Monday night and it's almost ten. Not much open other than maybe a couple drive thrus."

"Okay, co-pilot. Get me to somewhere with a greasy burger then."

I direct him through town and we wind up at McDonald's. We're waiting for them to bring the food to the car as they need to cook the McNuggets.

"I promise you a much better wedding feast when we have the second ceremony, little bunny." He caresses my face with his fingertips.

"Please don't subject me to a second ceremony," I grumble.

"You don't want another day in that beautiful dress? With Alannah at your side? Your father walking you to me?"

"To you?" I mutter, then scoff. "I didn't want to walk to you today; you really think I want to go through that again?"

"Ouch. Not nice."

"Whatever."

"Fuck, you looked beautiful today. I'll never forget it, Chloe."

The employee brings the food and saves me from having to reply.

Derek passes me my Big Mac and my fries. He puts the twenty-pack of nuggets between us, saying, "To share," and digs into his double quarter pounder.

"You're back to your old self," I muse, reaching for a French fry.

He sips his Coke.

Things go quiet as we eat under a parking lot lamp. I turn the radio on, self-conscious about the potential sound of my chewing.

I've got a mouth full of Big Mac when Derek casually says, "My mother tried to kill herself when I was a kid. I found her in a bathtub, unconscious."

My head turns in his direction, and I grab a napkin and put it to my mouth.

"When I saw you were underwater, not moving, it took me a while to shake it off. Turns out you needing me to act in a crisis snapped me out of it."

He takes a chicken nugget and pops it into his mouth, then fiddles with the station taking it from news to Smokey Robinson's *Cruisin'* before he turns his attention back to working on his burger.

He sips his Coke again and asks, "Mind if I start driving back now or you want to finish first?"

I finish chewing and wash it all down with a sip of my root beer. "I can eat while you drive," I say.

He steals one of my fries and then turns the vehicle on.

Derek has endured a whole lot of early life trauma, hasn't he? Finding his mother unconscious in a tub. Kidnapped and held for ransom? Living in that highly dysfunctional family environment while dealing with those things?

I abandon half my burger but finish my drink. The food is sitting in my gut like a rock.

I make the mistake of trying to distract myself by pulling out my phone. The number of notifications is staggering. Text messages.

Cheater

Social media tags. Missed calls. I start with the text messages, going back to first thing this morning.

Frank (work): Congratulations! Hope you have a long and happy marriage. Look forward to talking to you when you're back.

I read this in a snarky tone, hearing Frank's disapproving voice in my head. He's been a good boss, very understanding considering all the drama in my life in the past seven months, but how could he not feel snarky about this. Just days ago I told him I hadn't met with Derek and was going home with a migraine. Now Derek tells him that not only is he marrying me, but also he's buying the company and that I'm Frank's new boss? Maybe I'm wrong about the snarkiness. But if I were Frank I might be a little salty.

Alannah: Love you. Cya at city hall. I'm bringing something borrowed and BLUE.

I wonder if the blue in caps was a code that referred to Craig, a boy in blue.

Coraline: Girl?

Craig: We need to talk.

Maddie: What's happening, chica? Methinks we need a ketchup!!!!!!

I almost smile. Maddie loves her puns.

Craig: Get ahold of me, no matter what time.

Paul: Hi Chloe. Sorry to do this by text but Gran

passed at 8:40 tonight. Thought you'd want to know. I know things must be weird right now and I don't expect you to come but in case you want to know, I'll let you know the funeral details when it is arranged.

Adam's brother Paul might not know about the wedding today yet. And I'm sure Adam won't want me to come, considering that he didn't want me at the hospital. Not to mention getting held by another gun-toting person today because of me.

I take a moment to think about their grandmother. Lovely lady. Loved desserts. Great cook. Enjoyed reading mysteries and watching true crime and court TV. So kind. Never had a bad word to say about anyone.

I decide against opening any social apps. I'm not remotely interested in seeing how the drama has continued to unfold in terms of comments and shares. I don't want to know what people are saying about me, particularly because Jeannie is trying to control the narrative and make me the bad guy. I'm not a bad guy. I was just gullible enough to get reeled in by a hot guy not realizing the far-reaching impact a hall pass could have on my life.

Hall passes are supposed to be without consequences, aren't they? Well, I want a refund.

The way it's gone, though, even if I hadn't gone home with Derek after the gym that night, this would've eventually happened. Because he was determined, wasn't he?

I can't answer anyone tonight. I'll deal later.

"What's wrong?" the actual bad guy asks, turning the radio down after Smokey is done singing.

"Where do I start?" I mutter.

"Start. Maybe I can help."

"You're the cause of all my problems, though."

"Right," he says. "But I'm also the solution to all your problems. You just don't realize it yet."

Cheater

It takes me a minute to gather my thoughts. I take the hair tie out of my hair and fluff it out with a sigh. I catch sight of myself in the reflection of the windshield. I'm still wearing Grace's diamond earrings. I'll have to return those to her.

"Come on. Try," Derek prompts.

"Adam's grandmother is gone for starters."

"That's sad," he says but he says it without real emotion and finishes the last bite of his burger. He crumples the paper and hands it to me. I drop it into the fast food bag beside my feet.

"That's lip service, Derek."

"I didn't know the woman," he replies. "What do you want me to say?"

He's taking no responsibility for his part in it, either. He hasn't said he had nothing to do with it, so clearly he's admitting that he is responsible for Adam's uncle's death.

"How can I help otherwise, Chloe? I'm gonna deal with Hallman's ex. She'll stop slandering you. Not to worry."

"Don't take care of it with violence, Derek," I warn. "Violence is never the answer."

"I beg to differ, but what else beyond that? Anything?"

"Okay, first: how about if you let Craig off the hook?"

"Ah. Why are you worried about Officer Jenkins? He's a big boy that can take care of himself, I'm sure."

"He's Adam's best friend; he's my friend. A part of my life. He's into Alannah and might be in my life going forward. Even if he wasn't, I still give a shit."

"Okay..." He lets that hang.

"And he's just doing his job. Alannah pulled him into this ... this *thing* with us today because she cares about me and because her and I try to help one another when one of us is stuck. And now you're gonna try to force him to be a dirty cop? You're punishing him for simply being who he is, trying to help me when he thought I needed help. He's a good guy."

He snickers. "He's not been made to do anything. Yet. He's on standby to help me, should I need the help."

"He's an *actual* good guy and there aren't many of those around."

"So..."

"So I'd like you to let him off the hook."

"And I'd like you to give me a shot at making you happy," he fires back.

"More blackmail? Great. Great way to start a marriage."

"Is this going to be a marriage, Chloe? It is to me, but what about you? If it is, there won't be any blackmail required. Because you'll be giving me what I want."

"Which is for me to pretend I'm okay with all of this?"

He shakes his head. "Which is for you to let me do my job. I wanted to be your husband and now I am. Now I have a daily goal and checklist for that. I really think that'll go a long way for both of us if you let me do my thing. Needing to deal with the gossip blog tonight snapped me out of a bad mindset. Will doing my job as your husband help me stay out of a bad headspace? Maybe."

I cross my arms and stare out the window.

"Think about it," he requests. "You're attracted to me. The sex is incredible. That's a basis for a relationship to develop, right? Let it develop. Be open-minded."

I continue staring out the window.

"Think about it," he repeats.

A while later, I pull my phone out and reply to Craig.

I'm so so sorry about today. I'm trying to talk sense into him to get him to leave you be. Thank you for trying to help.

My phone almost immediately rings. *Craig calling.*

I answer it.

"Hello?"

"You alone?"

Cheater

"No." Though it wouldn't matter if I was since he's got my phone bugged.

"Right. I'll make this quick and I'll do the talking. Not your fault. Don't worry about me. I knew exactly what I'd be wading into, and I made the choice to do that. I'll figure things out. I wanted you to know Adam didn't push Jeannie to do any of that blog stuff. She works at City Hall and saw you guys when you got your marriage license and went apeshit. The only thing I will ask is for you to please request Derek gives me 24 hours to get her to back off before he retaliates. We don't need any other casualties. I was instructed not to reach out to him directly, ever, and I wouldn't normally put you in the middle, but I needed to do that just this once. My dad and Jeannie's mom are first cousins. They're close. I can't just stand by and let her get on the Steele shit list."

"I'll talk to him," I say.

"Who is that?" Derek asks.

"It's Craig."

He gestures for me to give him the phone.

"One sec." I hand it over.

"Jenkins," Derek greets, changing the phone to his left hand and taking the steering wheel with his right.

I knew Craig and Adam had been friends since they were kids. It's hitting me now that Craig knows Adam's history. Another person from his old life that he didn't cut off when he tried to move on from the childhood trauma. Did they all grow up in Michigan and move here? Did Adam move here to be closer to Craig and Jeannie followed? Did Adam and Jeannie live together, too? Whatever. It doesn't matter. It's all moot now. Adam is no longer in my life.

Derek listens for a minute, then says, "Well, my wife is being pretty adamant about the fact that she doesn't want your squeaky-clean record and conscience sullied, so if my wife plays her cards right, maybe she'll get her wish."

I fight the urge to gawk at him. Instead, I bite my lip and fix my gaze on the dark road ahead.

"Well..." Derek says after a moment, "I need to see just what she's written first, but if you ensure Ms. Gilligan deletes her blog post and any and all negative content about my wife as well as refrains from hassling her any further, ensuring she stops slandering Chloe or anyone else with the name Steele, I'll consider letting it go. Right. And hear me right now, Jenkins, this is the one time you get away with using Chloe to get to me. Clear? Bye for now."

"How does your family force cops to turn dirty?" I ask.

"We gather information and use it to our advantage. If there's a big need and nothing to find, we fabricate. With evidence to back it up."

"That's despicable."

"I know." He shrugs.

"Your father came from a wealthy family. Why turn to crime if there's already money there?"

"Most successful people have some degree of corruption attached to them. People just don't always find out about it. My grandfather and likely his grandfather before him had to get his hands dirty along the way to maintain power and wealth. My father inherited not only the family wealth, but also all those strategic relationships. My dead brother had issues. He was hotheaded and jealous of everyone. Especially Elijah. Thaddeus had substance abuse problems and got sloppy while he had a sometimes public battle with Eli, so it's just in the past five years or so that the Steele name got enough negative attention to create whispers and rumors. We all run clean businesses. But to do that, sometimes we have to create unsavory relationships and occasionally get our hands dirty."

"A dick swinging contest," I mutter.

He laughs. "Sometimes, yeah. I run clubs in business districts, near airports, and in blue collar areas in the three big cities in the state. I have a team that sifts through the gathered intelligence, and it helps my family keep us ahead of things. Eli does things in his business that benefit the family. So does Jonah. Ash isn't as involved, but he's had to get his hands dirty, too, a couple times. I'm not close with

Cheater

my brothers, but we all work toward a common goal of protecting what matters to us collectively."

I'm thrown for a loop when he turns off early but realize we're going to the house. That beautiful home that I haven't let myself enjoy. It's only been a day since he brought me there but today has felt like dozens of days all rolled into one.

I'm suddenly bone-tired.

44

Derek

Despite her protests, I carry her over the threshold.

"You can put me down now," she complains.

"No, I'm taking my bride straight to bed," I tell her, lock the door, set the alarm, and move us up the stairs.

"What's the alarm code?" she asks. "In case of emergency."

"The date we met. Four digits. Month, then day."

Her eyes change and I'm thinking she's counting back, so I tell her the code.

"That's different from what you gave the chauffeur."

"That's a garage and gate only code. That won't get anyone into the house."

"Oh."

I flick the light on and set her on the bed. "I'm sorry our wedding day was dramatic."

"Traumatic," she corrects.

"That, too. You should know I don't feel much empathy outside of for you. Didn't feel that at first but I'm feeling it more and more, day by day. It's inconvenient."

Her eyes flash with surprise.

I lean over, about to kiss her, when she crab crawls backwards. "I don't feel up to anything physical right now. I'm very tired."

"I'll do most of the work," I advise, yanking her sneakers off as I kick my own off while pressing my knee to the foot of the bed between her parted thighs. I advance, overtaking her, resulting in her back hitting the mattress.

Pinning her wrists above her head, I kiss her, then say, "I want to make you come over and over."

She swallows, affected, but tries to hide from me by shutting her eyes.

"You're mine now. It's my job to make you come. Look at your husband, Chloe."

Her eyes open.

"I told you I get what I want, didn't I?" I caress her face with my fingertips.

She doesn't answer.

I peel the sweater off her, leaving her in a tank top. That goes, too, then my mouth is on hers. "And you're mine. Until death do us part, baby. And I wanna make you happy, make you love me. So those are next. Now... take your pants off for me." I drop kisses on her throat, down to her breasts, unclasping her bra and freeing her beautiful tits.

I kiss one, then the other.

"Now, Chloe Steele. Show me your sweet, wet little hole. Show me what's mine."

She doesn't move.

"I'm gonna take what I want from you anyway. And you'll enjoy it. You always do."

She stays still. Quiet.

I lean back onto my knees between her parted legs and grab the pants and pull until I get them removed. I throw my hoodie and T-shirt, then strip the rest of my clothes off.

"How wet are you right now?" I ask. "Let's see..."

I push her knees apart and inspect visually, watching her face go pink. She didn't even try to keep them closed.

I spread her pussy wide and plunge two fingers in. "Drenched for your husband? I like that a lot."

She bites her lip and I watch her nipples harden before my eyes. Her pupils are large. She wants this. She wants me.

Cheater

I weave our fingers together, pinning her hands over her head and as I line up, her legs wrap around me.

"There's a nice hug," I say against her mouth. "You're not making this difficult. That's good. I'm a little tired, too."

"Then hurry up and get it over with," she says looking sassy.

I laugh, then I slam my hips forward and fill her.

She cries out, arching.

"Suddenly, I'm not so tired anymore. Suddenly, I have the urge to fuck my wife for the next several hours."

She lets out a sound of exasperation, but she arches her back. She's not trying to fight me off.

"Wanna spar with me?" I ask, staring into her eyes.

She closes them. "Not tonight honey, you're giving me a headache."

I laugh. "Fun. I like it..." I press my fingers between us against her clit and work it until she's panting, then I stop short, just before she's about to come and flip her to her belly, yank her hips up and slap her beautiful bare ass, pulling a yelp from her.

"Let's make it even more fun, shall we?"

I hold onto one hip, then the other hand slides down over her soaking wet cunt. I stick my finger in, then pull it out.

She's still, breathing hard, on her hands and knees and waiting for her climax.

I smile as I kiss her shoulder and then run both hands up and down her back, down her arms, across to cup her tits for a minute, pinching both nipples lightly.

She makes a sound of need. I grip my cock at the root and slide it down her ass cheeks, prodding then pushing it three inches into her heat before pulling back, dragging it through the wetness, then backing up.

She waits.

I wait.

She looks over her shoulder at me and fuck is she beautiful. She's got a wanton look in her eyes. She wants my cock back.

"Ask for it."

She frowns.

"Ask for my cock. Ask me to let you come."

"No," she whispers.

"No?"

"No," she confirms.

"Over," I grab both hips and she turns over onto her back.

I spread her legs wide, throw them over my shoulders, and press a kiss to her clit, then slide my middle finger through her wetness, getting it good and wet before prodding at her ass, then sliding it in.

Her body tightens for a moment, then relaxes as she looks at the ceiling, blinking. Frowning a little.

I caress her clit with my thumb while my middle finger is still in her ass. She's waiting for it.

I dip my tongue into her cunt and slide my left hand up her soft skin, pinching her nipple again while wiggling my middle finger inside her.

She squirms. She wants more, but I'm keeping her on the edge for the moment, enjoying watching her seek more.

"Maybe you should beg me for it, Chloe," I say.

"Not gonna happen," she pants, gripping the sheets.

"We'll see," I whisper against her inner thigh. It's out in goosebumps.

My phone rings.

I ignore it.

It rings again with my father's ringtone. Fuck. There are three ringtones on my phone. My basic one. My father's. And Chloe's. Chloe's only rang once, last Friday when she arrived at the office for our meeting. Thankfully I rarely get my father's tone, but you don't ignore my father's ringtone if you're one of his children.

I back off Chloe and grab the phone from my pants on the floor.

"Hello," I answer with obvious irritation.

"Are you dealing with this online gossip bullshit, or should I have someone else do it?"

Cheater

Chloe slips into the bathroom.

Shit.

"I'll deal with it," I bark, not hiding my irritation.

"I've got Gil saying you're not answering his calls."

"I'm busy fucking my wife," I state.

"I don't need bullshit right now, Derek. Neither does your mother."

"When do you ever?"

"She's not very happy you went the city hall route and now to see negativity about your new wife and her past?"

There went my hard-on.

"I told everyone yesterday that this was what I'd be doing, Dad."

"You also said it'd be kept quiet. It's not been kept quiet."

"I canceled our honeymoon to deal with it. We just got back from Chloe's parents' house as I had to do damage control there."

"Good. I'll tell Gil you'll be here in the morning. Your new wife needs to meet with your mother's media assistant tomorrow while you meet with Gil. Make sure she understands the importance of outward appearances. Bring her to the house at nine o'clock. Have breakfast with us first. We'll do a photoshoot, too, so clear your morning."

I grind my teeth.

"I've had to clear my morning, too, Derek, for your shit, so do not be insolent when you get here. Make this up to your mother."

I pull in a deep breath and let it out slowly.

"You there?" he snaps.

"I'm here."

"Nine o'clock," he says and ends the call.

I toss my phone to the dresser and put my ear to the bathroom door.

The shower is running.

I quietly slip in and catch my gorgeous wife under the shower with her hand between her legs. Her eyes hit me, and she looks at me with challenge.

I'm hard again.

"Nuh uh," I grab her wrist, place her hand on my shoulder, and lift her up, pressing her back to the wet tiled wall while I bring her down on my dick.

She whimpers in time with my groan as I fill her.

"You naughty little thing," I reprimand, grabbing her hair and bringing her mouth to mine. I dip my tongue in and then say, "You don't sneak off to come by yourself while I'm edging you. Now what should I do with you?" I flex my hips a couple times while she whimpers again.

Fuck, yeah.

"Should I make you come or edge you for the rest of the night?" I ask.

"Make me come," she whispers against my mouth.

"Yeah?" I ask, liking this a fucking lot. She's right on the edge and she wants it enough she might actually beg me. "Make you come over and over?"

She nods. "Yeah."

"Beg me," I demand, tightening my grip on her hair.

She whimpers, holding onto both my shoulders, looking straight into my eyes with those beautiful blues.

"No," she denies me.

I let go of her hair, lift her halfway off my cock by her hips, then slam her back down.

"Derek," she whines.

"Not gonna beg? You sure about that?"

She reaches between us and tries to go for her clit. I shove her hand away, turn the shower off, and carry her back to bed before pinning her wrists over her head.

I pull my cock out, line up and slam it straight in. To her asshole.

She screams and grabs my shoulders with both hands.

I stay rooted. "Now, ask nice."

"Ow, ow, ow," she cries out, burying her face into my neck. I back

Cheater

up so she can't but not far enough that I'm not still inside her. "No hiding from me."

I pull part way out.

Her legs tremble and she whimpers some more, discomfort all over her pretty face.

I haul her legs up over my chest, so her ankles are balancing on my shoulders and lick droplets of water off her leg as she protests, saying, "No, Derek, ow!" and I put my fingers to her pussy, shoving one in while pressing my thumb to her clit.

"Ask me to let you come."

She shakes her head.

My free hand goes to her mouth, and I press my thumb in.

"Okay, then suck. Suck my thumb while I fuck your ass and look into my eyes while you do and maybe I'll make you come with my fingers to your clit."

Her mouth tightens and she sucks just a little, but it's enough that I'm even harder.

"Good girl," I tell her, picking up the pace fucking her ass, seeing the discomfort in her eyes, so I pull out and not only gather wetness from her soaking wet pussy, I also spit in my hand and lube my cock up before I slide back in, much easier this time.

My beautiful girl swallows around my thumb and spreads her legs even wider for me, one dropping off my body, so I catch it and hold on while applying friction to her sopping wet clit. Her head rolls back.

"Suck!"

She obeys.

Just as she's almost there, just before I'm there, I pull my thumb out and go deeper as I put my mouth to hers.

"Beg, Chloe," I demand against her lips.

"Please, Derek," she whines in a tiny voice and immediately, I'm coming.

I'm coming in her tight ass, rubbing her clit fast, the sounds of the wetness like music to my ears. She comes, whimpering, clutching me in a hug that frankly surprises me. In a good way. My spent cock slips out while she's still whimpering, so I manage to keep circling on her clit until she goes rigid, then lax.

I roll to my back and take her with me, gathering her close. She's melted into me. Sated. Warm. Feeling perfect.

"I love you, wife," I say into her hair, then close my eyes, knowing I'll sleep good tonight. Because she's mine. And I know I'm on the road to having her realize it, too.

45
Chloe

Carson opens the front door to the Steele residence just like last time. I'm wearing the other blue dress Derek had gotten for me for the anniversary brunch.

I woke up snuggled with him and he fucked me as soon as his eyes were open. He fucked me sweetly, holding my face and staring into my eyes with a sleepy, sexy look. I didn't fight. I actively participated, even kissing him back, and then I felt mortified afterwards, and didn't hide that.

I don't know why I kissed him back; I tell myself it's just sex. At least I'm getting something good out of this craziness. But of course I feel guilty for it.

While I got ready, he explained what I'd be dealing with here today, which doesn't sound like my idea of a good time, but it also wasn't optional. He told me he understood my trepidation, that he would've gotten me out of it if he could, and I guess I believe him. He made me coffee while I dried my hair and then he shaved at the sink beside me, which I tried to ignore – because I got wet watching him do it.

I've been in my head all morning, but he was quiet on the way here, too, so seems like he's also in his head. God, what is it even like in there?

"Good morning, Mrs. Steele. Mr. Steele," Carson greets.

"Carson," Derek greets.

"Hello," I say. "Chloe, by the way."

"Thank you, but that wouldn't be..." Carson stops speaking and goes rigid in the doorway before continuing, speaking fast, "Mr. Steele, your parents are in the semi-formal dining room. Would you mind if I don't escort you there? I need to deal with an urgent matter."

I look over my shoulder and see a young landscaper wearing headphones, trimming a hedge while obviously feeling the song by the way he's erratically doing his work while his lips move like he's singing along. He's kind of slaughtering the hedge.

"Go ahead," Derek waves and we watch Carson rush to the young man trying to get his attention with waving arms. Derek tugs my hand and leads me in and down the hall the same way we went on Sunday. Only we walk past the solarium and I'm thinking semi-formal dining room? Why have multiple dining rooms with levels of formality? Especially for breakfast with your son.

"And you called my parents formal," I mutter. "Yours are, I guess, semi-formal."

"What's more formal than formal?" he asks.

I shrug. "Ceremonialistic?"

He laughs, taking me into a room that looks beyond formal.

"This?" I try.

He laughs harder.

His parents are seated at a table for twelve, dressed up, and looking at us curiously.

∞

By the time we're back in his SUV, I'm itching to rant.

But I won't rant to him since he's the enemy.

As we leave the property, he looks at me. "You good?" he asks, and he's amused.

"Fine," I say through tight teeth.

He laughs. He knows how frustrated I am.

Cheater

"I don't know what's funny," I mutter.

"You're funny," he says, leaning over and trying to kiss me.

"Drive the car, sheesh," I lean away so he can't get me. He brakes and grabs my face with both hands and plants a wet one on me. "That was fuckin' funny. I think my father wants to fire my mother's media bitch and hire you. But no matter how much money and perks he offers you, don't accept."

"Oh, there are Steele family members I'm allowed to say *no* to?" I ask, haughtily.

"You can say no to anyone, wife, but if you say it to me there might be consequences. If you feel strongly about the need to say no to my father, chances are that I'll back you up."

"What if he offers me an annulment and the ability to not have to deal with your nonsense anymore?" I quip.

Derek's expression darkens. "Do you wanna watch your husband commit patricide?"

I immediately lose every ounce of smartass. Because he looks serious.

His grip tightens on the steering wheel.

I stare out the window. Uncomfortable.

∞

It's halfway through the afternoon by the time we get back to the house. I was starting to wonder if I'd ever get out of there.

During breakfast, Derek's mother seemed sober. And kind of bitchy. She wasn't nearly as fun as she was when she was drunk. She was not happy about the gossip blog, about people finding out we'd gotten married, about not getting to organize a bunch of hoopla for her son's wedding, and at first seemed like she had plans to take it out on me.

Derek quickly set her straight about that. Despite that the offending blog post had apparently already been taken down, she inundated me with questions about Adam and his accident and that seemed to me like it was out of concern for how someone in the Steele family would be seen, not about any semblance of concern for Adam.

Any question or comment from her that was even remotely bitchy, Derek would answer, sticking up for me and assuring her none of this was my fault.

If she was even-tempered with a question, he'd let me answer.

I hate to admit it, but it was kind of refreshing to have someone stick up for me.

He declared, "I saw her and wanted her, Mom. I've already explained that I made it happen. Me. All this is on me. Except for the bitch that posted about it – I'm dealing with that. Chloe's innocent in all of this."

Derek's father vacillated from being preoccupied with his phone to paying close attention to me and how I was handling everything. His eyes were cold the entire time except that each time his attention strayed to his wife, that coldness vanished. It was intriguing to watch.

When Derek's mother switched gears and began talking about the upcoming anniversary party, asking what I would be wearing and letting me know I would be photographed with the family, Derek told her Grace's friend Nicola was going to outfit me. She seemed decided she's have her designer work with Nicola to make sure I was dressed well. She requested that if I'm unhappy and want to change my outfit, I should reach out to Carson with that information and that Carson would interface with her assistant. Talk about a waste of resources. But it wasn't a bad thing that I wouldn't have to deal with my new mother-in-law directly all that much outside of public Steele family functions, which Derek already assured were few and far between.

She had quite the preoccupation with whether or not I was capable of presenting myself as a member of the Steele family. I was ready to remind these people that I was now only a member of their family by a marriage I'd been forced into and the word family did not come to mind as a group descriptor, but didn't think that me biting

Cheater

back at a mother who was disappointed she didn't see her son get married would be productive, so I kept my mouth shut.

"Is Sabrina going to come? Have we found out?" Mrs. Steele asked her husband.

"Eli's working on that," he replied.

She sighed heavily. She'd been doing that a lot.

"You should just order her to be there, Michael. That'll settle that," she stated, examining her manicure.

"Eli has asked me to allow him the courtesy of dealing with his own wife. So I'm going to do that, my love."

"Well hopefully Elijah handles things with her soon," she snapped and then turned her gaze to me. "Appearances are important in a family such as ours. The media looks for the smallest thing to create sensational headlines." She aimed that remark at me and then added, "This is why you're here today, so we can adequately prepare you." She looked at Derek then. "I think you should have taken her on that trip, Derek, given them zero access to you two."

I knew from the little I had read about Sabrina Steele as Elijah's estranged wife that the local media was frothing at the mouth for the facts around the split.

"They won't gain access to Chloe," Derek told his mom. "The sooner we wrap up here, the sooner I can get her back home."

"There are two paps outside the gate," Derek's father piped up. "I suspected they'd be here this morning, expecting you both to show up, but they arrived ten minutes after you got here. Our pilot says there are also a few hanging around at the airport."

Derek replied, "We're not leaving the state this week after all. We'll probably head to Vermont next week for a little getaway. We'll wait for things to die down before we take an official honeymoon."

At that point, Carson came in to announce the photographer was ready when we were, and we went to Mr. Steele's office and then outside to the gazebo where they'd renewed their vows on Sunday.

Copious pictures were taken of the four of us. Derek and myself. Derek and his father. Me and Derek's mother. Derek and his mother.

And many photos of just me from multiple angles, with my hair up and then down again. I was also given a black power suit to change into with a blue shirt that they said made my eyes really pop. The photographer told me people find you more genuine if you wear your eye color. Who knew? And then they did several more headshots inside Mr. Steele's office by his fireplace and while that was happening, Derek was in a closed door meeting with some PR people and Derek's father had to duck out to get to a meeting, so I was left with Derek's mom and her media person, Donna.

Derek's mom was preoccupied with her phone for a chunk of the session with the media person, but then her mood shifted, and she became friendly, happy, almost girlish.

She said she had to dash, that she had a salon appointment and that she was meeting her husband after his meeting later this afternoon to join him on an impromptu New York City trip that they decided to take since we'd canceled our trip, freeing up the jet. She gave me air kisses and left me with Donna, who then worked hard to run me through my paces with quizzes and fake interviews, trying to trip me up and getting increasingly frustrated with my lack of tripping. The entire thing was recorded, which I found extremely annoying. She wanted me to mess up, wanted to correct me and tell me how I should respond instead, but I felt like she was frustrated by the fact that I didn't make any big enough blunders. She probably wanted to prove her worth but needed me to be a bumbling buffoon.

As Derek came into the doorway of his father's office, he leaned against the doorframe and watched as I informed Donna that I work in marketing, that I took media studies in school, and that I'm not about to trip over my words and make myself look stupid in public. She very bitchily informed me that there was more than just my reputation at stake here. At that point, Derek intervened instead of continuing to stare at me like a lovesick puppy, and told her we were done.

She looked me over with a miserable "hmpf" and handed me a handbook on media etiquette, asking me to memorize it to the letter.

Cheater

I have no intention of speaking with the media. If they paint me as a bitch, so be it. I'm telling myself this, but I'm terrified that I'll be spineless when it comes down to it. Because I feel like that. Like I should be stronger. Like I should know my way out of this situation I'm in.

Derek is just... overwhelming. Relentless. Maddening. What's most maddening is what he does to my body and that little part of me that would love to believe I can have what he wants to give me without it meaning I've lost my mind, too.

And I just can't come to grips with the talent that man has with his mouth, that hypnotizing gaze, those ten talented fingers and Lord, that male appendage. The right shape and size to drive me wild – with an air of danger because it's just a touch too big. Which seems to make it extra good for him, because the face he makes when he sinks in that final overwhelming inch? That expression he makes is tinder for the explosions he manages to detonate from the core of me.

When he's not threatening people I love, he says so many of the right things. He does romantic things. And I feel like I might be slipping because I keep catching myself thinking about an alternate universe where I might let myself slip into the madness with him.

∞

We pull up to the house and Derek gets out, leaving his SUV running.

I'm about to ask about that when he opens the door, so I follow him inside.

He disarms the alarm and turns to me, taking my face into both hands.

"I've got some shit to deal with. I'll be back later. Be good." He presses his lips to mine briefly, then wraps me up in a tight hug.

I stand still trying to ignore how warm and strong he feels, wondering why I can't shut off the attraction despite all the crappy things he's done.

"Am I under surveillance here?" I ask.

He smiles. "Maybe."

I scrunch my face up. He pokes my nose playfully.

"It's Tuesday, baby."

"And?"

"And how about tacos tonight? I'll get the fixings delivered."

I shrug. "I don't know if I want tacos."

"But you always say every day should be Tuesday."

I sigh and fold my arms.

He mocks me, copying my stance.

"Anyway..." I mutter.

"Okay, have food delivered if there's something you want then? I'll send you Carson's details. He can arrange it."

"Carson seems to be a busy guy. I'm sure I can manage groceries for us."

He smiles. Wide.

I roll my eyes because I realize I've just said "us".

"Oh," he says, "I just remembered, the rest of your belongings from the rowhouse will be here at about 5:00. I'll try to be back by then. If not, here, look." He gestures to the security panel on the wall by the door and shows me how to let the delivery guys in.

"I put the app on your phone yesterday, too, so you can deal with it from anywhere in the house."

"Are the movers bringing my Cherokee?" I ask.

"That's already here," he tells me, pointing over his shoulder.

"The garage?"

"Yep."

"Oh."

"Don't go out though. Stay here. Nobody knows where we live yet. There was media outside the apartment by The Fifth this morning. Just a matter of time before this address gets figured out. Meanwhile, best you stay here behind the gates."

We left his parents' place via the service entrance so missed the camped out photographers on our way home. I mean *here*.

Cheater

Here I am thinking in 'us and 'home' terms, as if that's my reality. But it is my reality, isn't it?

He kisses me again, then rubs his nose against mine. "Be back soon. Maybe think about paint colors. Other things you want to replace. If I don't run out of time, I'll be stopping by the bank today to get you copies of some cards."

"Cards?"

"Bank and credit cards."

"I have bank and credit cards."

He smiles. "I know that, bunny, but you get copies of mine now."

I roll my eyes. "Maybe I'll take my frustrations with you out on your cards."

He shrugs. "Won't bother me a bit. Back soon."

He leaves.

∞

I'm not sure what to do with myself. I don't have work since I'm technically on my honeymoon. And I'm not sure I even want the job anymore. I can't imagine what Frank thinks of me. I don't have work friendships with anyone else since everyone is remote and there's no bricks and mortar office, but we do monthly team video calls and I can only imagine how surprised everyone will be when they find out the new owner of Cavalier who gave me a $10K bonus, married me, bought the company, then gave it to me.

I decide to crawl into bed with the shifter romance and finish the last chapter and epilogue.

46
Derek

I decide to make my first stop my bank to get cards for Chloe. I've already called my lawyer in Cleveland and told him of my marital status change and requested my will be set up for Chloe to inherit everything. My next stop is the drug store where I've had my pharmacist connection do some custom work, providing me with two birth control pill packages that consist of just the sugar pills. She's got two packs in her bathroom bag, and I'd sent a photo text to show the package.

After this, I show my face at both clubs and get some shit done, talk to the managers, and when I'm ready to head out to pay a visit to Jeannie Gilligan, I see Alannah Fisher walking out of her office entrance in the Downtown nightclub building.

Alannah isn't paying attention; she's fishing through her handbag as she walks toward the street, and before she sees me, I've shackled her wrist with my hand, and her eyes widen as I back her up about half a dozen paces to the brick wall.

"Hello, Alannah," I greet.

"What are you doing?" she hisses bitchily, but she's afraid. It's all over her body language.

"You really should pay attention when you're out in public. Anyone could grab you, throw you in a van," I gesture toward a white sprinter van that just so happens to be parked out on the street, "and you might never be seen again."

Her eyes boing to almost comical levels.

"By the way, don't attempt to fuck with me again," I warn, making sure there's no mistaking my seriousness. "Your little game yesterday cost a lot of unnecessary headaches."

"If you think you're above the law, you're wrong. I'm not finished fighting for Chloe."

"I know. I've seen your phone records, your internet activities, and I've got access to a whole lot more information about you than you want me to have. Cancel your coffee date with Sabrina Steele on Thursday. The only way you get to meet my sister-in-law in person is if it's because you get to be part of our extended family and she becomes friendly with my wife."

She glares at me.

"Your quest to keep digging for dirt about us is stupid, Alannah. If you keep it up you'll have more than me from my family to deal with and believe me, you don't want that. And I happen to have a file in my possession with a good chunk of Fisher family dirt, particularly yours."

Her eyes narrow.

I continue. "I'm playing as nice as I am because Chloe loves you. Don't push me any further. Cease and desist, Breastie, or you'll be out of Chloe's life. You've already missed her wedding and I'm sure that later on, you'll both look back at that with regret. Do you want to be cut out of her life entirely? Do you want new problems in your personal and professional life? Or do you want to be part of her new and improved happier life?"

She continues to stare at me defiantly, but her lip trembles.

"Fuck around and find out," I warn through gritted teeth and then let go of her wrist.

Alannah storms to her car and peels out.

I get into my car, check my phone for the message from Kenny with the address for Jeannie Gilligan, then punch it into my navigation system.

I already know Craig Jenkins spent time with Jeannie yesterday.

Cheater

Kenny followed him to her house. He was there over an hour, and he clocked being tailed on the way home. Kenny's good. Jenkins must be good, too. Would be nice to have him in our pocket, but if he keeps his end of our bargain and doesn't cause me further hassles, I'll grant my wife's wish and let him continue to wear his white hat.

∞

I had Kenny do a quick background check, nothing too deep, but seems like there's not much to tell of her life. Jeannie Gilligan moved here after high school, and reconnected with Hallman the freshman year of college. Enrolled in his school, likely to rekindle their thing. She grew up on the same street as Adam *Hallman* (formerly Dalton), dated him long distance for a year in high school, they split, and she's been carrying a torch ever since. She has a 9-5 clerical job at the courthouse, has very few friends, is trying to make money with a side hustle as an online influencer, and has a steady routine.

On Tuesday nights at seven o'clock, she goes to a thirty-minute hot yoga class six blocks from her apartment. I kill time in the bookstore, buying a couple of books for Chloe, then five minutes before class is set to finish, I park near the yoga studio and watch the door.

Yeah, I've got people that can do this for me, but in a situation this personal, a situation that involves slandering Chloe's name? It'll be more impactful coming directly from me.

She steps outside the yoga studio with another woman, and they stand outside talking for a good ten minutes. I'm ready for this to be done. I want to get home to my wife. I also haven't eaten since breakfast at my parents'.

Finally, they go separate ways.

She walks about a hundred feet and then cuts right down a side street. I jog until I get to the turn and then slow down, keeping thirty or forty feet behind her.

She hasn't looked back for a good block and a half, so I squat, nab a small rock, and pitch it. It pings off the side of her head and bounces off her shoulder.

She startles, grabs the side of her head, and looks over her shoulder. It takes a solid three seconds before her body language tells me recognition has hit. I pick up my pace. Anger burns hot in my system. *This bitch.*

She rushes forward, holding her head, but power-walking away from me, digging through her bag, likely going for her phone and maybe some pepper spray. She breaks into a jog, still rifling through the bag, and so I rush her. She stumbles, falling to her hands and knees on the sidewalk.

She squeaks out a sound of pain and looks up at me with giant eyes.

She's generically attractive. Dainty. Probably used to getting her own way. Just has that look about her.

After a quick scan of my perimeter, I lift my foot and put my boot to her shoulder. I'm putting next to no weight on it, but she immediately loses her balance and now her cheek is pressed to the pavement. And the urge is there to kick her in the face, to stomp on her head.

How fucking dare she go after Chloe.

I resist the urge.

"Chloe Steele, formerly Turner, does not exist."

She whimpers.

"At all. Understand? You don't speak her name. You don't type it. You don't discuss her whatsoever. Not with anyone."

I pause for a few beats, then add, "Yeah?"

She whimpers and nods. She's crying. There's snot coming out of her nose.

I back off just two paces and spit. The spit lands on her face.

∞

I walk into the house at nearly eight thirty and the aroma of food lingers. I'm fucking starved.

Cheater

The sight of Chloe's bare feet on this kitchen floor in the house I bought for her? I'm hard. I take in her skintight blue yoga pants, her little white crop top showing me her belly button. The look on her face? I can't be sure, but she might be looking at me differently.

I'm harder.

She's got her hair tucked behind her ears, her teeth are chewing her bottom lip, and she's drying a frying pan with a look in her eyes I don't recognize. Almost like she *might* be happy to see me.

I set the bookstore bag on the counter, taking an exaggerated whiff of the air as I wrap both arms around her waist and take her lips with mine. She tastes like wine. The whites of her eyes are so bright white. Her eyelashes are so full. The shape of her mouth is fascinating. I never grow tired of watching it move as she talks.

I caress her face, thinking about the fact that she's mostly quiet around me. I want her lips moving, want her telling me things, want to hear her wants. I want to know that she's happy. I want to know that she loves that I give that to her.

"Guess I missed Taco Tuesday."

"I... um..."

"It's okay. Were they good? Did they make you happy?"

She tilts her head, regarding me.

"I bought you some books. The next two in that series you're reading."

Her eyes bounce to the bag on the island and her lips part. She looks surprised in a good way, instead of being panicked like usual with my surprises.

"Um... I made you some. Err, I mean, there are still tacos." She pulls free of my embrace to open the fridge door. She gestures to a covered dish with half a dozen compartments. I move up and get a better look. There are compartments with taco fixings in them. I look at her face. She gestures with her chin to the counter behind me.

"There's a plate with shells in the microwave. You just have to zap them for just ten or twenty seconds and then pull the two meat compartments out of that tray there and nuke those too, for maybe forty-five seconds to a minute. Then your other toppings in the platter are cold, so –" She shrugs. "ready to eat."

"You made dinner for me?" I ask.

She looks away shyly. "I made dinner. There was some left."

"You made dinner for us," I repeat and advance, backing her up until she's against the wall at the edge of the kitchen. My hands sift into her hair, and it feels fucking great woven through my fingers. Our mouths collide again and fuck me, but she's not recoiling. Not pushing at my chest. Not trying to turn her head away.

"I'm sorry I'm late," I say. "I would've loved to eat with you."

If she wasn't thinking of me, she wouldn't have set those taco shells into the microwave on a plate. She wouldn't take the time to explain the set-up which was done in a way to make it easy for me to eat when I got home.

Fucking love this.

Her here, waiting for me, having cooked for me? It makes this place feel like something I haven't had for a long time. An actual home. I've spent most of my life moving around. Between boarding schools and my parents' many homes. College was in the same place for four years, but it was just a crash pad. After that, jumping between cities staying at my two condos or a furnished rental apartment for the occasions I'm in Cincinnati. But this place? This is already starting to feel like a home. Like a place I'll look forward to after a busy day. Like a retreat.

She's now clutching my shirt with both hands. I hike her up by her hips and grasp her ass as her legs wrap around me. I walk her to the nearest soft piece of furniture, the couch in front of the island that faces the fireplace. After putting her on her back, I run both hands up her ribs until they cup her tits, then nibble my way down her jaw to her throat and suck.

She arches into me.

"Gonna mark you," I tell her, my voice coming out gruff as I latch onto her neck.

She arches further. It's like she's welcoming it. *Fuck yeah.*

Cheater

My hand dives into her waistband, straight to her bare skin and then glide through that wet silk of her. Now fingers hook inside my wife, and I press against her G-spot.

She licks my tongue with hers, letting out a sexy, needy little moan.

"Too many clothes," I tell her, hauling her yoga pants down before immediately whipping the white crop top sweatshirt over her head.

"Go for mine," I direct, dropping her shirt.

She freezes.

Fuck. I've pulled her out of the moment.

"Nuh uh, I'm not losing you." I point at my eyes. "Right here, Chloe."

She swallows, looking unsure.

"Thank you for making me dinner, baby," I say, getting my own jeans down enough and quickly filling her. She arches, eyelids lowering, moaning, pressing her tits to me. It's like she's been waiting all day for this. Like she couldn't wait for me to get here. But her eyes are closed now, so I move in and press a kiss to one eyelid, then the other.

"My good girl," I praise her. "Milk my cock with your sweet pussy. I fuckin' love being inside you."

My wife buries her face in my neck, but she complies, so I flex my hips and then jerk back almost all the way out before slamming home again. I see just a slight discoloration on her neck. I acted like a horny teenager, trying to mark her multiple times now. But I've never wanted to mark someone before. I want her to mark me, too. How long before she's willing to do that?

I stay rooted.

Her nails dig into my back.

"More?" I ask.

She clutches me tighter.

"Shit. There's not enough room on this couch; we need a bigger one for this room."

I lift her and put her on her back on the rug, but immediately change my mind about the position and turn her to her belly.

"Knees, Chloe. Lift that sweet ass in the air for your husband."

She does it and her breathing has quickened. On my knees now, I grab her hip with one hand and guide my way inside with the other. She's even wetter now. For me. As soon as I hit the end of her, I grab her tits and raise her to the same position as me, kissing the side of her neck.

She whimpers as my right hand slides down and cups between her legs. I work her bundle of nerves, fucking into her from behind, now tonguing the ridge of her ear as her head rolls back onto my shoulder.

I catch sight of her wedding rings on her finger and feel fierce affection in my chest. Love. Love for her.

I have marked her with those. Those rings on her finger, my name attached to hers? She's mine. This is what I want. Making her come. Making her want me. Making her want to look after me, though I'm going to look after her first.

"I love you, Chloe," I tell her, kissing her neck, then wrapping my hand around it while continuing to slam into her over and over. "And I want you. I want to do this to you every single day until I can't."

She falls forward, crying out while trembling through her climax.

I knee-walk us forward enough to prop her torso on the couch cushion while I increase my pace and intensity, chasing my own climax, fucking her until sensation trills from my spine to my nuts, my vision blurring as I spill my load inside her, tightening my grip on her throat just a little.

She's whimpering non-stop for a good ninety seconds when she finally goes slack.

Not long until she's on the sugar pills instead of birth control. I run my hand up her flat stomach.

I put my mouth to her ear. "I can barely wait to breed my sexy, smart, irresistible wife. Want you round, and tied to me forever." I kiss her neck. "How many babies you want me to put inside you?"

Cheater

She's panting. Breathless. Sated. Boneless. Quiet.

"Maybe one of these days, my wife will answer the question. I look forward to it."

I pull out and turn her into my arms, lifting her up and putting her on the couch. Her eyes are closed. She's hiding from me again.

I pull the soft blanket from the basket on the floor beside it and drape it over her, lean down, kiss her, haul my underwear and jeans back into place, then go down the hall to use the john.

When I'm back, she's still curled up on the couch, eyes open now and pointed at the fireplace. I grab the fireplace remote and start it up, so she's got something to stare at. She now wears a face full of regret.

And I feel an unpleasant twinge in my chest.

"I'll get you there," I say. "I promise."

And I mean that. I'll get her to a place where eye contact will mean I get her smiles, her promises, sweet words.

I turn the microwave on and when it beeps, pull out the warm taco shells. I heat up the meat, and carry the whole platter to the coffee table in front of the couch she's on. She's filled the compartments with salsa, cheese, sour cream, and one with shredded lettuce and diced tomato. I fetch a bottle of beer and join her at the couch, setting my plate on the table. She bends her legs to make room for me.

"There's taco sauce in the fridge. And squeezable guac," she says.

"Mm, good. Want anything?" I ask.

She shakes her head.

I go get them and ask, "Mind if I catch the news?"

She shakes her head again.

I flick the television on and dig in, putting away four tacos. She's asleep after my third. Looking angelic.

When I'm done with my food, I wash and put away my plate and the platter. I sit down again, take her ankles, and put them in my lap so her legs are stretched out. She doesn't stir.

A while later, I'm lifting her up and her eyes pop open. She looks disoriented.

"Fell asleep on the couch, baby. Gonna tuck you in."

"I can walk," she says.

"But you don't have to, do you?" I ascend the stairs with her.

When I put her on the bed, I kiss her on the temple. "Be with you in a minute. Grabbin' a shower and have to make a couple calls."

She doesn't answer, so I flick the lamp off and go shower.

When I join her in bed a while later, she's now under the covers and seems like she's out again. I pull her into my arms. She snuggles into me and lets out a sweet little sigh. She's sound asleep so it's not a sound she's aware she's making. But it's mine. Like her.

It's a happy sound even though I know she's not happy. I know she's holding my actions against me, still, but I'm also sure that she's gonna get where she needs to be.

I can't seem to fall asleep for hours. Because I can't wait to see if her eyes are gentler in the morning. But I'm also afraid they won't be. She didn't fight me tonight. She made me dinner. She wasn't entirely open, but she was more open than she has been. The most she's been since the first night I spent with her. The idea that it could be like that again? Like that all the time? I can't wait to see if this is a turning point. But if it isn't, I know I'm closer than I was yesterday. Maybe today alone was good for her. Maybe I should give her some space tomorrow, too.

I'm finally able to drift off thinking I'm looking forward to tomorrow night, to seeing if she's happy to see me, if she's made food again.

47

Chloe

I wake up alone and immediately face an onslaught of my own guilt with a heavy dose of mortification. Rolling over to the middle of the bed, I stare at the ceiling, giving myself a moment with my shame.

I can't believe I let him jump me when he got home. And I felt a little palpitation when he came in because I was kind of hoping he'd jump me. So stupid. Why? After everything? Why?

I was thinking about him all evening as I busied myself making dinner, wandering around the house, the yard. Running the vacuum after the movers tracked some dirt in. They came a few hours before Derek got in and I had them load all my things into one of the bedrooms on the second floor. Clothes, my desk and bookshelves. The sofa bed from my office. Boxes marked with the contents of each. Boxes of kitchen stuff. I don't know what's in any of them; I'm not about to unpack or have a look. Because what would that say about my opinion on this situation? At least I have access to the rest of my toiletries; I made sure the box I noted said *Chloe Steele, bathroom* didn't get buried.

Chloe Steele. I'm sure if Adam was home when those movers packed and marked my belongings, seeing that name in the black Sharpie block letters must have stung. Or maybe it didn't. There was even a woman as part of the crew, for packing my personal things. And that seemed like something my thoughtful, possessive, swoony psycho stalker would do.

I guess he's now technically my swoony psycho *husband*. Argh.

As the movers were coming in with the last box, there was a grocery delivery, so I got to cooking and saved food for Derek, not realizing it would get me a reaction even bigger than when I made him a sandwich.

He looked so warmed by the fact that I did something as simple as consider he might be hungry. And somewhere in his travels yesterday, he went out and bought me books. Books I'd have bought for myself. Because he pays attention. And I'm annoyed by how much I liked that he did that.

Yes, he pays attention. He tries to anticipate what might make me happy. He looks at me like I'm his dream girl. He fucks me like he can't get enough. And like he wants me to enjoy it even more than he wants to enjoy it. But he also wants to enjoy it. And he does. He makes sure we both get off. And then snuggles my feet on the couch while he watches TV and eats the food I made, as if tacos are the most gourmet and delicious thing ever. I woke up with his strong, warm hand on my foot and then drifted off again.

Then I wake up again being carried to bed with him looking at me while he carries me like I'm precious. Something wonky happens in my belly whenever he carries me somewhere. He's tall. Has those big muscled arms. And when he carries me he looks at me. Really looks at me.

He stood up for me with his mother yesterday. He had a look of pride on his face when I stood up for myself with that media monster lady.

He tried to make a point with my parents the night before last by gushing about what he feels are some of my qualities.

He bought me the company I work for so that it's mine.

And he's insane. Obsessed. Dangerous. He's put me through all sorts of mental turmoil after spying on almost every aspect of my life. And there's what he's done with Adam! And he all but admitted to being responsible for Adam's uncle's death, which caused Adam's

Cheater

grandmother's death! Having people held at gunpoint? Threats of forcing a cop to turn dirty?

Could I get him to go on medication? Would that help? Would that be a way to justify easing into this life in this dream house with the most gorgeous man I've ever been with? With the best sex I've ever had? With all those promises that make him sound like a dream husband? Would medication make him less dangerous? Would it also make him less... Derek? Because if he's just another hot guy that's not obsessed with me, would he be like most every other hot, rich guy out there that's instead obsessed with themselves? Maybe he'd let me go live my own life if I got him on medication. Maybe he'd realize just how fucked up all of this is.

I pick my phone up and see a text message from him.

Gone to work early. Sorry, baby. Know it's our honeymoon but I'll take the rest of the week off. My turn to take care of dinner so don't cook. I love you.

His turn to cook? A husband who shares the domestic load? A mythical creature indeed. Not unlike the mythical unicorns I was worried about being sacrificed when I lady-scaped for no good reason. Maybe there was a mythical creature meeting and they sent Derek to me so no more of their babies would dissolve.

Speaking of mythical creatures, I have two more sexy novels to read, and it's been eons since I gave myself a whole day on a couch reading a book. I decide that's what I'll do. After coffee. After an Alannah catch-up.

While I'm showering, I can't help but wonder what he's going to do for me for dinner today. And that's crazy. I can't be entertaining these sorts of thoughts.

∞

It's mid-afternoon and I'm lying on the couch with a fire going. Leaves are rapidly descending from their trees in the back yard. And this room would look absolutely incredible with a soaring Christmas tree. A real one. Filling the house with the scent of fir. I love that smell.

I've been enjoying my book, but I've been frequently assaulted with random thoughts or images to do with Derek, with a future. A future here in this house. One that has kids. That giant Christmas tree. Snowman-building. And me making dinner while watching him out back raking leaves into a giant pile and jumping into it with kids. And a dog, maybe. Not a purebred from a breeder, either. A rescue dog who gets his forever home with us.

Yeah, I've been crafting pie-in-the-sky fantasies today. And I feel a little stupid for it.

And just like in the first book in the series I read, the main male character morphs into Derek in my mind during the sex scenes. I've put the book down three times already when that's happened, but found myself picking it back up a few minutes later.

My phone rings and I sit up, feeling so absolutely lazy it's not even funny. Alannah's calling me. I called her first thing this morning but got her voicemail so texted to say,

All is okay here, just wanted to say Hi. Call when you've got time.

I did that so she wouldn't worry. She's most likely quite worried about me. And I'm not exactly okay. But I am.

"Hi you," I answer.

"Hey," she says.

"Everything good with you?"

"Everything good with you?" She answers my question with the same question. But her voice sounds funny.

"I mean... yeah. I guess. It's weird. We were gonna go on a honeymoon but with that dirty laundry blog thing, it got canceled. Not that I wanted to go, of course, and I don't even know where he was planning to take me. We saw my parents that same day and that was beyond weird. Derek took charge and tried to put their minds at ease,

Cheater

telling them he's handling the gossip and not to let it get to them. Talking about inviting them to the Swiss Alps for a do-over wedding and having them come here for a weekend."

"God," she mutters.

"Yeah. It was bizarre. Then yesterday we had to go to his parents', and I spent the morning being grilled, lambasted, and raked over hot coals by their media monster. A judgy woman who tried her hardest to trip me up in an effort to make sure I'm ready for any media attention. It was bizarre. And a photoshoot for any other media releases that go out. I'm afraid to look at social media. Is there still buzz about me?"

She makes a funny sound.

And the line is dead-quiet for a long minute, so I'm thinking I've lost her. I look at the screen to make sure we're still on a call, then call out, "Hello?"

"I'm here," she says. "So, you're okay?"

"Yeah, I mean, I'm not but I am. I don't know. This whole thing is crazy. Like... really crazy."

"Beyond crazy," she agrees.

"Are you okay? That was pretty stressful for you on Monday at City Hall, I'm sure. I'm trying to get him to leave Craig alone. He... I don't know if you know but he was planning to make Craig a dirty cop, force him onto their payroll. God knows how many other cops they've got, but I think I've talked him out of it."

She makes that funny sound again. Is that a sarcastic, throaty scoffing noise?

"Is Craig okay? Have you talked to him? I talked to him for a minute later that night, and he was trying to let me off the hook. He's such a good guy. And I don't know if I'm even supposed to talk about it. I'm sure I don't have to tell you to keep everything I say about Derek between us."

"Oh no, you don't have to remind me of that. Though if I forgot, I'm sure he'd remind me again. In a dark alley, probably."

She sounds absolutely pissed.

"I'm okay, Alannah."

"None of this is okay, Chloe. Don't go getting Stockholm Syndrome here, okay?"

I flinch. "I'm not. Definitely not." My face is suddenly burning hot. "I just... I wanted to make sure you're okay. Because that was beyond amped the other day."

"I am. No thanks to the heart attack I nearly had yesterday after work when he made it clear that bad things will happen to me if I intervene again."

"What?"

"He showed up. Cornered me after work and threatened me. He said, 'Fuck around and find out.' And I think he did something to that Jeannie girl. I had lunch with Craig today and he told me they're related. That he stopped by there this morning to check on her and she's terrified. Wouldn't tell him why but I have a feeling she got the same message I got. He said there was a bruise on her face, and she said she 'fell'. Maybe she got an even stronger message than what I got. And Craig said Adam is so distraught he won't even leave his house. He's shutting everyone out. So, who knows what else he's done to Adam."

I swallow down what feels like broken glass, then ask, "Tell me what happened after work yesterday. What did he do exactly?"

"He grabbed my wrist and pinned me to the wall and got in my face."

"He hurt you?"

"Not physically, no. He scared me. That's what he wanted to do. And mission accomplished."

I feel sick.

"Chloe, this guy is really fucking cracked. I don't know what I can even do to help you."

"You can't help me. I have to figure this out myself," I say softly.

"Well, he's warned me against trying to intervene again, so what am I supposed to do? Just leave you to him? Craig is backing off, too. Craig says his hands are tied. We wound up arguing at lunch about

Cheater

this and that's when he told me about that Jeannie. He's frustrated, but he's stuck. And I'm frustrated so I took it out on him and now I guess I'm taking it out on you, too, because I hate being powerless and I feel like that's what's happening here. This guy forced you to marry him by having three of us held by a dirty cop with a gun pointed at us. From what you said, he had some other guy hold you and Adam with a gun to make Adam break up with you. Something has to be done. I might be getting myself in big trouble here because he's probably listening in on this call, but Chloe, what the fuck? When does the gun actually get used? Do I wind up in that unmarked van he threatened with and then disappear without a trace?"

I've been holding my breath, so I let it out in a hard exhale.

"I don't know how I can sit back and watch this happen to you, Chlo. It's already like you've lost so much of yourself because of Adam's accident. If we can't get you away from this guy, you're going to disappear completely, and I don't want to lose my best friend."

Tears are streaming down my face now. And I'm angry, too. He threatened her. Scared her. After everything he's done already, after me granting his marriage demands while she was held at gunpoint he goes and threatens her some more?

And to think where my mind was going today. And how I didn't even try to stop him last night. I even kissed him back when he kissed me. He'd come back from terrorizing her and I let him fuck me and fed him dinner!

"Fuck. This is so fucked up." I reach for the box of Kleenex and pull one out.

"You sounded okay when you called, and I just ruined your mood. It must be so hard being in that situation 24/7. I'm sor-"

"No. Stop."

She's right. I needed a reality check. Not that I'm about to say that aloud because I don't want him to get pissed off with her.

"I don't have Stockholm Syndrome. Believe me. I've just been trying to decompress because all this is so, so stressful. And he was out all day yesterday and he's not here today, so I've had a chance to decompress a little. But the fact that he threatened you after he already made me marry him to keep you safe? Not okay."

"He doesn't want me interfering again. If I hadn't done that, I'd have been there for you for your wedding day. As if you even wanted to be there. He's completely off his rocker anyway, but if he thinks me being there would've made the day somehow more magical for you, I don't even know what to say about his delusions."

"He has a whole lot of delusions," I mumble. "I... I need to go. I'll call you later."

"Yeah. Be safe, honey."

"You, too," I say.

Fuming, I go upstairs and quickly get dressed, put a jacket and shoes on, pocket my phone, my charger, and grab my purse.

Once I'm at the front door, seeing the security panel says the house alarm is armed, I take my phone out, disarm it, then go outside and press the app button to open the garage door. I see my Jeep sitting there and my keys are in the cup holder.

48

Derek

Where is she?

I came in, noticing the house alarm wasn't armed and I didn't like that. Now I know why.

I walked in with dinner, flowers, and when I didn't find her, I checked the security app and saw that two hours ago, the house was disarmed, the garage was opened and closed, and then the gate was opened and shut.

I don't have to go look to know that her car is gone.

I haven't put any surveillance in the house. Didn't want to do that. I also hadn't had cameras installed on the exterior either.

I still have access to her phone logs including calls and a key logger and I've got tracking on her Jeep. While I'm relieved to see her toothbrush and face stuff is in the bathroom, and that one of the books I bought her yesterday is on the couch with a bookmark in it showing she's already halfway through it, I don't know what to think.

I don't have her other belongings catalogued and the bedroom next to ours is full of the contents of her old place so I'm not sure if she took anything with her.

I grab my phone and turn on the tracking app and I'm tweaked by the sight of her location. Her car is parked at the airport. Her phone is at the same location. But it's turned off. I dial it anyway and leave her a voicemail message.

"Chloe? Call me. As soon as possible."

I dig in to her logs and check today's internet searches. Her emails from today. Nothing pointing to answers until I play the recording of the phone call she had with Alannah. And by the end I want to throw my fucking phone.

I didn't seek out Alannah to threaten her last night; I just had a word with her when I ran into her.

But it seems from the call I listened to like Chloe's attitude took a turn after Alannah told her about last night.

I push down the anger I feel bubbling up toward the surface. It'd be aimed at Alannah if I let it rise. I can't. Because reacting genuinely here won't do anything to help this situation. If I aim my anger in Alannah's direction, Chloe would find it unforgivable. Alannah simply told Chloe what happened, and Chloe is reacting.

I'm kicking myself for taking Kenny off Chloe detail. Putting her here behind the gates to keep her safe left me with a false sense of security. I hadn't bargained on her leaving. Especially not after her spending half the day alone yesterday without incident. But my sense of security was more about how she was with me last night.

I count backwards from fifty as I leave the house and drive toward the airport to find my wife. Before getting to twenty, I decide to contact Kenny. I tell him to check her bank account and her personal credit card and let me know if she's bought a plane ticket.

Twenty minutes later, just as I'm pulling up to her car, he calls.

"She withdrew three grand from an ATM inside the airport," he says.

"Fuck!" I snap. "Keep watch on her accounts, yeah? Try to find out if she booked a flight somewhere."

"Got it, Derek."

"And pay attention to Alannah Fisher. Put someone on her and monitor her calls live until I find my wife."

"On it."

I end the call.

Her car is empty, and the hood is cold. She left her phone in the car at the airport and withdrew what's probably her daily limit in

Cheater

cash. Three grand won't give her too many options, but it could make things pretty fucking inconvenient for a minute.

∞

Three hours later, I'm ready to lose my fucking mind. Because it's been churning over possibilities. Has she left town? What's her next move? More cash tomorrow? If so, I'll at least know where she withdraws it from.

I've driven by Hallman's house. I've driven by Alannah's condo. I've checked the tracker at least thirty times to see if she's moved her car or used her phone. I've been assured by Kenny several times that there's no change, no sight of her, and that she hasn't called or been called by Hallman or Alannah. I've also checked the app for security at the house just in case she took a taxi back. But nothing is showing up there.

Where else would she go? She's not close enough to her parents to call them to ask them to pick her up, is she? If I call them, I could set off alarm bells with them, so no, I won't do that.

∞

I'm at the house. Pacing. Checking the trackers repeatedly. Waiting on Kenny. Waiting. Fucking waiting while repeating all my earlier checks. He's checked some of her other friends' places. The lawyer Jeff is at his place with her friend Coraline. Her friend Madison is out of town for her job and Madison's husband is home alone. I don't know anyone else Chloe interacts with in Columbus.

Fuck, but I fucking loathe this feeling.

I don't like being out of control. My trigger finger is jumpy. It's never a good thing when I get spasms in that finger.

She can't hide for long. I'll get the cops in our pocket on it if I don't have news by noon tomorrow. My father's guy can run facial recognition checks to find matches for airport security or for other high-traffic spots around the city. But I don't know how the fuck I'm going to keep my shit together if it comes to that, if I need to wait another fourteen hours to act. But everything inside me tells me I need to wait until then because activating anyone outside Kenny will mean my father hears about this.

49
Chloe

I'm in the bathroom of the bar in the hotel, fishing around in the pocket of my purse for some lip gloss when I've suddenly got Derek's business card in my hand. And seeing it, holding it, I shudder from my head to my toes.

I tucked it in here when I found it in my dress after the night we met. It has his cell phone number on it.

It's after ten o'clock and I'm a little drunk.

I'm actually more than a little drunk. Maybe I found this for a good reason. That reason being that I should call him and tell him what I'm planning to do. I'm planning to do the shittiest thing to him that I can think of given the predicament he's put me in. Maybe what I'm about to do will be the way out of this mess.

There's a guy here who bought me two drinks. He's cute. He's tall. He's been a little persistent. I mean, nowhere near the Derek Steele level of persistent, but even though I came down here to get a glass of wine with the plan to maybe do this, I probably would've chickened out if he hadn't been so cute and persistent.

His name is Aaron. He has blue eyes, short dark hair and a mustache and beard. He talked about the beautiful blue-eyed babies we'd make together. But in a funny way, not a skeevy way. He's in tech. He's wearing a suit. I mean, no one wears a suit like Derek does, but this guy does look good in a suit.

He's visiting from Kansas City. And I think if Aaron Blue Eyes buys me one more drink, I could work up the nerve to suggest he invite me to his hotel room. There's also my room that I paid for in cash so my psycho stalker "husband" can't find me with a credit card transaction, but I think it would be better if it's *his* room because then I can leave when it's all over and go back to my own room. I already bought condoms in the hotel gift shop and they're in my bag.

He says he's here on business. I lied and told him I was, too. He remarked that my wedding rings are beautiful. My reaction to that had him asking me if my marriage was in trouble. I told him my marriage was nothing but trouble. That it was a marriage of inconvenience. He laughed and we clinked glasses as he told me this was why he was a confirmed bachelor. If only I'd used my hall pass on Aaron Blue Eyes.

I'm going to undo the top two buttons of my blouse, take my hair down from this ponytail and up my flirting game.

But maybe first I'll call my psycho stalker "husband" and tell him that I'm going to cheat on him tonight.

Yeah, that's exactly what I'll do. Letting him know what I'm about to do before I do it should make it even more impactful. Maybe this will get me my life back. If it doesn't, maybe it'll at least let him feel some modicum of the agony he's been putting me and the people I care about through.

∞

On my quest for a payphone, I find a courtesy phone in the lobby of the hotel. I don't know if it'll work to block my location, but figuring it's worth a try, I press *67 and then punch in Derek's cell phone number.

He blackmailed me into cheating on my fiancé by making me break the rules. Maybe if I do this, he'll realize actions have consequences. And maybe if I do this, he'll let me go. Maybe he'll agree that this isn't a real marriage, and we can get out of it without divorcing. I can try to get an annulment since it's only days since we got

Cheater

married. I believe there's grounds for an annulment in the state of Ohio if one of the parties was forced into the marriage.

He answers on the first ring.

"Hello?"

I open my mouth, and nothing comes out.

"Hello?" he repeats with irritation.

All the crap he's pulled. All the turmoil. I summon my bravery, straighten my spine, and slur, "Hey there psycho stalker husband."

"Chloe," he breathes. And he sounds so relieved I find my forehead crinkling.

No. No! I'm not going to chicken out. He's gone too far too many times and no!

"Where are you?" he demands, voice definitely bossy.

I laugh. I laugh loud. And obnoxiously.

"Chloe?"

"You made me a cheater."

"Chloe, what–"

"You are the one that made me break all the rules, meaning I cheated on Adam."

"Baby, are you drunk?"

"I'm a cheater. Because of you. And I'm about to break those vows you forced me to make. Know why? Because I'm about to cheat on you, Derek."

"You're about to what?" His voice has gone dangerous.

And damn it, it sounds sexy.

Focus, Chloe.

"Yep. This time, it's my decision. No one else's. You're a psycho prick and I've had enough. You force me to marry you to keep people safe and they're still not safe, Derek. Because nobody is safe from you. Certainly not me, but I don't care about me as much as I care about innocent bystanders like Alannah. And Adam's grandmother! And Craig! And you started this whole fucking thing by manipulating me into cheating on my fiancé. So yeah. I'm a cheater because that's what you made me so I'm about to cheat on *you* now."

"You'd better not," he growls through what sounds like gritted teeth. "What did I tell you? Nobody but me. And what did I tell you about making me worry about you?"

"You threatened me. Because that's what you do. You think threatening me gives you full control over me. Right?"

And it gives me a thrill to hear him angry. Because he deserves to feel angry that someone is doing something he doesn't like!

"But I'm tired of doing what's expected of me. I'm tired of being the good girl. So guess what, Derek? I'm not your good girl. I will never be your good girl. And there's a good-looking guy here at this bar who's into me. He's been buying me drinks. And I'm gonna go back to where he's sitting waiting for me now and invite him to invite me to his place. What do you think about that?"

There's no immediate reply, so I check. "Hello?"

"You fuck that guy, Chloe, and it'll be his death sentence."

I snort. "You don't even know where I am. You won't know who I did it with. He's not from here."

Shit. I need to guard my words. I'm too drunk. Can't let him figure out where I am by saying the wrong thing.

"You think I won't find out? You think I don't have the ability to have security footage checked all throughout the city to find out where you've been and exactly who you've been seen with?"

"You don't even know if I'm still in Columbus. So *there*."

"You're still in Columbus, Chloe. You just fuckin' said he's not from *here*."

I scoff. "Maybe I am and maybe I'm not. Maybe, but I do know one thing."

I pause.

He doesn't say anything.

So I start talking again. "I know that I'm fucking finished being that good girl, Derek. I'm d-o-n-e *done*! What has it gotten me? Huh? I'm so done letting you do whatever you want to do to me with no repercussions."

Cheater

"You do this, you're responsible for that man's death. Because I will fucking kill him. I'll kill him and guess what, wife? You'll watch."

I'm losing bravado. My knees are wobbly. I think the air just got sucked straight out of this place. I brace with my hand on the wall beside the phone.

He starts speaking again. "Decide if you're coming back to me, ready to work hard to make up for this or..." He pauses for effect, and he achieves his goal because I'm chilled to the bone. "doing something you can't undo. Doing something that you'll regret. Because, Chloe... are you there?"

I'm frozen in place, my heart hammering so hard it hurts.

"Are. You. There? Wife?"

"I'm here," I somehow manage to rasp.

He's The Ice King, delivering his frigid blow through the phone line. "Not only will I end him if you, my bratty wife, are unfaithful to me, you will watch me do it and then you'll find yourself writhing around my cock for so long you'll think you're being fucked to death. And that won't be the end of your punishment either. Because we both know how much guilt you'll suffer if you're the reason I end a man's life and ruin both our happiness, don't you? Choose wisely, Chloe Steele. Think long and hard about this before you do something that'll change everything between you and me. Has he put his hands or his mouth on you yet?"

My shoulder gets tapped and Aaron with the blue eyes is smiling. Close.

"Hey, beautiful! Wondered where you'd gone to."

I abruptly put the phone receiver back onto the cradle, hanging up on Derek.

50
Chloe

I somehow wake up hangover-free. Shocker, since I started with wine, drank some vodka, and then finished with several different minibar bottles back in my hotel room.

My period has arrived and thankfully, I've got two tampons in my purse.

I leave the hotel two minutes before check-out time, get a cab to my car at the airport, unlock and then get into it and start it up. Five minutes later at a stoplight, I see the familiar blue SUV behind me at the stoplight.

Bile rises at the back of my throat.

Ken follows me all the way to Dublin, to my dream house. The sight of it right now makes me so, so sad. I press the app on my phone and get the gate opened, then tap the app and close it behind myself. The SUV parks directly outside the gate. Blocking it, in fact.

I press the app command to open the garage. Not only is the driveway empty, the garage is also empty. Derek isn't here.

And I don't know if I'm relieved or not because although I don't want to see him or talk to him, waiting to see him for however long it takes for him to come back is going to fry my nerves to a crisp. I stayed gone all night, leaving him to worry and wonder.

Waiting, worrying, and wondering must be part of *my* punishment. Because it's midnight when I hear the sound of footsteps coming down the hallway.

I'm in bed, the television on, the bedside lamp on.

He stops in the doorway and stares at me.

I stare at him, frozen.

Our eyes lock. Like they always do.

And my blood suddenly runs cold.

His mouth is in a tight line, and it twitches, looking like he's about to erupt into pure rage.

My heart is racing now and I'm feeling very, very afraid.

He warned me the night he broke in and fucked me in my and Adam's bed not to push him. But I finally broke and did that. I've pushed him pretty hard judging by the look on his face.

He takes purposeful strides toward me and then he puts a knee to the bed and climbs up and hovers over me, caging me in with one knee between my parted thighs, his palms propped on the bed on either side of my shoulders as he stares, nostrils flaring, fire burning in his dark gaze.

I'm frozen in pure terror.

"Did you?" he demands.

I must not answer fast enough, because he moves in even closer, eyes burning into mine.

"Did. You?" he repeats through his teeth.

And before I get a chance to answer, to tell him that no, I didn't, he knifes off me and leaves, slamming the door behind himself.

And I immediately spring into action. Because if he thinks I did that, he's going to hunt down poor, innocent Aaron and kill him. I don't doubt he has the resources to find out who I had two drinks with.

I run down the hall after him.

"Derek!" I shout as he gets to the stairs. He looks over his shoulder at me and he's clenching and unclenching just his right hand.

Cheater

"I didn't," I say. I shake my head fiercely. "I didn't."

He stares at me like a raging bull, nostrils flaring, chest rising and falling, hand clenching and unclenching, and I'm sure he's about to charge at me.

But he doesn't. He shoots ice from his gaze at me and then he goes down the stairs, disappearing from my view.

My knees give out or something, because I'm now sinking to the carpet, holding onto the banister, feeling like my heart is breaking. Why does it feel like that? He did *me* wrong. *He* pushed *me*. He did all the bad things that drove me to almost doing something in retaliation and here I am feeling like... like I'm the one that fucked up royally.

∞

I wake up alone. I didn't sleep much. I think it was the *not* knowing what might happen that kept me up. Or maybe I would've slept if he'd come back in, taken me into his arms and held me. Not because that's what I want; because that's the norm for Derek. To try in his warped way to look after me.

I hear noise, so I peek into the hallway and it's just as he's coming out of the bedroom at the other end of the hall, the farthest away from the master. He's in just a towel. His hair is wet. His eyes burn into me as he approaches so I back up into the room, but not fast enough because suddenly he's directly in front of me.

He stops. He stares. I look down at my bare feet and bite my lip.

He passes me, which shocks me, so I stare at his back as he goes into the walk-in closet and rifles through his suits.

He shoots a glare over his shoulder at me and it kind of burns, so I quickly slip into the ensuite bathroom and lock the door, then put my back against it. My heart is racing. My stomach hurts. My head hurts.

After too long of standing like a deer in the headlights, I decide to wash my face, brush my teeth, use the facilities, and when I cautiously come out to an empty bedroom, I shakily make the bed before tiptoeing down the hall to investigate. The door to the room he came out of is open. The bed is unmade, there's an empty bottle of bourbon on the bedside table.

Downstairs, there's no sign of him. I go back up, put on my pink robe and slippers, slip my phone into my robe pocket, and walk outside. His car isn't in the driveway. I use the app to open the garage and his car isn't there either. He left.

I hear something though. I look and see the blue SUV inch up closer to block the gate.

Not that I had plans to go anywhere. But still. I resist the urge to give Ken *the finger*.

∞

I spent time looking through the boxes in the spare room today. I wondered if Adam might have tucked a note into a box or something. Something, anything. But he didn't. He's done. And that's not the only reason I looked in the boxes. I guess I took a little journey through my time with him, my time before him, too.

And I'm not sure why I even considered that he might have something to say to the woman he said he wanted to spend the rest of his life with. I don't know where things go for me from here and I've been pondering it all day.

Since Steeles don't divorce, maybe I won't ever get free of Derek. But maybe Derek also won't get over what happened yesterday. Maybe he doesn't believe me. Maybe he's trying to find out if I'm telling the truth or not. Maybe he's punishing Aaron anyway. That thought makes me ill, so I can only hope that my walking away from him directly after hanging up on Derek means that Aaron is safe and sound if he's still in the city and preferably, that he's already gone back to Kansas City.

∞

Cheater

The day drags on with being alone with my thoughts. Or maybe feeling like I'm alone is an illusion because maybe I'm under surveillance. I don't bother to unpack anything other than some more clothes.

I send a text to Alannah at five o'clock.

Proof of Life Request?

She immediately responds

Alive.

I send a heart. She sends one back. And I'm glad it ends with that because I don't know that I want to talk about my train of thought with anybody.

∞

At midnight, I'm in the kitchen getting a glass of juice when I hear footsteps.

He comes in. His eyes give me a dark sweep that generates a feeling of static in the air. He walks to the pantry and pulls out another bottle of bourbon, then walks down the hall away from me.

When I go up, I notice the door is closed to the room he stayed in last night.

I toss and turn in bed alone, still wondering if there's been any fallout from my outing the other night beyond my "husband" giving me what is evidently the silent treatment.

51

Chloe

I've ascertained he left extra early today by looking at the alarm app and seeing the garage and gate opened and closed before six o'clock. And I've been left with the babysitter again. Ken's blue SUV is inside the gates now alongside a van with the logo of a security company. Unsure of what this might mean, I start coffee.

It doesn't take long to realize external surveillance systems are being installed. What I don't know is if they plan to come inside or not. My thoughts are that either everything is being upgraded or maybe there's no internal surveillance yet. Is that about to change?

After drinking a third coffee by the fireplace while watching more leaves fall, I'm feeling jittery. I start spending my pent-up energy by getting to work on vacuuming with the new-looking fancy vacuum I find in the hall closet. Not far into mopping the kitchen floor, I hear the doorbell.

I'm thinking security techs are about to come in, but instead, it's Grace Steele. Ken is behind her with garment bags. There's no security van outside now.

"Good morning," she greets, looking at me with what feels like scrutiny. I'm not sure if it's because of how I look or if it's got to do with her brother's current feelings about me, which I'm assuming are just... disdain?

I step aside for Ken who walks into the dining room and sets the garment bags on the table. He gives me a nod and backs out, closing the door behind Grace.

She's dressed in a pretty blue pantsuit, face full of makeup, jewelry, her blonde curly hair loose and flowing down her back.

I'm wearing shorts and a tank top. My hair is in a top knot, my face is makeup free. I've got bags under my eyes due to three nights of very little sleep.

"Derek's not here," I tell her.

"I came to see you," she advises. "And bring you some options for the party tomorrow." She gestures to the garment bag stack.

The party tomorrow. Shit. *Shit.*

"I'm not sure that I'll be coming tomorrow," I tell her.

She shakes her head curtly. "It's mandatory. Even Sabrina is coming. Do I smell coffee?"

I gesture down the hallway and start walking. She follows me to the kitchen.

"So, this is the house, then. This is adorable, Chloe," she says, looking around. "Can I have a tour? Then we'll have coffee and go through the clothes."

"I mean, sure you can have a wander if you want. I'll make a fresh pot for you. I'm already juiced past my usual max, and this is old."

I go to the kitchen and fetch the carafe, then pour the remnants into the sink. Grace moseys around, looking out windows, then disappears from my view.

A party for about four-hundred people to celebrate Derek's parents fortieth anniversary is the last thing I want to attend. The idea of coping with that makes my stomach churn unpleasantly. I'm not sure Derek would even bring me, considering we haven't spoken.

My phone chimes with an incoming text so I pull it out of my back pocket.

Cheater

Mom: Hope everything is well with you. Just wanted to say hello and ask if you and Derek would like to come over for dinner. I know his parents' party is this Saturday so this Sunday you'll likely be tired but I was thinking maybe next Sunday. Or even Saturday? If Saturday we could have game night and you two could sleep over if you like.

I need to put my phone down because my hands are trembling. I'm about to burst into tears. I take a few deep breaths, my sinuses burning.

I read the text message again.

We haven't had a game night since Bryan got really sick. It was a Turner tradition most Saturday nights. We would pull out board games and order pizza or pick up fast food. Make sundaes. When we were small, we'd play Snakes and Ladders. Trouble. CandyLand. Sometimes we'd play Pictionary. Sometimes we'd play cards. Or Monopoly or The Game of Life once we got a little older. None of us has even suggested a game night since Bryan died. Because it was one of his favorite things.

I'm not going to cry. I'm not I'm not I'm not.

"You okay?" I hear.

Grace has walked back in, seeing me braced with both hands on the counter, taking breath after breath. I shake it off and straighten up.

"How do you take your coffee?"

"Black with stevia is good if you have it, but... the coffee isn't on yet, so... are you sure you're okay?"

The coffee pot is sitting in the sink overflowing with the still-running water.

I turn the tap off.

I'll answer my mother in a bit. Once I peel my jaw off the floor, I guess.

"Forget coffee. Let's sit." She takes my hand and tugs a little. I let her lead me to the couch on the other side of the kitchen island.

"Talk to me," she requests once we're sitting down.

"No offence, Grace, but I don't even know you."

"I'm your sister-in-law. We're family now. I care about my family."

I shake my head. "Your brother blackmailed me into an ongoing sexual relationship after manipulating me into bed with him and that quickly turned into me being blackmailed into marrying him. Into entering a sacred contract not only in the eyes of the church but also in the eyes of your family, evidently, because divorce is not an option. So... that doesn't make us family. I'm not trying to be mean. Maybe under different circumstances we could be genuine friends, but–"

"We can be friends anyway," Grace says. "Just because things are complicated with you and my brother doesn't mean they have to be with you and me."

I'm not sure how to respond.

"You need someone to talk to, to ask questions, to get history or Steele insight? I'm your girl."

She gives me a loaded look.

Is she expecting me to ask questions? To pick her brain for information? I don't want information. What difference will that make?

"Okay, so you don't take hints," she says with humor.

And I'm not in the mood for this, so I rub my eyes, exasperated.

"Chloe, Derek is a complex individual. Nobody gets close. I'm probably the closest, only because I don't typically respect boundaries."

I give her a pointed look. She shrugs, looking amused.

My shoulders jiggle with silent laughter.

"You're sworn to secrecy here as part of this family, okay?"

"I'm not making promises, Grace. Please don't tell me anybody's secrets. I can't deal with that kind of thing right now. I'm on absolute overload, I have been for weeks and-"

"Derek is who he is mostly due to trauma response," she states,

Cheater

cutting me off, letting me see just how little respect she has for boundaries. "He was kidnapped by someone he trusted. He saw our chauffeur murdered and was taken for ransom. When the time ran out and the kidnapper was getting twitchy, Derek got the kidnapper's gun and shot him in the head. Just like he'd seen the kidnapper do to our chauffeur. He was eleven, Chloe."

My throat goes dry. She's not done talking.

"The child psychologist was already treating him for some severe behavioral issues. He was already a problem child. And I think part of that was because our mom attempted suicide and Derek found her. He tried to help her and was covered in her blood so our Thad blamed Derek for it. He kept saying Derek did something to Mom. But that wasn't true. Dad sat Thad down and told him Derek had nothing to do with Mom being hurt and going away for a while to get better, but Thad got even more nasty and hard on Derek. Thad was... a lot. And he was a couple of years older than Derek, a lot bigger at that point. When Derek was about ten, he finally snapped and put Thad in the hospital with broken teeth, a concussion, broken ribs. It was extreme. That's when Derek went into counseling with the child psychologist."

"Oh boy," I mutter.

"On two more different occasions that I know of in their teens, Derek came very close to killing Thad. Their relationship was beyond contentious. Thad was in therapy most of his life. Lots of different therapists. It didn't do anything for him. I think Derek equates therapy with negativity because it didn't help Thad and certainly didn't help him."

"I guess I can see why he'd draw that conclusion," I say.

"He's always been distant. Only comes around the family when our father or mother pretty much mandates it. He never wants to let Mom down, though his relationship with Dad has always been strained. Anyway, I wanted to sort of explain some of Derek's history because I had a feeling you didn't know and thought it might help you understand him."

"Thank you for taking the time to tell me, but I don't think it'll help in any way. Derek reeled me in and then pulled the rug out from under me. My fiancé lost use of his legs and we weren't intimate. Adam pushed me to seek that intimacy elsewhere. I didn't want to do it. Derek overheard me talking about it with Alannah and went on a quest to get me to use my hall pass on him. You kind of know the rest, so... our entire relationship is based on manipulation and blackmail. It's not a real relationship and I don't think it can be."

She grabs my hand and squeezes it. "I know you didn't sign up for this, but I think you're so, so good for him. He's the most human I've ever seen him. He's... he's seen something in you that has made him reach for some sort of normal life, a normal relationship. Marriage, Chloe! I didn't think it would ever happen. He wants you. He could be willing to work on his issues in order to have that. Thad's also gone now and maybe that has something to do with Derek wanting to find normalcy in his life. To move forward in a healthier way."

"Or he could just spiral further and further away from reality, Grace. And he's threatened people I love. He's also done some frankly unforgivable things."

"He courted you in a fucked up way, I don't deny that. But you could help him."

"He's hurt people I care about. He's... he's done some heinous things to me. I know you care about your brother's happiness but so much has happened. I don't know what sort of miracle it would take for me to be able to wipe the slate clean, Grace, but I can't fathom it."

"So what's the alternative, Chloe? Living your life being miserable?"

"Finding a way to get my life back. I'm thirty years old. What am I going to do? Just start getting drunk at breakfast in order to cope and decide I'm done fighting for what I want in life?"

She gives me a sad smile. "I hope not. I like you. I hope you and Derek find a way forward. Somehow."

I sigh. "Things are even worse now than they were just a few days ago. I tried to fight back and crossed the line in his books, even

Cheater

though he has respected zero lines in my books, and now he's not even speaking to me. I don't know where he and I can possibly go from here. He might not even bring me with him tomorrow."

"He will. I told him last night I'd be over today to bring you some dresses. He said he wouldn't be here, but that I should come over."

I shrug. "Maybe he's letting you bring them so he can avoid the conversation with you but has no intention of me coming tomorrow."

"That's something he would do, yes. But my parents would lose their shit if he showed without you, and he knows that. They're still in New York, but Mom was messaging me this morning about some party details she wants me to check on and said herself that everyone, even Sabrina, would attend. With the press about you, the media will expect you to be there. The PR team wouldn't want speculation about why you're not there. It'd make you look weak."

I shrug, unsure of what else I can say.

"So, should we have a look at the dresses then? All Steele women are dressing in ruby red. All Steele men will have ruby swatches and ties or probably shoelaces in Ash's case. All guests have been instructed not to wear anything red since that's the family theme."

"Sounds like your mom is very particular."

"You have no idea. Yet. You're about to, though." She smiles. "It'll be nice having another female family member who's local. Nay stays away a lot. She and Ash have... issues and he's here in Columbus these days, so she only shows when she has to."

We go upstairs, each with an armful of red dresses for me to try on, and before getting to the master, Grace wanders in the other direction and looks into each room.

"What's going on here?" she asks, poking her head into the last room at the end of the hall.

"Derek has slept in here the last two nights."

The bed is unmade, there are now two bourbon bottles on the nightstand, one empty, one half-empty. And there's laundry on the floor.

"But it's a mess."

I shrug.

"Derek never leaves a mess. He's meticulous for a man. Meticulous in general."

"So that wasn't just an act for my benefit?"

"He's a neat freak. When he was found with his kidnapper's body, the guy was a hoarder. We all think that's why Derek is so neat. The place was piled high with newspapers, books, all sorts of rubbish. This... this does look like some sort of spiral. How bad was your fight?"

"Bad," I say.

She looks very concerned.

"The master is this way," I gesture.

"Ow! My eyes!" she complains when she's inside the master bathroom.

"When I fell in love with this house I knew I'd want to change the color this and the closet," I say.

"It's loud in here. It hurts my brain."

I laugh. She sets the stack of red dresses in her arms down. I do the same.

"Most of these look kind of like prom dresses," I say.

"Mom told Nicola the styles she wanted for you, Sabrina, and me. She sent a dress to Nay directly since Nay doesn't generally do flashy and Mom does." She shrugs. "Nay isn't happy. She already texted me. These are all pretty, though. Nicola wouldn't saddle us with hideous dresses."

"What's the story with Elijah and Sabrina?" I ask before I can stop myself. I quickly add, "And Naomi and Asher?"

She sighs, looking frustrated. "Eli and Sabrina? Those two have a rather combustible relationship. Really passionate. She thinks he stepped out and I asked but she won't say why she thinks that. He swears he didn't. She doesn't believe him. You'll like her. She's great. I mean, she might not be all that great tomorrow if she's been summoned against her wishes, so don't hold it against her if she's bitchy."

Cheater

"Seems like you haven't held it against me, so..." I let that hang.

She smiles warmly.

"And Asher interfered in Naomi's love life once. Pulled the brother card when one of his friends tried to date her. She wouldn't forgive him for it."

"That's it?" I ask.

"It was a guy that meant a lot to her. And Ash did some very not-nice things to get the guy out of Nay's life. That's all I can reveal. Sisterly vault. You can trust me with the vault, too. Like I said to Sabrina, it applies to sisters by blood and by marriage to my blood."

We decide together on an off-the-shoulder trumpet style lace applique dress that touches the floor. She tells me she hasn't decided on her own dress yet but we're the same dress size, so she figured she'd choose hers with me. I sit back as she tries all of them on and we both agree that she looks amazing in a tulle dress with a sweetheart neckline and a ruffled high-low hem.

"Your Mom's not worried about other women showing her up with these princess dresses?" I ask.

She shakes her head. "Nope. One of her best qualities is that she never feels threatened by other women. My mother is very comfortable with her own level of beauty."

"She's a beautiful woman," I say. "She has every right to feel confident."

"Dad always makes sure she feels beautiful. She might be a bit of a high maintenance diva, but she wants everyone else to feel beautiful at all times, too. Wanna go for lunch? I'm hungry."

"I can make us some lunch," I offer.

"If you're not busy..."

"I was only planning to clean today."

"Derek hasn't hired a housekeeper for you yet? I'll get on him for you."

"No, don't. I don't mind cleaning. It'd be weird to have someone here when I've got nothing to do."

"Are you going back to work? Or are you going to take some time off? You don't strike me as a lady of leisure."

"I don't know what I'll do. He bought the company I work for and says it's mine now. It'll be weird going back. I might find something else."

She laughs. "He's going out of his way to give you things that'll make you happy. Tell me that's not attractive. This house that he said you wanted. The company you worked for. Does he try to give you other things you want, too?"

I blow out a long breath. "Everything from my job, to clothes, to food I like, to books I like, to knowing what I like on my pizza because he stalked all my social media profiles. It's extreme."

"And you're not sopping it up like a dry sponge? Not letting him treat you like a princess? Do you want to get kicked out of the sisterhood?"

I lower my voice, maybe because there might be surveillance. "Before I met my ex I used to write an anonymous sex fantasy blog. He's even trying to deliver on all of that. Or... he was until we had a big fight and I finally fought back. Oh shit, sorry... you don't want to hear that about your own brother." My face flames.

She waves her hand. "If I don't respect other peoples' boundaries, I can't exactly draw my own with those people, can I?"

I laugh nervously. "Still. He's your brother."

"Yeah, and every friend I've ever brought around him has developed an instant crush on him. I have had more than one friend hook up with him, too, and drive me nuts afterwards with talk of how good he is in bed, so I've had no choice but to become immune."

She looks at me and smiles big. "Is that a little bit of jealousy I see on your face at the idea of your husband hooking up with my friends?"

"No, not at all," I say, but I might not be being entirely honest. I can't let my brain even ponder this notion for a minute, so I keep talking. "You do have a very good-looking family. But looks aren't everything. Neither are sex skills."

Cheater

"No, not everything but they do count, don't they?"

I'm about to protest when she waves her hand, "I know, and it's not my business. But I wanted to share some insight and hope it'd help. If it doesn't, I tried."

"Something tells me you're the type to keep on trying."

"And that tells me either Derek warned you about me, you're intuitive, or both."

"What are you doing?" I ask.

She has my phone in her hand.

"Programming myself in your phone. I'm your favorite sister-in-law. Not Nay. Okay?"

I tip my head and smile. "Let's go find something for lunch."

52

Derek

I answer my ringing phone. "I'm busy, Grace."

"I love her. Love her!"

"Huh?"

"Chloe, Derek. I love her."

I scrub my itchy jaw with my fingernails. I should've shaved this morning.

"Derek?" Grace inquires.

"What?"

"I think marrying her was very smart. And I also think that if you play it smarter, you can win her over, too."

"Oh yeah?" I mutter, sounding bored. But I'm not really bored. I'm actually interested in learning what my sister might suggest here, though I'm not about to feed her interference or she'll run rampant with it.

"She's having a lot of difficulty with some of your tactics."

"No shit?" I volley sarcastically.

"Brother, you need to focus on showing her your good side. Keep doing what you're doing in terms of showing her that her happiness matters to you, but ease up with the threats. Don't do anymore of that if you can help it. Just do the other stuff. Show her what a life with you would be like if you didn't feel like you had to make threats. You follow?"

"I follow," I confirm.

"And lots more of the sexy stuff. She goes to a happy place when she thinks about that stuff with you."

I say nothing to that, not remotely willing to talk sex with my sister, but now I'm wishing the house had cameras so I could rewind to see what Grace is referring to.

"Gonna dash," she says. "See you tomorrow night then. We got her dress and shoes all picked out. She's going to look stunning. I dropped off your pocket square, too."

She always looks stunning. Especially when she first wakes up in the morning. Sleepy. Fresh-faced. Hair fanned out.

"Oh, and Derek?"

"Yeah?"

"Get home. It's only days since you got married. You shouldn't be at work. She said you guys aren't speaking but you can't fix that if you're not home."

"Did she tell you why we're not speaking?"

"No. Do *you* wanna tell me?"

"No," I say, scratching my jaw some more. "Gotta go, Grace."

"Okay, love you, bye!"

She hangs up.

∞

It's after nine o'clock when I walk in to a quiet house that smells like lemons.

I go upstairs and see the light filtering around the door to the master bedroom. I walk the opposite way to the spare room I've been in the last two nights, but I stop in the doorway, surprised. The bed is made, and the room has been cleaned. The room smells like laundry soap. She must have washed the bedding. The clothes that were on the floor earlier are now folded on the chair. She did my laundry.

A half bottle of bourbon still sits on the table beside the bed, but the empty one is gone.

My stomach nags at me for food and it hits that I haven't eaten for

Cheater

twelve hours, so I back out of the room, intending on going downstairs to see what might be there, but here she is, in the hall, in a pink tank top and matching short shorts. Very short shorts. No fucking bra.

Something primal rises in my system. Something else also rises. Immediately.

She startles. She must not have heard me come up. She hangs onto the doorframe, eyes dropping to point at her toes, and before I can calculate it, I'm in her space, using my index knuckle to tip her chin up so our eyes meet.

She backs up a step. I follow with a step, which makes her back up some more. This goes on again and again and now we're deep into the bedroom. It's lit with a soft glow from the lamp. It smells fresh in here, too.

Her phone is lit with a cooking video on the bed beside the paperback she's now reading. A book I bought her the other day.

My eyes scan her face, her body, assess her body language. She seems afraid. And I don't like it.

"You're acting afraid of me," I say.

"That's because I am," she whispers.

"I'd never hurt you, wife."

She frowns. "But that's all you do, Derek."

An unpleasant sensation grips my insides and squeezes.

"And you're obviously mad at me," she says, "which is also scary."

"I don't *just* hurt you. Did buying you this house hurt you?"

"Yes," she whispers.

I shake my head. "Did buying you that book hurt you?"

"Yes."

I shake my head again, giving her a confused look.

"You don't get it," she says. "Because you're not well." She points to her head.

"I get it, Chloe. But I don't think *you* get it."

"You're right; I don't get it. I don't understand any part of this obsession with me. At all."

"Why do you think I'm mad at you, Chloe?"

While she moistens her lips and swallows, my eyes are glued to her mouth. Wanting to take it. Wanting to slam my cock into it. Wanting her to give me what I want, for fuck's sake. Devotion. Loyalty. Unwavering love. I want what she gave him. He didn't deserve it and I want it so fiercely it makes me want to drive over there and beat the living shit out of him for having something he didn't deserve, something I want, something I'm working to earn.

"You're mad because I left you wondering where I was all night. You're mad because I made a threat. And you get to make threats against me, Derek, but clearly while you dish it out, you don't like to take it. Do you?"

My eyes snap up to meet hers.

"I'm not mad at you, Chloe. And my threats are never empty. Was your threat empty?"

"It wasn't going to be empty. Because I was very much wanting to strike back at you. But I didn't follow through because I..." She doesn't finish her sentence. She swallows in a way that looks painful as she looks away.

"Because that's not who you are," I finish for her. "Don't try to be anyone other than who you are."

"Because I didn't want you to murder someone. If you're not angry with me, why are you staying in another room? Why do you *seem* like you're angry?"

"I'm not mad at you," I repeat. "I'm mad at me. I'm denying myself you because I don't want to hurt you."

"And you're afraid you will?" She bristles, taking another step back.

I take another step forward. "No. I already *did*. I hurt you by trying to make you love me."

"You can solve that by stopping with the threats. By letting me walk away and make my own choices about who to marry, who to be with."

I shake my head. "If keeping you makes me bad, Chloe, oh well. Because nobody and nothing will take you from me. And I might

Cheater

have to keep making threats if I think you'll do something that'll destroy me. And now maybe you're starting to understand that the threats aren't empty. The threats will stop when I don't feel the need to make them."

Her face turns exasperated. Tears fill her eyes. And I hate it. Tears never affected me before. From anyone. Chloe's tears started to do things to me not long after we met.

I move in, ready to reach for her and she backs up faster, shaking her head. "Don't."

I grab her anyway and pull her against me. Tight against me. Her big, blue eyes widen. My eyes rove her pretty mouth as I absorb how she feels. So soft. So right, so fucking right. I can't believe I voluntarily went days without touching her. Hours without touching her is too much as it is.

"If keeping you makes me bad, I'll be bad. But the problem is how much I hate myself right now. That's why I've stayed down the hall. It hurts me that you're hurting, and I don't like the way it feels in here." I thump my chest. "I fuckin' hate the way this feels when I see how sad you are. I want to make you happy."

"Then stop hurting me," she whispers.

"I don't think I can. And right now I know I'm about to hurt you some more."

"How?" she asks, looking afraid.

"Not in a violent way. Never, baby. Nothing beyond what you can handle."

"Meaning?"

"Meaning I'm about to fuck you. And it might get a little rough."

"Derek, don't."

"I need to," I inhale her hair. "I need to feel you. I need those sounds you make for me, Chloe." I grab the back of her neck and put my nose to her throat. "I need that feeling that comes over me when you give in to how it feels, when you stop fighting me for a minute and hold onto me, writhing in what I make you feel. When you let yourself be mine."

She whispers, "No."

But she's melting into me just enough that I feel the change.

I nod. "Yeah." I back her up a few more paces so she falls onto the bed. I climb over her, fingers threading into her hair, mouth fusing with hers, tasting her, grinding my rock-hard cock against the heat between her legs.

"I need you."

"Stop it," she whispers, and it feels like a game. Because I'm sure by the way she feels that she actually wants me.

"Are you playing a game saying *no?*"

"No," she whispers, but she's biting her lip while looking away and the fast way her chest is moving tells me she's worked up like I am. "You don't want me tonight. I have my period."

"I don't care." I kiss her.

Surprise lights in her eyes.

I grab the shorts and rip them down, taking her plain white bikini brief underwear with them. I use my knee to push them further and they fall.

"You want this too. It's okay that you don't want to admit it. So I'll hold you down, take it, and then you don't have to feel guilty about enjoying it."

"That's not what I'm doing," she protests.

"You're full of it, Chloe Steele, but we'll play it that way, anyway. Are you gonna be my good girl immediately tonight, or do you want me to wrestle you into submission first?"

"Maybe I'll just lie here like a corpse," she snaps.

"You never do, though. Do you? I don't think you can," I say. "Because unlike everyone else you've ever been with, I've got the playbook. Don't I? I know how to make you feel good. I know what gets your motor running."

Between kisses and nips, I pin her wrists over her head with my left hand as I fumble to get my shirt unbuttoned, snap my fly undone, rip the zipper down and quickly free myself before I guide it through her folds.

Cheater

She wasn't fibbing. I run my erection over the dangling string. I smack her clit with my cock. She jumps, closing her eyes tighter at the same time as she opens her legs wider.

I grab the string and carefully tug. It resists, so I pull a little harder. The white clump has just a little pink tinge on it, so I toss it to the floor.

"Derek. The carpet!"

I laugh darkly. "It barely had a spot, Chloe. But even if it was sopping wet with blood, I don't give a fuck. Because I need to fuck you. Now."

I thump the crown of my cock against her clit again, loving how she jolts. I do it several more times while I attack her throat with my teeth, nibbling all the way down to her rock hard nipples.

"Struggle baby. Fight me. But this ends with me inside you. We never end, though. This is us, Chloe. You loving me back? That's my end game."

I fist my cock and line it up. Her slit is soaking wet for me.

"Yeah," I whisper against her mouth as I slip in just an inch or two.

She blows out a slow breath.

I pull out and thump it against her clit again. "Maybe I won't fuck your wet little slit. Maybe I'll just fuck your mouth and leave you on the edge."

She stares into my eyes and the heat there? It's been too long since I was inside her. I slam my hips forward, hitting home.

She arches, gasping, and I'm kissing her again.

"I'm not ever letting you walk away. You're my wife, Chloe. You're my life now. You..." I slam forward, "are..." another thrust. "everything to me. And goin' back to what you said on the phone the other night? I didn't *make* you cheat on Hallman. He gave up on you. I won't ever, will *never* do the same. You don't let anybody in this body but me, Chloe. Nobody. If you even dare to even consider it again, do it knowing I'll fucking kill them. And it'd destroy me. I would never, not ever be okay again. The very idea of someone else touching you this way fills me with so much fury I can't even fathom. The reality of it actually happening?" I glare. "No. Don't fucking do it, woman. Never." I slam in again, letting go of her wrists, bracing so I can caress her throat. "You're my wife. You're mine. Yeah, I'm a thief who stole you from him so I could keep you for myself, but he didn't fight back. He'd already given up. Nothing and no one will take you from *me* without me fighting to the death. The only way you get away from me is if I'm dead. Do you understand?" I grip her chin and say it again. "Do you?"

She doesn't answer me. She also doesn't look away. I know she sees just how serious I am.

"I want to make you happy, wife. I want you to love me back. I'm not gonna stop trying to get that. But I'm telling you right now that if you let anybody have what's already mine, what you promised at that altar..." I shake my head, "I don't care that I threatened you and made you make those promises. You made them. You're keeping them. Or I will rip that person limb from limb and yes, I'll make you watch. Because maybe then you'd get it. That I won't ever be done with you. That my threats are never empty. But if it comes to that, know that you'd have ruined me, Chloe. Ruined. Me. If anybody else touches you like this? Like I'm touching you now? Lava will run in my veins until the end of my days. And I still won't let you go. Do you understand me?"

I pull my hips back and snap them forward again, making her whimper.

I grab her left hand and kiss her wedding rings. "You're mine. Don't run away from me again without telling me where you are. It made me half-crazy."

"Half-crazy?" she mutters defiantly, her chin trembling.

"If you do it again, you'll see me go full-on crazy. I'll chain you to this bed and fuck you so rough you'll swear I'm rearranging your guts with this cock, and I'll do it for a week straight before I unchain you."

She sniffles.

"I wanna make you happy, woman. I love you and I want you to

Cheater

love me back. Nothing you can think to do will mean I'll let you go. But what you do *will* impact how the rest of our life together will go. Tell me you understand."

She nods, tears streaming down her face. She sniffles and makes another shuddering sobbing sound.

I bury my face in her neck and breathe her in as I continue to fuck her in a hard, bruising way. Skin slaps skin. Hips bruise hips. I fuck her so hard I know I'll be bruised in the morning, which means so will she.

I come. But it's barely satisfying, because I'm not remotely ready to be done. When I pull out, I take her over my lap and finger fuck her hard, alternating between twisting her clit and her nipples until she cries into the sheets. And now I'm hard again, so I give her ass one wallop of a slap before I fuck her again. And I fuck her for so long, in several different positions, that I'm exhausted by the time I finish.

On our sides, I wrap both arms around her from behind, burying my face in her soft hair. I pass out, clinging to her.

∞

I'm woken by the phone ringing. I try to ignore it. It rings again. And stops. And starts again. I slept like absolute shit the last two nights and don't want to let go of her. She's so warm, soft, and cuddling me, too.

"Derek?" she whispers. I tighten my hold on her.

The phone is again ringing.

"Derek, she repeats.

I kiss her and snuggle her closer.

It keeps ringing and she's tense, so finally I roll over and reach to the floor for my jeans and fish out the phone.

Why is Carson calling me at four AM?

53
Chloe

"Carson?" is how Derek answers the phone. "Tell me," he snaps a second later.

And the way his body seizes up seconds after this has me turning the lamp on.

His jaw is slack, his face looks stricken. It takes an unnaturally long time for him to even blink.

I hear Carson is still speaking, but Derek's hand drops and the phone falls to the bed as he sits the rest of the way up, throwing his legs over, putting his elbows to his thighs, his head into his hands.

"Derek?" I call.

He's frozen.

I lift the phone from the blankets.

Carson is talking. "Mr. Steele? Derek, are you there?"

"Carson, hi, it's Chloe. What's wrong?"

"Where's Derek, Mrs. Steele?" Carson asks.

Derek doesn't try to take the phone from me. He's not even looking at me.

"He's right here. He's visibly upset. What's wrong?"

"There was a terrible accident, Mrs. Steele," Carson says softly, but his voice wavers. "He... he should get to the airport as soon as possible. I've contacted his siblings and have the jet on the way here to pick all but Naomi up to bring them to New York, so they can get to the hospital."

"What happened?" I ask.
"His parents were in a terrible car accident in New York."
"How terrible?" I ask.
Derek is just hunched over. It's bad. Really bad.
What Carson says next has me shocked. So shook, I find myself putting my hand on Derek's back.
"Mrs. Steele died on scene. Mr. Steele has been in surgery for a couple of hours already. The hospital staff says it doesn't look good."
"Oh God," I whisper.
"Can you help by getting him to the family jet? I'll send you the details by text message."
"Yes," I say. "I'll do that. And if there's anything else I can help with, please call me or text me."
"Thank you, Mrs. Steele."
"Chloe," I correct softly. Even though he told me before that he wouldn't be able to call me Chloe.
But he answers with, "Thank you, Chloe."
I press *end* and climb over to sit beside Derek, who's got his face in his hands, still.
"I'm so sorry about your mom," I whisper.
He lifts his head a little bit and scratches his stubbled jaw on both sides, staring straight ahead.
"I can drive you to the airport," I tell him, putting my hand on his back again, rubbing it with my palm.
He flinches as if it hurts or something like that and gets up. He walks into the bathroom and shuts the door.
I swallow down a lump of sadness and feeling my bladder nag at me, throw my robe on, grab a pair of underwear from the closet, and go down the hall to another bathroom.
Trying to ignore the bruised feeling between my legs as well as on my breasts, I also notice I'm still bleeding, though only lightly, but I might have ruined the sheets. He's still in the bathroom where my pads and tampons are so I stuff a wad of Kleenex into my underwear,

Cheater

then begin throwing a bag together with a change of clothes for each of us. Jeans for each. Sweatshirts. T-shirts. Socks and underwear. I pull on a bra, then a pair of yoga pants, a tank top and a hoodie. As my head emerges from the hoodie, I see he's come out of the bathroom and is pulling on clean underwear and then he pulls a dress shirt suit off a hanger.

I go to the bathroom and fix my period situation, grab some tampons and toss them into my toiletries bag, then zip to the bathroom down the hall to grab his shaving stuff, his deodorant and hair brush, and meet him back in the bedroom.

He looks at the bag.

"In case we need to be there overnight." I say, quickly pulling his brush through my hair, before dropping it into his bag.

He shakes his head, staring at me with a look of confusion. "You don't have to come."

"You shouldn't drive, Derek. You've just had terrible news; it's not safe to drive when you're upset. And..." I stop for a second and ask, "Do you want me to come with you?"

He's frowning. And I know he's in shock but the series of frowns on his face is painful to watch. It's like I'm watching his thoughts crumble one by one. He's breathing hard as he grabs a pair of socks from the drawer, looking like he's ready to blow his top for a second as he pulls them on before his expression changes again to one of confusion. "You don't have to come," he repeats, squatting and grabbing a pair of brown dress shoes from the closet, dropping them and getting them on. He moves toward the door, carrying his blazer.

"You shouldn't drive. You're upset," I call.

He pauses and looks over his shoulder at me.

I'm getting into a pair of sneakers. "I'll come," I tell him. "I'll drive."

I grab my phone and charger and put them into the bag and zip it up, grab my coat and put it on, then lift the bag I packed and jog down the stairs. I catch up to him when he's almost to his SUV.

It's snowing. The driveway and lawn are covered in fallen leaves. It's like I'm not even here as he opens his car door.

"Derek," I say, touching his arm.

He looks at me with a perplexed expression, eyes darting to my hand on his arm.

"Let me drive. Please?"

He holds out his fob, so I take it as he goes to the passenger side.

I toss the bag in the back seat and get in, put the seatbelt on and adjust the seat so that I can better reach the pedals.

When I pull out and the gate closes behind us, he says "Rickenbacker, not John Glenn."

And he stares out the windshield at the falling snow saying nothing until we get to Rickenbacker airport, when he says, "Just drop me here."

"Drop you?"

"Just here." He presses his seatbelt button and pulls it off.

I had been about to park.

"You don't want me to come?" I ask.

"You don't have to," he says, his voice coming out hoarse.

He gets out, closes the door and walks toward the terminal without looking back. He didn't take the bag, he didn't say goodbye. He didn't even take his laptop bag, which he put on the floor on the passenger side when he got in.

I stay still, idling for a minute in case he turns back around, but he disappears into the building.

Shannon Steele shouldn't have been in New York City. It was an impromptu trip. She should be in Columbus, at home and getting ready for the big party tonight. The big party for four hundred *plus* guests that now won't happen.

If we'd gone on that honeymoon she wouldn't have gone to New York.

I spot Jonah and Grace walking toward the building and am about to get out of the car and approach, but Grace looks devastated,

Cheater

red-eyed, crying. Jonah has his arm around his sister, leading her inside. They don't see me, so I leave.

∞

I'm back at the house and putting coffee on when I send a message to Carson, whose earlier message indicating which airport to go to and what time the flight would leave, I missed.

Can you please keep me posted on things? And please let me know if there's anything I can do to help with canceling tonight's event.

He responds promptly.

Thank you, Chloe. Elijah just arrived, so we've boarded and are about to taxi. Thank you for the offer. The company's team is working on notifying all guests of the anniversary party's cancellation, though there is media coverage now. I shall keep you updated.

I turn the local morning show on, and it doesn't take long before something pops up on the ticker.
Local CEO Michael Steele in critical condition after car crash in NYC. Wife: (Continued...)
My sinuses burn at the sight of the next ticker line:
socialite, model, actress Shannon Steele, 59, pronounced dead on scene.
Derek's family is dysfunctional. But most people only get one family. And now he's lost his mother and is facing losing his dad.
I think about my own parents and realize I didn't answer my mom's text message yesterday.
I message her, knowing she's probably getting ready for work.

Hi Mom. Sorry I didn't reply yesterday. I'd love to visit but Derek's parents were in a bad car accident and his mom didn't survive. It's on the news. His dad is in surgery. I'll keep you updated.

My phone rings not even a whole minute later and it's my mom calling.

I answer.

"Hi, Mom." My voice cracks.

"Oh Chloe, I'm so sorry."

I hold the phone a second, feeling choked up. Feeling like a little kid who just wants her parents to make everything all better. There was a time when a hug and kind words from either of them did make everything in my world right again.

I feel for Derek and Grace. And the other Steele family members. And also, I feel exceedingly emotional that my mom is calling me. That she sent me that text at all yesterday, wanting to spend time together, wanting to do something we haven't done in a decade in a half. Emotional that she's currently acting like... well... a mother toward me.

"I've got the news on now," she says. "Dad isn't awake yet, but I'll tell him and if there's anything we can do, please let us know. Please give Derek our condolences for his mom and let him know we'll be thinking good thoughts for his father."

My phone makes a text alert noise.

"Thanks, Mom. I'd better go," I say.

"Keep me posted. Text me if you're too busy to call. Just... text over some updates. Okay?"

"I will."

"We'll be thinking of you both."

"Thanks, Mom," I say, "Lah-love you. B-bye for now."

"Love you, too, honey," she says softly.

Cheater

When I press end, my hands are shaking. I can't remember the last time she and I exchanged *I love yous*.

The text I missed was from Alannah.

WTF? I just saw the news. Where are you?

I call her.

She answers right away.

"Hey," she says softly. "Where are you?"

"Hey. At home."

"Home?"

"The house in Dublin," I say, feeling strange at referring to this place as *home*.

"You okay? What's happening right now?"

"I took Derek to the airport. He's on his way to New York. His mom died at the accident scene, but his dad is in surgery, apparently. That's all I know. I'm here by myself just waiting for updates."

"Want me to come over and hang out with you?"

"Could you?"

"Of course I can."

"Oh God, yes, please." I'm feeling immense relief.

"I'm on my way. I'll bring coffee and donuts and... some flotsam and jetsam. I'll be there, soon."

Flotsam and jetsam means she'll bring things to occupy us. Alannah has always been immensely good at distracting you when you need it most.

∞

It's forty-five minutes later and I've had no choice but to phone Derek.

He doesn't answer, so I send him a text message.

Hope everything is okay there. Sorry to bother

you, but Alannah came to keep me company and Ken isn't allowing her past the gate. Can you have a word with him?

I didn't bother bitching Ken out when he wouldn't let Alannah in. He wasn't rude about it, simply said he'd only open the gate on Derek's orders.

I don't get an answer to my text, but just two minutes later, Alannah is allowed in with a stern look from Ken, who I'm pretty sure communicates silently that he will make sure I don't leave.

As if I'm going to cause any problems when Derek's mother just died.

∞

It's about four hours later, and Lan and me are in the family room, curled up in front of the fireplace. The snow is falling and we're in the midst of a chick flick marathon. She brought four DVDs, nail polish and remover, a deck of cards, and a bunch of junk food with her.

I get a text message, so I reach for my phone with a sinking feeling.

Carson Shields: Hello, Chloe. Mr. Steele is out of surgery and in serious but stable condition.

I read it aloud to Alannah, then reply.

Good news. Thank you for the update.

Alannah and I ponder whether or not Derek will come back tonight. She decides to stay the night and says she doesn't care if he comes back – she's in my life and she's not about to hide from him.

Cheater

I don't hear anything else from Carson. And I don't hear anything at all from Derek.

∞

Alannah has to leave by nine in the morning to go set up for her cousin Claudia's baby shower. I feel bad because I'd normally go with her, I know and like Claudia and I'm so happy she's having twins after trying for four years to get pregnant. Alannah tells me she already signed my name to her gift as I hug her goodbye.
"Be safe. Be smart. I love you," she says softly.
"Same, same, and love you more," I tell her, hugging her tight.

∞

Not even ten minutes after she goes, my phone rings.

DS Cavalier calling.

I guess it's time to change his display name.
"Hello?" I answer, feeling shaky.
"Keep the house alarm armed," Derek says tersely. "Kenny is staying there to keep you safe until I get back."
"Pardon?"
"He slept in his car last night. He's switching out with one of his people so he can go home and shower, but then he's coming back. He'll stay parked outside until I get there."
"Why, um... why? You don't have to think I'm about to cause any problems while you're dealing with what you're dealing with, because I-"
He cuts me off. "It wasn't a car accident. It was a hit and run. They were coming out of a restaurant when they got run down. Don't know if it was an enemy or if it was random. Keep the alarm on. Stay home. Ken said she left. Is she coming back?"

"She has plans today. How's your dad?"

The line sounds dead, so I eventually call out, "Hello?"

"Still unconscious," he answers.

"I'll say a prayer for him. My mom sends her best for your dad and condolences for your mom."

There's more silence on the line for a long minute so I'm not sure if he's still there.

"Are you there?" I ask.

"Gonna go. Bye."

He ends the call.

Wow, was he cold with me. It's not about me, of course, but it still doesn't feel nice to be on the other end of coldness from Derek. And I have no desire to dissect my emotions on the issue.

My day with Alannah yesterday was somewhat therapeutic, especially with all my *alone* time lately. She did her best to keep me distracted. Of course she wanted to know how things were with me and Derek when she first got here, but because I was pretty clammed up, she let it go instead of launching into her typical non-surgical information extraction mode. I told her I had no idea if the house was wired for surveillance or not, so she let it go and pampered me by making me cream of cauliflower and broccoli soup and an extra bougie grilled cheese for lunch. She also gave me a manicure and we watched some old favorite chick flick movies and hung out, showing one another stupid memes and videos on our phones.

She ordered pizza at about ten o'clock at night and got Ken to bring it in after giving him two slices.

"He's kinda hot, isn't he?" she asked after shutting the door.

"He's the guy that held me and Adam at gunpoint. He's been following me around for weeks. Following you at points, too."

She was offended. "I should go take that pizza off him."

She didn't.

She slept in the guest room I'd changed the bedding for yesterday and told me she loved the house, thought it was even better in person than it had been on the real estate website listing

Cheater

from several months ago, and while we didn't talk much about Derek given the likelihood that the house was wired, she did bring up running into Derek the other day, telling me she thought he planted a white van there, insinuating she could be abducted by it and never to be seen again... but she went on to say it was there again the next day, that when she was leaving at the end of the day, she saw men going in and out for flooring materials. She realized he'd probably used that to his advantage rather than planted it himself.

This confused me, so I asked her to explain and give me a play-by-play of that entire exchange with Derek. By the time she recounted all that had happened in that encounter, it seemed plausible that Derek had run into her instead of seeking her out.

Maybe the van thing was a coincidence that he took advantage of. We debated it and she admitted she wasn't sure if he'd just seen her while at his club or if he'd waited to run into her. Regardless, it didn't make what he did okay. He made sure to intimidate and threaten her. The way she described it from start to finish sounded slightly less horrific than I'd first imagined it. But only slightly. I wasn't giving him a pass; he'd made direct threats about her being part of my life. Or not.

He wasn't getting a pass on anything he'd done, including punishment sex the other night. Or emotion-affirming sex. Or... *me Derek, you my woman* caveman sex. Whatever it was... it was memorable, that's for sure. But then again, sex with Derek always is. As usual, I do my best to push those thoughts away. And as per the norm, I fail.

∞

I've gotten stuck in a sort of loop of thinking frequently about all the things Grace told me about his history.

And for a moment I allowed myself to ponder whether or not cooperating with all of this would change anything. Would it be me throwing in the towel and letting him win at this game I've been an unwilling participant in? Or would there be any sort of shot at happiness in a marriage with him?

And big question: would having kids with him mean I've got a chance of having a kid with a genetic predisposition to mental illness? Is what Derek has become due to trauma? Or is it in his DNA? The stories I've heard about Thad Steele make me think it might be a little of both. I berate myself for considering having kids with him, of course, but my thoughts repeatedly flit to the visions I had of him with kids here in this house, in this yard, in that treehouse out there.

54

Chloe

I wake up touching someone and startle, moving away.

It's Derek and I've been snuggled into his back. I reach over to the bedside table and touch my phone. Two o'clock in the morning.

I stare at the back of him for a solid minute before a familiar unpleasant, lonely twinge twists in me.

"How's your dad?" I ask softly, not sure how long he's been here or if he's even awake.

"Alive," he answers.

I sit up and take a long drink of my water. He keeps his back to me.

If everything that has happened between us hadn't happened, I could try to comfort him right now, offer an ear so he could talk out his emotions.

But that's not where we are. It's nowhere I can fathom getting to.

I lie down again and blink into the darkness, listening for his breathing to even out. I drift off before it happens.

∞

I try to move but I'm sort of trapped. And uncomfortable. By the faint light peeking in through the blinds, it must be near dawn. I've got Derek wrapped around me. Tight.

As my eyes adjust I realize he's awake. Staring into space. But the grip he has on me feels like he thinks he needs to hold on otherwise I'd float away.

"I have to pee," I whisper.

His grip loosens and he moves away just enough for me to get up.

When I come back and climb in, he's looking at me. It's still kind of dim in here, but it looks like he's staring at me with surprise. Maybe he's surprised I've gotten back into bed.

"Did you sleep much?" I ask.

He stares at me with his brows knitted. "Not much."

"What time did you get back?" I ask. Not like it matters. I guess I'm making conversation. Seeing if he wants to talk.

"Back?"

"From New York."

"I got back from New York on Sunday night."

It's now Thursday morning. I frown.

"I stayed at the apartment," he explains, obviously reading my confusion.

"Is Grace back, too?"

"She's at their Manhattan apartment."

"Anybody else back?"

He shrugs.

So he was there by himself for the last few days. And this means he's been half an hour away for three days.

"You're upset with me for that?" he asks.

I try to clear my expression.

I've got a lot to be angry with Derek for, but I shouldn't be upset about being left here. He lost his mother. But he does have me under guard, doesn't he? Has he been watching me? I don't bother to ask. Instead, I ask, "Do you... wanna talk about it?"

The frown lines on his forehead deepen.

He finally says, "No."

"Okay," I whisper, about to turn back over to see if I can find sleep again.

"Could you..." he starts but doesn't finish.

Cheater

"Could I?" I repeat, letting it hang.

I wait.

"Never mind."

I wait anyway, eyes on him.

He clears his throat. "When Carson called with the news, you... rubbed my back."

I nod a little.

He doesn't say anything else, but the pain in his features intensifies.

"Do you... want me to do that now?"

He swallows without answering, but his eyes say it all. He needs comforting; it's why he's here. He's been alone, probably, with his grief for the past few days and now he wants comforting.

"I have no right to ask you for that," he adds, looking sad.

"Come here," I invite.

He scooches over and puts his head on my chest, looking up at me with an almost boyish expression.

I reach around and run both hands up and down the warm skin of his back.

He's lying still, tense though, and it's not entirely comfortable for me with his weight on me like this, but I keep running my hands up and down his back. He wraps an arm around my waist and twists us so that we're face-to face on our sides. So I keep one hand moving up and down his back.

It goes on for what feels like a long time, me trying not to look at his face, his gaze pointed at me like usual.

Why did I agree to do this for him after all his sins? I think he senses my desire to retreat. My hand halts and drops.

"Thank you," he says.

"If you decide you want to try to talk about it, you can," I say. "With me, I mean."

He doesn't answer. But warmth floods his expression as he lifts up onto one elbow and puts his free hand to my jaw.

His mouth lowers and his lips are just about to mine when his phone rings.

He looks annoyed, but folds away from me and fishes his phone out of the pants on the chair beside the bed.

I'm relieved. Because although I know he wouldn't care, it would be predatory for him to kiss me when I know he's grieving and upset. Does he realize I wouldn't have stopped him? I might not have participated, but I wouldn't have stopped him because he's upset, and I don't want him to feel worse. And I'd feel bad about myself for it. This isn't the first time I've wished I was selfish and could treat him how he deserves based on his actions instead of based on empathy for him losing his mother. Even though he felt next to nothing about Adam's grandmother.

I get up and put my robe on over my pajamas, then slip out so I can get some coffee into me. And get some distance.

I notice a text message on my phone.

Frank: I was planning to reach out today to say I hope you're enjoying your honeymoon and to let you know all is running smoothly with work so you wouldn't worry. But I'm now reaching out to say I'm very sorry to hear about the loss of Mr. Steele's mother. Everything here is smooth-sailing, but as you're the new owner and payroll needs to go in today to be processed I was going to ask for some guidance on your salary. It's being processed at the usual amount unless you advise otherwise. Everything else can wait until you're ready to discuss. Thanks.

After I get a few sips of coffee into myself, I decide to rip the bandage off by phoning Frank.

"Hello Chloe," he greets.

"Hi Frank."

Cheater

"My condolences. And my congratulations, too. I don't know what the etiquette is for a conversation like this."

"Same. And thank you. It's been a whirlwind. I... um... everything right now can run as usual if that's okay. I'm going to need to take a bit of time to figure out exactly how things will work for me going forward."

"I was wondering if I should update my resume, expecting that you'd likely have all sorts of plans I might not fit with. Or wait for you to decide. I don't mean to pressure you; I won't pressure you, but a clue would... help."

"Of course you have every right to wonder, Frank. I didn't mean to leave you feeling like you're in limbo."

"It's all right, Chloe. I can keep things running while you deal with your family matters there and then we can talk when you're ready."

"I had no idea I was getting married and certainly had no idea my husband would give me the company. To say all this has been a shock is the understatement of the century."

"Okay?"

And I fill the awkwardness with more words. "I'm not sure what I want to do about any of that. It all sort of blindsided me. Would it be okay if things run as usual for the time being? If you're not down with lack of security and that's why you thought about looking for something else, I'd just like to say I would love if you'd stay. If you have more responsibilities because you now technically report to me and I don't know what owning the company entails as of yet, I am happy to increase your salary. Can you handle the running of things for now?"

"Well-"

I cut him off, "If it's too much, I'd give you approval to hire someone to replace me so you're not covering me. Hire an assistant if you need to, or promote within if you think someone else on the team is capable of helping you run things. I don't know what the company's financials are like but I'm sure Derek wouldn't have bought it if the company was in trouble, so... you've got my approval to do what you need to do for the good of the company until we can talk about the direction and what involvement I might have. You've been a wonderful mentor and very, very accommodating with these last tumultuous months of my life." I take a big breath and finish with, "I wasn't sure if the owners had anything to do with that or if it was all you, but either way I'd love if you'd stay and keep doing exactly what you already do as well as looking after things until I can figure out what my role could be."

"I would be happy to stay, Chloe. Happy to keep mentoring you. I have a lot of ideas and our previous owners were rather resistant to change. And all the accommodations for you were all me. Because you're smart, talented, and a good worker, so of course we wouldn't have abandoned you when things got tough."

I smile.

He takes a big breath and keeps going. "When you're ready I'd love to talk about my ideas and a role for both of us that would likely work very well and would give you flexibility if you'd like to focus on other things while still being involved. I'm a signing officer so I can handle everything until you're ready to talk further."

"That's a huge relief, Frank. Huge. Thank you very, very much."

"My pleasure, Chloe."

"Okay, so like I said there's a lot happening here with my husband's family, so I'd appreciate it if you could keep things running and I'll be in touch if and when I'm ready to jump back in. I'm just... not ready to make any big decisions right now."

"You could decide to boost my salary by, say, twenty per cent, and know that I'll take very good care of your company. Though I'd do that anyway, Chloe. Financials are good so you can afford to give me this raise. And we can talk performance bonuses when you're ready."

I smile. "How about thirty per cent?"

"I like the way you think. I've always liked the way you think."

I laugh.

Cheater

"Take care, Chloe. Please send your husband my condolences. I hope his father makes a full recovery."

"Thanks, Frank. I'll talk to you soon." I hang up.

"Your husband," I hear.

Derek is in the doorway of the kitchen.

Our eyes meet. He stands there in a pair of gray sweatpants. Nothing else.

"There's a lot happening here with your husband's family, you said. I loved hearing you use that word for me. Love hearing it come from your lips. Love hearing you talk. You don't talk to me."

"I made you a cup of coffee." I gesture to the counter.

He's looking at me like he wants to eat me alive.

"Frank sends his condolences," I add.

And Derek's expression drops, but he reaches for the cup.

"That conversation sounded like it went well," he says. "Sounds like you and Frank make a good team."

His phone rings. He sets the mug on the counter and pulls it from his sweatpants pocket, looks at the screen and answers it.

"Eli," he greets, leans over and kisses the top of my head, then walks away.

I spend the morning in the office upstairs, scanning articles online about Derek's family. They all talk about Shannon Steele's extensive modeling career, the few TV sitcoms she was on, and her involvement in charity.

There's talk of Michael Steele's success and some history about his family along with each article mentioning a paragraph about Thaddeus Steele being gunned down a while back. All the articles I read from local sources seem like they've been approved by the Steele family. Nothing salacious or gossipy, though there is speculation on one article from a New York paper about whether or not the accident was really an accident and pondering about whether or not it's connected with Thaddeus Steele's murder.

I decide to send a text message to Grace. I see she sent herself a message from me with my name on it the other day, so I know I'm in her phone and probably don't need to sign the text with my name.

I'm so, so sorry about your mom. If you need anything, please reach out.

I send a group text message to Maddie and Cor and include Alannah just because we usually don't leave one another out of the loop when it's a group text. Though I'm already aware from Lan that they have had some group texts about me lately.

Hi Coraline and Maddie. Sorry I've been out of touch. Life has been beyond crazy as I'm sure you can imagine from the various headlines. Never imagined anything related to my life would make headlines unless it was that I died trying to win a taco-eating contest, but I promise we'll catch up as soon as possible. Love you guys.

When Alannah stayed over, she told me they were asking questions. She told me she told them the truth. And this horrified me. She didn't give them a lot of detail, only that Derek Steele had set his sights on me and essentially stolen me from my life, had seduced me and become extremely possessive. But she said as far as she knew it was all mostly very swoony. She's also kept Jeff in the loop but with only the truth, which has me a bit nervous. I message him next.

Hey Jeffy. Sorry I've been out of touch. I just wanted to send my love and tell you I appreciate you. Hope everything is good.

Cheater

Jeff writes back right away.

Hey Chlo. I'm now employed by the Steele family. They just recruited* me into their legal team.

Recruited? With an asterisk?
I pick up the phone and call him.
He answers right away.
"Hello, beauty," he greets.
"Recruited you? As in... asterisk?"
"Technically, yes. I start in two weeks. I'm working out my notice here."
"Oh Jeffy. I'm so sor-"
"Hey. Stop. I stuck my nose in and got too close to a few things. I took that chance, because I love you like a sister. Like a sister!" he exclaims, loudly, then his tone returns to normal. "There, I said that loudly in case your spouse happens to hear this. I don't want there to be any mistaking my love for you. Absolutely platonic and sisterly only."
I drop my forehead to the desk.
"I'm good, Chlo. Don't sweat it. They're paying me a fucking fortune. It's all good."
"But is it... asterisky?"
"Not expecting it'll be any riskier than the work I do now. But it pays better and one of my dearest friends has the last name Steele now, so I know you'll look after me."
"Of course I will. I mean, if I have any control whatsoever, which I'm not sure if I do, but I would absolutely walk across hot coals barefoot for you; you know it."
"I do know it. And I also suspect you have more control than you realize. Ponder that, will you? Anyway, gotta get into a meeting but I'm here for you. I love you. Like a sister! And by the by... Coraline and I are an item."

I'm frozen for a beat before I squeal.

Jeffy chuckles.

And then I ask, "Exclusive?"

"I'm not sure I'm an exclusive kind of guy. We'll see where it goes."

"Be good to her."

"She's quite possessive," he says. "But I dig it. I might not have a choice but to go exclusive if I wanna keep my balls. And I do like my balls. Anyway. Talk later. Bye, Chlo."

"Oh shoot. Wait. Cor doesn't know from Alannah the truth about Derek but if you lie to her too, that'd be a dealbreaker for her. So um..."

"I've already given her the truth. She won't breathe a word to a soul. Don't let the Steeles force-recruit her to work for them or she'll have my balls. And once again, I'd like to keep them. Please tell your husband Coraline can be trusted. I'll tell him the same."

"Good, because he and I aren't on the best terms."

"Well, I hope that changes because it doesn't sound like he's willing to walk away," Jeff says. "But like I said, ponder your power, baby girl. You have more than you realize here. Okay?"

"Hm," is my reply.

"Bye for now, lovey. Gotta dash."

"Bye Jeffy. And I love you too."

"You love me like a brother," he adds and is laughing as the call ends.

My office door opens, and Derek is in the doorway, looking concerned.

"Is everything okay?" I ask.

"I heard you scream, so I rushed up and then you were laughing."

"Oh, it was Jeff. It was a happy scream. He and Coraline are a thing. She kind of knows a little but he swears she'll keep quiet. I swear it, too. Coraline is solid. She's my second-best friend; I've known her over a decade and she won't do a thing to put me in jeopardy."

Cheater

Derek doesn't say anything.

I clear my throat and ask, "How's your dad doing?"

His lip curls. "He's conscious. He'll likely be released next week. Then we'll have a... service for my mother."

"You said it was a hit and run. Any details about that?"

His lip curls.

"If you don't want to tell me, it's okay." I look back at my laptop to show I don't need him to elaborate if he doesn't want to.

"Don't have details yet on who or why. He's conscious, but he's too doped up. Not makin' sense. Broken arm. Broken ribs. Busted ankle. Punctured lung. Head injury. Lost his spleen. Suffered some other internal damage. He's a mess. We're trying to get to the bottom of it."

"Oh," I say softly. "He's going to make a full recovery, though?"

"Looks like it," Derek mutters, but his eyes are on me and they're active.

I feel like I'm being assessed; it feels awkward.

I open my email and scan the inbox, which has no new messages.

His eyes are still on me.

I meet his gaze and wait. "Is there something else?" I ask.

He says nothing but continues to stare and it might be ten seconds or something, I don't know, but it feels like thirty or longer and each one of them feels uncomfortable.

"I love you," he finally says.

I say nothing.

He waits.

My phone rings and it's a relief.

Alannah calling.

I answer, hoping he'll walk away.

"Hey. How are you?" I greet.

"Craig's cousin, Adam's ex Jeannie?"

"Uh huh..."

"She's dead."

My eyes bulge.

And I immediately look at him.

"Are you there?" she asks.

I try to pull in a breath. It's not easy.

Derek is still leaning against the doorframe, watching me.

"How?" I manage, my gaze dropping to my desk.

"Found floating in the Scioto. They figure she either jumped or was pushed off a bridge."

"What?" I whisper.

"Yeah. You alone?"

"No," I say, continuing to examine the wood grain on the desk.

"They're searching her place to see if there's a note. I don't think there's gonna be a note."

"No," I whisper.

"That's all I've got. You good?"

"No. Yeah, but no."

"Yeah," she says softly. "Call you later. Love you."

"Love you," I whisper.

I put the phone down, my vision blurring around the edges briefly, my heartrate picking up speed. I look up at him. I'm shaking.

He has a look of concern on his face.

"D-did you kill..." I force down a swallow and shake my head.

He's straightened up. "Did I kill?"

"Jeannie?"

"Did I kill Jeannie?" he parrots.

"Adam's ex."

He stares blankly.

I shove my chair back and bolt upright and point. "You monster."

His eyes narrow and his forehead crinkles.

"I will never, not fucking *ever* love you. Do you hear me? Never. Please get that through your sick head."

His eyes turn so cold it chills me to the bone. I keep going, louder.

Cheater

"No matter what you buy me, no matter how good you fuck me. Never. Because you're a sick, demented individual. And I hope you get caught and put away for the rest of your psychotic life."

I storm past him, but he catches my arm, which halts me.

"Chloe," he starts to say, but I shout, "No!"

And then I repeat it in a near shrill scream. "No! My voice trembles as I say, "You can't make someone love you this way. You can't do these things like you're above the law, Derek. I don't care how much money your family has, how many shady connections. I hope you do get caught. I'll be so relieved. So fucking relieved that I'll finally get my life back. Because you'll be behind bars. You said the only way I get rid of you is death, well there's also prison. And prison works for me. Let go of me!"

"Tell me exactly what you're accusing me of," he requests with an eerie calm that makes my scalp prickle.

The sign of a sociopath, right?

"Fuck off!" I struggle and he subdues me, like always. "Let go!"

"Chloe, stop." He lifts me up, carries me down the hall into the master bedroom. As soon as he puts me down, he pins me to the bed. "You're hysterical right now and you're also wrong."

I'm writhe uselessly, unable to find any semblance of logic or control. "Don't play stupid, Derek. You swore you wouldn't lie to me. Not that I should believe anything you say. Not only have you raped, threatened, stalked, and blackmailed me, you're responsible for the death of at least three people just since you met me? How can you think I'd ever love you?"

"Settle down!" he demands, and he's beginning to lose his cool.

"It's her fault you canceled the trip with me, but you were supposed to be out of town with me and if you were, your father wouldn't have taken your mom to New York, right? Your mom got killed because Jeannie's blog made you cancel our trip. So you chose to punish her by ending her life."

"I didn't kill her. I had no idea she was dead until now."

I scoff.

"I've been busy trying to figure out what happened in New York, who ran my parents down and killed my mother. That and dealing with my fuckin' head over my mother and of course... you."

"I'm sorry about your mom, Derek, I said that already and I meant it."

"I know you do, baby."

I'm talking over him before he finishes his sentence, saying, "But the person who is the reason your mom is in New York is found dead. A person you probably threatened. Did you threaten her when you threatened Lan?"

"Yes."

"You're admitting you threatened her?"

"Yeah, of course I fuckin' did. She needed to be stopped."

"So you stopped her permanently."

"No. Told her she doesn't say your name, doesn't type it out, you do not fucking exist to her. She was smearing your name in defense of that fuckin' asshole who didn't deserve you."

"So you stopped her permanently, right?" I demand.

"Scared her, but that's pretty much it."

"Pretty much?"

He shrugs. "She tripped and fell."

"Oh and did she also trip and fall into the river and die?"

"Chloe, I didn't."

"Get off me. I hate you. I hate how you make me feel. You make me feel ten times worse than Adam ever did. No, a hundred times worse."

His expression falls and he backs off me.

"I won't ever love you. Never," I whimper, wiping my eyes.

He clenches his jaw.

I roll off the bed and grab Kleenex from the table and dab my eyes.

"I had nothing to do with her death, Chloe."

Cheater

"Whatever."

I storm out of the room, down the hall, down the stairs, to the covered porch, and sit down on the chair. It's cold in here. And I welcome it.

55

Derek

Rage floods my system while I stare at the rumpled bed where she told me just what she thinks of me. After what might be a long time of staring, of feeling more than I want to feel, I realize I'm flexing my right index finger over and over. It's not her I want to hurt, but I can't seem to stop flexing. My heart is beating too fast. Blood pumping too hard.

I need to leave.

56

Chloe

Almost a Week Later

It's 10:30 in the morning and I'm getting into the Town Car Carson messaged about by myself. The driver who introduced himself as Neil, who also drove us on the day Derek forced me to marry him shuts the back door and gets in, asking, "Would you like music? We'll arrive at your destination in forty minutes, Mrs. Steele."

"No, thank you," I say.

"I'll give you privacy," Neil offers. "If you require anything, feel free to open the window or use the intercom."

"Okay," I reply.

"Please don't hesitate to make any requests."

"Thank you."

The privacy glass closes, and while I smooth out the skirt of the ruby red gown I catch sight of my reflection. My hair is done in big curls and I'm wearing dramatic matte ruby-red lipstick that doesn't feel matte. I rub my lips together. Feels great. Grace Steele sure knows how to pick lipstick.

She sent it over with matching nail polish and instructions that funeral garb was not allowed. She coordinated with her sister and other sister-in-law as well as her aunts and female cousins. All Steele family women would wear this color today in honor of Shannon Steele and Michael Steele's ruby anniversary.

The funeral would be somber, but Grace said it would also observe many of her favorite things. Fashion. Family. Friends. Instead of being the four-hundred person affair her anniversary shindig had been planned to be, today would be for family and close friends of the Steeles and Grace requested we all do our best to look as lovely as she wanted us to look for her anniversary party.

I've spoken to Grace via text a few times over the past few days and once on the phone. The funeral clothing conversation happened in a group text conversation with her, Naomi, and Elijah's wife Sabrina, not that Sabrina replied.

Grace called me a few days ago when I responded to Carson's text about the funeral arrangements and the part that said he would send me a car. It was clear by the phrasing in his message that he knows Derek and I aren't in contact.

Five minutes after my response stating I couldn't make it, Grace was phoning and working on me via emotional blackmail. The Steeles are evidently good at blackmail.

I have neither seen nor heard from my psycho husband since I unleashed my frustration on him verbally. Ken has stayed close.

I told Grace I hadn't seen Derek for a few days, I also told her I think Derek is a monster and I hope he stays away.

"He said as much," she admitted. "And well, first, that makes me very sad."

"I'm not responsible for how your brother's actions make you feel."

"And second... you're family," she said softly.

"By involuntary marriage," I reminded her.

"And... you're my friend," she said, choked up. "I need friends close right now. And we need as many ruby red dresses as possible. For Mom."

I relented and said I'd come to the cemetery, but would not come to a reception afterwards.

She seemed satisfied with that.

Yesterday, I ventured off the grounds, and Ken didn't stop me. I

Cheater

grocery shopped and stopped into a flower shop in my old neighborhood, requesting a tasteful floral arrangement for the funeral done in white with some red accents. I stumbled over what to sign on the card, but inevitably decided on

Sincere condolences,
Chloe

Although I'm technically married, I haven't changed my last name and have no intentions of doing so. But for all I know, Derek pulled strings and did it without my knowledge. I suspect as much since I found an unsealed envelope on the kitchen counter with a credit card and debit card that were both made for "Chloe Steele" with pin number details that match the front door code Derek gave me. The day we met. The day he started fucking with my life.

Will we speak today? I really have nothing to say to him. I don't even want to set eyes on him, but again, Grace guilted me.

The media will be around, I'm sure, so it's not like I can sit at the back, away from him. I'm sure it'll be awkward to sit together, for me at least. Derek doesn't have normal reactions to things.

I've been glad for the space, though I haven't been sleeping well. I've been having bad dreams about him throwing Jeannie off a bridge. About Jeannie throwing *me* off a bridge. I've also woken abruptly multiple times a night wondering if he's in the house, sometimes checking the security app to see if anyone has disarmed it.

Bottom line, he either pushed her or ordered someone else to do it, just as he likely did with Adam's incarcerated uncle. And regardless of the chain reaction Jeannie's blog post and "Smear Chloe" campaign caused, it's absolutely, abhorrently unforgivable.

My phone rings, pulling me from my dark thoughts. I half-expect it to be Alannah, who I've only had brief 'proof of life' text conversations with over the past few days as she's in Pittsburgh for work the rest of this week.

But it's not her; it's Craig calling me.

I answer, feeling dread spread through my belly. Craig just lost his cousin and God knows what he's doing about it.

I also don't know if Derek has kept his word, sticking to what he said to Craig on the phone on the way back from my parents' place or if he's making Craig do unsavory things for the Steele family.

After I shouted my head off at Derek about Jeannie's death, I group messaged Adam and Craig to offer my condolences. Adam didn't answer. Craig sent me a reply that simply said, "Thank you Chloe."

"Hey Craig," I answer.

"Can you talk?" he asks.

"I'm being driven to Shannon Steele's funeral. I'm alone in the back of a car with privacy glass up, but my phone has been bugged for a while now so...I guess I'm never truly alone."

"I'm not a fan of any male member of the Steele family, first off. I had a truce with Jonah for a while because we had some common goals, but other than that, I can't stomach these elitist asshole types who think their money can buy their way out of anything."

"Okay..." I say, wondering what he's prefacing.

"But I had a conversation with Gracie yesterday that led to this phone call. At her request."

Gracie?

"I wasn't aware you and Grace know each other."

"There's history," he says.

"History?" I ask. "Together? You two?" I blink a couple of times, shocked.

"Not relevant to this conversation."

"Wait, what?" I'm thrown.

"History. The past. Can I just tell you what I need to tell you?"

"Uh... okay," I say, noting the hostility in his voice, which isn't something I'm accustomed to getting from Craig.

"Jeannie called Adam from the bridge before she jumped."

What? I blink hard.

He takes a big breath and goes on, "She called him and wanted him to leave town with her. Start a new life. She was troubled. Really troubled, Chloe. She followed him twice to different cities,

Cheater

constantly trying to get with him. He wanted nothing to do with it. She was clingy and unstable and even finagled an engagement when he did give it a shot, but she wasn't for him. She was a constant reminder of his uncle and all that abuse because of her sister's murder. I think Bell's death opened up old wounds and she clung to Adam as her hero since Adam was the one that got him put in prison. The uncle molested Jeannie, too. It was all... ugly. I know he gave her shit for dragging your name through the mud and we suspect Steele also threatened her. She was manic when I saw her last. Probably off her meds along with reeling from getting put on Derek's shitlist."

"She was medicated?" I ask.

"Has been for years."

"Oh."

"She threatened to kill herself on the phone to Adam. Told him it was imperative they get out of town and start a new life together, away from you, away from Derek Steele. Said if he didn't want to, she wouldn't survive the night. He wasn't in a good headspace. About you and Derek. About his uncle. His grandmother. All of it. He hung up on her. She's made self-harm threats before."

"Oh," I whisper.

"Gracie said you're blaming Derek for Jeannie. Now... I have no respect for Derek, barely know him, but based on what I do know of that family and what he's pulled in the last several weeks, I do not give two shits about him or what you think of him."

"Okay..."

"Gracie asked me about Jeannie. Said you're blaming Derek for her death. Asked me if I thought her brother *did* have anything to do with it. That lead to this call. A witness also provided dashcam footage. She jumped; nobody was with her. You blaming Derek for this means you're also blaming yourself. Because you think Derek did it because Jeannie lashed out at you. It was a hundred per cent suicide."

I don't bother to add the fact that I think Derek blames Jeannie for his mother being in New York as part of the reason I assumed it was Derek. Because that doesn't matter at this stage.

"Thanks for telling me that, Craig. I'm still so very sorry for your loss. She was a member of your family and I'm sorry you lost her."

"Thanks, Chloe. And thanks for trying to get him to leave me alone."

"Has he?" I ask.

"So far."

"Good," I whisper with relief.

"You hangin' in there all right?" he asks.

"I... um... not really. But anyway, you're a good guy, Craig. A good cop. I would've hated someone forcing you to be someone you're not."

"Wouldn't have happened, Chlo. Being dirty just ain't in me. Gotta go. Take care, okay?"

"Okay. You, too."

I stare out the window, deep in thought for the rest of the drive to the cemetery.

∞

"You'll wait here to bring me back home afterwards?" I ask the driver.

"No, Mrs. Steele. I was told your husband would be taking you home."

"That's not... I... can you wait? Or come back for me in about an hour?"

"Sorry, ma'am. I have another client to pick up."

"Thanks," I say.

"One moment, I'll open your door for you."

57

Derek

I watch her step out of the car looking glammed up like an old Hollywood starlet, ready for a red carpet. Red lips. Dark hair falling to her bare shoulders in soft curls. Cat's eye makeup. Body looking incredible in that gown.

My mother would approve. I assume my mother chose it for her. I know I approve.

Her eyes scan the crowd to find me immediately. And it's satisfying as fuck.

Only the sight of my wife could soothe me right now. I need her. And more than that, I need her to need me. I need her to want me. To let me do what I want most to do – take care of her every want and need. So I can feel like I'm not powerless, the way I've felt the last few days. How the fuck do I get her to need me? To want me? To forget about the way I've gone about trying to be everything she wants.

Despite everything, I know I'd do it all again. Again and again. Because she's *it*. *The one*. The one who makes me feel the closest to human, I guess.

A lump of something gross forms in the middle of my throat. I swallow it down and move toward her. Her eyes scan my face and then drop as her front teeth catch her bottom lip.

She's not looking at me the way she did the last time I saw her.

But that expression of hatred is already burnt into me; haunting my thoughts whether I'm asleep or awake.

I hold my arm out and she hesitates, but takes it. I press my lips to her temple and inhale her scent, hearing a shutter clicking in the distance. *Fucking vultures.*

I lead her to the front row of chairs reserved for the family. Jonah and Grace are already here. They rise. Jonah hugs her. My back straightens and my eyes narrow.

Jonah doesn't notice, which helps because it shows me he's not trying to rile me up. Though that's more Ash's style, not Joe's.

"I'm so sorry for your loss, Jonah," she says softly.

I grind my teeth at the soft tone for him, at the nothing I got.

Jonah says something under his breath, releasing her.

She wraps her arms around Grace next and Grace squeezes her tight.

"You look beautiful, Grace," Chloe says into my sister's hair, looking like she means to share affection instead of it being simple good manners.

More jealousy flares in my system.

"Not as beautiful as you," my sister returns. "You understood the assignment. Mom would gush over you right now. Thanks for being here." Grace kisses Chloe's cheek.

"Of course," Chloe says softly.

Irritated that I'm so fucking jealous of my siblings, I gesture to the empty seat beside Grace.

My wife sits. I sit beside her and wrap my arm around the back of her chair, giving in to the urge to run my thumb along her clavicle.

She shivers, then goes stiff at my touch, but says nothing.

Her eyes land on the casket and I watch as sadness seeps into her features.

Sadness. For my mother. Kindness to my brother and sister.

Despite everything, she's still so good, so caring. Because it's who she is. I chose well.

Cheater

In actuality, it feels more like I was chosen. Chosen to make her happy. To give her everything she wants.

If only I had more of her goodness in me. I seem to have it only where a few people are concerned, mostly her. My eyes land on the exorbitantly priced and decorated box containing the empty shell that used to be one of the other few people that I give an actual shit about.

This ceremonial nonsense solves nothing. I don't know how it can bring anyone closure to put their loved one's remains in a box and stare at it.

I want this over. I want to take my wife home and resume my plan of winning her over. I want to fuck her. Plant a baby in her. The math tells me she should be fertile around now. I've been thinking about this fact non-stop for the past twenty-four hours. The idea of planting my baby in her might be what has kept me from spinning out of control these past few days. Imagining my hands on her belly, feeling our child move. Imagining holding her while she holds a little bundle.

I've given her some space after her fury the other day, but I'm done. No more space. The less space the better.

I walked away from her fury the other day, partly to simmer my anger at her reaction, at her accusation despite the fact I've been up front about who I am and what I've done.

I started to feel impatient, started to get angry at her for resisting, for shouting at me in anger. For accusing me of lying. I'd never, ever physically hurt her; I know that in my gut. But in the moment, I needed to get away to make absolute sure. Because Chloe actually made my trigger finger twitch, and I didn't like it. I didn't like it and I didn't fuckin' trust myself. But the moment I was away from her, I felt like I was too far away.

I have no intention of staying away. She might think of me as a murderer, a psycho she wants nothing to do with, but tonight I'm going to do my very fucking best to get what I want most right now. What I need most.

Planting my child in her could give me some measure of my own closure for losing one of the few people I care about. Creating a new one to care about. One that will tie me and Chloe together permanently. I'll show her how good of a husband, father, and provider I'll be.

I'll love my own child, won't I? I think so. A piece of me, yeah, but more importantly, a piece of both me *and* Chloe.

I'll never give up on my goals, on working at convincing her. But the past few days, I've asked myself, what if it never happens? What if I find myself doomed to want something in my grasp but still out of reach? My trigger finger starts to twitch now at these thoughts. I frown at it and sit on my hand. It's been happening a lot the last few days, since my mother died, especially since Chloe screamed in my face that she'd never love me.

I need to hold steady, get through this funeral, get home and make love to my wife. Make our baby. Find my center. Daily goals. Is Chloe happy? Does Chloe love me? Once I get checkmarks on all of that, the twitching will stop.

I'll make her the family she's been wanting. She'll have a man who will desire her endlessly. A group of people around her that she can shower with love while having it reciprocated. I've done the math, and it has to be the answer.

It's not only the answer for Chloe. It's my answer, too. My mother didn't share the love she got from her husband with us, her kids. She kept my father's affection like a hoarder; all for herself. The second he aimed any of it in our direction, she suddenly needed more from him.

If she acted like she might spiral, he'd turn from anything and everything to focus solely on her.

I looked at Chloe that first night and sensed such thirst. So much *need*. But she didn't seem like another emotional vampire. She gives. If only Mom had what Dad gave her but shared it with us. Rewarded him for giving it to all of us instead of hoarding it all for herself.

But... if I give my wife a baby, what if she only showers that baby

Cheater

with her love? What if she only focuses on the child like my father only focused on my mother?

The twitching in my finger starts again and I see Chloe staring at my hand.

Elijah and Sabrina arrive and both her and my focus moves to them.

Sabrina is dressed in black, despite Grace's request. Sabrina is probably making a statement about being in grief, but not for her mother-in-law, I don't think. Those two butted heads; Sabrina never hesitated to play my mother's game right back.

Those who don't know her might think she's grieving, hiding under those big sunglasses, her mouth tight, but I'm sure it's because she doesn't want to be here. I can relate.

Eli has his hand on her lower back and she's stiff.

Grace handled all the arrangements including choosing the casket, flowers, set up, even wardrobe for everyone. She channeled our mother for certain, becoming almost manic about precision. She won't be happy at Sabrina's rebellion, but unlike my mother who would make cutting remarks about it, knowing Grace, she'll let it slide out of relief that Sabrina came.

Grace ran through today's details with us repeatedly, driving the point that she needed to create the perfect event to honor our mother as part of her own grieving process. The rest of us were more concerned about security. Particularly me and Jonah. With everything pointing to Eli's enemies in New York running our parents over and only succeeding in killing one of them, of course we believed we should have a more lowkey funeral to keep the rest of the family safe.

My father balked, insisting my mother's wishes for her funeral be carried out. To mimic that of other Steele family members. My dead brother's. My grandfather's. My grandmother's. Because Steele family members belong in the Steele family section of the cemetery near their home.

We were all invited to arrive early by the funeral home, to "visit" with my mother privately in order to say our goodbyes. As far as I know, each of us declined. Nobody would dare set eyes upon her for the last time with her looking less than her best. She made this request in a drunken monologue after Thad's funeral. Nobody would be permitted to look upon her dead body with sadness, lying about her looking like she was at peace when we would know there would be no peace for us because she'd haunt us, shrilly screaming to remember how she looked when she was alive instead of frozen in death. She wanted the casket closed and for no one who knew her in life to see her body.

Ash didn't show up for last night's meal and pre-funeral meeting. Grace has had several phone chats with him, but none of us has seen him since the day we landed in New York, at the hospital.

Security won't be seating any of the guests that aren't part of the immediate family until all of us are in our seats and I can see clusters of people waiting beyond security. Attendance is by invitation only, photo identification required.

Eli and Sabrina step up to greet Jonah, Grace, then Chloe.

Eli also hugs my wife, then shakes my hand and I pull my hand back early because my finger is twitching. He eyes my hand and our eyes meet. He wraps both arms around me and claps my back once.

"Easy, brother," he says into my ear.

I return the back slap, though I say nothing. I want him to move along. Sabrina has just hugged Chloe without exchanging words, but the two of them exchange loaded glances that I find peculiar since they haven't met.

I've given my wife space the past few days, doing my best to resist the urge to check trackers, bank accounts, or external surveillance. Either they've spoken on the phone or simply feel a commonality at the moment. Ken hasn't reported her having company. She shopped two days ago, and he followed her. He'd have reported it if she had met with Eli's wife.

I give Sabrina a perfunctory hug as she moves in front of me, expression unreadable under her sunglasses. I've never embraced my brother's wife before, not even on their wedding day. She's a curvy

Cheater

beauty with a curtain of long, black hair. I'm not sure I've ever even exchanged more than hellos and goodbyes with her in the year and a half they've been married.

These hugs are all phony, all a show for the shutters that are undoubtedly clicking in the distance. Grace and my father are the ones most concerned that we appear to be a close-knit family leaning on one another in our time of grief, because it's *what Mom would've wanted.*

I've heard that phrase too many fucking times in the past week. Too many times in my life, in fact.

Sabrina moves past me, past my brother, and sits in the next empty chair.

A moment later, a gust of cold wind blows through us and Chloe shivers and is about to put a wrap from her lap around herself, but I immediately remove my blazer and settle it over her bare shoulders. The sun was out this morning, an extra-warm late-autumn day. The few light snowfalls we've had so far haven't stuck. But I suspect this sudden chill speaks of things to come. Not only due to the weather but my father's arrival, which is happening now.

Carson appears at Grace's side and hands out thick red blankets to Grace, Chloe, and Sabrina, reserving one for Naomi who is approaching, walking beside her husband Josh. Chloe settles the blanket across her lap but she's shivering under my coat. I put my arm around her.

Josh pushes the wheelchair my father is in. He's in it just temporarily and despite his casts and arm sling with his other visible injuries, he still looks ten feet tall. Nothing frail about the man. His eyes are hard as they lock on the fire lily-covered casket.

He was released from the hospital yesterday, but didn't come down for the family meal last night. I haven't seen him since I left the hospital, shortly after he regained consciousness.

The first thing he uttered was, "Shan?"

Elijah broke the news that she didn't make it. Dad's eyes coasted across the five of us that were there before they closed and pain flooded his face. Grace and Naomi climbed onto the edge of the bed he was in and wept, failing at trying to comfort him, but comforting one another.

It was one of the ugliest moments of my life, and I've had quite a few.

His next question was, "Where's Asher?"

"He was here until a few hours ago," Grace answered. "We'll call him and ask him to come back."

Our father said, "Don't bother," then the nurse and doctor came in and ushered us out of the room. He wanted to be alone after that, so we all went back to their local apartment.

At my father's arrival, we all rise as he's wheeled past our row of seats to the end, directly in front of a tall easel holding a large collage of photos beside the casket. Photos of them. Of us. Of Mom's modeling campaigns. Childhood pictures of her that I don't think I've ever seen. I know there aren't many. My wife's eyes are on that collage. Naomi and Josh double back and greet everyone one by one.

I catch the look of surprise in Chloe's eyes as Naomi introduces her husband. Because Josh is a near spitting image of Asher. No tattoos, ten years older than my brother and not as fair, but he could pass for being Ash disguised with a darker wig and facial hair. This is not discussed, not since Thad died. Thad made cracks every chance he got, enraging Naomi who categorically denied the resemblance.

I'm vaguely aware of movement in my periphery as the crowd thickens behind the velvet ropes. Still no Ash.

Snow begins to fall in fat flakes as the man who presided over their vow renewal stands at the podium beside the casket and talks about my mother as if he knew her well.

I pay no attention to the words he says. Instead, I think about the people that need to pay for this. My father, due to his arrogance. Maybe also my brother Eli due to his negligence in letting his enemies fuck with him repeatedly. Though I guess I can relate somewhat as I know his resistance to dealing with that problem sooner involves his wife.

Cheater

Eli has moved his wife back into their home to keep her safe, against her wishes. He also arranged today's security and went over the details at the dinner Grace arranged last night. Eli said this team had the cemetery reconned yesterday and that there would be twenty-five skilled security team members guarding the event. Jonah and I both argued we shouldn't have it out in the open, in public. That it would be better to have it in a church. Eli and Grace had met with Dad just before dinner and said he insisted we have the funeral Mom would have wanted.

"Go ahead, seat everyone," Grace says to Carson who is leaning over her, whispering.

Grace is stuffing her phone under her thigh, looking irritated. But I almost immediately see a flash of relief on her face and follow her gaze to Ash, standing under a tree near our grandmother's headstone. He's unshaven, hands in his pockets, and with the same pained look on his face as when I saw him in New York.

I heard Grace fighting with him on the phone this morning, warning that if he didn't come not only would he never be forgiven, would never forgive himself.

He's even wearing a suit.

I see Naomi has spotted him, too. They're staring at one another. Naomi's chin quivers and she tries to keep it together. They were so close when they were kids. Inseparable. I wonder if this tragedy will help them get over their beef. Looking at how they regard one another right now, I think it might be possible. I know Ash misses her, but Naomi is stubborn in her grudge-holding.

It's odd; I don't generally ponder shit like this. Don't generally give a fuck. Maybe my wife is rubbing off on me after all.

But whether Ash and Naomi repair their relationship or not, this family is not only fucked, it'll be beyond fractured after this. Without our mother there won't be much reason for us all to be in the same room. My father won't organize family dinners and holiday celebrations. Grace will try to be the glue, will try to carry on the way she knows our mother would have wanted, but looking at Ash and Naomi now looking away from one another, I'm sure I'm not the only one with no desire to keep playing the game.

Something catches the corner of my eye. One of the security guards pointing to the sky, looking at another guard.

There's commotion beyond the trees where Ash stands and Naomi shouts, "Asher!" as a ball of fire erupts in the branches of the big oak tree directly behind him. The spark is quickly a fireball as Ash dives out of the way, disappearing behind our great grandfather's headstone just in time to miss a bunch of fiery branches falling to where he was standing.

Before any of us can fully digest what we're seeing, another fireball erupts to the left of that, behind a concrete fountain.

"It was a drone!" Josh gasps.

What the fuck?

People move fast and security guards surround my family as I turtle over Chloe while the sound of another explosion pierces the air.

What the fucking clusterfuck bullshit is this?

And now it's also blizzarding. The air is filled with smoke, snow, and sparks. And I'm on the ground amid all the chairs, on top of my wife, and I need to get her the fuck out of here. And now!

Her frightened eyes hit my face as I help her to her feet, but crowd her, herding her through the human security guard wall toward the cluster of vehicles outside the perimeter of the service area. I lift her up and hold her close, glancing over my shoulder to see Josh pushing my father's wheelchair as five suited guards form a wall around them.

"Don't protect me, protect my fucking daughters you goddamn dimwits!" he cusses.

Guards surround all of us, so his statement doesn't make sense to me.

I move faster but catch the fury on my father's face as he's wheeled away from his wife's casket. A fiery tree branch lands on the

Cheater

ground beside it and sets the easel holding the collage of photos on fire.

Grace cries out in hysterics from Jonah's embrace and Jonah pushes her in my direction so he can go stomp the fire out before it gets to my mother's casket.

"Stay close, Grace," I advise. "Hold onto my shirt."

Ash joins Jonah, but Naomi grabs Ash and tugs on his arm, pulling him out of the way as another branch falls, just missing him. Eli is putting a crying Sabrina into my father's limo. He rushes back to my mother's casket. I have Chloe and Grace, but Ash, Jonah, and Carson along with two male cousins and Eli grab the handles for my mother's casket and act as pallbearers, carrying her away from her gravesite as the fire spreads. Naomi rushes and puts her hand on the same handle as Ash, helping.

She's already dead. No way am I leaving my wife unattended during this shit in order to rescue a dead woman.

"What the fuck!" My father shouts hoarsely as he's helped by Josh and his driver into his stretch limo. "Fucking deal with this. You hear me, boys? Elijah!"

Dad stares at Eli with murder on his face.

"We will," Eli vows with a mirrored expression as he backs away from the Hearse.

My eyes hit my own wife, who is where she belongs. In my arms. But she's terrified. Pale. Also crying.

"I've got you. Nothing's gonna hurt you," I swear to her, pressing my lips to hers. I move us and get her into the passenger seat of my car. Grace gets into my father's limo.

"Stay together. Convoy, Derek!" Eli shouts at me.

Carson pipes up. "Back to the Steele homestead everyone, please. And carefully."

∞

Chloe stares over her shoulder at the flame-engulfed cemetery as I drive away, hearing the sirens of the coming emergency responders.

58

Chloe

I don't want to go to the Steele homestead, but I don't speak as Derek drives. Both of his hands are on the steering wheel, but his right hand is jerking as if he's having muscle spasms. This was happening at the cemetery, too. I think it's some sort of PTSD-related tremor. I can't remember the exact terminology but do remember that people can have involuntary body responses because of trauma. I'm no expert, but Coraline minored in psychology, and we spent many hours quizzing one another during exams.

He's breathing hard, staring ahead, mouth alternating between jaw clenching and lip curling.

My heart is racing, and I've got a tension headache.

What in the world was that? Someone said drones. Drones causing fires and explosions in a cemetery? I'm shook. It was horrific. People were running, screaming, and crying. Security was trying to get people to their vehicles in an orderly fashion, but it was chaotic. And Derek's single-minded focus, as always, was me. He covered my body with his. He focused on getting me to safety. And his hand won't stop twitching as he drives, but he seems to be in command of the vehicle.

It's just a short drive back to Derek's parents' home and a valet gets into the driver's seat before I'm out of the passenger seat. Derek is already grabbing my hand before the shoes that Grace sent me, black and red versions of the ones I was admiring like hers from the day of the anniversary brunch, touch the ground and we're moving toward the house. My eyes scan the sky. Derek notices and grinds his teeth.

Once in the house I see Carson, still wearing his coat, some dirt on his cheek. He waves us down the hallway to his father's office, where I spent a chunk of a day dealing with that media woman.

I signal to my own cheek with my eyes on him. He nods his thanks and pulls a handkerchief from his inside pocket.

Elijah and his wife as well as Grace and Derek's father are already in the office. Naomi and her husband as well as Jonah are behind us.

"Police will be here soon. I'll announce before bringing them in," Carson advises me and Derek as well as the family members behind us. "We want the immediate family together in the office for that. After that, we'll receive guests in the solarium where Mrs. Steele will be for those who want to have a moment with her."

"What's the plan for her, Dad?" Jonah asks. "Since the cemetery is up in fucking flames."

"Your mother will stay in the solarium tonight," Derek's father says from his office chair where he sits, looking every bit like a CEO, though with a look in his eyes that's so angry, cold, and also griefstricken that I don't think I'll forget it for the rest of my life.

"She'd want to be there. It was her favorite room in the house," Grace says softly.

She looks stricken, pale, traumatized. So does Naomi. And Sabrina. I probably do, too.

My chin trembles. This is so awful. Derek wraps his arms around me and holds me closer. His body is trembling. I don't know if it's adrenalin, anger, the tremor, or all of it.

Asher arrives, swiping a hand through his hair as he comes in. His tie is gone, his top few buttons are undone, and he moves straight to the bar cart in the corner. There's a discordant clang making all eyes

Cheater

in the room move in his direction and we watch as he opens a decanter and starts pouring a drink.

"I'll have some of that," Jonah says, walking that way.

Elijah follows.

Ash carries a large glass of amber liquid straight to his father, who accepts it without speaking. He goes back and sets up several glasses and pours.

Derek shakes his head as Elijah holds a glass out.

Elijah's eyes hit my face with question, still holding the glass.

"Brandy instead, ladies?" Carson pipes up.

"Yes, please," I say.

"I'll have a bourbon, too," Grace answers.

"Me, too," Sabrina says.

"Nothing for me," Naomi whispers, arms wrapped around herself before she goes to the fireplace and turns a button on the mantle, making it spring to life. She sits down on one of the big, comfortable-looking leather chairs there, giving the rest of us her back.

Her husband moves over there and squats, talking softly to her.

I can't get over the uncanny resemblance between Josh and Asher. It can't be just me that thinks it.

Asher passes me a brandy.

"Thank you," I say.

Michael speaks up. "Get yourselves together, kids. I'll talk to the police with all of you here, so you all know the exact script, then go out there and receive our guests. It's what your mother would have wanted."

Script?

"If I had a dollar every fuckin' time I heard that," Derek mutters under his breath.

Asher scoffs and I'm pretty sure it's in agreement.

"What's that, Derek?" Michael calls over, looking absolutely pissed.

"How about you give us five fucking minutes before we have to worry about appearances, Dad?" Derek snaps.

Michael's gaze goes even colder. "Who do you think you're talking to, son?"

"Oh shit," Grace mutters.

Derek shakes his head with disgust. "Who gives a fuck what the guests think? You think they might understand that we need a minute when we lost her, and her funeral got attacked with drone *fucking* warfare."

"The last thing I need right now is bullshit from you, Derek," Michael points at him.

"Bullshit from me?" Derek asks, then laughs. Dangerously. All eyes in the room are on him. His arms are still around me, but his whole body is trembling now.

I take a big gulp of the brandy in my hand.

"Whoa, let's settle d-down," Grace gets between us and their father, visibly upset.

"Who's trying to hurt us?" Naomi asks, no... demands. She's looking at Elijah.

"We're dealing with it," Elijah answers. "Derek, cut it out."

"Fuck you, Eli," Derek snaps.

"Whoa," Jonah says. "We're all on the same side here. Can we try to remember that?"

Naomi gets louder. "Someone ran over Mom and Dad and now tried to... what... kill all of us in the cemetery? Who out there hates us enough to want to ruin the graves of all our dead family members, too?"

"It's more of the same, isn't it?" Ash calls out, pouring another drink and then downing it. "Not sure how we'll spin *this* in the media though."

"Watch it, Asher," Michael warns.

Carson speaks up. "Might I suggest we speak to the police, then after we receive guests and spend an hour or two with them to honor Mrs. Steele, that you all stay here tonight, where we all know we're

Cheater

under one roof? And safe. I've already asked the team to prepare all of your rooms."

"Good plan," Grace says.

"I agree," Michael says. "Thank you, Carson."

"All of us under one roof where we can all be taken out in one fell swoop? I don't fuckin' think so," Derek states. "No way am I keeping Chloe here."

I look up at his face. Our eyes meet and his are frighteningly angry.

His hand at my lower back jerks some more.

"It was a public place; there was only so much we could do," Grace defends. "But-"

"Bullshit," Derek clips. "Did me and Jonah not both try to convince you people it was a bad idea to be out in the open like that? Lotta good that recon did when enemies can strap explosives to drones."

Michael keeps going. "We'll go out there, present a united front, and deal with all the bullshit tomorrow. How's that?"

"Did I not just fucking speak?" Derek snaps.

"Do I give a fuck?" Michael returns.

"You really gonna continue acting like I'm not here, Dad?"

"Me, Derek? You say practically nothing to me for decades and now you've got all sorts of shit to say to me? Now you want attention? Here. During all this?" Michael pauses and then sourly finishes with, "I think given the circumstances, it can wait one more day, son." He gulps back the contents of his glass and sets it down hard.

"I've got shit to say that should've probably been said a long fuckin' time ago," Derek snaps. "Maybe I don't wanna wait until tomorrow. Maybe I can't swallow it down for one more fucking minute."

"In case you haven't noticed, we're supposed to be burying my wife today, Derek."

"She's dead and gone. And she's still your biggest priority, isn't she?"

Michael's face is red, but like stone.

A staff member comes in and speaks low to Carson.

"The police are here," Carson states.

"Make them wait. We're busy," Derek snaps.

"I don't know what the hell is wrong with you all of a sudden," Michael says.

"Of course you don't know; you haven't given a fuck for most of my life, Dad."

"My wife is dead!" Michael shouts gutturally.

I wince.

"My mother is dead!" Derek counters. "And you didn't protect her when Elijah told you shit was too amped for you to be wandering around in New York. All because she wanted to see a fucking play and you didn't want to burst her fragile bubble by revealing that shit was dangerous. And now again today... again... your ignorance put *my* wife, my brothers and sisters, their spouses in jeopardy."

"And I have to live with all that, don't I?" Michael fires back.

"You have a history of not paying attention to anybody who says anything you don't wanna hear, don't you? Until big shit happens to wake you up, right? Oh... wait... except when it comes to your kids."

Michael bares his teeth, but Derek isn't done.

"Did sweet fuck all for your family unless it was throwing money at staff to look after them for you... until she almost died when we were kids and then she was *all* you gave a fuck about. And now she's dead. What'll you give a fuck about now, Dad?"

"You've lost your mind, Derek."

"I think I lost it a long time ago, man. Around the time my father didn't give a fuck that I was being held for a ransom he could easily pay."

"Here we go," Michael mutters. "I need another fucking drink."

Carson rushes over with the decanter, looking stressed out.

I'm still standing in Derek's embrace, trembling along with him.

Grace is crying, Naomi's crying, and Sabrina has sat down in the

Cheater

chair beside Naomi, has her arms wrapped around herself, and she's staring at the fireplace, looking broken.

Elijah moves over and stands beside her, looking frazzled. Looking like he wants to comfort her but is afraid to touch her.

"I say we shouldn't have the funeral at a cemetery out in the open and Elijah insists you won't listen. Jonah calls you to talk about it and you sluff him off, too. So Ash nearly gets blown apart, then the whole fuckin' place is being attacked and shit is on fire just five feet from my wife and my fucking sisters and still all you care about is what she would have wanted in terms of appearances. She's gone, Dad. Bullshit ceremonies and fake receiving lines and fucking nonsense for the clicking shutters to make the press think we're the perfect all-American one percent family? Why don't you tell everyone to go the fuck home so we can help clean up Elijah's mess and take out his fuckin' enemies?"

"What is your fucking problem?" Michael retorts, full of venom. "You-"

Derek cuts him off. "What's been my problem my whole life, man? Maybe your lack of giving a fuck has something to do with it. Probably figured the good doc was helping you weed that garden, huh? Too bad I shot him and came back."

"Bro..." Ash mutters, shaking his head.

"You pick now to do this?" Michael snaps.

Derek seems manic. Unglued. And it's scary. And upsetting. His father looks just as ready to lose it.

"Okay, I think we need to all take a minute," Naomi's husband says.

"Fuck that. Sick of shit not being said. Standing on ceremony. Used to say nothing, barely gave a fuck. All you wanted was to make her happy. Didn't bother doing sweet fuck all about Thaddeus, let him and his bullshit stomp all over this family to keep the peace for her, but guess what? I do actually give a fuck, Dad. Shocks the shit out of me, but I do. Too bad you don't."

587

"I was told it was too late. That you were probably already dead," Michael says, frowning.

Derek stares at his father with icy fury.

Michael sniffs and shakes his head, looking lost in thought as he keeps talking. "Wanted to throw every fucking dime I had at that situation to get you back. Cops said it was probably already too late. They found your blood in the limo and figured you were already gone, said your blood was on the ransom note too. That he was probably lying about you being alive. But it *was* too late. You were alive but you took matters into your own little hands and it fuckin' ruined you."

Derek's mouth twists in a grimace.

Michael continues. "...to shoot that man in cold blood when you were just a child. If you hadn't have killed him, son, I would have. I wanted to inflict pain on a dead man for years after that was over. But it was never over because you never looked at any of us the same after that. I felt like a fucking failure. It destroyed me and your mother. Nearly ended our marriage. Did you know that? Fucked up the entire family for years. Do you know what we went through for those long days and nights? Both your sisters bawling all day long for you. Thaddeus banging his own head against the walls in frustration crying out that his little brother is dead. And then we get you back and you were different. Completely different. You were already troubled after your mother's mental health crisis and after the abduction..." He lets that hang.

"Too different, right? Ruined. You probably wished he took me out. Aren't you glad I didn't become an embarrassment like Thad?"

"Stop it," Naomi weeps.

"But yet Thad would embarrass you repeatedly and you'd do nothing about it. Letting him terrorize most of the family in order to keep your wife happy. Pretend nothing was wrong. Because Thad knew how to hide his bullshit from Mom, didn't he? But the rest of us saw it in glorious technicolor."

Cheater

I'm stuck, glued in place watching pain take over Derek's features. Immense pain. His father wears the same pain.

Elijah and Jonah stare at their father with hard expressions, like they want the same answers Derek wants. Ash is pouring another drink.

"You didn't hide it though, did you, Derek?" Michael asks. "You have any idea how much sleep you cost her? Cost me?"

"Aw, poor you, Dad. Fuck this. We're leaving. I'm done with you."

"Derek..." Grace tries.

"Derek wait," Michael says as he rises slowly, with difficulty. He takes a big breath and clears the anger from his face. "Son, please don't go. I'd really like it if my family would all stay under this roof tonight. We'll talk tomorrow. About everything you want to talk about. But don't go out there with this threat. I don't... I'm asking you not to. Please. Stay." His voice cracks. "Not because it's what your mother would have wanted, it's what I want. I don't want you to be done with me. I want all of you here tonight. It's what *I* need." He clears his throat. "I need you all under this roof tonight. To know we're all together. Safe. I know it's a lot to ask. I'm sorry, but I'm asking anyway."

Derek stares at his father who suddenly looks utterly broken.

"Please, son," he tacks on.

Grace chokes on a sob. Asher hugs her.

I reach for Derek's twitching right hand behind my back and squeeze it.

Derek looks from his father to me. I squeeze his hand again and hold tight.

He flinches and stares at me with confusion in his pained eyes.

I put my other arm around him and rub his back.

He looks ready to break down in tears. From his father's speech? From my back rub? Both? Everything? Probably everything.

"Let's stay," I say.

Derek swallows, then looks back to his father. "Fine," he says,

"But I'm not participating in a circus out there. Receiving lines and bullshit like that. No. Me and Chloe will stay in my old room, and I'll see you all in the morning."

"Thank you," Michael breathes, sounding relieved. "All of you do what you need to do today, just please do it here. Stay. And let's meet for breakfast in the morning. Nine o'clock in your mother's morning room. I'd like to have breakfast with my children tomorrow. And your spouses. My family. Have a meeting with my sons about security and cleaning up after today, but after breakfast. Is that all right?"

"Okay, Daddy," Grace says quietly, dabbing her wet eyes with a Kleenex.

Derek moves toward the door, taking me with him.

My eyes meet Derek's father's.

"Thank you, Chloe," he says softly.

I give him a small, sad nod as we move out of the room.

Derek walks too quickly, meaning I need to jog to keep up, taking us down a hall through a room full of mourners eating and drinking, staring at us, and then down another hallway until we're approaching a grand, winding staircase.

"You're walking too fast," I manage to rasp, a stitch in my side.

He slows and we climb the stairs together, then move down a hallway of doors before turning down another hallway leading to a short staircase and yet another hallway of doors.

Three doors down, he opens a door.

A large bedroom with multiple doors including sliding patio doors that lead to a balcony. Done in dark wood furniture, gleaming hardwood floors, blue and green plaid bedding. A large desk with leather chair. An adjoining bathroom. A sitting area as well as a wet bar with a fridge microwave.

He closes the door, locks it, and turns to me, taking my face into both hands.

I gasp in surprise as his mouth touches mine gently, sweetly.

"I've missed you so much," he whispers. "I need you right now. I need you so fucking much I think I'll die if I don't have you."

Cheater

"Derek, no," I whisper. "I can't..."

"I can," he says, a gleam in his eyes. "And I will. Please, little bunny, don't try to deny me. I need you more than air. I need to feel my wife. I need to hold you. I need you to numb the pain for a while. Please, baby. Please. You're the only one that can stop it."

"Stop it?" I query.

"The pain. The trigger finger."

I stare at his hand.

He's not flexing it right now.

He pulls me close and the zipper on the back of my dress descends.

"I was trapped with that doc for nine days as he sank deeper and deeper into psychosis. As I watched the timer on the wall count down while he ranted for hours at a time about things a kid couldn't comprehend, telling me he'd have to kill me. Because my father had to be the bigger man with the bigger balls, not giving in to ransom demands because it was a shot at his manhood. He talked to me about life, death, fuckin' taxes, revenge, baseball, betrayal, sex..." He shakes his head. "Made me work through mind and guessing games for food and water. And then when it was clear the timer was about to go off and I knew no one was coming to pay him the ransom, I got my hands on the gun and pulled the trigger." He mimics the action again and I can see it's what he was doing. Squeezing an imaginary trigger over and over.

"I squeezed, and it was over. The guy was dead on the floor, bleeding out, and I knew it was over. I had nightmares for months about pulling the trigger over and over, watching the blood, gray matter, flesh and bone shards explode from his head. But even though what I saw was horrific, that one squeeze of my finger made it over."

Shit.

"And maybe that's why when I get stressed out, something in me thinks if I pull a trigger, it'll all stop. I couldn't trust another doctor after that. I spent two hours a week with that guy for months before he kidnapped me."

"I understand," I say softly.

"You do, don't you?" He caresses my face.

His eyes have softened. His hand is steady as he finishes unzipping me, then he takes the sleeves that rest on my biceps and tugs. The dress pools at my feet, leaving me in a flesh-colored strapless bra, a white thong.

"You make me feel the closest to human I've felt since then."

"This isn't the answer," I tell him. "You're upset. You're grieving, and-"

His mouth is on mine, his hot hands are on me.

I go weak in the knees.

He says, "I know you hate me, Chloe. I know you're sure you'll never love me. But you're so, so fucking good, so caring, so loving and sweet. You took care of me when I got the news. You were offering to help. Contacting Carson. Grace. You're so, so good. You'll give me what I need right now, won't you? You'll let me make love to you, you'll let me make you come. Because you're my good girl, my beautiful wife, who cares even if she doesn't want to. Even if she shouldn't."

I squeeze my eyes tight.

He was so upset down there I couldn't help but feel for him. And what happened at the cemetery was so terrifying, and it was moving to me the way I was his priority. It penetrated some sort of shield covering me, I think. I think I understand him. His motivations. The hand tremor. The trauma. It's all so twisted, but he's been through so, so much. The sum of his experiences and his environment have made Derek who he is.

"Please, baby. I need you." He walks me backwards and I stumble, tripping on the pool of red lace at my ankles. But I don't fall, because he scoops me up and then he stumbles and falls onto the bed with me, smiling, eyes alight with amusement.

"Oops," he quips.

"I don't think you're being fair here. Trying to use your grief to manipulate me into sex."

Cheater

"Of course I'm not being fair. I'll do whatever I have to do to get inside you. Don't you know that by now, wife?"

I sigh and roll my eyes. "Seriously, you're upset about things and what you're trying to do right now isn't going to solve anything for you. In fact, all it's gonna do to me is make me feel bad afterwards."

"But why do you feel bad afterwards?" He touches my face again. "I fuck you and it feels good, doesn't it? You know it does. And you deserve to feel good." He runs his fingers through my hair and bites his lip, eyes on my boobs, which are spilling out of the strapless bra. "I'm gonna fuck you, Chloe."

"No, Derek."

"Yes. It'll feel good and make us both happy."

"There's so much wrong with this... I can't even."

"Wrong with me you mean?"

I sigh again.

"I didn't kill Hallman's ex. I didn't order it."

"I know that now," I whisper. "Craig told me. I'm sorry I didn't believe you. But this isn't the answer; it won't fix things. You just had a really big and important conv-"

He covers my mouth. "Shh. I know you want this. Your eyes tell me even if your mouth denies it. And this..." He smiles and then his free hand dips between my legs and fingers slide through to hook the crotch of the thong to the side just a little, which is all it takes for him to find that I'm slippery. "This..." he chuckles darkly, "tells us everything we both need to know. Doesn't it?"

I can't answer with my mouth covered.

"The only problem here is your mouth, wife. So... let's take that out of the equation, yeah?" He lets go of my mouth so he can yank on his tie, then he loosens it, pulls it over his head and shakes his head smiling. "Shoulda thought of this weeks ago."

"No," I protest, giving him an expression that irrefutably shows that I mean business. "Don't you dare gag me."

But he does dare. He moves lightning fast and secures the tie by looping it over my head and quickly pulling the tail to make it taut between my teeth.

I struggle, but he effortlessly pins my hands and holds both my wrists with one fist, then snaps his fly undone and can barely wait to get his dick into me. I writhe and grunt with frustration, but he smiles. He smiles a smile that belongs to a man half angel, half monster. And damn it, but I'm wetter. My heart is racing with excitement now. And it feels so, so wrong.

"Give in, listen to your pussy. Give it what it wants. It wants to be pounded. It wants to help your husband forget how fucking much it hurts for a few minutes."

I stop writhing.

"God, I love seeing these rings on your finger." He kisses my ring finger just above where the rings rest.

I see the flash of his ring on his hand and a flash of something in his eyes. This along with the sound of his voice, the way he feels holding me, impaling me, wanting me... makes me nod.

He stills, eyes scanning my face.

I nod again and he flinches. He's looking at me with disbelief.

I nod again, harder. He pins me harder, daring me to change my mind with just those expressive eyes.

I grunt, pulling my right hand hard. He releases it. I pull at the gag and he helps me, releasing it.

His eyes are full of questions. He's aching to know what I'm trying to say.

As the gag is lowered to my throat, I squeeze my inner muscles around him. His expression shows me he feels it.

"Just go," I rasp. "Just go! Fuck me. Fuck me as hard as you want me. Take me, Derek. Do it!"

His nostrils flare and he slams his hips forward, letting out a snarling, animalistic sound as he grabs a fistful of my hair, using it to get my mouth to his.

"I fucking love you, love you so much, baby. This is what I need. You. You make me feel and I hate and love it at the same time. You

Cheater

say I'm psycho. I am, Chloe. But you have the power to get me as close as I can get to normal. Just use it. Use that power and get whatever you want, baby. Give yourself to me and take me. Take me as I am. Know that yes, I'm fuckin' cracked, but I'm yours. I'll do anything for you, as long as it's not you asking me to stop being your husband."

He pinches my nipple hard, but it hurts so good. I squeeze around him, tight as I can while I attack his mouth with my teeth, biting him, licking his lips, sucking on his tongue.

He comes. Explodes. He pulls my hair harder, roaring into my mouth as he trembles. He slams his palm against the headboard and growls.

"Fuck, yeah, Chloe. I fucking love you. I'm gonna give you everything, baby. Everything. Make you happy..." He kisses me. "Make you laugh, smile, make you wanna take care of me. But I won't stop taking care of you while you do it, okay?"

I whimper.

"How the fuck do you feel this good, wife? I can't fathom becoming less obsessed with you. I promise I'll never forget how much I want you, how hard I've fought for you. If you love me back, I don't even know how I'll hack it. My fucking chest'll explode with how it feels. Just you being here for me today, I can't even tell you how much it helps. I've been twitching off and on for days, almost non-stop today, and you made it stop, baby."

He cups my jaw tenderly. This feels so foreign and yet so real at the same moment. His hand slides down to the tie that's loosely around my neck and he holds it, his other hand cupping me between my legs as he slides his fingers through the wetness, and then slaps between my legs. I jolt. He slaps me three times quickly and then circles it before using three fingers to penetrate me.

My back leaves the mattress and I whimper.

"I love watching my cum leak out of you," he says, pressing a kiss to the inside of my thigh. His voice is sweet, almost hypnotizing.

Despite everything, for some reason, my mouth splits into a smile.

"Oh, a gift for your husband, wife? A smile?"

A giggle escapes my mouth. Maybe I'm going a little crazy, too.

He lets go of the tie, laughing. And it's a beautiful sight, one I don't feel bad about taking in. It's a sight I actually lap up for once. "But I need you to hold it all in, Chloe." His fingers play in the mess, then he cups me firmly. "Because I want my seed to grow our baby inside you."

I say nothing. What can I say? He's had an emotional episode today that was huge for him. His mother died. The funeral had explosions. His mother's coffin isn't in the ground, it's in a room downstairs because of the explosions. He's just had some sort of partial breakthrough with his father. I don't know what the next moments hold. I only know that this guy looking into my eyes right now, playing in the mess between my legs, yes, he needs psychiatric help. Definitely, he's done some unforgivable things. But also... in some ways he's kind of fucking magical.

"A baby for next summer sounds pretty fucking great," he says. "Doesn't it?"

I stretch, feeling languid from the ginormous orgasm. I don't answer the ridiculous question, though.

Yeah, maybe he is crazy, but he sure does know how to make me come. A girl could get addicted to physical satisfaction on a daily basis.

I think back to Jeffy's words in our last phone call, when he told me to ponder my power. How Derek himself pretty much just said the same thing to me. How Grace and Naomi also suggested it.

"Thought of any baby names?" he asks.

"You're crazy," I whisper. "I'm on the pill."

"Kiss your crazy husband, good girl."

I don't move, so he does, and I melt as he kisses me, as he touches me, looking at me like I'm making all his dreams come true. I can't fuck Derek into being mentally well, but can I ponder my power to find a way to help him find some semblance of wellness?

Cheater

I get why he's never wanted to trust another therapist. The trauma he went through as a child at the hands of a child psychologist was beyond extreme.

He never saw therapy do anything good for anybody in his life. He was surrounded by mental illness. The trauma of finding his mother unconscious and bleeding in the tub from self-inflicted wounds imprinted on him from a young age. Him wanting to look after me and solve all my problems is obviously related.

What would be the best way for him to get some help?

Yes, I need to ponder my power here some more.

But right now I can't think anymore, because he's lifting me, turning onto his back, and planting me on top of him. I look in his eyes, at the joy on his face as he gazes at me, looking at me like I'm the one and only woman in the world. Like he can't get enough. Like he really, truly loves me. Like I've helped take the pain away.

It's kind of heady.

I take his jaw into both hands and slowly move in, staring into those eyes until our lips touch. My eyes close as I kiss him, holding his face, absorbing the scent and feel of him. Giving myself something I've, at some level, wanted since the very beginning.

Letting myself feel the reality of what this *could* be. Me and Derek. Together. Really together.

He guides his hardness to my opening, and although his eyes look gentle, he slams me down hard, making me whimper. He grasps my hips. I squeeze tight and begin to rock, still kissing him.

His hands release my hips and capture my breasts.

"I love you so much," he tells me between lip touches. "I'm gonna make you so fucking happy. Please let me make you happy. Please, baby, please."

"Okay," I relent.

"What?" He stills.

"I said okay. But Derek... don't fuck it up."

He jolts in surprise and stares, chest rising and falling rapidly as his eyes rove my face.

"I won't," he vows, eyes fiery.

"Don't fuck it up, or you won't like what happens," I warn.

His body goes perfectly still. His expression goes completely cold. I hold his stare. He pulls his cock out and warmth overtakes his features as he flips me to my back and slams inside me.

"I won't."

And he's fucking me, fucking me like a jackhammer, pinning me with his strong body, bruising my hips, but although I'm on my back, being fucked hard, I feel strangely powerful.

59

Derek

I lift her out of the shower, our mouths fused together, and carry her back to the bed. It's got to be approaching dusk. We've been at it for hours. Not just fucking, either. Making out. Like teenagers. Groping, kissing, and... of course fucking. And I am not done. I want to fuck her until the end of time. I'll keep fucking her as long as my cock keeps going hard tonight.

It's soft right now, so maybe I'm done. Or maybe I'll be good to go again in another ten minutes, so I arrange her so I can get ready to feast between her thighs, but my phone chimes with a text alert from my suit pants. I lean over, dangling off the edge of the bed in order to get to it.

"That's Carson. Food plates from the buffet are outside the door. You hungry?" I ask, sending a thumbs up.

"Starving," she says in a sultry voice, and I feel a nip on my ass cheek.

I jolt in surprise.

"Did my wife just bite my ass?" I ask.

She laughs.

I roll to my back, dropping the phone. She's naked, wet, and on her hands and knees, at waist level. She drops a kiss on my hip, staring directly into my eyes.

"Another gift. My wife's laughter."

She winks.

My dick twitches. She eyes it and leans over, running her hot little tongue from the base to the crown, waking it up entirely.

I fold my arm and cup the back of my head with my palm, watching the show.

"You're so fucking hot," I tell her, joy welling up inside me as she grips my dick and squeezes, swirling her tongue around the crown. She kisses her way up and down, squeezing, and then whispers. "Open up."

I don't immediately move because I'm not sure what she means, but when she nudges my inner left thigh, I catch her drift and part my legs so she can fit between them better.

"More," she requests, slowly running her tongue along my cock.

I shuffle to give her more room, but realize it's not so she can tuck her body there and keep licking and sucking my cock, her tongue moves lower.

Lower.

Lower still, and now she's tonguing my sack. I sink my teeth into my lower lip watching the show, torn between wanting to watch and wanting to reciprocate.

She licks my taint, and I lift up on my elbow so I don't lose sight of her eyes. She stares straight into my soul and does it again.

"My dirty fucking girl. Fuckin' love it," I tell her. "I love *you*." I grab her by the armpits and turn her to her back, pressing my mouth between her thighs.

She whines, "But it's my turn!"

I chuckle.

"What my bunny wants, she gets. As long as I get what I want, too." I maneuver her so she can ride my face while sucking me. Not long later, we're coming into one another's mouths and I'm pretty sure I'm done for the night.

"Did you say something about food plates?" she asks as I'm drifting, holding her, feeling her, feeling *right*.

"Yeah. I'll go and–"

"I've got it," she offers and rolls away from me.

Cheater

After not sleeping well for more than a week, I'm sinking into slumber before she's back.

∞

I wake up in the dark and she's asleep on my chest. The TV is on the screensaver. I go to the bathroom, take a leak, and wander to the fridge in the kitchenette. I see it's stocked with water, Coke, beer, root beer, and a covered platter.

Chloe put this in the fridge for me. I see a matching platter and lid in the sink. She ate, saved my meal for me, and snuggled up in bed and watched television until she fell asleep.

She's mine. She's letting herself be mine.

Is this real?

"Don't fuck it up or you won't like what happens."

I let the feeling wash through me. It's real. And I'm not gonna fuck it up.

I almost smile at the contents of the plate. But sadness twinges in my gut, too. My mother was a fancy bitch. She loved all things upper crust. But she came from humble beginnings and this meal pays homage to not only that, but also to one of the best childhood memories I've got.

I was maybe eight or nine and we spent a summer at the New Hampshire place. Mom fired a maid for flirting with my father right before the cook took sick and wound up hospitalized for a weekend. This left our parents to fend for themselves. And us.

This was the meal we made. All of us. Together.

Mom told us it was her favorite summer meal growing up: a cold plate. Cold plates became a New Hampshire tradition.

That first time, she got Thaddeus and Elijah peeling potatoes for potato salad, me and Jonah passing her ingredients and then rolling the cold cuts into cylinders and arranging them on a platter. Nay and Ash were her stirring squad. My father watched all of this with a smile on his face, keeping Grace, who was too little to help on his lap, joy in his eyes as he watched us all work together to make dinner.

Because he got the easy job, he washed the dishes afterwards. Me, Thad, and Eli dried and put them away. Motown played on the radio. My parents slow-danced in the kitchen.

I feel a lump of emotion in my throat that Grace chose this meal for today. We recreated it many times at the New Hampshire place, but it was never as magical as that first time. That first time when Mom acted like a mother and the rest of us sopped it up like little sponges.

I wolf down some potato salad, pasta salad, a couple crustless sandwich quarters, and some cold cuts wrapped around cheese. I wash it all down with a cold beer and climb back into bed with my wife. She's asleep in my white dress shirt.

60

Chloe

"You scare me," I tell him. "Honestly. Deep in my soul, I feel like I should be terrified to let my guard down with you."

"Why?" Dream Derek asks.

"It's hard to explain," Dream me says.

"Try. You can be real with me."

"You sure about that?" I ask.

"Entirely." He smiles that dazzling wide smile of his.

We're in our bed, but it's on a cloud. There are a mated pair of unicorns on the next cloud over, nuzzling noses. Their little baby unicorn sleeps curled in a ball beside them, but close to the edge.

I smile at the baby, knowing she's safe. Because she has little pink wings.

I look away from the unicorns, back into Derek's eyes and say, "You definitely scare me."

"Why?" he asks.

"You could be everything I ever wanted. But it might be an illusion. I'm telling myself to try to believe, but I'm so, so scared."

"I'm real. Fall, Chloe. Open your arms wide, tip your head towards the sky. And lean back. Way back. Okay? Let go. Feel me catch you. Take what you deserve. You have to. I'm gonna make you, anyway. Let yourself have it early. Save yourself the angst. You don't want more angst. Do you?"

DD Prince

Derek plucks a piece of cloud up and feeds it to me. It's the sweetest cotton candy on my tongue.

I swallow the cotton candy and the bed vanishes, the cloud evaporates, Derek's not here, and I'm suddenly plummeting. The unicorns lean over and watch from their cloud as I fall.

My eyes bolt open. I'm disoriented. My heart is racing. But I remember where I am. Derek's childhood room. But, I'm alone. I hear distant male voices. They're coming from the balcony. I slip into the adjoining bathroom and use the facilities, wash my face with a new bottle of top-shelf face wash I find in the medicine cabinet along with a new toothbrush. There's already a wet toothbrush sitting on the vanity, a wrapper in the trash bin.

I start on my teeth, feeling strange. And emotional. I stare in the mirror and tell myself once again to ponder my power here. Use it. Could I get everything I want? Is it possible? Is it safe to tip my head back and let myself fall?

Am I making lemon meringue pie out of lemons? Or am I getting drunk on lemon drops? Delusional, thinking I can somehow wield things in my favor and not have this end in a fiery, messy end that's statistically speaking, likely to only end with one of us dead or him in prison.

With Derek, it feels like I won the lottery, but with a caveat. That he's crazy. That he'll go to extremes to have what he wants with no fear of consequences and that's the price I have to pay to have what I want.

Where will the crazy go if he gets all he wants? Sure, the twitching stopped yesterday, and he credits me with that, but what if I can't always stop it?

I don't know; I guess I'll find out.

I peer out the sliding doors. He's sitting on some patio furniture beside Jonah. He's wearing trackpants and a hoodie. His feet are bare. Jonah is dressed in jeans and a cable knit sweater. Grace stands at the railing that overlooks the pool area, that gazebo. She's in a thick robe and slippers. I see coffee mugs out there with them.

Cheater

Derek sees me and his eyes light up in a way that has butterflies fluttering in my stomach. I wave. It looks nippy out, but I see a patio heater out there, too.

I go to the tall dresser in the closet and open the top drawer, hoping there are some socks I can wear to go outside. There's a suit hanging in the closet and a pair of shoes on the floor for him as well as a pair of womens' slippers with the tags still on. The drawer is full, four piles organized with two stacks of socks and underwear for men and another two stacks for a woman. All with tags on them. The women's ones are basic bikini briefs in size medium. Three pairs, black, white, flesh-toned. Two bras. One black, one white. My size as well.

I check the second drawer. Left side, mens' T-shirts, right side, womens' tops.

The next drawer down has a *his* stack of track pants and gym shorts and a *hers* stack of yoga pants and shorts.

The bottom drawer has two pairs of mens' pajama pants and two pairs of womens' flannel pajamas.

The sliding door opens.

"I'm impressed," I say. "When did Carson do this?"

I snatch a pair of ladies undies and a pair of socks.

"Probably the day I brought you for the anniversary brunch," he says, eating up the distance between us. "I gave him your sizes and some of your favorite foods and drinks. He makes it a practice to keep all our old rooms ready in case we ever stay."

"Well, I'm impressed. I'm coming out for coffee. More coffee out there?"

"There's a coffee maker in Grace's room. She stays over often. I'd rather have you to myself right now, though, wife."

"Does everyone's room lead to this balcony?"

"Boys. Girls on the other side. No balconies for them, so they've often made use of ours by slipping into Ash's room at the end of the hall."

"That must have been fun growing up," I say.

He looks at me like I'm an alien. "Maybe if I had a different family."

My expression drops. "Sorry. I didn't think. I just... verbal diarrhea."

He pulls me close. "Good morning, wife," he says and kisses me.

"Good morning," I reply.

"Good morning, wife," he repeats, smiling.

My heart skips a beat. I know he wants me to say *good morning, husband*. I'm not sure I can form the word with my mouth right now.

"Slept great," he finally says. "you in my arms. Can't remember the last time I slept here and been a while since I slept so well while I was here. Or... in general."

He doesn't look disappointed that I didn't say what he wanted me to say. And that's refreshing.

"I'm gonna get dressed. Can you possibly get me a coffee from Grace's room?" I ask.

"On it," he replies and kisses me again.

"Are the track suits packed here okay for breakfast? Or are we expected to be dressed up?"

"Wear whatever the fuck you want, little bunny. I'd say stay just like that if I could keep you to myself all morning, but I definitely don't want my brothers or the staff catching sight of these sexy legs."

I laugh and slide the patio door open a couple inches and call out, "Grace?"

She turns away from the railing and looks surprised.

"You gonna dress casual for breakfast?"

"I... don't usually do casual."

"There are yoga clothes in here and I don't want to wear the red ballgown, so..."

"I'll do casual for you, sis," she says, smiling.

"Do you have casual clothes here? If not, there are some new yoga pants in the drawer in there."

"I've got workout clothes here. No worries. I'll text Nay and Sabrina and tell 'em to wear the same."

Cheater

"Thanks, Grace. Mornin' Jonah."

"Mornin' Chloe," Jonah replies with a little smile.

"Get back here, wife; your bare legs are showing, and you've got no panties on."

I shiver and I swat Derek's arm with my hand passing him to go back to the dresser to grab more clothes. When I come out, Derek is coming in with a mug of coffee in his hand.

"For you," he says.

"My hero," I whisper.

He gives me a soft kiss before he hands it to me.

This all feels so strange.

"Wanna have a quick conversation with the cook if you're all right here."

"I'm good," I say.

"Be back," he advises, kissing me again.

I take a mouthful of coffee and savor it. He knows just how I like it.

I look around, taking the space in more thoroughly, able to do so now that I'm not engaged in sex (that he also knows how to do the way I like...) and now that the sun has come up.

This room doesn't have childhood or teenaged Derek memories in it. No old trophies, pictures, or anything to mark milestones. It's just his old room, all his old memories and mementoes cleared away at some stage. And I'm disappointed that it's not a shrine to a younger Derek. I'm wishing I'd gotten a better look at that photo collage yesterday before it caught fire.

I can't fathom what his childhood entailed. And to not have support through it, instead to have all the division.

These siblings weren't there for one another the way you'd think they'd be. At least some of them weren't. Thad was a pot stirrer. Seems like Derek behaved like an outsider. Naomi and Asher were close, but I don't know when that changed. And no wonder Grace ignores boundaries. She's trying to bridge gaps all the time, for people she cares about. They grew up mostly apart at different boarding schools. Eli as the first born likely has a lot on his shoulders, seems to be the first one Michael hollers at when things go wrong. I hate the idea of this. If we ever get to a point where we choose to have children, I already know that I don't want nannies to raise my kids, I don't want boarding schools to ever even enter the conversation. I want my future kids to be with me until they choose to go away to school or move off on their own.

I also don't want my kids to sit at a stuffy table in a stuffy room watching all the adults get drunk in order to tolerate being together.

It's too soon to think about kids, so I decide to push it out of my mind. Derek and I have a long way to go before I can think about that. A very long way.

∞

Derek comes to get me just before nine o'clock, a smile on his face.

"I was wondering where you got to," I say.

"I made pancakes," he says.

"Pancakes?"

"We gave the staff the morning off. Me and my brothers made breakfast. It's ready."

He leads me through a maze of hallways to a humongous kitchen that's a cross between a residential and commercial kitchen. So many counters. Walk-in fridge, freezer, and pantry. In the corner is a large butcher's block table set for everyone. Platters of pancakes, bacon, sausage, and home fries are in chafing dishes. Everyone is dressed casually, including Sabrina, who is at the table in the corner, sipping from a mug. Grace waves to me from the counter where she's grinding coffee beans.

I wave back and give Sabrina a hesitant smile. She doesn't return it, but her eyes warm slightly.

"Morning," I greet.

"Hi Chloe," she says.

Cheater

Introductions weren't necessary yesterday, so they obviously aren't now.

Carson wheels Michael in and he's frowning.

"Why here and not Shannon's morning room?"

"No ceremonial bullshit, Dad," Jonah calls over, setting cutlery at each place setting. "Just a regular family having breakfast around their kitchen table."

Michael's expression changes and his features relax a little. Maybe he's ready to listen to his children and what they want.

"Mornin', Dad," Naomi greets, hugging him.

"Hey Dad," Grace waves from the counter and continues working on making another pot of coffee.

Michael moves himself from the chair to the head of the table, a table I suspect is usually used by the staff.

"You jokers cooked all this?" he teases, looking at Ash who's taking off a white apron with pancake batter and other stains on it.

"We sure did. Staff has the morning off. Car?" Ash looks to Carson, "You've got the rest of the day off. We've got Dad. We've got everything."

Carson smiles. "Very well."

"Unless you'd like to join us?" Naomi asks. "You're a non-blood member of this family, after all."

"I'd be a real family member if Asher would let me set him up on a date with my niece," Carson quips.

Asher laughs.

"I'd love to join you all," Carson goes on, "but truthfully, I could use a few hours to run some errands."

"You don't have to work today, Car," Naomi says. "You do so much for us and the last several days have been a lot."

"The errands are personal, actually."

"Oh. Okay then. Leave it to a Steele family member to assume absolutely everything is about them, huh?" Naomi laughs at herself.

Carson opens his arms, and she steps into them. He gives her a big hug.

"That's nice. You give good hugs. Always have," she says, smiling.

"Where's Joshua, Naomi?" Michael asks.

Her smile vanishes. "He had something urgent at the hospital, so he took a late flight out."

She's upset. It's all over her face. I'm thinking either she's upset he's gone or she's fibbing about why he's gone.

"Load up your plates, family," Jonah orders, bringing a large jug of orange juice over.

Grace brings a bottle of champagne. "Mimosa anyone?"

"Mimosas for everyone and a toast to our beautiful mother," Ash announces, and Jonah and Grace take turns with the orange juice and champagne, filling all the glasses.

Once all the glasses are full, we all raise them.

"To Shannon," Michael says, "A true beauty. She loved her family. She did, more than you'll know. She carried a lot of pain. From her childhood. From her regrets. But she loved her children very much."

"We know," Elijah says, sounding a little choked.

"I loved her so much it hurt," Michael adds. "Never dimmed in forty years. Loved her so much it seems it hurt some or all of you. But... I saw so much strength in all of you that I guess I leaned on you to help me make her happy. I..." He swallows. "I never claimed to be perfect, I'll never be perfect. I have high expectations of my children. You've all been given more blessings than most and I wanted you all to work hard anyway, for you to be solid people, hard workers, to make your mother proud. I wanted to give her a beautiful life, a beautiful family, and I might have failed in some regards, but I know I gave her all of you."

"We're pretty awesome," Grace quips.

Michael smiles. "I want to do better in this next chapter of my life. Be in your lives. All of your lives. I don't want the loss of your mother to mean you don't bother. Please. Give me a chance to be in your lives." He looks directly at Derek. "I promise I'll try to be more

Cheater

open, more approachable. Is this too much to ask? Have I hurt you all too much?"

"No, it's not," Grace says. "Is it?"

"No," Asher answers.

"No," Jonah chimes in.

"No, it's not," Derek puts in.

"Love you, Dad," Naomi says, voice shaky.

"Love all of you so much," Michael replies, gruffly.

I reach under the table and squeeze Derek's thigh, then rub up and down his leg. His eyes close as a smile spreads across his face. He puts his hand on top of mine.

"We're a family. We'll continue to be a family," Naomi says.

Elijah speaks up. "Let's eat, family. This looks amazing and I'm famished."

Everyone sips their mimosas.

Me and Sabrina exchange looks, and she unfolds her napkin and spreads it across her lap. "I'd love some scrambled eggs," she says.

"Pass me some pancakes, please," I speak up.

"Blueberry or chocolate chip?" Derek asks.

"Yes please," I nod.

He laughs. So do a few others.

Derek forks up a stack of two of each type of pancake and drops them on my plate with a flourish. They're huge. No way can I eat them.

"I don't think I can eat four," I tell him. "Take two for your plate."

"Of course you can," he counters. And then he drinks my mimosa. The whole thing.

I gawk at him. "Hey!"

He laughs and pours me a fresh orange juice.

"You forgot something," I say as there's no room for champagne. I reach for the bottle.

Derek pushes it out of my reach.

"I'm sure you don't need a boozy breakfast, do you, wife?" he states.

"Trying to tell us something?" Ash teases. "Food for two and whisking away her alcohol?"

Derek laughs and wiggles his eyebrows.

I roll my eyes. "No, he's not trying to tell anyone anything. Don't be silly, Derek." I laugh. "Pass me the butter and syrup."

"Gladly," he says, a big smile on his face.

Everyone is staring.

"Are Derek and Chloe going to be the first to give me a grandchild?" Michael asks, lightness in his voice. "I thought it'd be Eli and Sabrina. Then I thought maybe Nay and Joshua. But the newlyweds might beat you all. How about you all race and see who can give me the most grandchildren?" He smiles as Naomi fills his plate for him.

"I'm not ready for kids," Nay says. "Sorry to burst your bubble, Dad."

"Don't look at me," Sabrina grumbles and takes a big sip of her mimosa.

Eli doesn't look happy. Things are still tense with them.

"Guess it's down to us, little bunny," Derek says and drops far too many slices of bacon onto my plate.

I roll my eyes and decide to ignore the comment.

Breakfast is mostly jovial, somewhat playful, except that Elijah and Sabrina are quiet and I can't help but notice how he keeps looking at her. He looks at her with an intensity that's not unlike what I've seen from Derek, pointed at me.

Michael comments that Derek's pancakes are almost as good as his. From that conversation it's obvious that this is why Derek makes pancakes sometimes. His father did it a few times when they were kids at their family vacation house in New Hampshire.

Naomi and Asher don't interact, but there's also no apparent awkwardness that I can read.

Derek is all about public displays of affection, making sure I have plenty to eat, and even participates in a few conversations with his siblings. Grace seems like she's in her glory, like she's gotten the family she's been waiting forever for.

Cheater

I catch Michael staring at me.

I smile.

He gives me a sad smile and then seems to shake off his dark thoughts.

As the meal winds down and people stop eating, Grace pipes up. "We should do Christmas at the New Hampshire homestead!"

"I like that idea," Michael says.

"I'll decorate, arrange Christmas dinner. Maybe with some help from my sister and sisters-in-law?"

Sabrina puts her napkin down. "Excuse me, please." She leaves the table and walks out.

Tension crackles in the air as Elijah watches her leave, frustration etched into his features.

"She'll come around. You'll work at it, right?" Derek claps his brother's shoulder.

"Yeah," Elijah mutters and then looks at his father. "If everyone's done, can we meet now and strategize on our security issues?"

Michael puts his napkin down. "Good idea. Thank you, to all of you for being here. I appreciate it. I have something to say before we split up here."

"Should I go?" I ask.

"No, Chloe. You're part of this family. Seems like you're settling in?"

"I..." I'm not sure how to finish the sentence.

Derek puts his arm around me. "Seems like she's giving me a shot. I'm not gonna blow it."

"Good," Michael says. "That's really good." He clears his throat and takes a moment before he speaks, looking like he might be fighting emotion. Everyone waits.

"I... just want to tell you all that... that I appreciate you being here. It's not going to be easy adjusting to life without your mother. She was the light of my life. Truly. But at the same time..." He swallows hard. "I don't want you to take this the wrong way because... you all know how much I adored her."

"We do," Grace asserts firmly.

"I'll never forgive myself for allowing that to happen. For assuming it was safe to take her on an impromptu trip to a play she wanted to see. She found out about it last minute, it was an old modeling protegee's opening night on Broadway, and when we found the jet was free, she... we... we just lived in the moment. We don't know how those enemies pulled it all off, don't have all the details yet, but I don't want any of you to make that same mistake of assuming you're safe. Please be cautious. Vigilant. Very. I also want to say..." He swallows. "I want to take some time off. Recover from my injuries. Golf. Go fishing. When we've gotten justice, of course, but I still have a lot of life left in me, I think, and... while I loved looking after your mother, love my work, it took a lot. A lot. Running the companies, being a husband. I could use some help with the company so I can have a chance to..." He lets that hang, looking for the right words.

"Worry about just yourself for a while?" Naomi offers. "It makes sense, Dad. Don't feel bad about it. She was very high maintenance. We would all want her back in a heartbeat... but... I understand how you might want to take some time for yourself for a change. Take a breath. It must have been exhausting."

"You don't think that's selfish?"

Grace answers, "You can be a little selfish if you want, Dad. You just had a very real brush with death. It makes sense that you're reassessing your priorities."

Ash adds, "You've spent your whole life building your empire, providing for your family. Taking care of your wife. You only live once."

It's like Derek's father is a different person. I'm sure his wife's death and his own injuries fundamentally changed him, but this seems like a different man. More humble. More open. Warmer. I really hope it's a turning point for this family.

Cheater

"Don't take this the wrong way, but... did losing his wife help him put his own life, his priorities into perspective?" I ask.

"Good possibility," Derek says, turning off onto our street.

"Can you two repair your relationship?" I ask.

"I don't know. We haven't ever had a real relationship from my perspective. He was a workaholic and a Shannon-oholic. End of."

"I hope you can."

"I have all I need right here with me right now," Derek says.

Heat creeps up my cheeks.

He kisses my hand and holds onto it between us.

I spent almost an hour in the kitchen with Grace and Naomi, while the Steele men had their meeting. We cleaned up after breakfast and while the Steele men cooked a great meal they totally destroyed the kitchen in the process.

Derek told me he'll be stepping up with helping with his father's company. He said his clubs are running well with the current management and he doesn't mind stepping up for a few months, helping to recruit some additional C-level team members to help lighten his dad's load. Asher, who previously vowed to never work for the family business, is planning to step up as well.

Derek told me Grace is moving home with her father for a while to help run the household and take on her mother's charitable work. Derek feels comfortable with the safety of where we live, but tells me he's hiring extra security short-term while things get sorted with Elijah's enemy and wants me to use personal security when I leave the house, until all this is over with.

I tried to ask questions, but he asked me to trust him, to not worry about any of that.

∞

He scoops me up into his arms as we approach the front door of the house.

I laugh.

"Feels like a new beginning for us. Wanted to do this again. Crazy?"

"Batshit crazy," I quip.

He laughs, pushes in the door code and crosses the threshold.

And I stare straight ahead. At my dream house. That Derek bought for me.

Tears spring up in my eyes.

"Bunny?" he asks.

I try to blink them away. But he's seen them.

"It's been a whirlwind. A whirlwind and a half. I think I'm just feeling it."

He nods, seeming to understand, and carries me upstairs.

"Why are we going upstairs?" I ask.

"Why do you think?" he returns.

I giggle as I'm dropped on the bed. He pounces.

And he doesn't fuck me. He makes love to me. Slow, unhurried, passionately. I cry when I come and he holds me tight, whispering that he loves me.

∞

I'm cooking when Derek comes into the kitchen. His eyes light up.

"What is this delicious scent I'm smelling, wife?"

"Mongolian beef," I reply.

He kisses me and looks into the pan. "What's the occasion?" he asks with a big smile.

"Uh... dinner?"

"Dinner is the occasion?" he asks.

"We need to eat."

He wraps both arms around me and backs me up against the counter and tugs on my ponytail.

"Thank you for making dinner for us, Chloe. I can't wait to eat it."

Cheater

I feel like I'm beaming. And I feel a little silly for it, but the praise feels nice.

"How about if you set the table?" I suggest.

"You've got it, baby. My sister gave me a hard time for not hiring staff. I wanted to leave it up to you. If you want to hire someone to cook and clean, if you want to use my sister's chef friend for our meals, whatever you want, okay?"

"Okay."

"I love this, you cooking for me, but don't want you to feel like you have to do it just because you're a female."

"I don't know when I might go back to work, I might like to take another few weeks off," I say.

"Whatever you want," he says, and it seems like he means it.

"I can handle some domestic things for now. When I decide, maybe we can have someone come in once a week for the deeper cleaning. But day to day, we're both pretty tidy and I like to clean. I find it relaxing."

He smiles. "Your decision. I don't want live-in staff. Unless you decide differently when the baby comes, and you need help for that... you know. I mean, I'll help as much as I can of course."

I roll my eyes. "You're really fixated on this today, aren't you?"

He moistens his lips and looks like he's weighing what he wants to say.

"I do eventually want kids, Derek, but let's not jump the gun. I'm on the pill and-"

He squints a little.

"I don't want to burst your bubble here," I continue, "but let's table it for at least a year."

"Why?" he asks.

"We're very... new."

"You don't know if you're fully in this?" he asks.

I feel uncomfortable. "Derek, a whole lot has happened. How about if we just take one day at a time? If this were a traditional relationship, a year would probably pass before the conversation came up. You know?"

I can't decipher his expression. He sets the dinner table.

∞

"This is delicious," he says for the third time.

"Thank you." I reach to grab the wine bottle and top my glass off. "There's more. You look like you're ready for a second helping. Want me to grab it?"

"No, I'll do it," Derek says, giving me a strange look. He fishes his phone out of his pocket and does something on it, looking concerned as his eyes scan the screen.

"Everything okay?" I ask.

He looks conflicted.

"Something wrong?" I ask.

He blows out a breath slowly. His face is full of uncertainty.

"Is this about the baby stuff? If you're looking for a declaration, if you're asking me about the future, you have to be patient with me, please."

"I've got all the patience in the world for you, wife," he says, smiling, but it's not touching his eyes. Derek's smiles always touch his eyes.

"Hey," I reach for his hand and squeeze. "Think about where we were just twenty-four hours ago. Relax, okay?" I'm not trying to sound condescending, but something is clearly on his mind. "Or is this about the security concerns. Have you found out more information?"

He shakes his head.

I lift my glass of wine and take a sip.

And the look on his face has me even more on edge.

"I'm here. I'm trying to navigate the strange waters of not just being married to a man who forced me to marry him, of being here through your grief after a whole lot of things including the loss of

Cheater

your mother and the danger around us with what happened at the cemetery yesterday and now feeling like this might be a reality, this marriage, a real one, because you've made me want to explore this with you. You turned things around in a big way, and that's something good, right?"

"Right."

"Can we take things one day at a time? Things don't have to move at the speed of light, do they? Is this about the baby stuff you've been like a dog with a bone about?"

"Okay, here goes. I told you I'd always be honest with you, right?"

"Right..."

"Well, honestly I'm here fretting about you drinking wine, trying to decide how to tell you what I did with your birth control pills, looking up alcohol consumption in early pregnancy because I don't want you upset with me, but also don't want to put our baby at risk because of me not saying anything, so there. That's why I'm fixated."

"My birth control pills?"

"I swapped them. Had my pharmacist switch them out with packs of sugar pills."

I'm like a jack-in-the-box, popping up to my feet abruptly. My stemmed glass beside my plate topples, making the rice, beef and vegetables swim in red wine.

I try to blink away the haze of shock as I process what he's just said to me. Sugar pills. Sugar pills?

"When?"

"Just the other week."

I turn away and storm to the kitchen where I know my purse is on the counter. I rifle through it to find the blister pack, doing the math in my head. I think I only started this package just over a week ago, but I'm having trouble thinking straight. I'm shaking, on the verge of what... crying, shouting? I don't even know.

"Chloe?" He's behind me, hand landing on the back of my neck, squeezing with affection.

I whirl around and glare at him. I'm so angry I'm shaking, I don't even know how to form words right now. He's staring at me with wide eyes, worried eyes. Like he's realizing the ramifications of me finding out he did this.

"You...you..." I pull the package out of my bag and look. Eight pills in. I'm eight days into the package. This means I could be ovulating right now. We've had so much sex in the past twenty-four hours. So much sex. "Omigod." I cover my mouth, the pills falling to the floor.

Derek's eyes are wider. "Chloe," he whispers, and drags his hand through his hair, looking flustered.

"You did that to me?" I ask, my voice coming out hoarse.

He flinches hard. "Please, let's sit. Talk through this. I'll explain."

I back away.

He lunges and grabs me, clutching me tight to him, his mouth to my ear. "I love you. I love you so, so much. I want a family with you. I want you tied to me for the rest of your life and want you to love me. I wanted to give you a baby. I want you to give me a family. The kind of family I know we can make. A beautiful family."

"Derek..." Tears stream down my cheeks.

He loosens his grip just enough to look at my face, to assess it.

"I love you," he repeats, swiping tears away with his thumbs.

I'm shaking my head, bawling, crushed.

"Talk to me, baby," he requests.

"You fucked up, Derek. You really fucked up here."

He swallows.

"Do you have any idea how big of a breach of trust this is? All the things you've done to me, all the choices you took away, all the heinous things..."

He flinches again.

"Now you've gone and done this? Fucked with my choices like this? This is betrayal."

"No," he says gruffly and points at me. "I love you. I want to spend the rest of my life with you. You use a word like heinous when describing having a family with me? No."

Cheater

"Heinous," I repeat. "Yes, *this* is heinous. You knew what you were doing last night, didn't you? You were determined to fuck me last night hoping I'd get pregnant because I'm a week into fake pills which is perfect timing and... and... what? Knocking me up would magically make me agree to be your wife?"

"You *are* my wife."

"Until yesterday afternoon, that was in name only. It was blackmail, plain and simple. I was married to you only because I was terrified of what you'd do, what you threatened to do."

"Baby..."

"You fucked up, Derek. You can't sweet-talk me into being okay with this. You can't fuck me into submission here. You switched my birth control pills!" I can't even fathom this. "You manipulative asshole." I shove him. He doesn't budge. "How can you think I'd be okay with this? How can you think I would ever get past this sort of deceit?"

"You're angry with me, but baby, I'll take care of you. I'll be a good father. We might have made a person sometime within the last day and that beautiful little person is me and you and-"

"And maybe genetically predisposed to being a fucking psychopath!"

He jerks back like I've struck him across the face.

"How dare you? I can't believe I let myself believe for even five minutes that giving in to you wasn't insane." I back away. "I can't believe you. There's zero hope for us." I dash tears off my face with my sleeves. "Zero. I'm done, Derek. I'm so, so fucking done." I pull the rings off my fingers and throw them at him. They bounce off him and fall to the floor.

He squats to pick them up and I grab my purse, find my phone on the other counter, and storm away. I look over my shoulder and he's leaned against the wall, slowly sliding down, face full of remorse.

I walk out, not even shutting the door behind myself.

My phone is ringing, Derek is calling and I'm ignoring it. I'm pulling out of the Walgreens. I know Ken is following. I also know Ken saw what I bought because he followed me into the drug store.

I told him to go away, and he said, "You know there are security concerns. Can you please drive home? I'll follow you back. Not comfortable out here with everything that happened at the funeral, Mrs. Steele."

Where am I going? Where the fuck do I go?

I can't believe I thought this might actually work. That I had any power here. A marriage with a crazy, unhinged psychopath.

As soon as my phone stops ringing, it starts up again.

61

Derek

"Sorry to tell you this, boss, but she bought a box of Plan B and a sports drink."

My chest hurts.

"Did you stop her?"

"How?" Ken asks.

"You didn't fucking stop her? Did she take it?"

"You said follow her, keep her safe. I've followed her. You didn't say stop her."

"Did she take it?"

"I don't know, Derek."

I'm pacing. Bile keeps hitting my back teeth. I'm out of my fucking mind with a storm of emotions that feel like they're burning a hole in my gut. I've called her phone over and over. She won't answer.

Plan B and a sports drink. She's going to take it and erase the possibility of the link that's probably forming right now between us. And she's not going to forgive me. I saw it in her eyes. I saw something I'll never forget. I had it for a day. I fucked it up. If I'd waited, it would've happened naturally. She was falling for me. She started to believe. And I fucked it up.

"Derek?" Ken checks.

"I don't give a fuck how. Just get her here. Now!"

I get a text ten long minutes later.

Kenny: ETA, 5

I breathe out relief. He has her. He has her. Maybe she didn't take it. Maybe she didn't. Maybe I can fix this. Maybe I can...I can't fix this. I saw it in her eyes. The utter pain and betrayal. I had it for a day and it's gone. It's gone. I burnt it to ash.

My hands are shaking. Bile rises again, this time with an even more rancid taste. My stomach contracts hard and I hurl into the sink, losing the dinner she cooked for me. I hold onto the counter, white knuckled, staring at her rings that I put there, feeling in my gut like I've lost everything that matters.

The doorbell rings.

I open the door to Ken holding Chloe's arm. Her face is red and she's looking at me with hatred.

"Get your fucking hands off her!" I snap.

He jerks back in surprise. "You said get her here. It required some force."

He's got scratches on his face.

"Did you fuckin' hurt her?" I shout. "I'll fucking kill you." I grab his throat and back him up.

"No man, she just struggled. I just subdued her and got her here."

"You put her in danger?"

"Derek. Fuckin' relax."

I growl in his face and release him.

"Where's her car?" I demand.

"It's on the highway. I remote disabled it. Chuck is bringing it."

I growl.

"I did it safely, Derek. Chill out! It'll be here in a while."

"How'd you get her here?"

"I had to pull my weapon to get her out of the car. She didn't

Cheater

believe, so I fired a shot into the ground. Then she tried to run for it so caught her in the ditch and carried her to my car. Threatened with the gun again… just to get her to cooperate."

"You did not pull a fucking gun on my wife."

"You told me to do what I had to do, Derek."

I hear her mutter something under her breath. She's scowling at us both from the foyer.

I move in her direction but before I get all the way there, she slams the door in my face and locks it.

"Did she take it?" I ask.

"I don't know," he says.

"Fuck!" I shout.

I key in my entry code and find her upstairs in the master bedroom, a mess of clothes thrown on the bed. She's stuffing things into a suitcase.

"Chloe…"

"No!" she shouts, pointing at me. "Fuck you. Fuck off. Fuck you, Derek Steele. Fuck off! A fuckin' gun pointed at me again, one of your goddamn goons abducting me?"

"Did you take it, baby? Please tell me you didn't take it." I drop to my knees in front of her and grab her hands. She tries to pull away. I hold tight. "Did you?"

She's bawling.

"You didn't. Please tell me you didn't take it."

"Go to hell," is how my beautiful wife replies. And she says it without venom, she says it in a voice that echoes through my raw gut, making it feel even worse.

I can't hack this. I can't.

62
Chloe

"I didn't mean to fuck it up." He looks up at me pleading with his eyes, hands holding mine way too tight while on his knees. "Please, baby. Forgive me."

"Fuck you, Derek," I repeat with difficulty.

"I'll do whatever I have to do to show you that I won't fuck this up. If you took it, we'll try when you're ready. When you tell me you're ready, only then." He holds on tighter.

"You fucked it up already," I say, chin trembling. "You fucked it so hard, it can't be fixed."

"I'll fix it."

"You can't fix it!" I shout.

"I will!" he shouts back, entire body trembling, the pain stark and raw on his face.

He really looks remorseful for once. And I don't fucking care.

"You deceived me from day one, you blackmailed me, stalked me, you hurt Adam's family, you threatened Alannah, I've had guns pointed at me more than once, had guns pointed at people I care about. You threatened to have Craig and Adam shot, to have Craig forced to be a dirty cop. You've made my promises mean nothing because you forced me to say things to you that I only intended to say once, that I swore I would only say once, and now you've taken my choices about my own body, about the rest of my future away? No. No way is any of this ever going to be okay."

He gets to his feet. "I'll fix it, Chloe."
I scoff.
He lifts me up into his arms.
"Put me down!" I push at his chest and struggle.
"No. I'm gonna fix this."
"No, Derek, put me down!"
"I'm gonna fucking fix it!" he shouts, hollering it in my face with such fury on his face that I'm immediately terrified, wishing I could turtle into myself.

He lays me on the bed and is about to speak when his phone chimes from his pocket. He pulls it out and rushes out of the room.

Hearing him run down the stairs, I decide to follow. He's outside, walking toward Ken who is with another guy. My Cherokee is parked out front.

I gasp as Derek punches Ken in the mouth. They shout in one another's faces for a moment and then Ken and the other guy leave in Ken's blue SUV.

Derek gets into my Cherokee, leaving the driver's door open. He's bent over on the seat, looking around.

He turns, sees me and makes his way to me with the half-drank bottle of Gatorade in his hand. My handbag.

He storms past me, shooting me a look of murder. He dumps my purse upside down on the kitchen island. "Where is it? I need to know if you took it."

I say nothing.

He drops the Gatorade and now has the Plan B box in his hand.

He shakes the empty box and then drops it, staring at me with his mouth open.

I choke on a sob.

"No, no, no, no..." He falls to his knees and thrusts his hands into his hair, staring at me in disbelief. "I just want to fucking make you happy!" He shouts. "Give you a family. Give you everything you want. Why is that so fucking bad? I've never wanted to give these things to anyone and I'm trying so fucking hard, Chloe, and nothing I

Cheater

do is enough for you. Or it's too much. I can't fucking take it! I can't win with you, can I?" He grips his hair on both sides of his head. His face is beet-red. "What can I do to fix it? Tell me!"

"You need to fix yourself!" I choke out. "Please, please, please, just leave me alone. Just let me go. You have to stop this. Let it go, Derek, or it'll end in death."

"In about sixty years, yeah, Chloe. It'll end in death then."

"No. Not sixty years. Probably soon. Everything is falling apart. Everything. You're not right up here." I point to my temple. "And I don't trust you won't lose it and snap my neck or something."

"I know down to my bones it's you and me. It's possible. You know it. I fucked up before you gave me this chance and you just gotta please, please give me the chance you agreed to give me. I switched the pills out weeks ago, knowing you'd start a new pack soon. If you'd given me a chance sooner I wouldn't have resorted to that and–"

"Oh, it's my fault you deceived me?"

"No, baby. No."

"This is going to end badly. So badly, Derek."

"No. It's not," he says, shaking his head, raking his hands through his hair.

"Please let me go. Please let me leave. Please just... please let me go."

I sit on the couch and curl tight into a ball.

"Please let me go," I repeat. "I want my life back."

He sits beside me and tries to pry me out of the ball I'm in. I hold on tight.

"How do I fix myself, Chloe? Tell me what to do and I'll do it. Just don't tell me to let you go because I can't. I won't."

"It's gonna end with one of us dead, because either you're gonna snap and kill me or you're gonna go postal and wind up shot by a fucking SWAT team. I know it down to *my* bones. Ken said you told him to do whatever he had to do to bring me here? He pointed a gun at me, Derek. He fired a shot and scared the shit out of me and then dragged me kicking and screaming back to you. And you're scaring me now. I'm fucking terrified of you. Terrified one or both of us is going to wind up dead because you're so unhinged, so out of touch with reality. You want me to bring a baby into this? An innocent life coming into this? I know you're crazy but seriously?"

He stills.

I sniffle and after a few long minutes, I uncurl from the ball I'm in, roll over and get a Kleenex and blow my nose.

"Please let me go," I plead.

He says nothing for a minute, just stares into space.

"Please," I whisper. "If you really do love me, realize what you're doing here. Please, Derek."

"It's not too late to fix this. I love you."

"You don't. You don't act like this when you love somebody, Derek."

"I'll prove it. Watch me."

I roll my eyes. "Too late."

He pulls his phone out of his pocket.

I blow my nose again and get up to go to the bathroom. As I'm closing the door, I hear him on the phone.

"Carson?" he says, "I want to check myself in for a psychiatric hold somewhere. Can you help me?"

I put my back to the door and slide down to the floor, feeling relief, feeling like my heart is going to pound its way out of my chest.

I shakily reach into my bra and pull out the sealed small pill packet that I pulled from the Plan B box before Ken got to my car. I stare at it. I stare at it for a long time.

I've been on the pill for years. I might not have even ovulated yet after just a week into a new cycle without the hormones. I might not have.

But I might have.

Cheater

I hear nothing outside the powder room door for a long time. Finally, I come out. I look out the front door and see a silver Audi hatchback idling. Derek is in the passenger seat, sitting in a pose of defeat.

There's a knock on the door.

I stiffen.

It opens.

"Mrs. Steele?" I hear.

I see Carson in the doorway.

"Yes?" I rasp.

"I'm taking Derek to the hospital. If you need anything at all, please call me. I'll update you once he's admitted."

I swallow hard and frown at my feet.

"Okay?" he prompts.

"Okay," I barely whisper.

The door clicks shut.

∞

Two Hours Later

I pull the drain plug and get out of the bubbled water. I put on the fluffy robe Derek bought me and go downstairs to the counter and find my phone in the spilled contents of my purse.

Alannah should have gotten back from her work trip last night.

I send a group text message to Alannah, Coraline, and Maddie.

I really REALLY need you guys.

I tap out the address.

In forty-five minutes, Alannah is over with her flotsam and jetsam kit. Half an hour after that, Cor and Maddie arrive, too.

Ken's SUV is parked inside the gates. He doesn't stop them from coming in.

63
Chloe

Two Months and Two Days Later

I park my Cherokee and walk up to the entrance with the intercom. Before I press the buzzer, curiosity gets the better of me, so I change my mind, go to the other door, and press my thumb against the reader. It clicks unlocked.

I guess if it didn't, I would have my answer about whether or not my access has been disabled.

I got a text message the day before yesterday from Grace, asking me if I knew Derek had been discharged. I didn't.

I laid awake all night expecting him to show up.

He didn't.

I thought maybe he'd show up or call last night. He didn't. His SUV is still parked in the garage where he left it. I don't know if he has other vehicles or if any of his other siblings are currently staying here, but five of the eight parking spaces in front of the building where Grace and Derek would typically park are full. But she said she's still staying with her father so I'm not sure if one of them is her car or not.

I haven't talked to him in two months and two days. Not a word has been exchanged between us, verbally or in written form.

I've stayed in the house. I've been keeping busy. I've been back to work for almost six weeks. I felt a little claustrophobic so I rented a little office in Columbus because I felt like I needed to snap my brain out of a funk and thought it might be good for the company to have a physical location. And I needed to get out of that house. Away from the ghost of my so-called marriage.

So, I hired two local people and brought in the rest of the team for a team meeting two weeks ago. The company name has been changed to Amplified Marketing and Frank and I run it together. I've made him a partner.

Getting into a routine has helped, but I've still spent a whole lot of time pondering my situation. Thankfully, I've been busy, I've had people I care about around me, and I've been working on healing. From a lot of things. I've been in weekly counseling appointments and I'm sure that helped me face Adam last week without getting angry.

I was out with Coraline and Alannah. He was about to be seated at a table next to us. He was with an attractive woman. He looked at me with panic and requested to be moved.

It didn't even ruin my evening.

I've spent countless hours considering all that's happened. With Adam and me. With Derek and me. With Derek and everyone.

I saw Carson again the night he took Derek to the hospital. He came by while I was with my friends and packed a bag for Derek, telling me that Derek wanted him to tell me to please stay in our house, ensuring I'm safe. Please use my bank cards linked to his accounts for anything I need, and he wanted me to know the household bills are being taken care of by his accountant. Carson told me to let him know if there's anything I need. To please continue to be vigilant about my safety and let Kenny continue to watch over me.

I told Carson I wanted someone else to watch over me. Having "Kenny" point a gun at me more than once, having him carry me kicking and screaming to Derek? I wasn't in the mood to set eyes on him again. Carson didn't ask why I didn't want it to be Ken, just said

Cheater

he'd take care of it. Security for the house and for me is now generally handled on rotation between two guys, Chuck (during the day) and Fen (in the evening). I occasionally see Ken's blue SUV out there at night, so he's obviously still involved, but he hasn't bothered me.

I was paid a surprise visit by Derek's father and Grace about a week after Derek left. We had coffee. Michael tried to get a beat on where I'm at. I didn't give him much. He reminded me that Steeles don't divorce. I told him I knew that. I told him Derek needed help, that I hoped he would get well. I reminded him that I made this clear the first time I met them.

Michael reminded me that it's important that I not speak to the press. Grace got annoyed with him and defended me, telling him I'd never do something like that. He looked me over with scrutiny and, if I'm not mistaken, a little bit of a threatening manner, but let it drop.

A few weeks later, Michael phoned me and told me that the security issues for the family have been dealt with.

"Do I want to know what that means?" I asked.

"You don't," he replied. "Just know that the people who attacked us are no longer threats. That doesn't mean there are no threats, just not those ones."

"How reassuring," I muttered sarcastically.

He went on, "My son might not be prepared to cancel your security until he's back in his regular life, but I want you to feel more at ease about your safety."

"I appreciate that," I said. "And how are you doing?"

He was silent for a moment, then replied. "I'm getting there, Chloe. I've had two joint counseling sessions with Derek and his counselor. I think they helped. Helped us both. We have another one next week."

"Oh," I said, "That's good."

He held the phone. I think he hoped I'd ask questions about that. Or give him clues about what I thought about Derek at this point. When I didn't say anything, he said, "Thank you for asking."

"Take care of yourself, Michael," I replied.

DD Prince

He hesitantly said goodbye. But I suspected he wanted to ask me about my relationship with his son.

After that call, I scanned the papers for any news in New York, for any follow-up about Shannon's funeral, but nothing. Then again, I already knew the Steele family had a way of sweeping things under the rug.

I've been to my parents' place twice.

And both visits were quite therapeutic. The first one was the three of us for an overnight visit. We went to dinner and a movie.

I had to explain why I had a security detail. I told them there were still unresolved issues related to Derek's mother's death.

Mom and I did some antique store hopping the next day and had so much fun that she invited me for another weekend to go to an antique and craft show with her while Dad was away at a dental convention.

I fibbed, saying Derek was away for work both times. I don't feel good about fibbing, but was not remotely prepared to share the details of my Derek saga with them.

On my last visit, she insisted that she and Dad soon come spend the weekend at our house with me and Derek. She said she wants to give us the family collection of board games, for us to play some together.

I got weepy. So did she. We hugged it out and we talked about Bryan.

She opened up a bit, too, telling me that she felt like there was a distance between us for the past decade or so, that she felt like I didn't want much to do with them, like I had moved on with my life and left them behind. She didn't do it with accusation, she chalked a lot up to grieving after Bryan, saying she knows she wasn't very present for my last few years before going away for college.

I assured her I want her and Dad in my life, that I'm thrilled to be spending time with them. I also told her that Derek ran an investigation and found information on my birth parents. Mom looked hurt and upset about that. I told her I had no desire to open the file and

Cheater

read it. She told me that she sent my birth mother annual birthday pictures for four years and that the last year she did that, the letter was returned to her as my birth mother had moved and not given a forwarding address. Mom and Dad remained at my childhood home all this time and had never heard from her. She obviously moved on with her life.

In a roundabout way, it kind of feels like Derek gave me my family back. There was some sort of turning point when he took me there to talk about us getting married that made my mom decide to put in some effort. And I'm so glad she did.

Grace has invited me to lunch twice, the second time with her and Naomi. I made excuses both times. She told me they think I'm a miracle worker and wanted to know how I did it, how I convinced Derek to agree to get help.

My response was that I would be happy to stay in contact if she didn't ask me about Derek. She asked if I wanted an update about him. I declined. She gave me one anyway, saying he was in a rigorous program and that she'd visited him at the thirty-day mark. I didn't ask how he was. She told me he was doing well anyway.

Alannah has been here for me, as always. We do dinner together at least twice a week. I've told her everything. She has strong opinions on the Derek matter, and though she mostly keeps them to herself she made a point of saying that although she plans to hold a grudge, she would not hold it against me if I gave him a chance, since he went to the trouble of getting help and the fact that he's left me alone for all this time might mean he's taking his treatment seriously. The way she laid it out, I know she thinks I should give him a chance.

She told me she'd hold her grudge silently if I do. So long as she sees that I'm happy. If not, there's no chance she'll be silent.

Maybe he's well enough to realize how utterly over-the-top and unhinged he was. Maybe reason and logic have returned. I guess I'm about to find out. The elevator stops on the top floor and my thumbprint still unlocks the apartment door.

I knock anyway. And wait, holding the legal-sized envelope I plan to hand him.

I give it about two minutes before I open the door and peek in.

I don't see anyone, but it's clear someone's here. There's a pair of black high heels in front of me, one standing up, the other on its side. There's a pink scarf on the console table. Some keys. A Louis Vuitton clutch. Straight ahead, I see a Christmas tree by the wall of windows. Christmas is next week. It's about half-decorated. There are open ornament boxes on the floor. It smells like pine and like sugar cookies.

I startle in surprise and back away when I hear, "Who's there?" from a female voice.

Stunned, I back out and rush to the elevator, which is mercifully still on this floor, stab the button about twenty times, willing the door to hurry up and close before whoever *she* is comes down the hall. Or... before *he* does.

Thankfully, the door shuts before I have to face anyone and I exhale hard, heart pounding hard as the elevator descends to the main floor.

I book it out of there, pulling out and seeing – I think – Ash pulling in.

∞

I drop the envelope on the kitchen counter and down a half a bottle of cold water from the fridge. I stare into space after this for a good two minutes before I spontaneously burst into tears.

64 ♥ Derek

Stepping into the coffee shop, I immediately catch her scent. Daisy by Marc Jacobs. She wore it the night we met. I smelled it in the bedroom in that rowhouse when I visited her there that night while Hallman was gone. She's got her back to me. She's reading a book. She has soup in front of her. A bag that probably contains a chocolate éclair. Her briefcase is on the floor. She's in a business suit.

I wave at Mr. Nguyen and move to her table in the corner. She looks up from her book and startles.

"Chloe," I greet.

Her eyes bounce from the page to my face.

"You were looking for me yesterday?" I ask.

65

Chloe

My face is hot; I'm sure it's red.

He looks good. Really good. He's wearing a winter coat. Gloves. His hair is a little longer, in his eyes a little. He's clean shaven. In jeans and boots.

But the eyes are different.

Maybe because he's not looking at me the way he usually does.

"I... yes. I... have something for you. I have it with me." I fumble through my leather bag on the floor and find what I'm looking for, though I'm not sure here out in public is the place I want to be doing this.

His expression goes hard. Or I should say *harder*.

He takes a step back before I even have it out of the bag fully. He glares at it with an expression so insidious I'm surprised it doesn't burst into flames in my hand.

He turns around and walks out without looking back.

I look at the envelope in my hand and realize what he thinks it is. And of course he doesn't want it if he thinks it's divorce papers. Steeles aren't allowed to divorce. No, he's not allowed to divorce me but there are no rules against him having a woman in his condo with her stilettos off, are there?

Sour-faced, I stuff the envelope back into my bag, put the lid on my soup, sop up a few droplets of mess with my napkin, gather my things, and put my coat on.

I jolt awake in the pitch dark. I touch my phone screen on my bedside table. It's three o'clock in the morning.

A shadow moves in front of me, and I gasp and lunge for my phone.

I touch 9, 1, and am about to hit 1 again when light floods the space and temporarily blinds me.

It's Derek.

My heart trips over itself.

"You scared me," I breathe.

His mouth is tight. His eyes are cold. And not pointed at my face. He's looking past me.

"I saw you come out of the bakery down the street from Downtown. Who did you have lunch with that day?"

I frown. "The other day? Carlos. He works for me. I lease an office space in your father's office building above Downtown."

Carson organized that for me.

Derek's expression doesn't change.

I ask, "Who was in your apartment with you yesterday? Someone you're putting a Christmas tree up with?" My voice wobbles, betraying my emotions about this fact, damn it.

His eyes narrow, but still point at the wall. "I'm not staying in the apartment. That was Paulina. The chef. She's renting it while her house is being renovated."

"Oh. Where are you staying?" I ask shakily.

"I've been at the homestead."

"Oh," I say.

"You're not getting a divorce," he informs.

"Did I miss the part where I asked for one?" I ask.

"Chuck's log says you were in a lawyer's office last week for two hours," he accuses.

"Chuck's log?"

"I never got the chance to ask Kenny to stop having logs made."

Cheater

"And of course you read them anyway."

He doesn't respond.

"That was a corporate lawyer, not a divorce lawyer. I was making Frank a partner."

"I bought that company for you," he says with accusation.

"He's got a lot of experience and connections in the industry. He's got a lot of great ideas, too. Besides... I need the help."

He says nothing.

He made the company completely mine. And when I started working there again, the fact that he put it in the name Chloe Steele is how I found out he had my name legally changed, too. It's how I have to sign things, which I found extremely annoying as I got used to it.

"It's three in the morning, Derek. You left the hospital three days ago. So, why are you here now?"

His eyes move to me, and he stares at me for a long, uncomfortable moment. But he doesn't say anything, and my bladder is nagging at me, so I get out of bed, pull my robe on, and go to the bathroom.

When I come out, he's still standing in the same spot. He's staring at the bed.

I walk out, go down the hall to my office and grab the envelope from my briefcase.

His eyes are on what's in my hand when I get back. And they're like dark glaciers. Colder than I've even seen on his father or his brother Elijah. I feel the chill straight through to my marrow.

"Don't you wanna know what this is?" I ask.

"Do I?" he fires back.

I shrug. "Okay, forget it." I toss the envelope to the table.

He stares me down with the stone-cold expression.

"Is there something else?" I ask.

He doesn't answer.

"It's three in the morning. I'd like to try to get some more sleep, so if you just came here to mean-mug me, mission accomplished."

"Mean mug you?"

"Stare meanly. Intimidatingly."

He turns away and leaves.

I don't know what the hell that was, but I lie in bed pondering it, pondering him, until the sun is up, and I decide that although it's the weekend, I'd might as well get up and make myself useful. More useful than staring into the void pondering the facts, especially the obvious one – Derek went into the hospital vowing he loves me, but came out looking like he now despises me.

∞

When I get to the kitchen, I startle. Derek is drinking milk from the carton. He's in a pair of track pants, a white T-shirt. Bare feet.

And there, on his left hand, is his wedding ring.

He's still wearing it.

My heart skips a beat at the sight of it.

"I didn't know you were still here," I say.

"I live here," he mutters, not looking at me, tossing the empty milk carton into the trash.

I frown as he walks away. "You drank all the milk?"

"I needed to wash down my meds," he mutters without turning around.

∞

I don't know where he's been all day, don't know where he slept last night, but by eight o'clock, I'm dead on my feet from not having slept much the night before. When I get into bed, uncertain if sleep will elude me or not, I hear noise. Footsteps getting closer, then receding. Getting closer, then receding again. I step into the hallway and see Derek's back. He's walking down the hall.

"What are you doing?" I ask.

He whirls around and looks at me with a curled lip. He storms toward me and the intensity on his face, his body language, they make

Cheater

me back up. I stumble a little, but catch myself and plaster myself against the wall beside the door to the bedroom.

"Stopping myself," he rasps, thrusting a hand through his hair.

"From what?" I ask.

He gets four or five feet away and stops.

"They're not working," he tells me.

"What?" I ask, trying to shrink.

"The pills."

I blink a couple of times.

"What are they supposed to do that they're not doing?"

Is he having violent thoughts? He looks so angry.

He's not answering my question.

"Your hand isn't twitching," I observe. It looks steady to me.

He lifts his hand, turning it to first examine the front, then his palm.

He abruptly lunges, caging me in against the wall with both palms.

I gasp and stare at him wide-eyed.

He's breathing hard. He's got beads of sweat above his eyebrows, above his upper lip. His pupils are huge. What's happening here? Is Derek having a psychotic break?

"They're not stopping my thoughts, they're not stopping my urges."

"Derek, you're scaring me."

"Know what my urges are, do you?"

I shake my head.

"Do you want to know?" he demands.

He's so close I feel his body heat. His eyes are so angry, so cold.

"You're really scaring me."

"I want to throw you on the nearest surface and fuck your brains out. Fuck you to death. Fuck you until I'm dead. I want to fuck you until there's nothing left of either of us."

I somehow manage to swallow.

He's breathing even harder, practically breathing fire.

"If I touch you, I'll explode into full-blown madness."

My heart hammers hard in my chest.

His voice gentles just slightly. "If I don't touch you..."

"What will happen?" I ask in a whisper.

"The same."

I work down a swallow and ask, "So, what will you do?"

He flinches. "I've been trying not to touch you. Was trying to stay away, not sure what would happen when I saw you. Then you went looking for me and I saw how upset you were on the security footage in the hallway when you thought I was with another woman."

I nod slightly.

"So I tracked you. To the soup place."

I nod again.

"Smelled your perfume. Saw your face. Looked at you..."

I wait.

He moistens his lips. "And I knew the time apart, the counseling, the meditation, the medication... they didn't help."

My heart is about to take flight, leave my body; it's pounding that fast.

"At all. Because I want to fucking devour you. I want you, maybe even more than before."

He's so close. His face is just inches from mine. His hands are pressed to the wall just inches from my body.

Despite the chill in his gaze, I feel the radiation of his body heat, and it's like it's caressing my skin.

I bite my lip and tentatively reach for his face. He backs up as if I've got a communicable disease.

His nostrils flare.

I take a step forward.

"Chloe..." he warns.

"Derek," I whisper and reach for his jaw. He steps back out of my reach.

"I'm scared, bunny," he whispers.

"Why are you scared?"

Cheater

"They didn't fix me, baby."

"I was scared, too. But what you just said... it helped."

"I don't wanna hurt you anymore, Chloe."

"Then don't hurt me anymore, Derek."

His gaze softens just a little as his eyes travel my face.

I step closer and reach for his jaw again. This time he doesn't stop me.

He closes his eyes tight, like my hand on his skin burns.

I put my free hand on his back. I move it up and down.

He's shaking now. Hard.

His eyes open and pain slashes across his features as he grabs my face with both hands. He's holding me a little rough, his grip is a little too hard. His chest moves up and down with heavy breathing as I sidestep and begin to back up into the open bedroom doorway.

He follows, looking conflicted, still holding my face.

His eyes land on something. I look over my shoulder. The envelope lying on the nightstand.

"Do you want to see what's inside?" I ask.

"Maybe," he says carefully.

He still has my face in his hands. I try to move away, but his grip tightens.

"Open it," I urge, gently.

Uncertainty is in his eyes as he lets go of me and lifts the envelope.

He pulls out the cardboard sheets and the lined sheet of paper, frowning.

"The book report I owe you."

He jerks in surprise, eyes scanning the lined sheet of paper. He sets it down and looks at the three cardboard color charts in his hand.

"That's for ideas for the closet and the bathroom. I didn't want to just pick a paint color without you, but I can't take that green that much longer. And the other–"

I'm rendered speechless, because my nightgown is ripped from my body, and I'm thrown on the bed. The book report flies off the nightstand and the paint charts are on the floor.

My husband is on *me*.

His shirt is flying over his head. The clothing south of his waist is all falling and now he's covering me, mouth on mine, slamming his hips forward, filling me. Our needy sounds fill the space around us. They fill our room, in our house, where we're going to grow old together. Where we'll raise a family.

I clamp around him and weave my fingers into his hair, about to say something, but his tongue is in my mouth, then he nips my bottom lip, and it smarts. I jolt with the pain, and he pulls out, flips me to my stomach, and drives back inside me.

"Mine. My wife. My Chloe. Mine. Fuck." His teeth clamp down on my shoulder.

I whimper, fisting the bedding as his hand slips beneath me and cups me between the legs. His fingers work magic while he slams into me over and over again, grunting like a wild animal. *My* wild animal.

I'm flipped again and he's glaring into my eyes now.

"Never. Never want to be away from you again. Never."

I shake my head. "Never."

He grabs my face.

I notice the necklace he's wearing.

My wedding and engagement ring are dangling there.

I burst into tears, and he looks confused for a second until I fit my palm under them and sniffle.

"I've had them close to my heart this whole time," he says.

He's still wearing his wedding ring. And he's worn mine close to his heart.

My heart…

"Put them on me, Derek."

He's too lost in sensation, too focused on fucking me. My legs are lifted up to rest on his shoulders and he slams back into me, putting his thumb to my clit, running his other hand up and down my leg.

Cheater

He sets about a rhythm with his fingers and with his pelvis that have me shuddering out in ecstasy in no time at all.

I cry out his name, digging my nails into his skin, and as my legs fall, he spills inside me, collapsing on top of me. I can feel that his heart is beating as fast as mine is. I hang on tight to him, holding him with my arms and my legs. Reaching for him from somewhere deep inside me as our gazes lock.

He looks distraught. Torn up inside. I see so much pain on his face and I want to fix it. I long to fix it. Maybe what I'm about to say next will help.

"Which one do you like the most?"

His forehead crinkles. "Which what?"

"Paint color."

"Paint it whatever color you want. I'll even live with the green."

"I can't live with that green, husband."

He swallows.

"Can you reach them?" I ask.

He stares blankly at me.

"The paint swatch thingies." I stretch, signaling I want him to move.

He doesn't budge.

"Get me the paint things?"

"That's what you wanna talk about right now?" he asks, looking at me like I've lost it. "Paint it whatever color you want. I think there are other things we should talk about."

"What things?" I ask.

He looks like the weight of the world is on his broad shoulders.

"I don't know," he admits.

"Let's start with the paint. How about that?"

"The paint," he repeats.

"Yes. Can you grab those thingies?"

He rolls off me and halfway off the bed to reach them from the floor.

"Which one do you like?" I ask as he holds up the three cardboard sheets.

I take them from him and drop the purple and blue sheets to the bed beside me and hold the sheet with all the blue-gray shades.

"I like this one." I point to a bluey gray square. "Which one do you like?"

"Chloe, I don't care what color you paint the bathroom."

"Okay, we'll paint it this color then." I put the paint thingie down and lift the other two.

"Do you care what color we paint the baby's room? I like this one if it's a girl. If it's a boy, I'm not sure which blue I like. Maybe this one?"

His eyes are on me with laser-focus. "The baby's room?"

"My room was purple when I was a little girl. I just loved it. I didn't want pink. If it's a girl and she wants it to be pink, it'll be pink, but I was thinking a soft lavender first and go from there. If it's a boy... this blue is kind of nice." I point to the one closest to robin's egg. "Though if he or she wants it pink or purple or heaven forbid... neon green – blech – we'll paint it that."

Derek jumps up. Not to the floor. He's standing on the bed, looking down at me.

"Baby's room?" he repeats.

I bite my lip and nod.

He stares at my naked body and frowns.

"My belly hasn't popped yet. It probably will in a couple of weeks, though. I haven't had morning sickness yet, but I've been super-tired, and my boobs have been sore."

"You..." He gives his head a shake. "Wait. What?"

"The pill was in my bra, Derek. I didn't take it. I thought about it. Believe me, I did. I even unwrapped it. But I couldn't do it." I shrug.

"There weren't any doctor's appointments in the logs."

I shake my head. "I called my doctor and she said to start taking prenatal vitamins and to come in at twelve weeks for my first official appointment. I'm not at twelve weeks yet. Do you want to come?"

Cheater

At least no one was listening to my calls while he was in the hospital.

He falls to his knees on the bed. I sit up and reach to undo his necklace.

"You're carrying my baby?"

"That's why you can't finish all the milk, Derek."

He closes his eyes and lets out a long sigh. "I drank all the milk."

"Yeah. Don't do that."

He winces. "I threw you on this bed."

"It's okay. I landed on my back. I bounced. Put these on me." I pull the rings off the gold chain.

"Fuck, Chloe." He puts his forehead to mine. "Fuck, baby."

His hand splays across my stomach, then he moves down, kissing his way down to my stomach.

When he gets there, he presses a kiss just above my belly button, then just below it, before resting his chin there, love shining in his eyes.

"When you were here for me when she died and at her funeral, it meant so much. When you finally started to let me in, let yourself fall that afternoon, it was everything. I... I'm sorry I fucked it up," he says.

I swallow down a lump of emotion, eyes filling with tears.

"I'm sorry for all the times I made you sad, scared, angry."

I nod, chin trembling.

"And you should know... I'd do it all over again to be right here, you looking at me like this, my child growing inside you."

"I know," I tell him, handing him the rings.

He carefully puts them on my ring finger and kisses it.

"I love you, Derek," I tell him. "I've missed you so much. I'm so ready for you to make me happy. I'm so ready to make you happy, too."

"The doctors didn't fix me, Chloe," he reminds me.

"Good," I say.

Epilogue

Derek

Two Weeks Later, Portsmouth, NH

"Oh wow. It's gorgeous," she exclaims, as we pull up to the house. "And it's on the water!"

"Wait till you see it in the summer, little bunny. It's a great place to unplug."

"It's amazing."

Grace wanted us to come for Christmas. Dad came. So did Ash and Jonah. Grace laid the guilt on thick, but I couldn't bear to share Chloe with anyone.

Her company shut down from Christmas Eve until New Year's Day, so we spent most of that time in bed, other than putting up a Christmas tree together, and then painting the closet and master bathroom together, which devolved into painting my name on my wife's naked body with my fingers.

I shared her on New Year's Eve: with her parents, who came and spent the night, ringing in a new year with a cutthroat game of Monopoly. It was my throat that got cut the most.

The love and light in her eyes as she played a board game with me and her folks told me even more about the woman I'm obsessed with.

Now she smiles for me. She reaches for me. And as much as I

can't get enough of fucking her, she initiates fucking almost as often as I do. My dirty girl. My greedy girl. My good girl.

The Turners are cutthroat at the game of Monopoly, which I never played before New Year's Eve. So is Chloe Steele, who bankrupted me without hesitation. I want her bringing that game here to the New Hampshire homestead next summer. Grace has already begun organizing a family week where we're all here at the same time. I want Chloe to challenge my father to a game so he can see who he might be smart to leave his real estate empire to.

Chloe said she didn't want to announce the pregnancy until after her twelve-week appointment, but she blurted it to her mother not five minutes after Pam and Hal arrived. She did it with so much excitement that if I hadn't already fallen in love with my wife, that would've done it. Pam almost immediately got on her phone and began ordering baby gifts.

I found Chloe and her mother hugging and crying on New Year's Day morning. I was concerned, but found out they were playing Yahtzee, a dice game Chloe's folks brought, and it was discovered that the very last time the game was played, it was a game between Chloe and her late brother. The last used scorecard was in a teenaged Chloe's purple marker, but her brother won the game and circled his name, writing "winner", circling Chloe's and writing "loser." He drew a male stick figure with a winner trophy in his stick hand and a sad faced stick figure with a bow in her hair beside Chloe's final score.

While it hurt to see the emotion on my wife's face at these memories, those tears transitioned to laughter as memories of family game nights and stories of Bryan Turner's competitive and irreverent humor were shared.

I saw love between Chloe and her parents. Not neglect, formality, or indifference. I saw a family trying to heal after enduring pain of losing one of their own. I think they're still healing.

So am I. So is the rest of my family. Healing from wounds. Healing from trauma. I don't miss my dead brother. Good riddance. I

Cheater

do miss my late mother. More than I thought I would. And the rest of us might not all be on the same page about everything; we might still be considered corrupt and elitist rich pricks, but I'm on speaking terms with everyone including my father, who is making an effort. So am I.

Naomi and Ash haven't bridged the gap in their relationship, but they were much less hostile toward one another at that family breakfast the day after my mother's funeral. It was their birthday on New Year's Day and Grace told me Naomi sent Ash a happy birthday text. The first one in about a decade. It's a start. Grace told Chloe during a one-hour phone call on Christmas Eve that Nay and Josh's marriage is in trouble. My wife and sister seem like they're getting close. Good. Gets Grace off my back.

Speaking of marriages in trouble – I don't know what the deal is with Elijah and Sabrina. He dealt with his enemies while I was in the hospital, thankfully. He took her on a trip for Christmas, so I haven't spoken with him since I've been out. Whether Sabrina went kicking and screaming on this trip or not, I'm not sure.

As for my state of mind, I haven't had much stress, so I don't know yet how I'll react to it. I've got some stress management tools from my time in the hospital, so we'll see. I agreed to continue to do one-hour weekly therapy sessions. For now.

My two months in the hospital wasn't fun. I probably got worse before I got better enough for the doctors to not balk about me leaving. Between missing Chloe and feeling triggered by being in therapy, I very nearly walked straight through plate-glass windows every day for the first three weeks I was there in order to get out, in order to get back to my wife.

I didn't know if Chloe would ever speak to me again without venom, hatred, and fear, and unlike when I first became focused on her as a goal, it bothered me deeply that she didn't think there was any hope for us. I started to believe it. I was haunted by the notion she was terrified of bringing a child into this marriage because of me.

And I knew that my remorse might mean there might be hope for me. My developing feelings meant I might not be a complete sociopath.

I knew I wouldn't be able to stay away from her forever. I knew I wasn't done with her. At no point during the two months apart did I think I would ever let her go. I fought my urges hard, dreading seeing the hate and fear in her eyes again. But when I finally set eyes on her again on the surveillance feed for the building after Ash's text telling me he saw her in the parking lot, hatred and venom is not what I saw.

She was distraught, no *devastated*. Devastated that when she came looking for me, she saw another woman there.

She told me she was a wreck for the first few days that I was gone, traumatized from my meltdown, from everything we'd been through. But then she began to miss me. She couldn't stop envisioning a family with me in the house I bought for her. She didn't want to be anywhere else but in that house, with me, making memories together. And a few weeks after I committed myself, she was late for her period and got Alannah to bring her a pregnancy test. She said she couldn't wait to tell me the test was positive. She decided to do that as soon as I got out. And then sought me out when I didn't come to her.

She told me that even before she thought I'd replaced her, she was ready to give me another shot, which terrified her. Which still does. She didn't just want to give our marriage a chance because I wouldn't divorce her. She didn't just want to give it a real chance because she thought the doctors fixed me.

She tells me she loves me for who I am instead of loving me in spite of it. How I love her is what she wants. And that's good, because I don't know how to love her any other way. She still has fears. I'm probably still far from mentally well, but maybe I'm closer than I was before her.

I asked her yesterday if she wanted me to pay Adam Hallman out the million bucks early. So we can close the book on him. She told me she didn't want me to pay him at all. I've done all I agreed to do. The suits. Hooked him up with Josh who is looking at clinical trials for him. He's been given all the things I told him he'd get,

Cheater

including a publishing contract for his book series. Chloe says that's more than enough. She wants me to take out the cameras, stop tracking his online activities, and donate the million dollars to medical research. I'll make the donation, but I'll have to think about the rest.

∞

I've shown her the house, we've unloaded the groceries we shopped for on the way here, and it's time for me to tick another one of my little bunny's sexy bucket list line items.

"This is nice," she says as she looks around the bedroom. "I love how big it is. We can come back next summer and fit a pack n' play right here." She gestures beside the bed.

I wrap my arms around her. "I don't think we want our baby this close to the bed."

She looks at me curiously, tilting her head to the side.

"Don't want to scar him or her with all the naughty things we'll do in that bed, bunny."

She wrinkles her nose. "I'm not sticking our baby into a nursery down the hall. We'll paint and decorate the room next to ours at home, but he or she will probably sleep beside or even *with* us for the first year."

"Don't think that'll cramp our sex life?" I ask.

"Knowing us, we'll be able to get creative," she replies, looping her arms around my neck.

She gets up on her toes and presses her lips to mine.

"I love you, little bunny," I murmur against her soft lips.

"I love you, too, swoony stalker."

I chuckle, loving the light in her eyes.

"I'm about to make you swoon for the next forty-eight hours, Chloe Steele."

"Oh yeah? Bring it on," she invites and gives me another look I've worked hard for. *Longing.*

"Your fantasies or mine?" I ask, then whisper. "You picked mine last time you were asked."

She moistens her lips with her little pink tongue, looking intrigued. "I like the idea of some more of yours."

She's a miracle. My wife.

But I advise, "Pick yours, wife."

She lets go of me. "Now, husband..." She puts her hand to her waist and says, "it's not *my* choice if you manipulate me into choosing what you want me to choose."

"You want this sort of manipulation, believe me," I inform.

"Okay, Derek. I choose mine."

I give her a smile as I reach for the small suitcase I brought, that she quizzed me about when I packed the car for this trip. I told her she'd have to wait and see.

I set the suitcase on the trunk at the foot of the four-poster bed and my wife watches me unzip it.

Her eyes boing when I flip the top, revealing what's inside.

"Holy fuck," she whispers.

"Ready for a weekend of total power exchange, Chloe?" I ask. "For the next forty-eight hours, I make you do absolutely everything I want. Do whatever I want to your body."

She blinks at the sight of the handcuffs, the wrapped set of straps and small bench that make up a sex swing. I've got a leather sensory deprivation suit, nipple clamps, a ball gag, blind fold, some restraints, and some sex toys.

"Are you... are you interested in bondage?" she asks.

"Sure."

"Have you... dabbled before?"

"Do you really wanna know?" I ask.

She frowns. "No," she whispers.

I laugh. She mean-mugs me for laughing.

"Have you?" I ask.

"I'd ask you the same question you just asked me but... no, I haven't dabbled. I've always wanted to, though."

Cheater

"I know, baby. Let's have some fun," I say.

"Do I need a safe word?" she asks.

I smile wider. "Probably. But you aren't getting one."

My wife bites her lip as arousal lights in her eyes.

I'm going to fulfill another sexy bucket list item the day after tomorrow, too. Sunday sundaes. In bed. We'll be licking the ice cream and toppings from one another.

∞

A Month Later

"You don't get to tell me who I do and don't fire, Derek," she sassily informs. "Carlos is good at his job. You're just still holding onto unnecessary hostility because you saw me go to lunch with him before you came back home. He's dating Coraline. He likes her a lot. Also, I happen to be happily mated for life."

I smirk. She's referring to that line in the book report about the book I bought her that day I approached in the soup place. I read her book report the day after I found out she was pregnant. I love how she compared the love story in the book to ours.

"Wait. I thought Jeff was dating Coraline."

"That only lasted two weeks before Jeffy told her he didn't want to be tied down," she tells me. "Now she's dating Carlos. Though, it's not exclusive yet because Cor is still kind of hooking up with Jeffy."

"I don't give a fuck who Carlos is or isn't dating. If I catch him looking at your tits again, Chloe, you won't like what happens."

Her mouth drops open.

I tack on, "It's probably best that you fire him."

She doesn't look pregnant yet, but she looks curvier and her tits sure are bigger. Courtesy of growing my baby inside her.

I'm looking forward to it being obvious that I've impregnated her. I want the world to see her belly rounded because I made it that way.

"I told you I love you just the way you are, but Derek, I don't want to live with the fear of threats," she warns, poking my chest with her index finger. "That's still not okay with me. Okay?"

"Then you'd best be my good girl, Chloe," I fire back. "Unless you want a punishment."

The wicked gleam in her eyes right now at the idea of a punishment? It makes me love her even more.

But I'm absolutely serious. If she doesn't fire Carlos, I might have to get rid of him myself.

The End

Want More?

Want more of the Steele family? YES — I have plans.
Sabrina and Elijah? YES.
Jonah? Grace? YES.
Naomi? Asher? PROBABLY.

Book Report

Prepared for Derek Steele, By Chloe Steele

The Wolf Shifter Book.

What was it about?

Despite the very sexy cover and titillating description, this book also had substance. It explored the building of a relationship between a woman and a supernatural man. Not only was he a wolf shifter, he also hadn't been around people or other wolf shifters in several years due to trauma in his life. This meant for an interesting dynamic.

 The wolf shifter caught her scent and had to pursue her; he was sure she was the one meant to be his mate. Alpha wolf shifters mate for life so he was unwilling to give her up no matter how much she protested. And protest she did!

 She's extremely resistant to this idea, not understanding the way he thinks, confused and afraid of him because of his intensity, but she absolutely finds herself smitten by some of his actions as well as his prowess in the bedroom. This book had some interesting sexual dynamics including knotting (he is locked inside her during copulation and the knot vibrates against a very sensitive part inside her) and the fact that the mate mark becomes an extra erogenous zone on the neck. The wolf shifter vows he will do whatever he needs to do to convince her of his unconditional love.

What I loved so much:

 I enjoyed that the story had some laugh-out-loud moments, some heartwarming ones, some frustrating and angry moments as well as some emotional moments. This book made me feel a lot! Most of all, I

Book Report

loved that it had a lot of descriptive, panty-melting sex and some unexpected heart-warming moments.

Beyond their relationship, he develops relationships with his pack. The pack structure was interesting and watching him connect with and find his place in his family was beautiful.

What I didn't love as much:

He did some extreme things in order to try to convince her they were meant to be. Some of these passages were difficult read. Some of these things hurt her. A lot. He went quite feral a few times. I felt her pain through the pages. But I also felt his pain when he realized how bad he screwed up. I felt how misunderstood he was because of his upbringing, his biology, his trauma. I could feel how much he loved her despite the fact that he was so intensely primal about it.

In Conclusion:

I was gripped by this story, invested in hoping they'd somehow find their way to a happily-ever-after. We all want to believe that's possible. Don't we? I loved the fact that characters in this universe mate for life. Marrying only once, just like I believe it should be.

Even though what they went through was beyond tough at points, it was easy to see that despite it all, they had the ingredients for a strong relationship. Not only the desire to make one another happy, but also the determination to satisfy one another in every way.

Sometimes we hurt the people we care most about. Sometimes love isn't easy. Families can be messy. But it's all worth believing in, making an effort for, especially when the person you love and who loves you tries really hard to show you that you and your happiness really do matter.

End of Book Notes

Sign up for my newsletter at http://ddprince.com/newsletter-signup to be notified of sales, giveaways, and new releases as well as bonus scenes for my characters.

I do have several series ongoing right now so don't know when I'll write Elijah and Sabrina's story, but if you subscribe to my newsletter and join my reader group DD's Chickadees on Facebook, you'll be among the first to find out. The facts about their relationship that have spilled into the cauldron have me very excited.

I first 'met' the Steele family when writing Bad Girl, Alphahole Roommates book 3 (books best experienced in order). Ally was running from Jonah and Thad. I knew I'd tell Jonah's story some day. And probably not Thad's, but definitely Grace's. Her story is definitely in the cauldron, too. What's the story with her and Craig, anyway? (wink)

I might tackle Asher's and Naomi's stories, too. The ideas are flowing into the cauldron as I write this.

Love over-the-top possessive alpha male book boyfriends? Cheater was my 26th release so there are LOTS Of bad boys in the backlist for you to meet and fall for.

End of Book Notes

Those who loved this story might also love:

My Savage Alpha Shifters – Fated mates wolf shifter romances. (Book one, Wild, might be the same book Chloe wrote a book report for)

My Beautiful Biker series – possessive, protective biker book boyfriends that put their woman first.

The Nectar Trilogy – dark and taboo fated mate vampire romance.

The Dominator Series – The Dominator was my debut release. This arranged marriage mafia romance series is dark. To show people how over-the-top Derek was, I told my readers he made Tommy Ferrano from The Dominator look well-adjusted and this shocked them. If you love Derek, you might also love Tommy. Their story has a lot of feels. Those who prefer the cinnamon-roll type alphas prefer Dario, Tommy's brother, but please read book 1 before embarking on Truth or Dare.

Saved – A dark romance for the readers who aren't afraid to delve into the dark. It's a story for those who find themselves rooting for the bad guy sometimes. He's not the hero in this book. She is. This is a story about unconditional love from a naïve and pure soul who saves him. But he definitely doesn't deserve it. Can be read as standalone but if you plan to read The Dominator Series, read this after that.

The Devious Games Duet – Kill Game and Dirty Stack - Morally gray bookie uses a gambling debt to TAKE the girl he wants from her abuser. Killian is swoony AF, stalks, tosses birth control pills, and seeks revenge against those who've hurt Violet. I definitely took a little of his best qualities and transplanted them into Derek.

For something lighter but equally as dirty, check out my Alphahole Roommates enemies-to-lovers series and my Hot Alpha Alien Husbands books. The Alphahole Roommates series will introduce you to the Steele brothers in book 3.

My entire reading order and list of books with a link to trigger warnings is pinned to the home page of http://ddprince.com.

Sign up for The Scoop, my newsletter which goes out when I

End of Book Notes

have sales, new releases, and free book promotions - https://ddprince.com/newsletter-signup/

If you loved this book, a review is a HUGE help. Recommending it to your book-loving friends is also amazing. Supporting indie authors by reading our books the legit way, by reviewing and recommending, helps us bring you MORE stories to fall in love with.

Thanks for reading!

HUGE thanks to my beta and ARC team, my street team, and DD's Chickadees – my Facebook reader group.

The idea for this story hit me while I was digging in to work on my fourth shifter romance. And I tried to put this aside, to stick to the plan, but the muse wants what the muse wants. It wanted to explore Derek and his obsession with Chloe. I had to stop fighting it and let the story flow. Derek grabbed me by the proverbial throat and refused to let go.

I hope you enjoyed it.

Incidentally, if you're ever in Niagara Falls, Ontario, Country Fresh Donuts on Victoria Avenue is outside the tourist district. A rougher neighbourhood, and it isn't fancy, and although I don't know the owners' names and they never did get hurt and wounded if I failed to come in for a while, they do have the best won ton soup and chocolate éclairs I've ever had. Ever.

I left Niagara Falls in 2022 to move to the east coast of Canada. But if I go back, I'm definitely going for some soup and an éclair. At about 1:00, hoping that's still when the daily batch comes out. Because they sell out FAST. But all their donuts are good.

SAVE The Baby Unicorns:

Does my reference to *zero baby unicorns being hurt during the writing of this book* mean that I got lucky every time I lady-scaped? Sadly, no. But I'll explain.

I had already started writing this book and had the baby unicorn reference in it when I re-released The Dominator, my debut release (that's been banned multiple times and is now available again).

Something glitched during publishing on the book retailer's end

End of Book Notes

and somehow the book's paperback edition first got published with a unicorn coloring book cover that doesn't belong to me. I've been fighting with that e-book retailer for months to try to get this glitchy, non-existent cover deleted. I'm getting nowhere.

Are the unicorns fighting back? In case it appeases them, I wanted to say I meant no harm.

About the Author

DD Prince is a Canadian romance author who loves to write about alpha males, often antiheroes. Check out the full list of DD's books on http://ddprince.com.

Follow on social media:
Facebook: http://facebook.com/ddprincebooks
Instagram: http://instagram.com/ddprincebooks
Amazon: http://bit.ly/ddprinceonamazon
YouTube: http://www.youtube.com/@ddprincebooks
TikTok: https://www.tiktok.com/@ddprincebooks

Reader group: DD's Chickadees (http://facebook.com/groups/ddprincefangroup or search by the name on Facebook. Be sure to answer the membership questions).

Discord Server chat: http://bit.ly/ddprinceondiscord
Goodreads: http://bit.ly/ddprinceongr
BookBub: https://www.bookbub.com/authors/dd-prince